sharjah biennial

بينالي الشارقة

This catalogue accompanies the Sharjah Biennial 8, April 4 - June 4, 2007

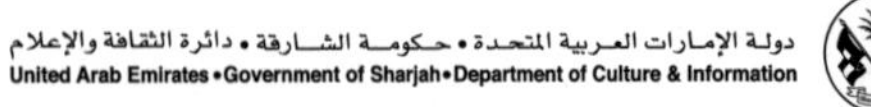

ART, ECOLOGY & THE POLITICS OF CHANGE

STILL LIFE

Sharjah Biennial 8

06
5567655

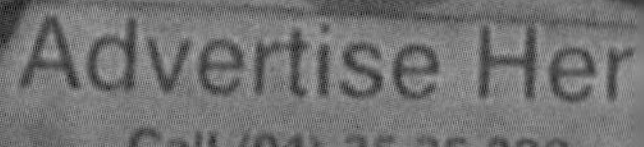
Advertise Her
Call (04) 35 35 222

H 75485

ابو شغارة
Abu Shagara
الشارقة
Sharjah
عجمان
Ajman
المجاز
الخان
ميناء خالد
Al Majaz
Al Khan
Khalid Port
300m
EXIT
K610i
D DUBAI 49640

DALLAS DISCOUNT CENTER

SHARJAH BIENNIAL 8

Biennial Director
Hoor Al Qasimi

Artistic Director
Jack Persekian

Assistant
Farah Shawar

Curators
Mohammad Kazem
Eva Scharrer
Jonathan Watkins

Jury Committee
Negar Azimi
Charles Esche
Geeta Kapur

General Coordinator
Hisham Al Madhloum

Biennial Office Secretary
Fatima Ahmad
Mariam Ali

Biennial Coordinator - Communication & Logistics
Mahita El Bacha Urieta

Logistics Assistant
Firas Audeh
Alia Al Sabi

Administrative Manager
Reem Shadid

Artists' Coordinator
Lara Khaldi

Exhibition Layout
Mona El Mousfy (architect)

Assistants
Samar El Mousfy (architect)
Mays Nafookh
May Mirza
Rasha Daher

Exhibition Production
Hassan Al Jidah (engineer)

Technical & Installations coordinator
Nikolaj Benedix Skyum Larsen

Assistants
Iman Al Sayed
Lateefa Maktoum
Nasser Abdul Karim bin Hashim

Arabic press liaison
Ismail Al Rifai

Financial Manager
Ahmed Kamal

IT
Noaf Yousif

Data Base Entry
Hussam Abu Basha

Web Designer
Hani Sharaf - Curious Design
Ghassan Al Soudani

Photographer
Peter Riedlinger
Alfred Rubio

Education Programme & Exhibition Guides
Zekryat Matouk
Hind Darwish
Alya Al Mulla
Anoud Al Khadar
Bassem Saleh Al Sayyed
Fatima Ali Mohammad
Haleema Sulaiman
Ismail Al Suwaidi
Jawaher Alsuwaidi
Mohammad Ahmad
Mohammed Fayez
Suad Ismail Taresh
Wafa' Abdullah Ali
Walid Said Al Baghdady

Workshops supervisor
Talal Moualla
Secretary
Dina Al Ghoussain

Trainers
Jaafer Duelah
Mohamed Bader
Riad Maatook
Wissam Haddad
Yaser Safi

Volunteers Coordinator
Yosra Saleh

Installers and Technicans
Ahmed Abdel Jabbar
Kanookaran Solaiman ShaJahan
Kamal Said Mohamed
Atlas Khan Amir Dawar Khan
Abid Amir Dawar Khan
Abdul Rahman
Anil Kumar. C
Habib Ullah Sultan
Hassan Derwish
Khalid Sami
Mohammad Khan Mira Khan
Mohammed Atiq
Ramadan Mohamad
Rashid Hassan
Sakeer Puthyya
Sameer K.P.
Seraj Ali
Mohammad Iqbal

Logistics
Ali Al Nemr
Saif Uddin. K. V.
Mansour Ahmed Zia
Mohammad Ghaleb
Amjeth Khan
Mohammed Kan Fadel Kul

Stores
Youssef Taha

Librarians
Mariam Abdullah
Huda Salim El Nassir

Design of Medals and Awards
Carlos Marinas

PR Consultant (international)
Brunswick Arts
Maria Finders
Ben Rawlingson-Plant
Joanna Boulos
Katie Taylor
Alex Robat

PR Consultant (regional)
JIWIN
Ma'moun Sbeih
Majid Wasi
Jane Meikle

Communication Consultants
Curious Design
Abir Barakat
Hani Sharaf

Outdoor advertising
Golden Balloon
Fahed Al Sharif

Shipping & Art Handling
Crown Fine Arts
Arnaud Bouzinac

Insurance
Al-Buhaira National Insurance Co.

Hospitality - Transportation, Accommodation & Ticketing
Orient Tours
Tito Mathachan
Sanyal Vijayal

Ticketing
Skyline Travels
Sadia Pasha

Hotels
Sharjah Rotana
Ayman Gharib
Manna' Al Eid
Holiday International Sharjah
Nasser M. Nassef
Marbella Resort
Anil Singh
Asim Bader

Catering
Albert Abela Co. Shj. LLC
Lyndon Mark Ananda

DEPARTMENT OF CULTURE & INFORMATION, GOVERNMENT OF SHARJAH

SPECIAL THANKS

Sheikh Issam bin Saqer Al Qasimi
Head of the Ruler's Office, Sharjah

Sheikha Bodour Al Qasimi
Chairperson of Qanat Al Qasba Development Authority

Salim bin Mohammad Al Owais
Chairman of the Sharjah Municipal Council

Mohammed M. K. Al Swaidi
Director General - Ruler's Office, Sharjah

Saleh Ali Al-Mutawa
Director General of Sharjah Police

Salah Taher Al Haj
General Manager of Sharjah Municipality

Randa Kamal

THANKS TO

Abdallah Al Shwaikh
Abdellah Karroum
Abdulrahman Abubaker Ahmad
Abdulrahman Mohamed Bukhatir
Adel Al Metwali
Ahmad Abdel Salam
Ahmed R. Abou Naja
Al Hur Mohammed Al-Nur
Alwalid bin Khadim
Anas Shomal
Andrea Rose
Anneka Lensen
Arwa Lootah
Cesar Espada
Chantal Crousel
Chris Dercon
Colin Reaney
Derek Ogbourne
Diana Stevenson
Ebtisam Abdul Aziz
Faten Haj Ibrahim
Fatima Yousif bin Sandal
Ghazi Baqjaji
Haidar Al Amin
Hammad Nasar
Hazel Page
Hazem Sawaf
Hind O. Kheir
Hisham Abdel Kareem
Inas Abu Sido
Iris Lenz
Irit Rogoff
Ismail Al Bishri
Jassem Al-Madhloum
John Martin - DIFC Gulf Art Fair
Judy Bullington
Juma' Ibrahim Alsuwaidi
Jumana Abboud
Khadijeh Kanambo
Khalid bin Butti Al-Muhairy
Khalid Ismail Safar
Leanne Mella
Mariam W. Al Dabbagh
Marwan Al Sirkal
Meera Al Suwaidi
Michael Bray
Moataz Mohammad Hussein
Mohammad Al Amiri
Mohammad Hassan Awad
Noor Omran
Nuria Oscoz
Osama Mohamed Samra
P. Ravi
Raeda Saadeh
Raymond Prucher
Rina Carvajal
Roberto Lopardo
Rubali Karnak
Saif Mohammad Al Midfa
Salah bin Butti Al-Muhairy
Salah Taher Al Haj
Samer Kamal
Siham Mohammad Sharif
Sue Underwood
Susan Roberts-Manganelli
Tarek Al-Ghoussein
Tariq Sultan A. bin Khadim
Tawfiq Al Kamati
Terry Evans
Thani Al Shamsi
Thilo von Debschitz
Walid Demas
Windy Chang
Yakub Abdallah
Youser W. Al Dabbagh
Zeina Farhat
Ziad Sobeh

Ministry of Interior - General Directorate for Naturalization and Residence
Ministry of Interior - Sharjah Police
Ministry of Education & Youth, Sharjah Educational Zone
Municipality of Sharjah
Municipality of Al-Zhaid
United Arab Emirates Television & Radio Station - Sharjah
Directorate of Town Planning & Survey, Government of Sharjah
Sharjah Electricity & Water Authority
University of Sharjah - College of Fine Arts & Design
American University of Sharjah
Sharjah Museums Department
Expo Centre Sharjah
Qanat Al Qasba
Al-Ma'mal Foundation for contemporary Art - Jerusalem
Dar Al-Khaleej Press Printing & Publishing
American University in Dubai
Al-Shifa' Bint Al-Hareth School
UAQ Aquarium & Marine Research center
Sea Club for Arts & Tourism

CATALOGUE

Catalogue Editor
Serene Huleileh

Assistant Editor
Lara Khaldi

Translators
Bassma Al Far
Diala Khasawneh
Etidal Osman
Hasan Abu Laban
Hatem Hussein
Mohammad Al Wadhah Aidabi
Murad Ramdani
Sulafah Hijjawi

Arabic Language Editor
Ismail Al Rifai
Ghazi El Khalili

English Language Editor
Anne Rodford

Photos
Jack Persekian
English section pp. 4-5, 6-7, 8-9, 28
Arabic section pp. 4-5, 24-25

Artists' names are listed alphabetically by family name. Artists' groups are listed alphabetically by the name of the first artist in the group as per their order. Credits are listed alphabetically by first name, except in particular cases.

Catalogue Design
Lena Sobeh

Assistant Designer
Khalid A. K. Mezaina

Print Management
Mohamed Khalil

Printing & Binding
Emirates Printing Press

Catalogue
Title: *Sharjah Biennial 8, Still Life: Art, Ecology and the Politics of Change*
360 pages, 233 x 165 mm
Cover: 300g. Conquerror Texture
- Stonemarque Diamond White
Paper: 80g. offset woodfree and
135g. ArtMatt

Published by the Sharjah Biennial

ISBN 9948-04-328-6

Address:
Sharjah Biennial
Box 19989, Sharjah
United Arab Emirates
Tel. +971 6 5685050
Fax: +971 6 5685800
Email: info@sharjahbiennial.org
www.sharjahbiennial.org

The Sharjah Biennial gratefully acknowledges the support extended by the artists and writers. The excerpts selected by the artists and / or their agents are considered intergral to the representation of each artist project - they are considered to be an important educational aspect of the exhibition. Every effort has been made to contact all writers, artists and copyright holders of the articles, essays and images forwarded to us by the artists and / or their agents.

All dimensions are stated in centimetres in order of height, width, depth.

SPONSORS

مصرف الشارقة الإسلامي
Sharjah Islamic Bank

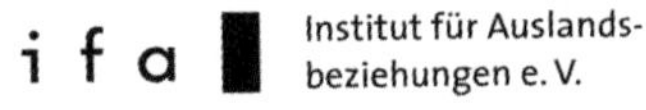

IKON

MEDIA SPONSOR

Mark Nash
Curator
This is a programme that takes a long view on art, ecology and the politics of change. On the one hand the eloquent documentary *Darwin's Nightmare* addresses the immediate issues of climactic and ecological change. On the other hand artists' films address a wide range of issues from the sensuous and symbolic materiality of water, (Zdravic), the state of the coalmining industry in China (Shaobin) to more poetic meditations on the legacy of independence and liberation struggles (Shahani & Julien).

Film list

Andrej Zdravic
Riverglass - A River Ballet in Four Seasons, 1997
The rhetoric of water in experimental, fiction, and documentary film, examines human relations to particular lands/places by focusing on the representation of water and of struggles over water rights in experimental, non-fiction, and activist cinema.

Riverglass is a 41-minute video that visually immerses viewers into the emerald waters of the Stocha River in Slovenia. The demands that the video's length and approach ask of viewers transform their awareness and experience of the natural world. *Riverglass* opens up a space in which they might meditate on their relationship to the natural world and how that world has come to function in representation, and in reality.

Viewers are conditioned to experience beautiful landscapes in film as something that does not deserve their sustained attention. It challenges this conditioning by offering nothing else on which to focus except for the flow of the river-from within the river-through the span of the four seasons. In these 41 minutes, either the river comes to matter or it does not. *Riverglass* compels the viewers to make that choice, and to acknowledge it as a choice.

Bregtje Van Der Haak
Lagos Wide and Close, 2002
This film is based on research by the Harvard Project on Lagos City under the direction of Rem Koolhaas.

Lagos is home to an estimated fifteen million people. Despite crime, drainage problems, relentless traffic jams, water and electricity shortages, Lagos is growing so quickly that by 2020 it is expected to be the world's third largest city. Architect Rem Koolhaas decided to study Lagos in order to understand what makes a dysfunctional city function. Loosely based on the trajectories of a bus driver, this film gives us a glimpse into the lives of eight Lagos inhabitants and the creative relationships they have developed with their complex city. Koolhaas adds his reactions and interpretations of five years of research on Lagos. Filming has long been prohibited in Nigeria so very few images of Lagos exist. This film separates the distant (wide) and intimate (close) views of the city allowing the viewer to switch between these perspectives interactively. There are also three different audio-tracks - commentary with Rem Koolhaas, talks with inhabitants and sounds of the city.

Hubert Sauper
Darwin's Nightmare, 2004
Darwin's Nightmare is a tale about humans between the North and the South, about globalization, and about fish.

Some time in the 1960's, in the heart of Africa, a new animal was introduced into Lake Victoria as a little scientific experiment, which in return had caused the ecological disaster of the lake. The Nile Perch, a voracious predator, extinguished almost the entire stock of the native fish species. However, the new fish multiplied so fast, that its white fillets are today exported all around the world.

Huge hulking ex-Soviet cargo planes come daily to collect the latest catch in exchange for their southbound cargo; Kalashnikovs and ammunitions for the uncounted wars in the dark center of the continent.

This booming multinational industry of fish and weapons has created an ungodly globalized alliance on the shores of the world's biggest tropical lake: an army of local fishermen, World Bank agents, homeless children, African ministers, EU-commissioners, Tanzanian prostitutes and Russian pilots.

Igloolik Isuma / Zacharias Kunuk, Norman Cohn
The Journals of Knud Rasmussen, 2006
Zacharius Kunuk and Norman Cohn, the team behind Atanarjuat: The Fast Runner -the first film in the Inuit language of Inuktitut- bring another groundbreaking film set within and produced by the Inuit community.

Director Zacharius Kunuk was inspired to make the film - *The Journals of Knud Rasmussen* - for a first audience that is Inuit: elders who are still alive and young people looking for a future beyond boredom, unemployment and suicide. It tries to answer two questions that haunted me my whole life: Who were we? And what happened to us?

This time their focus is on a pivotal moment in Inuit history when the people first encountered European explorers and Christianity. Around 1922 the Danish explorer and anthropologist Knud Rasmussen journeyed to the Canadian Arctic to record the stories and beliefs of the local tribes, and this quest forms a springboard from which their stories are told within this film. Focusing on the Inuit leaders, Avva the last great shaman (played by his descendent, Pakak Innukshuk) and Umik the Inuk who led the conversion to Christianity; the stories are narrated by Avva's daughter Apak. Viewed completely from the point of view of the Inuit, Kunuk and Cohn create a compelling vision of the recent past, and of a time which was both strange and familiar, where nature and spirituality determined behavior, and magical elements were part of daily life. Drawing on oral histories they learned from current Elders, and with astonishing cinematography Kunuk and Cohn create a poignant, thought-provoking yet thoroughly absorbing film.

Isaac Julien

Fantôme Afrique, 2005

Fantôme Afrique weaves cinematic and architectural references through the rich imagery of urban Ouagadougou, the centre for cinema in Africa, and the arid spaces of rural Burkina Faso, and is punctuated by archival footage from early colonial expeditions and landmark moments in African history. Renowned choreographer and dancer Stephen Galloway (Ballet Frankfurt) and actor Vanessa Myrie (Baltimore) figure as 'trickster/phantom' and 'witness' in this carefully composed meditation on the denationalized, de-territorialized spaces born of the encounters between local and global cultures, where the ghosts of history linger amid the realities of the day.

Kumar Shahani

Char Adhyay, 1997

Based on Rabindranath Tagore's novella written in 1934, Shahani's film is set in the terrorist phase of the Indian freedom movement. A woman 'Ela' allowed herself to be turned into a walking, talking, living mascot for a group of terrorists; a comforting female presence for youth whose self-respect has been lacerated by the experience of colonial domination. The ideologue uses Ela's beauty and dignified bearing to project the resurgent spirit of the country.

Having abandoned their own mothers, sisters and wives, these `knights-errant' are ready to loot and to commit suicide and murder for the sake of the cause. At first Ela exults in her glorification, but then begins to question it when one in the group, Atin, resists indoctrination. He refuses to sublimate his feelings for Ela and is filled with revulsion at the terrorists' deeds. They reach for simple happiness, but by then they are both in too deep and must play their roles to the hilt.

Oki Hiroyuki

The Form of the palace of Matsumae-kun's Brothers 1, 1988

The series originated with the work, "The Diary of Matsumae-kun" (1988). This work, a city plan for Matsumae-city in Hokkaido, was submitted as Hiroyuki Oki's graduation project while studying architecture in college. In addition to the architectural draft, the design was displayed alongside various media, presenting the landscape in a manga-like panel layout from the point of view of the fictional character "Matsumae-kun". The following year, the inaugural film "A Film of Matsumae-kun" (1989) was created. The early works in the series were captured on film in the form of a diary beginning on New Year's Day. It was marked by in-camera edits, creating a very physical sense of improvisation. The annual series was interrupted in 1996, but recommenced in 2002 with "Vision for Matsumae-kun's Death". These newer works reflect changes in progress, such as a shift to the use of video cameras, and bringing the actors to Matsumae-city for shootings. In terms of editing, material from previous series was incorporated to expand the films, giving them different forms than of those in the past.The filming for "The Form of the Palace of Matsumae-kun's Brothers 1", 13th in the series, took place over one month beginning January 22, 2006, and featured settings in Hakodate, Sapporo, Tokyo and Kochi in addition to Matsumae-city.

Yang Shaobin

800 meters under, Aboveground-Underground, 2005

The film is composed of two poles of the life of a coalminer, the depths of the coalmines and their communities and dwellings. "Underground" focuses on the process of production of the coal mines, while "Aboveground" presents a haunting look on the lives of coal miners once above the surface of the earth, a life which is still enshrouded in darkness, absent the possibilities of escape. Through personal experience and travel, the artist sensitively engages with the complexity of issues, revealing the humanity within this cycle of production.

This is both a historical and prescient issue concerning political organization, rapid shift in social system, survival, and power. The project re-examines the history of industrialization and urban spaces, socialist memory and their connection to contemporary Chinese art history.

OFFSET of 70 TONNES of CARBON

Symposium
5–7 April 2007
An RSA Arts & Ecology/Latitudes programme in collaboration with the American University of Sharjah (AUS)
Venue: Expo Centre, Sharjah

SYMPOSIUM ORGANIZERS
Michaela Crimmin
Royal Society for the encouragements or Art, Manufactures & Commerce, RSA, London
Max Andrews & Mariana Canepa Luna
Latitudes
Roderick Grant & Amir Berbic
American University of Sharjah, AUS
Symposium Coordinator: Sharon Ahimaz
Sharjah Biennial

The Symposium, which forms part of the Sharjah Biennial, aims to explore specific aspects of the relationship between culture and ecology – not least the challenges and the contradictions. The event will profile the extraordinary work taking place in architecture, the visual arts, across new technologies, in design and on screen. Discussions will involve artists, academics and students, architects and designers, people living locally and a number of key contributors from other continents. It draws from and will build on previous discourse – capturing the perspectives of people who are addressing ecological issues on a daily basis. The Symposium bravely takes place in a country which is prepared to look to the future and the changes we are all going to have to make.

Thursday 5 April

KEYNOTE SPEAKER
Bruce Sterling. 'Ecology and the Politics of Change'
Author, journalist, editor and critic (Texas and Serbia)

Panel Discussion
THE LURE OF THE 'ECO'
Eco-art, eco-fashion, eco-tourism, eco-politics, eco-activism, eco-village ... In almost every aspect of how and where we live, work and play, the eco has embedded itself. How has what we mean by ecology transformed and evolved through the practice of everyday life?
Chair: Jeremy Bendik-Keymer (Philosophy teacher in the Department of International Studies, AUS)
Sarah Rich (Managing Editor, Worldchanging and inhabitat.com, a weblog covering sustainable design and green building, Seatle)
Sergio Vega (Artist, Gainesville; participating in Sharjah Biennial 8)
Siobhan Leyden (producer and presenter of the daily talk show 'Siobhan Live' on Dubai Eye radio, 103.8 FM)
Stephanie Mahmoud (Marketing and Management student, AUS)

FILM PROGRAMME EXCERPT
Riverglass: A River Ballet in Four Seasons
Andrej Zdravi, 1997 (41 mins)
"Riverglass presents the 'materiality' of the river Soca. A symbol of importance in Slovenian culture, the film presents the force and clarity of the water from the point of view of the river itself, a Gaian perspective possibly. In its content and development of specialist filming equipment it recalls other film-makers landscape interventions (for instance Michael Snow's La Region Centrale (1970) or Robert Beaver's The Stoas, (1991-97)."
Mark Nash

Parallel Seminars
I. EMERGENCIES AND RISK
What is the role of architects, designers and artists concerning housing and communities? With increasing pressure on resources and space, and an increasingly volatile political climate how can we move from coping with aftermaths to try to mitigate risk before crises? Can design and architecture be a political act?

Moderator: Mehdi Sabet (Associate Professor, Architecture & Interior Design, School of Architecture and Design, AUS)
Susi Platt (Architecture for Humanity's leading post-Tsunami reconstruction designer, Sri Lanka)
Michael Rakowitz (Artist, New York; participating in Sharjah Biennial 8)

II. RESOURCES: TRUTH AND MATERIALS
How far are recycled or sustainable materials a consideration for artists, designers and architects? How do such considerations affect our experience/ percepetion of materiality in art and the built environment? And how does this relate to wider questions of resources– water, energy, etc.?

Moderator: Mona El Mousfi (Sharjah Biennial architect and Assistant Professor, School of Architecture and Design, AUS)
Michael Braungart (Designer and Chemist, co-author of 'Cradle to Cradle. Remaking the way we make things', Hamburg/ Charlottesville)
Tomás Saraceno (Artist and architect, Frankfurt; participating in Sharjah Biennial 8)

IN CONVERSATION
Kumar Shahani: Politics and the ecology of change
Mark Nash (curator of Sharjah Biennial 8 film programme; Director of the MA Curating Contemporary Art at the Royal College of Art, London) and Geeta Kapur (Critic and Curator, New Delhi, and member of the Jury for the 2007 Sharjah Biennial 8 Art Prize) in conversation about the work of Indian filmmaker Kumar Shahani.

Friday 6 April

Panel discussion
OFFSETTING / UPSETTING. 'ART VS ISSUES'
Much work in the field of art and ecology has emerged in the field of remedial actions in industrial sites. Today carbon trading and offsetting are, more abstractly, being proposed as a way of restoring the balance of the atmosphere. How might these two motions be linked? How or should the work of some artists might generally be regarded as a form of offsetting or redressing? How do some artists desire tangible palliative results, while others offer strategies of friction or resistance? What is more important, the issues or the art?

Chair: Stephanie Smith (Director of Collections and Exhibitions, Curator of Contemporary Art, Smart Museum of Art, University of Chicago)
Koyo Kouoh (Critic and curator, Dakar)
Peter Fend (Artist, Berlin; participating in Sharjah Biennial 8)
Charles Esche (Director, Van Abbemuseum, Eindhoven and member of the Jury for the 2007 Sharjah Biennial 8 Art Prize)

Jonathan Watkins (Co-curator, Sharjah Biennial 8; Director Ikon Gallery, Birmingham) and Cornelia Parker (Artist, London; participating in Sharjah Biennial 8) to introduce Parker's project for Sharjah Biennial 8:
VIDEO INTERVIEW WITH NOAM CHOMSKY
Followed by Q+A from the audience.

Saturday 7 April

ARTISTS' PRESENTATION
e-Xplo with Ayreen Anastas (Artists, US/Austria; participating in the Sharjah Biennial 8)

Panel discussion
URBAN PLANNING AND THE FUTURE CITY
What is the future of the city as a habitat for humanity? Increasingly dense housing, commercial, cultural, infrastructural and civic spaces seem to contradict our desire for space, openness and freedom. What lies ahead for the city as a living, symbiotic form of inanimate structure and animate inhabitants?

Chair: George Katodrytis (Architect; Professor of Architecture, School of Architecture and Design, AUS)
Samir Srouji (Artist, Palestine; participating in Sharjah Biennial 8)
Rula Sadik (General Manager, Design and Planning, The Design Group, Nakheel, Dubai)
Samer Kamal (Founder, Bee'ah, Sharjah Environmental Company, Sharjah)

SB8 SYMPOSIUM PARTICIPANTS
Bruce Sterling *Keynote Speaker, Author, Journalist, Editor and Critic*
Jeremy Bendik-Keymer *Assistant Professor of International Studies, AUS College of Arts and Sciences*
Sarah Rich *Managing Editor, Worldchanging and inhabitat.com, a weblog covering sustainable design and green building*
Sergio Vega *Artist; participating in Sharjah Biennial 8*
Siobhan Leyden *producer and presenter of the daily talk show 'Siobhan Live' on Dubai Eye radio, 103.8 FM*
Stephanie Mahmoud *Marketing and Management student, AUS*
Mehdi Sabet *AUS School of Architecture and Design, Associate Professor, Architecture & Interior Design*
Susi Platt *Architecture for Humanity's leading post-Tsunami reconstruction designer*
Michael Rakowitz *Artist; participating in Sharjah Biennial 8*
Michael Braungart *Designer and Chemist*
Mona El Mousfi *Sharjah Biennial architect and AUS School of Architecture and Design, Assistant Professor*
Tomas Saraceno *Artist; participating in Sharjah Biennial 8*
Mark Nash *curator of Sharjah Biennial 8 film programme; Director of the MA Curating Contemporary Art at the Royal College of Art, London*
Geeta Kapur *Critic and Curator, New Delhi, and member of the Jury for the 2007 Sharjah Biennial 8 Art Prize*
Stephanie Smith *Director of Collections and Exhibitions, Curator of Contemporary Art, Smart Museum of Art, University of Chicago*
Koyo Kouoh *Critic and curator, Dakar*
Peter Fend *Artist; participating in Sharjah Biennial 8*
Charles Esche *Director, Van Abbemuseum, Eindhoven and member of the Jury for the 2007 Sharjah Biennial 8 Art Prize*
Jonathan Watkins *Co-curator, Sharjah Biennial 8*
Cornelia Parker *Artist; participating in Sharjah Biennial 8*
George Katodrytis *Architect; AUS School of Architecture and Design, Professor of Architecture*
Samir Srouji *Architect & Artist; participating in Sharjah Biennial 8*
Rula Sadik *General Manager, Design and Planning, The Design Group, Nakheel*
Samer Kamal *Founder, Bee'ah, Sharjah Environmental Company*
Michaela Crimmin *RSA Arts and Ecology Director*
e-Xplo *Artist; participating in Sharjah Biennial 8*
Ayreen Anastas *Artist; participating in Sharjah Biennial 8*

UNESCO programme

The Sharjah Biennial had partnered with UNESCO to stimulate wider involvement in particularly the main issue of sustainable urban environment and its inter-cultural interpretation. Young artists around the world have been invited to conceive and design creative projects that are integral to their unique observations and reflections on urban spaces and its communities and that cultivate artistic transformation with new forms of digital expression. In this regard the UNESCO had dedicated the UNESCO Prize for the Promotion of the Arts to recognize an outstanding art work among the projects submitted by the commissioned artists of the Sharjah Biennial 8, under the theme of "STILL LIFE: Art, Ecology and the Politics of Change".

The selection of the UNESCO Prize winner will be undertaken by an international jury, officially appointed by the Director-General of UNESCO, assembling five jury members representing 5 geo-cultural regions (Asia/Pacific, Latin America/Caribbean, Africa, Arab States, Europe/North America) with the support of respective representatives of the co-organizers UNESCO and the Sharjah Biennial.

UNESCO coordinators
Tereza Wagner
Doyun Lee

International Jury Members
Abdellah Karroum (Morocco)
Berni Searle (South Africa)
Eugenio Tisselli Vélez (Mexico)
Jean Gagnon (Canada)
Soh Yeong Roh (Republic of Korea)

Within the framework of the cooperation between UNESCO and the Sharjah Biennial, an international educators' workshop will be organized in line with the 8th edition of the Sharjah Biennial.

The workshop will run for 5 days by the professional media artist-trainer who is the laureate of the UNESCO Prize for the Promotion of the Arts 2007 in the category of "arts related to technologies". The participants of the workshop will be 3 local/regional Arab educators and 3 international educators with the following profile: teachers of upper secondary schools teaching subjects of English, history, geography, arts, music, computer science, etc, as well as educators in youth clubs, ICT training centres.

Participating teachers
Ahmed Nabli
Francisca Marques
Joumana Abboud
Nilgun Arikan
Sherine Said
Sudesh Mantillake

Intellectual and creative identities are as diverse as human cultures and environments. However, creative discourse generally seeks to find a common ground between different people. It is a discourse that transcends restricted identities, one that is closely knit to the core of human existence on the face of this Earth.

The department of culture and information, within its overall directives, is attempting to contribute to this creative human scene in accordance with the comprehensive, wise, and humanitarian initiatives of his Highness Sheikh Dr. Sultan Bin Mohammed Al Qasimi, Member of the Supreme Council and Ruler of Sharjah. The Sharjah Biennial clearly reflects the constant wish to open up to modern creative structures, hoping to achieve a cultural harmony, while constantly searching for the quintessence of new visual arts and their intellectual propositions.

The Biennial, every two years, adopts a theme closely connected to international human concerns and urgent issues. Such is the theme of Sharjah Biennial 8: *Still Life: Art, Environment and the Politics of Change*, a vital and important topic, especially at these crucial times of the history of humanity, where life is threatened by several environmental dangers and catastrophes. This Biennial attempts to make its own contribution to the issue at hand, in an aesthetic, spiritual, and intellectual sense, connecting social, creative and international issues with the specific local environment.

Department of Culture and Information
Government of Sharjah

CONTENTS

AN ECOLOGY OF CHOICE...

Hoor Al Qasimi

The theme of this year's Biennial stems out of a need to re-negotiate and re-locate the issues of both art and ecology to a touchable realm, almost to appropriate both by bringing them together; an attempt to invite to this act of pondering a public that has been alienated from both. We aspire that this Biennial will aggravate a common questioning; where everyone simultaneously will have the chance to at least think difference, if not will it. As pondering is located in this void between action and surrender, it trembles in that space where one does not have to act, but also where one takes action to no limit. Let us slip in that place between sleep and awakening, that transitory moment that allows for interference and consider this Biennial a brief historical moment of hesitant intervention.

We all have different approaches to the issues at hand; and the urgency is to gather around this theme, to exchange not only ideas but roles, to negotiate the difference not only without but also within. Let us form an ecology of choice, let this biennial be an invitation not to find "the solution", but to understand what is at stake, why and how we can create an alternative discourse to an otherwise official stance.

It is no coincidence that Sharjah embraces this great event, for our Emirate is built on the respect of its local traditions and culture, and is committed to employing a humanitarian culture capable of bonding with wider common concerns and worries, and capable of posing new questions. In this context the Biennial attempts to expand the limits of traditions and austere ideas into a wider international horizon and a stronger humanistic weave. We hope that this space allows for a dialectic between traditions and new values, promoting a mechanism of critique. It is for this reason that the Biennial has become the platform for an open discussion for various parts of the Arab region and the world.

We attempt at the Sharjah Biennial 8 to entwine hesitance with action and to seek alternative creative narratives that weave into our desire to change this destructive and totalitarian approach towards this quilt of water and soil. In this sense this Biennial wishes to transcend the air of a fleeting art exhibition, and open up to be more than a visual space, or a transit station for art lovers and artists... It becomes a space and means for contemplation, reconsideration, and reluctant interventions. It is an attempt to offer a harmonious disruptive site for an intellectual and creative discourse that is simultaneously receptive to the various components of this age and its pressing issues.

(NOT DELIVERANCE)

Jack Persekian

The Sharjah Biennial 8 has undertaken the exigent task of addressing some of the ecological challenges confronting the world today, from the perspective of art and through the involvement of artists in various areas and on several levels: environmental, social, political, cultural, individual, etc. At first glance, this might seem restrictive and insensitive, or powerless in the face of the pressing issues and calamities presently raging in our region (the Middle East and the Arab world). It is the winter of 2007 and the list is hefty: Palestine, Lebanon, Syria, Iraq, Iran, Afghanistan, Sudan, the "War on Terror," nuclear armament, disarmament, sectarian and factional violence, assassinations, corruption, renditions, lawlessness, illiteracy, poverty, child labour, human rights, democracy, and on and on. As Jean-Luc Nancy wrote in the summer of 1995 in the introduction to his book *Being Singular Plural*:

> *It is an endless list, and everything happens in such a way that one is reduced to keeping accounts but never taking the final toll. It is a litany, a prayer of pure sorrow and pure loss, the plea that falls from the lips of millions of refugees every day; whether they be deportees, people besieged, those who are mutilated, people who starve, who are raped, ostracised, excluded, exiled, expelled.*[1]

In this part of the world, even the simplest terms we use to discuss ecology and the environment are elusive. In Palestine, for instance, the signifier "land"—ever precious and revered, and, more often than not, the motivation for people to kill or die—has become like a landfill, its original content emptied and replaced with detritus; thus debased, the word now exists as merely a strategic idiom in political speech, granted valour and respect only in games of rhetoric or nationalist sloganeering. Moreover, most of the signifiers that coin our existence, the environment in which we live, the paradigms that underpin our humanity, have become "landfills" as well. Organised crime corrodes social relations; violence, aggression, and treachery dominate the lived experience of our everyday. Auditory and visual pollution are rampant. "Post-political cynicism,"[2] as Gary Genosko phrased it, spreads torpor amongst citizens, and the body of ethical principles that we set as cornerstones on which to build our world has been usurped so casually that the moral fibre of social systems threatens to collapse.

When witnessing a calamity, whether natural or human-induced, my mother tirelessly rants, "The end of the world is near." Beyond wide-scale apathy towards the consequences of our deeds on our environment and ever diminishing prospects for an equitable sustainable existence for all on this planet, my mother's prophecy of doom unmasks the more sinister face of our humanity, namely, the desire for sheer destruction. Speaking of destruction, Mona Al Mousfi, the architect for the Sharjah Biennials 7 and 8, noted in one of our conversations that the body of threats from which humanity needs to be protected has changed markedly in the last hundred years, from hazards or dangers caused by nature to those caused by human beings. Man needs to be protected from man. From a psycho-emotional perspective (hence deterministic to the point of fatalism) one could revert to Jean Baudrillard's postulate that human beings' destructive tendencies stem from a desire to witness the end, given that they were not present at the beginning.

> *We will never get to know the original chaos, the Big Bang... because it is a classified event. We had never been there. We could retain the hope however, of seeing the final moment, the Big Crumb, one day. A*

1 *Being Singular Plural*. Trans. Robert D. Richardson and Anne E. O'Byrne. Stanford, California: Stanford University Press, 2000, p. xiii

2 "Prospects for a Transdisciplinary Ecology." Paper delivered at the RSA, London, 27 April 2005

spasmodic enjoyment of the end to compensate for not having had the chance to revere the beginning [l'origine]. *These are the only two interesting moments, and since we were frustrated with the first one, we invest all the more energy into the acceleration of the end, into the precipitation of things or events towards their ultimate loss...*[3]

The brave new world that we were supposed to achieve with scientific and technological progress has, in the end, served only to subdue nature, exploit its resources, devour its flesh, and forecast its outbursts. And if one tries to elucidate where things went awry, the answers invariably go back to the human agent, whose greed and unbridled exploitation of nature and its resources has driven colonialism, imperialism, racism, and capitalism.

We can illustrate this point with the example of oil spills (mindful, of course, that this project, this Biennial, is fuelled by the vast oil resources of the Emirates). We *know* that tankers are prone to accidents, that they are driven to breakdown by the unquenchable thirst for oil. Yet, in incidence after incidence, we regard oil spills as accidents, acceptable happenstances of the economy of the oil trade and of our lifestyles. Worse yet, the consequence of an oil spill is regarded matter-of-factly, with a "life goes on" shrug of indifference.

While the grand and visible issues of ecology (such as natural catastrophes and global warming) ought to be addressed, they should not eclipse or diminish issues on the level of social relations, culture, and politics. In his book, *The Three Ecologies*, Félix Guattari proposed a "transversal" approach for thinking about the ecologies he identified:

Now more than ever, nature cannot be separated from culture; in order to comprehend the interactions between ecosystems, the mechanosphere and the social and individual Universes of references, we must learn to think "transversally."... Just as monstrous and mutant algae invade the lagoon of Venice, so our television screens are populated, saturated, by "degenerate" images and statements [énoncés].[4]

These intersecting, cross-fertilizing forms of pollution–mental, visual, auditory–still go unnoticed by official and non-official bodies mandated with protecting the living environment. They are not yet very visible, and thus their harmful impact on people, habitats, and societies is not yet measurable, but they need to be identified and brought to the fore. The ecology of the social sphere, or "social ecology," calls for attention as well. Using the example of real estate developers, Guattari rather hyperbolically warned that:

...men like Donald Trump are permitted to proliferate freely, like another species of algae, taking over entire districts of New York and Atlantic City; he "redevelops" by raising rents, thereby driving out tens of thousands of poor families, most of whom are condemned to homelessness, becoming the equivalent of the dead fish of environmental ecology.[5]

We are living a historical moment when things are changing quickly, unpredictably it would seem. References generated by globalization replace modernist and post-modernist ones. The software age transforms ideas of nature and artifice, and relations of space and time are renegotiated. We can now digitally detach from the once constitutive elements of our subjectivity (as, for instance, avatars on the internet or in computer games). We are propelled into a "chaos-world", as Édouard Glissant observed, "a kind of universal erratics, an anti-systemic celebration of chaos and *errance*."[6] Such is the new world order.

[3] Jean Baudrillard. *Hystericizing the Millennium, L'Illusion de la fin: ou La greve des evenements.* Trans. Charles Dudas. Paris: Galilee, 1992, http://www.egs.edu/faculty/baudrillard/baudrillard-hystericizing-the-millennium.html, (12/12/06).

[4] Félix Guattari. *The Three Ecologies.* Trans. Ian Pindar and Paul Sutton. New Brunswick, New Jersey: The Athlone Press, 2000, p. 43

[5] Ibid.

[6] Quoted in Peter Hallward. *Absolutely Postcolonial.* Manchester, England: Manchester University Press, 2001, p. xvii

FURNISHED APARTMENTS

"We live in a time in which we can no longer impose conditions on the world," Glissant wrote.[7] Where does this leave us and what is to be done? Between the notion of trying to change the world, give it a future, and going with the flow, we, the Sharjah Biennial team, see our role as opening possibilities, providing the means, and establishing the platform for individuals and groups (artists, intellectuals, thinkers, activists, politicians, bureaucrats, scientists, people at large) to raise awareness of pressing ecological issues and sound the alarm. It is high time these issues were taken seriously, not only by specialists and interested parties, but also by the general public. These issues should "stop being associated with the image of a small nature-loving minority or with qualified specialists,"[8] as Guattari advocated. We intend to build a critical mass of unpretentious propositions that aim at disturbing prevailing complacency, and eroding the lustre of fake progress and its fictitious promise of paradisiac bliss on earth. At the same time, we intend to present works that embody alternative methodologies in thought and assessment, and models compatible with increased awareness of our endangered ecology. We want to bring art back into the process of social, economic, cultural, sustainable development without relinquishing ethical and aesthetic considerations.

We see the role of the artist as fundamental, pivotal. In contrast with scientists and analysts, artists have the freedom to experiment with intellectual inquiry beyond the pressures of market imperatives, where models "do not need to be tested, and found wanting, in terms of profitability or market share because [they have] no purchase on these terms."[9] The artists' autonomous free zone is, nevertheless, tied to a market economy (which rides the tide of every booming wave in the stock market and every gush of millionaires and billionaires) but articulated under different terms. Unbound by the narrow purviews of fields of specialization and the rigid adherence to equations and formulas, artists can bridge and connect between disciplines transversally. And they can propose networks and models that interrogate lifestyles and practices critically.

Our premise for this Biennial was simple and straightforward: we invited a number of modest proposals addressing issues of ecology in the social, economic, political, and environmental contexts. We expected to receive a barrage of criticism and indictments of the excessively consumerist lifestyle, apathy, and inconsiderate urban development in the Emirates. This has been invariably the case with all artists who have come here on exploratory visits. Our challenge is thus to sustain an ongoing dialogue with profoundly critical works and remain positive, to continue to invest in the creative ability of artists to innovate and imagine bold, sustainable, and engaging work. One possible response came to us from outside the Biennial's immediate sphere of activities and exhibitions, namely, carbon off-setting. When I met with one of the artists participating in the Biennial, she posed carbon off-setting as a condition to her boarding a plane to travel to Sharjah. She mentioned a few companies that calculate the cost of the amount of carbon spewed in the air by the plane for the length of the flight, and identify projects in which an equivalent sum is invested into "off-setting" by increasing carbon dioxide absorption. We also were motivated to raise awareness amongst the wider public of the environmental imperatives that call for immediate action at the most basic levels of the conduct of everyday life, and so we sought contact with Samer Kamal, a local entrepreneur, whose endeavours to introduce the practice of recycling in Sharjah seemed to have a meaningful connection to our desire to offset our contribution to global pollution. Kamal was looking for an aesthetic approach to render recycling bins attractive to Sharjah residents and had managed to earn the endorsement of official bodies for his project, as well as to win over partners in the private sector to his cause. The artist concerned with carbon off-setting and Samer Kamal, whose endeavours could only intersect in the context of the Biennial, emblematise how we envision the Biennial as proposing scenarios with positive outcomes and modalities for dealing with the ecological imperatives that press on our lives.

7 Ibid.

8 Guattari, op. cit., p. 52

9 Charles Esche, Modest Proposals, Selected Writings (ed. Sercan Özkaya), Baglam Press, Istanbul, 2005

10 Hallward, op. cit., p. 7

But it may seem naïve to believe that a biennial of art could reverse the trend or bring tangible positive impact. We are aware that the exponential increase of populations (particularly in underprivileged areas) eclipses all attempts to mend the damage or to reverse apathy and the mindset of "feudal anachronism, the opacity of local customs, and stubborn nativism."[10] Therefore, to side with Baudrillard's psycho-emotional outlook, yet stay tethered by rational assumptions, and in light of the current state of unpredictability, I would think that whatever we do–be it damage, deplete, erode, consume, exhume, pollute, destroy, derange, deface, despise, contain, constrain, occupy, terrorise, harm, spoil, spill, litter, corrupt, contaminate, or attempt to mend, amend, alter, fix, change, improve, condition, control, glue, develop, secure, repair, revamp, renovate, better–the world has its own safeguards and logic of sustaining equilibrium that transcend the actions and abilities of man. Yet systematically tipping the balance and disrupting the mechanisms of this self-sustaining equilibrium will (if it has not already) overwhelm the universe's ability to self-adjust. So if we would refer back to Newton's Third Law–that every action has an equal and opposite reaction–then our reprieve (not deliverance) from the wrath of the earth is through doing whatever we can to defer the end, denying what Baudrillard referred to as our "spasmodic enjoyment," and hoping against hope for salvation from apocalypse.

I am greatly indebted to Rasha Salti for reading this essay and pointing out several weaknesses and errors of thought, and to Joseph R. Wolin for editing the text.

ENVIRONMENTAL CONTEXT

Mohammad Kazem

The population of Earth is increasing daily. The resources and natural materials in the world are being severely drained to the degree where they no longer suffice to support the needs of human beings on the planet. All living creatures, small and large, have become severely exhausted because of war and political and economic instability at the international level. Natural power reserves are continuously diminishing. The general environmental climate is polluted. Diseases of all shapes, types and various names are not only attacking humans but also animals, birds and fish. Even iron, copper and other natural resources are threatened. The seas, forests, valleys, and rivers are all polluted, as are the clouds and the rain. Numerous issues relating to the environmental problem not only concern the surface of Earth but have also caused calcification of the human brain. Human beings have various intellectual capabilities - not everyone is able to digest and understand intellectual and cultural matters that affect the political, social and economic environment of society. This concerns the individual's ability to present issues of the self, and the ability of social institutions, in their different branches, to re-form this self-ness into social accomplishments. Furthermore, there is the pollution of space and the hemisphere with images, information, chats, talks, and news which are mostly fictitious and terribly cheap as they float through exterior space and appear before us like genies, day and night.

It is known that nature, "Planet Earth", is the source of all wealth. It is well stacked with materials in many different places. There are places that we like and visit, and we legitimise them as sacred locations that we make holy for religious reasons. Therefore, we protect them, love them and adorn them with gold, precious stones and attractive perfumes; we defend them and fight for them; we stand close to them. There are harsh locations on Planet Earth which are a part of nature we cannot escape, such as high mountains, waterfalls, frightening deserts bare of plants and water. There are locations we try our best to avoid, such as volcanoes, and others threatened by earthquakes and floods, and there are other dangerous natural places. We destroy some of the sites in this natural environment we live in, such as mountains, hills, valleys and natural beaches, in order to build in their place new structures like high towers, ports, high-tech farms, modern cities and all that follows to cope with modern life.

We dismantle the environment of the traditions and old myths of human anthropology by studying the origins of the human race, its development, races, customs, and beliefs and reformulating them anew in order to withstand self-criticism and create an interactive relationship with the environment we live in. We explain all environmental issues in the context of modern language and values and of new human experiences. We study the science of "prophecy" in order to understand the relationships between living creatures and their environment.

The surroundings of Planet Earth contain in themselves the meaning of life and death, and the beautiful and sad moments. We live out our youth, along with other creatures, after which we die and rot in the heart of this mother planet. We strive to leave behind our traces and etchings; we carve and write our notes, suggestions and hopes on the face of the planet, and we combine them with natural scenes. Yet, despite all this, we violate the space of this environment in which we find ourselves.

Since the beginning of the twentieth century until today, more than fifty schools or genres of art or cultural modes ending in "ism" have appeared. Have these "isms" brought about an environment suitable for the life of individual humans or other creatures? Will isolation and being shut away in a closed workshop, immersed in painting a tragic scene depicting the present situation, save humanity from ruin?

The issue of the environment is a complex one. There are political, economic, psychological, health-related, commercial, and consumer environments. We live in different risky environmental spaces; do we expect a new environmental event? Can the context of contemporary art create a seemly environment? The answers to all these questions lie in the fact that the environment itself is venturing into and being immersed in the process of the experiment, to intentionally choose contemporary aesthetic missions.

Between the 18th and 19th centuries, technological inventions were booming. They were intended to relieve human toil. Among such inventions were the steam engine, electricity and the train. Radical social change and the emergence of new ideas in human history totally revolutionised humankind's attitudes and understanding. The work of art became compatible with the other sciences.

Such change cannot be achieved without hard struggle or comprehending the contamination of culture prevalent in society. It requires an overhaul of the education system: the education authority decides the future of coming generations. The development of cultural and educational institutions, along with the introduction of the cultural statement of contemporary art into the education curriculum, guarantees that coming generations are able to welcome and embrace all that is new.

GLOBAL WARMING READY?[1]

Eva Scharrer

It might sound somewhat ironic - it is certainly a real challenge - to organise a biennial on the subject of "Art and Ecology" in the U.A.E. This is at a time when global climate change is no longer future prophecy but has long replaced global terrorism in the daily headlines as the new big threat facing the world today - the latest official proof of which came out on February 2nd 2007 with the publication of the IPCC's UN climate report. And this biennial happens at a place that was basically conjured out of the desert, whose economy and wealth is mainly based on fossil fuels, and where in nearby Dubai gigantomanic constructions are underway, interfering in existing ecosystems with as yet unpredictable consequences. Why care about the earth if you can build your own?[2] And that's not to speak about the increasing amount of art-world air travel, especially in a year when cultural mega-events like the Moscow Biennial, the Venice Biennial, Documenta 12, Sculpture Projects Münster, the Istanbul Biennial, and countless other biennials and art fairs accumulate to a global art marathon, more frantic than ever. I have myself just recently joined, as a result of my field trips to Sharjah, the frequent-flyer league - and I have to admit, it was not without feeling guilty. The dilemma stares us in the face, and it clearly cannot be faced simply with good intentions. Or put differently: how to conceptualise ecological consciousness (I assume we all do have it somewhere) with the joyfulness, the critical distrustfulness, and the aesthetics of contemporary art?

Recently, various exhibitions have shed light on the different ways in which art engages in ecological concerns: "Groundworks: Environmental Collaboration in Contemporary Art" at the Carnegie Mellon University in Pittsburg featured artworks as "case studies in social, ecological change"; "Beyond Green. Towards a Sustainable Art" at the Smart Museum of Art in Chicago explored sustainable strategies in contemporary art and design, with a focus on collaborative and community-based works; entitled "Ecotopia", the 2nd ICP triennial of photography and video in New York presented contemporary artists' views of the natural world in a climate of change; while for "The Ship: the Art of Climate Change" at London's Natural History Museum a group of artists were invited on a voyage to the melting glaciers in the Arctic at Cape Farewell (all exhibitions took place 2005/2006). More recently, "More than this: Voices and Expressions on Sustainability" at gallery KIT in Norway once more aimed to explore the role of art in relation to sustainable development. Furthermore, initiatives like the R.S.A.'s Arts and Ecology Programme brought together artists and scientists to discuss possibilities of ecologically and socially responsible practices in the fields of art, architecture and urban planning via symposia and publications.[3]

"Can Art save the Planet?" was the appropriate headline on the front page of last year's August issue of *Art Review*, also referred to as "the green issue" Interestingly enough, having languished on the fringes of social attention for a long time, a new wave of popular environmentalism or eco-chic has recently swept through the media.[4] After sustainability was the new hype in design, various life-style and high-gloss fashion magazines like *Elle*, *Vogue*, or *Vanity Fair* also launched their "green issues" in 2006. So if politicians and environmentalists have failed to save the planet so far, perhaps the fashion lobby will, for having the better arguments, as futurologist Bruce Sterling tartly analysed.[5]

No matter how *vogue* or *non-vogue* the topic may be, beyond that it is quite serious. Unfortunately, the answer to the above question will most likely be no. But even if art does not necessarily change the way in which people behave - and we are not quite in the position to tell anyone what's right or wrong - it might have the potential to infiltrate and provoke people's thoughts. We like to believe in

1 Title borrowed from the recent Diesel campaign, which quite cynically featured fashion for hipsters in the times of climate change.

2 For the „World" islands by the Dubai waterfront alone, one billion cubic feet of sand are being moved, and whole mountains are carried from one side of the country to the other. Read also Mike Davis, *Sinister Paradise* (2005), http://www.tomdispatch.com/index.mhtml?pid=5807

3 The R.S.A.'s Arts & Ecology Conference "No Way Back?" took place at the London School of Economics in December 2006, on the occasion of which also the book *Land, Art: A Cultural Ecology Handbook*, edited by Max Andrews and published by R.S.A. in partnership with Arts Council England, London 2006, was launched. Part two of the conference will follow at the American University of Sharjah, organised in collaboration with the R.S.A., London, and Latitudes, Barcelona, in April 2007

4 Just one example is Al Gore's *An Inconvenient Truth*, which everybody I know has seen on board a plane, to make the irony perfect.

5 Bruce Sterling, "Hot Trends: Climate Change in the Glossies", in *Land, Art: A Cultural Ecology Handbook*, ibid, pp. 111-15

the role of art as a trigger for emotional understanding, a catalyst and "a framing device for visual and/or social experience."[6]

Contemporary art practice has become a continually expanding, interdisciplinary and multiple science-embracing field of activity, which is in itself as diverse and trans-disciplinary as the cultural understanding of the term "ecology" (in its plural sense) has become during the past decades. The French philosopher, activist and psychoanalyst Félix Guattari in his *Three Ecologies* distinguishes between environmental, social and mental ecology[7] - a range from the macro to the micro level, which could be further extended to multiple other fields, such as the political, cultural etc. - and thus pleads for a transversal approach of dealing with ecological issues. Pollution is not just a gas in the air, it is something that inhabits and affects all aspects of human existence. In a similar transversal understanding, artist Joachim Koester refers to his contribution to SB8, a film based on animated mescaline drawings by Henri Michaux, as "ecology of the mind" - a journey into the outskirts of the inner world. Furthermore, along with the breaching of the term "ecology", also the concept of "environmentalism" and "the environment" per se have been scrutinized and fundamentally challenged:

> *The concepts of "nature" and "environment" have been thoroughly deconstructed. Yet they retain their mythic and debilitating power within the environmental movement and the public at large. If one understands the notion of the "environment" to include humans, then the way the environmental community designates certain problems as environmental and others as not is completely arbitrary. Why, for instance, is a human-made phenomenon like global warming – which may kill hundreds of millions of human beings over the next century – considered "environmental"? Why are poverty and war not considered environmental problems while global warming is?*[8]

Artist Gustav Metzger already stated in 1992 that the term "environmental" today means "everything and nothing", and therefore would be better dropped in favour of more precise definitions.[9] In short, we are confronted with a mess of interrelated terminology, multiple meanings, confused concepts, failed ideologies and the recent phenomenon of fashionably "going green" - or lucrative "green-washing" - while facing a global situation where the hands of the virtual clock point at five to twelve - or is it past twelve already?

In these frenzied times, when the urge for fundamental change is hindered by stubborn politicians, global power players and their lobbies, and environmentalists who still see the environment as a "thing" to be protected, but one which is detached from everything else, perhaps artists have the ability to tackle things differently. Within its own, however limited means, art can sometimes take a short cut by circumventing or slipping through institutional barriers, employing science without the burden of scientific stringency, or slowing down the pace by introducing a sense of poetry, or poetic disobedience, to the ways of global economics. It is not about presenting ad-hoc solutions for saving the planet; it's about creating an image and an experience to sharpen sensibilities with regard to our relationship with and our impact on the earth - bearing in mind the social, political, economic and mental dimensions of "ecology".

Will the Sharjah Biennial 8, entitled "Still Life: Art, Ecology and the Politics of Change", hence establish itself as "the green biennial", as some magazines have already quipped? It's doubtful. In fact, it might at times even appear to be the opposite, and the sincere environmentalists will probably disagree with us. Just as the still life genre in art history is a memento mori as much it is in praise of the gifts of nature, SB8's title alludes to more than just one single reading. And if art is said to be a potential mirror of society, then perhaps this biennial might not even

6 The expression was borrowed from Lucy Lippard, "Beyond the Beauty Strip", in *Land, Art. A Cultural Ecology Handbook*, ibid, p. 14

7 Félix Guattari, *The Three Ecologies*, London (2000) (orig. *Les trios ecologies*, Paris, 1989); see also: Gary Genosco, "Prospects for a Transdisciplinary Ecology", paper delivered for the R.S.A.'s Ecology and Artistic Practice Symposium, London, April 2005

8 Michael Shellenberger and Ted Nordhaus, "The Death of Environmentalism: Global Warming Politics in a Post-Environmental World" (2004), www.thebreakthrough.org/ images/ Death_of_Environmentalism.pdf, p.12

9 Gustav Metzger suggests dropping the term "Environment" and instead to speak of "nature" and "damaged nature" in his essay "Nature demised resurrects as environment", in Gustav Metzger, *Damaged Nature, Auto-destructive Art*, London (1996), from which an excerpt was used here as the artist's statement.

be (self-)destructive and contaminating enough to fulfil this function.

Of course this thought is hypothetical. Arguably, as organisers and curators, we do have a certain responsibility when addressing such a threateningly serious and hyper-actual subject. Issues like sustainability should - ideally - be primary thoughts in every step of conception, production and transportation. Not only for SB8, but also for all museums, art fairs and biennials, and indeed, for every company and every human being from now on. Without question, this asks for a radical u-turn and provides an immense challenge when operating within pre-fabricated conditions and within an always too tight time-span. Accordingly, the selected artists and projects raise questions rather than come up with solutions. Or they might present solutions for questions that have not even been articulated.

The projects commissioned for the Sharjah Biennial 8 range from the utopian to the disturbing, from the invisible to the spectacular, from ephemeral gesture to critical mass. They take off into the clouds, and dive down into the sea. Via strategies of deconstruction, reconstruction, and contamination, by applying research, activist and documentary methods, but also through the use of metaphor, humour and play, the selected artists comment on our ways of production and consumption, and make visible some of the daily absurdities within which society today exists.

Having a theme superimposed, which is so challenging and uncompromising at the same time, the choice of artists was not an easy exercise. There were obvious choices and less obvious. Some of the artists I have invited for SB8 have addressed issues like the destruction of nature, recycling and sustainability, eco-systems and global economies for a long time, with different foci and strategies, though none of them has the desire to be necessarily labelled as an "eco" or "green" artist. Many of the selected artists have worked in an expanded field on the intersections of art, activism and design, however, the focus here was on the individual work of art, rather than on putting together a fair for alternative energies, community gardens, sustainable design and new building methods. We are aware some relevant individual and collaborative artistic attempts (e.g. groups like Free Soil, Futurefarmers, Learning Group, Superflex, Vitamin Creative Space) concerned with ecological issues are not represent here, also due to the fact they have been featured already in some of the before mentioned shows and publications.

And though many relevant predecessors and art historical movements of the 1960s and 70s here had to be left out (I am thinking, for instance, of Land Art, and of artists like Robert Smithson, Richard Long, Gordon Matta-Clark, Joseph Beuys or Hans Haacke...), the lineage of an ecologically concerned art practice goes back even to pre-environmentalist times.

An artist like Gustav Metzger, who already in 1959 had developed the term "auto-destructive art", by definition "a form of public art for industrial societies",[10] as an answer to the post-war and cold war conditions of his time, today appears almost prophetic. Mierle Laderman Ukeles has performed her "Touch Sanitation Handshake Ritual", where she personally thanked each individual NYC sanitation worker for keeping New York City alive, between 1977 and 1980, and still keeps up a vital engagement in the issue of labour and the use of landfills. Peter Fend, founder of the Ocean Earth Development Corporation in 1980, has long since dedicated his ongoing, in-depth research on water and natural resources to the Gulf Basin. Chicago-based artist Dan Peterman has also developed an ecological and socially engaged art practice since the early 1980s, and has been influential for a younger generation of artists like Tue Greenfort, who answers complex economic and ecological coherences with playful, minimal, yet sharply analytic gestures. Notions of energy and entropy are central thoughts also in the poetic-conceptual work of Simon Starling, who proposed a literally self-engulfing (nevertheless quite comedic) boat trip to SB8's sombre theme.

[10] Gustav Metzger, "Autodestructive Art", London, 4th November 1959 in *Gustav Metzger*, Catalogue, Museum of Modern Art, Oxford 1999, p. 26

Artists Marjetica Potrc, Michael Rakowitz and Tomas Saraceno work on the intersections of art, design, and architecture: Potrc with a focus on self-sustainability and field work; Rakowitz intertwining architecture, historical fact and physical air-flow as metaphors for political and economical power-play; and Saraceno following the visions of architectural ideologists like Buckminster Fuller to create utopian - though eventually possible - future living scenarios in space.

Henrik Håkansson and Ilana Halperin both focus on different aspects of the natural world - Håkansson with his meticulous yet poetic investigation of endangered species and their man-fabricated living conditions, Halperin with her deeply personal, almost intimate engagement with geology - while Lara Almarcegui explores and documents as yet undefined spaces in flux in the urban landscape.

Other artists and artists' groups were invited to engage with the theme and the local context of Sharjah, and during their visits and excursions - most of them have been to this part of the world for the very first time, and one of them consciously decided to make the journey without boarding an airplane - some thrilling projects emerged, which not only address the subject at hand from an external, globalised point of view, but are engaged with the city, its infrastructure, surroundings and multiple communities, proposing it as a broad field for poetic investigation and experimentation. Gerda Steiner and Jörg Lenzlinger use the waste-product of Sharjah's desalination facility to create a wondrous salt garden, Luca Vitone portrays the city and its environment by means of the traces that settled down on blank canvases for the duration of months, and Dan Perjovschi scribbles his humorous but sharp comments on walls, informed by private observation and the daily news. Finally, the artists' group e-Xplo (in collaboration with Ayreen Anastas) gives a voice to the workers, who physically help build the U.A.E. as it is, by collecting their songs and poems in the many different languages spoken in this country.

In the end, however, we will not have reduced the amount of carbon emissions in the air with this biennial. Instead we have accumulated quite a bit of a carbon footprint. The artworks on view will not have contributed much to solve the global warming problem, nor that of social injustice, and they will not just self-compost either. Most of them will have to be crated and shipped back - just like the artists, curators and the international guests will board airplanes and head further towards other destinations. But we hope that they will carry some images with them that, despite art's alleged powerlessness in the face of the challenges posed by environmental change, are strong enough to survive beyond and make people think more about the footsteps we all leave when we move on and around this planet's surface.

CONFESSIONS OF A CURATOR, 1 December 2006

Jonathan Watkins

I am sitting in a Boeing 747 as I write this, flying from London to Miami. On this occasion I haven't paid a tax to counteract the carbon emissions that are my contribution to global warming. I drink tomato juice from a plastic cup, having just eaten a savoury snack from a plasticated foil sachet - now the cup and sachet are little bits of rubbish on my tray-table. And my meal to come? It will be eaten probably with plastic cutlery from various disposable containers, accompanied by doubly wrapped items including napkin, salt, pepper, toothpick, sugar and refreshing towelette. When this meal is finished, what I haven't consumed gets cleared away. Then what happens to the stuff? As one would expect in these enlightened times, a lot gets recycled, but surely something ends up in landfill, or is incinerated. I don't know, and I will not make enquiries about this particular detail in my life.

I'm flying to Miami to join in a roundtable discussion, a sort of trailer for the next Sharjah Biennial. The theme: ecology and contemporary art. It's not a little ironic, of course, to be flying around in preparation for such an event - a fact that has not eluded the organisers - especially as this exhibition will take place in a city thriving on the proceeds of fossil fuel.

Doubly ironic was the Emirates flight that last took me to Sharjah for a site visit, featuring in its entertainment programme Al Gore's extraordinary film debut, *An Inconvenient Truth*. It was a little bit like homework - a chance for me to brush up on our subject - and a lot like watching a revivalist chapel meeting. The format and rhetoric of *An Inconvenient Truth* is very familiar, instilling a sense of guilt, whilst offering salvation through a sequence of commandments in the form of handy ecological hints coming into focus as the credits roll. Non-joiners, like me, tend to feel uncomfortable when manipulation is so transparent, no matter how right the message might be, and so I exited the entertainment programme with a kind of bolshie disquiet. Ordering another drink - a little bottle of red wine, with another wrapped snack, plastic cup and napkin - I returned to my paperback novel, Michel Houellebecq's *Possibility of an Island*.

Houellebecq casts his spells in ways quite unlike Al Gore. His characters are often unsympathetic, his descriptions of decadent behaviour spliced with geekish science in an overall appeal to perversity. At the end of *The Possibility of an Island* this perversity is manifested in a subtle rant against "ecologism", characterising the ecological movement we are now witnessing as the result of some masochistic religious impulse, more about denial than the application of common sense. His vision of the future is bleak, comprising a world where the oceans have evaporated, more or less, and our descendants roam in scavenging packs while human clones live out lives of essential sterility.

I confess, I much preferred reading Houellebecq to watching Al Gore, perhaps because Houellebecq invites us to imagine something rather than believe. To reiterate, Gore might be right, but Houellebecq is pushing and pulling us through fiction to understandings that square with a philosophical scepticism that suits me more; that, on the whole, makes for the best contemporary art.

In this vein, the best art exhibitions are not didactic. They are like conversations in which the participants are not all agreeing, not "on message", illustrating other people's ideas. For the right reasons, it would be wrong to expect that the 8th Sharjah Biennial will be a model of good ecological practice. Any such claims for it will result in inevitable charges of hypocrisy, and any wholesome identity it assumes will be contradicted by countless works of art on display. Art history is not a history of saints, and so I hope, in this context especially, I'm not the only one wanting to confess.

Hisham Al Madhloum
General Coordinator of Sharjah Biennial
Director of directorate of Arts

One of Art's main priorities, since the dawn of history, has been, and continues to be, the enhancement of commonalities amongst humans in all four corners of the earth, towards expanding social and human communication. Art is the message that speaks to everyone, using the first global language awaiting to erupt each and every time an existential question is posed, or an obsession is expressed in human terms.

At the department of culture and information and in the directorate of arts, and since the establishment of this Biennial, we have been attempting to attract a certain quality of artists and intellectuals who will contribute to enhancing the intellectual and aesthetic vision of the Biennial, and provide the opportunity to present artistic constructs of high creative value. Based on the vision of His Highness Sheikh Dr. Sultan Bin Mohammed Al Qasimi, Member of the Supreme Council and Ruler of Sharjah, the Biennial, over the years, has expanded its objective, ambitions, and enhanced its visions towards developing human, intellectual, and creative links amongst different nationalities, and consolidating intellectual potential, allowing everyone to participate in its unfolding.

The discourse of His Highness was exemplified in the Biennial's humanitarian dimension, and His Excellency's directives guided our planning, and determination in sustaining various artistic and cultural events with great profoundness. The Sharjah Biennial has reached new heights ever since Her Highness Sheikha Hoor Al Qasimi became its director, as it assumed a central position within the latest developments in contemporary art, taking up its rightful place amongst other international world-class Biennials.

This Biennial's theme, *Still life: Art, Ecology and the Politics of Change*, further proves Her Highness's concern with urgent humanitarian and social issues, both a human necessity and an aesthetic need. This theme finds fertile ground in the Emirate of Sharjah, where the infrastructure and wise directives ensure the preservation of a safe environment. The large number of natural reserves as well as bodies concerned with the environment help to keep a watchful eye on it, and maintain its resources. Given the various factors and circumstances that impact the environment, such as wars, desertification, negligence, or depletion of human resources, this biennial becomes a social, human, and creative event that addresses the core issues of human existence, and tries to shed some light, through the various art projects, exhibitions, workshops, and seminars, on aspects pertaining to the preservation of the environment. The Biennial poses the question of ecology in its relation to art from various perspectives: visual, social, cognitive, and natural hoping to bring the question of ecology closer to our daily worries and concerns.

The Biennial has several tasks to address simultaneously, maintaining its connection to humanity, its concerns, and aspirations, and reflecting at the same time its structure as a comprehensive, intellectual, and artistic space, interconnected in a manner that combine to express its overall vision.

EXHIBITION DESIGN

Mona El-Mousfy

But among all these sites, I am interested in certain ones that have the curious property of being in relation with all the other sites, but in such a way as to suspect, neutralize or invent the set of relations that they happen to designate, mirror or reflect. These spaces, as it were, which are linked with all the others, which however contradict all the other sites, are of two main types. First, there are the utopias... There are also, probably in every culture, in every civilization, real places - places that do exist and that are formed in the very founding of society- which are something like counter-sites, a kind of effectively enacted utopia in which the real sites, all the other real sites that can be found within the culture, are simultaneously represented, contested and inverted.

Michel Foucault[1]

Introduction

The Sharjah Biennial 8 brief proposes art as a way of creating a better understanding about our relationship with nature and the environment, while considering its social, political and cultural dimensions in an interdisciplinary way. In response to the theme, we looked at ecology as a system of cohabitation and cooperation and opted for conceiving the exhibition design as a field of negotiation and cooperation between the various actors: artists, curators and designers. Sharjah Biennial 8 has three main venues: Sharjah Art Museum, the expo center and the Sharjah heritage area. It is in the expo center that the above strategies were more fully developed, for there the breadth of the open space presented a real challenge for all the actors involved. The architectural concept for that venue is to follow through with the idea of an interior urban space begun in Sharjah Biennial 7. Yet, rather than creating a pristine representation of an urban fragment with fully enclosed or open spaces, we have developed strategies of a negotiable decentralized interior site.

Strategies of Negotiation

The concepts of decentralization, distribution and self-organization are linked to an idea of urbanism. Adapted to exhibition design, a scenario was developed to engage artists in decisions related to the spatial needs and spatial implications of their work. Within that scenario, curators and designers become like sensors and facilitators mediating between artists as they participate in drawing their own territories and their relationships with neighboring installations.

Architectural Elements

The above strategies are supported by a fluid morphology that takes place through artists' participation. The resulting freely inhabited and easily regulated sites are materialized by a series of 9m wide and 4.5m high free-standing elements. Scattered yet in a flexible order along five wide mega strips of the same width, they are frontally perceived and define as needed spaces of different scale and lighting intensity. A translucent stretched fabric plane placed 9m above the ground and a meter below the building space truss diffuses both daylight and artificial lighting. It is pierced along a shifted geometrical pattern, echoing the plan below to allow the suspension of railings supporting additional electrical lighting. The rectangular openings into the ceiling plane also allow glimpses into the space truss beyond.

1 The concept of Heterotopia was the subject of a lecture given by Michel Foucault in 1967. Published in 1984 as 'Des Espaces Autres' in the French Journal *Architectures/Mouvement/Continuite*, no. 5 Paris, 1984, the text has been translated to English with the title 'Of Other Spaces', *Diacritics 16*, no. 1, Maryland, John Hopkins University Press, 1986

Weaving Movement

The exhibition's spatial strategy takes shape through its performance. Visitors can establish their own route, and it is as they weave freely through the exhibition space that they tangibly perceive the fluid morphology of the scheme and discover at every turn a new layering of installations. As the visitor walks towards a specific installation, the first dispersed distant viewing is gradually transformed into close-up focused viewing and, at times, full immersion in a partially defined or fully enclosed space. A field of tension, relationships and questioning is thus created around heterogeneous installations. Each visitor interacts differently with the familiar and less familiar works as he or she engages both their known and projected content. Implying a mega weave and a web structure, metallic bridges running perpendicularly to the free-standing elements at 4.5m above ground level offer the visitor wide-angle and close-up plunging views into the installations below and a direct linear route back to the entrance.

Scaffolding Structure

Linking to the location and its surrounding urban context, a febrile mega construction site, we opted to use a construction scaffolding system as the skeletal structure of the exhibition. Deviated from its original use, it is only partially visible along the 1.2m edges of most free-standing elements. The scaffolding system is rented from scaffolding contracting companies or recuperated from Sharjah public institutions. This gesture becomes a small contribution towards a sustainable awareness and a symbolic gesture towards slowing down the febrile construction outside by evoking with the SB8 artists the possibility of different future construction sites.

Conclusion

We share with many contributing artists the awareness that architecture can do its share by stretching to a wider scope beyond the relationship with the formal and symbolic, challenging and enriching economical, political and socio-cultural dimensions. Through the various cooperation strategies adopted to generate SB8's decentralized negotiable exhibition site, we have attempted to engage a particular aspect of the ambitious biennial theme.

Detailed view of SB8 Expo venue model showing the spatial weave. Model: Mays Nafoukh, photo: Plamen Galabov

Maha Mustapha
chael Rakowitz

TO NURTURE HOPE...

Serene Huleileh
Editor

This is the age of a million standards, the age of the masses, where politicians and the media no longer question the statement George Orwell made decades ago: all men are equal, but some are more equal than others. Artists alone stand as proof to that, after all the dust has settled, there remain a few principles that cannot be misinterpreted or twisted: i.e., the value of humanity and human life, and the need to act for the future and not for today.

The essays and artists' statements in this catalogue are a modest attempt to "put on knowledge with power"[1] before the audience/reader/artist can leave the show. Various possibilities are reflected on, questioned, and re-evaluated.

To have an impact, that's everyone's prerogative. It could be negative or positive, but simply by being born and surviving, we leave an impression on the face of the earth. This is the underlying theme of the essays and artists' statements in this Biennial. What impact do we have? What are the consequences of our actions? If they are not visible, then we will inflate them beyond all proportion so that no one can really miss the point. How can we make these consequences less harmful, more positive? - That's the million dollar question, answered in more than a hundred ways in this Biennial.

To make a difference, that's our responsibility. That's what everyone here is saying. We want to make a difference; we are here to do just that, whether out of a sense of responsibility, or duty, or simply as a survival technique.

A brief search on the internet will produce: 50 ways to save the planet, 101 ways, 12 ways, 10 ways...16 pain-free ways to help save the planet. All of them assume you have a car, credit card, shower, and money to buy in "bulk". So the responsibility obviously lies with the rich, both for the polluting and for the saving... What should the rest of us do? Selected essays in this catalogue present some answers that their writers are currently trying to explore in various parts of the "southern hemisphere" of our world.

It is not only life, the environment and our commitment to the physical or natural environment that we are covering. What we are also stressing in this Biennial is that human energy is the most valued renewable resource in the process of being depleted by the way we live our lives today; by war and conflict; by constant travel and worry; by the media and other diverse occupations. If there are truly so many ways to save the world, at the end of the day we need only apply three: think peace, get active, and nurture the hope that we can be saved.

1 The reference here is to the question that Yeats poses about the Greek Myth of the rape of Leda in his poem "Leda and the Swan", where at the end he asks:
Being so caught up,
So mastered by the brute blood of the air,
Did she put on his knowledge with his power
Before the indifferent beak could let her drop?

ARTS and PERCEPTIONS

Munir Fasheh

The concept paper starts by asserting that "SB8 takes for its theme the *ambiguous* topic of *Man's relationship* with the *planet*". Words in italics sum up the main ideas I would like to discuss in this article. Dominant contemporary ideology stresses the "science of certainty, control, and one path for progress", rather than the "art of living with ambiguity, conviviality, and plurality". Dominant ideology perceives every person as an individual detached from their surroundings rather than as part of a web of relationships. *This paper perceives the arts as a crucial way of preventing, remedying, and reversing the damage and harm done to human relations and to the planet by the sciences in their triumphant march - unchecked by wisdom - during the past 400 years.* The fundamental and crucial challenge we face today is not so much political, social, and economic change as the transformation of the perception of self, of one's relationship to the world of science, knowledge, tools, and of the logic and values that govern our actions and interactions. Without such a transformation, changes at other levels are, at best, technical and shallow. Arts are crucial in initiating and nurturing such transformation. I use 'arts' in this article in the way that they flourished in Arab Islamic culture - in the sense of being intimately connected to literature and to people's worldviews.

Arts start from a point which is the inverse of man as employee and consumer (consumer of ready products, solutions, meanings, measures, and formulas applied in a mechanical way). I will use an analogy to clarify this inverse. A Palestinian friend once told me how his peasant father used to go to the field every morning and look - with loving care - at every tree, and see what its needs were. This is a beautiful manifestation not only of the harmony between mind, heart, and action, but also of the man's relationship to the place, the land, trees, history, and culture - as well as to his family and community. The expression of that relationship was found in the flourishing plants and trees. The relationship formed the man's source of meaning, knowledge, understanding, and survival. It "taught" him how to live with uncertainty and helped him have a personal image of the future. It formed the basis of his attentiveness and aliveness, both of which were manifested in his daily concern to protect the trees from harm, and provide a healthy environment for their nurturing and ability to give. He did not try to control their growth and shape. Unlike employees and consumers, my friend's father was free. He was free in the sense that his work was self-defined, and in the sense of listening to nature and being in harmony with its laws - instead of listening to officials and professionals and following formulas and arbitrary rules and regulations. He perceived his role as providing healthy conditions for plants and trees to grow on their own, by respecting that natural ability. Like a good painter who lets their hand be driven by "mature natural impulses", my friend's father let the hand of nature draw the emerging creation.

In contrast, contemporary scientists - following Francis Bacon's conception of science - want to control the growth and shapes of plants and trees. According to Bacon, the purpose of science is "to conquer and to subdue" nature.[1] Within this perspective, science is not a "friend" of wisdom, and has no interest in respecting nature. Its purpose is to discover the laws of nature and use them to further certain interests (along with the interests of those in power) - which means in practice serving control, victory and greed. Chemistry, nuclear physics and genetic engineering are manifestations of this conquering and subjection of nature. We witness today the disastrous consequences of such a conception and practice of science in the form of chaos, disintegration, and rebellion (including that of Nature). It is worth stressing that such consequences are due to the dominant conception and perception of science and not to their bad application. Dominant forms of science, technology, and knowledge have no doubt solved many problems but, at the same time, have created

[1] See Carolyn Merchant, *The Death of Nature* (New York: Harper Collins, 1983). See also Yusef Progler in http://www.multiworld.org/m_versity/articles/yusef.htm

many more and much more serious problems. The threat of nuclear annihilation of all life on Earth, the almost irreversible degradation of the environment, and the quest for global domination are the biggest threats we face today. The pollution of the body and environment, for example, by the science of chemistry during the 20th century by far exceeds all pollutions since the beginning of history! In this sense, people like Einstein need to be presented in schools not as 'models' to be emulated but rather as scientists who followed a conception of science that lacked wisdom, ethics, and responsibility - a path we need to reverse. They did what they did fully aware of the consequences. Trying to justify what they have done, or to explain it differently, is nothing but a sign of the corruption of minds.

What makes things worse is the fact that most people believe that this dominant path is the only way to perceive science. Anyone who strays away from it is brushed aside as a romantic and idealist - as one who refuses to compete, as one who wants to "stay behind". Freeing the self from the belief in one path is for me the most basic challenge we face today in relation to human survival - a challenge that the arts can play a crucial role in responding to. But the arts would not be able to do this if we continued to conceive of science as subduing nature. We need to understand the purpose of science as remedying the wrongs we inflict on physical and human nature rather than deepening and adding to them.[2] In other words, we need a science whose conceptions and tools would help clean up the mess produced by the dominant sciences - including "cleansing" our perceptions, conceptions, and practices.[3] The sun and the wind are examples of sources of energy that do not pollute or harm life. In other words, science can be regarded as increasing people's ability and understanding in a way that protects and remedies nature from the onslaught and harm we inflict on it. It can be conceived as creating tools that make our lives more comfortable without harming human or physical natures.

I would like to choose an example from the SB8's concept paper to illustrate the point I am expressing here. We read in the paper, "We are using our resources to try and create a kind of man-made Garden of Eden, in other words turning our dry, arid desert into a lush, green land for our citizens and others to enjoy." For a European not to see the beauty, inspiration, richness, clarity, simplicity, and profundity in a desert is understandable. But for Arabs not to see it is inexcusable. The way Arabs perceive the desert is reflected in the beautiful word they used to refer to it: *al-badiyah* (the beginning - with all its purity, simplicity and clarity). Transforming *al-badiyah* into something other than its nature, which makes it dependent on being constantly fed from outside, is an example of science subduing nature rather than of the art of living in harmony with her and protecting her. Transforming *al-badiyah* into a Garden of Eden is like putting legs on a snake: we cripple the snake! By transforming *al-badiyah* into a Garden of Eden, inhabitants become crippled, unable to live and survive in their own environment without it being constantly fed with "foreign" elements. People would be adopting a way of life that is not sustainable in the long term. They would be ignoring the wisdom embedded in the story of the crow (in *Kalila wa Dimna*) that wanted to imitate the pigeon's walk and, when it failed, couldn't return to its own walk! Living in harmony with nature does not mean not trying to make life more comfortable but doing it in ways that are self-generating and in cooperation with nature - ways that are in harmony with the integrity of creation. Science without wisdom can be destructive. Part of the reason as to why dominant science did not follow this path is due to the fact that it was conceived in the womb of the empire, as a means of control, domination, and stealing continents. Living in harmony with nature is contrary to the consumption pattern of living and to its core values of profit, control, and competition.

Just imagine - as a clarifying suggestion - schools in the UAE designed around sailing as a basis of the educational system. Students would learn things that no current "world-class" school can provide! They would acquire radically different meanings to words such as knowledge, learning, competition, and evaluation.

[2] See Ivan Illich, *Shadow Work* for the seeds of this idea.

[3] Some tools of dominant forms of science and knowledge can, of course, help in this process.

They would learn how to live with uncertainty and harmony at the same time - competencies ignored in educational institutions (which usually follow lifeless one-dimensional curricula controlled by expensive foreign experts). In addition, the sea and people's relationship to it would be a natural lively inspiration for their arts. (It is revealing to think of the two radically different worlds represented by sailing boats and motor boats...)

In a world that is increasingly dominated by science and technology, whose purpose is to "conquer and subdue nature", arts can provide paths of living, perceiving, understanding, and relating that embody values other than competition, profit, control, winning, and greed. Dominant perceptions, conceptions, practices, and values have *used* the human body, *torn apart* the social spiritual fabric in communities, and *polluted* nature. The arts can provide different perceptions and values. First and foremost is the value of health - health of the body, of relationships, and of nature. In addition to health, arts can embody goodness, joy and pleasure as fundamental values in living. Nature is to be enjoyed rather than subdued, to be admired rather than abused. We need to regain the feeling of joy in the miracle of creation and in our expressions of it. This, for me, is the essence of art. It was beautifully expressed by a Chinese potter, who said: "it is not the pot I am interested in; it is in what remains after the pot is broken." I once watched a woman who was making beautiful shapes in the sand, and people would stop and watch what she was doing with admiration. Every time the woman finished a certain shape, she gently flattened the sand with her hands and started a completely new configuration!

Art is embedded in the relationship we have with our surroundings, in the relationship between the inner and the outer world; it is embedded in the joy and meaning achieved from creative expressions stemming from that relationship. It best happens when we are not conscious of it, when it is not commissioned, when we are inseparable from the experience or from the expressions we create. I am not talking about joy and pleasure that can be sold and bought, but about them, these feelings that are felt in spontaneous surprising ways - in ways that are not planned but stem from being attentive and alive. For art to embody respect for life, nature, people, and culture, the artist needs to remain in touch with the pain in the world. The two periods that were most inspiring in my life were the 1970s and the first Intifada, both in Palestine. People lived with full attentiveness to their surroundings and with full awareness in their dealings with them. They lived with what was available to all people, including their abilities and their own energies, under their own control. There is still much more room for people to manoeuvre in the arts than in the sciences in this regard. Thus, we need to protect the arts from falling into the pitfall of surrendering their lifeline to institutions, professionals, and commercialisation. Freedom that is connected to art does not mean feeling free from having connections but free from pre-packaged frames, meanings, and symbols. Art happens when respect shifts from following instructions and regulations to being true to one's connection to life; when one's life is not separated from what one is doing, creating, or expressing. There is a difference between a storyteller who tells a story the same way every time and a storyteller who is fully in touch with their surroundings. There is a difference between a teacher who prepares details of their lesson plan and presents it in a mechanical way and a teacher who - like an artist - is surprised by what s/he creates. There is a difference (as I mentioned earlier) between sailing and driving a motor boat; between an organic farmer and one who follows formulas and depends on machines... In general, there is a difference between living as an "artist" and living in a mechanical way.

The above is related to a characteristic of institutions that is worth mentioning here: when learning is happening, we don't notice it and we do not use the word "learning" to refer to it; and when learning is not happening, we use the word "learning" to describe it! If, for example, children are playing with sand, or walking in the woods, or cooking, conversing, swimming, riding bicycles, planting, praying or sailing - through which they learn a lot - we say they are playing, cooking, planting, or sailing but we rarely use "learning" to refer to what they are doing. "Learning" is reserved for what takes place in educational institutions, where it is controlled, measured, and evaluated by licensed professionals. Within such settings, people don't mean what they say and they don't say what they mean; learning becomes - at best - technical and mechanical, following formulas and techniques.

Just as institutional education monopolises learning and suppresses life-related learning, fine arts monopolises the arts and suppresses people's creative expression. The challenge is to recognise the arts that are part of people's ways of living and to protect their rich and diverse cultural expressions from the onslaught of institutions and professionals. Any aspect of life (whether a language or an art or a science) that depends for its continuity on being taught by institutionalised professionals would soon lose its spirit and vitality. Art reflects one's relationship to what is around. The Iranian poet, Hafiz, lived most of his life in the city of Shiraz. Yet, the beauty of the city shaped his understanding and made him one of the eternal poets who described human and physical nature in ways that continue to inspire people around the world. Similarly, Sayyed Darwish, the Egyptian composer and singer, continues to nurture and please Arabs everywhere.

In 1978, I was a member of a committee that was in charge of overseeing the establishment of the school of "arts/cultural expression and communication" at Birzeit University. Unfortunately, it never saw the light (mainly because of the refusal of the Israeli occupation to give a permit to build the school). However, it is worth mentioning here that the school was designed around people who embodied, in their lifestyles, various Palestinian expressions - where people with degrees would build on that. (*Al-Warsha* Theatre in Egypt is the closest that embodies this philosophy.)

A most urgent and important challenge in the contemporary world (in the arts as well as in other fields) is how to protect and create spaces (both real and virtual) where people live, act, interact, express, and create outside the control of institutions and professionals; spaces where people and what they create are not treated as commodities. "Professional" classes in arts are usually stacked with books and art materials of all kinds (which are usually very expensive). Such classes are usually blind to artists, who make beautiful creations out of things that are considered by others as waste. Such artists are like organic farmers who look at a heap of garbage and see roses growing out of it.

Art is not a profession but a way of living, an attitude, a lifestyle, a relationship; it is a way of seeing and expressing the world honestly as one experiences it - with all its beauty and pain. Without art, one would easily believe that life can be fully comprehended by the mind and totally driven by market forces. Again, I find myself compelled to cite my illiterate mother as an example. I wrote about her as a "mathematician"[4], as a "teacher", and as an embodiment of the beautiful spirit of religion. Writing this article, I am seeing her as an artist in her dealing with shapes and measurements. As a seamstress, she had to deal with shapes and measurements that could not fit any tools made by mathematicians and engineers, who basically deal with rigid measurements: straight lines, angles, and shapes that have formulas. What my mother had to work with were the curves and shapes of a woman, which were uniquely characteristic of that woman. She did not use patterns - which made every dress she put together (during the 45 years she worked) a unique creation. Her creations were works of art rather than mechanical applications of formulas and measurements. It is the competence of an artist rather than of a mathematician or engineer - a competence that cannot be gained through formal instruction or cognitive knowledge. Yet, no one ever referred to my mother as an artist. This is what I meant when I said that people's arts are invisible to professionals.

***

4 I wrote about my illiterate mother as a "mathematician" (see, for example, my article "Community education is to regain and transform what has been made invisible", in the *Harvard Educational Review*. February 1990). Writing this article is making me aware of her as an artist.

I perceive what is happening in the world today (in spite of many appearances to the contrary) is the crumbling of the dominant logic of control, competition, winning and domination. The crises we witness are basically the crises of dominant institutions and of the consumption patterns of living. The threats I mentioned earlier (that are the result of dominant logic and lifestyle) - nuclear holocaust, degradation of the environment, and global domination - are very real. Although increasing numbers of people are becoming aware of these threats, they feel helpless before them. Impoverishment of the imagination contributes to such helplessness. Arts are crucial in enriching the imagination and providing healthy methods of transition.

Within this perspective, arts are crucial in enhancing each person's range of freedom - not freedom to own and consume but to create things, meanings, expressions, and spaces. People in rich countries may have access to more things and services, but always with instructions on how to use them, which degrade them into the status of mere consumers. Freedom means autonomous and creative interactions between persons and with their environments and communities. As such, freedom embodies a social ethical value. Freedoms that are crucial but ignored include the freedom to co-author meanings and measures, and to define images of the future. When I visit schools, I am usually directed to the computer room (computers are perceived as symbols of modernity and progress). I usually ask, "I want to see the *tablah* room" (Just as in the case of sailing boats and motor boats, the *tablah* (Oriental percussion instrument) and the computer represent two worlds that are worlds apart!)

When I talk about the importance for the arts to free themselves from the subordinate and dependent state and status they were confined to, I am not talking just about their importance in people's lives but also - and more importantly - about their importance to human survival in today's world. Culture, art, and lifestyles that embody wisdom are again inspiring people everywhere. I will briefly mention a few examples to illustrate this. The first example is that of the Zapatista movement of indigenous peoples in southern Mexico. After 500 years of being oppressed, the Zapatistas emerged recently as a most inspiring hope for many people around the world.[5] Samuel Huntington's book *Who are we?* - to cite another example - points to what he considers to be the biggest threat to the US way of life: the Hispanics! Obviously, their threat is not political or economic; it is cultural. Huntington's worry stems from the way Hispanics conduct their lives, and the ways in which they relate, converse, dance, sing, and bring up their children - and the fact that their source of worth resides within them. (In light of this, one can see how much the TV programme *Sesame Street* is imbued with colonial values!) Similarly, the backbone of Africa, Central Asia, the Indian subcontinent, and the Arab world is cultural. Arts need to be seen through this lens.

***

A central aspect in every person's life is the source of their value. I would like to end this article by mentioning the principle that guides the thinking and practice of the Arab Education Forum - and which I would like to propose as the principle to guide the estimation of artists (rather than international committees). The principle is embedded in Imam Ali's statement: *qeematu kullimri'en ma yuhsenoh* (the worth of a person is what s/he *yuhsen*). *Yuhsen* in Arabic has at least 5 meanings: the first meaning refers to how well the person does what s/he does - the knowledge and skills dimension; the second refers to how beautiful and pleasing to the senses it is- the aesthetic dimension; the third meaning refers to its value to the community - the ethical dimension; the fourth refers to how much of the self is given- the emotional/giving dimension (as opposed to only taking or, what is worse, consuming); and the fifth meaning refers to how respectful (of people and ideas) the person is in discussion - the social spiritual fabric dimension... It is hard to think of an aspect of life where this principle is more appropriate.

[5] In 1970, I visited Cuzco, Peru (the capital of the Inca Indians). In the museum at the centre of town, there was a sculpture of a man on a horse pushing his spear into a man kneeling in front of him. The guide explained that the man on the horse was Spanish and the one who was kneeling was a Moor. The face and clothes of the kneeling person were like the Incas. It seems that the artist (who was an Inca Indian), who had never seen an Arab or a Moor, assumed that since the Moors had the same relationship with the Spanish as the Inca Indians, they must have looked like Incas! The guide (an Inca himself) proudly pointed out to another aspect of the sculpture: how the Moor was holding the spear and looking straight into the eyes of the horse-rider in a way that embodied resistance and defiance. Obviously, the subtlety of the art escaped the soldiers who were overseeing the work!

HOPE IN THE ERA OF *KALYUG*

Manish Jain

In the West, the experts talk of the age of globalisation - the opportunities and crises brought on by the unprecedented size and speed of the global economy. Our elders and sages in India refer to the present times as the era of *Kalyug*. By this they mean, the Dark Ages, or the time when people are furthest away from "God". It is the most difficult period for the human race and it is predicted that many atrocities will become commonplace in society. The ancient scriptures warn that during this age: "Those who act like tyrants are accepted and approved." "And men with false reputation of learning will, by their acts, cause Truth to be contracted and concealed."

I have often thought about what *Kalyug* means for me apart from these scriptures. Some days I feel it is symbolised by the total disconnection that modern wo/man has from Nature (and the complete arrogance which drives any kind of interaction that *homo economicus* initiates with Mother Earth). Today, our children do not know where their food, water, clothing, fuel, etc. comes from or where their plastic bottles, batteries, old video games, etc. actually get dumped. They are taught that they are good citizens if they throw things in the recycle bin - without asking what happens to them after they leave the bin. Modern schooling and mass media have rendered them unable to see the connections and consequences of their choices, e.g., how the oil that they are so dependent on is linked to war. Ironically, countries with the so-called best education systems have the highest ecological footprints.

Other days I think that *Kalyug* is symbolised by the great loss of the value of one's *jabaan* - the chasm between what we say we believe in and what we do - and along with it the loss of one's *izzat* (dignity) and sacred sense of Being. Our own sense of human agency and personal responsibility for our actions and choices has been eroded in the face of massive institutions. Many years ago, Lewis Mumford observed quite perceptively that the humanisation of the Machine will lead to the mechanisation of humanity. What is really scary is that we are not able to (or, more disturbingly, *do not want to*) tune into our conscience, our internal and eternal compass, that nagging voice of common sense within that thwarts our delusions of self-grandeur and helps us set our own self-imposed limits.

Our capacity to value things or assess choices from a long-term perspective has also become totally distorted. We have been trained to believe that everything valuable in life can be measured accurately and effectively by money. Our children are trained through schooling to believe that success is about being able to get money without an honest day's labour; the more people one can exploit, the better. We put a price tag on forests, water, mountains, entire ecosystems, and we think that we can financially account for their destruction. Our lives only matter when it comes to increasing consumption and GNP; otherwise our existence is a burden for governments and planners. Perhaps this can shed some light on why we continue to let the logic of the Market and the Nation State dominate our decision-making and our relationships - why we consider violent militarisation, unsustainable economic growth and sadistic technologies the equivalent of Progress.

It is interesting to note that in the face of *Kalyug*, particularly the devastating ecological crisis that it brings, the world's leaders are calling for a global agenda of Millenium Development Goals, Human Rights, Education for All, Information and Communication Technologies, etc. - all legalistic-technocratic solutions which keep us well-tamed within the frameworks of modernity and its institutions. We are told over and over again to believe that someday the benefits will "trickle down" to everyone; or that new technologies will be developed to clean up all the messes created by the economic juggernaut; or simply that there is no alternative.

Even so-called radical forums are mainly focused on fixing American foreign policy or the WTO laws. The nature of the crisis before us, however, seems to point to the need for a more profound shift of consciousness which can inspire us to see hidden/new possibilities. As Albert Einstein once said, you cannot solve a problem using the same frames of reference that created it in the first place. So we must move beyond thinking in terms of isolated issue-based, problem-solving approaches. In other words, a longer view with a larger perspective is needed.

With this in mind, I would like to posit that the severe ecological catastrophes which face planet earth today cannot be solved simply by legalistic measures or by technological gimmickry. It is essentially a cultural issue, and needs to be approached in this light. As Margaret Wheatley describes, "The world doesn't change one person at a time. It changes when networks of relationships form among people who share a common cause and vision of what's possible. This is good news for those of us intent on creating a positive future. Rather than worry about critical mass, our work is to foster critical connections." Diverse efforts towards cultural regeneration require that we nurture intercultural dialogue. Consciousness grows and evolves as we learn to interact with different realities – both internal and external. Intercultural dialogue is a critical tool for uncovering and exploring different perspectives of reality. To understand the realities that others experience requires the skills of reflective conversations, in which we can test our own assumptions and inquire into those of others.

Gustavo Esteva describes, "Intercultural alludes to a dynamic situation wherein there is a consciousness that other people, values and cultures, exist and that isolation is impossible. This awareness implies acknowledgement of the limitations of every culture and an understanding of all that is human. Instead of taking refuge in one's own culture - trying to isolate oneself, taking distance from the other or suppressing it - one is inspired to interact with the other recognising its radical otherness... It implies opening up to the concerns of the other, to guidance, suspicions, inspiration, ideals or any element that both parties can share and neither of them controls."

Today, this intercultural dialogue is not just about East vs. West or North vs. South. The Other is not just an external phenomena, it has been created within each of us. Intercultural dialogue has, then, to start with ourselves - between our rational, analytical selves and our intuitive, creative selves, between our ancient, timeless beings and our modern selves. It also has to take place within our families and communities, between our urban and our rural communities, between men and women, across generations, classes, castes, etc. There is an urgent need to think more deeply about how to shift the scale and the speed of our interactions to make more time for the intimate, the subtle, the hidden.

The artist has a critical role to play in creating and co-hosting such intercultural dialogue. Sadly, the role of the artist has been neglected and maligned in most circles on social change. This domain has been captured by politicians, management activists, media propagandists and activists. I have taken great inspiration from Ananda Coomaraswamy's words that "an artist is not a special kind of man. Rather, every human is a special kind of artist." At the same time, I believe that realising one's specialness as an artist comes with a higher kind of social responsibility. In other words, saying that everyone is an artist in life does not necessarily mean that the "artist" is devoid of any social role. In fact, the artist should be held to a higher standard. Each of us, as artists, must actively participate in co-creating - not just observing or passively fitting into - these learning communities. Otherwise, we risk falling into another trap of the ready-made world if we expect others to create these learning communities for us.

The arts, however, are a powerful instrument of both personal and collective transformation and must be reclaimed from the domain of "luxury item". Humanity has reached the limits of the analytical and logical mind. Immersion into art helps to facilitate clarity about individual identity (who am I?), meaning (why is my life worth living?) and relationship (how am I interconnected with others?). The arts can help us move beyond slogans and propaganda and into, as Rumi once said, the worlds that exist beyond "right" and "wrong". The arts can help us to break the black and white mechanisation of humanity - the frameworks of efficiency, standardisation, monoculture - and start to see again the spaces of grey in all fields of life. We can then view uncertainty as an opportunity to make higher level connections for expansion and evolution of consciousness, rather than as something to be feared, controlled, or wiped out.

I would like to highlight two seemingly contradictory domains - unlearning and re-membering - on which those involved with the arts could focus in order to promote more learning communities for intercultural dialogue.

Unlearning is essential if we wish to regain our faith in the goodness of others and in the belief that many new possibilities exist and can be created - two essential conditions for intercultural dialogue to take shape. By unlearning, I mean those processes which help us to re-examine our mental models or our conditioning. To see freshly we must become aware of and step back from the mental filters which govern our ways of making sense.

It is not the same as forgetting. In order for unlearning to open up possibilities for intercultural dialogue, we will have to understand that many of the obstacles can be found within us, including: fear of criticism, lack of confidence, competitiveness, fragmented thought and big egos. Other deep obstacles stem from our "schooled" inability to tolerate ambiguity or see more holistically (beyond artificial disciplines). We have been conditioned into thinking in either/or bivalent categories (e.g., capitalism vs. communism, community vs. Nature). Our capacity to dialogue is also weakened by certain labels that we attach to ourselves and others. These identity labels - most often based on professions, caste, gender, class, schooling level, etc. - create artificial barriers which limit our exploration and growth. We become afraid to interact with certain people because of whom we think they are (or we think we are). Unlearning will involve confronting these obstacles and barriers.

In terms of re-membering, we must reconnect to our members - our hands, our hearts, our spirits, our different generations, our sacred links to fire, water, earth, soil. We all possess deep and timeless intuition, wisdom and imagination. We must try to reclaim from factory-schooling our own individual learning styles, paces (learning things faster is not always better for our creativity), multiple intelligences, emotional states, experiences, knowledge systems, etc. We must also re-member to see power outside the institutions of the State and the Market. This can inspire us to be able recognise creative spaces and opportunities that are in front of our eyes but we have never appreciated before - in other words, seeing again what has been forgotten.

Simultaneously, we must re-member how our capacities can be enhanced by engaging in collaboration and sharing with others. Most importantly, we must re-member how to connect knowledge and technology with wisdom and ethics. This will provide us with the humility to know our limits and with the common sense to understand that we should not do all things just because we can (i.e., not all "creative" scientific and commercial initiatives should be pursued).

Re-membering is essential to fuel us with the inspiration to start dreaming our own dreams again (and not someone else's ready-made dreams) and with the self-confidence to put them into action. When we begin to re-member, we will once again begin to see that each of us is deeply part of co-creating the universe together. This co-creation is in deep harmony and interdependence with all life. In India, we call this *Tat-twam-asi* (Thou art that).

Udaipur as a Learning City (ULC)

Over the past six years, we have been exploring in various ways how to regenerate intercultural dialogue within our own lives and the local learning ecology as part of the "Udaipur as a Learning City" process/project. We see the city is a living organism, with natural, cultural, spiritual and physical elements, in which people are active co-creators of meanings, relationships, and knowledge. The city provides a variety of contexts for expanding our consciousness and bolstering our capacities to appreciate our strengths and talents, to address ecological and psychological problems associated with rampant urbanisation and to build trusting and convivial friendships. ULC is an open invitation to people of all ages and all backgrounds in Udaipur, to explore ways of living and learning that are more organic. We seek to restore control over learning back in the hands of the person who learns. This has led to the work of ULC to span everything from zero waste tourism to working with traditional healers to producing community theatre and video.

ULC focuses on families, homes and neighbourhoods as radical spaces of social change. We recognise that intergenerational interactions are critical if wisdom is to emerge and profound action is to take place. A key guiding principle for us is that people freely share what they have with each other in the spirit of gratitude, thus aligning with an ancient Indian principle condemning the commodification of knowledge. There is no compulsion. No separate building has been especially constructed for ULC; rather, we have chosen to creatively utilise what already exists: peoples' homes, empty lots, public gardens and parks, art galleries, temples, mosques, ashrams, businesses, or local organisations' offices. ULC is trying to transcend institutionalised categories of public and private and to appreciate and integrate the authentic concerns and energies of local people. In other words, in Udaipur as a Learning City, individual people and real contexts are the starting point - not abstract ideas, cookie-cutter projects or results-based indicators.

ULC is not geared to the demands of the Market, as much as to personal understanding and intercultural dialogue. This does not mean that questions of livelihood do not exist but rather that they are in the context of understanding and relationship. ULC enables us to be alive to surprises and to feel a constant excitement in journeying into the unknown.

Over the course of working in the ULC process, I have had several opportunities to engage with the arts in various situations in Udaipur and around India. There are several trends that I have observed to be of great threat to the radical generative energy of the artist and his/her capacities to open up intercultural dialogue. First, I have seen that promotion of children's art is continually being placed within the framework of competition. This has created an unhealthy situation where many people, including myself, believe that they are not "good" artists. It also pushes children to remain within the box of what is "safe" so as to please the judges and discourages them from taking risks with their art. This spirit of competition later manifests itself within the art world to limit the way artists interact with each other.

Second, I have seen a serious disconnection of the professional artist from the local community in favour of either tourists or wealthy people. I have heard many artists comment that "local people do not understand or appreciate our art, so what's the point of interacting with them?" It is a bizarre situation in which the de-rooted artist is drawing ideas, motifs, images from the local surroundings but not sharing these back with the local people and not helping to replenish the local culture and community life.

Third, there is a severe fragmentation of the artist into three separate roles: the designer, producer and the marketer. For example, I recently visited a family in India who has been creating hand-made paper and hand-made paper products for over four hundred years. The design, production and marketing were all done in-house by the family members. Now, however, that is changing in the era of specialisation and mass production. There is a separate person who comes from the US to create the designs, a separate group of workers who do only the production, and separate people who do the marketing or sharing. With all three of these trends, the art products are being produced but the artist as holistic Being, as a framer and convenor of intercultural dialogue, is lost.

In our work, we have been trying to counter these trends through a variety of activities in Udaipur. I should clarify at the outset that much of our thinking and strategies have been inspired by the spirit of the Outsider Art Movement. The term Outsider Art is used to describe art that is loosely understood as "outside" of official culture (for more information, see www.rawvision.com). Typically, those labelled as Outsider Artists have little or no contact with the institutions of the mainstream art world (universities, galleries, museums, etc.). They have no professional art degrees. Their work grows out of their own intrinsic motivation and experimentation, often employing unique materials or fabrication techniques. We would like to encourage more artists to re-emerge in the community without any professional training or certificate.

We have been hosting various Unlearning Workshops around the arts with children and youth. These take place both within schools and neighbourhoods. There is no compulsion, fees, examinations or certificates. The underlying intention of such workshops is to actively nurture people's capacities to identify, resist and say "no" to the consumerist, competitive and compulsory institutions/attitudes/behaviours/structures that enslave us and, instead, to start and construct again, organically, spaces and relationships that serve to foster self-initiated learning and intercultural dialogue. Such workshops seek to explore: *How can we authentically share our feelings, experiences and ideas with each other through our own expressions?*

When we started hosting these workshops, one of the first things we noticed was the deep conditioning of each child that is taking place in schools. Children have been taught to follow the teacher's instructions and to rely on adults to provide them with moulds to fit into. For example, on the first day of one workshop, 21 out of the 25 children drew exactly the same subject – mountains, a sun, a hut, and a river – exactly what they've been trained to draw in school. The second day most of the children said that they did not know how to draw anything else. The children also required constant praise, approval and reassurance from the external facilitator: that they knew how to draw, that they could make whatever they wished to, and that what they drew was "good". We noticed that the children often ridiculed their peers' artwork; they did not know how to support or appreciate each other. We found that children who had not been schooled were more open to expressing and experimenting with diverse forms and images.

Within the context of the workshops, there are certain themes that have emerged as critical. One is having the space to respectably "get one's hands dirty again" – away from sterile middle-class notions of "cleanliness". Another theme is to open up space for engaging in critical questions about the dominant media forms such as textbooks, TV and newspapers. We spend time discussing who creates the images we see and how different agendas and stereotypes are promoted through specific images.

A third theme explores how we understand the "resources" or "roots" of our art. This has several dimensions. We try to encourage young people to share different personal experiences as well as favorite local stories. We also spend time delving into traditional forms of local art and design. The easiest way to do this is to interact with our local illiterate mothers and grandmothers (who have been discredited as legitimate teachers by the school). They are the holders of many traditional styles such as *mandanas* which were painted on cowdung and mud houses. We also tap into the subconscious memory of vernacular aesthetics and *lokavidya* (people's knowledges) through working in the local language (which is usually banned in schools) and through local festivals. In terms of resources, we have focused on using local colours (made from everyday natural household materials such as tumeric, henna, charcoal, etc.). We also promote upcycling of waste. A key aspect of this has been to rebuild relationships with people like the tailor (for used cloth pieces), the bicycle mechanic (for rubber tyre tubes), the shop owner (for cardboard boxes).

A fourth theme tries to explore our willingness to make mistakes rather than hide them. Overcoming the fear of punishment or ridicule is critical to exploring new ideas and engaging in new experiments and relationships.

Another initiative that we have undertaken is to reconnect children and youth with artists and artisans. We try to take children to the sites of artists rather than just calling the artists into school. One of our hopes is to demystify galleries as something only for the rich. Also, the children get a chance to engage artists more about their work, inspirations and experiments. They also spend considerable time asking the artists about the meaning behind their art, particularly more contemporary styles. Most importantly, they experience that there are many different styles of art besides realism. We also visit more traditional spaces such as a potter's village called Molela. In these settings, children live with the families in order to experience more integrated ways of living - the artist living within the wisdom of community, the artist in harmony with Nature. Ultimately, taking a page from these experiences, we hope to dissolve the gallery back into the home and neighbourhood. What has been particularly exciting so far is that some of the artists have started venturing out of the safe confines of their galleries and universities and are volunteering their time at local community events.

To create more opportunities for self-organised learning interactions between local people and artists, we have also published two books for children and their families. One book, *Rang Bharay Jeevan Mein* (Life is Filled with Colour), shares interviews about various artists and art forms in Udaipur. The book highlights the work of 12 artists whose styles range from traditional miniature to tribal to contemporary. It also features the addresses of different artists' galleries along with invitations to visit. What is particularly interesting about this book is that it was totally researched by youth who had no background in the arts. The last chapter of the book features their reflections on how their perceptions about art and artists has shifted.

A third initiative that we have been experimenting with is to bring art back into public spaces such as parks as well in front of local houses and shops. We have been asking local artists to work collaboratively with local neighbourhood children and families to create murals, mosaics and sculptures using local materials, particularly waste materials. In several of the projects, we have been using appreciation techniques with local families to explore interesting moments in people's lives as well as the important knowledge, questions, passions and skills that they have. We have also engaged in many discussions about the changes taking place in their communities and in Udaipur.

Where these various initiatives have left us is that art as a product and the artist as a producer of art relics must shift to questions of artistic living i.e., what we eat, what we wear, how we move about, how we choose to communicate, how we take care of our health, how we raise our children, how we take care of our natural resources. We must understand that the arts is not about our output but rather about our lifestyle - our ways of exploring and connecting to new places, people and ideas; of understanding ourselves and developing our infinite talents; of nurturing our sensitivity to others and Nature. As Carlos Petrini, founder of the Slow Food movement, discusses, "Being Slow means you control the rhythms of your own life. You decide how fast you have to go in any given context. If today I want to go fast, I go fast; if tomorrow I want to go slow, I go slow. What we are fighting for is the right to determine our own tempos."

IRREVERSIBILITY, DISSIPATION, CHAOS AND NOISE MACHINES

Francesco Manacorda

Man, in degrees beyond all other creatures known to him, consciously participates - albeit meagrely - in the selective mutations and accelerations of his own evolution. This is accomplished as a subordinate modification and a component function of his sum total relative dynamic equilibrium as he speeds within the comprehensive and complex interactions of the universe (which he alludes to locally as environment).

Buckminster-Fuller

It is hard to avoid the impression that the distinction between what exists in time, what is irreversible, and, on the other hand, what is outside of time, what is eternal, is at the origin of human symbolic activity. Perhaps it is especially so in artistic activity. Indeed, one aspect of the transformation of a natural object, a stone, to an object of art is closely related to our impact on matter. Artistic activity breaks the temporal symmetry of an object. It leaves the mark that translates our temporal dissymmetry into the temporal dissymmetry of the object. Out of the reversible, nearly cyclic noise level in which we live arises music that is both stochastic and time-oriented.

Ilya Prigogine and Isabelle Stengers

Visual art's flirtation with systems theory and cybernetics has a strange trajectory that starts in the Fifties, namely with Independent Group founder John McHale's interest in ecology related to design and architecture (directly mediated by Buckminster-Fuller), and comes back in the Seventies in the core of conceptual art's relationship with information theory, in the work of Hans Haacke or Martha Rosler for their sculptural simulations of living systems and of Stephen Willats for its more openly cybernetic approach. Artist and critic Jake Burnham has been the most prominent translator of such an approach in the aesthetic field; his seminal text *Systems Esthetics* was published in *Artforum* in 1968, setting a solid theoretical framework: "the specific function of modern didactic art has been to show that art does not reside in material entities, but in relations between people and between people and the components of their environment.'[1] Such a long-term interest is perhaps based on a somehow metaphysical fascination with an all-encompassing model, which would demonstrate how all the different sections of life as well as the different domains of knowledge are connected and interdependent, exactly like any living organism in its environment. This figure of theoretical rhetoric ignited man's understanding in the dream for a holistic vision of the human condition in connection with the universe. Similar to a religious belief, systems theory - and to a much greater extent its 'second cousin' structuralism - aimed at a linguistic framework able to explain the large amount of biological, intellectual and social phenomena in a single bird's-eye view. The unprecedented advantage of the systemic approach was rooted in its relationship with biology, which would give it a grounding far from any metaphysical claim, as it based itself on the translation of formal observable models from science into theoretical speculation. It allowed both to rephrase old problems and to explain the newly born information theory, linking past and future in a synergic approach. This was the dream of one single universal code that can be used to translate across disciplines as well as different organisms and environments.

For John McHale, contemporary art - not dissimilarly from contemporary architecture - was a tool projected towards tomorrow, an accessory that would

1 Jack Burnham, 'Systems Aesthetics', republished in Jack Burnham, *Great Western Salt Works - Essay on the meaning of Post-Formalist Art*, George Braziller, 1974 p. 16; In relation to Haacke's early work Burnham specifies: 'Some recent tendencies in Haacke'swork intrigue me. One is the willingness to use all form of organic life - from the most elementary to the most complicated. This seems a logical extension of his philosophy of natural systems. A work of last winter [this text was publishedin 1969] involved the incubation of chicks as an ongoing process. Already Haacke is planning more complete animal "ecologies" where information is derived from the normal activities of aanimals in their environment" Jack Burnham, 'Real Time Systems', in Jack Burnham, *Great Western Salt Works*, Op. Cit, p. 30; see also Burnham's exhibition *Software, Information Technology: Its New meaning for Art*, Jewish Museum, New York, 1970

2 John McHale, 'Are they Cultured?', in *This is Tomorrow*, The Whitechapel Art Gallery, 1956, p. 30. For McHale's more advance investigation on design art and ecosystemic approach see John McHale, *The Future of the Future*, Studio Vista Limited, 1969 as well as John McHale, *The Ecological Context*, Studio Vista Limited, 1971

allow man to integrate into the cultural and biological landscape of the future. In his contribution to the catalogue of the seminal exhibition "This is Tomorrow", he spells out the function that art and architecture share: "at a point in human affairs where the actual nature of such reality as traditionally evidenced by the senses is under question, to depict tomorrow in the guise of today's artefacts, perceived and embroidered according to our present assumptions about their relevance to man, becomes pointless. Any change in man's environment is indicative of a change in man's relation to it, in his actual mode of perceiving and symbolising his interaction with it.'[2] Man will finally reach a better understanding of his present and future condition in the world through the application of technology only if situated in the larger economic system that does not just consider short-term advantages, but rather places human activity in the middle of a net of biological, social and cultural interrelations. The future represents the field of action for a long-term ecological commitment towards man and his universe, and the time/space for projecting aesthetic energy.

The dark side of the same urgency to address time and its asymmetry inevitably revolves around the notion of entropy and dissolution that obsessed the mind and imbued the practice of artists from Robert Smithson to Gustav Metzger. The second law of thermodynamics - according to which entropy in a closed system increases over time, increasing the system's disorder - is the most fascinating postulate, which again cuts across disciplines and is related to any systems theory, from biology to information theory to economy and recycling. Its implications go so far beyond its merely factual application, that this has opened space for metaphorical speculation of such religious subjects as inevitable catastrophic future, death, and the problem of the irreversibility of time, with which every theology as well as teleology have to come to terms. If the genealogy of the purely systemic approach can be traced back to protagonists of diverse disciplinary applications such as Buckminster-Fuller (architecture and technology), Ludwig von Bertalanffy (biology), Gregory Bateson (psychology), Margaret Mead (anthropology), and Norbert Weiner (the founder of cybernetics), the protagonists of the entropic side such as George Bataille, Ilya Prigogine and Michel Serres surrender to a deeper fascination with[?] chaos, disorder and accursed dispersion.

In a deeper look at system theory, the interrelatedness of the ecosystem as a methodological notion is easily abstracted into the generalised living structure through which all sorts of distant natural and artificial phenomena, as well as man's mind itself can be interpreted: "let me now begin to talk about the individual organism. The entity is similar to the oak wood and its controls are represented in the *total* mind, which is perhaps only a reflection of the total body. But the system is segmented in various ways, so that the effects of something in your food life, shall we say, does not alter your sex life, and things in your sex life do not change your kinesic life, and so on. There is a certain amount of compartmentalisation, which is no doubt a necessary economy."[3] In the cybernetic model, art has a reiterative function, its mission would be to point to the interconnectedness that we tend to forget.[4] Taking the full advantages of the ecosystem approach, the similarity can be extended to artistic practice not only to illustrate a point about the artwork's content level, but also to apply understandings and theoretical findings to the art discourse as an ecosystem in its capacity system for the production of meaning.[5] The further breakdown of systems within systems would then be useful in the study of the interaction of single works as systemic units whose meaning and functioning is strictly dependent on art discourse as a living organism in constant dynamic adaptation.[6] Can we consider then the ecosystem model as a 'medium' used by artists to construct their work? Could we push this idea as far as importing some ecosystemic evaluation into aesthetic theory and attempt to formulate aesthetic judgements thanks to this, perhaps inappropriate, 'translation'?

3 Gregory Bateson, *Steps to an Ecology of Mind*, Jason Aronson, 1987, p. 437-438

4 "There is what Freud called the royal road to the unconscious. He was referring to dreams, but I think that we should lump together dreams and the creativity of art, and the perception of art, and poetry and such things. And I would include with these the best of religion. These are all activities in which the whole individual is involved. The artist may have a conscious purpose to sell his picture, even perhaps a conscious purpose to make it. But tin he making he must necessarily relax that arrogance in favour of a creative experience in which his conscious mind plays only a small part. We might say that in the creative act man must experience himself - his total self - as a cybernetic model." Ibid, p. 440 This approach is furthermore reinforced by the openly cybernetic practice of Stephen Willats: "As a counter force to perceptual conformity the art work provides the audience with a symbolic environment in which connections, and interactions can be made between disparate Information, in ways which would not be permissible within the reality of their own world." Stephen Willats, 'The "Group" as Social Analogue in Art Practice', in Stephen Willats, *Attitudes within Four Relationships*, Southampton Art Gallery, 1977, p. 4. This was the way in which art could be at the avant-garde of trans-disciplinarity: "Cybernetics - the catalyst for the development of computer sciences - offered sets of ideas (feedback, system of self-organised control, similarities between scientific and social pehomena) which enabled the artist of constructor to make models (mathematical or otherwise) for works which actively involve the audience." Richard Francis. 'Stephen Willats', in *Stephen Willats - Three Essays*, ICA London, 1986, p. 7

5 "We also need to extend the physical and biological concepts of ecology to include the social behaviours of man - as equally critical factors within the ecosystem. The earth has not only been changed by scientific and technological transformations for particular economic and industrial functions - but these have spurred by specific value attitudes, by politico-ethical systems, by art, by religion, by the need for social contiguity and communication expressed in cities, by highway systems, and so forth." John McHale, *The Ecological Context*, Op. Cit., p. 3

6 In a matrioska fashion we could endlessly analyse systems containing other system, perhaps ending up in an blinding cybernetic infatuation that already occurred in the 1970s: "A major illusion of the art system is that art resides in specific objects. Such artefacts are the material basis for the concept of the 'work of art'. But in essence, all institutions which process art data, thus making information, are component of the work of art. Without the support system the object ceases to have definition" Jack Burnham, 'Real Time Systems', in Jack Burnham, *Great Western Salt Works*, Op. Cit, p. 27

According to Rosalind Krauss, who limpidly phrased what could be considered the canonical definition of medium-specificity, "in order to sustain artistic practice, a medium must be a supporting structure, generative of a set of conventions, some of which, in assuming the medium itself as their subject, will be wholly 'specific' to it, thus producing an experience of their own necessity"[7]. This definition of medium (leaving aside for a moment its own specificity) has the advantage of opening up if we expand the definition of "supporting structure", extending its boundaries from what could be considered a technical support (a canvas, marble, photography, text) as well as from the work's prominent feature (such as the work's content or the issues or the set of concerns it refers to, e.g contradiction in the work of Marcel Broodthaers). A supporting structure can indeed be an idea, a concept or a concern, providing that it is treated through the conventions it generates and that it is addressed recursively. It seems legitimate to compare the notion of supporting structure with that of system and Krauss's definition is not dissimilar from the definition of living structure, especially in Maturana and Varela's notion of autopoietic machine.[8] Likewise, an ecosystem is defined by the interaction of its organisms exchanging energy and materials with their surroundings in a state of dynamic stability and harmony.[9] A work of art with ecosystemic connotation could be considered one able to generate a visible or partly implied four-dimensional map functioning - metaphorically or literally - as a living organism in interaction with its cultural and art historical environment. If we accept this definition, we can explore further how to judge an artwork 'ecosystemically' and investigate if the values activated by this judgement can be tentatively delineated.

So, what exactly constitutes a four-dimensional map and how does it become intelligible? A work of art consciously or unconsciously inserts itself into a network of meaning that has historical, social and symbolic values and implications as well as interconnections. A work that employs the notion of ecosystem as its supporting structure succeeds in delineating a set of relations and the prospect of their changing over time (the fourth dimension). As with the 4D design of Buckminster-Fuller's *dymaxion* or the time-based architecture of Cedric Price, time represents a key factor in the creation of adaptable structures in a constant state of dynamic equilibrium. The addition of the fourth dimension nonetheless brings us back to two important factors: on the one hand, the issue of reversibility connected to the second law of thermodynamics, on the other hand, the four-dimensional map, bothseem ultimately to testify to the notion of complexity rather than of didactic simplification as one of the indicators through which to judge an artwork ecosystemically. A complex work is one that is opposed to transparent communication and illustration: it might not be the role of art to communicate an issue or a state of affairs but rather to make it more complex and obscure, articulating its multiple, sometimes ambiguous and multifaceted implications. Ludwig Von Bertalanffy reminds us that "it has been said that energy is the currency of physics, just as economic values can be expressed in dollars or pounds"; in yet another act of translation we wonder if we could establish complexity as the currency of a provisional eco-aesthetics.[10] Such attitudes lead us to value works that, rather than pointing out solutions, pivot within their inner supporting system on a total dynamic ever-changing equilibrium - sometimes nurturing it, at other times concentrating on its disruptions (and here Smithson magically reappears to rescue us) as it is exactly here that we can find a more complex key with which to locate ourselves in our 4D map.[11]

Pointing to the relations inherent in a system is therefore not sufficient; this was the dream of the early application of cybernetics to art and perhaps ambiguously related to its technocratic infatuation with the implication of computer science.[12] Reversibility and its entropic implications must remain central to the aesthetic debate because of their symbolic potential. When time enters the picture, the teleological approach often verges into the theological one as the

[7] Rosalind Krauss, *A Voyage on the North Sea: Art in the Age of the Post-Medium Condition*, Thames & Hudson, 2000, p. 26

[8] *"An autopoietic machine is a machine organised (defined as a unity) as a network of processes of production (transformation and destruction) of component that produces the components which: (i) through their interactions and transformations continuously regenerate and realise the network of processes (relations) that produced them; (ii) constitute it (the machine) as a concrete unity in the space in which they (the components) exist by specifying the topological domain of its realisation as such a network.* It follows that an autopoietic machine continuously generates and specifies its own organisation through its operation as a system of production of its own components, and does this in an endless turnover of components under conditions of continuous perturbations and compensation of perturbation" Humberto R. Maturana and Francisco J. Varela, *Autopoiesis and Cognition*, D.Reidel Publishing Company, 1972, p. 78-79

[9] The systemic approach to ecology pioneered by Howard T. Odum in particular generated this simple definition: "Living organisms and their nonliving (aboitic) environment are inseparably related and interact upon each other. Any entity or natural unit that includes living and nonliving part interacting to produce a stable system in which the exchange of materials between the living and nonliving parts is an ecological system or ecosystem." Howard T. Odum and Eugene P. Odum, *Fundamentals of Ecology*, W. B. Saunders Company, 1953 p. 9; in art theory the system introduced by Burnham as a key to understand conceptual and information art was described as: "we have considered the system - a complex of seen and unseen forces in stable relationship - as becoming ascendant form of visual expression. The system, like the art object, is a physical presence, yet one that does not maintain the viewer-object dichotomy but tends to integrate the two into a set of shifting interacting events" Jack Burnham, *Beyond Modern Sculpture - The Effects of Science and Technology on the Sculpture of this Century*, Allen Lane The Penguin Press London, 1968, p. 372

[10] Ludwig von Bertalanffy, *General System Theory*, Op. Cit., p. 41

[11] "Of course, by the early 1970s, numerous artists were already investigating questions of ecological intervention and reclamation - people as variable in style and attitude as Helen and Newton Harrison, Hans Haacke, Betty Beaumont and Alan Sonfist. There seems to be little evidence in his writing or public comments that Smithson felt any particular affinity to this strand of work. After all, his primary ambition - and this in fact unifies all his other impulses - usually seemed less to suggest how a particular site might be fixed, but rather to consider the ways in which it

temporality brings along the notions of death and dissolution. In his book *The Accursed Share - Essay on General Economy*, George Bataille identifies energy circulation as the key force of biological as well as human activity. He calls it a cosmic phenomenon that regulates life on the planet and in the universe. His deep fascination is directed towards the excess of energy that cannot be used, and has to be spent with no profit in a dissipative gesture.[13] In his grand schema, energy gets used in normal economic consumption, while its surplus is dissipated in extreme conditions such as war or is channelled into exuberant luxury. In the latter category he gathers three natural modes of luxurious squandering": eating, death and sexual reproduction, to which he contrasts two modes set to control energy expense: labour and technology.[14] Entropy and its irreversible necessity become in Bataille's vision a fascinating theoretical metaphor for man's unavoidable tragic condition. Bataille values dissipation on a symbolic level as a paradoxical and glorious state of exuberance; his belief turns what is valued as morally reproachable - namely waste - into a symbolic operation in which meaning is created by excess and dissipation.

Bataille is not the only thinker who tried to change our acquired comprehension of the loss of order (entropy) from a negative effect into a positive resource. The outbreak of non-linear thermodynamics allowed for the scientific notion of "dissipative system" to emerge. This definition, delineated by the Nobel Prize chemist Ilya Prigogine and philosopher of science Isabelle Stengers, includes any open system, such as hurricanes or cyclones, exchanging energy and matter with the environment in a condition "far from thermodynamic equilibrium", which could roughly be translated into a positively chaotic system.[15] This occurs when a system is fluctuating in such a powerful way, because of positive feedback, that it destroys the pre-existing organisation; the unpredictable result of this bifurcation could be chaos or organisation of a higher order. In these conditions, stability and equilibrium - the much valued factors of old general systems theory - lose their teleological status of unquestionable superiority to leave some space for positive action to chance, chaos, necessity and disorder. If Bataille values excess and dissipation as a necessary symbolic activity in which life's exuberance is ritually celebrated, Prigogine is far from making moral and aesthetic value judgements over chaos, waste and entropy. In his understanding there is no scientific loss in disorganisation but on the contrary there might be gain in complexity, which is the value that gets produced - in a logical paradox - through chaos far-from-equilibrium. Loss is not a negative value for Prigogine. Differently from Bataille who values it on a symbolic level (poiesis), he values it on a practical level (praxis), grounding his judgement in scientific evaluation[16].

Can an artwork be a dissipative structure rather than a general system? Can such structure be a medium? Here might lie the main difference with the hopes of Burnham's *Systems Esthetics* and of cybernetics art of the Seventies. Then, values such as stability of the system and control of its components gave its protagonists the possible ultimate filter to dominate the real, one that accepted the dream of information technology and the quasi-religious underpinning of structuralism: "the stabilised dynamic system will become not only a symbol of life but literally life in the artist's hands and the dominant medium of further aesthetic ventures."[17] Far from placing the same optimism in the ultimate systemic approach, we can approximate, and possibly add the value of disorder to complexity as a key factor in our aesthetic judgment, confident - bearing in mind the model of dissipative structures - that if we do not deem it a negative factor it might lead the artwork to a higher degree of organisation, certainly a more *complex* nonlinear system.[18] In the second incipit quotation, Prigogine and Stengers place man's symbolic activity precisely on the cusp between order and disorder, between reversible and irreversible, between eternity and entropy's time arrow. According to them, art's achievement would consist in translating our temporal dissymmetry (entropy's

was broken. And always how these breaks, these disruptions, might serve to instantiate the resonant entropic residues he flavoured." Jeffrey Kastner, 'There, Now: From Robert Smithson to Guantanamo', in Max Andrews (Ed.) *Land, Art - A Cultural Ecology Handbook*, Royal Society of Arts, 2006, p. 28

12 "To use another cybernetic analogy, artists are 'deviation-amplifying' systems, or individuals who, because of psychological makeup, are compelled to reveal psychic truths at the expenses of existing societal homeostasis. With increasing aggressiveness, one of the artist's functions, I believe, is to specify how technology uses us." Jack Burnham, 'Real Time Systems', *Op. Cit.*, p. 38

13 "I will begin with a basic fact: The living organism, in a situation determined by the play of energy on the surface of the globe, ordinarily receives more energy than is necessary for maintaining life; the excess energy (wealth) can be used for the growth of a system (e.g., an organism); if the system can no longer grow, or if the excess cannot be completely absorbed into its growth, it must be necessarily be lost without a profit; it must be spent, willingly or not, gloriously or catastrophically." George Bataille, *The Accursed Share - An Essay on General Economy*, Zone Books, 1988, p. 21

14 The volumes of Bataille's *The Accursed Share* are famously divided into Volume 1: Consumption, Volume 2: The History of Eroticism and Volume 3: Sovereignity.

15 "Entropy increases only because of irreversible processes. During the nineteenth century the final state of thermodynamic evolution was at the centre of scientific research. This was equilibrium thermodynamics Irreversible processes were looked down as nuisance, as disturbance, as subject not worthy of study. Today this situation has changed. We now know that far from equilibrium, new types of structures, new types of structures may originate spontaneously. In far-from-equilibrium conditions we may have transformation from disorder, from thermal chaos, into order. Newdynamic states of matter may originate, states that reflect the interaction of a given system with its surroundings. We have called these new structures *dissipative structures* to emphasize the constructive role of dissipative processes in their formation" Ilya Prigogine and Isabelle Stengers, *Order Out of Chaos - Man's new Dialogue with Nature*, Heinemann, 1984, p. 12

16 "Increasing entropy is no longer synonymous with loss but now refers to the *natural processes* within the system. These are the processes that ultimately lead the system to thermodynamic "equilibrium" corresponding to the state of maximum entropy." Ilya Prigogine and Isabelle Stengers, *Ibid.*, p. 120

17 Jack Burhnam, *Beyond Modern Scupture*, Op. Cit. P. 376

18 A nonlinear system is one whose behaviour is not equal to the sum of its parts.

irreversible linear timeline) and inserting it into the object's dissymmetry, by the way of including in such a gesture all the paradoxes and contradictions embedded in the process. Good art is, therefore, a symbolic activity that inscribes its multi-layered implications in the process of transformation/translation of energy, matter, and concept, without sanitising it of the noise that such a conversion process produces.

Is disorder then another currency value of aesthetics? Perhaps we can allow the aesthetic field to be the one in which more than a single currency is spent, one in which a particular combination of continuous exchange generates singular, non-replicable episodes combining many currencies together amongst which 'noise' is certainly one. We could then gather disorder, noise, and complexity under the many possible translations of entropy and its symbolic and material consequences. It is precisely in the interference produced while constructing a four-dimensional dynamic system striving for its equilibrium that we can identify an indicator of aesthetic transformation: in the politics of change, noise and interference should be valued as additional means of transport rather than the unusable waste of the translation or transformation process. Such means of transport will activate yet another communication, at times dealing with symbolic activity, at others transmitting a more crystalline message. The work of art concentrates on the disruption of equilibrium of any kind, investigating asymmetry and aiming at contradictions as valuable manifestations of positive disorder.

In the view of post-structuralist philosopher Michel Serres, poetry is the noise of science. On the cusp between order and disorder, human creativity is able to produce new meaning, a new order, a more complex one: "noise destroys and horrifies. But order and flat repetition are in the vicinity of death. Noise nourishes a new order. Organisation, life, and intelligent thought live between order and noise, between disorder and perfect harmony. If there were only order, if we heard only perfect harmonies, our stupidity would soon fall into a dreamless sleep; if we were always surrounded by shivaree, we would lose our breath and our consistency, we would spread out among all the dancing atoms of the universe."[19] It is in the ambivalent non-equilibrium status between noise and harmony that ecosystemic art should be positioned. Serres advocates the translation between disciplines as one in which a message is transformed through the use of a particular channel. This transformative activity is bound to produce interference, a noise that could be valued rather than considered waste. The operation set up by this very essay as well as by the art that the essay is advocating are both such noise machines, translations producing interference conceived as a symbolic activity that seems peculiarly located in the art discourse.[20] A noise machine refuses to serve as a channel tackling issues directly and unequivocally. It rather leaves the task of appropriating clear communication to efficient graphic design and transparent journalism. We leave to artists the mission to construct appropriate noise machines, generating opacity rather than communicating efficiently, finally complicating with ambiguity and complexity our vision and our understanding of man's position, within and not outside the ecosystemic four-dimensional nonlinear model.

[19] Michel Serres, *The Parasite*, John Hopkins, 1982 p. 127

[20] "Cela était déjà vrai de la notion méthodique de symbole: si l'analyse symbolique était le fait de ce que nous avons appelé en gros la critique romantique, tout le XIX siècle savant, mathématicien, physicien, etc., pratiquait ce type de pensée, calcul symbolique, modèles physiques, économiques, etc. Merleau-Ponty, dans *L'Oeuil et l'esprit*, a deviné ce genre de translation des procedés méthodiques, mais il a affaibli sa généralité en alléguant la mode et en donnant que l'exemple peu significatif du gradient. De fait, il n'y a vraiment mode que lorsque joue *une certaine loi d'entropie* dans la suite des importations successives et qu'en un point donné de cette suite, l'acception rigoureuse du concept s'est perdue, en partie ou en totalité, et qu'on ne parle plus de lui qu'en oui-dire, comme un enfant essaye les mots des grandes personnes." Michel Serres, *Hermès ou la Communication*, Edition de minuit, 1968, p 28

BETWEEN HUMAN DESIRE AND THE LAW OF NATURE: SOME EXAMPLES OF MAN'S RELATIONSHIP TO THE PLANET IN CURRENT ARTISTIC PRACTICE

Akiko Miki

Man's relationship with the earth is not a new theme in the history of art. Since the time of mankind's appearance on the planet, and from the paintings of 19th century Romanticism to the large-scale Land art and Environmental art projects of the 1960s and 1970s, to the more recent Ecological art activities, many artists have explored this fundamental question.

This theme, however, has become absolutely crucial in recent years and the artistic propositions in problematising related issues such as excessive urban development, pollution, the misuse, abuse and exhaustion of the earth's natural resources, etc. are taking increasingly diversified directions. Quite recently, some specialists have anticipated the displacement of 200 million people because of an increase in ocean levels, as well as the future extinction of 40 percent of animal species.[1] Others warn of frequent heat waves in 2040, outbreaks of dengue fever even in the temperate zones in 2080, or the disappearance of the tropical forests and their desertification one hundred years from now. In such horrendous circumstances, no one living on earth, including artists, can ignore completely the question of man's relationship with the earth: how are we to treat our planet? What do we owe the earth, and what does it owe us? What is our place in the world? What are our responsibilities and our privileges?

Many artists have actively taken on projects to confront these problems. One example is " Wind Caravan - Observation of Our Planet " by the Japanese artist Susumu Shingu. This time-long project is an attempt to find out, through artistic activities and cultural exchange with local people, how we can live in harmony with nature and what true happiness is. Another example is "Cape Farewell" by the British artist David Buckland. Buckland organised expeditions to the High Arctic, inviting artists such as Gary Hume, Antony Gormley and Rachel Whiteread, as well as scientists and educators to address and raise awareness about climate change. Meanwhile, others, particularly some younger generation artists, raise these questions in more indirect or abstract ways by blending critical analysis and the formal quality of plastic art and presenting them in an artistic context. Here, I would like to discuss some of the latter examples of artists from different corners of the world, separately from those artists participating in this year's Biennial.

Symbiosis

It may sound odd for me to start talking about Ikebana, the Japanese tradition of flower arrangement which was much developed in the 14th century and is still widely practised in my country today. However, some ideas of Ikebana seem to be particularly meaningful when thinking about the current artistic practices of some younger generation artists. It is often said that Ikebana is an artistic practice, but not a main player. Its artistry lies in the positioning of the arrangement in relation to the flower vase, and the harmony of these elements. The basic attitude of the practice is to do with appreciating what the god Nature has created. In other words, no human activity can be isolated from its environment or from nature, and nothing can be created entirely by man alone. Such sensibility and attitude can be found at the core of the activities of Swedish artist Henrik Håkansson.

Håkansson is probably one of those artists who come first to mind when viewing Man's relationship with the earth, especially with nature. Since the very beginning of his career in the early Nineties, Håkansson has actively employed real plants as principal materials, as well as focusing on the daily lives of animals,

1 Nicholas Stern, "Review on the Economics of Climate Change", The Treasury, UK, October, 2006

birds, and insects in creating his artworks. A wall entirely covered with lush vegetation providing a suitable habitat for insects, an upside-down tropical forest in which the spectators are invited to walk beneath and amongst the plants, or a forest of one hundred epiphytic orchids each growing on a fragment from a tree limb suspended in the air are some of the best examples. They are equipped with watering, heating, and solar systems so that each forms an autonomous living unit. Håkansson observes, documents and films them using the most sophisticated technological devices in the way of pseudo-scientific research. His works do not offer an idealised depiction of nature, nor do they propose a didactic analysis. Rather, the artist simply extracts the fragments from nature and presents them in an artistic context, but in a very specific way, in the guise of the world of spectacle - with stages, beam lights, posters, vinyl records, etc., as though the decaying plants and the species in process of extinction are pop stars. His attention often settles on scenes that are foreign to us, like the film of a sleeping anaconda recorded by a surveillance camera, a vision that certainly exists, but is far removed from our daily urban lives. Is the way that Håkansson slowly shows the destruction of nature by putting plants in absurd and stressful conditions a metaphor for how man treats nature? And do the animals in his works, who seem so close but impossible to communicate with, suggest to us the isolation of the human species from nature? Many questions arise. Through these questions, the artist both awakens our sensibility to natural phenomena and diversity, and reminds us that we are part of a broader biological system, i.e., the planet.

Everything Interacts

In the case of Swiss artists Gerda Steiner and Jörg Lenzlinger, the connection between the different elements is even more important. Their art-making starts by their travelling to various parts of the world. As one can clearly see from their book *Stupid and Good Miracles* (2003), which mixes the scenes/oddities they have come across and the installations they have realised during their travels - often extending over long periods of time - the duo believe that the way to create art is to receive inspiration from the various subjects they encounter and further develop relationships between them. Whenever they visit a place to conceive and create a specific artwork, they learn about the local culture as well as the different planting techniques, local systems of gardening, and what the scientists of each different region discover through the plants. The artists see all the world's secrets in what surrounds the plants and different materials, and by continuing to learn about them and their diversity, they try to understand the world in a more profound way.

Steiner and Lenzlinger collect all sorts of things from local people, including waste materials such as electric cords, broken toys, etc., and integrate them into complex and poetic installations together with vegetation and other materials they purchase on site. In their recent installation "Night Moths in the Whale Belly" (2006) in Japan, both new and old materials, such as a bird's nest they found in Africa, a fishing net and discarded styrofoam from a nearby beach, as well as food samples and artificial flowers bought at local shops, were all mixed together. What interests them in the creating process is the method of 'recycling'. Not only do the artists recycle the waste materials that are transformed into a mysterious existence by being put in a different context, but they also recycle their past works, for example, making wallpaper from the details of the earlier installation shots. Organic materials like crystal are often chosen by the artists. Crystal grows over time, manifesting different aspects at different locations and periods. One artist connects to the other continuously in their works. The artistic practice of Steiner and Lenzlinger may be described as weaving a fabric or gathering together the threads of a never-ending story. Their installations create metamorphosic effects and a playfulness between imagination and reality, exterior and interior, intimacy and openness, macroscopic and microscopic, and order and chaos. Indeed, the accumulation of detail in the works of Steiner and Lenzlinger itself represents the world. Through delicate strangeness and gentle beauty the artists tell us that the world may be full of charm if we look at our environment differently.

Source of Healing and Energy

Cai Guoqiang is best known for his large-scale art projects that use fireworks, an unconventional medium of expression invented in his native China. Cai's works are based on critical observation of the contemporary world and give direct commentary. They often take the form of ephemeral events creating mushroom clouds (directly evocative of the atomic bomb), by the means of fireworks. In the 90s, he realised a number of events in various areas of the United States, including the nuclear testing site at Nevada. The photographs of the events were distributed on postcards - thus the nuclear weapon became the speciality of the United States. A more recent installation work of a herd of ninety-nine wolves rushing blindly into a wall, thus killing themselves, points critically to the rise of nationalism as well as to animal extinction.

Cai's art revolves around a sensitivity to nature, and spiritual and cultural history, and is characterised by bold scale, Eastern wisdom, and unique humour; but more importantly we should not forget that he often intends it to be a source of healing and energy for those who experience it. This is clearly shown in his early work "Bringing to Venice what Marco Polo Forgot" (1995). This work includes an installation that merges imagery from the practice of acupuncture with local Venetian geography concerning the water from the Grand Canal, which is said to be among the most polluted in the world. Viewing Venice as a living organism, the artist offers remedies to cure the modern ills of the city. Cai talked about the project: "Marco Polo brought back to the West many new and rare things and interesting stories; but he did not bring back the important spirit, the Eastern view of the cosmos and of life. By using Chinese medicine as one of the symbols of this spirit, I will bring the things that Marco Polo could not."[2] A more recent work, "Caretta Fountain" (2002), is a fountain in the form of a tortoise shell placed at the very centre of the business and commercial complex in Tokyo, and it emphasizes connections with nature by bringing natural stone into the city and actively applying feng shui ideas. In fact, the number of projects using fireworks should also be interpreted as an intention to create a source of energy. Fireworks have been widely used for weapons over time. But Cai does not use them for violence. Instead, he uses them for the coexistence of nature and human beings by transmitting the accusation of nuclear arms, visualizing sympathetic vibration between the mother earth and the artist ... and more.

Creating a Platform

"Land Mark", a project that American artist Jennifer Allora and Cuban artist Guillermo Calzadilla developed together in 2003-06, deals with the question of Man's relationship with the earth in a very particular way, by considering the multiple and complex ways in which land is 'marked.' The project has been realised by taking as a sort of a case study the problems of the Puerto Rican island of Vieques with reference to the occupation of its land by the American military for around six decades. The use of the land as a US Navy bomb-testing range had considerable impact on the economic, social, cultural and ecological situation of Vieques, which used to be an island of tropical beauty inhabited by local fishermen. Although the land has not been used by the American military since 2003, following the efforts of the civil resistance movement, its future is still uncertain. Basing their work on the real story of Vieques, and in close contact with the activists of the land reclamation campaign and local people, the two artists realised their artistic propositions in videos, a book, a series of photographs

[2] Conversation with the curators, including the author. Exhibition catalogue, *Transculture*, Venice Biennale, 1995

and a floor sculpture. They remind us of the fact that all land is marked by a history of human presence and raise the questions: what does it mean for land to be marked? How does land get marked? Who decides what is worth preserving and what should be destroyed?[3]

For the photographic series, the two artists designed custom-made soles to be attached to the shoes of people involved in the land reclamation campaign. By the way that the protestors walked through the military land, their presence was marked in the form of footprints. Allora and Calzadilla's intention was that the footprints depict territories (geographical, bodily, linguistic, etc.) and function as counter-representations of the site's function at that time. They are also reminiscent of the mark left on the moon as a result of the space race and of the prints of colonisers first setting foot on new territory. Another piece, the large-scale floor sculpture, is an aesthetic and conceptual representation of part of the bomb-testing range; it utilises the same imaging technologies that the military uses - a critical re-appropriation of the military-used media.[4] The geometric beauty of the pattern is what strikes the spectators first of all. However, once they realise that they are physically experiencing the destruction of the land by walking directly onto it (in the same way that its destruction is caused by the bomb-tests), they are made to feel uncomfortable at the thought that the beautiful tropical lagoons that once covered the shallows of the seabed have now almost disappeared. Furthermore, this floor is not fixed. It is composed of a number of parts, simply arranged side by side, that can be fragmented, re-structured or re-configured; it conveys the instability of the present situation, yet functions as a kind of a platform for the future. The artist explains:

"All in all, the work considers how to make a testing ground for weapons of resistance against forces such as colonisation, globalisation, militarisation, and ecological destruction. It is a platform from which to stage fundamental debates about ethics, human rights, and justice in a global society increasingly prone to greater and more destructive forms of violence and aggression. Thus, the representation of this wounded territory can become a fertile ground, raw material with which to imagine, develop, and explore these issues, an intermediary transitional geography, between destruction and recovery."[5]

Truth of the Earth

Rockets against the blue sky, diverse views of an industrial rocket launch facility, a diver in a training pool, a seaside crane, a team of men and women who swim together in freezing conditions… these are the subjects that the Japanese photographer Rika Noguchi captures through her camera. With some exceptions, the photographs are set in the expansive views of broad horizontal bands of ground, sea and sky with little or no human presence. The images documenting the simple scenes are taken following a method that is similar to that of German conceptual photography. Contrary to the masters of this genre, however, the photographs of Noguchi are not at all enhanced or altered by manipulation. They are simply lit by mild everyday light; but this direct method paradoxically gives a strange effect to her images. Moreover, the scenes she captures do not seem to be of much importance to our contemporary eyes. Consequently, her photographs are often described as a vision of the earth by aliens.

In her images, two opposite atmospheres curiously co-exist: ordinary and extraordinary, dirty and beautiful, worldly and spiritual, or industrial and heavenly like the landscapes of Tanegashima Space Centre, a complex from which the Japanese Space Programme launches nearly all of its flights and located on the south island of natural beauty. Whereas the images tend to be calm and full of ethereal beauty, Noguchi's visions often focus on places at the four corners of the earth, as well as harsh landscapes, or at the limits of human reach, such as a sky, a high mountain, a lake in freezing conditions. In fact, firing rockets, diving

3 Jennifer Allora & Guillermo Calzadilla, Land Mark", Palais de Tokyo, site de création contemporaine/Paris Musées, 2006

4 Ibid.

5 Ibid. p. 54

6 Press document, Exhibition Rika Noguchi, *Somebodies*, Ikon Gallery, 2005

or swimming, all these are acts that defy the earth's gravity. By focusing on such landscapes and activities, the artist may be reminding us that planets, the sky, or underwater are not our natural habitat, whilst still being the realm of our desires and dreams. In spite of the fact that the images of such simple subject matters are available through the mass media, Noguchi insists on capturing the subjects herself. In order to photograph a diver, she took a divers licence; for the photos of the Space Centre, she worked at the local restaurant in exchange for sleeping at the owner's house, as there were no hotels available; for a series of photos of a blurry rocket and its smoke trail, she even made paper rockets and launched them herself. Noguchi's photographs are derived from her own curiosity and a wish to explore the truth as she sees it, in direct contact with the environment; she explains: "I wish to photograph the truth, to find new ways of looking at the earth...."[6] Her photographs suggest that there are still wonders, mystery and beauty on our planet and these may be seen simply through one's own will and effort.

The period in which we are living, at the beginning of the 21st century, is often described as a period of uncertainty, anxiety and impasse. In the 1960s Jean-Paul Sartre questioned what literature can do to overcome the critical condition . Now, many artists question what art can do to change the situation, as the artist may be the one who can provide the solution from a dimension that is different from, say, politics or science. Indeed, art is one of the few supranational domains that Humanity has succeeded in building and may have more power as a media than politics, which is still country-focused. As long as no action is taken, such as creating a kind of planetary government facing the ecological problem (despite numerous propositions made by society's intellectuals), each artist discussed here is exploring our living environment in his/her own way and trying to reveal the contradictions and complexities of the reality from historical, political, social, economic and cultural points of view. And more importantly, the artists' voices often reach more directly to the public than those of the politicians.

If the result of human desire has brought excessive urban development, pollution, the misuse, abuse and exhaustion of the earth's natural resources, it is also human desire endlessly to find earthly paradise. Desire represents worldly attachment, as well as karma from the religious perspective. But it is also a wellspring for human progress and potential. Everything has to be viewed from multiple perspectives. Perhaps the reason that these artworks particularly appeal to our eyes today is that they beautifully visualise and unify the industrial and the heavenly, the spiritual and material, the natural and artificial, destruction and recovery, and human desire and the law of nature – all of which may provide the keys to our future.

IN PRAISE OF OUR LIMITATIONS

Trevor Smith

> *To articulate the past historically does not mean to recognize it the way it really was. It means to seize hold of a memory as it flashes up at a moment of danger. In every era the attempt must be made anew to wrest tradition away from a conformism that is about to overpower it.*
>
> Walter Benjamin[1]

Lately an image of my younger self has been haunting me.

Twenty years ago, in the late 1980s, I was in my early twenties and had recently moved to Vancouver to study art history. The image that occurs to me now is not of a particularly momentous occasion or traumatic event; rather, it is more of a detail of daily life. I am walking between classes, spinning and twirling my umbrella - maroon with a wooden handle.

Having left the arid and extreme climate of my prairie childhood, I am revelling in the mild rain of this West Coast city and the novelty of an umbrella. If today, like many alienated urbanites, I associate umbrellas and sodden skies with bad moods and a deep desire to stay indoors, this connection had not yet occurred to me. The fecund sodden scent of the forest floor and the slow steady rain that could last for days contrasted sharply to the sudden breaking of a prairie thunderstorm, my nostrils burning as the cumulus clouds became thunderheads in the heat of the afternoon.

The looming environmental consciousness addressed by the 8th Sharjah Biennial was well understood by the late 1980s in Vancouver. I remember my fellow students and even professors hurrying between classes with insulated mugs attached to their bags. Everyone knew that it was not such a good idea to be throwing out endless paper and plastic cups. Grocery stores were encouraging the use of re-usable bags. Public transport was promoted. There was a strong environmental movement protesting the clear-cutting of large sections of rainforest.

One weekend, my friends and I travelled to the front lines driving slowly for a couple of hours down rutted logging roads. I remember moving through an incredibly dense forested landscape until we arrived at the site of a vast clear-cut, the anthropomorphic power of which it is difficult for me to articulate, except to say that it was as close to being in a war zone as I ever expected to be. In hindsight, I wonder why the pesticides and fertilisers that allowed farming monoculture to replace the great seas of native prairie grasses never struck me with the same force. Perhaps because the life cycle of grasses seems to be measured in annual cycles, rather than in the decades and even centuries that it might take a tree to reach maturity.

The tree has long been an important subject for artists in Vancouver. In the early 20th century Emily Carr depicted the rainforests of a remote Canadian province and many of her most famous images showed abandoned First Nation (Aboriginal) villages and rainforest landscapes. One of her most moving paintings was *Scorned as Timber, Beloved of the Sky*, 1935, which depicted a single crooked tree left standing in the middle of a clear-cut.

The contemporary artists of my generation depicted Vancouver less as a metropolitan centre than as a city of infinite margins; endless suburbs swallowing up rural acreage or coming to an abrupt stop at the forest edge. That the tree, almost more than modernist office blocks and bank buildings, has been a critical emblem in Vancouver's urban consciousness is something that Jeff Wall details in an essay written about the same time that I was still smelling the forest and twirling my umbrella in the rain:

1 Walter Benjamin, "Theses on the Philosophy of History", *Illuminations*, (New York: Schocken Books, 1969), p. 255

"In the same social process in which the beautiful productive trees of the forest are counted out of existence by unplanned overharvesting, the unproductive trees of the cities are strategically marshalled into position in the ideological struggle. How easy it is to fall back into the belief in the still-existing harmony of city and country when Vancouver seems nestled in the cyclic life of thousands of these decorative sentinels. Urban planting emphasises ensembles of greenery, composed of numbers of tree-emblems arranged repetitively along streets or clustered picturesquely in open spaces and parks. Rarely do we see an isolated tree in the city. The reason for this is profoundly ideological. The lone tree is the great ancient symbol of the mortal individual, rooted in the totality of nature yet suffering its solitary destiny. In an epoch when the totality of nature begins to suffer mortally, we begin to be able to see it as an individual".[2]

One of Rodney Graham's signature motifs has been precisely this lone-tree emblem turned on its head. Inaugurated with *Camera Obscura*, 1979, Graham returned to the subject on several occasions over the next 25 years. In Wall's *Pine on the Corner*, 1990 it is also possible to see an example of just such an individual tree in the city, "rooted in the totality of nature yet suffering its solitary destiny". A lone pine tree towers over the modest two family homes to its left. Another work from 1990, Ken Lum's *A Woodcutter and his Wife*, is a dryly humorous depiction of the economic and social relationships in British Columbia's resource-based economy. The couple are wearing plaid checked shirts, work boots, hats and jeans, and standing in front of the base of a tree wider than the pair of them put together. Around the same time Roy Arden began producing his photographs depicting the "landscape of the economy" such as *Tree Stump, Nanaimo, B.C.*, 1991 in which a tree stump is seen lying on the ground, the cut where the trunk has been severed facing the camera, like a decapitated body. Slightly later Ian Wallace's series *Clayoquot Protest (August 9, 1993), 1993-95*, depicted the massive protests triggered by the provincial government's attempt to open over half of the pristine wilderness area of Clayquot Sound on the west coast of Vancouver Island to logging operations.

If I were to look through rose-coloured glasses I'd like to say that these artists inspired my environmental awareness - though I think it more accurate to say that they inculcated in me a sense of the political contradictions and cultural ironies that perpetuate the misuse of the environment. The relationship between these works of art and the environmental movement was not one of direct engagement; instead art provided the much needed emblems of critical reflection absent from media sound bites and strident calls to mobilise public opinion. While reduce, reuse, recycle was not a bad mantra to live by, it was certainly more of a palliative than a cure. Through the works of these artists I gained more of an understanding of the complex cultural ecoystem within which ethical and aesthetic choice is bound in a complex relationship to the environment.

In spite of the fact that several of the artists in Vancouver had substantial international reputations and others were beginning to be so recognised, what strikes me most clearly in my recollection is not how worldly I felt but how inevitably limited my horizons were. However provincial I was, this was not - as would often be assumed - a barrier to gravitating towards the most ambitious vanguard art I could see around me. Quite the reverse, I think such limitations were critical to my hunger for new explicitly cosmopolitan knowledge - such as I felt to be represented by artists, their works and writings.

Having now lived in six cities on two continents and having had the opportunity to work and travel extensively around the world, it is strange to remember that in the late 1980s Vancouver was the largest, most cosmopolitan city I had ever

[2] Jeff Wall, "Into the Forest: Two Sketches for Studies of Rodney Graham's Work" in *Rodney Graham* (Vancouver Art Gallery, 1988), p. 16

lived in - many times larger than Regina, where I was born and grew up. I had never been to the Venice Biennale or Documenta. There was not yet the intense proliferation of Biennials that we have seen over the last decade - the Sharjah Biennial was itself founded in 1993. It would be another year before I would even visit New York for the first time.

Naturally, when speculation ensued about how New York was losing its position at the centre of the art market to cities like Cologne, I had no perspective whatsoever. While I was beginning to encounter the contemporary art flourishing around me, I did so not through the art market - there was no local market to speak of for the kinds of conceptual and photo-based practices that built Vancouver's international reputation - but through the Vancouver Art Gallery and fellow students and colleagues who were involved in artist-run spaces where the most vital contemporary art was taking place.

Learning more and more about art, cinema, philosophy, politics and the usual brew of student experiences, I developed a hard-won but precarious sense of empowerment, as if confirming philosopher Michel Foucault's dictum Knowledge=Power. At the same time, the environmental movement's mantra, "Think Global, Act Local", only confirmed in me a sense of efficacy and purpose.

Exciting as this was, there came a point of diminishing returns where all this worldly knowledge seemed ultimately to complicate or to show up the contradiction in any action. The certitude with which I embraced the idea of "Think Global, Act Local" began to rapidly break down after moving to Australia in the early 1990s. There, I began to understand the profoundly conservative downside of this mantra. Acting locally, you can never contest your place in the world. If you are on the margins you remain more or less powerless and if you are in the centre it is too easy to become complacent in your own power and cultural efficacy. Yet, in an increasingly globalised market-place, even simple local initiatives like recycling can have a profound economic impact, just not always the one you might expect. Recently the photographer Zoe Leonard has been photographing bales of recycled clothing sitting outside industrial sorting centres in New York. Tracing their journey, Leonard has photographed the same clothing being sold in village markets in Africa. The used t-shirts, suit jackets and so on are sold so cheaply that they undercut precarious but long-term local textile industries, thus complicating a cycle of global dependencies. Next time you see a child in the Congo wearing a shirt with an American flag on it, realise it likely has nothing to do with a love for America (or Def Leppard or Slayer for that matter) and everything to do with economics.

For a time, I thought it might be possible to revise these terms to "Think Local, Act Global." I wanted to use specifically local concerns and particularities as the motivating factor in developing exhibitions while engaging in dialogues that would be more global in their scope - more or less the curatorial motivation for the development of many biennials over the last decade. While in Perth, I might have been on the margins of the global centres of contemporary art, I wanted to work and behave as if I was at the absolute centre. Every show not only had to feed some local particularity or concern but also had to try somehow to intervene in that larger discussion. I no longer saw myself as provincial and I wanted to provide a way into that larger conversation for those who were interested, much as the artists and professors had done for me in Vancouver a decade before.

Needless to say, this exhibition strategy could easily accommodate environmental concerns and themes - even if environmental praxis remained elusive. Singaporean performance artist Tang da Wu's *I'm sorry whale I didn't know that you were in my camera*, 1998 drew an impassioned response from visitors.[3] A lifesize effigy of a whale was constructed out of chicken wire and prayer papers onto which visitors were invited to place objects or notes that related to their involvement with or use of the environment. By the end of the exhibition that whale looked as barnacle-encrusted as any creature that ever arose from the deep.

3 Tang da Wu's work was presented in the exhibition "Divide and Multiply: Tang da Wu and Lucas Jodogne", Art Gallery of Western Australia, 1998

Presenting the *Macrolab*, a self-sustained living and communications unit, on a nature reserve on an island 18 km off the coast of Perth in 2000 certainly required a new level of engagement with environmental concerns.[4] The ironies of trying to site a work of art some 40 feet long by 10 feet wide and 10 feet high, not including solar panels and wireless infrastructure in a highly sensitive environmental zone, was both challenging and thought-provoking. Daily conversations via wireless Internet brought visitors at the gallery into the picture and those who were visiting the island could drop by at certain times of day to converse with the crew-members. As I have been writing this article I have been logging on to the Interpolar Transnational Art Science Constellation website (www.interpolar.org), a project which grew out of the *Macrolab*. Their team has been in Antarctica researching the feasibility of establishing a research facility there. This long-term project is partly interesting for the almost science-fiction type of image it presents - at once in the environment yet strangely alienated from it.

What are more interesting somehow are the conversations engendered among the crew, not for deep philosophical insight but for an honest attempt to grapple with the privilege and the contradictions of their short time on the last continent on earth. Early in their stay Amanda Rodriguez Alves, one of the crew members, posted her frustration with the double standards of the environmental impact questions raised by the project:

> *"In general I find it hypocritical when people say we must preserve Antarctica, because it is the last great wilderness, without being at least as preoccupied in preserving the environments where we come from. If we are going to be radical about Antarctica we have to be radical about our own home. It is very easy to want to preserve something that is almost not touched but it is very hard to preserve what we already destroyed."*[5]

Knowledge might be power, but clearly having more and more information and sophistication does not mean that you have any outlet or power to transform worldly knowledge into action. Recently I watched Al Gore's Inconvenient Truth from the ironical position of sitting in a plane 10 thousand metres above the Atlantic Ocean. Gore is smooth, persuasive, calm in the face of what seem to be unsurmountably grim statistics. He shows the first image of the whole world taken from space by Apollo astronauts and talks about how this image inspired a wave of environmental consciousness in the late 1960s. Seeing the whole earth at once somehow cut things down to size, makes the earth appear both fine and fragile. Yet, paradoxically, the great difficulty with all the worldly knowledge we have about both art and the environment is that the issues seem so big and intractable that you just want to throw up your hands and walk away. As Rodriguez Alves says "it is very hard to preserve what we already destroyed".

If my provincial self flashes before my eyes in this moment of danger, it is because I am remembering how sometimes innocence can be a spur to action. Sometimes we know too much and the tasks in front of us appear impossible. Despite our search for worldly wisdom through projects like the Sharjah Biennial, I think we are all ultimately provincial, partial in vision, deeply implicated in our own experiential horizons and all too often lacking the power to transform our insight into action. Great art can of course be made out of this gap between exalted ends and finite means, Thomas Crow has articulated this as virtually the definition of the pastoral genre.[6] The evidence is not so promising when it comes to the environment. The attempt to exercise pastoral care is largely confined to localised situations - thinking globally while acting locally. Yet when it comes to bringing larger forms of power and instrumentality - such as the Kyoto Protocol for example - to bear on these issues they are deliberately undermined by countervailing desires and

[4] *Macrolab* was presented as part of "Home" at the Art Gallery of Western Australia in Perth, Australia in 2000. It was curated by Tom Mulcaire, Gary Dufour and myself. Mulcaire has gone on to partner with Marco Peljhan in establishing I-TASC (Interpolar Transnational Art Science Constellation).

[5] www.interpolar.org The crew diary can be found under the link "Now". Rodriguez Alves' comments were posted on December 31, 2006

[6] Thomas Crow, "The Simple Life: Pastoralism and the Persistence of Genre in Recent Art" in *Modern Art in the Common Culture*, (New Haven and London: Yale University Press, 1996), p. 177

[7] I am paraphrasing here the words of Robert MacPherson, a great artist and inspiration and one of the reasons I keep doing what I do.

specific interests that think locally while acting globally.

It is something of a paradox that art, which I saw as my gateway to an expanded world, now seems a painfully weak force in the face of the challenges posed by environmental change. Whether it is the epistemological drive that marks many of the great Vancouver artists or the more participatory aesthetic that was driving the projects I was involved in presenting in Perth, art stands diminished before nature. Of course, it has always been thus. The great landscape traditions, even at their most bombastic, have always been, by definition, acts of miniaturisation. Set those paintings out in the landscape and watch even the greatest of artworks disappear as you drive by at a hundred kilometres an hour.[7] Of course we don't view those kinds of paintings at that speed. And that is one of the interesting things about accepting art as a weak social force. It is a reminder that we have to slow down and sometimes accept our limitations.

Each generation finds new ways of re-ascribing a sense of importance to sharing modest pleasures and small, even provincial insights. Gradually accumulated, such attempts represent our collective endeavour to survive an age of great hubris.

Trevor Smith is Curator in Residence at the Center for Curatorial Studies, Bard College.

ECOlogical?

Reflections on the Relationship between Art and Environmentalism

Raimar Stange

I. Deconstruction or Decoration?

A river, suffused in a bright green pool of light - the colour owes itself to the presence of "Uranium". It concerns the work *Currents in the Weser* (1998) by the Icelandic artist Olafur Eliasson. Yet what is it really about? A piece of fluid Land Art? A painterly intervention in the landscape? A "fleeting monochromatic image" that "the flowing of the river makes visible"? Or a warning about environmental destruction, of "oil pollution"? What's exciting about this work is that all of these readings are possible. Open-ended it retains its claim to aesthetic or environmental activism. Olafur Eliasson himself speaks about "a gentle terrorism". But isn't this really the weakness of the work? Doesn't the fleeting fluid installation unwillingly change between decoration and deconstruction, between kitsch and merely background critique? In order to answer this question, a look at a second work of the artist is necessary, namely the installation "Your Waste of Time" (2006): five blocks of ice are placed in the Berlin gallery Neugerreimschneider, six tons of ice from the South Coast islands, up to 15,000 years old. They were transported across Europe, so that there, in the middle of Germany, they could be exhibited and ultimately, with the help of an elaborate cooling system, be "kept alive". After the exhibition the expensive cooling system is shut off, the ice melts, and the work consists then "only" of its (re-enactable) concept, in spite of its "end" it is saleable. On the one hand, the work is entirely aesthetic with its shiny ice surfaces and well-positioned cubes; they immediately remind one of the images of the German Romantic painter Caspar David Friedrich or of the Hollywood blockbuster *Titanic*. On the other hand they raise questions about the absurdity of the "all-is-transportable" concept that has become so inexpensive that it's profitable for nearly any mobile-business in relatively poor-income nations; one of the current consequences of Neoliberalism. Or there's the question of glacier melt and climate catastrophe, an issue brought up not only by the removal and later melting of ancient glacier ice, but also by cooling machines that actually speed up this process with their elevated energy consumption. Thus, Eliasson again demonstrates the tension between aesthetics and engagement. Nevertheless, don't these works ultimately remain stuck in the intelligently interpretable and pleasurably enjoyable zones? Isn't the precision of the analysis and the aggressiveness of the approach missing - things that might just perhaps have political consequences? Or is this consequence perhaps today no longer thinkable; is it too late and the global neoliberal pressure too intense for an environmental rebound anyway? Is Eliasson's approach modest, perhaps harmless, but unfortunately the only one still possible?

II. Excursus: A Selected History of the Environmental Movement

Human civilisation, according to many, is wrested from nature, the technical and the artificial is therefore of human origin. From the middle of the 19th century this unnaturalness was celebrated as the "modern," above all in France. The brothers Edmond and Jules de Goncourt, for example, wrote in their journals on July 1st, 1856: "The setting sun poured gold over the large gilded advertisements hanging over the passageway of the panorama. Never before had my eyes and heart been so enchanted as by the view of the plastered, clumped together facades ... hardly a frail tree bloomed in an asphalt crack - and these hideous facades spoke to me, in a way that nature rarely ever has." Nature appears "frail" from this perspective, and, in contrast, the hideous artificiality is a source of enchantment. Charles Baudelaire later became the high priest of this modern way of seeing. But the critics of such nature-hostile utterances don't wait to respond: "Let us not, however, flatter ourselves overmuch on account of our human victories over nature. For each such victory nature takes its revenge on us. Each victory, it is true, in the first place brings about the results we expected, but in the second and third places it has quite different, unforeseen effects, which only too often cancel the first. The people who, in Mesopotamia, Greece, Asia Minor and elsewhere, destroyed the forests to obtain cultivable land, never dreamed that by removing along with the forests the collecting centres and reservoirs of moisture, they were laying the basis for the present forlorn state of those countries," wrote Friedrich Engels in 1876.

Nearly simultaneously, Art Nouveau and the German Wandervogel youth movement introduced an aesthetic or reform-oriented "back to nature" credo. As early as 1896 the latter movement consciously combined the appeal of Romanticism with anti-middle-class effects, and a pedagogical approach oriented to social reform with the cult of emancipated youth. Also important is the critique of civilisation put forward by Art Nouveau around the turn of the last century. Its overall linear ornamentation, stemming primarily from botanical motifs, and general thematic concerns presented a far-reaching critique of the "triumphal procession" of modern technology. The cultural critic and philosopher Walter Benjamin described it in view of the portrayal of women in Art Nouveau in his *Arcades Project* thus: "The basic theme of Art Nouveau is the transfiguration of infertility. The body is particularly present in the forms that pubescence foregoes". "Infertility" - that is the technology-induced out-of-balance state of nature.

Jumping ahead: after the Second World War, an increasingly critical environmental awareness entered the general consciousness. Early on, the themes were broached by social scientists and philosophy, like that of the "Frankfurter School" in the U.S.A. and Germany. However, such critical thinking didn't develop into mainstream environmental consciousness until the middle of the sixties with the so-called "flower power generation"- the hippies, and beatniks who sought to re-connect humankind's basic way-of-being with nature. Out of this movement the "Green Parties" and others were formed all over Europe in the seventies to fight against atomic energy and other kinds of environmentally damaging industrial activities. Also at the beginning of this decade, Greenpeace, the international environmental organisation, was founded. An activist group, it continues to protest against the problems of environmental destruction today.

III. Gustav Metzger and, later, Santiago Sierra

During the aforementioned 1960s, the artist Gustav Metzger - born in 1926 in Nürnberg, the son of Polish Orthodox Jews who emigrated to London in 1939 - developed his politically engaged art, which was also critical from an environmental perspective. Gustav Metzger's self-labelled "Auto-destructive Art" consists, as the name already states, of artefacts that are destroyed (by him) in an aesthetic process, such as the "Acid Action Paintings". One of the first of these was executed in 1961 on the South Bank in London. The artist gradually perforated the canvasses with the help of acid that was applied to the canvas, a process that undeniably produced painterly effects. However, in his *Manifesto of Auto-destructive Art* (10 March 1960), Metzger emphasised less the sensual beauty of this type of art than its analytical-cautionary character: "Auto-destructive art re-enacts the obsession with destruction, the pummeling to which individuals and masses are subjected. Auto-destructive art demonstrates man's power to accelerate disintegrative processes of nature and to order them. Auto-destructive art mirrors the compulsive perfectionism of arms manufacture - honed to the point of destruction. Auto-destructive art is the transformation of technology into public art." The artist came to the idea "to accelerate disintegrative processes of nature and to order them" whilst in the British Shetland Islands at the beginning of the 1960s. Metzger referred to this experience almost 30 years later: "It was so peaceful there, in a way that I've never experienced. I kept a journal. And during this time I also made notes that were important to me. One of these was that cars had to go. That was a kind of breakthrough in a new direction for me. It was really extreme: they had to go! I used the destruction of the car as a way of addressing the destruction of mankind and nature."

This very aspect concerning the destruction of the environment was also the focus of his project *Stockholm June* (1972) that had already been planned for Documenta 5 in Kassel in an earlier form, *KARBA* (1970/72). Like many of Metzger's projects, *Stockholm June* has never been realised. The project envisions arranging 120 cars around a square construction that is between two and four metres tall. The room-like construction is wrapped in transparent plastic that is perforated at regular intervals. The motors of the 120 cars run from morning till night and produce exhaust that is channelled to the inside of the construction, thereby transforming it into a grey, poisonous nightmare. A second phase of the project envisions that the cars, fully gassed up and running, are situated inside the room construction that is now wrapped in unperforated plastic. If the cars hadn't burst into flames by the following afternoon, small bombs were to be thrown on the entire installation. Overall, with this work Metzger discovered a highly provocative image for what takes place in "our" streets on a daily basis: the environment is knowingly being destroyed. In comparison to Eliasson, one can't speak of a "gentle terrorism" here, given the highly aggressive and destructive nature of Metzger's work. At the same time, and perhaps surprising at first view, Gustav Metzger makes artistic works that one might describe as "abstract, apparently completely non-aggressive, kinetic nature-sculptures." An example: in his solo exhibition *Art of Liquid Crystals* from 1966, Metzger showed his sculpture *Earth from Space* (1966) in the display window of the London bookstore, Better Books; the work was made out of small glass plates installed in the form of a cross with liquid crystals placed between them. A filament heated up the crystals, melting them. As a result, the liquid crystals first became see-through, then grey, and after finally cooling off, they took on an intensely colourful hue. Destruction does take place here, yet its visualised process has a more poetic-decorative nature. This "liquid crystal" technique, co-developed by Metzger, was later used consistently for similarly mounted projections as background decor at various concerts for rock groups like The Who.

The Mexican artist Santiago Sierra recently realised an installation in Spring 2006 that was based on the aforementioned project *Stockholm June* by Metzger: in the centre of the small German town of Stommeln, six cars were parked with their motors running. Hoses were attached to the tailpipes of the cars and channeled the exhaust inside a synagogue. At the entrance of the synagogue, gas-masks were available to guarantee safe passage.

The work had to be taken down after only a few days because of the high amount of public criticism. This criticism was based on a misunderstanding, however, since Santiago Sierra had in no way intended to belittle the suffering of Jews gassed by German National Socialists. For him, this pointed work has much more to do with showing that by driving an automobile today one knowingly gasses the environment (with fuel emissions) and thus consciously carries the responsibility for environmental catastrophe with disastrous consequences – just as nobody wants to acknowledge personal responsibility for the catastrophe that took place during the Third Reich -despite knowing about it. This is exactly what makes Sierra's parallelling of the gassing of the Jews and the emissions of cars provocative, but entirely logical.

To be sure, the targeted, mass scale and factory-based killing of the Jews was something other than what the conscious destruction of the environment is today. And yet now, just like then, there are victims who are being unwillingly affected without being asked. Also now, just like then, there is no escape from a global environmental catastrophe. Moreover there were then, like today, certain capitalist interests responsible for the catastrophe (and they're still partly the same ones!). It's no coincidence that the first highways were built in Germany by the Nazis. And even the legendary Beetle was built by Volkswagen. And, the fact that the visitor to the synagogue could put on a gas mask clearly shows that, for the artist, it's not about an endless belittling of the mass killings, but about the role of the protected perpetrator, because drivers represent the majority of those with gas-masks visiting the installation!

Metzger and Sierra both make environmental art that is not only explicitly political but also uncompromising and provocative. And in comparison to Eliasson, these aggressive strategies do raise questions - questions like: Does political art have to be explicitly problematic and pugnacious? Does it need provocative themes? When do themes become explicitly environmental? In the next section I would like pose these questions.

IV. What is an "Environmental Aesthetic?"

For a long time critically engaged "left-wing" art was abstract art. Let us briefly recall the "avant-gardes" from the first half of the last century: Dadaism and Surrealism, both, for the most part Communist-oriented, act out the uprising against the bourgeoisie. While these two movements might not belong to abstract art, realism is either aggressively taken apart, as by the Dadaists, or transformed into the surreal, into the "unreal". The most influential political art of that period is arguably (Russian) Constructivism and the German Bauhaus, both of which favour abstraction. As a rejection of bourgeois representational culture and politics, these two currents set their sights upon the direct formulation of the real, and consequently the field of abstraction appeared to be the optimal solution for them. Thus, Kasimir Malevitsch's "Black Square" (1929) stands only for a black square and therefore represents nothing, except itself. The almost "picture-less" picture becomes a model for an understanding between society and power, in which the czar no longer represents the people - rather the people stand for the people; they represent and govern themselves. Furthermore, the clear language of abstraction seemingly allows for the renunciation of the hated sentimentalism and ideology of the bourgeoisie, which ultimately led to the First World War. Later, aesthetic abstraction also acted as a critique of the authoritarianism of "socialist realism". Because the experiences of the Russian Constructivists with the actual realities of socialism and communism were disastrous - keyword: Stalinism - many of the Constructivists ultimately turned away from a politically engaged art.

The reduction- and abstraction-based language of Constructivism was picked up by U.S. American Minimalism à la Donald Judd and Robert Morris, among others. This artistic direction also thoroughly understood itself as anti-middle class and struggled against the decorative nature of representational art. It is the decorative element that turned such art, in what was then already a fully developed art market, into an inexpensive product that quickly found a home in living rooms and collections. Yet, Minimalism also quickly lost its ability to formulate political resistance and was implemented to the advantage of the capitalist system. Precisely because Minimalism rejected representational portrayal, it also refused to develop a critical counter-image, and this is exactly what enabled its formal language to be integrated into the aesthetic of capitalism. In short, Minimalism's cool aesthetic was good for conferring the impression of coolness on global business - Minimalism became "corporate design."

A consequential response by artists soon followed. On the one hand, reduction was pushed further in a *Dematerialization of the Art Object* (Lucy R. Lippard); out of this process developed Conceptual Art. On the other hand, the style of

Minimalism was shaken-up and loaded with narrative-disruptive structures - Gustav Metzger and Hans Haacke, above all, merit attention here, and later the aforementioned Santiago Sierra also worked in this vein. Like Gustav Metzger, Hans Haacke seemed to have two different work phases: an early, almost abstract one, including his *Condensation Cube* (1963-1965), a transparent cube in which water condenses. In this work a closed (environmental) system was envisioned in which biological processes communicated with one another. The second phase was the long-standing, well-known, politically disruptive one - exemplified by the work *Isolation Box, Grenada* (1983). Also a closed cube, the form was now made out of wood, perforated with slots and printed with the text "Isolation Box as used by U.S. Troops at Point Salines Prison Camp in Grenada". The purity of the form was thus contaminated by political consciousness-raising; Hans Haacke's notion of the system was taken a step further and applied to a political context.

Another aesthetic strategy escaping the cashing in of capitalism and arising out of conceptual art was "Projekt Kunst". Here, among others, Joseph Beuys and his politically environmental performances soon began to carry weight. Finally, typical of a younger generation of artists was the critical and evenly weighted use of all of these strategies in their work - the American Dan Peterman and the Dane Tue Greenfort (more on these artists in the next section) are good examples.

The open questions on the quality of political art in relation to the question regarding the quality of environmental art have still further implications: does environmental art have to be explicitly socially critical, in a narrower sense political? In this context, the German philosopher Burghart Schmidt already considers the "perception of nature" and the "natural encounter" to be environmental art. His colleague Gernot Böhme develops these thoughts even further in placing such "natural alliances" (Ernst Bloch) as "atmospheres" in the centre of an environmental art. In these "atmospheres" it's about "overcoming subjective points of view." The human being no longer perceives him/herself as isolated and egoistic, the crowning glory of creation, but rather recognises him/herself as bound to the environment that provides for life (survival). According to Böhme, this environmental worldview enables the human capacity for reflection and language. Böhme writes: "As an especially linguistic being, the human being is not only openly receptive to communication that is directed toward him or her, but to the articulation of presence as such. Sensitivity to the beauty of nature would thus not only be the co-perceiving of what is agreeable to him or her, rather the experience of one's own existence as moved and heightened by the surrounding nature in the expression of its presence." From this perspective, both the work of Olafur Eliasson that I previously took to task and the "abstract-aesthetic" bodies of work from Metzger and Haacke that I referred to would also qualify as environmentally political art.

VI. Dan Peterman and, later, Tue Greenfort

Alternative energy production and recycling lie at the centre of American Dan Peterman's art. The artist addresses some of these aspects in his *Chicago Compost Shelter* (1988): a typical Volkswagen is heated during an ice-cold winter with the help of horse manure from Chicago's mounted police and used as a life-saving sleeping shelter by the homeless. Here the setting serves as an actual model for the use of all possible energy resources - in this case bio-gas - but also as an engaged and humanitarian interaction with socially disadvantaged, so-called "groups on the edge of society".

For Dan Peterman, recycling takes several different avenues, including the form of recycled plastic that is then made into furniture. His *Running Table* (1997) that can be used by passersby on Chicago's Michigan Avenue is an example. At the same time, the work is also convincing minimalistic sculpture with its clear, geometric forms. The *Running Table* is simultaneously autonomous and useful art.

Since 1996 Dan Peterman has been working in a building complex that he named "The Building", which incorporates a recycling centre, artist's studios as well as the office of the leftist magazine *The Baffler*. Alternative agriculture rounds off the spectrum of activities. Peterman also runs a repair shop for junked bicycles here that works both as an art project as well as a totally pragmatic "real and functioning" activity. Young, jobless kids not only learn technical skills but they can make social contacts, and also receive a fully functioning bicycle as a reward. Here the artwork consists of, if one chooses to see it this way, the dematerialized concept of an alternative economy as well as the performative work of the young unemployed kids and their sculptural results, bicycles that can be ridden again.

In 2001, "The Building" burned down. Today it has been rebuilt and stands in the middle of Chicago's capitalistic metropole as proof that alternative forms of economy and ecology can exist together in the 21st century.

The young Dane Tue Greenfort, and with this I come to the end of my essay, also deals with recycling as a theme. For example, the title of his work *Producing 1 kilogram of PET plastic requires 17.5 kilograms of water* (2004) already plays off of Peterman's art. On view is a 1.5 litre mineral-water bottle heated up and melted down to only 0.5 litres. Here it is implied that the disposable bottle requires much more water to produce than it can later contain. The issues of consumption, recycling and related energy usage are, in this case, also at the centre of the artist's concerns, but entail a comparably cautious optimism that applies to a possible shift in the crisis situation that is coming to a head.

To put the rule to the test, Tue Greenfort made his project *From Green to Grey* (2006), with which he critically reflects upon the power supply of the Witte de With exhibition centre in Rotterdam. The point of departure is the artist's wish that during the period of his exhibition the centre is to run on "green", i.e. environmentally friendly, power. An exchange of correspondence between the Witte de With and its Dutch energy supplier over such a possible change in service yields that due to contractual grounds this isn't possible until 2007, and then only for the entire year. For his exhibition, Greenfort then arranged the following setting: Hall 1 of the centre, nearly 100 square metres in size, was left empty and thus presented as a pure white cube, brightly and expensively illuminated by all the neon lights from the ceiling. On view in this as much sterile as clear display is nothing more than the aforementioned correspondence, printed on grey, unframed DIN A3 format paper and mounted on the front wall of the room. Simple documentation and intelligent "dematerialisation" are thus united in the best tradition of Conceptual Art. Documented is an initial unsuccessful attempt to move from the "grey" period of unreasonable, "conventional" power to a "green" power supply with the help of an art project. What remains is the demand for actual and long-term environmental change – beyond the (closed) system of the art world.

HOOR AL QASIMI
Director
Co-curator of 'NEAR' - 1998, with Derek Ogbourne and Peter Lewis and Co-curator of 'Andy Warhol' - 2002, with Brigitte Schenk from Brigitte Schenk Gallery, Cologne, both at Sharjah Art Museum. Director and Co-curator of 'Sharjah Biennial 6' with Peter Lewis - 2003. Director of 'Sharjah Biennial 7' - 2005. Tutor of Painting and Drawing at Sharjah Fine Art Centre - 1997. Studied Fine Art at Slade School of Fine Art, London and is currently completing an MA in Curating Contemporary Art at the Royal College of Art, London.

JACK PERSEKIAN
Artistic Director
Curator and Producer, Founding Director of Anadiel Gallery and, the Al-Ma'mal Foundation for Contemporary Art in Jerusalem. Head curator of Sharjah Biennial 7 (2005). Recent curated exhibitions include: Reconsidering Palestinian Art, Fundacion Antonio Perez, Cuenca, Spain (2006); Disorientation - Contemporary Arab Artists from the Middle East, Haus der Kulturen der Welt, Berlin (2003); in weiter ferne, so nah, neue palastinensische kunst, Ifa Galleries in Bonn, Stuttgart and Berlin (2002); Official Palestinian Representation to the XXIV Biennale de São Paulo. Additional productions and directing include: The Palestinian Cultural Evening at the World Economic Forum in the Dead Sea, Jordan (2004), The Geneva Initiative, Public Commitment Event (2003), the Millennium Celebrations in Bethlehem - Bethlehem 2000. Short films and video works: 'A Ball and a Coloring Box', 'my son', 'the last 5 short films of the millennium' and 'the first 4 short films of the millennium' in collaboration with Palestinian filmmakers.

MOHAMMED KAZEM
Curator
A native of Dubai, UAE Mohammed Kazem was born in 1969. He has been a member of the Emirates Fine Arts Society in Sharjah since 1985, and has been a participant in 3rd, 4th, 5th, and 7th Sharjah Biennials. Kazem has exhibited on the international level as well, including 7th Havana Biennial, 1st Bangladesh Biennial, the Netherlands, and Moscow. Kazem was also curator of the Emirates Fine Art Society Exhibition, concurrent with the Sharjah international Biennial, Sharjah Art Museum (2005). Also curator of WINDOW Exhibition (16 UAE Artist), total Arts gallery, Dubai (2006). Kazem has been teaching painting at Art Atelier in the Youth Theatre and Arts in Dubai since 1999.

EVA SCHARRER
Curator
Independent curator and art critic, currently based in Basel, Switzerland. She has worked on shows in international art institutions, such as P.S.1 Contemporary Art Center, New York; Kunstverein Freiburg; and Kunsthaus Baselland, Muttenz/Basel. Exhibition projects include Submerge. New Art from New York at Kunstbunker Nuremberg (curator); and Insideout, 5th Festival of Young Art: Berlin, Prague, New York at Bunker Reinhardtstrasse, Berlin (co-curator). She has written catalogue essays on several emerging artists and is a regular contributor to Artforum International Magazine and Artforum.com, New York; Kunst-Bulletin, Zurich; C Magazine, Toronto; and BAZ, the Basel daily newspaper, among others.

JONATHAN WATKINS
Curator
Jonathan Watkins has been Director of Ikon Gallery Birmingham since 1999. Previously he worked for a number of years in London , as Curator of the Serpentine Gallery (1995-1997) and Director of Chisenhale Gallery (1990-1995). Jonathan Watkins was Artistic Director of the Biennale of Sydney 1998. He was guest curator for Quotidiana , Castello di Rivoli, Turin (1999-2000), Europarte La Biennale di Venezia (June 1997), Milano Europa 2000, Palazzo di Triennale, Milan (November 2000), Facts of Life an exhibition of contemporary Japanese art at the Hayward Gallery, London (Autumn 2001), and Days Like These, the Tate Triennial exhibition of contemporary British art (London 2003). Currently, he is on the curatorial team for the Shanghai Biennale (September 2006). Jonathan Watkins has written extensively on contemporary art, and recently was the author of a Phaidon monograph on the Japanese artist On Kawara.

MONA EL-MOUSFY
Architect
Architect Mona El-Mousfy has professional experience in France, Italy and the U.S.A. During her professional practice in Paris, she focused on residential renovation, and more recently on exhibition design. Mona has entered several exhibitions and museum design competitions, and participated in the design of the winning entry for the French Pavilion at the 1989 Seville Universal Exhibition. As the architect of the Sharjah Art Biennial in April 2005, she designed a changing interior urban landscape to support exploration, exchange and personal introspection around contemporary art installations and the biennial theme of "belonging." She has also been involved in the design development of the Al-Buhais 18 Archaeological Exhibition at the Sharjah Archaeological Museum. This project was conceived with archaeologists from Tubingen University to explore innovative strategies in archaeological exhibitions and to bridge the gap between teaching and practice.
El Mousfy's academic career has included teaching at the School of Architecture at Georgia Institute of Technology (Atlanta, USA) from 1991 to 1992, and for the school's Paris programme from 1993 to 2001. In Paris, she developed site-specific courses ranging from urban to interior spaces, allowing her to explore space continuum across scales. Since 2002, she has held a full-time position at the School of Architecture and Design at the American University of Sharjah (U.A.E.). Her present teaching and research interests focus on the discourse around 20th century post-modern space with an engagement in exhibition design, lighting and phenomenological perception.

SERENE HULEILEH
Editor
Cultural management consultant, journalist, and writer who has been involved in a variety of cultural projects mainly in Palestine and Jordan for the past 15 years. 1999 - 2000, Editor of "This Week in Palestine", monthly magazine promoting culture and arts in Palestine, and UNDP consultant for Ramallah and Jericho municipalities to set up a municipal cultural department. Since 2000, Regional Director of Arab Education Forum (Jordan), project established in 1998, focusing on learning and building knowledge upon indigenous experience. Initiator of pan-Arab projects: "*Azkadunya*" - website for the promotion and distribution of Arab cultural production, and "*Safar* - Arab youth mobility fund" - supporting Arab youth who are actively involved in community initiatives. Since December 2005, consultant for cultural affairs with the Greater Amman Municipality. Coordinator of Bethlehem 2000 millennium celebrations, developing major events including millennium New Year's Eve celebration. 1992 - 1998, Administrative team member of Palestine International Festival for Music and Dance and in 1999 produced the Jericho Winter Festival in cooperation with the Jericho municipality. 1990 - 1998, developed national reading campaign with Tamer Institute for Community Education (Palestine) in and in 1994 developed the Publishing Unit which publishes books for and by children and youth. Member of

Board of Trustees of El Funoun (Palestinian popular dance company) and of AIIC (International Association of Conference Interpreters).

MUNIR FASHEH
Essayist

Born in Jerusalem, Palestine, in 1941, Munir Fasheh was expelled from the city with his family in 1948 and settled in Ramallah. He studied and taught mathematics, physics, and education in both Palestine (mostly at Birzeit University) and in the U.S. He received his Ph.D in Education from Harvard University, and established Tamer Institute in Palestine in 1989. Munir Fasheh has been working on community education projects for over four decades in Palestine and in the Arab world. He has been Research Associate at the Center for Middle Eastern Studies at Harvard University since 1998, where he established the Arab Education Forum. Fasheh has several publications in Arabic on community education, mathematics, and colonialism, with special interest in the centrality of artistic expression in community development and learning. He has published articles in the *Harvard Educational Review* as well as in other international journals and magazines, and is an active member in the "learning societies" network of educators and community activists involved in an emerging discussion about the need to develop/connect different kinds of spaces and opportunities to nurture a fuller range of human potential.

MANISH JAIN
Essayist

Manish Jain currently serves as Coordinator /Co-Founder of Shikshantar: the Peoples' Institute for Rethinking Education and Development and as Chief Editor of the journal, *Vimukt Shiksha* ("Liberating Learning"). He has edited five books on the theme of Learning Societies, which explores the future of learning and ways to transform the current models of education. He is very involved in the Udaipur-as-a-Learning-City process, where he works actively with local children and families on community video and rooftop organic farming projects. Prior to founding Shikshantar, Manish spent two years in France working as one of the principal architects of UNESCO's Learning Without Frontiers global initiative. Manish has also worked as a consultant in the areas of educational planning, policy analysis, research, programme design and use of media/technology with the UNICEF, USAID, UNDP, World Bank, and Academy for Educational Development Centre in several countries in Africa, South and Central Asia. He has served as Assistant Editor of *The Forum for Advancing Basic Education and Literacy* with the Harvard Institute for International Development. Manish also spent two years as an investment banker (mergers & acquisitions and corporate finance) with Morgan Stanley focusing on the telecom and high technology sectors. For the past 12 years, he has been trying to unlearn his Master's Degree in Education from Harvard University and B.A. (Magna Cum Laude) in Economics, International Development and Political Philosophy from Brown University in order to see the world with more authentic and creative eyes. His interests include healthy cooking, chess, film-making, simulation gaming, basketball, organic farming and hiking.

FRANCESCO MANACORDA
Essayist

Francesco Manacorda is tutor in the Curating Contemporary Art Department at the Royal College of Art, London, and a writer and freelance curator based in London. In 2004 he curated the exhibition, "The Mythological Machine", at the Mead Gallery, Warwick University, on the impact of mass-media images, and, in 2005, "A Certain Tendency in Representation - Cineclub at Thomas Dane", Thomas Dane Gallery, London. He also organised the symposium, Ecology and Artistic Practice, for the programme Arts & Ecology at the Royal Society of Arts, London. In 2006 he curated "Subcontingent - The Indian Subcontinent in Contemporary Art" at the Fondazione Sandretto Re Rebaudengo, Turin and "Satellites" at Tanya Bonakdar Gallery, New York. He has just published a monograph on Maurizio Cattelan (Electa, 2006), and regularly contributes to *Flash Art, Metropolis M* and *Domus*.

AKIKO MIKI
Essayist

Akiko Miki has been Chief Curator at the Palais de Tokyo, Site de création contemporaine, since 2000. Some of the exhibitions she has co-curated and curated are: "TransCulture" at the 1995 Venice Biennale; "Immutability and Fashion: Chinese Contemporary Art in the Midst of Changing Surroundings" (1997); "Site of Desire" at the 1998 Taipei Biennial; "Art Life 21 - Spiral TV" (1999); "Twilight Sleep: Japanese Contemporary Videos" (2000); Tobias Rehberger: "Night Shift" (2002); "Rivane Neuenschwander: Superficial Resemblances" (2003); "Nobuyoshi Araki: Self, Life, Death" (2005). Akiko Miki has also served as co-director of the Dentsu Art Project (a number of commissioned artworks site-specifically installed in the new building complex designed by Jean Nouvel and Jon Jerdi in Tokyo - completed in 2002). Her various essays are included in a number of exhibition catalogues and Japanese and overseas magazines like *Bijutsu Techo, Paris Photos, Tema Celeste*, etc. Co-author of books such as *Very New Art* (2000), *World Artists File* (2004).

TREVOR SMITH
Essayist

Trevor Smith is Curator-in-Residence at the Center for Curatorial Studies, Bard College, New York where he recently co-curated *Wrestle*, the inaugural exhibition at the Hessel Museum. Previously he was Curator at the New Museum of Contemporary Art in New York City where he co-curated *Andrea Zittel: Critical Space*, which is currently nearing the end of its critically acclaimed tour of the United States. Smith was born in Canada and studied Art History at the University of British Columbia. From 1992-2003 he was based in Australia where he worked first at the Biennale of Sydney, then as Director of the Canberra Contemporary Art Space, and from 1997-2003 as Curator of Contemporary Art at the Art Gallery of Western Australia. Highlights among his previous exhibitions include "The Divine Comedy: Francisco Goya, Buster Keaton, and William Kentridge" and the presentation of the work of Robert MacPherson as the Australian representative to the 2002 São Paolo Biennial. He has published widely in exhibition catalogues and journals in Europe, Australia and North America.

RAIMAR STANGE
Essayist

Raimar Stange was born in Hanover in 1960 and is currently based in East Berlin as a freelance curator and critic. Selected curated shows include: "Just do it", Lentos Museum, Linz, 2005 (with Florian Waldvogel); "Location Shots", Gallery Erna Hecey, Brussels 2005; "Das große Rasenstück", City of Nuremberg (with Florian Waldvogel); and "Klartext Berlin", Kunstraum Niederösterreich, Vienna. He has several publications to his name including: *Sur.Faces*, Revolver Verlag, Frankfurt 2002; *Zurück in die Kunst*, Rogner & Bernhard, Hamburg 2003; and *International Galleries*, Dumont Verlag, Cologne/London 2005 (with Uta Grosenick). He is a regular contributor to *Parkett*, Zürich; *Flash Art*, Mailand; *Modern Painters*, New York; *Kunst Bulletin*, Zürich; Spike, Vienna; and *Neue Review*, Berlin. Stange is also Bassist in the Berlin-based Art Critic Orchestra.

IGNASI ABALLÍ

إغناسي آبالي

ولد عام ١٩٥٨ في برشلونة، أسبانيا
يعيش ويعمل في برشلونة

Born 1958 Barcelona, Spain
Lives and works in Barcelona
Faculty of Belles Arts, University of Barcelona

Selected Solo Exhibitions

2006 "0-24h.", ZKM, Karlsruhe; Ikon Gallery, Birmingham; Museu Serralves, Porto, Portugal
2005-06 "0-24h.", Museu d'Art Contemporani de Barcelona, Barcelona (MACBA), Spain

Selected Group Exhibitions

2006 "Entre la palabra y la imagen", Fundación Luis Seoane, Corunna, Spain
"Untouchable", Centre Nacional d'Art Contemporain, Villa Arson, Nice, France
"Identidades críticas", Museo Patio Herreriano, Valladolid, Spain
2005 "Salir a la calle y disparar al azar", Barcelona, Spain
"Pintar sense pintar", Centre d'Art La Panera, Lleida, Spain
2004 "Laocoonte devorado", Artium, Vitoria-Gasteiz, Spain
"Looking further - Thinking Thought", Marc, Islandia
2003 "En el principio era el viaje", Bienal de Pontevedra, Pontevedra, Spain
"Gestes", Printemps de September Festival, Toulouse, France

LIDA ABDUL

ليدا عبدول

ولدت عام ١٩٧٣ في كابول، أفغانستان
تعيش في كابول

Born 1973 Kabul, Afghanistan
Lives in Kabul
M.F.A. University of California, Irvine
B.A. Philosophy, California State University
B.A. Political Science, California State University

Selected Solo Exhibitions

2006 "Petition for Another World", Museum Voor Moderne Kunst, Arnhem, Netherlands
"Lida Abdul", Giorgio Persano Gallery, Turin, Italy
"Lida Abdul, Pino Pascali Contemporary Art Museum, Polignano, Italy
"Now, Here, Over There", FRAC Lorraine, Metz, France
"What we saw upon awaking", CAC Bretigny, Bretigny, France
2005 "Afghan Pavilion", 51st Venice Biennial, Venice, Italy
"Ursula Blicke Video Lounge", Kunsthalle Vienna, Vienna, Austria

Selected Group Exhibitions

2007 2nd Moscow Biennial, Moscow, Russia
3rd Auckland Triennial, Auckland, Australia
"Global Feminism-Feminism", Brooklyn Museum, New York, NY
2006 27th São Paulo Biennial, São Paulo, Brazil
"The First Chapter", Gwangju Biennial, Gwangju, South Korea
"Modern Painting as a Way of Living", Istanbul, Turkey
"Mens S.M.A.K Gent en K.U." Leuven, Belgium
"The UnQuiet World", Australian Centre for Contemporary Art, Victoria, Australia
"Courant Alternatifs", Centre for Contemporary Art, Parvis, Tarbes, France

Bibliography

Di Genova, Arianna, "Il Manifesto Visioni", Feature Article Lida Abdul, No. 135, Italy (June 2005)
Olofsson, Mikael, "Arkitekture i spillror", Goteborgs-Posten (18 June 2005)
Knofel, Ulrike, "Baumfaller und andere Monster", Der Spiegel, Frankfurt (13 June 2005): 138-41
Raza, Sara "Travelling Light", "Journeys", n.paradoxa - International Feminist Art Journal, Vol. 17 (2006)
Vorkoeper, Ute von, "Kunst fur die nächste Generation. Der Anfang danach", Die Zeit, Hamburg (5 February 2006)

JENNIFER ALLORA

جينيفر أيورا

ولدت عام ١٩٧٤ في فيلادلفيا، الولايات
المتحدة. تعيش وتعمل في بورتو ريكو

Born 1974 Philadelphia, U.S.A.
Lives and works in Puerto Rico
M.Sc. Massachusetts Institute of Technology; Whitney Independent Study Program, New York
B.A. University of Richmond, U.S.

GUILLERMO CALZADILLA

غييرمو كالزاديا

ولد عام ١٩٧٤ في هافانا، كوبا
يعيش ويعمل في بورتو ريكو

Born 1971 Havana, Cuba
Lives and works in Puerto Rico
M.F.A. Bard College
B.F.A. Escuela de Artes Plásticas

Selected Solo Exhibitions

2006-07 "Concentrations 50: Allora & Calzadilla", Dallas Museum of Art, Dallas, TX
2006 "Land Mark", Palais de Tokyo, Paris, France
"Allora & Calzadilla", Stedelijk Museum voor Actuele Kunst, Ghent, Belgium
2004 "Radio Revolt: One Person, One Watt", Artist in Residence Project, Walker Art Center, Minneapolis, MI
2003 "Chalk", 7th Annual ICA/Vita Brevis Project, Institute of Contemporary Art (ICA), Boston, MA

Selected Group Exhibitions

2006 Whitney Biennial 2006, Whitney Museum of American Art, New York, NY
2005 "Uncertain States of America", Astrup Fearnley Museum of Museum Art Oslo, Norway
8th Lyon Biennial of Contemporary Art, Lyon, France
"inSite 05", San Diego, California and Tijuana, Mexico
"Material Time/Work Time/Life Time", Kopavogur Art Museum, Reykjavik, Iceland
"Dialectics of Hope", 1st Moscow Biennial of Contemporary Art, Moscow, Russia
"Irreducible: Contemporary Short Form Video", CCA Wattis Institute, San Francisco, CA
2004 "A Grain of Dust, A Drop of Water", Gwangju Biennial, Gwangju, South Korea
"Ailleurs/Ici", Musee D'Art

Moderne de La Ville De Paris/Arc Au Couvent des Cordeliers, Paris, France

2003 "Common Wealth", Tate Modern, London, UK

Public Collections

Philadelphia Museum of Art, Philadelphia
Musee D'Art Moderne de La Ville De Paris, Paris, France
Tate Modern, London, UK
Centre Pompidou, Paris, France
Stedelijk Museum voor Actuele Kunst, Ghent, Belgium

Selected Bibliography

Bishop, Claire, "Remote Possibilites: A Round Table Discussion on Land Art's Changing Terrain", Artforum (Summer 2005)
Fyfe, Joe. "Jennifer Allora and Guillermo Calzadilla at Chantal Crousel", Art In America (November 2004)
Manacorda, Francesco, "Entropology: Monuments to Closed Systems", Flash Art, No.241, (March-April, 2005)
McKee, Yates. 'Allora & Calzadilla. The monstrous dimension of art." Flash Art, No. 240 (January-February 2005)
Obrist, Hans-Ulrich, "1000 Words: Allora and Cadzadilla talk about three pieces in Vieques." Artforum (March 2005)

Artist's Writings

Allora, Jennifer and Guillermo Calzadilla, "Land Mark", Paris: Palais de Tokyo (2006)
Allora & Calzadilla, "Questionnaire", Frieze, No. 96 (January-February 2006)

LARA ALMARCEGUI

لارا المرسيغي

ولدت عام ١٩٧٢ في ثارغوثا، أسبانيا
تعيش وتعمل في روتردام، هولندا

Born 1972 Zaragoza, Spain
Lives and works in Rotterdam, Netherlands

Selected Solo Exhibitions

2004 FRAC Bourgogne, Dijon, France

2003 INDEX The Swedish Art Foundation, Stockholm, Sweden
Art Centre, Le Grand Café, Saint Nazaire, France
Gallery Marta Cervera, Madrid, Spain

2001 Etablissement d'en Face, Brussels, Belgium

Selected Group Exhibitions

2006 "Frieze Projects", Frieze Art Fair, London, UK
"How to live together", 27th São Paulo Biennial, São Paulo, Brazil
"Momentum, Festival of Nordic Art", Moss, Norway
"The Unhomely", Biennial of Seville, Spain
"Project Rotterdam", Museum Boymans van Beuningen, Rotterdam, Netherlands

2004 International Liverpool Biennial, Tate Liverpool, UK
"VI Werkleitz Biennale", Common Property, Halle, Germany

2003 "Idealism", De Appel, Amsterdam, Netherlands

2000 "Scripted Spaces", Witte de With, Rotterdam, Netherlands

1999 Stedelijk Museum Bureau Amsterdam, Amsterdam, Netherlands

Public Collections

Kröller-Müller Museum, Otterloo (Arnheem)
Les Abattoirs, Toulouse, France
FRAC Bourgogne, Dijon, France
FRAC Alsace, Sélestat, France
Fundación La Caixa, Barcelone, Spain
MUSAC, León, Spain
CGAC, Centro Gallego de Arte Contemporáneo, Santiago de Compostela, Spain

Selected Bibliography

Bouman, Ole, "The Emancipation of Nowhere Land", Pasajes de Arquitectura y crítica, Madrid (February 2004)
Choi, Binna "A Statute of the Inhabitable", Reader: Contributions to a topical artistic discourse, Amsterdam: De Appel (2005)
Huitorel, Jean Marc, "Entropic Promise: Lara Almarcegui", Art Press, Paris (February 2005)
Sancho, Eva Gonzalez, "Raconter un lieu, raconteur la ville", Archistrom 'l'architecture, l' art, Paris (January 2004)
Smiededrecht, Thorsten, "Art and Architecture - a reciprocal relationship?", Architectural Design, London (June 2003)

Artist's Writings

Almarcegui, Lara, "Guide to the wastelands of São Paulo", São Paulo: 27th Bienal de São Paulo (2005)
Almarcegui, Lara, "Guide to Undefined Places in Lund", Lund: Lunds Konsthall (2004)
Almarcegui, Lara, "Wastelands Map Amsterdam: a guide to the empty sites of the city", Amsterdam: Stedelijk Museum Bureau Amsterdam (1999)

EL ANATSUI

إل أناتسوي

ولد عام ١٩٤٤ في أنياكو، غانا
يعيش ويعمل في إنسوكا، نيجيريا

Born 1944 Anyako, Ghana
Lives and works in Nsukka, Nigeria
B.A. University of Science and Technology, Kumasi, Ghana

Selected Solo Exhibitions

2006 "Asi", David Krut Projects, New York, NY
"Nyekor", Spazio Rossana Orlandi, Milan, Italy

2005 "Danudo", Skoto Gallery and Contemporary African Art Gallery, New York, NY

2003-07 "Gawu", Oriel Mostyn Gallery, LIandudno, Wales; touring: Djanogly Gallery, Nottingham, UK; Harn Museum of Art, Gainesville, FL; Fowler Museum, Los Angeles, CA

Selected Group Exhibitions

2006 "The Missing Peace: Artists Consider the Dalai Lama", UCLA Fowler Museum, Los Angeles, CA; Loyola University Museum of Art, Chicago, IL
DAK'ART, 7th Biennial of Contemporary African Art, Dakar, Senegal

2004-07 "Africa Remix", museum kunst palast, Dusseldorf, Germany; touring: Hayward Gallery, London; Centre Georges Pompidou, Paris; Mori Art Museum, Tokyo

1998 "Triennale der Kleinplastik", Stuttgart, Germany
9th Osaka Sculpture Triennale, Osaka, Japan

1995 "Seven Stories about Modern Art in Africa", Whitechapel Art Gallery, London, UK
"An Inside Story - African Art of our Time", Setagaya Art Museum, Tokyo

1994 5th Havana Biennial, Havana, Cuba

1992 "Arte Amazonas", Modern Art Museum, Rio de Janeiro, Brazil

1990 "Five Contemporary African Artists", 44th Venice Biennial, Venice

Public Collections
Asele Institute, Nimo, Nigeria
The British Museum, London, UK
Centre Pomipdou, Paris, France
de Young Museum, San Francisco, CA
Eden Project, Cornwall, UK
Jordan National Gallery of Arts, Amman, Jordan
Metropolitan Museum, New York, NY
Missoni, Milan, Italy
Musee Ariana, Geneva, Switzerland
museum kunst palast, Dusseldorf, Germany
National Art Gallery, Abuja, Nigeria
Smithsonian Institution, Washington DC
Osaka Foundation of Culture, Osaka
Setagaya Art Museum, Tokyo
The World Bank Art Collection, Washington, DC

Selected Bibliography
Preece, Robert,"Out of West Africa: interview with El Anatsui", Sculpture, (July-August 2006): 34-39
Rubinstein, Raphael, "Full-Metal Fabrics", Art in America (May 2006): 158-161

ROY ARDEN
روي أردن
ولد عام ١٩٥٧ في فانكوفر، كندا
يعيش ويعمل فانكوفر
Born 1957 Vancouver, Canada
Lives and works in Vancouver
M.F.A. 1990 University of British Columbia

Selected Solo Exhibitions
2006 Ikon Gallery, Birmingham, UK
"Against the Day", Richard Telles Fine Art, Los Angeles, CA
"Against the Day", Charles H. Scott Gallery, Vancouver, Canada
"Against the Day", Monte Clark Gallery, Toronto, Canada

Selected Group Exhibitions
2006 "Artist's Choice: Herzog & de Meuron, Perception Restrained", Museum of Modern Art, New York, NY
2005 "Intertidal", Muhka, Antwerp, Belgium
"Covering the Real - Art and the Press Picture from Warhol to Tillmans", Kunstnstmuseum Basel, Basel, Switzerland
"Roy Arden, Michael Krebber, John Miller", Richard Telles Gallery, Los Angeles, CA
2004 "Jede Fotografie ein Bild - Siemens Fotosammlung", Pinakothek der Moderne, Munich, Germany
2002 "Shopping - Art & Consumer Culture", Tate Liverpool, Liverpool, UK
2001 "Roy Arden, Scott McFarland, Howard Ursuliak, Stephen Waddell, Jeff Wall", Monte Clark Gallery, Toronto, Canada
"Superman in Bed, Kunst der Gegenwart und Fotografie", Schuermann Collection, Museum am Ostwald, Dortmund, Germany
1998 "Everyday", 11th Biennial of Sydney, Sydney, Australia
1996 "Roy Arden, Dan Graham, Ed Ruscha, Christopher Williams", Blum & Poe, Los Angeles, CA

Public Collections
Hammer Museum, Los Angeles, CA
Los Angeles County Museum of Art, Los Angeles, CA
Musee d'art contemporain, Geneva, Switzerland
Musée d'art contemporain de Montréal, Canada
Museum of Modern Art, New York, NY
Siemens Photocollection, Neue Pinakothek, Munich, Germany
Staatsgalerie, Stuttgart, Germany
Vancouver Art Gallery, Vancouver, Canada

Selected Bibliography
Alberro, Alex, "Between the Tides", Artforum, New York (January, 1997)
Chevrier, Jean-François, "Die Abenteuer der Tableau-Form in der Geschichte der Photographie, in Photo Kunst, Staatsgalerie, Stuttgart (1989)
Roelstraete, Dieter, "Negative Diagnostics - Vision and Discontent in the Work of Roy Arden", in Roy Arden, exhibition catalogue, Ikon Gallery, Birmingham, England (2006)
Steiner, Shep, "Aspects of the Rustic as Trope", in Terminal City, Ediciones Universidad de Salamanca, Salamanca (1999)
Wall, Jeff, "An Artist and his Models", Roy Arden Contemporary Art Gallery, Vancouver (1993)

VLADIMIR ARKHIPOV
فلاديمير أرخيبوف
ولد عام ١٩٦١ في ريازان، روسيا
يعيش ويعمل في موسكو
Born 1961 Ryazan, USSR
Lives and works in Moscow
Artistic self-education

Selected Solo Exhibitions
2006 "Functioning Forms Ireland", Burren College of Art, Ballyvaughan, Ireland, UK
2004 "Folk Sculpture", Kunstverein, Rosenheim, Germany
"I have been making a museum", Shchusev Museum of Architecture, Moscow, Russia
2002 "Post Folk Archive", Ikon Gallery, Birmingham, UK

Selected Group Exhibitions
2006 27th São Paulo Biennial, São Paulo, Brazil
2005 1st Moscow Biennial of Contemporary Art, Liga Gallery, Kolomna, Russia
2004 "Berlin-Moskau/Moskau-Berlin 1950-2000", State Historical Museum, Moscow, Russia
1998 11th Biennial of Sydney, Museum of Contemporary Art, Sydney, Australia

Public Collections
The Russian State Museum, St Petersburg, Russia

Selected Bibliography
Romer, Fedor, "Museum of Very Needful Things", Every Week Journal, No.48 (2002): 54-58
Subtil, Marie-Pierre, "Systeme D au temps des Soviets", Le Monde 2, No. 15 (25-26 Avril, 2004): 44-47

Artist's Writings
Arkhipov, Vladimir, "Born Out of Necessity" (105 thingumajigs, and their creators` voices, from the collection of Vladimir Arkhipov), Moscow: Typolygon (2003)
Arkhipov, Vladimir, "Home-Made: Contemporary Russian Folk Artifacts", London: Fuel Publishing (2006)

MIREILLE ASTORE

ميريي استور

ولدت عام ١٩٦١ في بيروت، لبنان

تعيش وتعمل في سيدني، استراليا

Born 1961 Beirut, Lebanon
Lives and works in Sydney, Australia.
M.V.A. University of Sydney

Selected Solo Exhibitions

2006 "Apparitions" Conny Dietzschold's Multiple Box, Sydney, Australia
"An Ungrateful Death", The Green Room, University of Western Australia, Sydney, Australia

2004 "When Gazes Collide - Tampa Introspection", Conny Dietzschold's Multiple Box, Sydney, Australia

2003 "Honourable Fears", Groundfloorgallery, Sydney, Australia
"Premonitions", Conny Dietzschold's Multiple Box, Sydney, Australia

Selected Group Exhibitions

2007 "Paranoia", Freud Museum, London

2006 "Paranoia", Leeds City Art Gallery, Leeds, UK; Focal Point Gallery, Southend, UK
"Selfportrait - A Show for Bethlehem", Casoria Contemporary Art Museum, Naples, Italy
"Coding/Decoding", Copenhagen Contemporary Art Centre, Copenhagen, Denmark; Museum of Contemporary Art, Roskilde, Denmark
"Nafas Beirut", Espace SD, Beirut, Lebanon

2005 "Art in the Age of Terrorism" Millais Gallery, Southampton Institute, UK
CinemaEast Film Festival, New York, NY

2003 "Sculpture by the Sea", Bondi, Sydney, Australia
"National Photographic Purchase Award Exhibition", Albury Regional Art Gallery, Albury, Australia

Selected Bibliography

Dunn, Abigail, "Paranoia", Catalyst, UK (7 July 2006)
Hutchings, Peter J., "Through a Refugee's Eyes" in Eyeline-Contemporary Visual Arts, No. 54 (2004): 11-13
Juchau, Mireille, Tampa Microcosm, "Featured Artist - Mireille Astore", Realtime No. 59 (2004)
Wood, Christopher, "The Art Attacks Heat Up in War on Propaganda", Times Higher Education Supplement, (5 November 2004): 22

Artist's Writings

Astore, Mireille, "In This House: A Conversation with Akram Zaatari", Eyeline Contemporary Visual Arts No. 60. (2006): 18-20
Astore, Mireille, "Focus Interviews: Steve Kurtz - Critical Art Ensemble", Artlink, Vol. 26, No. 2, (2006): 95-6
Astore, Mireille, "Tampa: When Gazes Collide", Art in the Age of Terrorism (ed.)

LARA BALADI

لارا بلدي

ولدت في بيروت، لبنان

تعيش وتعمل في القاهرة

Born in Beirut, Lebanon
Lives and works in Cairo, Egypt
B.A. 1990 Richmond University, London, UK

Selected Solo Exhibitions

2006 "Towards the Light", 20 screens (slide show), projections along a kilometre on the seashore for the opening event of "Image of the Middle East" Festival, Copenhagen International Theatre, Denmark
"Roba Vecchia", The Townhouse Gallery, Cairo, Egypt

2004-06 "Kai'ro", Lansmuseet, Harnosand, Sweden; Nikolaj Copenhagen Contemporary Art Centre, Copenhagen, Denmark; Pori Art Museum, Pori, Finland; Bildmuseet, Umea, Sweden

Selected Group Exhibitions

2006 Frieze Art Fair, London, UK, represented by the Townhouse Gallery of Contemporary Art
"Snap judgments", International Centre for Photography, New York, NY; Miami Art Central, Miami, FL

2005-06 "Regards de Photographes Arabes", Andaluz de Arte Contemporaneo, Sevilla, Spain; Institute du Monde Arabe, Paris, France

2005 "Water, water everywhere...", Scottsdale Museum of Contemporary Art, Arizona
"Remix", Moderna Museet, Stockholm, Sweden; Mori Museum, Tokyo, Japan; Centre Georges Pompidou, Paris, France; Hayward Gallery, London, UK; Kunst Palast Museum, Dusseldorf, Germany
"Some Stories", Kunsthalle Wien, Vienna, Austria

2004-07 I-dentity (ID magazine), Beijing, China; Long March Space, Tokyo, Japan; Spiral Garden, Hong Kong Cultural Centre, International Film Festival; Chelsea Art Museum, New York; Biennial of São Paulo; São Paulo, Brazil; Fashion and Textile Museum, London, UK

2003 "Disorientation", Haus der Kulturen der Welt, Berlin, Germany

2000-01 "The Desert", Fondation Cartier Pour l'Art Contemporain, Paris, France; Fundacion Caixa, Barcelona, Spain; Centro Andaluz de Arte Contemporaneo, Seville, Spain

Public Collections

Pori Art Museum, Pori, Finland
Audi Bank, Beirut, Lebanon
Joop van Den Ende, Stage Holding, The Hague, Netherlands
Museet For Fotokunst, Copenhagen, Denmark
Aesbek Gallery, Copenhagen, Denmark
Fondation Cartier pour l'Art Contemporain, Paris, France

Author's Writings

Baladi, Lara, "Territoire Mediterranee", Geneva: Labor et Fides (2005)
Baladi, Lara, "L'arabesque Aroussa Baladi", Madrid: Factum-Arte (2002)
Baladi, Lara, "Sleep", Paris: Coromandel Express (2000)

NOOR AL BASTAKI

نور البستكي

ولدت عام ١٩٨٥ في المنامة، البحرين

تعيش وتدرس في البحرين

Born 1985 Manama, Kingdom of Bahrain
Lives in Isa Town, Bahrain and studies in Bahrain

B.Sc. Banking & Finance, University of Bahrain

Selected Group Exhibitions

2006 "Performance of Light Language", Photography Exhibition at University of Bahrain
"Contemporary Curves", Al Riwaq Art Gallery, Manama

2005 "Contemporary Angles 2", University of Bahrain
"2nd Arab European Photo Festival", Hamburg Rathaus, Hamburg, Germany

2003-05 National Day and Annual Exhibitions, University of Bahrain

TAYSIR BATNIJI

تيسير البطنيجي

ولد عام ١٩٦٦ في غزة، فلسطين
يعيش ويعمل في فرنسا وفلسطين

Born 1966 Gaza, Palestine
Lives and works in France and Palestine
DNSEP 1997 Ecole Nationale des Beaux-Arts de Bourges, Bourges, France B.A. 1992 Al-Najah University, Nablus, Palestine

Selected Solo Exhibitions

2006 "Péres", Kasr el Basha and Centre Culturel Français, Gaza & CCF of Amman, Amman, Jordan

2004 "Transit", Witte de With Centre for Contemporary Art, Rotterdam, Netherlands

2002 "Voyage Impossible", Galerie K&S, Berlin, Germany
"Gaza, Journal Intime" Belgrade, Yugoslavia

2001 "Dépêche/Breaking News", Arts and Crafts Village, Gaza, Palestina

1996 Centre Culturel Français, Gaza, Palestine

Selected Group Exhibitions

2006 "Wanderland (Israel-Palestine)", Kunstmuseen Krefeld, Museum Haus, Lange, Germany
"Coding:Decoding", Nikolaj Copenhagen Contemporary Art Centre, Copenhagen, Denmark
"New Territories", Stadshallen, Brügge, Belgium
"Middle East News", Hebbel Theater, Berlin, Germany

2005 "KunstFilmBiennale", Kunst Station Sankt Peter, Cologne, Germany
"18émes Instants Vidéo Nomandes", Rencontres Internationales de la création vidéo et de la poésie électronique, Région PACA, France

2004 "17. Instants vidéo Nomades, Rencontres Internationales de la création vidéo et de la poésie électronique", Aix-en-Provence, France

2003 "Dreams and Conflicts. Utopia Station", 50th Venice Biennial, Venice, Italy

2002 "A Need of Realism-Solitude in Ujazdowski", Ujazdowski Castle Centre for Contemporary Art, Warszaw, Poland
"Rencontres International de la Photographie", Arles, France
"C'est pas du cinema", Studio national Le Fresnoy, Tourcoing, France; Public Collections Ursula Blikle Videoarchiv, Kunsthalle Wien, Vienna, Austria; Ursula Blikle Foundation, Kraichtal, Germany; Centre d'art de Tourcoing, France; Friche de Belle de Mai, Marseilles, France

Selected Bibliography

"C'est pas du cinéma", Tourcoing: Studio national Le Fresnoy (2002).
Rosen, Miriam, "Review", Artforum (Summer 2002): 184-85
Bédarida, Catherine, "Culture Portrait", Le Monde, Paris (19 January 2002)
"Rencontres International de la Photographie", Arles (2002)
"Palestinian Art", Stockholm: Royal Academy of Art (1998)

MARJOLIJN DIJKMAN

ماريولين دجيكمان

ولدت عام ١٩٧٨ في غرونينغن، هولندا
تعيش وتعمل في روتردام، هولندا

Born 1978 Groningen, Netherlands
Lives and works in Rotterdam, Netherlands
BFA, Gerrit Rietveld Academy, Amsterdam
Post-Graduate Piet Zwart Institute Rotterdam
Jan van Eyck Academy, Maastricht, Netherlands

Selected Solo Exhibitions

2005 "Rave Nature", Cementfestival/ Marres, Maastricht, Netherlands

2004 "Tunnel", Installation, Sign, Groningen, Netherlands
"Refuse dump", Nomads in Residence, Beyond Utrecht, Netherlands

Selected Group Exhibitions

2007 GHB, Van Abbemuseum, Eindhoven, Netherlands

2006 "Resonances", STUC Leuven Belgium; Artis Den Bosch, Netherlands
"Georgia here we come!", ERforS / Expodium / GEO-Air, NAC, Tbilisi, Georgia
"Hiscox Award", Arti Amiciae, Amsterdam, Netherlands
"Wat is/Wat zou kunnen", W139, Amsterdam, Netherlands

2005 "Plakatieren verboten!" K2H, Regensburg, Germany
"Enough Room For Space II", Filiale, Basel, Switzerland
"Basis", Artis Den Bosch, Netherlands

2004 "Een: 1", Pictura, Dordrecht, Netherlands

2003 "Proposition", Art & Nature, Symposium, Centre d'Art Contemporain, St-Colombe sur l'Hers, France

Public Collections

'Proposition', permanent work, St-Colombe sur l'Hers, France

Selected Bibliography

Bardoe, Megan and Vesna Madzoski, Hiscox Award, catalogue, Netherlands (2006): 9-5
Bik, Liesbeth, "Basis, is a process", Artis (2005)
Dijkman, M. and W. Osterholt, "Looking, Encountering, Staging", Netherlands: PZI, Revolver (2005): 243-56.
Dijkman, M., "Territorial Invasions in the Public and Private", Netherlands: PZI (2002): 28-30

MURATBEK DJUMALIEV/ GULNARA KASMALIEVA

مرتبيك جماليف

ولد عام ١٩٦٥ في بشكيك، كيرغستان
يعيش ويعمل بشكيك

جلنارا كاسماليفا

ولدت عام ١٩٦٠ في بشكيك، كيرغستان
تعيش وتعمل بشكيك

Muratbek Djumaliev

Born 1965, Bishkek, Kyrgyzstan

Lives and works in Bishkek, Kyrgyzstan
Academy of Fine Arts, Moscow
Kyrgyz State College of Arts, Bishkek

Gulnara Kasmalieva
Born 1960, Bishkek, Kyrgyzstan
Lives and works in Bishkek, Kyrgyzstan
Academy of Fine Arts after V.I. Muchina, St. Petersburg
Kyrgyz State College of Arts, Bishkek

Selected Solo Exhibitions

2007 Institute for Contemporary Art, Chicago, IL
2006 Plus Ultra Gallery, New York, NY
2002 Levall Gallery, Novosibirsk, Siberia
1999 Aytiev Memorial Museum, Bishkek, Kyrgyzstan
1993 City Hall, Odense, Denmark

Selected Group Exhibitions

2006 1st Singapore Biennial, Singapore
"Russia Redux 2", Sydney Mishkin Gallery, New York, NY
"Biennale Cuvee", O.K. Centre for Contemporary Art Oberösterreich, Linz, Austria
"Art from Central Asia", Ujazdowski Castle Centre for Contemporary Art, Warsaw, Poland
2005 "The Tamerlane Syndrome", Palazzo dei Sette, Orvieto, Italy
"Art from Central Asia.Actual Archive", Central Asian Pavilion, 51st Venice Biennial, Venice, Italy
"The Taste of Others", Apex Art, New York, NY
2004 "Pueblos I Sombras", CANAJA Gallery, Mexico City, Mexico
2002 "Trans-forma", Centre for Contemporary Art, Geneva, Switzerland
"No Mad's Land", House of World Culture, Berlin, Germany

Public Collections

Kyrgyz National Museum of Fine Art, Bishkek, Kyrgyzstan
Museum of Modern Art, Narva, Estonia
National Library, Tallinn, Estonia
National Library, Odense, Denmark
Odense Commune, Odense, Denmark
State Museum of Oriental Art, Moscow, Russia

Selected Bibliography

Iles, Chrissie, "Venice Biennial 2005", Frieze, (September 2005): 98-103
Li, Jennifer, "Kasmalieva and Djumaliev at Silk Road Chicago", Art Asia Pacific (December 2006)
McEvilley, Thomas, "Video comes to the 'Stans" - Report from Central Asia", Art in America (December 2005): 85-87
Moulton, Aaron, "The Tamerlane Syndrome: Art and Conflicts in Central Asia", Flash Art (November-December 2005): 53

Artist's writings:

Djoumaliev, Muratbek, "Others or other?", Moscow Art Magazine (2004)
Djoumaliev, Muratbek, "Will fighting return to Batken, Kyrgyzstan this spring?", Central Asia- Caucasus Analyst, Web-journal (2000)
Djoumaliev, Muratbek, "Stealing the Bronze Age in Kyrgyzstan" Central Asia- Caucasus Analyst, Web-journal (1999)

BRIGHT UGOCHUKWU EKE

برايت أوغو تشوكو إيكي
ولد عام ١٩٧٦ في نيجيريا
يعيش ويعمل في إينيغو، نيجيريا

Born 1976 Imo, Nigeria
Lives and works in Enugu, Nigeria
MFA, University of Nigeria, Nsukka
BA, University of Nigeria, Nsukka

Solo Exhibition

2006 Goethe Institute, Lagos, Portugal

Selected Group Exhibitions

2006 ACP (Africa, Caribbean and Pacific) Festival, Saint Dominique, Antilles
Trans-Cape Contemporary African Art Exhibition, Cape Town, South Africa
DAK'ART, 7th Biennial of Contemporary African Art, IFAN Museum, Dakar, Senegal
MFA Exhibition, Ana Gallery, Dept. of FAA, University of Nigeria, Nsukka, Enugu
2005 Founders' Day Anniversary Exhibition, Ana Gallery, Dept. of FAA, University of Nigeria, Nsukka, Enugu
5th Biennial Exhibition of the Pan African Circle of Artists, National Museum, Enugu
2002 Degree Exhibition, Ana Gallery, Dept. of FAA, University of Nigeria, Nsukka, Enugu

SOPHIE ELBAZ

صوفي الباز
ولدت عام ١٩٦٠ في باريس، فرنسا
تعيش وتعمل في باريس

Born 1960 Paris, France
Lives and works in Paris
1984-85 International Center of Photography, ICP, New York, NY
1982 T.O.E.F.L.E., Massachussets
1979-81 Law, Sorbonne, Paris

Selected Solo Exhibitions

2006 "How far along are you?" Raum Gallery, Bern, Switzerland
2005 "Caracaos", Museum of Contemporary Art, Maracaïbo, Venezuela
2003 "Caracaos", National Gallery, Fine Arts Museum, Caracas, Venezuela
"Origins", 5th Bamako Biennial, Mali
2002 "Memory of Theirs", French Cultural Centres in Bahrein, UAE; Qatar, and Art Centre, Baghdad, Irak

Selected Group Exhibitions

2005 "Origins", French Institute, Joannesburg, South Africa
"Origins", French Cultural Centre Kinshasa, Congo
2004 "Origins", City Hall of Saint-Denis, Reunion Island; Contemporary Cultural Centre of Barcelona, Spain
"Made in Africa", Porte Romana Museum, Milan, Italy; Kornhausforum Museum, Berne, Switzerland
2003 "Origins", with Alfons Alt at the Lhomond Space, Paris, France
"Buffalo Caravan", Modern Art Museum, Arhuskunstmuseum, Arhus, Denmark

Public Collections

Maison Européenne de la Photographie, MEP, Paris

Selected Bibliography

Krifa, Michket, "Recovered Images", Paris Photo Magazin, No. 24 (February/March 2003)
Paolucci, Marisa, "African Self-portraits", Il Manifesto 4 April 2004)
"Living in Exile", American Photo (September/October 1996)
Cier, Bernard, "The coming scene", text for

the exhibition, "How far along are you?" (2006)

Artist's Writing

Elbaz, Sophie, "Caracaos"(text and photos), ART SUD (November/December 2003): 50-55

TOUHAMI ENNADRE

تهامي النادر

ولد عام ١٩٥٣ في الدار البيضاء، المغرب
يعيش في باريس ونيويورك

Born 1953 Casablanca, Marocco
Lives in Paris and New York

Selected Solo Exhibitions

2006 Galerie Biedermann, Munich, Germany
Galway Arts Centre, Galway, Ireland
2005 Galerie Alain Le Gaillard, Paris, France
2002 "New York, September 11", Museum Villa Stuck, Munich, Germany
1999 Maison Européenne de la Photographie, "Black Light", Paris, France

Selected Group Exhibitions

2006 "Paris Photo", Carrousel du Louvre, Paris, France
"Arte Fiera", Bologna, Italy
2005 "Occident vist des d'Orient", Centre de Cultura Contemporània de Barcelona, Barcelona, Spain; Fundacion Bancaja, Valencia, Spain
2004 "Techniques of the Visible", Shanghai Biennial, Shanghai
"Speaking with hands. Photographs from the Henry Buhl Collection", Solomon R. Guggenheim Museum, New York, NY
"Periplo del Mediterraneo", Museo dell'Academia Ligustica di Belle Arti, Genoa, Italy
2002 "Platform 5", Documenta 11, Kassel, Germany
"Human Face", Artists Space, New York, NY
2001 "The Short Century: Independence and Liberation Movements in Africa 1945-1994", Museum of Contemporary Art, Chicago; P.S.1 Contemporary Art Center, New York, NY; Haus der Kulturen der Welt, Berlin, Germany; Museum Villa Stuck, Munich, Germany
2000 "Partage d'exotisme", 5th Lyon Biennial of Contemporary Art, Lyon, France

Public Collections

Maison Européenne de la Photographie, Paris, France
FRAC, Aquitaine, France

Selected Bibliography

Aubral, Francois, "Ennadre - Black Light", Munich/New York: Prestel Verlag (1996)
Rühle, Alex, "Dunkelkammer Manhattan, der Caravaggio der Fotografie: Touhami Ennadres dramatische Bilderreihe", New York (11 September 2001), Süddeutsche Zeitung (31 August 2002)
Spector, Nancy, "Ennadre - If you see something say something", Hatje Cantz (2004)
Stubenrauch, Bertram and Eva Karcher, "Geist in Stein - Der Regenburger Dom", Regensburg: Verlag Schnell & Steiner (2000)
Gattinoni, Christian, "La Photographie en France (1970-2005)", Paris: Editions Culturesfrance (2006)

e-Xplo
(Renee Gabri, Heimo Lattner, Erin McGonigle, in collaboration with Ayreen Anastas)

إي-اكس بلو

رينيه غابري، هايمو لاتنر، إرين ماكغونيغل، بالتعاون مع أيرين أنستاس

ولدت المجموعة عام ٢٠٠٠ في نيويورك
وسان فرانسيسكو والبندقية وبرلين

Born 2000 New York
Lives in New York, San Francisco, Venice, and Berlin
The School of Hard Knocks (1968-2006)

Selected Projects

2005 "Sleeping Dogs Lie, Part 1, Nyctalopia", organised by Wexner Center for the Arts, Claudine Isé, Columbus, OH
"Sleeping Dogs Lie, Part 2, Nights in Brasilia", organised by: BALTIC, FORMA, amino, & Michelle Hirschorn, Newcastle/Gateshead, UK
2004 "Something About Revolution Repetition", organised by Franciska Zsolyom, Budapest Autumn Festival, Átrium Theater, Budapest, Hungaria
"Roundabout - Love at Leisure: Help me Stranger", organised by MASS MoCA & Nato Thompson, North Adams, MA
"My Lodging and Some Others" organised by Transmediale, Club Transmediale & Oliver Baurhenn, Berlin, Germany
2003 "Found Wanting" organised by Lucia Farinatti & Goldsmiths College, London, UK
"Hidden Track" organised by DEAF Festival, Art In/Output & Adriaan Stellingwerff, Rotterdam & Eindhoven, Netherlands
2002 "Domestic Disturbance; Fight or Flight; or Shelter" organised by Inside/Out Festival & Eva Scharrer, Berlin, Germany
"Picnolepsy" organised by e-Xplo, Roulette & 16Beaver, New York City, NY
2001 "65MPH" organised by e-Xplo & Southfirst, Highway BQE & LIE, New York City, NY
2000 "Dencity" organised by e-Xplo & Parker's Box, Brooklyn, NY

MOUNIR FATMI

منير فاطمي

ولد عام ١٩٧٠ في طنجة، المغرب
يعيش ويعمل في طنجة وباريس

Born 1970 Tangier
Lives and works in Paris and Tangier

Selected Solo Exhibitions

2006 "Hard Head", La B.A.N.K Gallery, Paris, France
2005 "Bad Connexion", Saw Gallery, Ottawa, Canada
"Black Screens", Centre d'art contemporain, Istres, France
"Comprendra bien qui comprendra le dernier", Le Parvis centre d'art contemporain, Ibos, France
2003 "Obstacles, next flag reexistência cultural generalizada", Migros Museum, Zürich, Switzerland

Selected Group Exhibitions

2006 "Black Panther Party for Self-defense!", La B.A.N.K Gallery, Paris, France

"Courants alternatifs", Le Parvis centre d'art contemporain, Ibos, France
"Africa Remix", Mori Art Museum, Tokyo, Japan
DAK'ART, 7th Biennial of Contemporary African Art, Dakar, Senegal

2005 "Africa Remix", Centre Georges Pompidou, Paris, France
"Meeting Point", Stenersen Museum, Oslo, Norway
"Tourist Class", Konstmuseum, Malmö, Sweden
"Africa Remix", Hayward Gallery, London, UK
"Inventaire contemporain II", Galerie nationale du jeu de paume, Paris, France

2004 "A Drop of Water, a Grain of Dust", Gwangju Biennial, Gwangju, South Korea

Bibliography

Diec, Odile, Evelyne Toussaint, Nicole Brenez, "Mounir Fatmi", Edition le Parvis & Centre d'art d'Istres (2005)
Clot-Goudard, Bernadette, "Ecrans noirs", Arles: Edition Revue Semaine, (2005)
Cohen-Hadria, Michèle & Frédéric Bouglé, "Ovalprojet", Mantes-la-Jolie: Centre Culturel le Chaplin, (2002)
Miles, Roy & Mohamed Choukri, "Fatmi/Rabat", Casablanca: Edition Goethe Institut (1994)

PETER FEND

بيتر فند

ولد عام ١٩٥٠ في كولومبس، أوهايو، الولايات المتحدة
يعيش ويعمل في برلين ونيويورك

Born 1950 Columbus, Ohio
Lives and works in Berlin and NewYork
BA 1973 Literature/History, Carleton College, Northfield, Minnesota

Selected Solo Exhibitions

2006 "Beyond Petroleum, And Nuclear Too", Künstlerhaus Pappelhof, Rieseberg, Germany

2005 "Parallel Projects: Proposals for Condoleezza Rice", Galerie Christian Nagel, Berlin, Germany

2004 "Reverse Global Warming", Spacex Gallery, Exeter, UK
"Proposals for Arabia", Galeria Marta Cervera, Madrid, Spain
"Correspondence", American Fine Arts, New York, NY

Selected Group Exhibitions

2006 "Gletscherdämmerung", Eres Stiftung, Munich, Germany

2004 "Wonderful: Visions of the Near Future", Arnolfini, Bristol; Cornerhouse, Manchester; Magna, Sheffield, UK

2003-4 "Banquette", ZKM, Karlsruhe, Germany; Medialab, Madrid, Spain; Centro de Cultura, Barcelona, Spain

2003 "Global Navigation System (GNS)", Palais de Tokyo, Paris, France
"Ecovention: Current Art to Transform Ecologies", Contemporary Arts Center, Cincinnati, OH

2002 "Unplugged: Art as Scene of Global Conflict", Ars Electronica, Linz, Austria

2000 "Ecologics", Smart Museum of Art", University of Chicago, IL

1993 "Aperto", 46th Venice Biennial, Venice, Italy

1992 "Documenta IX", Kassel, Germany

1984 "Medien und Kunst", Kunsthalle Berlin, Berlin, Germany

Public Collections

FRAC, Provence-Alpes-Cote d'Azur, Marseille, France
Sammlung Hoffmann, Berlin, Germany
FRAC, Poitou-Charentes, Angouleme, France
Neue Galerie am Landesmuseum Joanneum, Graz, Austria
Musee d'Art Moderne et Contemporain, Geneva, Switzerland

Selected Bibliography

Crary, Jonathan, "Peter Fend's Global Architecture", Arts (July 1981): pp. 152-3
Getler, Warren, "UN Investigates Charge that Military Data was Passed on to Teheran", International Herald Tribune (20 October 1987): 8
Jones, Alan, "Thinking Big:Peter Fend's World Beach Party", accompanied by an interview with Jerome Sans, "Construction and Development", Arts (November 1991): 52-7
Nuttal, Nick, "Landslip was Factor in Chernobyl Blast, Expert Says", The Times, London (27 November 1989): 3
Trucco, Terry, "From Eyes in the Sky, Profitable Images", International Herald Tribune, (26 February 1986): 9

Artist's Writings

Fend, Peter, "H2Earth," Mute: The Art Issue, London (December 2001): 26-35
Fend, Peter, "New Architecture from Gordon Matta-Clark", Drawings of Gordon Matta-Clark, Vienna: Generali Foundation (1997): 46-55
Fend, Peter, "Video Art Inquiry", New Observations, No. 103, New York (1994): 24-26

FRANZ GERTSCH

فرانز غيرتش

ولد عام ١٩٣٠ في مورغن/برن، سويسرا
يعيش ويعمل في روشيج وبرن

Born 1930 Mörigen/Berne, Switzerland
Lives and works in Ruschegg and Berne
Max von Mühlenen Art School, Berne 1947-50; trained under painter Hans Schwarzenbach, Berne 1950-52
1997 Kaiserring Goslar award

Selected Solo Exhibitions

2006 "Retrospective", Museum Albertina and Museum Moderner Kunst (MUMOK), Vienna, Austria; Kunsthalle, Tübingen, Germany; Ludwig Forum Aachen, Germany; museum franz gertsch, Burgdorf and Kunstmuseum, Berne, Switzerland

2004 "Patti Smith", Pinakothek der Moderne, Munich, Germany; museum franz gertsch, Burgdorf, Switzerland; Gagosian Gallery, New York, NY

1998 "Landschaften und Porträts", Nationalgalerie im Hamburger Bahnhof, Berlin, Germany

1990 "Woodcuts", Museum of Modern Art, New York, NY; Hirshhorn Museum, Washington, DC

1980 Kunsthaus, Zürich, Switzerland

Selected Group Exhibitions

2003 "From Rauschenberg to Murakami", 50th Venice Biennial, Palazzo Correr, Venice, Italy
"Hyperréalismes USA 1965-1975", Musée d'art moderne et contemporaine, Strasbourg, France

2002 "Urgent Painting", Centre Pompidou, Paris, France

1999 "D'Apertutto", 48th Venice Biennial, Venice, Italy
"Face to Face to Cyberspace", Fondation Beyeler, Riehen, Switzerland
1997 Lyon Biennial of Contemporary Art, Lyon, France
Gwangju Biennial, Gwangju, South Korea
1978 Venice Biennial, Venice, Italy
1974 "Hyperréalistes Americaines - Réalistes Européens", Centre national d'art contemporain, Paris, France; Museum Boijmans van Beuningen, Rotterdam, Netherlands
1972 documenta 5, Kassel, Germany

Public Collections

Museum Franz Gertsch, Burgdorf-Berne, Switzerland
National Gallery, Berlin, Germany
Staatsgalerie Stuttgart, Germany
Pinakothek der Moderne/Bayerische Staatsgemäldesammlung, Munich, Germany
Kunsthaus Zurich, Switzerland
Museum Ludwig, Cologne, Germany
Ludwig Forum for International Art, Aachen, Germany

Selected Bibliography

Affentranger-Kirchrath, Angelika, "Franz Gertsch. Die Magie des Realen", Berne (2004)
Gramaccini, Norberto, "Franz Gertsch. Silvia - Chronicle of a Painting", Baden (1999)
Mason, Rainer Michael, "Franz Gertsch. Xylographies monumentales 1986-2002", with a catalogue raisonné of the woodcuts, Centre culturel Suisse, Paris (2001)
Ronte, Dieter (ed.), "Franz Gertsch", Berne (1986)
Spieler, Reinhard (ed.), "Franz Gertsch - Retrospective", with a catalogue raisonné of the paintings, Ostfildern-Ruit (2005)

Artist's Writings

Gertsch, Franz, "Zwischen tanzenden grünen und blauen Gräsern aus Malachit und Azurit ein rotes Zünglein chinesischen Bergzinnobers", Berne (2006)
Gertsch, Franz, "Meine Sonntagvormittage bei Hodler" in: Zeitmaschine (exhib.cat.) Kunstmuseum Berne, Berne (2002): 49
Gertsch, Franz, "Aus einem Gespräch mit Franz Gertsch", Franz Gertsch Landschaften, (exhib.cat.) ETH Zurich and Städelsches Kunstinstitut Franfurt (1993): 45

ABDULNASSER GHAREM AJLAN AL AMRI

عبد الناصر غارم عجلان العامري

ولد عام ١٩٧٣ في خميس
مشيط، السعودية
يعيش ويعمل خميس مشيط

Born 1973 Khamis Mushayt, Kingdom of Saudi Arabia
Lives and works in Khamis Mushayt

Selected Solo Exhibitions

2006 "Al Assirat - Video Art", King Fahad Art Village, Abha, Saudi Arabia
2004 "The white tongue who speaks slowly", King Fahad Art Village, Abha, Saudi Arabia
2003 "UN Inspector", Attileh, Jeddah, Saudi Arabia
"Mute", Attileh, Jeddah, Saudi Arabia

Selected Group Exhibitions

2006 "Son of Assir Exhibition", Abha, Saudi Arabia
2005 "Abu Dhabi Culture Council" Abu Dhabi, UAE
Exhibition in Bahrain, Al Rhuwak Gallery, Bahrain
Exhibition in Muskat, Oman
2004 "The 18th Contemporary Art Exhiition in Saudi Arabia", King Faisal Gallery, Riyadh, Saudi Arabia
"(Shattah) Group First Exhibition", Attileh, Jeddah, Saudi Arabia
"You are so far from earth (Shattah) Group Second Exhibition" King Fahad Art Village, Abha, Saudi Arabia
"Bahat Al Fenon Competition", Al Baha, Saudi Arabia
"Collectors Exhibition", King Fahad Gallery, Riyadh, Saudi Arabia
2003 "Saudi Maluan Competition" (Jeddah, Bahrain, Beirut & Dubai), Hilton Hotel, Jeddah, Saudi Arabia

SIMRYN GILL

سيمرن غيل

ولد عام ١٩٥٩ في سنغافورا
يعيش ويعمل في سيدني، استراليا
وبورت ديكسون، ماليزيا

Born 1959 Singapore
Lives and works in Sydney, Australia and Port Dickson, Malaysia

Selected Solo Exhibitions

2006 "Simryn Gill", Tate Modern, London, UK
2004 "Power Station", Shiseido Gallery, Tokyo, Japan
"Matrix 210: Standing Still", University of California, Berkeley Art Museum and Pacific Archive, Berkeley, CA
2002 "Simryn Gill: Selected Work", Art Gallery of New South Wales, Sydney, Australia
"A Small Town at the Turn of the Century", Contemporary Art Centre of South Australia, Adelaide, Australia
2001 "Dalam", Galeri Petronas, Kuala Lumpur, Malaysia

Selected Group Exhibitions

2006 "To see the world, to feel with your eyes", Lofoten International Arts Festival, Svolvaer, Norway
1st Singapore Biennial, Singapore
2003 "After Image", The Fruitmarket Gallery, Edinburgh, UK
2002 "Your Place or Mine? Fiona Foley & Simryn Gill", Institute of Modern Art, Brisbane, Australia
2000 "Delicate Balance: Six Routes to the Himalayas", Kiasma Museum of Contemporary Art, Helsinki, Finland

Selected Bibliography

Bolton, Ken, "Simryn Gill: A Small Town at the Turn of the Century", Broadsheet, CACSA, December 2002 - February 2003, Vol. 31, No. 4 (2002)
Brophy, Philip, "Singapore Biennial 2006: Simryn Gill's Station", Flash, Melbourne, No. 3 (2006)
Bush, Kate, "Simryn Gill: Portfolio", Artforum (February 2003)
Choy, Lee Weng, "The Spectre of Comparisons", Art AsiaPacific, No. 37 (2003)
Sambrani, Chaitanya "Other Realities, Someone Else's Fictions: The Tangled Art of Simryn Gill", Art and Australia, Vol. 22, No. 2 (2004)
"Simryn Gill in Conversation with Natasha Bullock and Lily Hibberd", Photofile 76, (Summer 2006)

TUE GREENFORT

توووه غرينفورت

ولد عام ١٩٧٣ في هولبيك، الدنمارك
يعيش ويعمل في الدنمارك وبرلين

Born 1973 Holbæk, Denmark
Lives and works in Denmark and Berlin
2000-03 Staatliche Hochschule für Bildende Künste (Städelschule), Frankfurt a. M.
1997-00 Academy of Fünen, Denmark

Selected Solo Exhibitions

2006 "Rococo Eco" Max Wigram Gallery, London, UK
Arts & Ecology Programme, Royal Society of Arts, London, UK
"Unravelling Rotterdam", Witte de With, Rotterdam, Netherlands
"Dänische Schweine und andere Märkte", Johann König, Berlin, Germany
2004 "Umwelt", Gallery Zero, Milan, Italy

Selected Group Exhibitions

2007 "Skulptur Projekte Münster", Münster, Germany
2006 "Momentum", Nordic Festival of Contemporary Art, Moss, Norway
"Jagdsalon", Kunstraum Kreuzberg/Bethanien, Berlin, Germany
"Inaugural Exhibition", Johann König, Berlin, Germany
"The Show Will Be Open When the Show Will Be Closed", Store Gallery and various locations, London, UK
"Jan Freuchen, Tue Greenfort", ALP Peter Bergman Gallery, Stockholm, Sweden
ISP residency, Oslo, Norway
"Stefan Thater, Frederike Klever, Tue Greenfort", Anna Helwing Gallery, Los Angeles, LA
2005 "Lichtkunst aus Kunstlicht", ZKM Zentrum für Kunst und Medientechnologie, Karlsruhe, Germany
2004 "L´attitude des autres", SMP, Marseilles, France
"Tuesday is gone", Tblisi, Georgia

Selected Bibliography

Andrews, Max, "Now Weirdy Beardy", Wonderland (January 2006)
Gray, Zoe, Jesper Hoffmeyer & Maria Muhle, "Tue Greenfort: Photosynthesis", New York: Lukas & Strenberg (2006)
Loch, Catrin, "Tue Greenfort", Frieze, No. 95 (2005)
Sladen, Mark, "First Take", Artforum (January 2006)
Stange, Raimar, "Die Kunst der ökologischen Praxis. Zu den ästhetischen Strategien von Tue Greenfort", Kunst-Bulletin (April 2005)

GROUP TUESDAY

مجموعة الثلاثاء

وليد صادق
ولد عام ١٩٦٦، يعيش ويعمل في بيروت
بلال خبيز
ولد عام ١٩٦٣، يعيش ويعمل في بيروت
فادي عبد الله
ولد عام ١٩٧٦، يعيش ويعمل في بيروت

Group Tuesday is a partnership between Walid Sadek, Bilal Khbeiz and Fadi Abdallah. Their first work entitled File: Public Time is a collection of short essays and aphorisms presented first in Beirut as part of Home Works III, a forum for cultural practices organized by Ashkal Alwan, November 2005. The project they propose for SB8 is their second collaboration.

Born in 1966 Walid Sadek is an artist and writer living in Beirut. He has exhibited Love is Blind, 2006; Les Autres, 2001; Al Kassal, 1999, with writer Bilal Khbeiz; Bigger Than Picasso, 1999; and Karaoke, 1998. He has essays published in magazines such as Parachute, Lettre Internationale, Al Adab and in the volumes Tamass, 2001, Territoire Méditerranée, 2005 and Notes for an Art School, Manifesta 6, Nicosia, 2006. He has also published a collection of essays entitled Jane-Loyse Tissier, 2003. Sadek is currently assistant professor at the Department of Architecture and Design at the American University of Beirut.

Born in 1963 Bilal Khbeiz is a writer, poet and artist living in Beirut. He is the author of two poetry books A Memory of Air, Perhaps, 1991; and Of My Father's Illness and the Unbearable Heat, 1997; three collection of essays, That the Body is Sin and Deliverance, 1998; Globalization and the Manufacture of Transient Events, 2002; and The Enduring Image and the Vanishing World, 2004. He has participated in various exhibitions including the 6th Sharjah Biennial, United Arab Emirates, 2003 and Dreams and Conflicts - The Dictatorship of the Viewer, Venice Biennial, 2003. He is an editorial secretary for the cultural supplement of the Lebanese daily Annahar.

Born in 1976 in Tripoli, Lebanon, Fadi El Abdallah is a poet and essayist. He has published two collections of poetry A Stranger with a Camera in his Hand, Dar Al Jadid, Beirut, 1999; and The Hand of Intimacy, Dar Al Intishar Al Arabi, Beirut, 2001. He is a frequent contributor to the cultural supplements of the local dailies Assafir and Annahar. He currently resides in Paris.

GRAHAM GUSSIN

غراهام غصين

ولد عام ١٩٦٠ في لندن، بريطانيا
يعيش ويعمل لندن

Born 1960, London, UK
Lives and works in London

Selected Solo Exhibitions

2006 "Illumination Rig", public work, Newcastle City Centre, UK
"Spill", Ikon 2, Birmingham, UK
2004 "Backdrop", Centre d'Art Santa Monica, Barcelona, Spain
2003 Lisson Gallery, London, UK
2002 Ikon Gallery, Birmingham, UK
2001 "States of Mind", New Media Space, New Museum of Contemporary Art, New York, NY; Goldie Paley Gallery, Moore College of Art and Design, Philadelphia, PA

Selected Group Exhibitions

2006 "5 Billion Years", Palais de Tokyo, Paris, France
"If it didn't exist you'd have to invent it", Showroom, London, UK
2005 "OK/Okay", Grey Art Gallery, Swiss Institute, NYU, New York, NY
2004 "From nowhere to somewhere without return: the knowledge", Coleman Gallery, London, UK
"Dazzling", Jeu de Paume, Paris, France
Pontevedra Biennial, Pontevedra, Spain
2003 "The Distance Between Me & You", Lisson Gallery, London, UK
"This was Tomorrow", New Art Centre Sculpture Park & Gallery, Salisbury, UK
2002 "Ferrotel, Fuoriuso 2002", Pescara, Italy

"En Route", Serpentine Gallery, London, UK

Artist's Writings
Gussin, Graham, "The Starry Messenger", Visions of the Universe, Compton Verney (2006)
Gussin, Graham, "Art works: Place", London: Thames and Hudson (2005)
Gussin, Graham, "Densite +0", Paris: Ecole superieure des beaux-arts (2004)

KHALED HAFEZ
خالد حافظ

ولد عام ١٩٦٣ في القاهرة، مصر
يعيش ويعمل القاهرة

Born 1963 Cairo, Egypt
Lives and works in Cairo

Selected Solo Exhibitions
2006 "North-East to South-West", Espace Doual'Art, Douala, Cameroon
"Between Sacred & Profane", Galleria Punto Arte, Modena, Italy
"Philadelphia Chromosome", Galleria San Carlo, Milan, Italy
2005 "Secret Works", Falaki Gallery, AUC, Cairo, Egypt
"French Memories", CCM Jean Gagnant, Limoges, France
"African Memories", Chantiers de la Lune, Toulon, France
2004 "Kartonopolis & Some 10 years later", Townhouse Gallery, Cairo, Egypt

Selected Group Exhibitions
2006 Coding:Decoding, video screening programme, Museum of Contemporary Art, Roskilde, Denmark
1st Singapore Biennial, Singapore
DAK'ART, 7th Biennial of Contemporary African Art, Dakar, Senegal
"Images of the Middle East", Danish Cultural Foundation, Copenhagen, Denmark
2005 "Mediterranean Encounters", Horcynus Orca Foundation, Messina, Italy
2004 DAK'ART, 6th Biennial of Contemporary African Art, Dakar, Senegal (Prize)

Selected Bibliography
Abu Nawar, Alia, "Recycling Culture: Khaled Hafez", SKIN Magazine (April 2006): 162-170
Grasso, Sebastiano, "Il Medico egiziano che dipinge Batman", Corriere della Sera (25 February 2006): 40
Corgnati, Martina, Khaled Hafez: Between Sacred and Profane, Milan: Edizione Galleria San Carlo (February 2006): 4-9
Lombardi, D. Dominick, "Mediterranean Encounters", NY ARTS Magazine, Vol. 10, No. 11/12 (November-December 2005)
Karnouk, Liliane, "Contemporary Egyptian Art" (AUC Press 2005): 240-241

HENRIK HÅKANSSON
هنريك هاكينسون

ولد عام ١٩٦٨ في هلسينبورغ، السويد
يعيش ويعمل في السويد ولندن

Born in 1968 in Helsingborg, Sweden
Lives and works in Köinge, Sweden, and Berlin

Selected Solo Exhibitions
2006 Isabella Stewart Gardner Museum, Boston, MA (artist-in-residence)
Palais de Tokyo, Paris, France (with Allora/Calzadilla and Sergio Vega)
2005 Galleria Franco Noero, Turin, Italy
2003-04 "Henrik Håkansson", The Dunker Culture Centre, Helsinborg, Sweden
"An Introduction to the birds", Villa Merkel, Esslingen, Germany; De Appel, Amsterdam, Netherlands; Bonner Kunstverein, Bonn, Germany; Moderna Museet c/o Riddarhuset, Stockholm, Sweden
2002 Secession, Vienna, Austria
1999 "Tomorrow and Tonight", Kunsthalle Basel, Basel, Switzerland

Selected Group Exhibitions
2006 "Where the Wild Things are", Dundee Contemporary Arts, Scotland, UK
Echigo-Tsumari Art Triennial, Niigata, Japan
2005 "Experiencing Duration", 8th Lyon Biennial of Contemporary Art, Lyon, France
2004 26th São Paulo Biennial, São Paolo, Brazil
Hamburger Bahnhof, Berlin, Germany
2003 "Utopia Station", 50th Venice Biennial, Venice, Italy
"Ars Viva 02-03 Landschaft", Kunstverein Hamburg, Hamburg, Germany; Städtische Museen Zwickau, Germany
2002 "Beyond Paradise", National Gallery, Bangkok, Thailand; National Gallery, Kuala Lumpur, Malaysia
"The Power of Art", Hyogo Prefectural Museum of Art, Kobe, Japan
"Ecovention", The Contemporary Arts Center, Cincinnati, OH
2001 2nd Berlin Biennale, Berlin, Germany
2000 "The Greenhouse Effect", Serpentine Gallery, London, UK

Selected Bibliography
Birnbaum, Daniel, "Openings", Artforum (May 1997)
Bradley, Will, "Henrik Håkansson, The world should listen then", exhibition catalouge, Vienna: Secession (2002)
Enwezor, Okwui, "Mirror's Edge", exhibition catalogue, Umea: BildMuseet (2001): 84-87
Gellatly, Andrew, "A Bug s Life", Frieze (September-October 2000): 100-103
Heiser, Jörg, "Bionic Feedback", Ars Viva 02/03-Landschaft, exhibition catalouge (2003)
Manacorda, Francesco, and Akiko Miki, "Through the woods to find the forest", exhibition catalogue, Paris:Palais de Tokyo (2006)

ANAWANA HALOBA
أنوانا هالوبا

ولدت عام ١٩٧٨ في ليفنغستون، زامبيا

Born 1978 Livingstone, Zambia
B.A. 2006 Oslo National Academy of Fine Arts
D.F.A. 2000 Evelyn Hone College of Applied Arts and Commerce
2000-08 Resident Artists at the Rijksakademie, Amsterdam

Selected Solo Exhibitions
2005 "The Salt licked Map", Gallery 21-25, Oslo, Norway
"Loud Silence", NSA Gallery, Durban, South Africa
2004 "Senseless Wars", Léopold

Senghor Gallery, Village des Arts, Senegal

Selected Group Exhibitions

2007 "Transcape" Biennial, Cape Town, South Africa
2006 Exposition d ´Art Africain Contemporain, Ateliers des Tanneurs. Brussels, Belgium
Avgangsutstillingen/Graduation show, Stenersenmuseet, Oslo, Norway
DAK'ART, 7th Biennial of Contemporary African Art, Dakar, Senegal
2005 "Prog Me", New Media Festival Rio, Rio de Janeiro, Brazil
2002 "Essence of a Women", Madison Insurance, Lusaka, Zambia
2001 African Union Summit, Lusaka
"Women's Eclipse of the Sun", Pamodzi Gallery, Lusaka, Zambia
"National Silk Screen" (AWW), Henry Tayali Gallery, Lusaka, Zambia
"National Visual Arts Show", Henry Tayali, Lusaka, Zambia
2000 "Camera as a tool of Art" photography, Henry Tayali, Lusaka, Zambia

Bibliography

Kerkham Simbao, Ruth, "Salt Licked Maps", The Harvard African (Vol. 1, No. 1): 25
Mbeye, Massamba, "Ces mains de l`indicible souffrance", Le Martin - Senegalese newspaper (17 December 2004)
Ngcobo, Gabi, "No Longer At Ease", exhibition catalogue, YAP (2005)
Sudheim, Alex, "Louder than Silence", Mail & Guardian (18th March 2005)
Polvo Art Magazine (Spring 2005)

ILANA HALPERIN

إيلانا هيلبرين

ولدت ١٩٧٣ في نيويورك، الولايات المتحدة. تعيش وتعمل في غلاسكو، اسكتلندا

Born 1973 New York, NY
Lives and works in Glasgow, Scotland, UK
M.F.A. Glasgow School of Art; B.A. Brown University

Selected Solo Exhibitions

2005 Doggerfisher, Edinburgh, UK
2004 Autori Cambi, Rome, Italy
2002 Tramway, Glasgow, UK

Selected Group Exhibitions

2006 "How I Finally Accepted Fate", Elizabeth Foundation for the Arts, New York, NY
"Where the Wild Things Are", Dundee Contemporary Arts, Dundee, UK
"Drawing Links", The Drawing Room, London, UK, touring
"Our House is a House that Moves", Living Art Museum,Reykjavik, Iceland, touring
2004 "The Dazzled Eye", Whitworth Gallery, Manchester, UK
2003 Institute for Drawing, Central Academy of Fine Arts, Beijing, China, touring
2002 "Art and Mountains - Conquistadors of the Useless", Alpine Club, London, UK
"Into the Abyss", Kettilhusid, Akureyri, Iceland
2000 "New Contemporaries 2000", MK Gallery, Milton Keynes, UK, touring
"A Day Like Any Other", Stavanger Kulturhus, Stavanger, Norway

Public Collections

Hunterian Museum, Glasgow, UK
Gallery of Modern Art,Glasgow, UK
Whitworth Gallery, Manchester, UK

Selected Bibliography

Barley, Nick, "Ilana Halperin", Map (Issue 3, Autumn 2005): 58
Campbell, Mungo, "Journey Through the Surface of the Earth", London: Camden Arts Centre (November 2006)
Gale, Iain, "Anniversary leap of faith into volcano of discovery", Scotland on Sunday (May 15, 2005): 8-9
Garbarino, Laura, "In the Vast Perhaps", Dromacroma, Autori Messa (February 2004)
Patrizio, Andrew, "Ilana Halperin: Emerging Properties", London: Drawing Room (2005)

Artist's Writings

Halperin, Ilana, "Emergent Landmass (a chronicle of disappearance)", Artist's publication, Dundee Contemporary Arts (2006)
Halperin, Ilana, "Ruins in Reverse (Nomadic Landmass)", Artist's publication, Doggerfisher (2005)

MONA HATOUM

منى حاطوم

ولدت عام ١٩٥٢، في بيروت، لبنان
تعيش وتعمل في لندن وبرلين

Born 1952 Beirut, Lebanon
Lives and works in London and Berlin
A.A.S. Beirut University College; D.F.A. Byam Shaw School of Art, London; H.D.F.A. Slade School of Fine Art, London
2004 winner of the Sonning Prize, the University of Copenhagen
winner of the Roswitha Haftmann prize, Zurich

Selected Solo Exhibitions

2004-05 "Mona Hatoum", Hamburger Kunsthalle, Hamburg, Gerrmany; Kunstmuseum Bonn, Germany; Magasin 3, Stockholm Konsthall, Stockholm, Sweden, and MCA Sydney, Australia
2003 "Mona Hatoum", Museo de Arte Contemporáneo de Oaxaca (MACO), Oaxaca, and Ex-Convento de Conkal, Yukatan, Mexico
2002 "Mona Hatoum", Centro de Arte de Salamanca (CASA), and Centro Galego de Arte Contemporánea (CGAC), Santiago de Compostela, Spain
2001 "Domestic Disturbance", Mass MoCA, North Adams, MA
2000 "The Entire World as a Foreign Land", Tate Gallery, London, UK

Selected Group Exhibitions

2006 "Zones of Contact", 15th Biennial of Sydney, MCA, Sydney, Australia
2005 "Always a little Further", Arsenale di Venezia, 51st Venice Biennial, Venice, Italy
2003 "Trans-cultures", EMST - National Museum of Contemporary Art, Athens, Greece
2002 Documenta XI, Kassel, Germany
2001 "El Mundo Nuevo/The New World", Biennale de Valencia, Valencia, Spain
1999 "Looking for a Place", SITE Santa Fe's Third International Biennial, Santa Fe, New Mexico
1997 Gwangju Biennial, Gwangju, South Korea
1996 "Distemper: Dissonant Themes in the Art of the 1990s", Hirshhorn Museum and Sculpture Garden, Washington, DC

1995 "Orient/ation", 4th International Istanbul Biennial, Istanbul
"Identity and Alterity", Italian Pavilion, Venice Biennial, Venice, Italy

Selected Bibliography

Archer, Michael, Guy Brett, Catherine de Zegher, Piero Manzoni, and Edward Said, "Mona Hatoum", London: Phaidon Press (1997)
Cameron, Dan and Jessica Morgan, "Mona Hatoum", Chicago: Museum of Contemporary Art (1997)
Garb, Tamar (interviews with Janine Antoni and Jo Glencross), "Mona Hatoum", Salamanca: Centro de Arte de Salamanca (CASA); Santiago de Compostela: Centro Galego de Arte Contemporanea (2002)
Panhans-Bühler, Ursula, Volker Adolphs, Nina Zimmer, Richard Julin, Elisabeth Millqvist, and Christoph Heinrich, "Mona Hatoum", Hamburg: Hamburger Kunsthalle (2004)
Said, Edward W. and Sheena Wagstaff, "Mona Hatoum: The Entire World as a Foreign Land"ß, London: Tate Gallery Publishing Ltd. (2000)

SUSAN HEFUNA

سوزان حفونة

ولدت عام ١٩٦٢ في مصر

تعيش وتعمل في مصر وألمانيا

Born 1962 Egypt
Lives and works in Egypt and Germany

Selected Solo Exhibitions

2006 Gallery Ralf Seippel, Cologne, Germany
2004 "xcultural codes", Kunstverein, Heidelberg, Germany
"xcultural codes" Townhouse Gallery, Cairo, Egypt
2004 "xcultural codes", Bluecoat Arts Centre, Liverpool, UK
2000 "navigation xcultural", National Gallery, Cape Town, South Africa

Selected Group Exhibitions

2006 2nd International Biennial for Contemporary Art, Shumen, Bulgaria
"Nomads of Nowadays", Lazina Centre for Contemporary Art, Gdansk, Poland
"The Third Line Gallery", Dubai, UAE
2006 "NETEROTOPIA", Palais de Tokyo, Paris, France
2005-06 "Regards des Photographes Arabes Contemporains", Institut du Monde Arabe, Paris, France
2005 Prague Biennial, National Gallery, Prague, Czech Republic
2004-05 "Contrepoints", Louvre, Paris, France
2003 "Photo Cairo",Townhouse Gallery, Cairo, Egypt
"Rencontres", Photo Biennial Bamako, Bamako, Mali
"Fantasies de l'harem i noves Xahrazads", CCCB Centre de Cultura Contemporània de Barcelona, Barcelona, Spain

Selected Bibliography

Biggs, Bryan, "Susan Hefuna - xcultural codes", Bidoun Magazine (Fall 2004): 108-09
Emmerling, Leonhard, "The Ethics of being Alien", INKA Journal of Contemporary African Art, Issue 15 (Fall/Winter 2001): 38-43
Emmerling, Leonhard, "Celelebrating Difference, Unpacking Europe. Towards a Critical Reading", Rotterdam: Museum Boijmans Van Beuningen, Nai Publishers (2001): 344-49
Murinik, Tracy, "Navigation X Cultural - Celebrate Life", NKA Journal of Contemporary African Art, Issue 14, (Spring 2001): 127

USCHI HUBER

أوشي هيوبر

ولدت عام ١٩٦٦ في بورغوسين، ألمانيا

تعيش وتعمل في كولون، ألمانيا

Born 1966 Burghausen, Germany
Lives and works in Cologne, Germany
B.A. 1992 Fine Arts, Brighton University, UK
M.A. 1995 Fine Arts, State Academy of Art, Düsseldorf

Selected Solo Exhibitions

2006 "Uschi Huber-Photographische Arbeiten", Photographische Sammlung, SK Stiftung, Cologne, Germany
2005 "Autobahn", Toll Collect Headquaters, Berlin, Germany
2004 Gallery Liquidation Totale, part of PhotoEspana, Madrid, germany
"OHIO e.V.", Kunstverein Düsseldorf, Düsseldorf, Germany
"Out of Print", IPS Gallery, Birmingham, UK
2002 Chelsea Kunstraum, Cologne, Germany

Selected Group Exhibitions

2007 "Darstellung/Vorstellung", touring photo exhibition, organised by ifa Gallery, Berlin, Germany
2006 "artconneXions", ifa-Gallery, Berlin, Germany; Singapore; Melbourne, Australia
"Found and Shared", Cube Gallery, Manchester, UK
2005 "Die Schweizer Krankheit", Kunsthaus Dresden, Dresden, Germany
2003 "Transfer", Kunstmuseum Bonn, Bonn, Germany
"Wonderlands", Museum Küppersmühle Duisburg, Germany
"Hotel Hotel", Landesmuseum Graz, Graz, Austria
2002 "Chilufim/Transfer", Israel Museum, Jerusalem and Herzlyia Museum of Art, Israel
"Ökonomien der Zeit", Museum Ludwig, Cologne, Germany
Manifesta 4, Frankfurt a.M., Germany
2001 "TRADE", Photomuseum Winterthur, Switzerland
2000 Opening of the Ohio-Vitrine in Cologne, Germany

Artist's Writings

Huber, Uschi and Jörg Paul Janka (eds), Ohio Photomagazin Nos. 1-14, Cologne (1995-2006)
Huber, Uschi, "Anlagen", Chelsea Kunstraum, Cologne: Thorsten Koch (2002)
Huber, Uschi, "Autobahn", Düsseldorf: Richter Verlag (2000)

MOHAMED AHMED IBRAHIM

محمد أحمد إبراهيم

ولد عام ١٩٦٢ في خورفكان، الإمارات

Born 1962 Khorfakkan, UAE
Since 1986 Member of the Emirates Fine Arts Society, Sharjah, UAE
1997 Founder of Art Atelier in the Khorfakkan Art Center, Department of Culture and Information, Sharjah, UAE

Solo Exhibitions

1991 Cultural Centre, Sharjah, UAE

Cultural Foundation, Abu Dhabi, UAE

Selected Group Exhibitions

2003 Sharjah International Biennial, Sharjah, UAE

2002 Ludwig Forum for International Art, Aachen, Germany
Dhaka Biennial, Bangladesh, India

2001 Sharjah International Biennial, Sharjah, UAE

2000 "Emirates Identities", French Cultural Centre, Dubai. UAE
7th Havana Biennial, Havanna, Cuba

1999 Sharjah International Biennial, Sharjah, UAE

1998 "UAE Contemporary Art", Institut du Monde Arabe, Paris, France
7th Cairo International Biennial, Cairo, Egypt

1997 UAE Artists Exhibition, French Cultural Centre, Dubai, UAE

1986 Participation in annual exhibitions of Emirates Fine Art Society, Sharjah, UAE

Public Collections

Arab Museum of Modern Art, Doha, Qatar
Sharjah Art Museum, Sharjah, UAE
Sittard Art Centre, Netherlands

ALFREDO JAAR

ألفريدو جار

ولد عام ١٩٥٦ في سانتياغو، تشيلي
يعيش ويعمل في نيويورك

Born 1956 Santiago de Chile
Lives and works in New York
Architecture, 1981, Universidad de Chile, Santiago
Filmmaking, 1980, Instituto Chileno-Norteamericano de Cultura, Santiago

Selected Solo Exhibitions

2006 Fundacion Telefonica, Santiago, Chile
Fotofest, Houston, TX

2005 Museum d'Arte Contemporanea, Rome, Italy
Musée d'Art Moderne et Contemporain, Geneva, Switzerland
Museum of Fine Arts, Houston, TX

Selected Group Exhibitions

2007 Trienal de Luanda, Luanda, Angola

2006 Fotofest, Houston, TX
Biennale de Sevilla, Seville, Spain
Brighton Biennial, Brighton, UK
Biennale de Canarias, Santa Cruz de Tenerife, Spain

2005 "Emergencias", MUSAC, Leon, Spain

2004 "En Guerra", Centro de Cultura Contemporanea, Barcelona, Spain

2003 Rotterdam Photo Biennial, Foto Institute, Rotterdam, Netherlands
"Black President", New Museum of Contemporary Art, New York, NY

2002 Documenta 11, Kassel, Germany

Selected Bibliography

Accatino, Sandra, "Chiuminatto, Cuneo, Jaar, Risco, Valdes and Zuniga", Jaar SCL 2006, Barcelona: Actar (2006)
De Lecco, Emanuela, Roberto Pinto, Annie Ratti and Gianni Vattimo, "Alfredo Jaar, The Aesthetics of Resistance", Barcelona: Actar (2006)
Denegri, Derksen, Smith, Pasolini, and Vattimo, "Alfredo Jaar", Rome: Electa (2006)
Princenthal, Nancy and Mary Jane Jacob, "Alfredo Jaar - The Fire This Time: Public Interventions, 1979-2005", Milan: Charta (2005)

MARYA KAZOUN

ماريا قزعون

لبنانية/ كندية
تعيش وتعمل في نيويورك

Lebanese/Canadian
Lives and works in New York

2004 M.F.A. School of Visual Arts, New York, NY

2000 B.A. Interior Architecture, Lebanese American University, Beirut

1999 B.S. Interior Design, Lebanese American University, Beirut

Selected Solo Exhibitions

2005 "Pull Christian, Pull, Pull", Roberta Lietti Gallery, Como, Italy
"Personal Living Space", 51st Venice Biennial, Venice, Italy

2004 "It's Me, It's Okay", Michela Rizzo Gallery, Venice, Italy
"The Intolerable Weightlessness", Tapper-Popermajer Gallery, Malmö, Sweden
"Tonight is The Full Moon, Trapeze Artists Crash and Break Their Necks", Xanadu Gallery, New York, NY

Selected Group Exhibitions

2006 "Facing 1200 Degrees", MMKK, Klagenfurt, Austria
"MFD", Casoria International Contemporary Art Museum, Naples, Italy
"Beijing Art Fair", Beijing, China
"Astarojna Stiklo", Pushkin State Museum of Fine Arts, Moscow, Russia
"Sei Artiste per un Territorio", Galleria Comunale d'Arte Contemporanea di Monfalcone, Monfalcone, Italy
"Art Miami", Miami, FL

2005 "Altre Lilith", Frascati, Italy
"In & Out", Museo Michetti, Chieti, Italy
"Art Palm Beach 3", West Palm Beach, FL

2004 "In a Bind", SVA West Side Gallery, New York, NY

Bibliography

Artes, Italy (November 2006)
Artes Magazine, Sweden (January 2006)
Espoarte, Italy (November/December, 2005)

Artist's Writings

Kazoun, Marya, "Personal Living Space", Catalogue - 51st International Art Exhibition, Venice Biennial (June 2005)
Kazoun, Marya, "Statement", Global Art Glass Triennial, Oland, Sweden (June 2005)
Kazoun, Marya, "Statement", Mizna, Vol. 6, No. 2 (December 2004)

AMAL KENAWY

أمل القناوي

ولدت عام ١٩٦٠ في القاهرة، مصر
تعيش وتعمل القاهرة

Born 1974 Cairo, Egypt
Lives and works in Cairo
B.A. in Painting, 1999, Faculty of Fine Arts, Cairo

Selected Solo Exhibitions

2006 Darat El Funun, Amman, Jordan
"You'll be Killed", video, space, Karim Francis, Contemporary Art Gallery, Cairo, Egypt

"Booby-trapped Heaven", video, Masharabia Gallery, Cairo, Egypt
2004 "The Journey", video/installation/sculpture, Townhouse Gallery for Contemporary Art, Cairo, Egypt
"Transformation", Grant of Pro-Helvetia Swiss Arts Council, Artist's Residency, Aarau, Switzerland

Selected Group Exhibitions
2007 2nd Moscow Biennial, Moscow, Russia
2006 1st Biennial of the Canaries for Architecture, Art and Landscape, Canaries
1st Singapore Biennial, Singapore
"Nafas", ifa Gallery, Berlin, Germany
2006-04 DAK'ART, Biennial of Contemporary African Art, Dakar, Senegal
2005 XX111 Biennale de Alexandre des Pays de La Mediterranee, Egypt
"Flight 406", Sfeir Semler Gallery, Beirut, Lebanon
"Some Stories", Kunsthalle, Vienna, Austria
2004-07 Africa Remix Exhibition, touring, museum kunst palast, Düsseldorf, Germany; Hayward Gallery, London, UK; Centre Georges Pompidou, Paris, France; Mori Art Museum, Japan
1998 7th Cairo Biennial, Cairo, Egypt

Collections
Darat Al Funun, Amman
Simdika Dokolo, African Collection of Contemporary Art

LEOPOLD KESSLER
ليوبولد كيسلر
ولد عام ١٩٧٦ في ميونيخ، ألمانيا
يعيش في فيينا، النمسا
Born 1976 Munich, Germany
Lives in Vienna, Austria
Diploma Academy of fine Arts, Vienna

Selected Solo Exhibitions
2007 Galerie Andreas Huber, Vienna, Austria
2006 "GRAZ", Studio/Neue Galerie, Graz, Austria
"Interventionen 02-05", Galerie der Stadt Schwaz, Tirol, Austria
2005 "Transportable works", Lombard-Freid Projects, New York, NY
"0", Kunstbüro, Vienna, Austria
2003 "Privatisiert", Galerie Corentin Hamel, Paris, France

Selected Group Exhibitions
2006 "One second/one year", Palais de Tokyo, Paris, France
"Wien Südbahnhof / Bratislava hl.st.", Galerie Nadine Gandy, Bratislava, Slovakia
"Société des nations", circuit, Lausanne, Switzerland
"On mobility", Trafo, Budapest, Hungary; and De Appel, Amsterdam, Netherlands
2005 "Lives & works in Vienna", Kunsthalle Wien, Vienna, Austria
"OKAY/O.K.", Swiss Institute, New York, NY
"Don't interrupt your activities", Royal College, London, UK
2004 "Manifesta 05", San Sebastian, Spain
"Beuys don't cry" Galleria Zero, Milano, Italy
2003 "Critique is not enough", Shedhalle, Zurich, Swizerland

Selected Bibliography
Dusini, Mathias, "Kritikerumfrage: Rueckblick 2005", art-Das Kunstmagazin, No.1, (2006)
Huck, Brigitte, "Reviews", Artforum, (December 2005)
Johnson, Ken, "Art in Review; 'OK/Okay'", New York Times (June 17, 2005)
Petresin, Natasa, "What to Do with Alternative/Artistic Knowledge?", Parkett, Issue No. 73 (2005)
Shaw, Francesca, and Lavinia Garulli, "Was will Europa", Flash Art, No. 237 (July-September 2004)
Wulffen, Thomas, "Manifesta 5", Kunstforum International, Bd.171 (July-August 2004)

Artist's Writing
Kessler, Leopold, "Akademiekabel", Paris: One StarPress (2005)

SUSHAN KINOSHI
سوشان كينوشي
ولدت عام ١٩٦٠ في طوكيو، اليابان
تعيش وتعمل في ماسترخ، هولاندا
Born 1960 Tokyo, Japan
Lives and works in Maastricht, Netherlands

Selected Solo Exhibitions
2006 "Das Fragment an Sich", Ikon Gallery, Birmingham, UK
"hoe langzamer hoe beter", Gallery Nadia Villene, Liege, Belgium
2005 "project room", Ellen de Brine, ARCO, Madrid2004 "Archives of Problems", Marres, Maastricht, Netherlands
2002-03 "Eerste Huwelijk", Museum van Hedendaagse Kunste Antwerpen, Antwerp, Belgium

Selected Group Exhibitions
2006 "Kleine Biennale", Utrecht, Netherlands
2005 "A Guest + A Host = A Ghost", Wijlre, Netherlands
"Depot des mots", Gallery Nadia Villene, Brussels, Belgium
2004 "Adaptive Behaviour", New Museum of Contemporary Art, New York, NY
2002 "Spring", Gallery Nadia Vilenne, Liege, Belgium
"HELLGRUEN", Stadt Düsseldorf, Germany
"Scenarien, oder der Hang zum Theater", Bonner Kunstverein, Bonn , Germany
2000 "Strange Paradise", Casino Luxembourg, Luxembourg
Biennial of Sydney, Sydney, Australia
1999-00 "Carnegie International", Carnegie Museum of Art, Pittsburgh, PA

Public Collections
Bonnefanten Museum, Maastricht, Netherlands
Van Abbe Museum, Eindhoven, Netherlands
SMAK, Ghent, Belgium
MUKHA, Antwerp, Belgium

JOACHIM KOESTER
يواكيم كوستر
ولد عام ١٩٦٢ في كوبنهاغن، الدنمرك
Born 1962 Copenhagen, Denmark

Selected Solo Exhibitions
2006 Galleri Nicolai Wallner, Copenhagen, Denmark
Lunds Konsthall, Lund, Sweden
Galerie Jan Mot, Brussels, Belgium

CASM, Centre d'Art Santa Monica, Barcelona, Spain
Palais de Tokyo, Paris, France

Selected Group Exhibitions

2006 "Prophets of Deceit", CCA Wattis Insitute, San Francisco, CA
Busan Biennial, Busan, Korea
2005 "Billion Years", Palais de Tokyo, Paris, France
Danish Pavilon, 51st Venice Biennial, Venice, Italy
"The Need To Document", Kunsthaus Baselland, Muttenz-Basel, Switzeland
"Black Market Worlds", 9th Baltic Triennial of International Art, Vilnius, Lithunia
2002 "Out of Place; Contemporary Art and the Architectural Uncanny", Museum of Contemporary Art, Chicago, IL
1990 "Nuit Blanche", Musee d'Art Moderne de la Ville de Paris, Paris, France
1997 Documenta X, Kassel, Germany
Johannesburg Biennial, Johannesburg, South Africa

Public Collections

S.M.A.K, Stedelijk Museum Voor Actuele Kunst, Ghent, Belgium
Metropolitan Museum of Art, New York, NY
Statens Museum for Kunst, Copenhagen, Denmark
KIASMA, Museum of Contemporary Art, Helsinki, Finland
Putaux, Fonds national d'art contemporain, Paris, France
Moderna Museet, Stockholm, Sweden
Malmö Konstmuseum, Malmö, Sweden
Museum of Fine Arts, Houston, TX
Musee des arts contemporains MAC's Grand-Hornu, Belgium
Museum De Verbeelding, Zeewolde, Netherlands

Selected Bibliography

Foster, Hal, "Blind Spots, The Art of Joachim Koester", Artforum (April 2006)
Nielsen, Henrikke, "Review", Flash Art, (March-April 2006)
Smith, Roberta, "Sandra of the Tuliphouse", New York Times (June 2005)
Staffan Boije af Grennas, "Review", Frieze, No. 99 (May 2006)
Wilson, Michael, "Review", Artforum (September 2005)

CHRISTINA KUBISCH

كرستينا كوبيش

ولدت عام ١٩٤٨ في بريمن، ألمانيا
تعيش في هوبغارتن قرب برلين

Born 1948 Bremen, Germany
Lives in Hoppegarten near Berlin and works in Saarbrucken
Academy of Fine Arts, Stuttgart
Academy of Music, Hamburg
Conservatories of Zurich and Milan.
Diploma in flute and composition.

Selected Solo Exhibitions

2006 Ikon Gallery, Birmingham, UK
Gasometer, Oberhausen, Germany
2005 Ettersburg Castle, Weimar, Germany (with Bernhard Leitner)
Art Museum Ystad, Ystad, Sweden
e/static, Milan, Italy

Selected Group Exhibitions

2006 "Invisible Geographies: New Sound Art from Germany", The Kitchen, New York, NY
2005 "B!AS International Sound Art Exhibition", Taipei Fine Arts Museum, Taipei, Taiwan
2003 "sounding spaces", ICC, Tokyo, Japan
2000 "Sonic Boom", Hayward Gallery, London, UK
1996-06 "Sonambiente", Akademie der Künste, Berlin, Germany
1990 Biennial of Sydney, Art Gallery of New South Wales, Sydney, Australia
1987 "Ars Electronica", Brucknerhaus, Linz, Austria
Documenta 8, Neue Galerie, Kassel, Germany
1980-82 Venice Biennial, Venice, Italy
1980 "Augen und Ohren", Akademie der Künste, Berlin, Germany

Public Collections

Skulpturenmuseum Glaskasten, Marl, Germany
Hamburger Bahnhof, Museum für Gegenwart, Berlin, Germany
MASS MoCA, Massachusetts Museum of Contemporary Art, North Adams, MA

Selected Bibliography

Christina Kubisch, "Works' 74/75", Milan: Giancarlo Politi Editore (1975)
Christina Kubisch, "Zwischenräume", Saarbrücken, Stadtgalerie Saarbrücken (1996)
Christina Kubisch, "Klang Raum Licht Zeit", Heidelberg: Kehrer Verlag (2000) (with CD)
Christina Kubisch, Bernhard Leitner, "Zeitversetzt/Shifted in Time", Heidelberg: Kehrer Verlag, (2004)
Christina Kubisch, "103 Arten Beethoven zu singen", Cologne: Verlag der Buchhandlung Walther König (2005)

Artist's Writings

Kubisch, Christina, "Ohne Scheidegruß. Vom Verschwinden der Klänge", Positionen. Beiträge zur Neuen Musik, 35 (1998): 43-44
Kubisch, Christina, "Klangkunst in Kirchen", Kirchenräume - Kunsträume. Ein Handbuch. Münster/ Hamburg/London: LIT Verlag (2002): 173-180
Kubisch, Christina, "Digital Arts' Black Sheep", Soundscape, The Journal of Acoustoc Ecology, Vol. 3, No. 1 (July 2002): 20-21

DEBORAH LIGORIO

ديبورا ليجوريو

ولدت عام ١٩٧٢ في برينديسي، إيطاليا
تعيش وتعمل في برلين

Born 1972 Brindisi, Italy
Lives and works in Berlin, Germany
MFA, Brera, Academy of Fine Art, Milan, Italy

Selected Solo Exhibitions

2007 Fondazione Sandretto Re Rebaudengo. Turin, Italy
2006 Büro Friedrich, Berlin, Germany
2005 with Mats Adelman, Signal, Malmö, Sweden
2004 with Laura Horelli, Galerie KunstBank, Berlin, Germany

Selected Group Exhibitions

2006 "Architecture of the Self", Chelsea Art Museum, New York, NY
2005 "M City - European Cityscapes", Kunsthaus Graz, Austria
"Imaginary is Potential", Halle Für Kunst, Lüneburg, Germany
"E-Flux Video Rental", KW Institute for Contemporary Art, Berlin, Germany
"Follow Your Shadow", Villa Delle Rose, Bologna, Italy
2004 "3 Fireplaces and 2 Bathtubs", MAK Center for Art and Architecture at the Schindler

House, Los Angeles, CA
"Was ist in meiner Wohnung wenn Ich nicht da bin?", Ausstellungsraum Greifswalderstrasse 212, Berlin, Germany

2002 "To The Lighthouse", GAM, Turin, Italy
"Fuzzy", Galleria Massimo Minini, Brescia, Italy

2001 "Strategies Against Architecture II", Teseco Foundation, Pisa, Italy

Public Collections

GAM, Turin, Italy
Montblanc Cultural Foundation, Hamburg, Germany
Ernst & Young, London, UK
BSI Art Collection, Lugano, Italy

Selected Bibliography

Cerizza, Luca, "An e-mail conversation with L.Cerizza, L.Horelli and D.Ligorio", Neue Review (September 2004): 8-9
Nicolin, Paola and Deborah Ligorio, Abitare, No.443 (October 2004): 134
Nielsen, Henrikke, "A bird's eye view of the dematerialized space", Art in Progress (Summer 2005): 62-65
Schlaegel, Andreas, "Love and Sustainability", Praesens - Central European Contemporary Art Review (2006/1): 68-73
Synapser and Barbara Casavecchia, "Interview with Deborah Ligorio", Follow your Shadow, exhibition catalogueß (2004): 64-69

CLAUDIA LOSI

كلوديا لوسي

ولدت عام ١٩٧١ في بياسينزا، إيطاليا
تعيش في بياسينزا
وتعمل في ميلانو، إيطاليا

Born 1971 Piacenza, Italy
Lives in Piacenza and works in Milan
Ph.D. (1994) Bologna Academy of Fine Art
Ph.D. (1998) Bologna University of Foreign Languages and Literatures

Selected Solo Exhibitions|

2006 Monica De Cardenas, Milan, Italy

2005 BALENAPROJECT | Ecuador'05, MACC de Guayaquil and Cento Cultural, Universidad Catolica de Quito, Ecuador

2004 Galleria d'Arte Moderna, Spazio Aperto, Bologna, Italy
BALENAPROJECT | e altre storie, Lerici, La Spezia, Italy
Ex Caserma dei Carabinieri (with Antonio Marras), Alghero, Italy
BALENAPROJECT | animazione, Viafarini, Milan, Italy
BALENAPROJECT | balena di fiume, The Beach, Murazzi del Po, Turin, Italy

2003 Monica De Cardenas, Milan, Italy

2002 Galerie Lindig in Paludetto, Project Room, Nuremberg, Germany
Spazio Mobile, Rocca Sforzesca, Imola, Italy

2001 Monica De Cardenas, Project Room, Milan, Italy
Galleria Primo Piano, Rome, Italy
Istituto Italiano di Cultura, Washington, DC

2000 Luigi Franco Arte Contemporanea, Turin, Italy
Galleria Zone c/o Graffio, Bologna, Italy

Selected Group Exhibitions

2005 "Generations of Art", Fondazione Antonio Ratti, Como, Irtaly
"Filoluce", Museo della Permanente, Milan, Italy
"TVB, from Italy with Love", Raid Projects, Los Angeles, CA

2003 "Innatura, X Biennale Internazionale per la Fotografia", Palazzo Bricherasio,Turin, Italy
"Il racconto del filo", MART-Museo di Arte Contemporanea di Trento e Rovereto, Rovereto, Italy

2002 "Utopie Quotidiane", PAC Padiglione d'Arte Contemporanea, Milan, Ialy
"Assab One", Ex tipografia GEA, Milan, Italy

2001 "Italian Studio Programme 2000/2002-P.S.1", Palazzo delle Esposizioni, Rome, Italy

1999 "The Equinox", Cairn Gallery, The Old Stamp Office, Nailsworth, UK
"Onufri 1999", National Fine Arts Gallery, Tirana, Albania

ANDRES LUTZ / ANDERS GUGGISBERG

لوتز وغوغيزبورغ

أندره لوتز

ولد عام ١٩٦٨ في وتينغين، سويسرا
يعيش ويعمل في ميونيخ

أندرز غوغيزبورغ

ولد عام ١٩٦٦ في بييل، سويسرا
يعيش ويعمل في ميونيخ

Born 1968 in Wettingen, Switzerland/Born 1966 in Biel, Switzerland
Both live and work in Zurich

Selected Solo Exhibitions:

2008 Kunsthaus, Aarau, Switzerland

2007 Kunstverein Freiburg, Freiburg, Germany

2006 Galleria Monica de Cardenas, Milan, Italy

2005 Institut für moderne Kunst, Nuremberg, Germany

2004 Kunsthalle, Zurich, Switzerland

2003 Anna Helwing Gallery, Los Angeles, CA
Villa Merkel, Esslingen, Germany

2002 Kunstmuseum, St.Gallen, Switzerland

Selected Group Exhibitions:

2007 "The Photograph as Canvas", Aldrich Contemporary Art Museum, Ridgefield, CT

2006 "Nothing but Pleasure", Bawag Foundation, Vienna, Austria
"Aller et Retour", Institut Culturel Suisse, Paris, France

2005 "Postmodellismus", Krinzinger Projekte, Vienna, Austria
"When Humour becomes painfull", Migros Museum für Gegenwartskunst, Zurich, Switzerland
"A Lucky Strike", Gesellschaft für aktuelle Kunst, Bremen, Germany

2003 "Buenos Dias Buenos Aires", Museo de Arte Moderno, Buenos Aires, Argentina

2002 "Sonsbeek 9", Arnheim, Netherlands

1998 "Freie Sicht aufs Mittelmeer", Kunsthaus, Zurich, Switzerland

Selected Bibliography

Carmine, Giovanni, "The vehicles of Lutz&Guggisberg", in: Lutz/Guggisberg, exhibition catalogue, Milan: Gallerie Monica de Cardenas (2006)
"Freie Sicht aufs Mittelmeer", exhibition catalogue, Zurich: Kunsthaus (1998)

"Swiss Made", exhibition catalogue, Netherlands: Waanders Publishers (2005)
When Humour Becomes Painful, exhibition catalogue, migros museum, Zurich: JRP | Ringier publishers (2005)

Artist's Writings
Lutz/Guggisberg, "I will Rest in Pieces", monographic publication (7007)
Lutz/Guggisberg, "The Queen at the Louvre", monographic publication (2007)
Lutz/Guggisberg, "The Great Unknown", monographic publication (2002)

TEA MÄKIPÄÄ
تيا ماكيبا
ولدت عام ١٩٧٣ في لاتي، فنلندا
تعيش وتعمل في فنلندا وألمانيا

Born 1973 Lahti, Finland
Lives and works in Finland and Germany
M.A. 2003 London Royal College of Art

Selected Solo Exhibitions
2006 "Catwalk", Künstlerhaus Bethanien, Berlin, Germany
2005 "Sexgod", Galleri21, Malmö, Sweden
2004 "Solitude", Akademie Schloss Solitude, Stuttgart, Germany; Galerie K&S, Berlin, Germany
2003 "Expert," Jerwood Installation Commission, Wapping Project, London, UK

Selected Group Exhibitions
2006 "Breaking the Ice", Kunstmuseum Bonn, Bonn, Germany
"More or Less", Maerz Galerie, Linz, Austria
"Art Projects", Art Basel Miami Beach 2006, Miami, FL
2005 "World of Plenty", Photo Installation, Expo 2005 World Fair, Aichi, Japan
"Passion of Collecting", Halle 14, Leipzig, Germany
"Irony is Dead. Long Live Irony!", ACC Galerie Weimar, Germany
"Unheimlich", De Warande, Turnhout, Belgium
2004 "Parasites - When Space Comes Into Play," Museum of Modern Art, Vienna, Austria
"Supermarket", Helsinki Art Hall, Helsinki, Finland

Public Collections
Helsinki City Art Museum, Helsinki, Finland
Collection Pentti Kouri, State of Finland
Akademie Schloss Solitude, Stuttgart, Germany

HASSAN MEER
حسن مير
ولد عام ١٩٧٢ في مسقط، عمان

Born 1972 Muscat, Oman
M.A, Savanna College of Art and Design, 2000
B.F.A. Savanna College of Art and Design, 1999

Selected Solo and Group Exhibitions
2006 Omani Artists at UNESCO, Paris, France
"Language of the Desert", Institut du Monde Arabe, Paris, France
"Hot and Cold", Berlin, Germany
2005 "Language of the Desert", Museum of Bonn, Bonn, Germany
"Trap and Labrant", Museum of St. Polaton, Austria
New Media from GCC Artists, Washington, DC
Doha Cultural Festival, Qatar
Annual Show, Emirates Fine Art Society, Sharjah, UAE
2004 ARTIADE 2004, Olympics of Visual Arts, Athens, Greece
"The Circle" video art, poetry, narration, Oman Society of Fine Arts, Oman
2003 The Art Studio Show, Al Harthy Complex, Muscat, Oman
Cairo International Biennial, Cairo, Egypt
British Art Exhibition, Oman Society for Fine Arts, Oman
"The Arabian Canvas: Contemporary Arab Art", Dubai, UAE
2001 "The Shining Spirit", solo show, Oman Society of Fine Arts, Oman

GUSTAV METZGER
جوستاف ميتسجر
ولد عام ١٩٢٦ في نيرمبورغ، ألمانيا
يعيش ويعمل في لندن

Born 1926 in Nuremberg, Germany
Lives and works in London, UK
Received Paul Hamlyn Grant in 2007

Solo Exhibitions
2006 "Gustav Metzger Verk", Lunds Konsthall, Lund, Sweden
"Gustav Metzger in memoriam, new works", Kunsthalle Basel, Basel, Switzerland
2005 "Eichmann and the Angel", Cubitt Gallery, London, UK
"Gustav Metzger: Geschichte Geschichte", Generali Foundation, Vienna, Austria
1999 "Gustav Metzger - Ein Schnitt entlang der Zeit", Kunsthalle Nürnberg, Nuremberg, Germany
1998 "Gustav Metzger", Museum of Modern Art, Oxford, UK
1997 "Gustav Metzger", Kunstraum München, Munich, Germany
1966 "Art of Liquid Crystals", Better Books, Charing Cross Road, London, UK

Selected Group Exhibitions
2006 "How to Improve the World? 60 Years of British Art", Hayward Gallery, London, UK
2005 "Summer of Love: Art of the Psychedelic Era", Tate Liverpool, Liverpool, UK
2004 "Art and the Sixties - This Was Tomorrow", Tate Britain, London, UK
2003 "C 'est arrivé demain", 7th Lyon Biennial of Contemporary Art, Lyon, France
2002 "Blast to Freeze - British Art in 20th Century, Kunstmuseum, Wolfsburg, Germany
"Live in Your Head - Concept and Experiment in Britain 1965-75", Whitechapel Art Gallery, London, UK
"Protest and Survive", Whitechapel Art Gallery, London, UK
1999 "Dream City", Kunstraum München, Kunstverein, Villa Stuck, Siemens Kulturprogramm, Munich, Germany
1998 "Out of Action: Between Performance and the Object 1949-1979", Museum of Contemporary Art, Los Angeles, CA
1996 "Life/Live - La scène artistique au Royaume-Uni en 1996", Musée d'Art Moderne de la Ville de Paris, Paris, France
1974 "Art into Society - Society into

Art. Seven German Artists", ICA, London, UK

1972 Documenta 5, Kassel, Germany

Selected Bibliography

Bowron, Astrid, and Kerry Brougher (eds.), "Gustav Metzger", Oxford: Museum of Modern Art (1998)
Breitwieser, Sabine (ed.), "Gustav Metzger, Geschichte Geschichte", Generali Foundation, Vienna: Hatje Cantz Verlag, Ostfildern-Ruit (2005)
Hoffmann, Justin (ed.), "Gustav Metzger, Manifeste, Schriften, Konzepte", Munich: Verlag Silke Schreiber (1997)
Stiles, Kristine, "Art and Technology", in Kristine Stiles & Peter Selz, "Theories and Documents of Contemporary Art: A Sourcebook of Artists' Writings", University of California Press, Berkeley, Los Angeles, London (1996): 384-96
Unterdörfer, Michaela (ed.), "Gustav Metzger - Ein Schnitt entlang der Zeit", Kunsthalle Nürnberg, Nuremberg: Verlag für Moderne Kunst (1999)

Selected Artist's Writings

Metzger, Gustav, "Damaged Nature, Auto-Destructive Art", London: Coracle Press (1996)
Metzger, Gustav, "Earth to Galaxies. On Destruction and Destructivity", Pavel Büchler, Charles Esche (ed.), Tramline No. 5, Glasgow School of Art, Glasgow (1996)
Metzger, Gustav, "Machine, Auto-Creative and Auto-Destructive Art", in: Ark. Journal of the Royal College of Art," London, no 32 (Summer 1962)

MINDBOMB

مايند بومب

الأفراد في مجموعة مايند بومب غير معروفين. لأن رسالتهم أهم من هويتهم

Members are anonymous
Their message is more important than their identity
All posters are group work and should not have a traceable authorship

Selected Projects

2006 "Street Postering Action - MindBomb for Rosia Montana!", 5 posters, 12,000 pieces. A protest against the planned open-cast gold mine at Rosia Montana. Disseminated in 18 towns of Romania

2005 "Street Art", Millenaris Park, Budapest, Hungary
"Street Postering Action - Freedom of Speech", 3 posters, 3000 pieces. Disseminated in Cluj-Napoca and Bucharest, Romania

2004-05 "Billboard Action", 3 Billboards, Claiming the Unirii Square as a Public Place. Cluj-Napoca, Romania

2004 "Street Postering Action", 12 posters, 12,000 pieces. The action addressed the issue of CORRUPTION. Disseminated in 10 major towns of Romania

2002 "Focus Romania", Museums Quarter, Vienna, Austria
"Street Postering Action", 7 seven bilingual posters, 1400 pieces. Cluj-Napoca, Romania and San Francisco, CA

Selected Bibliography

Dusini, Mathias, "MindBomb", Camera Austria. No. 82 (2003): 50-51
Mercea, Dan, "Exploding Iconography: the MindBomb Project", Budapest: Environment Conference, 13-15 October (2005)
Nastac, Simona, "MindBomb for Rosia Montana" Praesens, No. 1 (2006)

ABDUL RAHMAN AL MUENI

عبد الرحمن المعيني

ولد عام ١٩٧٥ في خصب، عمان
يعيش في الإمارات

Born 1975 Kasab, Oman

2005 Member of Emirates Fine Arts Society, Sharjah, UAE; Member of the Dubai Art Atelier, Youth Theatre & Art, Dubai, UAE

Selected Group Exhibitions

2006 Silver Jubilee Exhibition, Emirates Fine Arts Society, Sharjah, UAE
Window Exhibition, Total Arts Gallery, Dubai, UAE

2005 Youth Theatre & Art Exhibition, Sharjah Art Institute, Sharjah, UAE

2003 Youth Exhibition, Sharjah, UAE

MAHA MUSTAFA

مها مصطفى

ولدت عام ١٩٦١ في بغداد، العراق
تعيش وتعمل في كندا، والسويد وأمريكا

Born 1961 Baghdad, Irak
Lives and works in Canada, Sweden and USA
B.F.A. 1984 Academy of Fine Arts, Baghdad

Selected Solo Exhibitions

2005 Mösting Hus, Copenhagen, Denmark
"Check point X", Landskrona Art Museum, Landskrona, Sweden
Skovhuset, Konsthall, Vaerlose, Denmark
Växjö Konsthall, Växjö, Sweden

2004 "Beyond 100°C", Darat al Funun, Amman, Jordan

Selected Group Exhibitions

2004 "Arteeast", The New Space, New York, NY

2000 Brunei Gallery, London, UK

1999 Malmö Museum, Malmö, Sweden

1987 National Museum of Art, Baghdad, Irak

1985 Modern Museum of Art, Baghdad, Irak

Public Collections

"Turning Torso", Malmö, Sweden
A building of the Spanish architect Santigo Calatrava, in Malmö 2005-2006
Landskrona Art Museum, Sweden
Darat al Funun, Khalid Shoman Foundation, Amman, Jordan

Bibliography

Altgård, Clemens, "The Fire Within"
Altgård, Clemens, "Hanging Landscapes in the Border Zone", in Checkpoint X
Beyond 100° C, an art book on mankind and the environment, with pictures, essays, and poems by Adonis (2002) (English, Swedish and Danish)
Jönsson, Dan, Checkpoint: El Aleph - Checkpoint X, an art book with pictures, essays and poems (art project and mobile exhibition at several art galleries in Sweden and Denmark), (2005) (English and Swedish)
Lindboe, Ole, Earth, Light and Air. Man and Nature according to Maha Mustafa and Ibrahim Rashid
Söderberg Lässe (with Maha and Ibrahim), Art Catalog with pictures, essays and poems (1998)

JESUS BUBU NEGRON

جيزوس بوبو نيجرون

ولد عام ١٩٧٥ في باشيلونيتا، بورتو ريكو
يعيش ويعمل في باشيلونيتا وسان خوان في بورتو ريكو

Born 1975 Baceloneta, Puerto Rico
Lives and works in Barceloneta and San Juan, Puerto Rico
Studies at Escuela de Artes Plasticas 1997

Selected Solo Exhibitions

2006 "Picas/VIP Sketch", Art 37 Basel, Basel, Switzerland (with Galería Comercial, San Juan, Puerto Rico)
2004 "Jesús 'Bubu' Negrón 2001-2004", Galería Comercial, San Juan, Puerto Rico

Selected Group Exhibitions

2006 "MACO '06", México City (with Galería Comercial, San Juan, Puerto Rico), Mexico
Whitney Biennial 2006, Whitney Museum of American Art, New York, NY
"The Lovers" (Carolina Caycedo, Michael Linares, Jesús 'Bubu' Negrón, Chemi Rosado Seijo), CANADA, New York, NY
"35mm", Laboratorio 306, Chiapas, México
"S-Files", Museo del Barrio, New York, NY
2005-06 "The Pantagruel Syndrome", T1 Torino Triennale Tremusei, Turin, Italy
2005 "NADA '05", Miami, FL
"Tropical Abstraction", Stedelijk Museum Bureau Amsterdam, Amsterdam, Netherlands
"The Fourth Floor", Western Exhibitions, Chicago, IL
"Coordenadas del inconsciente", Colección Berezdivin, San Juan, Puerto Rico

Bibliography

Bonami, Francesco & Carolyn Christov-Bakargiev, "The Pantagruel Syndrome", exhibition catalogue, Turin (2005)
Gortzak, Roos, "Tropical Abstraction", exhibition catalogue, Amsterdam: Stedelijk Museum Bureau Amsterdam (2005)
Iles, Chrissie & Philippe Vergne, "Whitney Biennial 2006", exhibition catalogue, New York: Whitney Museum of American Art (2006)
Morton, Tom "Tropical Abstraction", Frieze, No. 96, U.K., (January-February 2006): 147
Ramírez, Mari Carmen et. al., Trienal poligráfica de San Juan, San Juan, Puerto Rico (2004)
Robayo, Olga, et. al., GPB 05, Finland (April 2005)

JACQUES NIMKI

جاك نيمكي

ولد عام ١٩٥٩ في بورت لويس، موريشس
يعيش ويعمل في لندن

Born 1959 Port Louis, Mauritius
Lives and works in London, UK
B.A Chelsea School of Art, 1986-89.
Postgraduate, Royal Academy School, 1989-92

Selected Solo Exhibitions

2006 "Woodlock", Fabrica Gallery, Brighton, UK
The Approach Gallery, London, UK
2005 "Magic of the East", Ikon Gallery, Birmingham, UK
2004 Camden Arts Centre, London, UK
2002 The Approach Gallery, London, UK

Selected Group Exhibitions

2004 Bolwick Hall, Norfolk, UK
"Art of the Garden", Tate Britain, London, UK
2003 "Into the Grey", Cover Up, London, UK
"Nature & Nation", Hastings Museum, Hastings, UK, touring
2002 "Life Everyday", Tablet Gallery, London, UK
2001 "Out of Line", Arts Council of England, London, UK, touring
1999 "Idlewild", The Approach Gallery, London, UK

CORNELIA PARKER

كورنيليا باركر

ولدت عام ١٩٥٦ في شيشاير، إنكلترا
تعيش وتعمل في لندن

Born 1956 Cheshire, UK
Lives and works in London
B.A. Wolverhampton Polytechnic
M.F.A. Reading University, Reading

Selected Solo Exhibitions

2006 "Brontean Abstracts", Broünte Parsonage Museum, Haworth, West Yorkshire, UK
2005 "Focus: Cornelia Parker", Modern Art Museum of Fort Worth, Fort Worth, TX
"New Work by Cornelia Parker", Yerba Buena Center for the Arts, San Francisco, CA
"Subconscious of a Monument", Royal Institute of British Architects, London, UK
Württembergischer Kunstverein, Stuttgart, Germany

Selected Group Exhibitions

2007 "Living in the Material World", National Art Centre, Tokyo, Japan
2004 "Speaking with Hands: Photographs from the Buhl Collection", Guggenheim Museum, New York, NY
2003 "From Dust to Dusk", Copenhagen Udstillingsbygning, Denmark
2002 "To Eat or not to Eat", Centro de Arte de Salamanca, Salamanca, Spain
"Continuitá: Arte in Toscana 1945-2000", Fattoria di Celle, Santomato di Pistoia, Italy
1997 "The Turner Prize Exhibition", Tate Gallery, London, UK
"Material Culture", Hayward Gallery, London, UK
1995 "Something the Matter: Helen Chadwick, Cathy de Monchaux, Cornelia Parker", Museo Municipal de Bellas Artes, Rosario, Argentina; touring to Centro Cultural Recoleta, Buenos Aires; Museo Nacional de Bellas Artes, Rio de Janeiro; Galeria Athos Bulcao, Brasilia, Brazil
1994 XXII São Paulo Biennial, São Paulo, Brazil
1992 "Through the Viewfinder", Stitching De Appel, Amsterdam, Netherlands

Public Collections

Arts Council of Great Britain, UK
British Museum, London, UK
De Young Museum, San Francisco, CA
Fundacio La Caixa, Barcelona, Spain
Government Art Collection
Henry Moore Foundation, Herts, UK
ICA Boston, MA
MAG Collection, UK
Milwaukee Arts Museum, WI
MoMA, New York, NY
Museum of Modern Art, Fort Worth, TX
Phoenix Art Museum, A

Tate Gallery, London, UK
Victoria & Albert Museum, London, UK
Yale Center for British Art, CT

Selected Bibliography

Picardie, Justine, "Is any Brönte there?" Sunday Telegraph (17 September 2006): 44-48
"Perpetual Cannon", Württembergischer Kunstverein Stuttgart, Bielefeld: Kerbeler Verlag (2005)
Ghose, Sumantro, "Destruction and Nostalgia- Cornelia Parker's Cold Dark Matter: An Exploded View", Modern Painters (Autumn 2004)
Blazwick, Iwona, Ewa Lajer-Buchart, "Sightings. Cornelia Parker", Turin: Galeria Civica d'Arte Moderna e Contemporanea (2001)

PABLO PATRUCCO
بابلو باتروكو

ولد عام ١٩٧٥ في ليما، بيرو
يعيش ويعمل ليما

Born 1975 Lima, Peru
Lives and works in Lima
B.A. 2006 Universidad Nacional Mayor de San Marcos, Lima
B.A. 2000 Escuela Superior de Arte Corriente Alterna, Lima

Selected Solo Exhibitions

2007 Galeria Kiosco, Santa Cruz, Bolivia
Galeria Arte Enlace, Lima
2005 ESPACIOS COMUNES, Galeria Lucia de la Puente, Lima, Peru
2004 iCONOS, Galeria Punctum, Lima, Peru

Selected Group Exhibitions

2007 ArteBA, Buenos Aires Contemporary Art Fair, Buenos Aires, Argentina
Feria Internacional de Arte - FIA, Caracas, Venezuela
The Latin American Art Fair ARTE AMERICAS, Miami, FL
2005 The Latin American Art Fair ARTE AMERICAS. Miami, FL
2004 "Arte Contemporaneo del Peru" (BID), Galeria Lucia de la Puente, Lima

DAN PERJOVSCHI
دان بيرجوفسكي

ولد عام ١٩٦١ في سيبيو، رومانيا
يعيش ويعمل في بوخارست، رومانيا

Born 1961 Sibiu, Romania
Lives and works in Bucharest, Romania
Graduate of Art Academy, Iasi, Romania

Selected Solo Exhibitions

2007 "Project 85", The Museum of Modern Art, New York, NY
2006 "On the other Hand", Portikus, Frankfurt a. M., Germany
"The Room Drawing", Tate Modern, London, UK
"Perjovschi", Van Abbemuseum, Eindhoven, Netherlands
2005 "Naked Drawings", Ludwig Museum, Cologne, Germany

Selected Group Exhibitions

2007 2nd Moscow Biennial, Moscow
"The Cloud", Centre Pompidou, Paris, France
2006 "Unhomely", 2nd Biennial of Contemporary Art of Seville (BIACS), Seville, Spain
"The Vincent - Biennial Prize for European Contemporary Art", Stedelijk Museum, Amsterdam, Netherlands
"Focusing Iasi/The Social Project", Iasi Periferic Biennial, Iasi, Romania
2005 "New Europe - The Culture of Mixing and Politics of Representation", Generali Foundation, Vienna, Austria
"Istanbul", 9th Istanbul Biennial, Istanbul, Turkey
"I still believe in Miracles. Dessins sans papier", ARC Musee d'Art Moderne de la Ville de Paris, Couvent des Cordeliers, Paris, France
2003 "Open City: Models for Use", Kokerei Zollverein, Zeitgenössische Kunst und Kritik, Essen, Germany
1998 "Manifesta 2", Luxembourg

Public Collections

Tate Modern, London, UK
Van Abbemuseum, Eindhoven, Netherlands
Ludwig Museum, Cologne, Germany
Ludwig Forum fur Internationale Kunst, Germany
Moderna Museet, Stockholm, Sweden
Moderna Galerija, Lublijana, Slovenia

Bibliography

Babias, Marius, "Self-Colonisation: Dan Perjovschi and his Critique of the Post-Communist Restructuring of Identity from Dan Perjovschi's 'Naked Drawings'", Ludwig Museum, Cologne: Verlag der Buchhandlung Walter Koenig (2005)
Krajewski, Michael, "Zeichen als Subversion", Kunst-Bulletin No. 9 (September 2005): 38-40
Lorch, Catrin "Writing on the Wall", Frieze (April 2006): 136-139
Obrist, Hans Ulrich, "Dan Perjovschi, Vitamin D: New Perspectives in Drawing", New York (2006)
Wilson, Michael, "Graphic Equalizer", Artforum (May 2006): 83-85

DAN PETERMAN
دان بيترمان

ولد عام ١٩٦٠ في مينيابوليس، الولايات المتحدة. يعيش ويعمل في شيكاغو

Born 1960 Minneapolis, Minnesota
Lives and works in Chicago
B.F.A. 1983 University of Wisconsin
M.F.A. 1986 University of Chicago

Selected Solo Exhibitions

2006 "Adaptations", Klosterfelde, Berlin & Andrea Rosen Gallery, New York, NY
2004 Museum of Contemporary Art, Chicago, IL
2002 Museum Abteiberg, München Gladbach; Klosterfelde, Berlin, Germany; "Parallel Excerpts from the Universal Lab", Andrea Rosen Gallery, New York, NY
2001 "7 Deadly Sins", Kunstverein Hannover, Hannover, Germany
Helga Maria Klosterfelde, Hamburg, Germany
1999 "Recent Economies", Andrea Rosen Gallery, New York, NY

Selected Group Exhibitions

2006 "Beyond Green. Toward a Sustainable Art", Museum of Art & Design, New York, NY
2005 "Beyond Green. Toward a Sustainable Art", Smart Museum of Art, University of Chicago, Chicago, IL
"Schrumpfende Städte 2 - Interventionen", Galerie für Zeitgenössische Kunst, Leipzig, Germany

"Alternatives", FRAC Provence-Alpes-Cote D`Azur, Espace Jean Giono, Le Beausset, France

2004 "Untitled (Vision Existence Resistance)", Franco Soffiantino arte contemporanea, Turin, Italy
"Prête à pêter 2", Frac Paca, Marseilles, France
"Dark Matters", curated by Chris Gilbert, Baltimore Museum of Art, Baltimore, ML

2003 Skulptur-Biennale Münsterland, Kreis Steinfurt, Germany

2002 "Die Kunst des Festes", Brixen, Italy
Skulpturengarten, Museum Abteiberg, Mönchen Gladbach, Germany

Bibliography

"Dan Peterman: Plastic Economies", exhibition catalogue, MCA Chicago (2004)
Jones, Jonathan, "Pyramids of Mars; The Barbican, London", Frieze (May 2001): 90
Möntmann, Nina, "Umweltsünden in ein Minimalformat gepresst" (Environmental Pollution Pressed into a Minimal Format), in: Bos, Saskia & Alice Koegel, "Skulptur Biennale Münsterland" exhibition catalogue (2003): 160-165
Piffer-Damiani, Marion, "Dan Peterman: Villa Deponie", in: "Fest Kunst", exhibition catalogue (2002): 114-23
Smith, Stephanie, "Beyond Green. Toward a Sustainable Art", exhibition catalogue, Smart Museum of Art, University of Chicago (2005): 100-5
Snodgrass, Susan, "Dan Peterman at the MCA", Art in America (March 2005)
Stange, Raimar, "An die Wand gefahren. Kalkulierter Vandalismus: Dan Peterman und Jeppe Hein in zwei Berliner Galerien", Tagesspiegel (19 October 2002): 26

MARJETICA POTRC

ماريتيكا بوترك

ولدت عام ١٩٥٣ في لوبليانا، سلوفينيا
تعيش وتعمل لوبليانا

Born 1953 Ljubljana, Slovenia
Lives in works in Ljubljana
B.A. Architecture, School of Architecture, Ljubljana
M.A. Sculpture, Academy of Fine Arts, Ljubljana

Selected Solo Exhibitions

2006 "Marjetica Potrc and Tomas Saraceno: Personal States/ Infinite Actives", Portikus, Frankfurt a. M., Germany

2005 "Drawing Cities", Max Protetch Gallery, New York, NY

2004 "Urban Growings", Stichting De Appel, Amsterdam, Netherlands
"Marjetica Potrc: Urgent Architecture", PBICA, Lake Worth, Florida; and MIT List Visual Arts Center, Cambridge, MA

2003 "Caracas: House with Extended Territory", Galerie Nordenhake, Berlin, Germany

Selected Group Exhibitions

2006 "How to Live Together", 27th São Paulo Biennial, São Paulo, Brazil
"What is positive? Why? Strategic Questions - Platform 6", Kunsthalle Exnergasse, Vienna, Austria; and De Appel, Amsterdam, Netherlands

2005 "M City, European Cityscapes", Kunsthaus Graz, Graz, Austria
"Farsites: Urban Crisis and Domestic Symptoms in Recent Contemporary Art", San Diego Museum of Art, San Diego, CA and Centro Cultural, Tijuana, Mexico
"Emergencies", MUSAC Museum of Contemporary Art, Castilla y Leon, Spain

2004 "International 04", 3rd Liverpool Biennial, Liverpool, UK

2003 "The Fifth System, Public Art in the Age of Post-Planning", 5th Shenzhen International Public Art Exhibition, Shenzhen, China
"Arte all'Arte 8", Associazione Arte Continua, San Gimignano, Italy
"Poetic Justice", 8th Istanbul Biennial, Istanbul, Turkey

Selected Bibliography

Basualdo, Carlos & Reinaldo Laddaga, "Rules of Engagement," Artforum International (March 2004): 166-170
Crowley, David, "Paradise Lost?" Piktogram (Warsaw), No. 2 (2005): 52-57
Heartney, Eleanor, "A House of Parts", Art in America (May 2004): 140-43
Higgie, Jennifer, "Form Follows Function," Frieze (May 2006): 136-41
Yang, Haegue, "Researcher in an urban-jungle: Marjetica Potrc", Space, Seoul (June 2006): 162-67

Artist's Writings

Potrc, Marjetica, "Strategies of Transition: Parallelism and Fragmentation in the Western Balkans and the European Union", Selforganisation - Counter-economic Strategies, ed. Superflex, Lukas and Sternberg, New York (2006)
Potrc, Marjetica, "Five Ways to Urban Independence", Urban Negotiation, Valencia: IVAM Instituto Valenciano de Arte Moderna, Spain (2003): 26-35; reprinted in "Structures of Survival', Dreams and Conflicts - The Dictatorship of the Viewer, 50th International Art Exhibition, Venice Biennial (2003): 272-273
Potrc, Marjetica, "Back to Basics: Objects and Buildings", Designs for the Real World, Vienna: Generali Foundation (2002): 82-89

MICHAEL RAKOWITZ

مايكل راكوفيتش

ولد عام ١٩٧٣ في غريت نيك، نيويورك
يعيش ويعمل في شيكاغو وبروكلين، نيويورك

Born 1973 Great Neck, New York
Lives and works in Chicago and Brooklyn
M.A., M.Sc. 1998 Massachusetts Institute of Technology
B.A. 1995 Purchase College SUNY, New York

Selected Solo Exhibitions

2007 "The invisible enemy should not exist", Lombard-Freid Projects, New York, NY

2006 "Return", Creative Time, New York, NY
"Enemy Kitchen", More Art, New York, NY
"The Visionaries", Trafo Gallery, Budapest, Hungary
"Endgames", Galleria Alberto Peola, Turin, Italy

Selected Group Exhibitions

2006 "Revisiting Home", NGBK, Berlin, Germany
"LESS - Alternative Living Strategies", PAC, Milan, Italy

2005 Tirana Biennial, Tirana, Albania
"The Pantagruel Syndrome", T1 Torino Trinnale Tremusei, Castello di Rivoli, Turin, Italy
"SAFE: Design Takes on Risk", MoMA, New York, NY
"Beyond Green: Toward a Sustainable Art", Smart Museum

of Art, University of Chicago, Chicago, IL
"Do Not Interrupt Your Activities", Royal College of Art, London, UK

2004 "The Interventionists", MassMOCA, North Adams, MA
"Adaptations", Kunsthalle Friedricianum, Kassel, Germany
"Inside Design Now", 2003 National Design Triennial, Cooper-Hewitt National Design Museum, New York, NY

Public Collections

The Museum of Modern Art (MoMA), New York, NY

Selected Bibliography

"Bidoun: Arts and Culture from the Middle East": Rumour, Issue 9 (December 2006)
"Can Design Prepare For Disaster?" (roundtable discussion on the MoMA show "Safe: Design Takes On Risk") New York Times (8 September 2005)
Christov-Bakargiev, Carolyn, "First Takes: Carolyn Christov-Bakargiev on Michael Rakowitz", Artforum (January 2005)
Christov-Bakargiev, Carolyn & Michael Rakowitz, Circumventions (monograph), Paris: Onestar Press/Dena Foundation (2003)
Eleey, Peter, "Michael Rakowitz: An import-export business, posters, shelters for the homeless and the smell of buns", Frieze (May 2006)
McClister, Nell, "Michael Rakowitz at Lombard-Freid Projects", Artforum, (September 2005)
Sinclair, Cameron, Design Like You Give A Damn, Metropolis Books (2006)

Artist's Writings

Fry, Tony "Interview between Tony Fry, Marjetica Potrc, and Michael Rakowitz" Revisiting Home, Berlin: NGBK (2006)

NOGUCHI RIKA

نوجوشي ريكا

ولدت عام ١٩٧١ في سيتاما، اليابان
تعيش وتعمل في برلين

Born 1971 Saitama, Japan
Lives and works in Berlin, Germany
BFA, Photography, College of Art, Nihon University, Tokyo

Selected Solo Exhibitions

2006 DAAD Gallery, Berlin, Germany
2005 D'Amelio Terras, New York, NY
2004 IKON Gallery, Birmingham, UK
Hara Museum of Contemporary Art, Tokyo, Japan
2003 Galerie der Stadt Schwaz, Schwaz, Austria

Selected Group Exhibitions

2006 "PHOTOESPANA2006 - Naturaleza: Experiencia", Museo San Roman, Toledo, Spain
2003 "Moving Pictures" Guggenheim Museum Bilbao, Bilbao, Spain
"Spread in Prato 2003" Dryphoto arte contemporanea, Prato, Italy
"Time After Time: Asia and Our Moment", Yerba Buena Center for the Arts, San Francisco, CA
2002 "Under Construction: New Dimensions of Asia Art", Tokyo; Opera City Art Gallery and The Japan Foundation Forum, Japan
"Photography Today 2- Site/ Sight" The National Museum of Modern Art, Tokyo, Japan
"Under Construction/ Fantasia" East Modern Art Centre, Beijing, China
2001 "Facts of Life: Contemporary Japanese Art", Hayward Gallery, London, UK
"The Standard", Naoshima Contemporary Art Museum (currently Benesse Art Site), Naoshima, Kagawa, Japan
2000 "Sensitive", "Le Printemps de Cahors", Cahors, France

Public Collections

Benesse Art Site Naoshima, Kagawa, Japan
Collection Lambert, Avignon, France
Hara Museum of Contemporary Art, Tokyo
Kiyosato Museum of Photographic Arts, Yamanashi, Japan
Marugame Genichiro-Inokuma Museum of Contemporary Art, Kagawa, Japan
Solomon R. Guggenheim Museum, New York
Takamatsu City Museum of Art, Kagawa, Japan
The Museum of Contemporary Art, Los Angeles, CA
The National Museum of Modern Art, Tokyo
The Vangi Sculpture Garden Museum, Shizuoka, Japan
21st Century Museum of Contemporary Art, Kanazawa, Ishikawa, Japan

BUDOOR AL RIYAMI

بدور الريامي

ولدت عام ١٩٧٧ في الكويت
تعيش وتعمل في سلطنة عمان

Born 1977, Kuwait
Lives and works in the Sultanate of Oman
BA in Art (with honors) from Sultan Qabous University, 1999

Selected Solo Exhibitions

2006 "The burning begins at the last smoke", Cultural Club, Muscat, Oman

Selected Group Exhibitions

2006 The Eighth annual exhibition of plastic arts and Arabic calligraphy for the GCC countries in Muscat, Oman
2005 The Circle group exhibition at the Cultural Club, Muscat, Oman
Guest of Honor at the first Youth Salon in Qatar
2001/04/05 The Youth Salon Exhibition in Cairo, Egypt
2003 Omani-British friendship week exhibition at the Omani Society for Plastic Arts, Muscat, Oman
1997/03 All annual exhibitions organized by the Omani Society for Plastic Arts at the Sultanate of Oman

RAEDA SA'ADEH

رائدة سعادة

ولدت عام ١٩٧٧ في أم الفحم، فلسطين
تعيش وتعمل في القدس، فلسطين

Born 1977 Umm Al-Fahem, Palestine
Lives and works in Jerusalem
M.F.A. Bezalel Academy of Art and Design, Jerusalem
B.F.A. Bezalel Academy of Art and Design, Jerusalem

Selected Solo Exhibitions

2003 "Immaterial", Gallery Anadiel, Jerusalem, Palestine
2000 "Eklil", A.M.Qatan Foundation, Ramallah, Palestine
"there", School of Visual Arts, new York, NY

Selected Group Exhibitions

2006 "Zones of Contact", Biennial of Sydney, Sydney, Australia
2005 "Mediterranean Encounters", Castello Ruffo, Scilla, Italy

2004 "Mediterraneans", Macro Museo d'Arte Contemporanea, Rome, Italy
"Unscene", University of Greenwich, London, UK
2003 "Art Focus 4", International Biennial of Contemporary Art, Jerusalem, Palestine
"Fantasies de L'HAREM I noves Xaharazads", Centrede Cultura Contemporania de Barcelona, Spain
2002 "Williamsburg Bridges Palestine 2002", Brooklyn, NY
Arles Festival, Arles, France
"In weiter Ferne, so nah", Neue palästinensische Kunst", ifa Galerie, Berlin, Germany

Bibliography

Lagarriga, Didac P., "Raeda Sa'adeh Versus Mahmoud Darwich", Masala (June 2003)

ABDULLA AL SAADI

عبد الله السعدي

ولد عام ١٩٦٧، خورفكان، الإمارات
يعيش ويعمل خورفكان

Born 1967 Khorfakkan, UAE
1986-89 Studied English Literature, Al Ain University, UAE
1986 Member of the Emirates Fine Art Society, Sharjah, UAE
1994-96 Studied Japanese Art, Kyoto Seika University, Kyoto, Japan
Member of the Emirates Society of Plastic Arts since 1986

Selected Solo Exhibitions

1999 Sharm Coffee Shop, Fujairah, UAE
1997 Emirates Fine Art Society, Sharjah, UAE
1994 Emirates Fine Art Society, Sharjah UAE

Selected Group Exhibitions

2006 Window Exhibition, Total ARTS Gallery, Dubai, UAE
Silver Jubilee Exhibition, Emirates Fine Art Society, Sharjah, UAE
2002 Ludwig Forum for International Art, Aachen, Germany
2001 Sharjah International Biennial, Sharjah, UAE
2000 Emirates Identities, French Cultural Centre, Dubai, UAE
1999 Two Artists Exhibition, Emirates Fine Arts Society, Sharjah, UAE
1998 UAE Contemporary Art, Arab Institute, Paris, France
1997 French Cultural Centre, Dubai, UAE
Sharjah International Biennial, Sharjah, UAE.
1986 Participant in the annual exhibitions of the Emirates Fine Art Society, UAE

Collections

Arab Museum of Modern Art, Doha, Qatar

HUDA SAEED SAIF

هدى سعيد سيف

ولدت عام ١٩٧٨، الشارقة، الإمارات
تعيش وتعمل في الشارقة

Born 1978 Sharjah, UAE
B.Sc. 2003 College of General Physics, UAE University

Solo Exhibition

2000 "Dark hole", UAE University

Selected Group Exhibitions

2006 Window Exhibition, Total Art Gallery, Dubai, UAE
2005 2nd National Exhibition For Plastic Arts, Abu Dahbi, UAE
2004 Sharjah Art Museum, Sharjah, UAE
Exhibitions of Youth Theatre & Art Summer Activities, Sharjah Art Institute, Sharjah, UAE
Emirates Cultural Festival, Bazaar of Art and Music, Al Ain Mall, Abu Dhabi, UAE
2003 Sharjah University Exhibition, Sharjah, UAE
Annual Exhibition at Creative Club
2003-04 UAE Association forIllustrative Art Exhibition, Abu Dhabi, UAE
2002 "Alone in the Dark", UAE University, Abu Dhabi, UAE

MICHAEL SAILSTORFER

ميخائيل سيلستورفر

ولد عام ١٩٧٩ في فيلدن/فيلز، ألمانيا
يعيش في برلين

Born 1979 Velden/Vils, Germany
Lives and works in Berlin
M.A. 2004 Goldsmiths College, University of London

Selected Solo Exhibitions

2007 U1-U13, Zero, Milan, Italy
2006 Johann König, Berlin
2005 Ursula-Blickle-Stiftung, Kraichtal, Germany
"Hoher Besuch", MARTa Herford, Herford, Germany
"Der Schein trügt", Jack Hanley Gallery, Los Angeles, CA
"Zeit ist keine Autobahn", Zero, Milan, Italy
2004 "Dämmerung", Attitudes, Espace d'arts contemporaines, Geneva, Switzerland
2002 "Und sie bewegt sich doch!", Museumsplatz, Städtische Galerie im Lenbachhaus, Munich, Germany

Selected Group Exhibitions

2007 "Made in Germany", Kestnergesellschaft, Hannover, Germany
2nd Moscow Biennial, Moscow, Russia
2006 "Momentum 2006", Nordic Art Festival, Moss, Norway
"Of Mice and Men", 4th Berlin Biennale for Contemporary Art, Gagosian Gallery, Berlin, Germany
"Inaugural Exhibition", Johann König, Berlin
"Bühne des Lebens, Rhetorik des Gefühls", Kunstbau, Städtische Galerie im Lenbachhaus München
2005 "Yokohama 2005", International Triennial of Contemporary Art, Yokohama
"Rückkehr ins All", Galerie der Gegenwart in der Hamburger Kunsthalle, Hamburg, Germany
"LIGHT LAB. Alltägliche Kurzschlüsse", Museion, Bozen, Italy
"Things Fall Apart All Over Again", Artists Space, New York
2004 Manifesta 5, San Sebastian, Spain
Biennial of Sydney, Sydney

Public Collections

Centre Pompidou, Paris, France
Städtische Galerie im Lenbachhaus, Munich, Germany
MARTa Herford, Germany

Selected Bibliography

Cotter, Holland, "We disagree", New York Times (February 4, 2005)
Haines, Bruce, "Michael Sailstorfer. Between te earth and the sky", Frieze, No 94 (October 2005)
Hüster, Wiebke, "Unerschöpfliches Rservoir, malerische Dichte", Frankfurter Allgemeine Zeitung (May 6, 2006)
Schaffhausen, Nicolaus, "Michael Sailstorfer. Für immer war gestern", exhibition catalogue, Ursula Blickle Stiftung, Nuremberg: Verlag für Moderne Kunst (2005)
Schwendener, Martha, "We disagree", Artforum.com (February 8, 2005)

TOMAS SARACENO

توماس ساراسينو

ولد عام ١٩٧٣ في سان ميغيل، الأرجنتين يعيش ويعمل مابين وما وراء الأرض

Born 1973 San Miguel de Tucumán, Argentina
Lives and works between and beyond the planet earth
B.A. 1999 Universidad Nacional de Buenos Aires, Argentina

Selected Solo Exhibitions

2006 "Cloudy Dunes Air-Port-City", Attitudes, Espace d'arts contemporains, Geneva, Switzerland
"Air-Port-City", Tanya Bonakdar, New York, NY
"Cumulus", The Curve, Barbican Art Gallery, London, UK
"Sehnsüchtig gleiten Ballone rund um die Welt", Berlin, Germany
"Personal Status - Infinite Actives" (with Marjetica Potrc) Portikus, Frankfurt a. M., Germany

Selected Group Exhibitions

2006 "How to live together", São Paulo Biennial, São Paulo, Brazil
"Infinite State", Portikus, Frankfurt a. M., Germany
"I still believe in miracles" ARC, Musee d'Art moderne de la Ville de Paris, Paris, France
"Luna Park-Fantastic Art", Villa Manin Contemporary Art Centre, Passariano, Italy
"Sudeley Castle Reconstruction 1", UK
Busan Biennial, Busan, South Korea
"Buenos dias Santiago", Museo de Arte Contmporaneo, Santiago, Chile
"On Mobility", BüroFriedrich, Berlin, Germany

2004 "Was ist in meiner Wohnung wenn ich nicht da bin?", Ausstellungsraum Greifswalderstrasse 212, Berlin, Germany
"Open Duende" Duende, Rotterdam, Netherlands

Selected Bibliography

Bayrle, Thomas "Overture" Flash Art, International Edition (2005): 112
Birnbaum, Daniel, Artforum (January 2004)
Obrist, Hans Ulrich and Stefano Boeri, Domus, No. 883 (July/August 2005)
Van Weelden, Dirk, "On Mobility", exhibition catalogue, Amsterdam: De Appel (July 2006)
Vettese, Angela, "Dialectic of hope", exhibition catalogue, Moscow: First Moscow Biennial of Contemporary Art (2006)

JOE SCANLAN

جو سكانلن

ولد عام ١٩٦٧ في سركليفل، أوهايو، الولايات المتحدة. يعيش ويعمل في نيوهيفن، كونتيكت، الولايات المتحدة

Born 1967 in Circleville, Ohio
Lives and works in New Haven, Connecticut
B.F.A. 1989 Columbus College of Art and Design

Selected Solo Exhibitions

2007 Kunstsammlung, Nordrhein-Westfalen, Düsseldorf, Germany
Galerie Chez Valentin, Paris France

2005 Galerie Micheline Szwajcer, Antwerp, Belgium

2003 Van Abbemuseum, Eindhoven, Netherlands
Ikon Gallery, Birmingham, UK

Selected Group Exhibitions

2006 "Broken Lines, Printemps du Septembre", Toulouse, France

2005 "BMW: The IXth Baltic Triennial", Contemporary Art Centre, Vilnius, Lithuania

2004 "BUY AMERICAN", Galerie Chez Valentin, Paris, France

2002 "DIY", Galerie Jan Mot, Brussels Belgium
"No Ghost, Just a Shell", Kunstalle, Zürich, Switzerland

1999 "Waste Management", Art Gallery of Ontario, Toronto, Canada

1998 12th Biennial of Sydney, Sydney, Australia

1996 "Art in Chicago: 1945-1995", Museum of Contemporary Art, Chicago, IL

1993 "Oppositions and Sister Squares", The Secession, Vienna, Austria

1992 "Documenta IX", Kassel, Germany

Selected Bibliography

Filipovic, Elena, "Joe Scanlan", Frieze No. 97 (March 2006): 166.
Lojecs, Anna (ed.), "Nesting Bookcase, the First Decade: 1989-1999", Brooklyn: Store A (1999).
Roelandt, Els (ed.), Aprior 13, Brussels: Aprior (2006)
Scanlan, Joe, et al., "Pay Dirt Birmingham", England: Ikon Gallery (2003)
van den Bossche, Phillip, Journal 4, Eindhoven, Netherlands: Van Abbemuseum (2004)

Artist's Writings

Scanlan, Joe, "Traffic Control," Artforum (Summer 2005): 123
Scanlan, Joe, "DIY or How To Kill Yourself Anywhere in the World for Under $399", Ghent: Imschoot Uitgevers (2002)
Scanlan, Joe, "The Ballad of Ed Ruscha", Parkett 55 (June 1999): 60-65

ZINEB SEDIRA

زينب سديرا

ولدت عام ١٩٦٣ في باريس، فرنسا تعيش وتعمل في لندن

Born 1963 Paris, France
Lives and works in London, UK
B.A. Saint Martins College of Art & Design, London
M.A. Slade School of Fine Art, London

Solo Exhibitions

2006 Photographers Gallery, London, UK
Galerie Kamel Mennour, Paris, France
Galerie Esma, Algiers, Algeria

2005 Fri-Art, Fribourg, Switzerland

2004 Cornerhouse, Manchester, UK

Selected Group Exhibitions

2006 "Around the world in 80 days", Institute of Contemporary Art, London, UK
"Une vision du Monde, la collection de Jean-Conrad et Isabelle Lemaître", La Maison Rouge, Paris, France

2005/06 "British Art Show 06", Baltic, Newcastle; Cornerhouse, Manchester; Arnolfini, Bristol; UK

2005 "Ficcions Documentals", Fundació la Caixa, Barcelona

2004/05/06 "Africa Remix", Centre Pompidou, Paris, France; Hayward Gallery, London, UK; and Mori Museum, Tokyo, Japan

2003 "Strangers", the First ICP Triennial of Photography and Video, Institute of Contemporary Photography, New York, NY

2002 "Self-Evident: Making the Self the Subject of Art from 1900 to the Present Day", Tate Britain, London, UK

2001 "Authentic/ex-centric: Africa In and Out Africa", 49th Venice Biennial, Venice, Italy

2000 "Insertion: Self and Other", Apex Art C.P, New York, NY

1999 "From Where-to Here, Art from London", Konsthallen Göteborg Museum, Göteborg, Sweden

Public Collections

Tate Britain, London, UK
Musée d'Art Moderne de la Ville de Paris, Paris, France
Centre Georges Pompidou, Paris, France
MUMOK (Museum Moderner Kunst Stiftung Ludwig), Vienna, Austria
Arts Council of England, London, UK
Fond National d'Art Contemporain, Paris, France
Victoria and Albert Museum, London, UK

ANAS AL-SHAIKH

أنس الشيخ

ولد عام ١٩٦٨ في البحرين
يعيش ويعمل في البحرين

Born 1968 Bahrain
Lives and work in Bahrain
Diploma in Architecture, Arab Collage, Jordan, 1989

Solo Exhibitions

2001 "Memory of Memories", Garage of Mohammed Abdulla Saif in the district of Al Gudaibiya, Manama, Bahrain

Selected Group Exhibitions

2006 "Contact Zones", 15th Biennial of Sydney, Sydney, Australia
"Nafas", ifa Gallery, Berlin/ Stuttgart, Germany
"Coding: Decoding", Copenhagen Contemporary Art Centre, Denmark

2006-05 "Regards des photographes arabes contemporains", Institut du Monde Arabe, Paris, France; Centro Andaluz de Arte Contemporaneo, Seville, Spain; Kunstforeningen Gl Strand, Denmark
"Common Ground", Bait Al Quran & Sharjah Art Museum, Bahrain

2005 "Contemporary Curves", Installation & New Media Exhibition, Al Rewaq Gallery, Bahrain

2005-04 "Nazar", photography exhibition, Fries Museum, Netherlands; Aperture Foundation, New York; FotoFest Gallery, Houston, TX; Langhans Gallery, Czech Republic; ifa Gallery, Berlin, Germany

2004 "The Circle 3", Cultural Club, Oman

2003 "More Darkness... More light", Installation & New Media Exhibition, Contemporary Art Association, Bahrain

2002 "Out to in!", Installation & New Media Exhibition, Contemporary Art Association, Bahrain

Public Collections

Bahrain National Museum, Bahrain
Institut du Monde Arabe, Paris, France
Sharjah Art Museum, Sharjah, UAE
Arab Modern Art Museum, Qatar
Jordan Fine Art Museum, Amman, Jordan

Selected Bibliography

Al Mannai, Wejdan, "Three artists from Bahrain", Jamini Art Magazine, Bangladesh" (August 2004): 70-75
Creations artistiques contemporaines en pays d'Islam, Editions Kime (Paris, 2006): 262
Mazmouz, Fatima, "Tendances de photographie contemporaine dans le monde arabe", Art Book

Artist's Writings

Al-Shaikh, Anas, "Art in the 21st Century", Awan, University of Bahrain (Autumn 2002): 38-43
Al-Shaikh, Anas, "Can Abdul Raheem Sharif Sell Water in the Water Seller Zone?", cultural supplement, Al Ayam, Bahrain" (14 January 2001): 16
Al-Shaikh, Anas, "The third generation in the art movement in Bahrain", Cultural supplement, Al Ayam , Bahrain" (4 July 1999): 14-15

RANJANI SHETTAR

رانجاني شيتار

ولدت عام ١٩٧٧ في بانغالور، الهند
تعيش وتعمل في بانغالور

Born 1977 Bangalore, India
Lives and works in Bangalore
B.F.S. 1998 College of Fine Art, Bangalore
M.F.A. 2000 Chitrakala Institute of Advanced Studies, Bangalore

Selected Exhibitions

2006 15th Biennial of Sydney, Sydney, Australia
Artist in Residence, ARTPACE, San Antonio, TX

2005 "J'en rêve" (Dream on), Fondation Cartier pour l'art contemporain, Paris, France
"Out There", Sainsbury Centre for Visual Arts, Norwich, UK
"Transition & Transformation", Fine Arts Center, University of Massachusetts, Amherst, MA
"Landscape Confection", Wexner Center for the Arts, Columbus, OH; and touring Contemporary Arts Museum, Houston, TX; Orange County Museum of Art, Newport Beach, CA
"(desi)re", Talwar Gallery, New York

2004 Talwar Gallery, New York, NY
Khoj International, New Delhi, India

2003-05 "How Latitudes Become Forms: Art in a Global Age", Walker Art Center, Minneapolis, MI; touring to Fondazione Sandretto Re Rebaudengo, Turin, Italy; Contemporary Arts Museum, Houston, TX; Museo Internacional de Arte Contemporaneo Rufino Tamayo, Mexico City, Mexico; Museo de Arte Contemporaneo de

Monterrey, Mexico
2003 "When Beads Converse", Gallery Smukha, India
2000 "Concept Shop", Synergy Art Foundation, Bangalore, India

SOI PROJECT

مشروع (اس او آي)

ويت بمكنشنبونغ

ولد عام ١٩٧٦ في بانكوك، تايلاند.
يعيش ويعمل في بانكوك

جيرو إندو

ولد عام ١٩٦٦ في طوكيو، اليابان. يعيش ويعمل في بانكوك وطوكيو

بتيبونغ شواكول (جاك)

ولد عام ١٩٧٥ في اوبونرتشاتاني، تايلاند
يعيش ويعمل في بانكوك

Wit Pimkanchanpong

Born 1976 Bangkok, Thailand
Lives and works in Bangkok
H.N.D. Architecture, Chulalongkorn University, Bangkok, Thailand
M.A. University of Kent, UK

Solo Exhibitions

2004 "The Odyssey", Visual Loft, Bangkok, Thailand

Selected Group Exhibitions

2006 "Platform: About Installation", Queen Sirikiti Gallery, Bangkok, Thailand
"SOI Project", Mairie de 6e, Paris, France
"Temporary Art Museum, Soi Sabai", Silpakorn University, Bangkok, Thailand
2005 "Politics of Fun", Haus der Kulturen der Welt, Berlin, Germany
"SOI Project", Yokohama International Triennale of Contemporary Art, Yokohama, Japan
"T1 Torino Trienniale Tre Musei", Turin, Italy
"Mirror Worlds", Australian Centre for Photography, Sydney, Australia
"Bangkok Bangkok", La Capella, Barcelona, Spain
2004 "-+- negative plus negative", Earl Lu Gallery, Singapore
"Have we met?" Japan Foundation Forum, Tokyo, Japan

Jiro Endo

Born 1966 Tokyo, Japan
Lives and works in Bangkok and Tokyo
B.A. Architecture Musashino Art University, Tokyo

Solo Exhibitions

2004 One Ten Gallery, Tokyo, Japan

Selected Group Exhibitions

2006 "SOI Project", Mairie de 6e, Paris, France
2005 "SOI Project", Yokohama International Triennale of Contemporary Art, Yokohama, Japan
2004 "SOI Music Festival from BKK", Tokyo, Japan
"SOI Music Festival from Tokyo", Bangkok, Thailand
2003 "SOI Music from BKK", Tokyo
1999 "The Museum of Soy Sauce Art" (exhibition design for Tsuyoshi Ozawa/artist), Tokyo, Japan

Pitupong Chaowakul (Jack)

Born 1975 Ubonratchathani, Thailand
Lives and works in Thailand, Bangkok
B. Arch, Faculty of Architecture, Chulalongkorn University, Bangkok, Thailand
M.Arch, Berlage Institute of Architecture, Rotterdam, Netherlands

Projects

2006 Exhibition design for "Living under the crescent Moon", a traveling exhibition from Vitra design museum, at Thailand Creative & Design Center, Bangkok, Thailand
Cheeze Studio, Siam Center, Bangkok, Thailand
2005 Pru Pop Live concert, Tossapak Arena, Bangkok, Thailand
Ghost transmission, multi-media performance with Duck unit, Met bar, Bangkok, Thailand
Ghost tower, A Statement on "on-hold" high-rise buildings in Bangkok. H-Gallery, Bangkok
2003 Paradox circus, Fat live 4, Bangkok, Thailand
Presently, Pitupong Chaowakul runs the architecture office in Bangkok, Thisdesign CO.,LTD which deals with a wide range in the design field, from architecture, interior, exhibition to product design

SAMIR SROUJI

سمير سروجي

ولد عام ١٩٦١ في الناصرة، فلسطين
يعيش ويعمل في بوسطن،
الولايات المتحدة

Born 1961 Nazareth, Palestine
Lives and works in Boston, MA
B. Arch. 1986 University of Oklahoma, Oklahoma

Selected Solo Exhibitions

1998 "Kibbutz Falafel", Kibbutz Gallery, Tel Aviv, Israel
1994 "Measures of Loss", Gallery Anadiel, Jerusalem, Palestina
"Samir Srouji", Centre Culturel Francais, Nazareth, Palestine

Selected Group Exhibitions

2006 "A Space of Light and Reflection", Andover Chapel, Harvard University, Cambridge, MA
1997 "Home", Gallery Anadiel, Jerusalem, Palestine
1996 "Three Territories", Artist's House, Tel Aviv, Israel

Architectural Installation

2000 "Eilaboun 1948", Memorial in Eilaboun town square
1998 "El-Kurum Outdoor Classroom", El-Kurum school, Nazareth

Filmography

2002 Art Director, "Divine Intervention", a film by Elia Suleiman
1996 Production Designer, "Chronicle of a Disappearance", a film by Elia Suleiman

SIMON STARLING

سيمون ستارلنج

ولد عام ١٩٦٧ في إبسوم، إنكلترا
يعيش ويعمل في كوبنهاجن، الدانمرك

Born 1967 Epsom, UK
Lives and Works in Copenhagen, Denmark
1990-92 Glasgow School of Art

Selected Solo Exhibitons

2006 "24 hr. Tangenziale", Galleria Franco Noero, Turin, Italy
"Wilhelm Noack oHG", Neugerriemschneider, Berlin
2005 "Cuttings", Kunstmuseum Basel, Museum für Gegenwartskunst, Basel, Switzerland
"Kakteenhaus," Portikus,

Frankfurt a.M., Germany
2001 "Inverted Retrograde Theme", Secession, Vienna, Austria

Selected Group Exhibitions

2006 "Strange I've Seen that Face Before", Museum Abteiberg, Mönchen Gladbach, Germany
"Ecotopia: The Second ICP Triennial of Photography and Video", International Center of Photography, New York, NY
2005 "The 2005 Turner Prize Exhibition", Tate Britain, London, UK
"Universal Experience: Art, Life and the Tourist's Eye", MCA, Chicago, IL
2004 26th São Paulo Biennial, São Paulo, Brazil
2003 Munsterland Sculpture Biennial, Germany
"Moving Pictures", Solomon R. Guggenheim Museum, Bilbao, Spain
Scottish Pavillion, 50th Venice Biennial, Venice, Italy
"The Moderns", Castello di Rivoli, Turin, Italy

Artist's Writings

Starling, Simon, "24 hr. Tangenziale", Turin: Galleria Franco Noero (2006)
Starling, Simon, "Cuttings", ed.
Philipp Kaiser, Basel: Museum für Gegenwartskunst (2005)
Volz, Jochen, and Simon Starling, "Kakteenhaus", Frankfurt am Main: Portikus (2003)

GERDA STEINER & JÖRG LENZLINGER

جيردا شتاينر ويورغ لنزلينجر

جيردا شتاينر

ولدت عام ١٩٦٧ في ايتسويل، سويسرا.
تعيش وتعمل في أوستر، سويسرا

يورغ لنزلينجر

ولد عام ١٩٦٤ في أوستر
يعيش ويعمل في أوستر، سويسرا

Gerda Steiner

Born 1967 Ettiswil, Switzerland
Lives and works in Uster, Switzerland
Studied at the School of Arts, Lucerne and Basel

Jörg Lenzlinger

Born 1964 Uster, Switzerland
Lives and works in Uster
Educated as a carpenter and by travelling

Selected Solo Exhibitions

2006 "Das Vegetative Nervensystem", Museum Kunst Palast, Düsseldorf, Germany
"Night Moths in the Whale Belly", Artium, Fukuoka, Japan
2005 "Seelenwärmer", Stiftsbibliothek, St. Gallen, Switzerland
"Le Méta Jardin", La Maison Rouge, Paris, France
2004 "Les Envahisseurs!" Jardin botanique and Musée d'histoire des sciences, Geneva, Switzerland
2003 "Cómo llegó la morsa a Madrid?", La Casa Encendida, Madrid, Spain
"Giardino Calante", 50th Venice Biennial, Venice, Italy
2002 "Die Heimatmaschine", Die Heimatfabrik, Expo '02, Môrat, Switzerland
2001 "The Seed Sounds of the Vegetative Nervous System at the Hydroponic Nectar-Lake", Contemporary Art Center, Cincinnati, OH
2000 "Pique-nique au bord de la Fontaine de Jouvence", attitudes, Geneva, Switzerland

Selected Group Exhibitions

2006 "Swan Lake", ARS '06, Museum of Contemporary Art, Kiasma, Helsinki, Finland
"Artificial Fertility", Shanghai Biennial, China
"Grottes sauvages sur forêt cérébrale civilisée, Tropico Vegetal", Palais de Tokyo, Paris, France
2004 "Fountain of Youth, La Alegria de mis sueños", Biennale de Seville, Seville, Spain
"Brainforest, Polyphony - Emerging Resonances", Kanazawa 21st Century Museum, Japan
"Wurzelbehandlung, Rose c'est la vie", National Museum, Tel Aviv, Israel
"Whale Balance, Empty Garden II", Watarium, Tokyo, Israel
2002 "Lift-Up, Public Affairs", Kunsthaus, Zürich, Switzerland
"Der Tag nach der Kiesgrube", Art Unlimited, Stampa, Basel
2000 "Oase 2000", Academy of Fine Arts, Berlin

RIRKRIT TIRVANIJA

ريركريت تيرافانيت

ولد عام ١٩٦١ في بيونس آيرس، الأرجنتين
يعيش ويعمل في شيانغ ماي ونيويورك

Born 1961 Buenos Aires, Argentina
Lives and works in Chiang Mai and New York
1985-6 The Whitney Independent Studies Program, New York
1984-86 The School of the Art Institute of Chicago

Selected Solo Exhibitons

2005 "A Retrospective - Tomorrow is Another Fine Day", Serpentine Gallery, London, UK; Musée d'Art Moderne de la Ville de Paris, Paris, France
2004 "A Retrospective - Tomorrow is Another Fine Day", Museum Boijmans van Beuningen, Rotterdam, Netherlands
2002 Untitled, 2002 (he promised), Secession, Vienna, Austria
Untitled, 2002 (the raw and the cooked), Opera City, Tokyo, Japan

Selected Group Exhibitions

2006 27th São Paulo Biennial, São Paulo, Brazil
"Peace Tower at the Whitney Biennial", New York, NY
2005 8th Lyon Biennial of Contemporary Art, Lyon, France
"Luna Park, Arte Fantastica", Villa Manin, Passariano, Italy
2004 DAK'ART, 6th Biennial of Contemporary African Art, Dakar, Senegal
"International 04", Liverpool Biennial, Liverpool, UK
2003 "Installation Art 1969-2002", Museum for Contemporary Art MOCA, Los Angeles, CA
"El aire es azul", Casa Museo Luis Barragan, Mexico City, Mexico
2002 "No Ghost Just a Shell", Kunsthalle Zürich, Zürich, Switzerland
"Points of Departure II: Connecting with Contemporary

Art", San Francisco Museum of Modern Art, San Francisco, CA

Public Collections
MUSAC, Museo de arte contemporaneo de Castilla y Leon, Leon, Spain
Kunsthalle Bielefeld, Bielefeld, Germany
Walker Art Museum, Minneapolis, U.S.
Sammlung der Bundesrepublik Deutschland
Migros museum, Zürich
FRAC Nord-pas de Calais, Dunkirk, France
Carnegie Museum of Art, Pittsburg, U.S.A.
Moderna Museet, Stockholm, Sweden

Selected Bibliography
"Une Rétrospective - Tomorrow Is Another Fine Day", exhibition catalogue, Paris: Musée d'Art de la Ville de Paris/ARC (2005); and London: Serpentine Gallery (2005)
Pareno, Philippe and Matthias Hermann, "Rirkrit Tiravanija, Interview/Conversation", exhibition catalogue, Vienna: Secession (2002)
Kataoka, Mami, "Rirkrit Tiravanija: Untitled, 2002 (the raw and the cooked)", exhibition catalogue, Tokyo: Tokyo Opera City Art Gallery (2002)

MIERLE LADERMAN UKELES

ميرل لادرمن

ولدت عام ١٩٣٩ في دنفر، كولورادو، الولايات المتحدة
تعيش وتعمل في نيويورك

Born 1939 Denver, Colorado
Lives in New York and works in New York and internationally
B.A. Barnard College in 1961
M.A. Inter-related Arts, New York University in 1973

Selected Solo Exhibitions
1989-14 "Percent for Art Artist of Fresh Kills Park", multiple permanent and temporary projects in progress, Staten Island, New York, NY
1989-08 "Turnaround/Surround", multiple part work in progress, Danehy Park, Cambridge, MA
2003 "Snow Workers Ballet", performance, Echigo-Tsumari Triennial 2, Echigo Tsumari, Tokamachi City, Japan
1998 "Mierle Laderman Ukeles: Maintenance Art Works, 1969-1979" (with Eleanor Antin), Ronald Feldman Fine Arts, New York, NY
1993 "Re-spect", performance work on the Quai de la Navigation and the Rhone River, Givors, France, October 28, 1993
1977-80 "Touch Sanitation Performance", citywide performance work with 8,500 sanitation workers, New York City, NY

Selected Group Exhibitions
2006 "The Downtown Show: The New York Art Scene, 1974-1984", Grey Art Gallery, New York, NY; Andy Warhol Museum, Pittsburgh, PA; Austin Museum of Art, Austin, TX
"Mapping the Studio", Stichting Stedelijk Museum, Amsterdam, Netherlands
2005 "Odd Lots: Revisiting Gordon Matta-Clark's Fake Estates", White Columns, New York, NY
2002 "Fresh Kills: Artists Respond to the Closure of the Staten Island Landfill", Snug Harbor Cultural Center, Newhouse Center for Contemporary Art, Staten Island, New York, NY
1997 "Uncommon Sense", Museum of Contemporary Art, Los Angeles, CA
1994 "Garbage! The History and Politics of Trash in New York City", Gottesman Hall, New York Public Library, New York, NY
1993 Blizzard of Released and Agitated Materials in Flux, permanent installation for the Recycling through Art Museum, Taedok Science Town, Art Pavilion, Taejon, Korea
1992 "Allocations", World Horticultural Exhibition Floriade, The Hague and Zoetermeer, Netherlands
1990 Landfill Cross Section, installation for self-curated "Garbage Out Front: A New Era of Public Design", Municipal Art Society, New York
1988 "Out of the Studio: Art With the Community", P.S.1 Museum, Long Island City, New York, NY
1976 "Art World", Whitney Museum of American Art, New York, NY

Public Collections
Recycling Through Art Museum, Taejon, Korea
Danehy Park, City of Cambridge, MA
Maine College of Art, Portland, Maine
Wadsworth Atheneum, Hartford, Maine
Department of Sanitation, New York, NY
Fire Department, New York, NY
Westside Light Rail Extension, Preposition Park, Tri-Met, Portland, Oregon

Selected Bibliography
Carr, C., "Waste. Not! Fresh Kills Becomes an Urban Artwork", Village Voice (May 28, 2002): 43
Finkelpearl, Tom, "Interview: Mierle Laderman Ukeles on Maintenance and Sanitation Art", in Finkelpearl (ed.) Dialogues in Public Art, Cambridge, Massachusetts: MIT Press (2000): 294-322
Kastner, Jeffrey, "The Department of Sanitation's Artist in Residence", The New York Times (19 May 2002), AR37 & AR39
Oakes, Baile, "Sculpting with the Environment - A Natural Dialogue", London: Van Nostrand Reinhold, ITP (1995): 184-93
Phillips, Patricia C., "Maintenance Activity: Creating a Climate for Change", in Nina Felshin (ed.) But Is It Art? The Spirit of Art as Activism, Seattle: Bay Press (1995): 165-93

Artist's Writings
Ukeles, Mierle Laderman, "Time Travel in Public Landscapes", Landscape & Art, No. 29 (Summer 2003): 21-22
Ukeles, Mierle Laderman, "Leftovers/It's About Times for Fresh Kills", Cabinet, No. 6 (Spring 2002): 17-20
Ukeles, Mierle Laderman, "Maintenance Art," in Hafthor Yngvason (ed.) Conservation and Maintenance of Contemporary Public Art: 'Materials, Maintenance, Change, and Community' London: Archetype; and Cambridge Massachusetts: Cambridge Arts Council (2002): 9-14

SERGIO VEGA

سيرجيو فيغا

ولد عام ١٩٥٩ في بيونس آيرس،الأرجنتين
يعيش ويعمل في فلوريدا

Born 1959 Buenos Aires, Argentina
Lives and works in Gainesville, Florida
M.F.A. Sculpture 1996 Yale University
Artist in Residence, Yale University, 2006-7

Selected Solo Exhibitions

2006 “Momentum 6: Tropicalounge”, Institute of Contemporary Art, Boston, MA
“Crocodilian Fantasies”, Palais de Tokyo, Paris, France
“Utopian Paradises: Modernism and the Sublime”, Umberto di Marino Arte Contemporánea ,Naples, Italy
2003 “High Art”, John Erickson Museum of Art, www.JEMA.US
2002 “Modernismo Tropical”, Harn Museum of Art, Gainesville, FL

Selected Group Exhibitions

2006 “ARS06, Sense of the Real”, Kiasma, Helsinki, Finland
2005 “Down the Garden Path: The Artist's Garden After Modernism”, Queens Museum of Art, New York, NY
“Always a little further”, Arsenale di Venezia, 51st Venice Biennial, Venice, Italy
2004 “‘Nous venons en paix...’ Histoires des Amériques”, Musée d”art contemporain de Montréal, Canada
2002 “Etnografía”, Museo de Bellas Artes de Caracas, Venezuela
2001 “Yokohama Triennale 2001: Dancing Matrix”, Red Brick Warehouse, Yokohama, Japan
“Sonsbeek 9: Locus Focus”, Kronenberg Mall and Arnhem Museum of Modern Art, Arnhem, Netherlands
2000 “Partage d'Exotismes”, 5th Lyon Biennial of Contemporary Art, Lyon, France
“Exotica Incognita”, 2nd Gwangju Biennial, Gwangju, South Korea
1997 “Alternating Currents”, 2nd Johannesburg Biennial, Electrical Plant, Johannesburg, South Africa

Public Collections

Fondazione Biennale di Venezia, Italy
KIASMA, Museum of Contemporary Art, Helsinki, Finland
Museé d'art contemporain de Montréal, Canada
Cisneros Fontanals Art Foundation, Miami, Florida
Museum Voor Moderne Kunst, Arnhem, Netherlands

Selected Bibliography

Smith, Valerie, “Heaven/Paradise, Sergio Vega, Roberto Burle Marx, Lothar Baumgarten, and Ingrid Pollard”, Down the Garden Path: The Artist's Garden After Modernism, exhibition catalogue, New York: Queens Museum of Art (June 2005): 14-16
Vetrocq, Marcia, “Venice Biennial: Be Careful What You Wish for”, Art in America (September 2005): 113
Rugoff, Ralph, “Venice Top Ten (In no particular order)”, Frieze, London (September 2005): 102-3
Foster, Hal, “In Venice”, London Review of Books, Vol. 27, No.15 (August 4, 2005)
Ichihara, Kentaro, “Biennale di Venezia, Sergio Vega”, BT (Bijutsu Techo), Vol. 57, Tokyo (September 2005): 30-32, 69, 88

Artist's Writing

Vega, Sergio,"Paradise in the New World", (2006): 152-55
Vega, Sergio, “Sergio Vega: 1000 words”, Artforum (September 2006): 215-16
Vega, Sergio, “Extraits de El Paraiso en el Nuevo Mundo”, Reemergence of Paradise, Paris: Palais de Tokyo, (June 2006)

LUCA VITONE

لوكا فيتوني

ولد عام ١٩٦٤ في جنوا، إيطاليا
يعيش ويعمل في ميلانو، ايطاليا

Born 1964 Genoa, Italy
Lives and works in Milan

Selected Solo Exhibitions

2006 “At Home Everywhere”, Casino Luxembourg, Luxembourg
2005 “Io, Roma”, Magazzino d'Arte Moderna, Rome, Italy
“L'Ultimo Viaggio”, Galleria Franco Soffiantino Arte Contemporanea, Turin, Italy
2004 “Prêt-à-Porter”, Centro per l'Arte Contemporanea Luigi Pecci, Prato, Italy
“Nulla da dire solo da essere”, Galleria Emi Fontana, Milan, Italy

Selected Group Exhibitions

2006 “Fuoriuso '06, Are you experienced?” Ex mercato ortofrutticolo COFA, Pescara, Italy
“Less, Strategie dell'abitare”, Pac, Milan, Italy
“The People's Choice”, Isola Art Centre, Milan, Italy
2005 “Nach Rokytnik. Die Sammlung der EVN”, MUMOK, Vienna, Austria
“Domus Circular”, Stadio Giuseppe Meazza, Milan, Italy
“Emergency Biennial in Chechnya”, traveling exhibition, Palais de Tokyo, Paris, France; Grozny, Chechnya; Matrix Art Project, Brussels, Belgium; Museion, Bolzano, Italy
“Fuori Tema”, XIV Quadriennale d'Arte, Galleria Nazionale d'Arte Moderna, Rome, Italy
2004 “Shake, Staatsaffäre”, O.K. Centrum für Gegenwartskunst Oberösterreich, Linz, Austria; Villa Arson, Centre National d'Art Contemporain, Nice, France
2003 “Stazione Utopia / Utopia Station”, nell'ambito di Sogni e Conflitti. La dittatura dello spettatore, Venice Biennial, Venice, Italy
“La Ciudad Radiante”, Centre Cultural Bancaja, Valencia, Spain

Selected Bibliography

Bucco, V., “Luca Vitone”, Tema Celeste, No. 112 (Nov.-Dec. 2005): 87
Damiani, D., “Luca Vitone, Casino Luxembourg”, Flash Art International (Jan.-Feb. 2007): 123-124
Iovane, G., “Luca Vitone, Immaterial Geographies”, Janus, No. 20 (2006): 14-18
Lauf, C., “Luca Vitone, at Magazzino Arte Moderna”, Art in America (May 2006): 198-99
Scharrer, E., “Luca Vitone, Casino Luxembourg”, Artforum International (Dec. 2006): 324
VV.AA., Luca Vitone, At home Everywhere, Bolzano: OK Books, Folio Verlag (2006)

Artist's Writings

Vitone, Luca, “Sounds Paths”, Dena Foundation Art Award 2002, Paris: One StarPress, (2002)
Vitone, Luca, “Wide City”, Comune di Milano: Progetto Giovani (1999)
Vitone, Luca, & Franco La Cecla, “Non è cosa - Luca Vitone, Non siamo mai soli”, Milano: Elèuthera (1998)

SHATHA AL WADI

شذى الوادي

ولدت عام ١٩٨٤ في المنامة، البحرين
تعيش في البحرين

Born 1984 Manama, Bahrain
Lives in Bahrain
B.Sc. University of Bahrain

Selected Solo Exhibitions

2006 Light language photographic exhibition, University of Bahrain
2005 Pictures from photographic exhibition, University of Bahrain
"Contemporary Curves", Al Riwaq Gallery, Bahrain
"Contemporary Angles", University of Bahrain

CAMILLE ZAKHARIA

كميل زخريا

ولد عام ١٩٦٢ في طرابلس، لبنان
يعيش ويعمل في البحرين

Born 1962 Tripoli, Lebanon
Lives and works in Bahrain
B.F.A. 1997 Nova Scotia College of Arts and Design, Halifax, Canada
B.A. 1985 American University of Beirut, Beirut

Selected Solo Exhibitions

2006 Art Gallery of Virginia Commonwealth University, Doha, Qatar
Art Gallery of St Mary's University, Halifax, Canada
2005 Art Gallery of Taib Tower, Manama, Bahrain
1999 Artemisia Gallery. Chicago, IL
Dalhousie Faculty of Architecture Art Gallery, Halifax. Canada

Selected Group Exhibitions

2006 "Middle East & North Africa Cultural Week", British Council Gallery, London, UK
"Common Ground", Sharjah Art Museum, Sharjah, UAE
2001-03 "The Lands within Me", Canadian Museum of Civilization, Hull, Quebec, Canada
2000 "Second Time 'Round", Matrix Gallery, Sacramento, CA
1999 "Appropriations", City Arts Gallery, Wichita, Kansas
"Proof", Gallery 44 for Contemporary Photography, Toronto, Ontario, Canada
1998-99 "Combined Talents, the Florida National 1998", Museum of Fine Art, Florida State University, Tallahassee, Florida; Appleton Museum of Art, Ocala, FL
1998-99 "Far and Wide, Third Biennial Exhibition", Art Gallery of Nova Scotia, Halifax, Canada
1998 "Skin A Political Boundary", Anna Leonowens Gallery, Halifax, Canada

Public Collections

Canadian Museum of Civilization, Hull, Quebec
Wichita Center for the Arts, Wichita, Kansas
St Mary's University, Halifax
Beit Al Qur'an, Manama, Bahrain
British Council, Muscat, Oman

Selected Bibliography

Al Moosawi-Hassanovich, Jamal, "Division Lines"' in Division Lines, exhibition catalogue (September 2006)
Barnard, Elissa, "The Art of Compromise", Chronicle Herald (7 October 2006)
Bullingtom, Judy, "Through the Prism: Camille Zakharia's Photo-Montage as Medium and Message", Elusive Homelands (October 2006): 13-19
Glazebrook, Mark, "Quest for Self", The Spectator, (18 February 2006): 53-54
Sokoly, Jochen "Diaspora and Displacement - The Modern Nomad", Elusive Homelands (October 2006): 6-9

Artist's Writings

Zakharia, Camille, "Stories from the Alley", Division Lines (forthcoming exh. cat.)
Zakharia, Camille,"We Immigrants", Elusive Homelands (October 2006): 11
Zakharia, Camille,"Where to start? A parent's soul searching", The Lands within Me (October 2001): 22-23

AHMED MATER AL-ZIAD

أحمد ماطر

ولد عام ١٩٧٩ في تبوك، السعودية
يعيش ويعمل في أبها

Born 1979 Tabouk, Kingdom of Saudi Arabia
Lives and works in Abha, KSA
Doctorate, Medical College, King Khalid University, Abha

Selected Solo Exhibitions

2006 Solo exhibition at the Saudi Arabian Embassy, London, UK
2004 "Standing in Front of You", project combined with shadow image inspired by Arab heritage, performed by the actor Saeed Af, Faculty of Medicine, King Khalid University, Abha, Saudi Arabia
2003 "X-ray", project at 6th Saudi Malwan contest in Jeddah, Beirut, Sidon and Manama, Saudi Arabia
2001 "Landing on the Earth's Surface", exhibition at Al Maseef Cultural Club, Abha, Saudi Arabia

Selected Group Exhibitions

2007 "New Art from Saudi Arabia and Yemen", Brunei Gallery, London, UK
2006 "Word into Art", contemporary art from the Middle East, British Museum, London, UK
Al Sharjah Calligraphy Biennial, Sharjah, UAE
2005 Curator of the Saudi Arts Exhibition, Hamburg, Germany
Saudi Arts exhibition in Tunisia
National Dialogue Conference in Saudi Arabia
2004 "So far you are from the earth", 2nd exhibition, sponsored by Shatta group in public park, Abha
"Shatta Group" 1st exhibition" at Jeddah Atelier, KSA
"Bayna-Ma'ayn", exhibition, Dammam

Public Collections

HRH Prince Khaled Al Faisal, Abha, KSA
The British Museum, Brooke Sewell Permanent Fund, London, UK
Abha Chamber of Commerce, Abha, KSA
Offscreen Education Programme, London, UK
Saudi Arabian Embassy, London, UK

IGNASI ABALLI

Malgastar

To come in through the door of a museum and see 20 large, open buckets of white industrial paint on the floor is somewhat perplexing. Our first feeling is one of hesitation, or misgiving, as if the museum were still being prepared and we have arrived too early for the Ignasi Aballi exhibition: after all, this is a modern museum, they must be adding the final touches to the white cube? Or else the exhibition is over and they've already repainted the walls for the next one? Whatever the case, we have the feeling there's been a hitch, a mistake: if we are not early, maybe the museum, the artist, the curator or the technical crew are running late? A few pots of paint left on the floor and seen from a distance are enough to generate uncertainty and misgiving, opening up a sort of time warp between too soon and too late. This work - because it is a work, and seemingly a very simple one, called Malgastar - possesses the strange power to suspend the present, the present of the work at the time of viewing it, and thus to suspend the work itself. And in so doing, it puts the viewer in the position of seeing something other than the work, of seeing what s/he's not supposed to see: a time preceding the work, the preparations for a work or an exhibition, the behind-the-scenes business of art and museums, a vertiginous temporal upsetting, in which the work of art becomes a machine for looking at the past. You could call this a "witches' brew", thinking back to the opening scene of Macbeth where, as if the curtain has risen too early, the audience surprises the three witches in "a desert place", making their deadly predictions - we should not have been there, should not have seen what happens before the actual story begins: a stolen vision in which we intrude on a secret not meant for us, an art secret, a magic moment. The works of Ignasi Aballí are written into time. The works of Ignasi Aballí write time. The works of Ignasi Aballí disturb time. Maps of the past, they rise out of time warps: between before and after, yesterday and today, between what's seen and what happens, between now, before and after. Or rather, offering themselves in the moment of seeing that is our present, it is they themselves that open up the time warps. In all their seeming immobility, the works of Ignasi Aballí are works in motion. For as Aristotle says in Physics, Book VIII, "Time is the number of motion" in terms of 'before' and 'after'."

Gérard Wajcman, Memory, Sight, Expectation, inside catalogue 0-24h, Museu d'Art Contemporani de Barcelona; Museu de Serralves, Porto; Ikon Gallery, Birmingham (2005-2006).

إغناسي آبالي

ملغاستار

أن تدلف من باب متحف لترى ٢٠ دلوا كبيراً مفتوحا من الدهان الصناعي الأبيض على الأرض، أمر يبعث على الحيرة والدهشة بعض الشيء. اللبس الأول - وكأن المتحف في طور التجهيز، ونحن الذين وصلنا مبكرين جداً لحضور معرض إغناسي آبالي. إنه أحد المتاحف الحديثة، ولا بدّ أنهم يضعون اللمسات النهائية على المكعب الأبيض، أو ربما، أن المعرض قد انتهى، وانتهوا فعلاً من إعادة طلاء الجدران لاستقبال المعرض التالي. مهما يكن الحال، يتكون لدى الزائر شعور بأن ثمة خطأ ما: فإذا لم يكن هو قد حضر مبكراً، فلربما المتحف، أو الفنان، أو قيم المتحف، أو الطاقم الفني، هم من تأخروّا؟ بضعة أوان من الدهان قد تركت على الأرض، كافية لأن تخلق الشك وسوء الفهم، وأن تفتح الباب أمام جملة زمنية معترضة ما بين مبكر جداً ومتأخر جداً. ولأن هذا العمل هو عمل، ويبدو عملاً بسيطاً جداً، ويسمى ملغاستار، فإنه يملك تلك القوة الغريبة القادرة على تعليق الحاضر، حاضر العمل عند مشاهدته، وبالتالي تعليق العمل بحد ذاته. وبهذا، يوضع المشاهد في وضع مشاهدة شيء آخر غير العمل، ورؤية ما لا يتوقع منه/منها رؤيته: وقت يسبق العمل، إعدادات العمل المهيأ للمعرض، وعمل الفن والمتاحف خلف الكواليس. إنه اضطراب يبعث على الدوران مؤقتاً، حيث يصبح عمل الفن آلة للنظر إلى الماضي. يمكنك أن تسمي هذا بـ "نقيع الساحرة"، وأنت تفكر بالماضي وبالمشهد الافتتاحي من مسرحية مكبث لشكسبير حيث - وكأن الستارة قد رفعت باكرا جداً- يفاجئ الجمهور الساحرات الثلاث في "مكان صحراوي" وهن يطلقن نبوءاتهن القاتلة. كان علينا ألا نكون هناك، كان علينا ألا نشاهد ما يحدث قبل أن تبدأ القصة الفعلية. إنها رؤية مختلسة، نكون فيها طارئين أو متطفلين على سر لم نكن نحن المقصودين فيه - إنه سر فنّي، لحظة سحرية.

لقد سطرت أعمال أغناسي آبالي على صفحات الزمن، أعمالها هي التي تكتب الزمن، وهي التي تقلقه. خرائط الماضي، إنها تخرج من أنواع مختلفة من التواءات الزمن: في فترة ما بين الآن وقبل وبعد، أو حتى، أنها تطرح نفسها في لحظة مشاهدتها على أنها الحاضر. إنها هي ذاتها التي تفتح تعرجات الزمن. أعمال أغناسي آبالي تضج بالحركة، وإن بدت وكأنها فاقدة لها. فكما يقول أرسطو في الفيزياء، الكتاب الثامن، "الزمن هو عدد التحركات" بالعلاقة ما بين "قبل" و"بعد".

جيرار وايكمان، الذاكرة، النظر، والتوقع، في الكتالوج ٠-٢٤ ساعة، متحف الفن المعاصر في برشلونة، متحف سيرالف، بورتو، جاليري آيكون، بيرمنغهام، ٢٠٠٥-٢٠٠٦.

Waste, 2001, 250 kg of industrial paint which has been left to dry and aluminium cans, variable, installation view "0-24h". MACBA. 2005-2006, Courtesy of the artist and the Estrany-de la Mota Gallery, Barcelona

LIDA ABDUL

Brick Sellers of Kabul

Lida Abdul's "Brick Sellers of Kabul" approaches the complex process of reconstruction in Afghanistan, producing a subtle reflection that could be perceived and considered as a comment on social negotiation and transformation.

In this work, the dynamic tension between the protagonists of such reconstruction comes to the fore through a penetrating synthesis. On the one hand, we confront, conceptually speaking, the necessary and basic elements embedded in every process of reconstruction: primary materials (bricks) and the future generation (children). However, on the other hand, the third protagonist is a man whose presence disrupts and marks this process of renovation and transformation with his constitutive role of authority.

The continuous enduring sequence of children playing and selling the stones gives us a sense of inescapability marking out the presence of an unwritten law that belongs to every moment of reconstruction, namely dynamisms of power that emerge from the everyday struggle for survival. The brick sellers that we encounter in this video are the children of Kabul, but their movements never speak about total resignation. Nonetheless, this fragment of everyday struggle testifies to a precarious indication of redemption.

Abdul's visual alphabet remains always straightforward, but there is never an intention of judging what is happening. However, at the same time, there is not an absolute detachment from issues concerning the everyday life of these children. Put differently, in Abdul's work there is a clear attempt to explore the way the various elements contributing to the rebuilding merge together, and this is accomplished through an act of suspension in which the situation is presented without additional elaboration.

Abdul's work puts forward the possibility of redefining the notion of public performance in relation to social and political questions, employing Kabul's people as the first protagonists of the process of reconstruction. Moreover, the artist confronts us with the question of how reconstruction could be investigated through a performative act in the public sphere avoiding, on the one hand, the stereotypes of mass media and, on the other hand, a documentarist investigation. Here Abdul faces, in a delicate and contemplative way, the recent and dramatic reality of her country and she touches truthfully the wounded skin of this reality. In this sense her video performances could be considered as imaginative re-appropriations that function as reflective gestures on the condition of existence of Kabul's people. These imaginative re-appropriations speak about a tendency of confrontation in which collective memory and imagination and their configuration become fundamental components of the process of reconstruction itself.

Roberto Cavallini

ليدا عبدول

بائعو الطوب في كابول

يقدم عمل ليدا عبدول "بريك سيليرز أوف كابول (بائعو الطوب في كابول)" مقاربة لعملية إعادة البناء المعقّدة في أفغانستان، من خلال تأملات مرهفة يمكن إدراكها واعتبارها ملاحظات على عمليتي التفاوض والتحوّل الإجتماعيين.

يضع هذا العمل الفني التوتّر الحيويّ بين أبطال عملية إعادة البناء هذه في المقدمة من خلال توليفة ثاقبة. فمن ناحية، نواجه أنفسنا، نظريّا، بالعناصر الضروريّة والأساسيّة المتضمّنة في أيّ عمليّة إعادة بناء: مواد أساسيّة (الطوب) وجيل المستقبل (الأطفال). بالرغم من ذلك، ومن الناحية الأخرى، نجد البطل الثالث وهو رجل يشتت ويؤثر على عمليّة الترميم والتحوّل هذه من خلال دوره الأساسي السلطويّ.

تمنحنا المشاهد المتتابعة المستمرة للأطفال الذين يلعبون ويبيعون الحجارة شعورا بالحتميّة يدل على وجود قانون غير مكتوب ينتمي لكلّ لحظة من إعادة البناء، ألا وهو ديناميكيّات السلطة التي يبرزها الصراع اليومي من أجل البقاء.

بائعو الطوب الذين نقابلهم في هذا الفيديو هم أطفال كابول، إلاّ أنّ حركاتهم لا تتحدّث أبدا عن الخنوع الكامل. بالرغم من ذلك، يقدم لنا هذا الجزء من الصراع اليومي شهادة على مؤشرات غير مضمونة العواقب للخلاص.

تبقى أبجديّة عبدول البصريّة صريحة دائما، إلاّ أنّها لا تقصد إصدار الأحكام على ما يحدث. بالرغم من ذلك، لا يوجد انفصال مطلق عن قضايا الحياة اليوميّة لهؤلاء الأطفال.

في إطار مختلف، هناك محاولة واضحة في أعمال عبدول لاستكشاف الطريقة التي تندمج بها مختلف العناصر المساهمة في إعادة البناء معا، ويتحقق هذا من خلال عملية تعليق للحدث، حيث يتمّ عرض الوضع دون توضيحات إضافيّة.

تطرح أعمال عبدول احتمال إعادة تعريف فكرة الأداء العام بالعلاقة مع القضايا السياسيّة والإجتماعيّة باستعمال أهل كابول كأول الأبطال في عمليّة إعادة البناء هذه. إضافة إلى ذلك، تواجهنا الفنانة بالسؤال حول كيف يمكن تقصّي إعادة البناء من خلال فعل أدائيّ في مساحة عامّة بحيث يتجنب الصور النمطيّة للإعلام الجماهيري من ناحية، ويكون تحقيقا توثيقيّا من ناحية أخرى. تواجه عبدول هنا، بطريقة رقيقة وتأمليّة، الحقيقة الراهنة والمثيرة لوطنها، وتتلمّس بصدق، الجلد المجروح لهذه الحقيقة.

يمكن اعتبار عملها الفيديو الأدائيّ من هذه الناحية إعادة استملاك خيالية تخدم كإيماءة تأمّلية حول ظروف حياة أهل كابول. عملية إعادة الاستملاك الخيالية هذه تشير إلى ميل نحو المواجهة، حيث تصبح الذاكرة الجماعيّة والخيال وتشكيلاتهما مكونات أساسيّة من عمليّة إعادة البناء ذاتها.

روبرتو كافاليني

Brick Sellers of Kabul, 2006, video still, 16 mm film transferred to DVD, 6'00'', courtesy Giorgio Persano Gallery

JENNIFER ALLORA & GUILLERMO CALZADILLA

Over the past five years, we have realised a series of site-specific projects informed by the working concept Land Mark, which unsettles the formal and ecological premises of earlier Land Art by posing the following questions: in whose interest is land marked, and to what ends? Which marks are deemed worthy of preservation, and which are subject to obliteration?

These questions were formulated in response to what we call the "transitional geography" of the Puerto Rican island of Vieques. In 2003, a long-term campaign of civil disobedience succeeded in forcing the U.S. Navy to quit the western half of the island, which for 60 years was used as a munitions testing ground. This was only a partial victory for activists - the bomb-scarred land was transferred from the military to the Department of the Interior and reclassified as a wildlife refuge, purportedly to restore the costal ecosystem and protect it from "disruptive" human activity. While claiming to heal the land in the aftermath of its violent usage, official environmentalism has inscribed a violence of its own, silencing the demands of island residents that the land be fully decontaminated and turned over to municipal management, which would enable the process of reconstruction to be debated democratically rather than dictated from above.

Returning a Sound is a project of vehicular re-engineering that addresses not only the landscape of Vieques, but also its soundscape, which for residents of the island remains marked by the memory of the sonic violence of the bombing. In this case, we follow a civil-disobediance activist named Homar as he takes a kind of "victory lap" around the demilitarised island on a motorcycle whose muffler has been supplemented by a trumpet. The noise-reducing device is thus diverted from its original purpose, becoming a counter-instrument whose emissions follow not from a preconcieved score, but from the jolts of the road and the discontinuous acceleration of the bike's engine as Homar acoustically reterritorialises areas of the island formerly exposed to ear-splitting detonations. The atonality of the trumpet's call - it variously evokes the siren of an ambulance, Luigi Russolo's Futurist *Intonarumori* and even experimental jazz - puts it at odds with the musical convention we might typically expect to mark a popular victory and an affinity with a "land", namely an *anthem*. Indeed, the title of the work excavates the etymological origins of the word order to unsettle it from within: *anthem* derives from the Greek *antiphonos* ("sounding in answer"), a composite of anti ("in return") and *phone* ("voice"). The anthem thus entails a kind of answerability to a sonic event that precedes the one who answers. This primitive definition marks a potential dissonance in a genre associated with the harmonious "voice of the people," a figure normally tied to the principle of territorial co-belonging. Yet in Viques, the future of the reclaimed land remains uncertain and is largely insulated from democratic claims - *Returning a Sound* at once celebrates a victory and registers its precariousness, calling for an unheard-of vigilance.

جينيفر أيورا وغييرمو كالزاديا

على مدى الخمس سنوات الماضية، قمنا بإنجاز سلسلة من المشاريع الفنية المرتبطة بمواقع محددة، معتمدين على ما تجمع لدينا من معلومات عن مفهوم "المَعَالم"، والذي يربك الفرضيات الرسمية والبيئية لفنون الأرض الأولى، من خلال إثارة الأسئلة التالية: لصالح من توضع المعالم، ولأي غايات؟ ما هي المعالم التي تستحق أن نحافظ عليها.

صيغت هذه الأسئلة استجابة لما نسميه بـ "الجغرافية الانتقالية" لجزيرة فييك، في بورتوريكو. في عام ٢٠٠٣، نجحت حملة عصيان مدني طويلة المدى في أن تجبر البحرية الأمريكية على مغادرة النصف الغربي من الجزيرة، والتي كانت تستخدمها طيلة الستين سنة الماضية أرضا لاختبار مختلف أنواع الذخائر والعتاد الحربي. ولم يكن هذا سوى انتصار جزئي للناشطين المهتمين - فقد نقلت ملكية الأرض التي شوّهتها القنابل من الإدارة العسكرية إلى وزارة الداخلية، وأُعيد تصنيفها كمحمية للحياة البرية، بما يعني ظاهريا استعادة النظام البيئي الساحلي للجزيرة وحمايتها من النشاط البشري "المدمّر". ولكن السلطات البيئية التي ادعت أنها ستعيد للأرض عافيتها، قامت بفرض شكل آخر من العنف اختصت به، إنه العنف المتمثل في إخماد مطالب سكان الجزيرة بتنظيف الأرض بالكامل من التلوّث وإعادتها إلى إدارة البلدية حيث يمكن أن تتم عملية إعادة الصيانة بناء على نقاش وتداول ديموقراطي، بدلاً من أن تفرض الإملاءات من فوق.

إعادة صوت، مشروع لإعادة هندسة الوسائط، لا يتعامل مع المسطحات الأرضية في فييك وحسب، بل مع الفضاءات الصوتية فيها، والتي ما زالت تحمل بالنسبة لسكان الجزيرة ذكرى العنف الصوتي الناجم عن انفجار القنابل. وفي هذه الحالة، نحن نتتبع ناشطاً في إطار العصيان المدني اسمه هومار، وهو يركض فيما يشبه "جولة المنتصر" حول الجزيرة التي تخلصت من وجهها العسكري، على دراجة نارية زودت ببوق بدلا من كاتم الصوت. هكذا، تم تعديل الغاية الأصلية من وسيلة تخفيض الضجيج بحيث تصبح آلة معاكسة الهدف تنتج أصواتا ليس حسب نوتة معدة مسبقا بل بناء على مطبات الطريق والتسارع المتقطع لمحرّك الدراجة. بهذا يقوم هومار بإعادة معالجة مناطق في الجزيرة، كانت معرّضة مسبقاً لانفجارات تصم الأذن. باستخدام نبرة نداء البوق - التي تذكّرنا بصفارة سيارة الإسعاف، وبعمل لوغي راسولو Intonarumori المستقبلي وحتى الجاز التجريبي - فيصبح متناقضا مع التقليد الموسيقي الذي قد نتوقع منه أن يكون وسيلة الاحتفاء بنصر شعبي وحب للأرض، ألا وهو النشيد الوطني.

يستكشف عنوان العمل في اشتقاقات نظام الكلمة ليقوضها من الداخل: النشيد الوطني، كلمة أصلها من الكلمة الإغريقية antiphonos ("رجع الصوت"). ويشكل هذا التعريف البدائي تنافراً في جنس يرتبط بـ "صوت الناس" المتناغم، وهو شكل يرتبط ارتباطاً طبيعياً بالانتماء المشترك للمكان. ولكن في فييك، يبقى مستقبل الأرض التي استعيدت مشكوكاً فيه، ومعزولاً بشكل كبير عن المطالبات الديموقراطية. رجع الصوت يحتفل بانتصار محفوف بالمخاطر، ويدعو إلى يقظة وترقب غير مسبوقين.

Returning a Sound, 2004, DVD, 5:42 min

04650-M
PUERTO RICO

LARA ALMARCEGUI

Demolitions, Wastelands, Empty Lots

I want to question urban planning through the study of places that escape a fixed definition of a city or of architecture: empty lots, wastelands, buildings before, during and after their demolition; places which, due to forgetfulness or lack of interest, escape a defined design and are open to all kinds of possibilities.

In order to present those places I make projects which involve physical actions with a very direct message about engagement with the site: such as the action of spending three weeks restoring a marvellous market that was scheduled to be demolished; or digging in an empty lot for 20 days in order to find out more about the place. Other projects consist of a long research that seems to never end and does not sound very useful: e.g to calculate the weight of all the buildings of the city of Sao Paulo; or when I spent years trying to integrate into a community of allotment gardeners in Rotterdam, in order to show an interest in self-constructed spaces. I rented a vegetable garden, cultivated it, built a shed and did everything the other gardeners did.

Often it is good to invite the public to come to the "place of interest" so that they have a real experience of the site by themselves. I like to identify the empty lots of a city and publish guides about them, pointing out the interesting aspects of each wasteland, describing them carefully as places different from the rest of the city as, for example, in *Wastelands Map Amsterdam: Guide to the Empty Sites of Amsterdam*. Other projects consisted in the simple action of opening the previously closed gate of an empty lot so that the public can visit it, in this way completely changing the use of the land. In my most recent projects, I am trying to convince the owners of different lots of land terrains to keep them empty and unbuilt upon. I made sure that a wasteland in Rotterdam harbour and another one in Genk stayed undeveloped for 10-15 years. This project is an experiment that consists of leaving a place undefined so that everything happens by chance, not corresponding to a predetermined plan. Therefore, nature develops its own way and interrelates with the spontaneous use given to the land and with other external factors like wind, rain, sun and flora. Wastelands are important as places of possibility, because one can only feel free in this type of land, forgotten by the town planners. I imagine that, in few years time, *those wastelands protected by the project will be the only empty land remaining*, once the surrounding land is built upon.

I would like to see as many empty lots as possible open and preserved for as long as possible.

لارا المرسيغي

الهدم، الأرض اليباب، الأرض الفارغة

أود أن أطرح أسئلة بشأن التخطيط الحضري من خلال دراسة الأماكن التي تنجو من تعريف ثابت للمدينة، أو الهندسة المعمارية: أراض فارغة، أراض يباب، المباني، قبل وخلال وبعد إزالتها، والأماكن التي، بسبب النسيان أو نقص الاهتمام، تنجو من تصميم معرّف، وتنفتح على جميع الاحتمالات.

وبهدف عرض تلك الأماكن، أقوم بتنفيذ مشاريع وأعمال تشتمل على إجراءات ملموسة ذات رسالة مباشرة جداً، حول الانخراط في المكان: مثل تمضية ثلاثة أسابيع في ترميم سوق رائع، كان قد وضع على قائمة الهدم، أو الحفر في قطعة أرض فارغة لعشرين يوماً، بهدف معرفة المزيد عن المكان واكتشاف تفاصيله.

وثمة مشاريع أخرى، تتكون من بحث طويل يبدو وكأنه لا نهائي، وغير ذو فائدة، مثلاً: حساب وزن كافة مباني مدينة ساوباولو، أو عندما أمضيت سنوات في محاولة للاندماج في مجموعة من قيّمي حدائق التخصيص في روتردام، بهدف إظهار الاهتمام في المساحات ذاتية البناء. قمت باستئجار حديقة خضروات، زرعتها وبنيت كوخاً، كما قمت بكل شيء كان قيّموا الحدائق الآخرون يقومون به.

في الغالب، يكون من المستحسن دعوة العامة للحضور إلى "المكان الملفت" بحيث يعيشون تجربة الموقع بأنفسهم. أود تحديد الأراضي الفارغة في مدينة ما، ونشر أدلّة خاصة بها، تبيّن النواحي الملفتة لكل أرض يباب، ووصفها وصفاً متأنيّاً، كونها أماكن تختلف عن باقي أجزاء المدينة، كما في: خريطة الأراضي اليباب في أمستردام: دليل إلى المواقع الفارغة في أمستردام. لقد تكوّنت مشاريع أخرى بإجراء بسيط، هو فتح البوابة التي بقيت مغلقة في الماضي، بحيث يمكن للعامة أن تزور الأرض الفارغة، مما يؤدي إلى تغيير تام في استعمال الأرض. وفي آخر مشروع أنجزته، أعمل على إقناع مالكي مختلف الأراضي بالابقاء على أراضيهم دون بنيان. وحرصت على إبقاء إحدى الأراضي اليباب في ميناء روتردام، وأخرى في جنك، بعيدتين عن التطوير لمدة ١٠-١٥ سنة. هذا المشروع، يمثل تجربة تنطوي على ترك مكان ما دون تعريف أو هوية، بحيث يحدث كل شيء فيه بمحض الصدفة، بعيداً عن تلبية متطلبات خطة موضوعة مسبقا. بهذا، تعمل الطبيعة على بلورة طريقتها الخاصة، وترتبط بالاستعمال التلقائي المعطى للأرض، كما ترتبط بالعوامل الخارجية الأخرى، مثل الريح، والمطر، والشمس، والنباتات. الأراضي اليباب مهمة كونها مساحة للاحتمالات. فالمرء لا يشعر بحريته إلا في هذه الأراضي التي غابت عن أعين مخططي المدن. أعتقد أنه خلال بضع سنوات، ستكون هذه الأراضي اليباب التي يحميها المشروع، هي الأرض الفارغة الوحيدة، حالما يتم إنشاء الأبنية على الأرض المحيطة بها.

أحب أن تبقى الأراضي الفارغة، بأكبر كم ممكن، متاحة ومحفوظة لأطول فترة ممكنة.

A Wasteland in Rotterdam Harbor, Rotterdam 2003-2018

WAGENBORG
www.contship.com
P&O

EL ANATSUI

The media I explore have certain things in common. They are sourced from my immediate environment. They have been put to intense human use. They are thought to have lost value. They are ignored, discarded or thrown away. They all have something to do with food consumption.

To me, their provenance imbues or charges them with history and content, which I seek to explore in order to highlight certain conditions of mankind's existence, as well as his relationship with himself and the environment. I therefore try to bring these objects back, to present them again in ways which seem to make them confront their former lives and the lives of those who have used them. Among these media, I count the old wooden mortars I worked with in the 1980s, broken pots, and old metal graters.

My engagement with the mortars sought to raise these objects to the vertical – in real use they are laid horizontally and violently rammed into – in an attempt metaphorically to empower them to stand up in order to see and be seen.

My broken pots series explored the idea of the inevitability of death, breaking, delapidation – not as ends in themselves but as conditions for renewal, new birth, just as rotting seeds sprout new plants .

Old rusty metal graters which I configured into expansive walls were constructs which, rather than hide, sequester or erase, revealed presences because of the intense curiosity they generated: when walls obstruct views the other senses (including imagination) tend to probe deeper.

The work for this biennial can be looked at from two perspectives: the medium and the process. Liquor bottle-tops to me represent the collective soul of the bottles of schnapps, rum, gin etc., which were brought to my continent several centuries ago, ostensibly by traders to establish a bridge between peoples, and their links with the infamous transatlantic triangular trade and subsequent impoverishment of parts of the earth. The process, consisting of manually and individually ripping, rolling, crumpling, twisting, folding, bending and piercing these tops and stitching them into a large continuous sheet, not only attempts to valorise an evolutionary pace of doing things but also references the commonalisation and cheap rating of labour – human labour, over the greater part of the planet.

Wrinkle Of The Earth could be saying several things, or is probably just a scroll essaying themes of permeation, binding, yoking, opulence, bleakness: the textures, patterns and complexions of the globe, resulting from age-long human actions and interactions.

إل أناتسوي

تشترك الوسائط التي استكشفها ببعض الميزات: فمصدرها بيئتي المباشرة، ويستخدمها البشر بشكل مكثّف، كما يعتقدون أنّها فقدت قيمتها. إنّها مهملة أو متروكة أو تمّ التخلص منها، وكلها لها علاقة بالطعام، بالاستهلاك.

ما اهدف إلى استكشافه هو أصلها، أو تشبعاتها، أو ما نحمّلها من تاريخ، ومضمونها، لأسلّط الضوء على شروط معيّنة للوجود الإنساني وعلاقة الإنسان مع ذاته وبيئته. أحاول بالتالي استعادة هذه الأشياء لإعادة تقديمها بطرق تبدو وكأنّها تضع هذه الأشياء بمواجهة مع حياتها السابقة وحياة أولئك الذين استعملوها. أعدّ من ضمن هذه الوسائط، مدقّات هاون خشبيّة قديمة استعملتها في الثمانينيات وأواني مكسّرة ومبشرة حديديّة عتيقة.

حاولت من خلال تعهدي لمدقّات الهاون أن أرفعها بشكل عموديّ (في الإستعمال الفعليّ توضع أفقيّا ويتمّ دقها بعنف)، في محاولة لأمنحها القوّة المجازية لتقف فتَرى وتُشاهَد.

أما سلسلة الأوانيّ المكسّرة فتستكشف فكرة حتميّة الموت، التكسّر، والتلف، ليس كنهاية بحد ذاتها، وإنّما كشروط من أجل التجدد وولادة جديدة، تماما كما تنبثق عن البذور العفنة نباتات جديدة.

أما المَباشِر (جمع مبشرة) الحديديّة الصدئة، فقد شكلت منها حيطانا واسعة لتصبح هياكل وبنى، وبدلا من أن تُخفي أو تحتلّ أو تمحو، تكشف عن حضور نتيجة للفضول الذي تُثيره: فعندما تُعيق الحيطان الرؤية تميل الحواس الأخرى (ومن ضمنها الخيال) إلى التعمّق في الإستكشاف.

يمكن رؤية العمل المعد لهذا البينالي من خلال منظارين: الوسيط والعمليّة. تمثّل أغطية زجاجات كحوليّة بالنسبة لي الروح الجماعية لزجاجات الشنابس والرّم والجن وغيرها، والتي أتى بها التجار إلى قارّتي قبل قرون عدّة، زاعمين أنّها تهدف لتجسير العلاقات بين الشعوب، والتي ترتبط بالتجارة المشينة ثلاثية الأوجه عبر الأطلسي، والفقر الذي لحق بأجزاء من الأرض تبعا لها.

لا تهدف العمليّة التي تتألّف من تمزيق ولف وتجعيد ولوي وطوي وثني وثقب هذه الأغطية يدويا، كل على حدى، ومن ثم خياطتها على شكل ملاءة متصلة كبيرة، إلى إعطاء قيمة للسرعة ثوريّة في إنجاز الأمور فحسب، بل تشير كذلك إلى الإبتذال والتسعير الرخيص للعمل – العمل الإنساني – في معظم أنحاء الكوكب.

تجعيدة كوكب الأرض يمكن أن تقول أشياء عدّة، أو ربما هي مجرّد لفيفة تطرح موضوعات مثل المسامية، التلزيم، وضع النير، الوفرة، اليأس: كلها نسيج وأنماط وشكل لوجه الأرض ناتجة عن أفعال وتفاعلات الإنسان عبر الزمن.

Hovor 2, 2004, 505 x 612 cm, aluminum and copper wire, courtesy of the artist

ROY ARDEN

Around 1990, I began to photograph my local surroundings. I was interested in how the forces of history, the economy and modernity, revealed themselves through the surface of the quotidian. At the time, I had a friend who had become a photojournalist and was documenting violent conflicts in Asia. I reasoned that one could also stay home in Vancouver and picture the slow war of the everyday economy. I was not interested in the rhetoric of the documentary, and decided instead to make Realist tableaux. I am as inspired by painting and cinema as much as by photography and see my work in a dialogue with other depictions and their traditions. My videos are non-narrative and I think of them as "breathing tableaux". After a time it became clear that the old problems of genre, and of the picturesque and the rustic, were central to my work. Today these problems seem no more resolved, nor less relevant.

روي أردن

حوالي العام ١٩٩٠، بدأت بالتقاط صور فوتوغرافية للمواقع المحلية المحيطة. وكنت مهتماً بتجليات قوى التاريخ والاقتصاد والحداثة، على سطح الحدث اليومي. في ذلك الحين، كان لي صديق أصبح مصوراً صحفياً، وكان يوثّق بالصورة الصراعات العنيفة الدائرة في آسيا. وقد قدرت أنه بإمكان الواحد منا أن يبقى في فانكوفر ويصور الحرب البطيئة للاقتصاد اليومي. لم أكن مهتماً بالبلاغة الوثائقية، وقررت أن أصنع لوحة واقعية بدلاً منها. فأنا أستلهم الرسم والسينما كما أستلهم التصوير الفوتوغرافي، وأرى عملي في حوار مع أشكال التجسيد الأخرى وتقاليدها. أفلام الفيديو التي أنتجها ليست سردية، فأنا أفكر فيها كما لو كانت "لوحات تتنفس". وبعد حين، اتضح لي أن المشاكل القديمة المتعلقة بنوع العمل الفني، وخصائصه الجمالية، كانت هي المحور الذي ترتكز عليه أعمالي. أما اليوم، فإن هذه المشاكل لا تبدو أقرب إلى الحل، ولكنها أيضا لم تفقد مغزاها.

D'Elegance #1, 2000, gelatin silver print, 101 x 127 cm, courtesy Monte Clark Gallery, Vancouver & Toronto

VLADIMIR ARKHIPOV

In the Russian language the word for "creative work" ("tvorchestvo") shares a root with the word for "Creator" ("Tvorets"). The word for "art" ("iskusstvo") shares a root with the word for "Tempter" ("Iskusitel"). Formerly, when artists still believed in God, they created. Today, when most artists do not believe in anything, they make art. There is no creation left in art. What is an honest artist to do? I have found a partial answer to that question. Since I require a viewer and I am doomed to self-conscious aesthetic reflection, I cannot be absolutely honest and sincere. But I know that every day hundreds of millions of people discover their connection with God in some way when they create. The act of creation has no need of evaluation and argumentation. It is self-sufficient. The visually most interesting traces left by creation are those that have not been subject to conscious aesthetic assessment by their creators. All that is required is to find them and present them in a skillful manner. The right of choice is mine. I spent a long time searching for and selecting a modern folk phenomenon (which as yet has no name) as an example: millions of people throughout the world create unique everyday items for themselves. I interview them, take photographs, show their things in exhibitions... In this way, I combine creative work that is someone else's (but is not anonymous) with my art...

فلاديمير أرخيبوف

تتشارك الكلمة "تفوركيستفو" التي تعني "العمل الإبداعي" في اللغة الروسيّة جذرها مع كلمة "خالق" ("تفوريتس"). الكلمة لـ "فن" ("إسكستفو") تتشارك جذرها مع الكلمة لـ "المُغوي" ("إسكُسيتل"). في السابق، حين كان الفنانون ما يزالون يؤمنون بالله، كانوا يَخلقون/يبدعون الأعمال المنية. اليوم، في الوقت الذي لا يؤمَن معظم الفنانين بأيّ شئ، فهم يصنعون الفن. لم يعد هناك خَلْق/إبداع في الفن. ماذا يمكن لفنان صادق أن يفعل؟ وجدت حلاًّ جزئيّا لهذا السؤال. بما أنّي أحتاج إلى مشاهد، وأنا نفسي محكوم بالتأمّل الجمالي الواعي بالذات، لا يمكنني أن أكون صادقا ومخلصا بالمطلق، ولكنّني أعرف أن مئات الملايين من الناس يكتشفون يوميا علاقتهم مع الله بشكل أو بآخر حين يخلقون/يبدعون شيئا ما. ليس لفعل الخلق/الإبداع حاجة للتقييم والنقاش. إنّه مكتف ذاتيّا. إن أهم الآثار البصريّة لعملية الخلق/التكوين هي تلك التي لم تتعرض للتقييم الجمالي الواعي من قِبل من كَوَّنها. كل ما هو مطلوب هو العثور عليها وتقديمَها بمهارة. أنا أمتلك حقّ الإختيار. قضيت وقتا طويلا في البحث عن، واختيار ظاهرة فولكلوريّة حديثة (لم أجد لها إسم حتّى اللحظة)، لأستخدمها كمثال: يخلق/يبدع ملايين الناس في أنحاء العالم أشياء يومية فريدة لأنفسهم. أقوم بإجراء مقابلة معهم، آخذ صورا وأعرض أشياءَهم في معارض. بهذه الطريقة، أدمج العمل الإبداعيّ الذي قام به شخص آخر (وهو معروف) بفنّي أنا...

Naming Forms / UAE, 2007, installation

Name: Mohammad Naeem
Title of object: Air fan
Place of production: Sharjah
Date of production: 2006

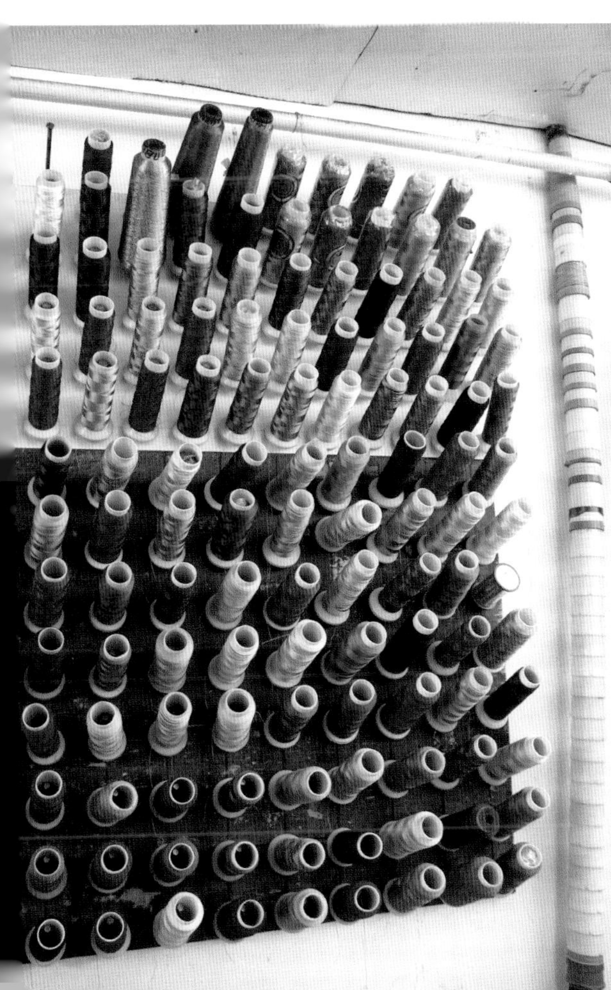

Name: Rashid Wahab Al Deen
Title of object: Thread stand
Place of production: Sharjah
Date of production: 2001

MIREILLE ASTORE

ميريي استور

Efface: Death Becomes Her is a body of work that examines eternal grief as a continuum between a desired state and the imminent and natural occurrence of death. It is an attempt to recognise the symbiotic links that bind the body to its pervasive representation and the elegiac quality of the natural environment. The paradoxical states of fantasy and evasion on the one hand and fetishistic constructions of instruments of destruction on the other seem to be a characteristic of modernity. Postcolonial cities and their latent myth of progress together with the incipient phantasm of wealth distribution in the era of emerging globalisation have culminated in the production of highly visualised but nevertheless exceedingly affective bodies. Deleuze and Guattari remark, "We know nothing about a body until we know what it can do, in other words, what its affects are, how they can or cannot enter into composition with other affects, with the affects of another body, either to destroy that body or to be destroyed by it, either to exchange actions and passions with it or to join with it in composing a more powerful body."[1]

As such, I believe destruction of the very crucible of our existence – that is the natural environment – is no longer in the domain of visuality and perception alone. However, very little is articulated on the role of the "destroyer within" or to put it as Deleuze and Guattari describe it: the role of the "affected body". The body as a site where nature and destroyer reside in the very same space and time is a difficult but nonetheless challenging concept to envisage and detangle. For example, through modernity, individuals are offered very little space for critiquing the construction of their sense of self in relation to existing categorisations of bodily appearance. This sociability of the body, which invariably signals communicability, is constructed within environments that individuals are born into, and that constrain their ability simply to "celebrate natural embodiments". The urban experience in particular evokes dialectical relationships such as between seclusion and sociability; ecstasy and horror; synthetic and natural. Each relationship, contaminated at its onset by representation, is a nuanced variation of artifice, mirage or nightmare. Further, the intensity of the illusive quality of urban living is proportional to the scale and density of the metropolitan experience and collective living.[2]

Efface: Death Becomes Her is an attempt to pose tangible questions such as "What do the living want to know? Is it what the dead would want to tell them?"[3] Finally, just as the sublime can be experienced as moral purity, it cannot be known without the necessary prerequisite of a particularly painful exigency.

تواري: الموت يليق بها، هو عمل فني يفحص الحزن الأبدي كاستمرارية، ما بين حالة مرغوب فيها وواقعة طبيعية ومحتومة هي الموت. إنها محاولة للاعتراف بالصلات الحيوية المتبادلة، التي تربط الجسد بكنايته والسمة الرثائية للبيئة الطبيعية. الحالات المتناقضة للخيال والتملص من جهة، والبنى الوثنية الرمزية (fetishistic) لأدوات التدمير من جهة أخرى، تبدو وكأنها سمة الحداثة. المدن ما بعد الكولونيالية، وخرافة التقدم مضافا إليها الوهم الأولي لمرحلة توزيع الثروات للعولمة الناشئة، توجت بإنتاج أجساد على درجة عالية من الطبيعة البصرية، ولكنها فعالة أيضا بشكل كبير. يعلق ديلوز وغوتاري بالقول، "نحن لا نعرف شيئا عن جسد ما حتى نعرف ما يستطيع القيام به، بكلمات أخرى، ما هو تأثيره، كيف يمكن له، أو لا يمكن له، أن يدخل في تكوين مع مؤثرات أخرى، مع مؤثرات جسد آخر، إما لتدمير ذلك الجسد أو يكون مصيره الدمار، إما لتبادل الأفعال والانفعالات معه، أو للالتحام به لتكوين جسد أقوى."[1]

بالتالي، أعتقد بأن تدمير بوتقة وجودنا – أي البيئة الطبيعية – لم يعد مساحة الإدراك والرؤية فقط. ولكن لا يتم التعبير كثيرا عن دور "المدمر من الداخل" أو كما يصفه ديلوز وغوتاري: دور "الجسد المتأثر". الجسد، كموقع تسكن فيه الطبيعة والمدمر في نفس المساحة والوقت، هو مفهوم صعب ويشكل تحديا في الوقت نفسه لتصوره وتفكيكه. على سبيل المثال، لا يتاح للأفراد من خلال الحداثة، مساحة كبيرة لانتقاد بنية إحساسهم بأنفسهم، بارتباطها مع التصنيفات الموجودة لشكل الجسد. هذه الصفة الاجتماعية للجسد، والتي تشير إلى القدرة على الاتصال، يتم بناؤها داخل البيئات التي يولد فيها الأفراد، والتي تقلص بكل بساطة، قدرتهم على "الاحتفاء بتجلياتهم الطبيعية". إن تجربة حياة المدينة تستثير بشكل خاص، العلاقات الديالكتيكية بين العزلة والاجتماعية، بين النشوة والرعب، بين الطبيعي والاصطناعي. كل علاقة ملوثة منذ البداية بعملية كناية، هي تنويع دقيق للتكلف، هي سراب أو كابوس. إضافة إلى ذلك، فإن كثافة الصفة الوهمية للحياة المدنية تتناسب، مع مدى وكثافة الخبرة المتروبولية والحياة الجماعية.[2]

تواري: الموت يليق بها، هي محاولة لطرح أسئلة ملموسة مثل "ما الذي يريد الأحياء أن يعرفوه؟ هل هو ما يرغب الأموات أن يقولوه لهم"؟[3] وأخيرا، فكما أن الجلال يمكن أن نختبره على أنه نقاء أخلاقي، لا يمكن أن نعرفه دون أن نعرف حالة طارئة مؤلمة بشكل خاص.

[1] Deleuze, Gilles and Felix Guattari. *A Thousand Plateaus: Capitalism and Schizophrenia* (trans.Brian Massumi), Minneapolis: University of Minnesota Press (1987): 257

[2] Rajeev Shridhar Patke, "Benjamin's Arcades Project and the Postcolonial City", *Diacritics*, 30 (4) (Winter 2000): 10

[3] Toufic,. Jalal *Over-Sensitivity*. Los Angeles: Sun and Moon Press (1996): 171

Efface: Death Becomes Her, 2007, video (5 min.), courtesy of the artist

LARA BALADI

Lara Baladi works the reproducible image in various media and formats. Her installations, videos and collages, which often stage culturally hybrid scenes, are dense with mythology and visual theory. She addresses memory, both collective and personal, in a codified and multicultural language articulated in a world of shifting boundaries. Symbolic appropriations, legible as representations of primeval dreams, contribute to the construction of her numerous visual landscapes.

The works exhibited in the 8th Sharjah Biennial are all enquiries into the notion of Paradise. They consist of two photomontages mirroring each other; *Perfumes & Bazaar, The Garden of Allah* and *Justice for the Mother* (working title); and her latest installation, *Roba Vecchia, The Wheel of Fortune* (Ragman).

The two photomontages are *trompe l'oeils* of walls in a living-room covered with wallpaper showing on one side a teeming garden of earthly delights and on the other a jungle. They are filled with iconography inspired by representations of the Chateau de Versailles, waterfall lightboxes - direct reference to a "made-in-China" aesthetic - and photomontage posters of idealised landscapes. From out of these landscapes - populated by a variety of objects and people, imagery of the jungle, the wilderness, war and sexuality - Baladi's father rides his motorbike: away from his youth, his roots and the politics of the Middle East, towards the viewer, but also towards the commanding photograph of the artist's mother, here representing the original paradise, the womb.

Roba Vecchia, The Wheel of Fortune, is a life-sized kaleidoscope, which the viewer can enter and become a part of. The installation presents viewers with fragments of the artist's work, recomposed into a shifting array of kaleidoscopic images. The piece evokes the accumulation and reworking of leftovers of the past in a continuous rewriting of history. The artist worked with a computer programmer to create software that organises the images in a pattern that mutates randomly so that the projected photographic images combine in an infinite and non-repetitive way. This is framed by the work's illusory, yet historically and culturally resonant sacred geometry, resembling stained glass windows, mandalas, arabesques, the microcosm of cellular life or the infinite night sky.

In the end, all three works are an invitation to the viewer to enter a transitional space and become the centre between opposite yet complementary poles and reconnect to his or her original "nature".

لارا بلدي

تتعامل لارا بلدي مع الصورة المعرضة لإعادة الإنتاج، بوسائط وأشكال مختلفة. تتطرق لارا في التراكيب الفنية وأفلام الفيديو والكولاج التي تنتجها، والتي عادة ما تعرض مشاهد مهجنة ثقافياً، تتكثف فيها الميثولوجيا والنظرية البصرية، إلى الذاكرة الجماعية والفردية، بطريقة مشفرة وبلغة متعددة الثقافات، يتم التعبير عنها في عالم متغير الحدود. عملية استيلاء رمزية، تقرأ ككناية لأحلام أولية، تساهم في بناء مساحاتها الطبيعية البصرية المتعددة.

أعمالها المعروضة في بينالي الشارقة الثامن، عبارة عن تساؤلات حول مفهوم الجنة، وتتكون من عملين عبارة عن مونتاج صور، يعكسان بعضهما البعض: "عطور وبازار، حديقة الله" و"حجة الأقوى" (عنوان مبدئي)، وعملها التركيبي الأخير، "روبا فاكيا، دولاب الحظ" (راغمان).

هذان العملان من المونتاج الصوري، هما انعكاس لحيطان غرفة معيشة مغطاة بورق حائط، يظهر من ناحية حديقة تحفل بمباهج الحياة الدنيا، ومن جهة أخرى غابة. يمتلئ العملان برموز مستوحاة من كنايات لقصر فرساي، علب إضاءة فيها شلالات - إشارة مباشرة إلى الجمالية المصنوعة في الصين - ومونتاج صور لملصقات فيها مشاهد طبيعية مصورة في غاية الكمال. من بين هذه المناظر الطبيعية - التي تملؤها أشياء وأشخاص ومشاهد من الغابة، البراري، الحرب، والجنسوية - نرى والد الفنانة (بلدي) يركب الدراجة النارية، مبتعداً عن شبابه وجذوره، والسياسة الشرق أوسطية، باتجاه المشاهد، ولكن أيضاً، باتجاه صورة مهيبة لوالدة الفنانة - التي تمثل هنا الجنة الأصلية، رحم الأم.

"روبا فيكيا، دولاب الحظ" هو (كلاديو سكوب) بحجم الحياة، يمكن للمشاهد أن يدخله ويصبح جزءاً منه. يقدم هذا العمل التركيبي للمشاهدين قطعا متناثرة من أعمال الفنانة، تم إعادة تشكيلها في كوكبة متحولة من المشاهد. يستحضر العمل تراكم وإعادة تشكيل بقايا الماضي، في عملية مستمرة من إعادة كتابة التاريخ. عملت الفنانة مع مبرمج كمبيوتر لإعداد برنامج ينظم الصور بنمط يتبدل ويتحول بشكل عشوائي، بحيث تجتمع الصور الفوتوغرافية بأشكال لا نهائية وغير مكررة. إطار العمل هو الهندسة المقدسة المخادعة، ولكنها في الوقت نفسه ذات صدى تاريخي وثقافي، بحيث تشبه نوافذ الزجاج الملون، (ماندالا)، أرابيسك، العالم الصغير لحياة الخلايا، أو سماء الليل اللانهائية.

في النهاية، فإن الأعمال الثلاثة هي دعوة للمتفرج ليدخل في مساحة انتقالية ويصبح المركز ما بين أقطاب متضادة، ولكن متكاملة، وأن يعيد التواصل مع "طبيعته/ها" الأصلية.

Justice for the Mother, 2007, photographic montage, 560 x 248 cm, printing material variable, courtesy of the artist

NOOR AL-BASTAKI

Steps and Paths... Youth and Future

Confident steps of youth, armed with knowledge and will, filled with determination and life, on a road fraught with difficulties, confusion and fear.

Steps forward or jumps high to surpass all obstacles standing in the road to the future...

Holding the torch of knowledge and dreams and climbing the rough mountains, armed with what he owns of oil wealth, to reach the peak, and plant the torch to lighten the paths of others...

So will this oil wealth determine the future and fate of youth? Or will youth's determination and ambition do that? Or Both?

نور البستكي

خطوات وخطوط، شباب ومستقبل

خطوات واثقة لشباب مسلحين بالعلم والإرادة وممتلئين بالعزيمة والحياة في طريق محفوف بالصعاب والحيرة والتردد والخوف.

خطوات إلى الأمام أو قفزات إلى الأعلى يتخطون بها كل العوائق في خطوط دربهم إلى المستقبل، حاملين شعلة التحدي والحلم، صاعدين الجبال الوعرة، متسلحين بما يمتلكون من ثروة نفطية داعمين بها خطواتهم لتحقيق أحلامهم.

فهل النفط هو ما يحدد مستقبل ومصير الشباب؟ أم إصرارهم وطموحهم؟ أم الاثنان معا؟

Steps and Paths, 2005, photography & video, variable, courtesy of the artist

TAYSIR BATNIJI

The documentaries of Taysir Batniji differ from sensationalised standard documentaries. Similar to Haikus, they are outstanding human aphorisms. In a simple and elliptical manner, the Gaza-born artist shields the Palestinian reality from the potent distorting media limelight. The dense political and social life of the country is not underrated; its human substance, subtly expressed, remains diffused. The artist acts mainly as a witness, hence his subtly subjective perceptions. Like an optic lens, he resists the fragmented report, at the same time remaining sensitive to the visions of the international media that focus on the Middle East without managing to objectively represent it.

In *Transit* at the border between Egypt and Palestine, the artist suffers endless days of waiting: chunks of time, *time freezes*, like a still photograph. As in *La Jete* of Chris Marker, photography and film overlap. A sequence of movements, right from the moment when the customs officer calls the names and throws the passports in the air, Batniji's camera starts rolling. The artist reproduces this sudden trajectory of passports in slow motion in an attempt to dilute its eloquent significance.

The work of Batniji presents a degree of poeticism, punctuated by temporal jolts. These accelerations also reflect a political time, unstable or syncopated. In *Me 2* he abruptly stops the news on TV and shifts the camera onto himself as he sings “I will survive”. These realities are either diluted beyond their normal time frame, or compressed to become of extreme urgency. In another performance the artist moves a mound of sand, a handful at a time, till no more sand remains, as in the myth of Sisyphus, until his finale: an impasse revisited endlessly in vain. Diffused or concentrated, this is the very reality of Palestinians held hostage, a reality that Batniji condemns. This work also symbolises this Catch 22 that splits the artist between Europe and Palestine. As for his constant “re-doing, undoing,”, “building, demolishing”, they are actions inherent in his creation. In Palestine, a series of imperceptible moments in time can suddenly be caught up in a bottleneck that makes the present moment both critical and highly dangerous. Only these desperate moments alert the media. For Batniji these jolts and plunges are subtle components of the long-standing process of normalisation fed with the patience of a lifetime. It is not only the space that is conditioned and conditional in Palestine, but also time. It is this fragmented absurdity of existence that the Palestinians see, “like an eclipse”, being gravely altered.

تيسير البطنيجي

تختلف الأفلام الوثائقية لتيسير بطنيجي عن تلك التي تعتمد الإثارة. فهي كما قصيدة الهايكو اليابانية، حِكَم إنسانية متميزة، بأسلوب بسيط وموجز. يعمد الفَنان، المولود في غزة، إلى حماية الواقع الفلسطيني من التشويه الذي يلحقه به الإعلام والأضواء. وهو بذلك لا يقلل من شأن الحياة السياسية والاجتماعية المتوترة في ذلك البلد. وتظل المادة البشرية التي يصورها بشكل مرهف، مستفيضة. يلعب الفنان دور الشاهد، فنشعر بإدراكه الذاتي المرهف. فهو يرفض التقرير المجتزأ، على النحو الذي تفعله عدسة الكاميرا، وفي نفس الوقت يحافظ على حساسيته لرؤى الصحافة العالمية التي تركز على الشرق الأوسط دون أن تنجح في التعبير عنه موضوعيا. "مفكرة غزة" تحبذ يوما عاديا "دون إثارة" في سوق غزة. باهتمامه الطبيعي، لا يغيّب بطنيجي الأخطار الكامنة، فهو يصور الأطفال العائدين من المدرسة جنبا إلى جنب مع الجزار الذي يفرم اللحم، والقوارب التي تمخر البحر ذهابا وإيابا، وأصوات باعة الخضار. يذكرنا هذا الإيقاع المؤثر بتردداته السلمية تارة، والدراماتيكية تارة أخرى، بسيف ديمقليس.

في "ترانزيت"، على الحدود الفاصلة بين مصر وفلسطين، يعاني الفنان أياما طويلة من الإنتظار الطويل. في كتل زمنية، يتجمد الزمن كصورة فوتوغرافية ساكنة. وكما في عمل "لا جيت" لكريس ماركر، يتقاطع التصوير الفوتوغرافي مع الفيلم. سلسلة متتابعة من الحركات، ابتداء من اللحظة التي ينادي فيها موظف الجمارك على الأسماء قاذفا بجوازات السفر إلى الهواء، تبدأ كاميرا البطنيجي بالدوران. يعيد الفنان إنتاج عملية انطلاق جوازات السفر في الهواء بحركة بطيئة، في محاولة منه لإطالة دلالتها البلاغية.

تتضمن أعمال البطنيجي قدرا من الشاعرية تستوقفها هزة وقتية تعكس تلك الحالة المتسارعة، زمنا سياسيا مضطربا متوالي الهبوط والارتفاع. في "أنا-٢"، يقوم فجأة بإقفال الأخبار على التلفاز ويدير الكاميرا نحوه ويأخذ بالغناء: "سوف أعيش I will survive". يمتد الواقع إلى ما بعد إطاره الزمني الطبيعي، أو ينضغط على نحو يتحول فيه إلى ضرورة حرجة. في عرض آخر، يقوم الفنان بنقل الرمل من تلة رمال حفنة إثر حفنة. تلك هي أسطورة سيزيف تتكرر. والمأزق ذاته يتكرر عبثا إلى ما لا نهاية. الاستسلام أو الإستنفار؟ ذلك هو واقع الفلسطينيين الواقعين في الأسر. وهو واقع يدينه البطنيجي الذي ترمز أعماله أيضا إلى العقدة-المطب الذي يقسم الفنان بين أوروبا وفلسطين. أما مواظبته على "العمل، التفكيك"، "البناء، الهدم"، فهي كلها أنشطة كامنة في تكويناته الفنية. ففي فلسطين، هناك سلسلة غير مكتنهة من الزمن، تقود إلى الإنحباس في عنق الزجاجة على نحو يهدد بالانفجار. هذه اللحظات اليائسة هي التي توقظ الإعلام فقط. أما في رأي البطنيجي، فإن تلك الهزات والمغامرات هي مكونات دقيقة لعملية التطبيع طويلة الأمد، يغذيها صبر يطول. ليس الفضاء هو الوحيد الذي يتكيف مع ويشترط الظروف في فلسطين، بل الزمان أيضا. وما يراه الفلسطينيون ليس إلا وجودا مبعثرا على نحو عبثي، و"هو أشبه ما يكون بكسوف" تم تعديله على نحو خطير.

Untitled, 2002, video, 2 min. Courtesy of the artist

MARJOLIJN DIJKMAN

Interventions

Developing works in an on-site manner, Dijkman reacts to a specific context by making temporary spatial shifts or adjustments to a given space. These gestures often manifest themselves as installations that alternate the architectonic characteristics of a building or site and as interventions into the social layers of public spaces. Raising questions as to the supposed neutrality of public space, Dijkman manages to provoke and activate the local population and officials to rethink discriminatory policies practiced through these particular uses of the public space. In a more formal way, her installations function as unexpected theatre stages that shine bright in the dark and bring out these usually hidden and invisible systems of control.

Working alone or in collaboration with various artists or collectives, Dijkman shows a strong belief in the efficiency of the artistic actions and interventions as ways to reflect on and improve the existing reality. These sometimes subtle and small interventions function as gigantic mirrors that reflect back the (hidden) image of the ones responsible for the establishment and practice of certain rules and regulations. Her definition of public space is wide and includes nature and urban environments in their totality.

Megan Bardoe and Vesna Madzoski

ماريولين دجيكمان

مداخلات

من خلال تطوير أعمال فنية في موقع ما، تستجيب دجيكمان لسياق معين من خلال إدخال تحويلات مؤقتة على الفضاء المعني أوتعديلات على مساحة ما. تتجلى تلك الإيماءات عادة كأعمال تركيبية تغير من السمات العمرانية لبناء أو لموقع ما، وكمداخلات في الطبقات الاجتماعية للمساحات العامة. بإثارتها للأسئلة حول الحيادية المفترضة للفضاءات العامة، تنجح ديجكمان في إستثارة وتفعيل سكان المنطقة والمسؤولين المحليين، لإعادة التفكير في السياسات التمييزية التي تمارَس لدى التعامل مع تلك الفضاءات العامة. وبشكل أكثر رسمية، فإن إنشاءاتها تبدو وكأنها مسرحا غير متوقع، يشع براقا في الظلام، ويفضح نظم السيطرة الخفية وغير المرئية في العادة.

وسواء عملت بمفردها أم بالتعاون مع عدد من الفنانين والتعاونيات الفنية، فإنها تعبر عن إيمان قوي بكفاءة العمليات والمداخلات الفنية، كوسائل للتأمل في الواقع القائم وتطويره. إن تلك المداخلات الغامضة أحيانا، والصغيرة، تعمل في بعض الاحيان وكأنها مرايا عملاقة تعكس الصورة (المخفية) لأولئك المسؤولين عن وضع وممارسة بعض القوانين والإجراءات. إن تعريفها للفضاء العام تعريف واسع، ويتضمن الطبيعة والمحيط الحضري برمته.

ميغان باردو وفيسنا مادجوسكي

Rave Nature, Maastricht, 2005, installation, M. Dijkman / M.T. Vanden Eynde

MURATBEK DJOUMALIEV & GULNARA KASMALIEVA

The Past, the Present and the Future. These words spell out our evolution and raise a variety of images.

As the generation compelled to live at the turn of two epochs, we became a witness of the history that was made in our presence.

We were raised during Soviet times when there was no past, the present was ordinary and mediocre, but nobody was worried about the future because it was predictable and predetermined.

The majority of our works are based on research of the past and the future. As there is no future without past, in our early works we wanted to touch our Kyrgyz historic roots, which is why our previous works were dedicated to the history of Kyrgyzstan.

Artists are called upon to depict their attitude to the environment and to record the changes in our everyday life and reality. We dare to draw the attention of humanity to the problems that do not seem important today, but that may become a threat tomorrow - and that is our humble message to everyone.

Our future is very vague and we want to represent everyday life in our works, because an artist, when critically depicting reality, influences the future, whether he wants to or not.

The problems that our country faces today are the sources for our works. They are universal problems and that is what makes them our prime focus, but most importantly, they are problems that radically break historic traditions, not only in our country but in the entire world.

مرتبيك جماليف وجلنارا كاسماليفا

الماضي، الحاضر، المستقبل: كلمات تعبر عن عملية تطورنا وتستحضر صوراً متنوعة.

نحن الجيل الذي عاش رغما عنه في الفترة الانتقالية بين عهدين، أصبحنا شهودا على التاريخ الذي صُنِع في حضورنا.

كبرنا في أيام حكم السوفييت، عندما لم يكن هناك ماض، والحاضر كان عاديّا وركيكا، ولا قلق من المستقبل إذ كان متوقّعا ومعروفا مسبقا.

تعتمد معظم أعمالنا على البحث في الماضي والمستقبل، فلا وجود لمستقبل دون ماض. أردنا في أعمالنا الأولى أن نتلمس جذورنا التاريخيّة القرغيزية ولهذا ركزت أعمالنا الأولى على تاريخ قرغيزتان.

يتوقع الناس من الفنانين عادة التعبير عن مواقفهم من محيطهم وإلى تسجيل التغيّرات التي تطرأ على الحياة والواقع اليوميّ. ونجرؤ نحن إلى شد انتباه الإنسانيّة إلى القضايا التي قد لا تبدو مهمّة اليوم، إلا أنها قد تشكّل تهديدا غدا، وهذه هي، بكل تواضع، رسالتنا للجميع.

مستقبلنا مبهم، ونريد أن نعرض الحياة اليوميّة في أعمالنا، لأنّ الفنان، عندما يصوّر الحقيقة بشكل نقديّ، يؤثّر على المستقبل، شاء أم أبى.

نستوحي أعمالنا من قضايا بلدنا الراهنة، وهي قضايا عامة عالمية، مما يجعلها همّنا الأوّل اليوم. لكن الأهم هو أنّ هذه المشاكل تكسر بشكل راديكاليّ تقاليد تاريخيّة، ليس في بلدنا فحسب، وإنما في العالم أجمع.

Into the Future, 2005, two channel video installation, 5'53", courtesy of artists

52

BRIGHT UGOCHUKWU EKE

In my country, Nigeria, many people rely on sachet water (popularly called "pure water") because of the lack of good drinking water. Such water is believed to have been processed before it is packaged in plastic sachets. However, the majority of Nigerians have always disposed of the sachet wrongly after use. This has resulted in widespread litter all over the country. Furthermore, in the Niger Delta region, the presence and activities of the oil companies have caused serious environmental pollution in the form of oil spillage, which has destroyed large land mass, aquatic animals and vegetation, and acid rain resulting from industrial emission and gas flaring. These environmental pollutions have directly and indirectly affected mankind, especially in my immediate environment.

Recently, I was attacked by acid rain while working at Port Harcourt, River State, one of the largest industrial cities in Nigeria. This bitter experience inspired my *Acid Rain* installation, which was presented at the recent Dak'Art Biennial 2006, in Senegal. Accompanying the work *Acid Rain* was another piece in which I explored a possible means of self-protection from the toxicity of acid rain. This I did by recycling the "pure water" sachets (one of the environmental menaces) into a "shield" of raincoats and umbrellas. The *Shields* installation was presented along with the *Acid Rain* installation at the Dak'Art Biennial.

It does appear that environmental issues are bound to occupy my creative purview or concern for a long time to come. This is because I have grown very sensitive to constant disagreement between man and man, society and society, man and nature, etc. But in all, my priority is the silent but fiery conflict between man and nature.

Indeed, man, as a result of his insatiable need for comfort and pleasure, has altered the natural appropriations of the earth. This alteration has no doubt occurred as a result of the production of hazardous waste, pollution, the production and use of dangerous chemicals, etc. What else could be expected as the consequence of the hyper-industrial revolution, urbanization, and the consumer society?

برايت أوغو تشوكو إيكي

يعتمد الناس في بلدي، نيجيريا، عادة على الماء المعبّأ (المعروف شعبيّا بالماء النقي) نتيجة لنقص الماء الصالح للشرب. والاعتقاد السائد أن هذا الماء قد تمّ تكريره قبل تعبأته في أكياس بلاستيكيّة. لكن، لطالما تخلّص معظم النيجيريين من هذه الأكياس بطريقة خاطئة. وهذا ما أدّى إلى وجود قمامة في كلّ زاوية من البلد. كذلك الأمر في منطقة دلتا النيجر حيث يتسبب وجود وأنشطة شركات النفط في تلوّث بيئيّ خطير على شكل رقع نفطيّة (دمّرت بقعا كبيرة من الأراضي والحيوانات المائيّة والزراعة) ومطر حامضيّ بسبب الإفرازات الصناعيّة واحتراق الغاز. لقد أثر هذا التلويث البيئي بشكل مباشر وغير مباشر على البشريّة، وبالذات على محيطي المباشر.

حديثا، تعرّضت للمطر الحامضيّ أثناء عملي تحت المطر في بورت هاركورت، ريفر ستيت، إحدى أكبر المدن الصناعيّة في نيجيريا. أوحت لي التجربة المرِيرة هذه بتركيبي الفنّي "آسيد رين" (مطر حامضي) والذي قُدّم حديثا في بينالي داك آرت ٢٠٠٦، في السينيغال. يصاحب العمل "مطر حامضي" عمل آخر استكشفت فيه طريقة محتملة واحدة ليحمي المرء نفسه من سموم المطر الحامضي. قمت بهذا من خلال إعادة تدوير أكياس "الماء النقي" التي تهدد البيئة، فصنعت منها "واقيا" ضد المطر على شكل معاطف ومظلاّت. قُدّم التركيب الفنّي "واقي" مع "مطر حامضي" في بينالي داك آرت.

تطوّرت أعمال أخرى لاحقة انطلاقا من هذه الفكرة ذاتها وحملت مفهوما رمزيا يحاكي منظوري ورؤيتي الناقدة لهذه القضية الملحة، ألا وهي هلاك البيئة. هذه الأعمال هي صرخات فنان شاب ملتزم، يؤمن إنّه حين يُسمع صوته سيكون من الممكن تجنب حتى أصعب المشاكل البيئيّة – خاصة إذا كان هناك من يسمع النداء ويتفاعل معه.

يبدو حتما أنّ قضايا البيئة ستحتلّ المرتبة الأولى في مداركي الإبداعية واهتماماتي لفترة طويلة جدا. إذ يبدو أنّني أصبحت حساسا جدا للخلاف المستمر بين الإنسان والإنسان، المجتمع والمجتمع، الإنسان والطبيعة وغيرها. ولكن بشكل عام، أولويّتي هي للصراع الصامت، المتأجج، بين الإنسان والطبيعة.

حقا، لقد غيّر الإنسان الخصائص الطبيعيّة للأرض من أجل إسرافه في طلب الراحة والمتعة. حدث هذا التغيير، بلا شك، نتيجة المخلّفات الخطيرة والتلوّث وإنتاج واستعمال المواد الكيميائيّة الخطيرة وغيرها. ولكن، ما الذي كنا نتوقعه كنتيجة للثورة فائقة-الصناعيّة، المدنيّة، والمجتمع الإستهلاكي؟

Shield, 2005-2006, water sachet, variable

SOPHIE ELBAZ

My work talks about the cradle of humanity contaminated, about the African continent as the world's garbage bin. I use my process to go behind reality in an attempt to reveal what cannot be seen: the endangering of humanity.

The work is articulated around a central piece, a metamorphosis: *I Accuse*. It shows an African man facing us as he is slowly transformed by his changing environment. He then partly disappears in the fourth image. From one negative, four images have been produced, and the last one will be revealed at the Biennial. Through its own transformation, *I Accuse* symbolises the progressive contamination of the human race.

The series is introduced by *Atomic Tree* and closes with *Facing Emptiness*.

Atomic Tree not only symbolises life, but also knowledge, and therefore wisdom. In its introduction, it forces us to wonder: are we using our knowledge properly today?

Facing Emptiness invites us to face our own responsibility considering our future. The image thus reminds us that we still have a choice.

صوفي الباز

يتكلّم عملي عن مهد الإنسانيّة الملوّث، القارّة الأفريقيّة كحاوية القمامة للعالم. أستعمل عملي لأذهب وراء الحقيقة، في محاولة لكشف ما لا يمكن رؤيته: تعريض الإنسانيّة للخطر.

يترابط العمل حول قطعة مركزيّة، المسخ:

"أنا أتّهم" يُظهر رجلا أفريقيّا يواجهنا وهو يتحوّل تدريجيّا بفعل البيئةَ المتغيّرة، ومن ثمّ يختفي تدريجيّا في الصورة الرابعة.

أنتجت أربع صور من نيجاتيف واحد، وسيُكشف عن الأخيرة في البينالي. من خلال تحوّلها، يرمز "أنا أتّهم" إلى التلوّث المتنامي للبشر.

يتمّ تقديم السلسلة بـ "أتوميك تري (شجرة نووية)" وتنتهي بـ "فيسنج إمبتينيس (مواجهة الفراغ)". لا ترمز "شجرة نووية" للحياة فحسب وإنّما للمعرفة أيضا، وبالتالي الحكمة. في المقدّمة، تجبرنا أن نتساءل: هل نستعمل معرفتنا بالشكل المناسب اليوم؟ يدعونا "مواجهة الفراغ" لمواجهة مسؤوليتنا الخاصّة بالنسبة لمستقبلنا. بالتالي لا تزال الصورة تذكّرنا أنّه ما يزال لدينا خيار.

I Accuse N°3, 2005, Kodak metallic paper mounted on aluminium, 100 x 70 cm

TOUHAMI ENNADRE

تهامي النادر

Touhami Ennadre: Black Light

On seeing Touhami Ennadre's work for the first time, you will be sure to experience strong feelings. You will not remain indifferent, calm. Either you will flee, refusing to contemplate your image and the world, or you will be rooted to the spot, paralyzed yet forced to react when faced with the tragic side of existence. The shock that moves you is not that of an evil eye. It is not complacent about suffering, but labours to set you free. Its cathartic aim is quite simply shattering.

The most striking thing about Ennadre's work is its plastic unity, the necessity that runs through it. He starts out, he says, from the principle that "you must give. You must be truly true. It's heart-rending. It brings to the surface all kinds of things you're not familiar with. It's either that or nothing." He tries to find out "what's really real": "Light is what's really real, it's the only thing that obsesses me." He also claims not to know "what photography is". "I'm not a photographer. Technique isn't important, at most it's a means." The important thing lies elsewhere: to ward off "violence, misery and death".

Just as light has a constant speed, everything in Ennadre's work is governed by a constant. We are in the presence, not of themes, but of variations on one and the same theme: death. But to limit oneself to this observation would be either too much or too little. Ennadre is certainly part of that gigantic tradition which puts death at the heart of every artistic creation. The dance of the Maccabees, the tombs, an entire literature stretching from Montaigne to Bataille (to limit ourselves in history and geography) marks out the terrain: it is man's mortal condition that gives rise to artists. True, but too general: the main thing still remains to be said: Death, then. But which death? How and why?

"I'm a painter in the dark", says Ennadre, whose palette is rich with the blacks he uses to define the subject and structure of the image with lines and surfaces. Black is the "other", the place occupied by the other, it allows our vision to get its bearings, to appreciate variations in density between different shades of gray and white. There is nothing funereal about it. It acts like a form of lighting that provides relief and contour, the desired depth, thanks to a skilful counterpoint of light and dark that is reminiscent at times of Caravaggio in painting and Murnau or Dreyer in cinema.

The image, then, concentrates all its energies - those of Ennadre, our own - and redirects them towards life: tensions, intensities, tragedy. No artifice, never any lighting from behind, only darkness and light, a counter-death. His world is inhabited by myth, the myth of origin and ends, of revival. The cosmic order demonstrates that indissociability of life and death that only a poetic vision can reveal.

So: is Ennadre a photographer or something else? It is a ludicrous question. He sculpts the light of catastrophes. His logic is that of a plastic artist who would found his work on the Principles of an Aesthetic of Death. He will pierce your eye to the brain in its very flesh.

François Aubral

From his book entitled *Ennadre Black Light*, Munich, New York: Prestel, 1996.

تهامي النادر: الضوء الأسود

عند مشاهدة عمل تهامي للمرة الأولى، ستختبر مشاعر قوية بالتأكيد. لن تبقى هادئاً أوغير مهتم. فإما أنك ستهرب رافضاً التأمل في صورتك والعالم، أو أنك ستتسمر في مكانك، مشلول الحركة، ومع ذلك تجد نفسك مجبرا على إبداء رد فعل عندما يواجهك الجانب المأساوي من الوجود. الصدمة التي تحركك هي ليست صدمة العين الحسود. إن أعماله لا تأخذ موقفاً متقبلا لمعاناتك، بل تجهد لتحريرك. هدفها الخلاص، وهو وبكل بساطة، أمر محطم.

يقول: "عليك أن تعطي، أن تكون صادقاً بالفعل. أمر يُقطع القلب. إنه يسمح لجميع أنواع الأشياء غير المألوفة بأن تطفو على السطح. إما أن يكون الأمر هكذا، أو لا يكون." إنه الوصول إلى "ما هو حقيقي فعلاً": "الضوء هو الشيء الوحيد الحقيقي، إنه الشيء الوحيد الذي يتملكني." كما أنه يدعي أنه لا يعرف "ما هو التصوير الفوتوغرافي." "أنا لست بالمصور الفوتوغرافي، والتكنيك ليس مهما، فهو عبارة عن وسيلة في أحسن الأحوال." الأمر المهم يكمن في مكان آخر: أن تتفادى "العنف، والأسى، والموت".

وحتى أثناء جنازة والدته، لم يكن في الصور الفوتوغرافية الأولى التي التقطها النادر شيئا قاتماً أو محزناً: لا دموع، لا كفن، فقط مقاومة الألم في جلد وعظام اليدين اللتين أتعبتهما المعاناة - إنه توكيد على الحياة، في تأصلها في ظرفها المأساوي. هكذا، يمكن التوسع في هذه التجربة الحرجة للموت، لتمتد على مساحة المكان والزمان.

نحن لسنا في حضور الموضوعات، بل التباينات في الموضوع الواحد والموضوع ذاته: الموت. ولكن، أن نقصر أنفسنا على هذه الملاحظة، يمكن أن يكون إما أمر مبالغ فيه أو مبسط. ويبقى النادر، بالتأكيد، جزءاً من ذلك التقليد العملاق الذي يضع الموت في قلب كل إبداع من الإبداعات الفنية. رقصة المكابي، والقبور، ومجمل الأدبيات التي تمتد من مونتين إلى باتاي.

يقول النادر: "أنا رسّام في العتمة"، وطبق ألوانه غني بدرجات الأسود التي يستخدمها لتعريف موضوع الصورة وهيكليتها من خلال الخطوط والأسطح. والأسود هو "الآخر". إنه المكان الذي يشغله الآخر، وهو يسمح لرؤيتنا بأن تكتسب تجلياتها المختلفة، وأن نقدر التباينات في الكثافة بين مختلف ظلال اللونين الرمادي والأبيض. ما من شيء جنائزي في العمل. إنه بمثابة شكل من الضوء يوفر لنا الراحة والخطوط، والعمق المرغوب فيه، وذلك بفضل تقابل الضوء والعتمة الحافل بذكريات من أزمان كارافاجيو في الرسم، ومورناو أو دراير في السينما.

بعدها، تركز الصورة كل طاقاتها - طاقات النادر وطاقاتنا نحن- وتعيد توجيهها نحو الحياة: التوترات، والكثافات، والمأساة. لااصطناع، لا ضوء من الخلف أبداً، العتمة والضوء فقط، شيء مقابل للموت. عالمه مسكون بالأسطورة، أسطورة النشوء والنهايات، والإنعاش. ويظهر النظام الكوني ذلك الانفكاك أو عدم الألفة بين الحياة والموت، والتي لا يمكن الكشف عنها إلا من خلال الرؤية الشعرية.

إذن: هل النادر مصور فوتوغرافي أم شيء آخر؟ إنه سؤال سخيف. فهو ينحت ضوء الكوارث، ومنطقه هو منطق الفنان التجميلي، الذي قد يؤسس عمله على مبادئ جمالية الموت. وهذا ما سيثقب عينك مخترقاً إيّاها وصولاً إلى عمق الدماغ.

فرنسوا أوبرال

من كتابه "الضوء الأسود للنادر"، ميونيخ، نيويورك، برستل، ١٩٩٦.

Fish, 1992-1993, photography, silver print, 120 x 150 cm, courtesy of the artist

e-Xplo

(RENE GABRI, HEIMO LATTNER, ERIN McGONIGLE) WITH AYREEN ANASTAS

Our very first work together was already our last. Or to put it as Deleuze may have preferred it, we started right in the middle. That work spelled out concerns that would haunt us in whatever work we would subsequently undertake together. And the task would be a monumental one. We aptly titled that work *Dencity*, fusing the words density and city. We hoped to call out to ourselves the task at hand: to look, listen to, recover, (re)present, and in some sense stay vigilant to the dense, vertiginous city – the city which is ever-changing, ever-elusive, reappearing and disappearing in a kind of dance between competing forces.

Our approach to studying the city and those disparate forces was, one could say, materialist in orientation. We physically explored, experienced, looked at and listened to the city. As much as we were concerned with the discourses enveloping it, we felt the need to confront those discursive sites with physical and material developments, locations, and manifestations. The ambition was to have the city stand in for itself, the manifest city, in its everyday*ness*, everyday shifts, slips, hiccups, tremors, stalls, orderings, and movements. For each question, there was a voice, a sound, a time and a part of the city that would offer us insight. All the while we began also to accrue a vocabulary for working together, for moving through spaces, for describing what we were seeing, for orienting our conversations with one another and with our public. The terms spanned psychological, economic, and social motivations and effects, including words like amnesia, blithe, corrosion, corruption, desire, exile-aration, flight, fear, neglect, oblivion, emigration, immigration, hope, memory, greed, gentrification, speculation, development and redevelopment, renewal, renovation, regeneration, resonance, property, power, silence, nostalgia, nyctalopia, speed, tremors, pollution, picnolepsy, private and public "good", Brooklyn, Manhattan, BQE/LIE, Torino, Eindhoven-Rotterdam, Berlin, London, North Adams, Budapest, Columbus, Newcastle-Gateshead. These are the physical terrains e-Xplo has covered in our short but intensive history together. But as has been our habit, we have always been attuned to the density of information and material that we are co-habiting with and co-exploring together.

إي-اكس بلو

(رينيه غابري، هايمو لاتنر، إرين ماكغونيغل) بالتعاون مع أيرين أنستاس

عملنا الأول هو ذاته عملنا الأخير، أو كما يفضل ديلوز صياغته، بدأنا في منتصف الطريق. لقد عبّر ذلك العمل عن قضايا ظلت تسكننا في كل عمل قد نقوم به بشكل مشترك بعد ذلك. المهمة ستكون شاقة. أسمينا العمل "دينسيتي" (الكثافة - المدينة)، بحيث دمجنا بين كلمتي الكثافة والمدينة، وكان أملنا أن نعلن عن المهمة بين أيدينا، ألا وهي أن ننظر، ونستمع إلى، ونستعيد، ونعيد محاكاة، وبشكل أو بآخر، أن نبقى متحفزين للمدينة المكثفة الدائخة المتقلبة: المدينة المتغيرة دائما، المتملصة، التي تعاود الظهور والاختفاء، في ما يبدو، كرقصة بين قوى متنافسة.

كانت مقاربتنا لدراسة المدينة وهذه القوى المتباينة مقاربة مادية في توجهها. قمنا باستكشاف واختبار مادي، نظرنا واستمعنا إلى المدينة. ومع أننا كنا معنيين بالخطاب الذي يغلفها، إلا أننا شعرنا بالحاجة لمواجهة هذه المواقع المتجولة (المنتشرة دون نظام) بالتطورات المادية والفيزيائية والمواقع والتجليات. كان الطموح أن تقف المدينة وتدافع عن نفسها، المدينة المتجلية، في يوميتها، في تحوراتها اليومية، في المنزلقات، الهزات، البسطات، الطلبات، والتحركات، لكل سؤال، كان هناك صوت إنساني، صوت، وقت، وجزء من المدينة يمكن ان يعطينا بصيرة. بدأنا طوال الوقت، نجمع المصطلحات، للعمل معا، للحركة ضمن المساحات، لوصف ما كنا نراه، لتوجيه حديثنا مع بعضنا البعض ومع جمهورنا. تراوحت المصطلحات ما بين النفسية، والاقتصادية، والدوافع الاجتماعية، والتأثيرات بما يشمل كلمات مثل، فقدان الذاكرة، الحبور، التآكل، الفساد، الرغبة، المنفى، الهرب، الخوف، الإهمال، النسيان، الهجرة إلى، الهجرة من، الأمل، الذاكرة، الجشع، التجديد الحضري، المضاربة، التطوير وإعادة التطوير، التجديد، الترميم، الانبعاث، الصدى، العقار، السلطة، الصمت، الحنين، العمش، السرعة، الهزات الأرضية، التلوث، المصلحة الخاصة والعامة، بروكلين، مانهاتن، BQE/LIA، تورينو، إيندهوفن-روتردام، برلين، لندن، نورث آدامز، بودابست، كولومبوس، نيوكاسل - غيتسهيد. هذه هي المساحات التي غطيناها في e-Xplo عبر تاريخنا المشترك القصير، ولكن المكثف. وكما هي عادتنا، فقد كنا دائما نميل إلى كثافة المعلومات والمواد التي نساكنها ونشترك باستكشافها معا.

Apparently Not a Worker was to be Seen, 2007, production still

MOUNIR FATMI

Underneath is a special project for the Sharjah Biennial 8 based on a former architectural work by Mounir Fatmi called *Ovale Project*, and a video entitled *Horizontal Fall*, showing the deconstruction of a building.

With *Underneath*, the main idea is to show the world literally upside down. Since 9/11, the balance has totally changed and a new force has emerged in the geopolitical landscape as we know it. The threat and the power come from the Eastern part of the globe and, for the first time in centuries, the Western countries have to adapt to this new situation. Everybody knows now that the Earth is cut in two by an invisible line, similar to that of the equator, which divides North (rich) from South (poor). In this unstable period, where money doesn't guarantee security, people are looking for new values to bequeath to the next generation.

For the installation, three tables are placed in a room and under each table people can see the wooden sculptures of the skyscrapers of a big modern city. Those cities generate a lot of pollution. When you look on the top, those are regular tables and they symbolise a discussion area for ecological topics. It's a very trendy subject. But it's uncomfortable to sit down at these tables, the sculptures beneath get in the way. On the wall, there are three video projections showing different landscapes (urban or natural). It's a geographical disturbance: you don't know when or where the pictures were taken and you don't know what "paradise" we are trying to reach.

Are we ready to change?

منير فاطمي

"أسفل" هو مشروع خاص لبينالي الشارقة، مبني على أساس عمل هندسي سابق قام به منير فاطمي، اسمه "مشروع أوفال (بيضاوي الشكل)، وفيديو عنوانه "السقوط عموديا"، يظهر عملية تفكيك مبنى.

الفكرة الرئيسة من العمل، "أسفل"، هي توضيح أن العالم مقلوب فعليا. منذ الحادي عشر من سبتمبر تغير توازن القوى كما نعرفه، وظهرت قوة جديدة على الساحة الجيو-سياسية. كان مصدر التهديد والقوة القسم الشرقي من الكرة الأرضية، ولأول مرة منذ قرون، أصبح على الدول الغربية أن تتأقلم مع هذا الوضع الجديد. الكل يعرف الآن أن الأرض مقسومة إلى نصفين بينهما خط غير مرئي، يشبه خط الاستواء، يقسم ما بين الشمال (الغني) والجنوب (الفقير). في هذه المرحلة غير المستقرة، حيث لا تضمن الأموال الأمان، يبحث الناس عن قيم جديدة يورثونها للأجيال القادمة.

في هذا العمل التركيبي، توضع ٣ طاولات في غرفة، وتحت كل طاولة يمكن للمشاهدين ان يروا منحوتات لناطحات سحاب في مدينة كبيرة حديثة. هذه المدن تولد الكثير من التلوث. حين نشاهدها من فوق، هي فقط طاولات عادية، وترمز إلى مساحة نقاش للمواضيع البيئية، موضة هذه الأيام. ولكن من غير المريح أن تجلس إلى هذه الطاولات، لأن المنحوتات في أسفلها تقف في الطريق. على الحائط ثلاثة عروض فيديو تظهر مناظر طبيعية مختلفة (حضرية وطبيعية). إنه شغب جغرافي: فأنت لا تعرف متى أو أين تم التقاط هذه الصور، ولا تعرف ما هي "الجنة" التي نحاول الوصول إليها.

هل نحن مستعدون للتغيير؟

Evolution or Death, 2004, photography, variable, courtesy of La B.A.N.K, Paris

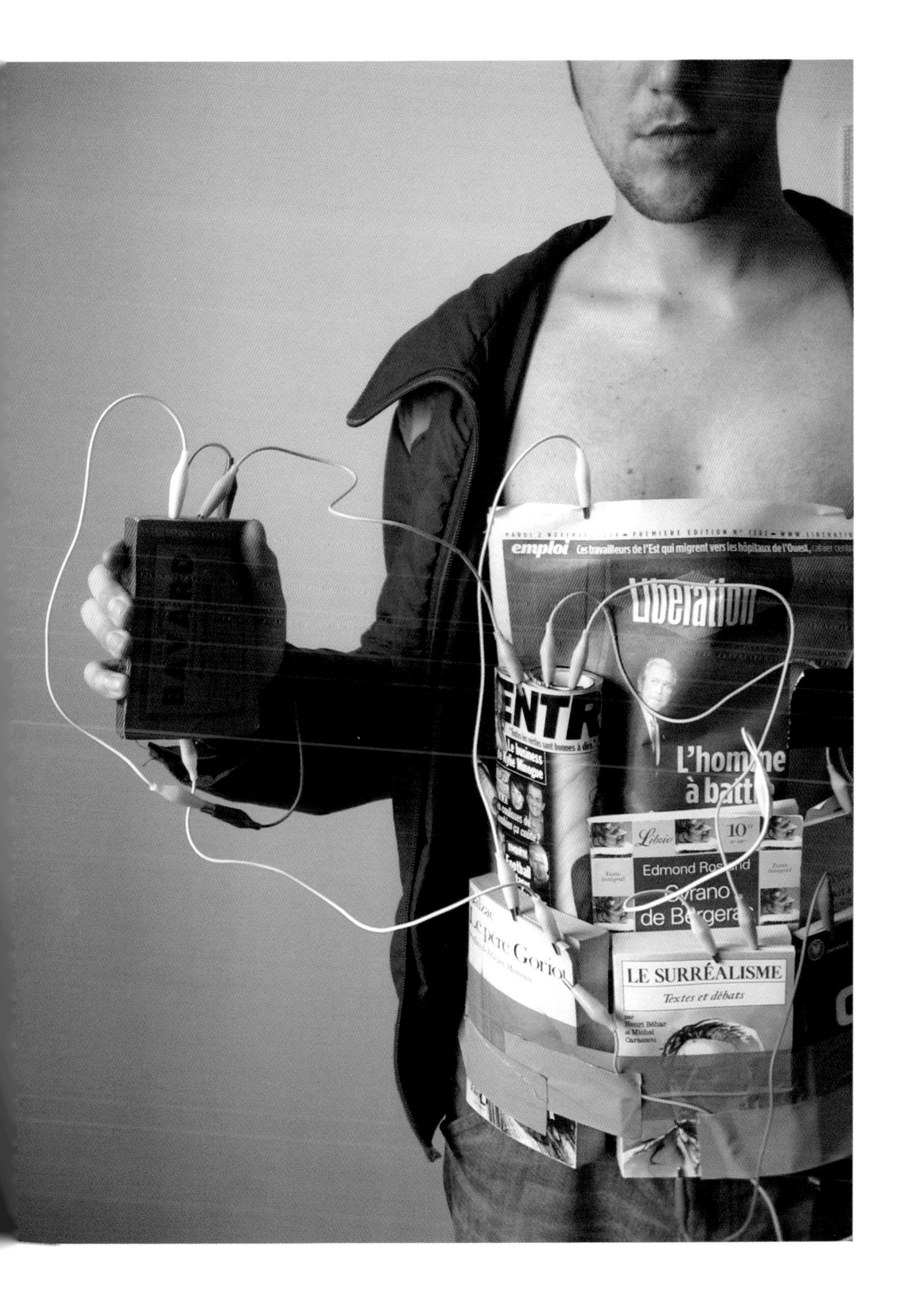
emploi
Ces travailleurs de l'Est qui migrent vers les hôpitaux de l'Ouest,
Le business de Kylie Minogue
Librio
Edmond Rostand
LE SURRÉALISME
Textes et débats
par
Henri Béhar
et Michel
Carassou

PETER FEND

The immense wealth from geological deposits of petroleum generated in the past century, and possibly still generated for another century, gives those living in most of the semi-arid or arid regions where petroleum is found – namely Arabia and Iran – an opportunity unique in human and geological history:

> to return what is now desert to savannah,
> to increase seaweeds and fishes in salt seas,
> to restore one-time hordes of wild-land animals.

This opportunity is available to the entire Arabian Gulf basin.

The wealth generated can be invested in a broad array of construction and engineering projects, inland, along the shore and offshore. Large structures can be built at the head of the Gulf, as recent history shows, most dramatically in the 1980s. But large structures can also be built along the rivers and wadis feeding the Gulf, from southeast and northwest, deep inside Saudi Arabia or Iran. And even with the concavity of lands tilting and, if watered, draining into the United Arab Emirates, into the south coast of the Gulf, a 10 or 20-year programme can be conducted to restore the water cycles, both in the air and in the ground, for a gradual recovery to ancient fecundity.

For Sharjah, physically, I focus on a very small concavity within the Arabian Gulf basin. The concavity is a small part of an intermediate basin, that of all lands draining into the coastal saltwaters of the United Arab Emirates. The concavity comprises just two ephemeral river basins, or wadis, flowing on occasion to the Gulf from the mountain ridge less than 100 km east of Sharjah. A thorough trek will be made over these two wadi basins: Wadi Yuddayah, sloping into Sharjah; Wadi Lamleh, sloping behind a low ridge northwards to the coastal shoals of Jazirat al Hamra. During the trek, I will be finding out where, how and in what sequence structures derived from Earth Art can be installed in the wadi basin or offshore, to induce more animal habitat, largely underground, stronger water cycles, and the return of nutrients offshore to human use as methane gas. The governing paradigm for continuous exchange between methane, oxygen and carbon dioxide comes from Joseph Beuys' sculpture *Fat Corner*. The molecule essential throughout this exchange is water. The means of assuring its presence, in line with *Water: A Natural History*, is provided by those activators of the soil with water: animals.

بيتر فند

توفر الثروة الهائلة المتأتية من المخزون الجيولوجي النفطي، التي تم جمعها خلال القرن الماضي، والتي قد تستمر على مدى قرن آخر، فرصة فريدة في التاريخ البشري والجيولوجي لمن يعيشون في المناطق القاحلة وشبه القاحلة التي يوجد فيها النفط، وبخاصة العالم العربي وإيران. فهي فرصة سانحة في التاريخ الإنساني والجيولوجي لتحقيق ما يلي:

> إعادة الصحراء إلى أرض خضراء،
> زيادة الأعشاب البحرية والأسماك في البحار المالحة،
> إستعادة ما كان موجودا من قطعان الحيوانات البرية.

هذه الفرصة متاحة لكل دول حوض الخليج العربي.

يمكن استثمار هذه الثروة في عدد كبير من المشاريع العمرانية والهندسية، في الداخل وعلى الشواطئ وفي المياه الساحلية. يمكن بناء هياكل كبيرة في رأس الخليج، على النحو الذي أثبته التاريخ الحديث، وخلال ثمانينات القرن العشرين، بشكل دراماتيكي. ويمكن أن تقام المشاريع الكبيرة على شواطئ الأنهار والوديان، وفي عمق المملكة العربية السعودية وإيران. ويمكن، حتى بالنسبة للأراضي المقعرة المائلة، فإذا ما تم ريها وصبت في الإمارات العربية المتحدة، نحو جنوب ساحل الخليج، من الممكن تنفيذ برنامج مدته عشرة أعوام أو عشرين عاما، يتم خلاله استعادة الدورة الطبيعية للمياه، في الهواء وعلى الأرض، من أجل استعادة الخصوبة القديمة.

إن الأموال المتأتية من النفط، تجعل هذه المشاريع ممكنة، إذا ما تم اتخاذ القرار بشأن التكنولوجيات الفعالة للموقع، وما يتطلبه ذلك من اختبارات، ثم نشر هذه التكنولوجيات على امتداد الحوض. يمكن وضع تلك التكنولوجيات على امتداد طرق الحيوانات المهاجرة، وخاصة الحشرات والأسماك والطيور.

أركز في الشارقة على تجويف صغير جدا ضمن حوض الخليج العربي، وهذا التجويف يشكل جزءا من حوض وسيط تنحدر مياهه نحو المياه الساحلية المالحة في الإمارات العربية. يتألف هذا التجويف من حوضين لنهرين غير دائمين، او واديين يتدفقان أحيانا نحو الخليج من سفوح جبلية تقع على بعد يقل عن ١٠٠ كم إلى الشرق من الشارقة. سوف أمشي في هذين الواديين: وادي اليودية المنحدر نحو الشارقة، ووادي لملة، المنحدر خلف سفح منخفض باتجاه الشمال، ثم إلى سواحل جزيرة الحمره، لأكتشف المكان والكيفية والسياق الذي يمكن به تطبيق البنى المستمدة من فن الأرض في حوض الوادي، أو بعيدا عن الشاطئ، من أجل توفير ملاذ حيواني آمن تحت الأرض بشكل خاص، ودورات هواء أشد قوة، واستعادة المغذيات لكي يستعملها الإنسان على شكل غاز الميثان. إن النموذج الأساس للتبادل المتواصل بين الميثان والأكسجين والكربون مستمد من مؤلف جوزيف بايوس: "الزاوية السمينة للبنيان". إن الماء هو الوحدة الضرورية لعملية التبادل هذه. فالوسيلة الضامنة لوجود الماء وفقا لمؤلف "الماء: تاريخ طبيعي". هم أولئك النشطاء الذين يمدون التربة بالماء: الحيوانات.

Installation view, 1996, migros museum für Gegenwartskunst, Zurich

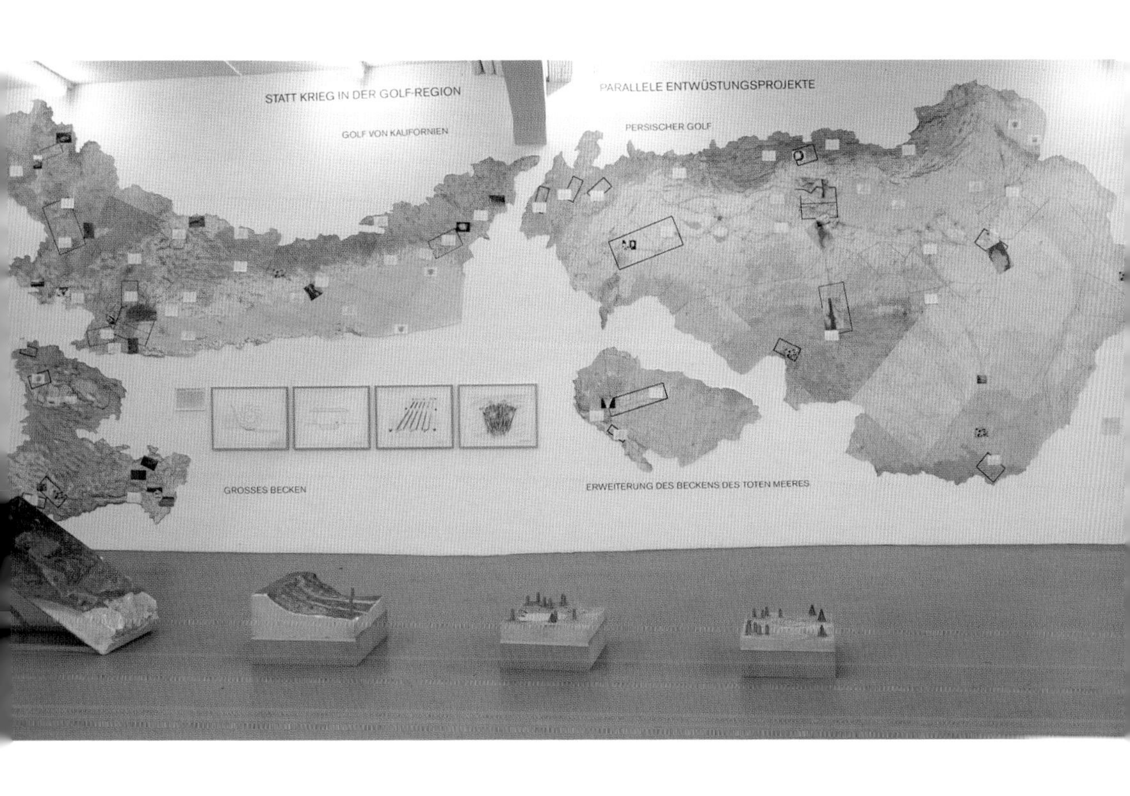
STATT KRIEG IN DER GOLF-REGION
PARALLELE ENTWÜSTUNGSPROJEKTE
GOLF VON KALIFORNIEN
PERSISCHER GOLF
GROSSES BECKEN
ERWEITERUNG DES BECKENS DES TOTEN MEERES

FRANZ GERTSCH

Grosser Waldweg **(The Big Forest Path), 2005/2006**

In the 1970s, especially after "documenta 5" in 1972 curated by Harald Szeemann, large-sized hyperrealistic group-portrait paintings featuring Bohemian hippy scenes had brought an international reputation to Franz Gertsch. Around 1985, he started to achieve a completely new and different body of work: the monumental woodcuts. For about seven years, Gertsch then concentrated exclusively on this medium. Since 1993, when he resumed painting on canvas, woodcuts and paintings have had the same importance in his work. Gertsch's woodcuts in their monumental size are not only equal to his paintings; although hand-printed in editions, they are produced as unique works of art: each print is made in a different colour.

Gertsch started to work with the woodcut technique at a point when the visual appearance of the world seemed to him no longer sufficient as pictorial language and as the subject of his art. The wish to go beyond visual reality led him towards an artistic concept that establishes a balance between the visual surface and the inner, spiritual nature of reality. The monochrome woodcut is the visual equivalent of this intention: the realism of the motif and the effect of the abstract monochrome colour field, completely independent of all descriptive ties to reality, are kept in a subtle balance.

The opposite effects of viewing from close up and from a distance support this concept. From afar, the viewer can detect the motif easily and clearly; coming closer, the figurative reality is being dissolved in myriads of abstract light dots, like a starry sky. This corresponds with the effects of depth and flat surface. The motive of the path creates an illusion of spatial depth, while the dots are pulling the view back to the surface, which is the reality of the paper and not of the forest. The huge size of the print gives the viewer the impression of being able to walk along this path into the forest. At the same time, the motif can be read in a highly metaphorical way, as a path of life.

With a stunning technique, Gertsch plays with the issues of positive and negative, defining objects sometimes by a concentration of dots, sometimes by a lack of dots. Material reality thus appears completely dematerialised. But beyond this, the real subject of this work is not the visual reality of a forest path, but the experience of nature. The enormous investment of time that is necessary to create such a work is embodied in it, giving an impression of what nature is: in essence, a manifestation of time.

Reinhard Spieler

فرانز غيرتش

ممر الغابة الكبيرة

خلال سبعينيات القرن الماضي، وبخاصة بعد "دوكيومنتا" الخامس عام ١٩٧٢ والذي كان هارولد زيمان هو القيّم عليه، أدت رسومات الصورة الجماعية التي تظهر مشاهد (هيبية Hippy) بحجم ضخم ومسرفة في الواقعية إلى اشتهار فرانز غيرتش عالميا. في عام ١٩٨٥، بدأ غيرتش مجموعة أعمال مختلفة كل الاختلاف عن سابقاتها: منحوتات خشبية ضخمة. وعلى مدى سبعة أعوام، ركز غيرتش على نفس الوسيط/المادة. وحين استأنف الرسم علي القماش في عام ١٩٩٣، احتفظ النحت الخشبي والرسم على القماش بأهمية متساوية في أعماله. إن منحوتات غيرتش الخشبية مماثلة في أهميتها لرسوماته، ليس فقط بسبب أحجامها الضخمة، فهي، وبالرغم من ظهور نسخ منها على شكل مطبوعات ورقية، تمثل إنتاجا فريدا كأعمال فنية، فكل طبعة كانت بلون مختلف.

بدأ غيرتش العمل على تقنية النقوش الخشبية (woodcut technique) في مرحلة بدا المظهر المرئي للعالم غير كاف كلغة تصويرية وكموضوع لفنه، وقادته الرغبة في تجاوز الواقع المرئي، إلى مفهوم فني يؤسس لتوازن بين السطح المرئي والطبيعة الداخلية الروحية للواقع. فالمنحوتات الخشبية ذات اللون الواحد، هي المعادل المرئي لهذا التوجه. إن واقعية المعنى، وأثر مساحة اللون الأحادي المجرد على نحو كامل الإستقلال عن أية روابط وصفية مع الواقع، قد وضعت في حالة توازن دقيق.

إن الأثر المتعاكس للمشاهدة عن بعد أو عن قرب، يؤكد على هذا المفهوم: فحين ينظر المرء إلى المشهد عن بعد، يستطع أن يتعرف على المعنى بسهولة ووضوح، وإذا ما اقترب أكثر، فإن الواقع الرمزي يتحلل إلى عدد لا يحصى من النقاط الضوئية المجردة، التي تشبه سماء نجومية، ويتساوق هذا مع أثر عمق وامتداد السطح. إن الهدف من المسار هو خلق وهم وجود عمق مساحي، بينما تجر النقاط المشهد إلى ما وراء السطح، الذي هو واقع الورقة وليس الغابة. فالحجم الكبير للمطبوع، يوفر للناظر الإنطباع بأنه قادر على المشي قدما فوق الممر نحو الغابة، ويمكن في الآن ذاته، قراءة المعنى بطريقة مجازية جدا، على أنه مسار حياة.

وبتكنيك مذهل، يلعب غيرتش بقضايا الإيجابية والسلبية، معرفا الأشياء تارة من خلال تكثيف النقاط، وتارة أخرى من خلال عدم وضع أية نقاط، هكذا يبدو الواقع المادي على نحو غير مادي تماما. ولكن وبمعزل عن ذلك، فإن الموضوع الحقيقي لهذا العمل، ليس هو الواقع المرئي لممر في غابة، وإنما هو اختبار الطبيعة، هكذا يتجسد الاستثمار الضخم للزمن في هذا العمل، وهو ما يلزم لمثل هذا العمل، موفرا الانطباع بأن ماهية الطبيعة في الأساس، هي: تجسيد الزمن.

راينهارد شبيلر

Graeser II (Grass II), 2004, woodcut, 1 block, 170 x 153 cm, Hand print on Kumohadamashi Japanese paper by Ivano Heizaburo, edition of 27, courtesy of the artist © Franz Gertsch 2007 © photo: Dominique Uldry, Berne/CH

ABDULNASSER GHAREM

عبد الناصر غارم

Flora and Fauna

Since the dawn of time nature has found a way to balance all its elements in order to live in a state of equilibrium. This state is known to us as the ecosystem. This system contains many elements that keep it in balance. Some are smart elements, others are less intelligent and most are task-oriented. All of them depend on each other to survive.

The smart elements in our ecosystem have found ways to introduce new elements into the already balanced equation in order to benefit themselves and in turn benefit other elements in this system. This approach, whether good or bad, is always based on selfish reasons. Beauty, riches, distraction, and also survival, are all selfish reasons used by the smart elements to manipulate nature's balanced equation.

The artist chose to show how using the tree does actually work in providing vital oxygen and water, contrary to the main image of Cornocarpus Erectus held by the residents of the region. The main use of the tree to the people of the region is in landscaping and the beautification of the city.

The work provided is to show that introducing foreign elements into our ecosystem, although beneficial, is not vital to the cause. Using indigenous elements has the same benefits, but doesn't in turn threaten the ecosystem.

Oxygen

The work comprises a plastic bag that covers the top part of a tree and a human head. There is obvious fusion between the two elements; the human being produces carbon dioxide, the main gas necessary for the survival of the tree, while the tree produces oxygen, which in turn is the principal gas for the survival of the human being. The water is the common component between the two and constitutes their "intellectual" spine, meaning that these elements emphasise the true relationship between the human being as a labourer, rather than a master, on the one hand and the environment as a friend on the other. Both are at the same level, the human being is a product of this unity.

فلورا و فونا

لقد أوجدت الطبيعة، منذ فجر التاريخ، وسيلة لتحقيق حالة توازن بين عناصرها. هذه الحالة معروفة لدينا باسم نظام التوازن البيئي (eco system). يحتوي هذا النظام على عدة عناصر تبقيه في حالة توازن.

بعض هذه العناصر ذكية، والبعض منها أقل ذكاء، وتعتمد كل هذه العناصر على بعضها البعض للبقاء.

تكرر غابة الأمطار الاستوائية ثاني أكسيد الكربون، تحوله إلى أوكسجين، وتنشره في الجو، ويساعد الأوكسجين على تكوين طبقة الأوزون، وتساعد طبقة الأوزون على حماية سكان الأرض من اشعة الشمس القاتلة.

تبخر الشمس مياه البحر وتحولها إلى غيوم مشبعة بالماء، وتسافر الغيوم وتسقط حملها على الأرض فتتكون الجداول، تحمل الجداول الحياة إلى النباتات، وتغذي النباتات والحيوانات، وكلاهما يغذي الإنسان...

الإنسان هو العنصر الذكي في الطبيعة، لذلك عليه أن يتأكد من استمرارية هذه المعادلة المتوازنة... أليس كذلك؟

وجدت العناصر الذكية في نظامنا البيئي طرقا لإدخال عناصر جديدة إلى المعادلة المتوازنة أصلا، ليتمكن الإنسان من تحقيق الفائدة لنفسه، وتبعاً لذلك، إفادة العناصر الأخرى. هذه المقاربة، سواءً كانت جيدة أو سيئة، تستند دائماً إلى دوافع أنانية: الجمال، المال، صرف الانتباه، والبقاء أيضا، كلها دوافع أنانية تستخدمها العناصر الذكية للتلاعب بمعادلة الطبيعة المتوازنة.

أوكسجين

لقد اختار الفنان أن يوضح لنا كيف أن استخدام هذه الشجرة قد ينجح في توفير الأوكسجين والماء الضروريين للحياة، بعكس الصورة السائدة التي يحملها سكان المنطقة والذين يرون فيها فقط وسيلة لتجميل المدينة. كما يوضح هذا العمل كيف أن إدخال العناصر الغريبة إلى نظامنا البيئي، مع الإقرار بفائدتها، ليس أمرا حيويا لقضيتنا الأساسية. فاستخدام العناصر المحلية يعطي نفس الفائدة ولكن دون أن يشكل تهديدا لنظام التوازن البيئي.

Oxygen, 2006, performance, photographic documentation, courtesy of the artist

Dolphin
PAINTS

SIMRYN GILL

"Power Station" is a series of 13 pairs of photographs recording the interiors of two buildings that have been neighbours for nearly 40 years. One is a power station and the other a residence. The oil-fuelled power station which was built in the 1960s had been recently decommissioned at the time that the photographs were taken in 2004. The residence, built in the late 1920s continues to be occupied.

I made this series of comparative photographs as a way to think about these two closed interiors which both generate different kinds of energy within them. I was also intrigued by their proximity as two very disparate structures; they literally share a fence. Over the decades they have moved from hostile cohabiting to neighbourly familiarity and now both look to the future with some uncertainty: both somewhat obsolete in their forms and their use of resources.

سيمرن غيل

"محطة الكهرباء" سلسلة من ثلاثة عشر زوجا من الصور الفوتوغرافية، تسجل دواخل مبنيين ظلا متجاورين لنحو أربعين عاما. أحدهما محطة لتوليد الكهرباء، والثاني بيت سكني. تم بناء المحطة المولدة للطاقة باستخدام النفط خلال ستينيات القرن العشرين، وقد أوقفت عن العمل قبل وقت قصير من التقاطي لهذه الصور في عام ٢٠٠٤. أما المبنى السكني الذي بني خلال عشرينيات القرن العشرين، فلا يزال مأهولا. لقد قمت بالتقاط هذه السلسلة من الصور المقارنة، كوسيلة للتفكير في دواخل هذين المبنيين المغلقين، اللذين ينتجان نوعين مختلفين من الطاقة. كما انشددت إلى واقع تجاورهما كمبنيين متباينين جدا، يشتركان بسياج يفصل بينهما. على مدى عقود، كانت العلاقة بينهما تنتقل من التساكن العدائي إلى الجيرة الأليفة، ويتطلعان الآن إلى المستقبل ببعض القلق: فكلاهما قد عفا عليه الزمن بعض الشيء، سواء في شكليهما أو في مقوماتهما الذاتية.

Power Station, 2004, 13 gelatin silver photographs, 13 type C photographs, 19 x 42 cm each, courtesy Albion, London & Tracy Williams Ltd, New York

TUE GREENFORT

When urban foxes are accidentally attracted to a photo-shoot by slices of sausage, when flies write poetic scores on panes of glass, or quite normal street-lamps do not switch on until someone passes them, then the young Danish artist Tue Greenfort is at work. His work looks at natural and technical cycles with a great deal of critical commitment and an equally large helping of profound humour, with an ecological awareness at the centre of his interest. At the same time, Tue Greenfort ties these complex cycles into the language of modern art - and so a whole variety of operating systems enters into an entirely productive dialogue.

One good example of Tue Greenfort's work is the sculpture *BONAQUA Condensation Cube* (2005). At first glance, this work is reminiscent of Hans Haacke's *Condensation Cube* (1963-1965); even the title suggests this historical reference. But here, Tue Greenfort makes a minimal but far-reaching modification: instead of using slowly condensing water, his cube sculpture is filled with Bonaqua commercial table water, a product from the global player Coca-Cola's stable. In so doing, the young artist places himself in the minimalist art tradition, but brings it up-to-date by charging it with ecological questions. The differences between "first and second nature" to use Karl Marx's terminology, and between genuineness and artificiality, are all available within the closed system of *BONAQUA Condensation Cube*.

Tue Greenfort's art constantly relates to his colleagues' approaches. The American artist Dan Peterman's recycling art is a case in point. In *Producing 1 kilogram of PET PL requires 17.5 kilograms of water and results in air emissions of 40 grams of hydrocarbons* (2004), which alludes to Peterman's work - even in the quantities of material mentioned in the title - Greenfort's piece features a 1.5-litre mineral-water bottle, which has been heated and melted down to offer a capacity of 0.5 litres. This work indicates that producing the throwaway bottle uses far more water than it can contain. Thus the necessity of recycling is presented dramatically. The complex situation in *Corner of the Month* (2005) is also absurd. Here the artist built a fridge, containing various kinds of yoghurt, combined with an oven. A high, contradictory use of power and a "cool" presentation are thus confronted as part of the aesthetic master plan in *Corner of The Month*, which, incidentally, is also the German name of a yoghurt-based product by the Müller brand. Instead of relying on oh-so-brilliant new creations and sensitive formal language, Greenfort invests everything in docking with aesthetics that are already in existence, therefore using them with commitment to address reality critically. His art is not based on the individualistic gesture of unique creations, but on a pan-societal, "objective" responsibility that always includes abandoning merely subjective authorship.

Raimar Stange

From *Flash Art International* No 250, October 2006

تووه غرينفورت

حين تنجذب ذئاب المدينة إلى جلسة تصوير بسبب قطع سجق، وحين يكتب الذباب أشعارا على النوافذ، أو حين لا تضيء مصابيح الشوارع إلا حين يمر شخص ما بجانبها، نعرف أن الفنان الدنماركي تووه غرينفورت يقوم بعمل فني ما. تبدو أعماله وكأنها تدور في دورات طبيعية وتقنية، بالتزام نقدي كامل ممزوج بكمية لا بأس بها من الفكاهة. فالوعي البيئي يتمركز في محور اهتمامه. وفي الوقت نفسه، يربط تو غرينفورت هذه الدورات المعقدة بلغة الفن المعاصر، بحيث نرى أنظمة تشغيل متنوعة تتداخل مع بعضها البعض في حوار منتج.

"منحوتة بوناكوا: مكعب التكثيف" (٢٠٠٥) هي أحد الأمثلة الجيدة لأعمال تووه غرينفورت. للوهلة الأولى، يذكرنا عمله بعمل هانز هاك "مكعب التكثيف" (١٩٦٣-١٩٦٥)، وحتى عنوان العمل يعطينا تلك الإحالة التاريخية. إلا أن تووه غرينفورت يقوم هنا بتعديل بسيط، ولكنه موسع: فبدلا من استخدام تكثيف المياه بشكل بطيء، يملأ منحوتته التكعيبية بمياه بوناكوا التجارية المعبأة، إحدى منتجات كوكا كولا. بعمله هذا، يضع الفنان نفسه ضمن تقاليد فن المنمنمات، ولكنه في الوقت نفسه، يعطي نسخة معاصرة من هذا الفن من خلال ملئه بأسئلة بيئية. الفارق ما بين "الطبيعة الأولى والثانية" باستخدام مصطلحات كارل ماركس، وما بين ما هو أصيل وما هو مصطنع، كلها نجدها ضمن النظام المغلق في "بوناكوا: مكعب تكثيف".

يرتبط فن تووه غرينفورت دائما بمقاربات زملائه. فن إعادة التدوير للفنان الأمريكي دان بيترمان هو أحد الأمثلة. "لإنتاج ١ كيلوغرام من PET PL نحتاج إلى ١٧,٥ كيلوغرام من الماء وينتج ٤٠ غرام من الهيدروكربون" (٢٠٠٤)، والذي يحيل إلى أعمال بيترمان - حتى في كميات المواد المذكورة في العنوان - يعرض عمل غرينفورت الفني زجاجة ١,٥ لتر من المياه المعدنية المعبأة، تم تسخينها وتذويبها لتصبح سعتها ٠,٥ لتر فقط. يمثل هذا العمل إعادة التدوير بشكل درامي. الوضع المعقد في "زاوية الفم" (٢٠٠٥) هو ايضا خارج عن المعقول. بنى الفنان هنا ثلاجة تحتوي على أنواع مختلفة من اللبن، معها فرن. إذاً هناك استخدام مرتفع ومتناقض للطاقة، وعرض "بارد" يتواجهان كجزء من خطة كبرى جمالية في "زاوية الفم". والتي هي بالصدفة، اسم منتج لبني من منتجات مولر. وبدلا من الاعتماد على التكوينات الجديدة الرائعة واللغة الحساسة الرسمية، يستثمر غرينفورت كل شيء في التفاعل مع الجماليات الموجودة، ويستخدمها بالتزام ليتصدى للواقع بشكل نقدي. لا ينبني فنه على الإيماءة الفردية للتكوينات المتفردة، بل على مسؤولية "موضوعية" اجتماعية عامة دائما ما تشمل التخلي عن فردية الفنان-الصانع.

رايمار شتانغه

هذا النص منشور في مجلة "فلاش آرت انترناشيونال"، ٢٥٠، أوكتوبر ٢٠٠٦

BONAQUA Condensation Cube, 2005, glass, silicone, BONAQUA - drinking water 45 x 45 x 45 cm, courtesy Johann König, Berlin

GROUP TUESDAY

(FADI ABDALLAH, BILAL KHBEIZ, WALID SADEK)

Group Tuesday:
Preliminary thoughts on a Project to Come

In our garden, trees stand aligned in rows of five. Much of our time is spent caring for their well-being. Even of late, when Israeli war planes were busy levelling apartment buildings in Beirut's southern suburbs, we kept at it: watering, pruning and cleansing - so much so that we seldom had the leisure to enjoy their perfect alignment, their subservience to our learned pleasure at seeing straight parallel lines converge. Endless care - the sort a parent knows well - is what these rows of trees require. It is the patient and erudite manufacture of a stand-still: branches extending along paths drawn by a judicious pair of shears. Our garden is small. But as an idea it stands as a monument to our despair. For we knew as early as when planting the saplings that, to survive, these rows of trees had to multiply. They had to colonise the buildings to their left and right, eastwardly claim the open plot of land and westwardly the road that passes by. For this to happen, we knew we had to care even more. We and the few rows we planted had to become trees walking; an expanding garden that would never grow to become adult, always a toddler moving about in expanding circles with foster gardeners trying hard to keep pace.

A small garden cannot suffice. If tending we started, then it must be to a whole world; a world more compliant than a toddler but just as frail and allergic - threatened by unexpected winds and bedridden by the slightest viral mutation; a world of aligned trees and for each a hospital bed. Our garden is a curse. And as I steal a moment to observe what we have done, I feel an urge to be like Cimon, that aged and unjustly imprisoned father, made to starve but kept alive by the nightly visits of his daughter Pero, who breastfed him secretly.

مجموعة الثلاثاء

(فادي عبد الله، بلال خبيز، وليد صادق)

مجموعة الثلاثاء:
أفكار أوليّة لمشروع قادم

في حديقتنا، يقف شجر في صفوف متوازية، كلّ صف من خمس شجرات. أمضينا من وقتنا الكثير نرعى هذه الشجرات. حتى أننا واصلنا عملنا في رعايتها، سقاية وتقليما وتنظيفا، في الوقت الذي كانت فيه الطائرات الإسرائيليّة مشغولة بتدمير البنايات السكنيّة في أحياء بيروت الجنوبيّة، لدرجة أنه نادرا ما توفّر لنا وقت لنستمتع بتوازيها الدقيق ومشاكستها لنا في استمتاعنا المُكتسب برؤيتنا لالتقاء الخطوط المتوازية. عناية لا نهائيّة – والتي يعرفها الأب أو الأم جيّدا – هي ما تتطلّبه صفوف الشجر هذه. تصنيع صبور وماهر لأمر ثابت: أغصان تمتد عبر طرق رسَمَها مقصّ حكيم. حديقتنا صغيرة، ولكنها كفكرة تقف مثل نصب ليأسنا. كنا على علم، منذ زرعنا هذه الشتلات، أنّها حتّى تستمر يجب أن تتكاثر هذه الصفوف من الشجر، أن تستعمر المباني من على يمينها ويسارها، وأن تستملك الأرض المفتوحة إلى شرقها والطريق التي تمر بمحاذاتها غربا. ومن أجل أن تفعل ذلك، كان علينا أن نهتم بها أكثر، وأن نصبح نحن والصفوف التي زرعنا شجرا يمشي. حديقة تتمدد ولن تكبر أبدا لتصبح راشدة، ستكون طفلا يحبو يتحرّك دائما في حلقات تستمرّ اتّساعا مع بستانيين يحاولون جاهدين أن يحافظوا على نفس وتيرة السرعة التي تتسع بها.

لا يمكن لحديقة صغيرة أن تكفي. إذا كانت العناية هي ما بدأنا به، إذاً لا بدّ أن تكون من أجل عالم كامل. عالم أكثر طواعية من طفل يحبو، إلاّ أنّه بالرقة نفسها ولديه الدرجة ذاتها من الحساسيّة. تهدده رياح غير متوقّعة وتقعده فراشا تشوّهات فيروسيّة. عالم من الأشجار المصفوفة ولكلّ واحدة منها سرير مستشفى. حديقتنا لعنة. عندما أسرق لحظة لأتأمّل فيما فعلناه، أشعر برغبة لأكون مثل سيمون، ذلك الأب العجوز المحبوس ظلما، والذي تُرك ليجوع ولكن أبقته زيارات ابنته بيرو الليليّة حيّا حيث كانت ترضعه سرّا.

"اللحظة التي تفتح فيها عينيك هي لحظة الفاجعة"؛ توطئة

بلال خبيز

درج تلفزيون "المستقبل"، قبل اغتيال رفيق الحريري، على تكرار الصورة الفريدة والوحيدة لصخب رواد المقاهي في وسط البلد ليلاً. في منطق الصور، هذه صورة مفحمة لكل اعتراض على خطة الاعمار السالفة الذكر. لكنها في منطق الكتابة والتفكر، على الاقل، لا تبدو كذلك على الاطلاق.

ما يؤلم في النظر بين الصورة التي يبني عليها وسط بيروت سمعته وصيته، والصورة التي كان يبثها تلفزيون "المنار" التابع لـــ "حزب الله"، هو هذا البرزخ الفاصل بين عالمين يصعب ان يلتقيا. عالمان نقيضان، واحد يجاهد بالروح والنفس والجسم، لانه، بحسب اقتناعاته الراسخة، اجبر على التضحية والجهاد. وآخر يستقبل ويستعد لاستقبال كل رموز المعاصرة واطيافها. في عالم الجهاد، الجسم حاضر بامتياز الى حد يستدعي غيابه كل هذا الضجيج. الجسم الذي هو هيكل الروح، نعم. لكنه الجسم الذي حين ننحره نتذكر كل الملامسات والهدهدات التي عرفها في طفولته، وكل المتع التي كان في وسعه ان يصنعها لنفسه وروحه وكل تلك التي صنعها على حد سواء. نتذكر الايدي التي تصافحت مراراً والملمس الندي للراحات وهي تجسد السلام باللحم والموت بالحديد. ونستطيع ان نفصل فصلاً قاطعاً بين الحديد واللحم. فكل سلام صفته اللحم وكل حرب صفتها الحديد. اللحم وليس الجلد، لأن المسلّم باللحم يعلن ان الفساد الذي يصيب الجسم ليس مرضاً جلدياً يخرج المواطن في الدول الحديثة من الاجتماع الى المستشفى ومن السوية العامة الى الفقر والعوز والجريمة والعيش في الضواحي المهملة. على النقيض تماماً، ثمة الجلد الذي يسكن الوسط التجاري وزواره. الجلد الذي يتطلب العناية والرعاية والفصل القاطع عن اللحم والاحشاء. الجلد الذي ليس وسيلة واداة لمتع الجسم او لثوراته. هناك، ثمة اصرار لا محيد عنه على جعل الاجسام جلوداً فحسب. ثمة اصرار على فصل قاطع بين الجسم وكل ما هو بري ومتوحش، تعرقاً وارتجافاً، توتراً او استرخاء. الاجسام في هذا المكان تحضر بوصفها خطاباً يدعي اتصالاً وثيقاً بروح العصر، بالعولمة على نحو ما. ليس هناك ما نريد ان نثبته غير هذا الاتصال. تلك الابنية التي تشبه كل ابنية العالم وتلك الشوارع والفضاءات التي نستطيع ان نراها في كل مدن العالم ايضاً. وهذا التعسف في حق الجغرافيا، الذي يجعل نعومي كامبل تزور بيروت فلا تجدها. لانها نامت في غرف وثيرة كتلك التي تصادفها في مراكش او باريس، وقابلت اشخاصاً يلبسون ويتكلمون ويسلكون ويتهذبون كأولئك الذين قابلتهم في بومباي او في نيويورك، وجلست في مقاه رأت بين جلاسها كثيرون يشبهون عشاقها وكثيرات يشبهنها الى حد التطابق. حسناً، ما الذي يبقى لنا هناك من اجسامنا؟ لا شيء غير الجلد الأملس والاصم.

"Tragedy in a Moment of Vision"; a preface.

Bilal Khbeiz

Aglow and alive; that is how Beirut's city center always appeared on Future TV. Images to quiet every attempted critique of Beirut's reconstruction plan. That was of course before the assassination of Rafic Harriri. Today, those images lie on one side of an unbridgeable chasm, separate from other images broadcast by Hizbullah's television station Al Manar. Two sets of images belonging to two worlds. The one zealously struggling, flesh and soul, to remain worthy of a chosen path marked by sacrifice while the other dolling itself up to welcome the symbols of contemporaneity and their retinues.

The distance that divides these two imageries is more than poignant. It sets up a costly dilemma. For the body that is called for in the world of sacrifice, namely the world of Jihad, is putatively a mere receptacle for a migrating soul. Yet, these receptacles when slaughtered summon their flesh and the warmth thereof. They summon also all the other bodies with which they inter-coursed: faces caressed, hips hugged and hands held. And at that moment they return to being bodies made of flesh not of iron. To be flesh, or be reminded of one's flesh, may call for pity. It may urge us to remember that every greeting is made of flesh while war lives in steel. Yet, it is precisely this flesh that fails to gain entrance into the world of contemporaneity. There, flesh is un-welcome. To enter one must shed it and wear only a well-tended and carefully fashioned skin; odorless and still. Such a skin is not only alien to perspiration; it is also as foreign to revolt as it is to pleasure. An impartial skin severed from its organic moorings. Such a skin announces its alignment with the spirit of contemporaneity, with globalization so to speak. Skins that ambulate in and around glass edifices denying any claim that geography might have. Practicing the hyper-traveling that allows a star like Naomi Campbell to sleep in an air-conditioned hotel in Beirut and mistake it for New York and speak with Beirutees as she would to Parisians. That much is demanded of us if we are to belong to this second imagery. And such is the dilemma: an impossible choice between a savage body and a specular skin.

GRAHAM GUSSIN

Illumination Rig starts with a basic premise, turning money into light; it is in this sense an event, an occasion where consumption and transformation are made conspicuous. But the piece works in other ways: the lights used are very specific, they are film lights, they have a particular architecture and quality and they bring about the sense that something is about to unfold within their throw; they imply some kind of narrative, something about to arrive or depart, something extraordinary. They turn whatever they illuminate into a possible film set and they are a way of orchestrating movement and architecture. They also light the audience, they become the subject in a fictional landscape. The nuance of the piece changes dramatically according to its location and the conditions around it.

Spill uses a cinematic device, or effect, in order to deal with notions of threshold, appearance and threat. It situates itself in a tradition of painting in the way it uses fog to evoke a feeling of the uncanny and the sublime, also referencing Horror and Science Fiction films of the 1950's and contemporary commercial music videos. Fog and mist were, and still are, used in Hollywood productions to designate a shift in aspect - a movement from the natural to the supernatural. I am interested in the way the dry ice both obscures and reveals in the way it is used, in one sense it is simply a process that we watch unfold but it also draws a screen over the present and visible and drops the viewer into a realm of suspense where things are semi-visible and shrouded. It is a hypnotic process yet threatening, acting a little like a narcotic.

غراهام غصين

تبدأ "عدة الإضاءة" أو illumination rig بفرضية أساسية، هي تحويل النقود إلى ضوء. بهذا المعنى، هي حادثة مناسبة، حيث يصبح الاستهلاك والتحويل ظاهرين للعيان. إلا أن هذا العمل الفني يعمل بطرق أخرى: فالأضواء المستعملة خاصة جداً، هي أضواء فيلم، لها هندسة وصفات معينة، توحي بأن شيئا ما سيظهر داخل دائرتها، تحيل إلى نوع من السرد، شيء ما سيصل أو سيسافر، شيء خارق. تحول هذه الأضواء كل ما تضيئه إلى مشهد من فيلم، وتصبح وسيلة لإدارة الحركة والهندسة. تضيء الجمهور أيضا، وتصبح موضوعا لمشهد طبيعي، متخيل. إن الاختلافات الدقيقة داخل القطعة تتغير بشكل درامي، حسب الموقع والظروف المحيطة بها.

أما "انسكاب" أو "spill" فيستخدم وسيلة سينمائية، أو مؤثرات سينمائية، للتعامل مع مفاهيم مثل العتبة، المظهر، والتهديد. يضع العمل نفسه ضمن سياق تقاليد الرسم، من خلال الطريقة التي يستخدم فيها الضباب ليستحضر شعور الغموض والوحشة والرفعة، ويحيلنا أيضا إلى أفلام الرعب والخيال العلمي في الخمسينات، والفيديو كليب الموسيقي التجاري المعاصر. لقد كان الضباب والرذاذ وما زالا، يستخدمان في أفلام هوليوود ليمثلا تحولا في المظهر - انتقالا من الطبيعي إلى ما هو خارق للطبيعة. أنا مهتم بالطريقة التي يحجب فيها الثلج الجاف الرؤيا، وفي الوقت نفسه يكشف، كل حسب الطريقة التي يستخدم فيها. فمن جانب، هو عملية نشاهدها وهي تحدث، ولكنها أيضا تضع حاجزا على الحاضر والمرئي، وتسقط المشاهد في عالم من الترقب، حيث تصبح الأمور إما شبه مرئية أو مغشاة. إنها عملية تنويمية، وفي الوقت نفسه خطرة، وكأنها مخدر.

Illumination Rig, 2004, 12 hour event, film lights, generator, cables, Whitstable, UK

KHALED HAFEZ

Visions of Contaminated Memory

I grew up in a different Cairo, the Cairo of the late sixties and seventies; at that time, to me as a child, people looked different, dressed differently, talked differently, and strangely enough, behaved differently. I had a bicycle; I climbed mango trees in the gardens of villas around the three-floor apartment block where I lived with my parents and kid brother.
Today, no wise parents allow their child to ride a bicycle in the streets of Cairo; there are no longer any mango trees to be seen. People today look different from in my childhood days; they dress differently, talk differently, and consequently behave differently. The openness, elegance and tolerance of the same citizens perished in a massive wave of cultural regression, noise, pollution and over-crowdedness of people, ideas, thoughts and distorted beliefs.

Extract from my diary, dated February 15, 2003

For slightly more than ten years I have been probing in my artwork the notion of *identity*; I personally believe that Egypt enjoys a polyvalent identity that influences in every possible way everyone and everything living on its land: Mediterranean, African, Middle Eastern, Arab, with several layers of culture, cumulative enough to create today *a cultural overload*, manifested in the last few decades by jammed and distorted streams of thought.

Visions of Contaminated Memory tries to probe, through the accumulation of created and stock sounds and images, the cultural contamination that is much represented in the state of identity confusion omnipresent today in many parts of the Middle East.

The visual part of the video works to juxtapose places and people of the past and of the present, through the use of a two-channel screen, one of which essentially carries stock images/video from the Egyptian past, while the other is a created video image of present-day places and people. The video exposes the environmental aggression seen today as the norm, as well as the change in the dress-code of the same social strata of people on the Egyptian street.

The audio part of the work accumulates and builds up throughout the video to climax with an aggressive mass of sound, reminiscent of what meets the average pedestrian in the crowded and noisy streets of Cairo today. The sound mass (more than ten audio superimposed tracks) represents, through violent tones and confounded speech, the identity confusion, jammed thoughts and distorted beliefs among other traits that accompany serious social urban contamination.

The accumulation of the audio tracks will be representative of Egyptian mainstream taste. The combination of audio + video will tentatively try to represent one of the most polluted cities in the world: Cairo.

خالد حافظ

رؤى لذاكرة ملوثة

في أواخر الستينيات والسبعينيات كنت طفلا، ومدينة القاهرة التي كبرت فيها كانت مختلفة، أشكال الناس حولي مختلفة، يلبسون بشكل مختلف، يتحدثون بشكل مختلف، والغريب أيضا، أنهم كانوا يتصرفون بشكل مختلف. كانت لدي دراجة هوائية، وكنت أتسلق شجر المانجا في حدائق الفلل المحيطة بمجموعة البنايات ذات الطوابق الثلاثة، حيث كنت أعيش مع أمي وأبي وأخي الصغير. اليوم، لا وجود لشجر مانجا في القاهرة، ولايوجد والدان يسمحان لطفلهم أن يقود دراجة هوائية في شوارع القاهرة. ويبدو الناس مختلفين عما كنت أراهم في طفولتي، يلبسون بشكل مختلف، يمشون بشكل مختلف، ويتصرفون بشكل مختلف. الانفتاح، الأناقة، والتسامح لنفس المواطنين، انطمست كلها تحت موجة جارفة من الانحطاط الثقافي، الضجيج، التلوث، واكتظاظ السكان والأفكار والمعتقدات المشوهة.

مقتطفات من يوميات، بتاريخ ٢٠٠٣/٢/١٥

منذ أكثر من ١٠ سنوات بقليل، وأنا أتفحص مفهوم "الهوية" في أعمالي الفنية: شخصيا، أؤمن بأن مصر تتمتع بهوية متعددة، تؤثر بكل الطرق الممكنة على الجميع، وعلى كل من يعيش على أرضها: متوسطية، افريقية، شرق أوسطية، عربية، مع طبقات متعددة من الثقافات، متراكمة بشكل كاف لتكون اليوم عبئا ثقافيا، يتجلى بجداول فكرية، مشوهة ومسدودة في العقود الأخيرة.

رؤى لذاكرة ملوثة عمل يحاول أن يتفحص من خلال تراكم أصوات وصور مبتدعة وأخرى جاهزة، التلوث الثقافي الذي يتمثل في حالة تشوش الهوية، الذي نراه اليوم في أجزاء مختلفة من الشرق الأوسط.

القسم البصري من أعمال الفيديو يصف الأماكن والأشخاص من الماضي والحاضر (من خلال شاشة بقناتين، إحداهما تعرض مشاهد فيديو جاهزة من الماضي المصري، الثانية تعرض مشاهد فيديو لأماكن وأشخاص اليوم) بحيث يظهر خلال مدى الفيديو، التعسف البيئي الذي نشهده اليوم على أنه قاعدة هذا الزمان بالنسبة للأماكن، بالإضافة إلى التغيير في طريقة اللباس، للطبقة نفسها من الأشخاص في الشارع المصري اليوم.

القسم المسموع من أعمال الفيديو، يراكم ويبني طوال فترة عرض الفيديو (مدة الفيديو)، ليصل إلى القمة بكتلة صوت تعسفية، تذكرنا بما يجده المشاة في شوارع القاهرة المكتظة، والتي تعج بالضجيج. كتلة الصوت هذه (أكثر من عشرة مسارات تسجيل صوتية فوق بعضها البعض) تمثل، من خلال نغمات صوت عنيفة وحوارات مشوشة، الهوية المرتبكة، والأفكار المسدودة، والمعتقدات المشوهة، من ضمن خصال أخرى تترافق مع التلوث الاجتماعي المدني. تراكم مسارات التسجيل الصوتية سيمثل الذوق السائد المصري، سيحاول الجمع ما بين الصوت والصورة، وأن يمثل مبدئيا، إحدى أكثر المدن تلوثا في العالم، القاهرة.

Revolution, 2006, video stills, experimental video, 4 min, courtesy of the artist

HENRIK HÅKANSSON

The first issue is to try and stay focused on the matters of survival. The purpose of the work is to seek out the possibilities for understanding and communicating on the environmental structures of the natural world that I, as do you, belong to dependently. The second issue is to register, save and expand all visions of it. The third issue is to change it.

Henrik Håkansson

Through his videos, sound works, and complex installations, Henrik Håkansson extracts fragments from natural cycles that he documents and recreates. Often with the aid of sophisticated technological means, the artist observes the growth of plants, birds, and insects, examining the possible forms that a dialogue between humans and nature can take.

Excerpt from Francesco Manacorda and Akiko Miki, *Henrik Håkansson. Through the woods to find the forest*, Paris 2006.

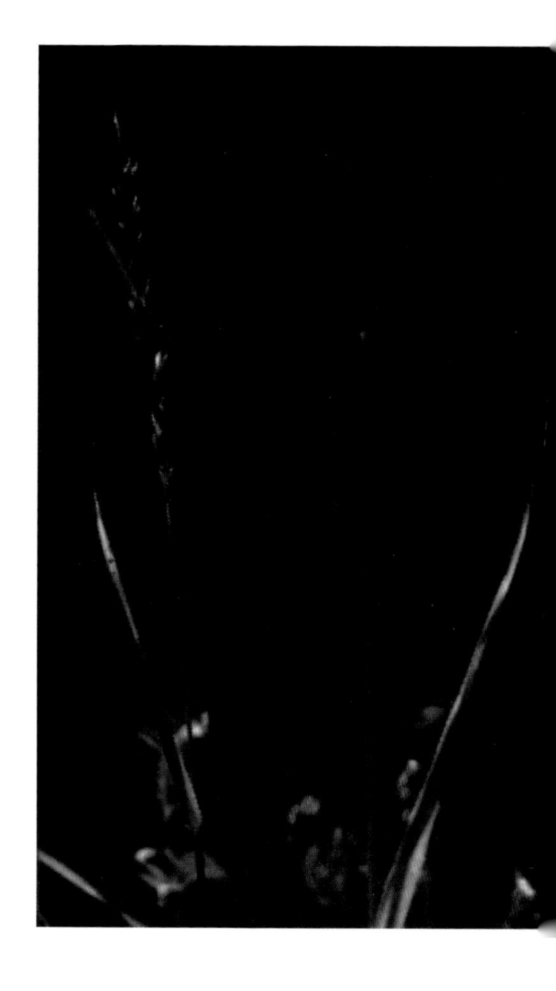

هنريك هاكينسون

القضية الأولى، هي محاولة التركيز للبقاء على قيد الحياة. قضية هذا العمل، هي البحث عن إمكانات الفهم والتواصل مع الهياكل البيئية للعالم الطبيعي الذي ننتمي إليه أنا وأنتم، بشكل معتمد على بعضه البعض. القضية الثانية، هي أن نسجل، نحفظ ونوسع، كافة الرؤى المرتبطة به. أما القضية الثالثة، فهي ان نغيره.

هنريك هاكينسون

من خلال أعمال الفيديو والصوت والأعمال التركيبية المعقدة، يستخلص هنريك هاكينسون أجزاء من دورات الحياة الطبيعية، يوثقها ويعيد تكوينها. يراقب الفنان، باستخدام أدوات تكنولوجية معقدة، نمو النباتات والعصافير والحشرات، ويفحص الأشكال المحتملة للحوار ما بين البشر والطبيعة.

من كتاب: مرورا بغابة الأشجار لنجد الغابة، فرانشيسكو ماناكوردا وأكيكو ميكي، باريس ٢٠٠٦

July 20 2004 (Pieris napi), 2005, 35 mm film mounted on loop, 1'20'', film still from Galleria Franco Noero, Torino

ANAWANA HALOBA

أنوانا هالوبا

My work is a result of the different thoughts going on in my mind, or, what I would call the noises in my mind. The way I react and place myself in this world is reflected in these 'mind discussions'. When I work I bring out my inner thoughts to interact with the outside thoughts. I am described as a feminist or political, but I would rather say I deal with social crises.

My body is an important medium through which to display these thoughts, with the intention of making a statement and being heard. I choose the specific materials I touch embracing, revealing, and in some cases, changing their meanings. Who names what and what right do they have?

To add thought and material to society and engage everyone in the debate allows me to create interactive pieces. I like directness, and maybe to be free and direct becomes an essential ingredient.

عملي هو نتاج عدة خواطر تمر ببالي، أو، ما أحب أن أسميه ضوضاء في ذهني. تنعكس طريقة رد فعلي وموقعي في هذا العالم في هذه "الحوارات الذهنية". وحين أعمل، أستحضر هذه الأفكار الداخلية لتتفاعل مع الأفكار الخارجية. يصفونني بأنني نسوية أو سياسية، ولكنني أفضل أن أقول بأنني أتعامل مع الأزمات الاجتماعية.

جسدي، هو أحد الوسائط الهامة التي أعبر من خلالها عن هذه الأفكار، بقصد أن أقول شيئا، أو أن يسمعني الناس. أختار مواد محددة ألمسها - أعانق وأكشف، وأغير معانيها في بعض الأحيان. من يسمي ماذا، وما الذي أعطاهم الحق بذلك؟

من خلال إضافة الفكر والمادة إلى المجتمع ودمج الجميع في الحوار، أستطيع أن أكون قطعا فنية تفاعلية. أحب المباشرة، وربما تصبح الحرّية والصراحة مكونان أساسيان لأي عمل.

Lamentations, 2006, video/sound installation, frog's view projection, 4 x 4 m

ILANA HALPERIN

Geologic Intimacy

My work explores the relationship between geological phenomena and daily life. Whether boiling milk in a 100 degree Celsius suphur spring in the crater of an active volcano, or celebrating my birthday with a landmass of the same age, the geologic history and environmental situation specific to the locale directly informs the direction each piece takes.

Recent projects take as a starting point a personal experience with an unexpected geological phenomenon. Increasingly interconnected events of a political, historical and everyday nature are progressively drawn together to form a narrative. Each story explores the changeable nature of landmass, using geology as a language to understand our relationship to a constantly evolving world.

The project Emergent Landmass (a chronicle of disappearance) takes the island of Ferdinandea as its starting point, charting the history of a territory that no longer exists. In 1831, the island appeared off the southern coast of Sicily, sparking an international dispute over territorial ownership of this strategically positioned heap of young geology. Before any serious conflicts developed, the island disappeared, crumbling back into the sea. Drawings attempting to describe the perpetual formation and erosion of new landmass, a text and the only remaining mineral samples of Ferdinandea, which were taken in 1831 when it was still above water, all feature.

Whilst searching for news of Ferdinandea, I discovered an early volcanologist named Angelo Heilprin. Though he may be a distant relative, it is definite that part of Greenland holds his name.

Towards Heilprin Land

Part one, the nature of love as explained by a geoscientist.
Part two, a voyage towards Heilprin Land.

During time I spent this summer with volcanologists, we discussed their long-term relationships with volcanoes from around the world. Seen from the deck of a ship in the North Atlantic off the coast of northeast Greenland, the aurora borealis fills the sky. From my porthole: icebergs, glacial walls, pack ice, which can only be likened to cracking bones.

Volcanic stories from the Smithsonian collide with polar encounters from a fragile landmass in the north in Towards Heilprin Land, a new project developed for Sharjah Biennial 8.

إيلانا هيلبرين

حميميّة جيومنطقيّة

يستكشف عملي، العلاقة بين الظواهر الجيولوجيّة والحياة اليوميّة. إن كان غليُ الحليب في ينبوع معدن الكبريت على ١٠٠ درجة مئويّة في فوّهة بركان ناشط أو الاحتفال بعيد ميلادي بصحبة جزيرة من ذات العمر، التاريخ الجيولوجيّ والوضع البيئيّ الخاص بالموقع مباشرة يحدّد الاتّجاه الذي تتخذه كلّ قطعة.

اتّخذت مشاريع حديثة من تجربة شخصيّة مع ظاهرة جيولوجيّة غير متوقعة كنقاط بداية. بشكل متزايد، تتجمع أحداث متقاطعة سياسيّة وتاريخيّة ويوميّة معا لتصنع حكايات. تستكشف كلّ قصة الطبيعة المتغيّرة للجزر باستعمال الجيولوجيا كلغة لفهم علاقتنا مع عالم يتطوّر بشكل مستمرّ.

يتخّذ مشروع نوماديك لاندماس (مذكّرات اختفاء) من جزيرة فيرديناندیس نقطة بداية، يرسم تاريخ أرض لم يعد لها وجود. في عام ١٨٣١، ظهرت الجزيرة بقرب شاطئ صقليّة الجنوبي، وأثارت خلافا عالميّا حول ملكيّة هذه الكومة الجيولوجيّة اليافعة ذات الموقع الاستراتيجي. قبل أن تتطوّر الصراعات بشكل خطير، اختفت الجزيرة، تهاوت عائدة إلى بطن البحر. يعرض المشروع أيضا رسومات قصدت وصف التشكّل والتآكل المستمرّين لجزر جديدة، ونصّا وعيّنات معدنيّة هي الوحيدة المتبقيّة من فيرديناندیس والتي أُخذَت في العام ١٨٣١ عندما كانت ما تزال فوق سطح الماء.

أثناء بحثي عن أخبار عن فيرديناندیس، اكتشفت عالم براكين من أوائل العلماء واسمه آنجيلو هيلبرين. بالرغم من أنّه يمكن أن يكون بيننا صلة قرابة بعيدة، من المؤكّد أنّ جزءا من جرينلاند يحمل اسمه.

نحو أرض هيلبرين

الجزء الأوّل: طبيعة الحب كما يفسّرها عالم جيولوجيّ.
الجزء الثاني: رحلة نحو أرض هيلبرين.

أثناء قضائي وقتا مع علماء براكين في هذا الصيف، تحدّثنا عن علاقتهم طويلة الأمد مع البراكين حول العالم. من سطح سفينة في شمال الأطلسي، قريبة من شاطئ شمال شرق جرينلاند، تملأ أورورا بوريالیس (الأنوار الشماليّة) السماء. من نافذتي - كتل جليديّة وحيطان جليديّة وجليد متراكم، تبدو وكأنها عظام متكسّرة.

قصص بركانيّة عن تصادم السميثسونيان مع لقاءات قطبيّة من جزيرة رقيقة في الشمال في تووردز هيلبرين لاند (نحو أرض هيلبرين)، مشروع جديد من أجل بينالي الشارقة الثامن.

Towards Heilprin Land, 2006 and ongoing, C-print, 50 x 76 cm, courtesy of the artist and Studio Matteo Boetti

MONA HATOUM

منى حاطوم

Hatoum's work is an outstanding example of the interweaving of ethical, political and aesthetic issues, whose beauty lies in the wit, economy, risk-taking and even mischief-making with which these issues are conflated...
In Hatoum's deceptively simple works, defiance cannot easily be separated from vulnerability, order from chaos, beauty from revulsion, the brain from the body, the self from the other, affirmation from negation, form from content, light from dark.

Guy Brett *Itinerary* in Mona Hatoum,
Contemporary Artists Series, London: Phaidon Press (1997)

I have recently created two works, both depicting a world map, that relate to environmental issues, in particular the concern over global warming.

Hot Spot (2006) is a cage-like steel globe, approximately the size of a person's height and arm span, which tilts at the same angle as the earth. Using delicate red neon to outline the contours of the continents on its surface, the work buzzes with an intense energy, bathing its surroundings in a luminescent red glow. It is both mesmerising and seemingly dangerous. On the one hand it suggests that the whole world is a political hot spot caught up in conflict and unrest; it also points to global warming, an impending concern.

The other map is a work on paper entitled *Projection* (2006) using the new 'Peters' projection, a more egalitarian map, as it shows all areas in true proportion and corrects the distortions of the traditional maps with their dominant northerly perspective. It is a white on white work that uses cotton and abaca to create a positive-negative reversal where the continents appear as submerged recesses, as if they have been etched or eroded. The title "Projection" was chosen to imply projecting or looking into the future. This again can be seen as a portrayal of an apocalyptic view of the world.

تشكل أعمال منى حاطوم "نموذجا بارزا لتداخل القضايا الأخلاقية والسياسية والجمالية، والتي يكمن جمالها في الفطنة والإيجاز والمجازفة، وأيضا بعض المداعبة المؤذية والتي تمتلىء بها هذه الأعمال.
لايمكن التمييز بسهولة في أعمال منى حاطوم والتي قد تبدو بسيطة، بين التحدي والهشاشة، النظام والفوضى، الجمال والنفور، العقل والجسد، الذات والآخر، التأكيد والنفي، الشكل والمحتوى، الضوء والعتمة."

غاي بريت: "مسار"، عن منى حاطوم،
في سلسلة فنانون معاصرون، لندن، فايدون، ١٩٩٧

أنتجتُ مؤخرا عملين يصور كل منهما خريطة العالم بارتباطها بقضايا البيئة وبشكل خاص بالقلق السائد إزاء ارتفاع حرارة الكرة الأرضية.

"نقطة ساخنة" (٢٠٠٦)، هو عمل يجسد كرة فولاذية تشبه القفص، حجمها بطول الإنسان وامتداد ذراعه، وتميل على الزاوية نفسها التي تميل عليها الأرض. يتم استخدام النيون الأحمر الخفيف لإضاءة الخطوط المحددة لأشكال القارات بهيئاتها المسطحة. يعج العمل بطاقة كبيرة تفيض على ما حوله بوهج أحمر براق. إنه مذهل حقا، ومرعب كذلك. يوحي وكأن العالم نقطة سياسية حارة غرقت في لجة الصراع وعدم الاستقرار، كما يشير إلى ارتفاع درجة حرارة الأرض، مشكلا تعبيرا عن مخاطر قادمة.

أما الخريطة الثانية، فهي عمل على الورق بعنوان "استدلال" (٢٠٠٦)، يستند إلى استدلالات بيترز الجديدة. هذه الخريطة أكثر ميلا للمساواة، فهي تظهر جميع المناطق بنسبها الحقيقية، وتصحح التشويهات الواردة في الخرائط القديمة، والموضوعة وفقا للرؤى الشمالية المسيطرة. إنها بياض في بياض، تستخدم القطن والأباكا (قنب مانيليا) من أجل ابتداع تناوبات إيجابية وسلبية، فتظهر القارات وكأنها قد غرقت في سديم، أو أنها تشققت أو تآكلت. لقد تم اختيار العنوان "استدلال" لكي يوحي بعملية توقع المستقبل استنادا إلى الماضي، كما يمكن اعتباره رؤية تنبؤية لمصير العالم.

Projection, 2006, cotton and abaca, 101 x 151,5 x 5 cm, courtesy Galleria Continua, San Gimignano, photo: Ela Bialkowska

SUSAN HEFUNA

In November 2006, as I was flying back from Dubai to Frankfurt, images appeared in my mind: buildings, grid structures, high-reflecting glass, in blue and green everywhere. I remembered a big billboard with an advertisement; the 3-dimensional billboard becomes a building in itself – a big photograph of a landscape, mountains, a street, all mounted on that billboard.

In December 2006, I saw the 3-dimensional billboard in Dubai again: an advertisement for Dubai Properties and Porsche Towers. Inspired by the billboard, I decided to install a glass building, 800 cm wide, 250 cm high and 150 cm deep, made of high-reflecting blue glass; the installation will be at a crossroads in the Heritage area of Sharjah. Only a part of the building will be transparent, the letters reading: MIRAGE 07. The crossroads where people usually walk will be blocked by this alien, reflecting-glass building.

In the museum I will present "Photographs", a kind of documentation of the trip through Sharjah in December, searching for crafts people. Finally we arrive at a cultural centre in Diba. Leaving Diba, I retain the image of the plastic trees inside the building of the cultural centre in my mind. My photographs will show, for example, the *afas* (a basket made of palmwood) in Sharjah and, next to it, photographs of *afas* structures I took a week later in Cairo and Alexandria.

The Egyptian *afas* is for me a modern, innovative design object with multiple functions, used for the transportation of fruits, bread, vegetables, and animals. On the street it becomes a table to display the fruits or bread for selling. The photographs capture the *afas* also amongst the garbage in Cairo streets, as well as showing the location where they are made by a craftsman, who is in fact blind.

I have observed these structures since my childhood. I used to see them everywhere on the streets of Egypt and for the last ten years I have wondered why they are still made of palmwood, without the use of any nails or glue. Why have they not yet been supplanted by plastic baskets, like, for example, the clay water bottles supplanted by plastic ones? Why have the horses and donkeys disappeared completely from Cairo's streets, which today, exceeding all pollution levels, are packed with cars, and human beings gasping for breath?

For some time, though, I have become aware that more and more *afas* are being replaced by baskets made out of plastic. On the streets of Egypt, the palmwood is slowly disappearing.

سوزان حفونة

بينما كنت عائدة من دبي إلى فرانكفورت في شهر تشرين الثاني من عام ٢٠٠٦، أخذت أتخيل صورا مختلفة: بنايات، هياكل شبكية، زجاج عاكس، باللونين الأزرق والاخضر في كل مكان. تذكرت لوحة إعلانية كبيرة، هذه اللوحة الثلاثية الأبعاد أصبحت بناية بحد ذاتها – صورة كبيرة لمشهد طبيعي، جبال، شارع، كلها كانت على تلك اللوحة الإعلانية.

أتذكر رحلتي بالسيارة عبر الشارقة، والبحث من الصباح إلى المساء عن حرفيين يستخدمون خشب النخيل. كانت الطريق ملأى بشجر النخيل، مشاهد طبيعية متغيرة، جبال جميلة، البحر، أزمة السير، شاحنات كثيرة تنقل أحجارا كبيرة من الجبال إلى دبي – للاستمرار في البناء.

كان هناك سوق الجمعة، وفيه سجاد للبيع ونباتات وفواكه وخضار، وكانت هناك سلّة – تسمى في مصر "القفة". هذه السلة المصنوعة في مصر من خشب النخيل مليئة بالبطاطا المستوردة. نستمر في طريقنا، وفي النهاية، لا نجد أي حرفي في ذلك اليوم.

في شهر كانون أول من عام ٢٠٠٦ رأيت مرة ثانية في دبي لوحة إعلانية ثلاثية الأبعاد، الإعلان لشركة عقارات دبي وأبراج بورش. وبإيحاء من هذه اللوحة الإعلانية، قررت أن يكون عملي التركيبي مبنى من الزجاج، من زجاج أزرق عاكس، بعرض ٨٠٠ سم وارتفاع ٢٥٠ سم وعمق ١٥٠ سم. سيعرض هذا العمل التركيبي في مفترق الطرق في المنطقة التراثية في الشارقة. سيكون جزء من هذا المبنى شفافا، ونقرأ الأحرف: ميراج ٠٧ (سراب). هذا الكائن الغريب، مبنى من الزجاج العاكس، سيقطع مفترق الطرق حيث يسير الناس عادة. .

في المتحف، سوف أعرض "صور"، نوع من التوثيق لرحلتي في الشارقة في شهر كانون الثاني، حين كنت ما أزال أبحث عن الحرفيين. في النهاية، وصلنا إلى المركز الثقافي في دبا. حين تركنا دبا، بقيت في ذهني صورة أشجار بلاستيكية داخل المبنى. ستظهر صوري ، على سبيل المثال، "القفف" في الشارقة وبجانبها الصور التي التقطتها للقفف، بعد أسبوع في القاهرة والاسكندرية.

القفة المصرية بالنسبة لي، هي تصميم معاصر مبتكر متعدد الوظائف، تستخدم لنقل الفواكه والخبز والخضروات والحيوانات، وفي الشارع تصبح طاولة لعرض الفواكه والخبز للبيع. تلتقط الصور القفة أيضا ضمن النفايات في شوارع القاهرة، وتلتقط موقع حرفي كفيف يقوم بصناعة القفف.

لقد لاحظت هذه الهياكل منذ صغري، وكنت أراها في كل مكان في شوارع مصر، وللسنوات العشر الأخيرة كنت أتساءل، إذا كانت ما تزال تصنع من خشب النخيل دون استخدام أي غراء أو مسامير. لماذا لم تستبدل حتى الآن بسلال البلاستيك، كما استبدلت على سبيل المثال، جرار الماء بالعبوات البلاستيكية؟ لماذا اختفت الأحصنة والحمير كليا من شوارع القاهرة، والتي تتجاوز اليوم كل مستويات التلوث، وتشهد ازدحاما بالسيارات والبشر الذين يصارعون لالتقاط أنفاسهم؟

لقد راودني الإحساس منذ فترة، بأن هناك المزيد من القفف التي تستبدل بسلال بلاستيكية في شوارع مصر. لقد بدأ خشب النخيل بالزوال.

Construction Dubai 2006, 3 x 40 cm, mounted behind plexiglass, courtesy of the artist and The Third Line Gallery, Dubai

الصفوة

USCHI HUBER

Uschi Huber's work centres around the use of photography and video, creating both her own series of images as well as working with already existing pictorial material.

In her photography, Huber depicts the often neglected and overlooked aspects of how the growing urban and post-industrial environment is defined and structured. The motifs of Huber's small format prints are often mundane and seem all too familiar. But with small shifts in the perception of reality, they allow for eye-opening interpretations of cultural and aesthetic phenomena. Huber's work process thus resembles that of a cultural researcher, not in a scientific sense, but through images that make complex relationships visible, reflecting at the same time how these images are constructed - a method that is also present in her video pieces and installations.

She is drawn to places that are defined predominantly by their function, as in her series on European Highways, "Autobahn" (1997/2000), photographed from the perspective of a pedestrian walking alongside the highways, observing details one would not normally notice whilst driving.

In the photoseries "Anlagen" (2001/2006), Huber deals with the fast-growing infrastructure of global tourism. Photographing in mass-tourism centres in Spain, Israel, Egypt and recently in Dubai, she looks at hotels and vast holiday resorts at an unusual moment: out of season or under construction. The pools are shown empty, the architecture is often in a state of imperfection and the deserted landscapes around the hotels are included in the overall view. Huber allows us to study these structures from a distance, as if presented with the remains of an unknown civilisation. She offers a non-polemical view, with no specific focal points or highlights in her motifs - nothing much to hold on to other than a strong but uncanny feeling of familiarity.

أوشـي هيوبر

ترتكز أعمال أوشي هيوبر على استخدام التصوير الفوتوغرافي والفيديو، بحيث تصنع سلسلة من الصور الفوتوغرافيّة من تصويرها هي، بالإضافة إلى استخدام صور موجودة أصلا.

في تصويرها الفوتوغرافي، تلتقط هيوبر الجوانب المهملة والمُتغاضى عنها والمتمثلة في كيف تتحدد وتتشكّل البيئة المدينيّة والمابعد-صناعيّة النامية. عادة ما تكون الأفكار البارزة (الموتيفات) في طبعات هيوبر الصغيرة الحجم عاديّة وقد تبدو مألوفة للغاية. ولكن بتغيّر صغير في إدراك الواقع، تسمح هذه الصور بتفسيرات تنويريّة للظواهر الثقافية والجماليّة. من هذه الناحية، تشبه العملية التي تنجز فيها هيوبر أعمالها الفنية ما يقوم به باحث اجتماعيّ، ليس من الناحية العلميّة، وإنما من خلال الصور التي تجعل العلاقات المعقّدة مرئيّة، وتعكس في الوقت ذاته كيفيّة تكوين هذه الصور. هذا الأسلوب حاضر كذلك في أعمالها الأخرى، الفيديو والتركيبات الفنيّة.

تنجذب أوشي للأماكن التي يتحدد معناها من خلال وظيفتها بشكل رئيسي، كما في سلسلتها عن الطرق السريعة الأوروبيّة، "أوتوبان" (١٩٩٧/٢٠٠٠)، التي صوّرتها من منظور أحد المشاة وهو يسير بمحاذاة الطرق السريعة، ويراقب التفاصيل التي لا يمكن للمرء أن يراها عادة أثناء القيادة.

في سلسلة الصور "آنلاجن" (٢٠٠١/٢٠٠٦)، تتعامل هيوبر مع البنية التحتيّة سريعة النمو للسياحة العولميّة. صُوّرت في مراكز سياحة-جماهيرية في إسبانيا وإسرائيل ومصر وحديثا في دبي، تلقي نظرة على فنادق ومنتجعات سياحيّة ضخمة في لحظات غير عاديّة: خارج موسم السياحة وقيد الإنشاء. تظهر برك السباحة مهجورة فارغة، والهندسة المعماريّة في حالة من عدم الاكتمال، كما تُدخل المشاهد الطبيعيّة المهجورة حول الفنادق في النظرة الشاملة. تسمح هيوبر بدراسة هذه الإنشاءات عن بعد، وكأنّما هي بقايا حضارة غير معروفة. إنّها توفّر مشاهد دون مماراة، بلا أيّ بؤر أو تركيز على "الموتيفات". لا شئ لإدراكه فعلا إلّا شعور غريب قويّ لما هو مألوف.

Anlagen, 2001/2006, photo series, C-prints, 38 x 38 cm and 43 x 38 cm

MOHAMMED AHMAD IBRAHIM

The Circles of Khor Fakkan - 2004

My son and I would ride our bicycles to this mountainous area in Khor Fakkan and there we made these six different-sized circles. In the future we might add more circles. The idea behind it is the bicycle: the motion of the bicycle. It is about the movement of ideas, of the bicycle, and the very act of carrying these little stones from one place to another. Art is motion; it is walking, riding a bike, realising, thinking, reacting, feeling... Motion! We don't want to stop, we are in perpetual motion, the geography, the social life of Khor Fakkan, they are all in perpetual motion. The circle has a musical ring; it rotates around a fixed axis. The rocks in Khor Fakkan are naturally round-shaped. Through this piece I want to break out of the circle and communicate my art and thought to the world. My art has everything to do with art history from Paul Cézanne to Richard Long. The circle has a very important geometrical value in our lives. It supplies new vision... the circle is earth; it is the sky; it is the universe.

Mohammed Ahmed Ibrahim

محمد أحمد إبراهيم

دوائر خورفكّان - ٢٠٠٤

كنّا نذهب أنا وابني بالدراجة الهوائية إلى هذه المنطقة الجبلية في خورفكان، وهناك صنعنا هذه الدوائر الست المختلفة الأحجام. قد نضيف المزيد من الدوائر في المستقبل. هذا العمل يعتمد على حركة الدراجة وحركة الفكر وحركة الإنسان في نقل هذه الأحجار الصغيرة من مكانها إلى مكان آخر. الفن هو الحركة، المشي، امتطاء الدرّاجة، الإدراك، التفكير، الانفعال، الإحساس جميعها في حركة دائمة! لا نريد أن نقف، نحن في حركة مستمرة، طبيعة خورفكان الجغرافية والاجتماعية في حركة دائمة. وللدائرة إيقاع موسيقي وهي تدور على محور ثابت. طبيعة الأحجار في خورفكان دائرية الشكل. من خلال عملي أريد أن أخرج من الدائرة لكي أوصل سياقي الفني والفكري إلى العالم. أعمالي لها علاقة وثيقة الصلة بتاريخ الفن من "بول سيزانٍ" إلى "ريتشارد لونج". للدائرة قيمة هندسية مهمة جداً في حياتنا وتمدّنا برؤية جديدة. الدائرة هي الأرض والسماء والكون كله.

محمّد أحمد إبراهيم

The Circles of Khor Fakkan, 2004, documentation photograph

ALFREDO JAAR

Muxima

If you want a sense of how utterly alive Africa is today, culturally and politically, listen to its popular music. That's what Alfredo Jaar does in his beautiful 30-minute film, *Muxima* (pronounced moo-sheem-AH), set in Angola and named for a local folk song.

Mr. Jaar is perhaps best known for another work inspired by Africa, a multipart project about Rwanda made in the immediate aftermath of the slaughter of Tutsi people. Unlike Thomas Hirshhorn's recent installation at Barbara Gladstone, with its gruesome photographs of Iraqi war casualties, Mr. Jaar's piece, a spartan, text-intensive installation, included no pictures of the Rwandan dead, as if he mistrusted the too-easy saturation effect of documentary images.

Muxima takes the opposite tack. A color film in 10 short sections, or "cantos", soaks us in images of Angolan life and history. Shots of crumbling commemorative sculptures refer to the country's past as a Portuguese colony; street signs with the names of Communist revolutionary heroes recall support from Cuba and the Soviet Union in the 1970s and '80s. Then there is life today in a land oil-rich and cash-poor: children cavorting at a beach; adults, as dignified as statesmen, traveling downriver in a boat; a patient languishing in a hospital; a land mine exploding.

Behind everything, like flowing water, is the song itself – "Muxima" means "heart" in the indigenous language of Angola – in several recorded versions. One is as sad and slow as a lament, another is peppy as a dance tune; a third, delivered in an exquisite high tenor by a singer seen in the film, throbs like a love song, which is what Mr. Jaar's clear-eyed film is.

Holland Cotter
Review of Alfredo Jarr's *Muxima* in The New York Times,
March 10, 2006

ألفريدو جار

موشيما

إذا أردت أن تشعر بنبض الحياة الثقافية والسياسية المتوقد في إفريقيا اليوم، عليك أن تستمتع إلى الموسيقى الإفريقية الشعبية. هذا ما قام به ألفريدو جار في هذا الفيلم الجميل الممتد ٣٠ دقيقة، "موشيما"، والذي تسير أحداثه في أنغولا ويحمل عنوان أغنية فولكلورية محلية.

السيد جار معروف بعمل آخر مستلهم من إفريقيا، وهو مشروع متعدد الأجزاء حول رواندا، قام بتنفيذه مباشرة بعد مجازر قبائل التوتسي. وبعكس العمل التركيبي الذي قام به هيرشهورن مؤخرا في باربارا غلادستون، بصوره البشعة عن ضحايا الحرب العراقية، فإن العمل الفني الذي قام به السيد جار، هو عمل تركيبي - نصي - اسبارطي، لا يحتوي على أي صور لأموات من رواندا، وكأنه لا يثق أبدا بالأثر الإشباعي للمشاهد التوثيقية.

"موشيما" يتخذ مسارا مضادا. فيلم بالألوان في ١٠ أقسام قصيرة، أو "كانتوات"، تغرقنا بمشاهد من حياة وتاريخ أنغولا. مشاهد لمنحوتات تذكارية منهارة تشير إلى الاحتلال البرتغالي الذي يشكل جزءاً من ماضي هذا البلد. علامات الشوارع التي تحمل أسماء أبطال ثوريين شيوعيين. وتستحضر دعم كوبا والاتحاد السوفياتي في السبعينيات والثمانينيات. ثم هناك الحياة اليومية المعاصرة في دولة غنية بالنفط، فقيرة بالسيولة النقدية: أطفال يتقافزون على الشاطئ، بالغون يتحلون بكبرياء الساسة يركبون قاربا في النهر، مريض يعاني في مستشفى، ولغم أرضي ينفجر.

وفي خلفية المشاهد كلها، كما الماء المتدفق، نسمع الأغنية - "موشيما" والتي تعني "القلب" باللهجة الانغولية - بتسجيلات مختلفة. إحدى التسجيلات حزينة وبطيئة كما لو أنها تندب الحياة، تسجيل آخر سريع وراقص، وتسجيل ثالث بصوت جهوري عال لمغن نشاهده في الفيلم، ينبض كأغنية حب، كما هو هذا الفيلم واضح الرؤيا للسيد جار.

هولاند كوتر
صحيفة النيويورك تايمز
١٠ مارس/آذار ٢٠٠٦

Muxima, 2005, digital video, 36 min, sound, courtesy of the artist and Galerie Lelong, New York

Canto IV
Pearl Jam

AVENIDA LENIN
MESTRE E GUIA DA REVOLUÇÃO DO
PROLETARIADO FUNDADOR DO
PRIMEIRO ESTADO SOCIALISTA DO
MUNDO 1870-1924
RUA
COMANDANTE
CHE GUEVARA
RUA
SALVADOR ALLENDE

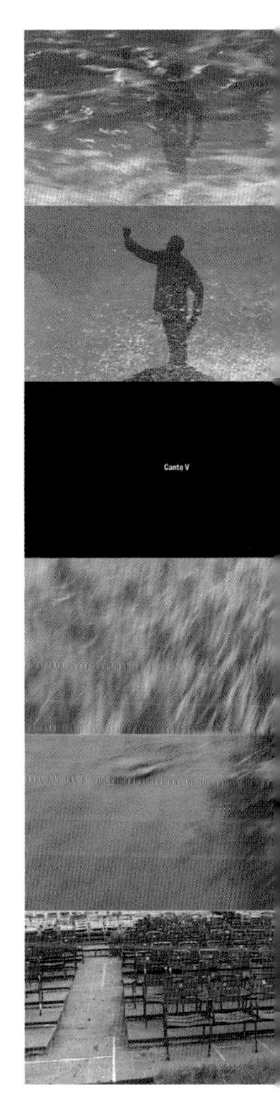
Canto V

MARYA KAZOUN

An artist's imagination, creativity, and transversely off-centre position leave behind a circumstantial trace that is linked to the artist's own individual sphere of influence. This concentration is channelled into their poetic dialogue with the world and the society they live in and which lives through them.

The tragic nature of the shapes sought out and created by Marya Kazoun are the point of contact between her emotivity and the conditioning framework of external activities.

The contingent dark moments in history regularly lead us back towards the thorny issues of life: time and death. But the fine line crosses over with life, with all its inevitable beauty and all its inevitable cruelty.

This moment is the backdrop for Kazoun's imaginative research into shapes in an oeuvre that seems to develop a questioning tension in the same way that human beings live and survive life. What might come across as a form of delirium is nothing other than love for the world, or sadness, or freedom from falseness. Kazoun acts with a broad strategy where she places the visible energy of what, every day, all over the world, our eyes refuse to see: to put the human being back in a central position.

Her work is a mirror in which we can see our own reflections. It may have a frightening soul, but Kazoun mends the rough edges to take care of us, to alleviate suffering and lead us back in the direction of thought.

Martina Cavallarin

A special thanks to Christian Minotto, for all his talent, perseverance and dedication and a special thanks to Andrea Busetto

ماريا قزعون

يخلف خيال الفنان وقدراته الإبداعية وموقعه التقاطعي البعيد عن المركز، أثرا ظرفيا مرتبطا بمجال نفوذه الفردي. يتدفق هذا التمركز عبر حوارياته الشعرية مع العالم، ومع المجتمع الذي يعيش فيه، والذي يحيا من خلاله.

إن الطبيعة المأساوية للأشكال التي تبحث عنها ماريا كازون، ومن ثم تخلقها، هي نقطة الإتصال بين قدرتها على ابتعاث المشاعر والإطار المكيف للأنشطة الخارجية. فاللحظات المظلمة في التاريخ تقودنا دوما إلى الوراء، نحو قضايا الحياة الشائكة: الزمن والموت. غير أن الخط الدقيق يعبر قدما مع الحياة، بكل ما هنالك من جمال محتم وقسوة محتمة.

تلك اللحظة هي الخلفية التي تنطلق منها كازون في استقصائها التخيلي للأشكال، وذلك في جملة أعمالها التي تبدو وكأنها تطور حالة من التوتر التساؤلي، على النحو الذي يعيش فيه البشر ويواصلون حياتهم. إن ما قد يظهر على أنه شكل من الهلوسة ليس إلا حبا للعالم، أو حزنا، أو تحررا من الزيف. فكازون تتصرف وفقا لاستراتيجية واسعة تضع من خلالها تلك الطاقة الرؤيوية التي ترفض عيوننا، كل يوم، وعلى امتداد العالم، أن تراها، والتي هي: إعادة الإنسان إلى موقع مركزي.

إن أعمال كازون مرآة نتمكن فيها من رؤية انعكاساتنا. قد تكون روح هذه الإنعكاسات مرعبة، غير أن كازون تصلح حواشيها لكي تواسينا، لكي تخفف من معاناتنا، ولكي تعود بنا إلى عالم الفكر.

مارتينا كافالارين

شكر خاص لكريستيان منوتو لموهبته، مثابرته وإخلاصه، وشكر خاص لأندريه بسيتو

Crumbling Desert Castle D6, 2006, drawing, mixed-media, 41 x 31 cm, photo: Francesco Ferruzzi

AMAL KENAWY

I try, always try, to create a space where I can probe my identities vis-á-vis the world around me. Using a wide range of mediums, I often attempt to explore the world of illusion against a background of memory, a memory nearly always based in reality. By sensing and exposing a metaphorical world that hides beneath the physical, I attempt to bring the unseen into a visual space. In the context of my work, I had come to sense the existence of a metaphorical room that hides behind the physicality of the body, a room that reflects the much bigger room outside, the one representing society, its customs, traditions, conventions and the factors conditioning it.

You Will be Killed is a video animation project. In the animation, my world depicts a person's self - their memories. Their dreams are shown on the walls of my surroundings. However, they are shown through symbolic representation instead of illustration. Some content corresponds to where a particular event (in the person's memory) is taking place, and other content corresponds to the person him/herself - hence the relation between a person and their surroundings. Therefore, any particular event in a person's life will not only represent a geographical location, but also their feelings, memories, and emotional drives.

The starting point for You Will be Killed is my visit to an old camp from the time of the English colonisation 30 years ago and the memories stirred by that location. To me, war is the easiest way to depict violence. However, my aim was to depict that violence in a circle of imagination far from war itself, and to show how it affects oneself and one's surroundings.

I plan to show memories of a person's self and their relationship with their surroundings in such a way that s/he is an absent viewer, or a static one, yet their surroundings are dynamic. The location, spaces as intimacy spaces, and their relationship with the person, all switch roles throughout the animation until they lose their original function. Then violence takes over and becomes the main drive of the story.

Non-stop conversation takes place through the overlapping artificial sounds of the machinery, until it reaches the point at which the sounds occur simultaneously and the place is reconstructed architecturally through a projection aimed at changing architectural constriction and rearranging it according to the extension, the overlapping and the violence of the voice performance in an inversely proportional method. The place becomes more constricted, chaotic and of unknown dimensions.

أمل القناوي

أحاول، دائما أحاول، أن أخلق مساحة أستطيع أن أتفحص فيها هوياتي من خلال العالم المحيط بي. وكثيراً ما أحاول أن استكشف، باستخدام وسائط متعددة، عالم الخيال على خلفية الذاكرة، والتي عادة ما تكون مبنية على أساس الواقع. من خلال عرض والإحساس بعالم مجازي يختبئ وراء العالم المادي، أحاول أن استحضر ما لا يرى إلى مساحة مرئية. في سياق عملي، بدأت أحس بوجود غرفة مجازية تختبئ وراء مادية الجسد، غرفة تعكس الغرفة الأكبر في الخارج، الغرفة التي تمثل المجتمع بعاداته وتقاليده والعناصر التي تشكله.

"ولسوف تقتل" هو مشروع فيديو صور متحركة. في الصور المتحركة يعرض عالمي "حياة" الشخص – ذكرياته. تظهر أحلامه على الحيطان المحيطة. تظهر من خلال رموز وليس رسوما توضيحية. بعض المضمون يحيل إلى موقع حادثة (في ذاكرة الشخص)، ومضامين أخرى تحيل إلى الشخص بحد ذاته. الحديث هو إذاً، عن العلاقة بين الشخص ومحيطه، وبالتالي، فإن أي حدث ما في حياة الشخص، لن يمثل موقعا جغرافيا فقط، وإنما سيمثل أيضا، مشاعر وذكريات ودوافع شعورية.

نقطة البدء لمشروع "ولسوف تقتل"، هي زيارتي للمخيم القديم من أيام الاستعمار الإنجليزي قبل ٣٠ عاماً، والذكريات التي ارتبطت مع ذلك الموقع.

بالنسبة لي، الحرب هي أسهل طريقة لعرض العنف، إلا أن هدفي كان أن أوضح ذلك العنف في دائرة من الخيال بعيدة عن الحرب بحد ذاتها، ولأوضح كيف تؤثر على الشخص ومحيطه. صورة الإنسان، الوجه، صورتي الشخصية، محاولة الرسم على حيطان الموقع، المخططات ترسم وتنمو في علاقة تبادلية تآكلية لا نهائية.

أريد أن أظهر ذاكرة الشخص نفسه، وعلاقته بمحيطه بطريقة يصبح فيها مشاهداً غائباً، أو ثابتاً، إلا أن محيطه ديناميكي متغير. الموقع، والمساحات كمساحات حميمة، وعلاقتها بالشخص، كلها تتبادل الأدوار عبر الصور المتحركة حتى تفقد وظيفتها الأصلية، حينها، يسيطر العنف على الموقف، ويصبح الدافع الأساسي للحكاية.

يصدر حديث متواصل من خلال الأصوات المصطنعة المتداخلة للآلات، حتى تصل إلى نقطة تصدر فيها الأصوات في نفس الوقت والمكان، وتتم إعادة هندستها من خلال عرض، يهدف إلى تغيير المحددات الهندسية وإعادة ترتيبها حسب امتداد وتقاطع وعنف الأداء الصوتي في مقاربة تناسب عكسي. يصبح المكان أضيق، ذو أبعاد فوضوية غير واضحة.

You'll be Killed, 2006, video animation, installation view, 1st Singapore biennial

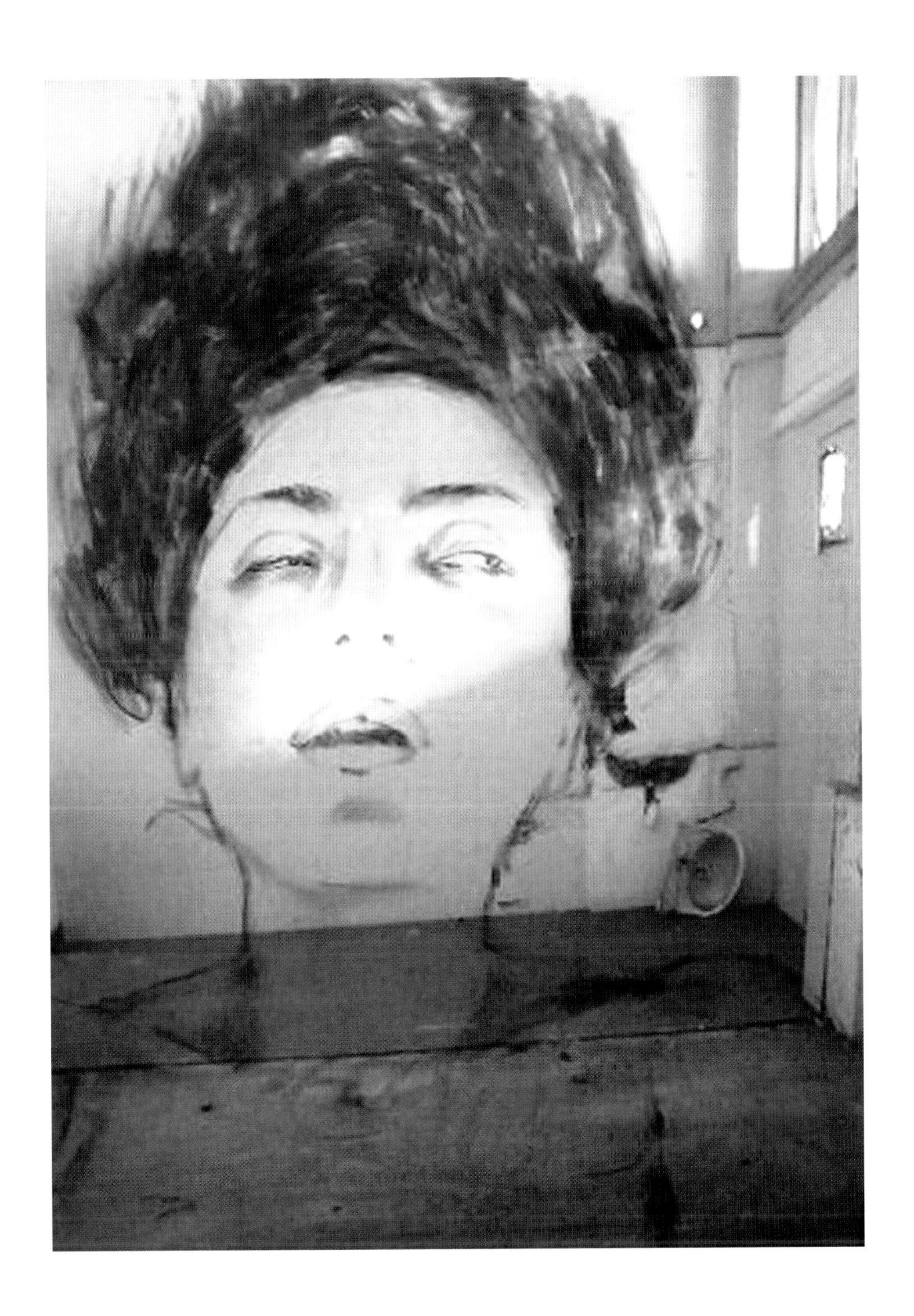

LEOPOLD KESSLER

In 2004, while still a student at the Akademie der bildenden Künste in Vienna, Leopold Kessler installed a 1,200m long electric cable from his studio at the academy to his private apartment – characteristically without seeking permission beforehand (*Akademiekabel*, 2004). For several weeks the artist obtained power parasitically from the institute's supply, until the day of his graduation, when he literally cut the cord. The only visual outcome of the project is a video, showing him (with the help of several orange-jacketed friends) dismantling and rolling up the cable all the way back round a gigantic cable-drum (*Diplom*, 2004). In this early work, Kessler playfully posed questions about our daily need for energy – where it comes from and to whom it belongs – through a simple yet circuitous, humorous yet subversive act of annexation. This strategy of gentle anarchism is integral to his artistic practice. Kessler's interventions in public space operate somewhere between service and sabotage, and explore the very relationship of the individual to his environment. Often disguised in blue workers' overalls, Kessler makes unauthorised interventions against public facilities, repairing things or altering them according to his own personal needs – or just for the purpose of creating a moment of absurdity, surprise or irritation in our daily routine. He has equipped street lamps with a remote control, allowing him to switch the lights off and on, as necessary (*Privatized*, 2003), used the letter 'O' in a police station lightbox as portal to a secret depot for storing money (*Depot*, 2005), manipulated the water pressure of public fountains in the Austrian city of Graz, so that they spat their water jets beyond their basins, eventually flooding a busy square (*Graz Hauptplatz*, 2006), and linked two soda machines via gsm-technique, so that if a coin were inserted in one machine, the selected can dropped out of the other, and vice versa; the machines could connect places around the globe (*Soda Machine a/b*, 2006). With his secret operations, Kessler takes simple given functions that are in the public domain into his own hands, and by altering them or reversing them, questions the way in which we passively interact with a given surrounding.

Eva Scharrer

ليوبولد كيسلر

ركّب ليوبولد كيسلر، وهو ما يزال تلميذا في أكاديمية دير بيلدندن كونسته في فيينا، في ٢٠٠٤، كابلاً كهربائيّاً بطول ١٢٠٠ مترا من موقع مشغله (الاستوديو) في الأكاديميّة إلى شقّته الخاصّة، دون أن يطلب تصريحا مسبقا (أكاديميكابل (كابل – أكاديمي)، ٢٠٠٤).

لعدّة أسابيع، "تطفّل" الفنّان على مصدر الطاقة الخاص بالمؤسسة، حتّى يوم تخرّجه حين قطع الحبل (إشارة إلى الحبل السرّيّ) فعليّا. الناتج البصريّ الوحيد لهذه التجربة هو فيديو فحسب، يُظهره (بمساعدة مجموعة من أصدقائه ذوي المعاطف البرتقاليّة اللون) وهم يفكّون الكابل ويلفّونه على بكرة بشكل كامل ومنظّم (دبلوم، ٢٠٠٤). في هذا العمل المبكّر، يطرح كيسلر متلاعباً، أسئلة عن حاجتنا اليوميّة للطاقة – من أين تأتي ومن يملكها – من خلال فعل تملّك بسيط ملتو ومرح إلاّ أنّه مشاكس. استراتيجيّة "الفوضويّة" الرقيقة هذه أمر جاد في عمله الفنّي. تدخّلات كيسلر في المساحات العامّة تعمل في مساحة بين الخدمة والتخريب، وتستكشف العلاقة ذاتها بين الفرد وبيئته. ينفّذ كيسلر، متنكّرا في العادة بزيّ عامل "ذو ياقة زرقاء"، أعمالاً غير مرخّصة في مرافق عامّة، يصلّح أشياء أو يغيّرها تبعا لحاجاته الخاصّة – أو من أجل خلق لحظة من العبثيّة فحسب، أو مفاجأة أو إزعاج روتين حياتنا اليوميّة. زوّد عواميد إنارة عامّة بأجهزة تحكّم عن بعد مما أتاح له التحكّم بالإنارة، إضاءة أو تعتيما، حسب الضرورة (برايفاتايزد (تخصيص)، ٢٠٠٣)، أو استعمل الحرف "O" في صندوق إضاءة في مخفر شرطة كبوّابة لمخزن سرّي من أجل إيداع الأموال (ديبو "مخزن"، ٢٠٠٥)، أو تلاعب بضغط الماء في نافورة عامّة لتلفظ الماء ما بعد الأحواض مباشرة وبما يؤدي إلى إغراق ساحة مكتظّة في مدينة كراز، النمسا (كراز هوبتبلاتس، ٢٠٠٦)، أو أوصَلَ آلتي مشروبات غازيّة من خلال تقنية (gsm) بحيث إن وضع أحدهم قطعة نقديّة في إحداهما سقطت العبوة التي تمّ اختيارها من الآلة الثانية وبالعكس (صودا أ/ب، ٢٠٠٦). يمكن للآلات أن توصل أماكن في أنحاء العالم ببعضها البعض. بعمليّاته السريّة يأخذ كيسلر بيده زمام وظائف بسيطة مسلّم بها في المجال العام، وبتغييره إياها أو عكسها، يتساءل عن الكيفيّة السلبيّة التي نتعامل بها مع المحيط المُعطى.

إيفا شارير

Red Sea Star, 2007, video, courtesy of the artist

SUCHAN KINOSHITA

They were different tribes. They did have one thing in common, I heard from his story. The people in that reliving of mine of his remembrance don't speak to each other the way do we in North Western Europe. They don't speak in our remarkably affected construction-like manner, whereby we exclude almost the whole world. The talking was a talking that was not practical for activists. Everyone said what was bothering him or her, the water supply, minor and major urgencies, activism too. Why not. For hours on end, until the conversation became a conversation by itself.

From such talk something approaching a consensus can grow, or something can grow which coheres in the way the world coheres, or an image of the world coheres.

An extract from Das Fragment an sich, written in collaboration between Bart de Baere and Suchan Kinoshita

سوشان كينو شيتا

قدموا من مختلف القبائل. وكان لديهم شيء واحد مشترك سمعت قصته. فالناس في ذلك الموقع الذي أعيد إحياءه من الذاكرة. لا يتحدثون إلى بعضهم بالطريقة التي نتحدث بها في شمال غرب أوروبا. إنهم لا يتحدثون بطريقتنا المتكلفة التأويلية التي نقصي بها العالم كله تقريباً. الحديث كان حديثا غير عملي بالنسبة للناشطين. فكل شخص عبّر عمّا يزعجه/ها - كمية المياه. الطوارئ الثانوية والرئيسية. والعمل الخالص. ولم لا؟ ولساعات عديدة. وحتى أصبح الحوار حواراً بحد ذاته.

يمكن أن ينبثق عن حديث كهذا ما يشبه الإجماع. أو يمكن أن ينبثق عنه شيء منسجم بالطريقة التي ينسجم بها العالم مع بعضه بعضاً. أو قد تنسجم أمامنا صورة للعالم.

اقتباس من Das Fragment an sich. كتب بالتعاون بين برت دو بار وسوشان كينو شيتا

Isofollies, 2006, wrapped rubbish from exhibition, 60 x 47 x 57 cm, 65 x 43 x 43cm, 60 x 50 x 39 cm, installation view Ikon Gallery, photo Jerry Hardman-Jones

JOACHIM KOESTER

From the Travel of Jonathan Harker

The Bargau Valley in Northeastern Transylvania provides the setting for much of Bram Stoker's novel Dracula (1897). Here Stoker situated Count Dracula's Castle, Jonathan Harker's wolf-haunted journey through the Borgo Pass, and the last part of the novel concluding with the beheaded Dracula evaporating into dust.

Bram Stoker never visited Transylvania but conducted extensive research in the reading room of the British Museum. Studying travel accounts and books on Transylvanian folklore, Stoker added excerpts from these to his story, anchoring his imaginary scenes in a geographic region which, at the time, was considered to be one of the "wildest and least known portions of Europe".

In Spring 2003, I was invited to Iasis, Romania, to participate in the exhibition "Prophetic Corners". Intrigued by the speculative nature of the exhibition's title and concept - that some places have the power of letting us see into the future - I went to Transylvania and travelled towards the Carpathians from Bistrita, just like Jonathan Harker in Stoker's book. My attention was equally divided between an interest in this region that had been re-created as a "landscape of the mind" in countless films and narratives, and the idea of "prophetic corners", which also implied a mapping of a somewhat invisible territory.

On the outskirts of Bistrita, which Stoker described as covered with "a bewildering mass of fruit blossom", I passed a development of suburban houses - enormous one-family houses in pastel colours, most of them newly built with the windows covered in black plastic. While the grey high-rises of Bistrita on the horizon and the absence of people gave a slight edge to the scenery, it also seemed very familiar. The houses looked no different from what I had seen in countless other places, pointing to a future of all-encompassing sameness.

My trip ended at Hotel Castle Dracula, built in 1982, to accommodate a steady stream of vampire aficionados visiting the region, at approximately the place where Dracula's Castle is located in Stoker's novel. The area was not being haunted by 'the undead' though, but by a series of scandals involving illegal logging with profits benefiting a group of corrupt government officials colluding with local entrepreneurs. Everywhere I looked, even on the most remote mountaintops, the landscape showed signs of the logging industry in the form of treeless spots. These spots did add a post-historic touch to the surroundings, but also pointed to something familiar from the (recent) past and present, the transformation of a landscape by the forces of market economy.

يواكيم كوستر

من رحلات جوناثان هاركر

يمثّل وادي بارغاو في ترانسيلفينيا الشماليّة الشرقيّة مسرحا لجزء كبير من رواية برام ستوكر دراكولا (١٨٩٧). فهناك وضع ستوكر قلعة الكونت دراكولا، وخط مسار رحلة جوناثان هاركر المسكونة بالذئاب خلال ممر بورغو، ثم ينتهي آخر جزء من الرواية بتحوّل دراكولا مقطوع الرأس إلى غبار.

لم يزر برام ستوكر ترانسيلفينيا قط، إلاّ أنّه قام ببحث معمّق في مكتبة المتحف البريطاني. درس سجلاّت الرحلات وكتب عن الفلكلور الترانسيلفيني، وأضاف ستوكر مقتطفات منها إلى قصّته، مثبّتا مشاهده الخياليّة في منطقة جغرافيّة كانت تُعتبر آنذاك إحدى "أكثر أجزاء أوروبا إثارة وأقلّها استكشافا."

دُعيت إلى إياسيس، رومانيا، في ربيع ٢٠٠٣، للمشاركة في معرض "بروفيتيك كورنرز (زوايا تنبؤيّة)." وقد أثارتني الطبيعة الوجدانية لعنوان المعرض ومفهومه - أنّ لبعض الأماكن قدرة تسمح لنا برؤية المستقبل. ذهبت إلى ترانسيلفينيا وسافرت نحو الكارباثيانز من بيستريتا، كما فعل جوناثان هاركر بالضبط في كتاب ستوكر. انقسم اهتمامي بالتساوي بين المنطقة التي أعيد تشكيلها في أفلام وروايات لا تحصى كما لو كانت "مشهدا طبيعيا وجدانيا"، وفكرة "الزوايا التنبؤيّة" والتي توحي كذلك بتركيب على مناطق غير مرئيّة إلى حد ما.

في ضواحي بيستريتا، التي وصفها ستوكر بأنّها مغطّاة بـ "كتلة مذهلة من نوار شجر الفاكهة"، مررت بمحاذاة بيوت الضواحي، بيوت ضخمة، كل منها لعائلة واحدة، مطلية بألوان باهتة، تم بناء معظمها حديثا ويغطّي نوافذها بلاستيك أسود. وفي حين تمنح مباني بيستريتا العالية الرمادية الظاهرة في الأفق وخلوّ الموقع من الناس جديّة ما للمشهد، إلا أنه يبدو مألوفا للغاية. لم تبد هذه البيوت مختلفة جدا عن مثيلات لها رأيتها في أماكن عديدة أخرى، وهو بحد ذاته مؤشر إلى مستقبل من التماثل الشمولي.

توجت رحلتي في فندق قصر دراكولا، الذي بُني في العام ١٩٨٢ في نفس موقع رواية ستوكر تقريبا، ليستقبل الأفواج المستمرّة من زوار المنطقة المغرمين بمصّاصي الدماء. ولكن المنطقة لم تكن مسكونة بـ "اللاّميّتين" على أيّة حال، إنما بفضائح عن تلاعب بصناعة التحطيب لصالح مجموعة من موظّفي الحكومة بالتواطؤ مع رجال أعمال محليين. أينما تجولت بنظرك، حتّى في أبعد قمم الجبال، يوحي المشهد الطبيعي بالتحطيب، بدليل البقع الخالية من الأشجار. تضيف هذه البقع صفة مابعد تاريخية للمنطقة، إلاّ أنّها دليل أيضا على أمر مألوف من الماضي (القريب) والحاضر، ألا وهو تحوّلات المشهد الطبيعي بتأثير قوى اقتصاد السوق.

From the Travel of Jonathan Harker, 2003, C-print, 50 x 60 cm, courtesy Galleri Nicolai Wallner

CHRISTINA KUBISCH

You may not fear these silences, you may love them

John Cage

What you see and what you hear often differ a lot. You may walk through a beautiful forest and hear the drone of the highways or explore a historic building and be surrounded by the noise of the electric airconditioner. Mostly we can accommodate these unwelcome neighbours, because we are used to them – or we pretend not to hear them. Sudden silence can be a shock because silence permits you to listen to unknown sounds, small sounds, fragile acoustic events that are usually hidden under the cloak of overall noise.

In the period of so-called Romanticism there are many paintings depicting solitary travellers gazing at the moon, sitting in the desert or contemplating the ocean.These visual paradises are easier to represent than the acoustic ones, at least in the Western tradition. Maybe many of these pictures are not very original, but they are easy to understand. Idyllic sonic landscapes are not so easy to imagine and much harder to build up from memory.

What do we remember of the sounds that could accompany a Romantic landscape? What do we hear when it is silent? Do we remember the reverberation of raindrops falling on a leaf or the early morning birdsong? Do we recall these sounds from our memory or do we remember them from the last movie we saw? Were they real or electronic sounds? Can we be sure? Does it matter? We do not question our acoustic memories, therefore it is easy to manipulate them.

In my artistic practice I like to play with the opposites of the true and the false. For example I use ultraviolet light or the high frequency sound of a tuning fork to create atmosphere, which seems artificial, but is based on natural phenomena. Familiar sounds give us security, daily protection from the unknown. But by implanting sounds out of context in a given situation a change of perception takes place. This is a chance to trigger a new relationship with what seemed familiar and which suddenly may become an unknown environment.

كرستينا كوبيش

لا يمكنك أن تخشى هذا الصمت. يمكنك أن تحبّه

جون كيج

غالبا ما يختلف ما تسمعه عما تراه. يمكنك أن تمشي في غابة جميلة وتسمع هدير الطرق السريعة. أو أن تستكشف مبنى تاريخيّا وتحيط بك ضجّة مكيف الهواء الكهربائي. يمكننا في الغالب أن نتأقلم مع هذه المجاورات لأننا متعوّدون عليها أو نتظاهر بعدم سماعها.

قد يكون الصمت المفاجئ صدمة. لأنّ الصمت يتيح لك الاستماع إلى أصوات غير معروفة. أصوات خافتة. أو أحداث صوتيّة رقيقة تختبئ عادة في عباءة الضجيج العام.

في فترة الرومانسية في الفن. ثمة صور عديدة تمثّل رحّالة منعزلين ينظرون نحو القمر أو يجلسون في الصحراء أو يتأمّلون المحيط. يمكن تمثيل الجنان البصريّة بسهولة أكبر من تمثيل تلك السمعيّة. على الأقل في التقاليد الغربيّة. قد لا تكون هذه الصور مبتكرة ولكنّها سهلة الفهم. ليس من السهل تخيّل مناظر صوتية شاعرية. أما استحضارها من الذاكرة فأمر أصعب بكثير.

ما الذي يمكننا تذكّره من الأصوات التي تتماشى مع المناظر الرومانسيّة؟ ما الذي نسمعه عندما تكون صامتة؟ هل نتذكّر صدى قطرات المطر وهي تتساقط على ورقة شجر. أو أغنيات الطيور الأولى في الصباح؟ هل نستحضرها من الذاكرة. أم من آخر فيلم شاهدناه؟ هل كانت طبيعية أو إلكترونيّة؟ هل الإجابة أكيدة؟ هل هذا مهم؟ لا تراودنا الشكوك أو التساؤلات بشأن ذكرياتنا الصوتيّة. وبالتالي من السهل جدا التلاعب بها.

أحبّ في أعمالي الفنية أن ألعب مع أضداد الصح والخطأ. أستعمل. على سبيل المثال. الضوء فوق البنفسجيّ أو الأصوات عالية التردد لشوكة الدوزان لأصنع أجواء تبدو اصطناعية. ولكنها تعتمد على ظواهر طبيعيّة. تمنحنا الأصوات المألوفة شعورا بالأمان. الحماية اليوميّة من المجهول. ولكن حين نزرع أصواتا خارجة عن السياق في وضع معيّن يحدث تغيّر في الإدراك. إنّها فرصة لإطلاق علاقات جديدة مع أمور مألوفة قد تتحول فجأة إلى محيط غير معروف.

Klangfeld, 2002, speakers, pigment, black light, multi-channel composition
Kunstverein Ebersberg, Germany, photos: Rolf Giegold

DEBORAH LIGORIO

"In an Irregular Configuration. Rapid changes: complex, turbulent, unpredictable. It's like moving into uncharted water; this is how I feel. Transformation brings melancholy. Conservation requires changes. Action calls for reaction. Reflux into flow. Trial generates error. Change brings uncertainty. Can anything be changed without being confronted? Or at least taken into consideration? I see it as a convincing signal that the danger has passed. A shift far from being peripheral brings with it a deep vulnerability. Whenever I am looking for a reference point, all is confirmed and then questioned again. Loss of pre-existing habitat during progressive shifts of conditions. Adaptation, migration, migration, adaptation. A different environment can profoundly change your personality. Many things make sense only in a given surrounding and can barely exist in other circumstances. Eventually in a different context you wonder how those things could have been possible. How difficult it is to adapt sometimes. Change and uncertainty are conditions occurring again and again. Maintaining an equilibrium is not easy, but why should I be pessimistic? I don't know enough. Tendency to preserve. Ability to improve. Developing a sustainable condition doesn't generate short-term gains. It requires a continuous redefinition."

Such are the words of the artist's voice-over on *Irregular Configuration* (2005), the video presented at the Sharjah Biennial 8. As in most of her videos, Deborah Ligorio uses her voice to take the viewer through images, forms and mental spaces. Here, images of landscapes are juxtaposed to Land Cover Animations, based on data from the European Commission programme to coordinate information on the Environment (CORINE), showing a survey of Europe's urban areas. After this information, more follows, in a nostalgic aesthetic that could be that of an old medicine book, with a list of information, abstracts from European Environment Agency reports on the impact of Europe's changing climate.

The artist often delimits a geographical or conceptual area over which she transposes other meanings, as in, for example, the videos *Wired Under Water* (1999) and *Donut to Spiral* (2004). Besides, a mental plot can be the original reason for shaping forms and figures, as in her drawings or collages and in several of her videos and animations, *Pattern* (2001), *SizeScape* (2003), *Landscape* (2002).

Deborah Ligorio's practice is characterised by a personal way of depicting surroundings through a rhythmic succession of narratives. Her work places the different layers of a subject side-by-side, playing with hierarchies and dimensions, making collective and personal stories overlap, which, in this context, often function as a metaphor for one other. A curious and specific mental chain emerges from her representations of a place. Ligorio thereby blends mental, social, cultural, and physical or geographical aspects while observing the environment in all its complexity.

ديبورا ليجوريو

"في تشكيلات غير منتظمة. تغيّرات سريعة. معقّدة. قلقة. لا يمكن التنبّؤ بها. كما التحرّك نحو مياه غير مستكشفة. هكذا أشعر. التغيّر يجلب الكآبة. المحافظة على شيء ما يتطلّب تغييرات. الفعل يدعو إلى ردّ فعل. التكثيف إلى جريان. التجربة تولّد الخطأ. التغيير يجلب المجهول. هل يمكن تغيير أيّ شئ دون مواجهته؟ أو على الأقل أخذه بعين الاعتبار. أرى، بإشارة مقنعة، أن الخطر قد مرّ. تحرّك بعيد عن الأطراف يجلب معه شعورا عميقا بالحساسيّة. في كلّ مرّة أبحث عن نقطة مرجعيّة، يصبح كلّ شئ أكيدا ومن ثمّ يصبح موضع شكّ مرّة ثانية. خسارة موطن موجود أصلا خلال تحولات متتالية للظروف. تكيّف، هجرة، هجرة، تكيّف. يمكن لمحيط جديد أن يغيّر شخصيّتك بعمق. تكون الكثير من الأمور منطقيّة فقط في سياق معيّن، وبالكاد تكون كذلك في ظروف أخرى. أخيرا، وفي سياق مختلف، تتساءل كيف كانت هذه الأمور ممكنة أصلا. يا لصعوبة التكيّف أحيانا. التغيّر وعدم الوضوح هما ظرفان يحدثان مرّة تلو المرّة. ليس من السهل المحافظة على التوازن، لكن لِمَ أكون متشائمة؟ لست أعرف ما يكفي. الميل نحو المحافظة. القدرة على التحسّن. تطوير وضع مستدام لا يولّد مكاسب على المدى القصير. يحتاج باستمرار إلى إعادة تعريف."

هذه هي الكلمات التي تتلوها الفنانة بصوتها في الفيديو المُقدّم إلى بينالي الشارقة الثامن بعنوان "شكل غير منتظم" (٢٠٠٥). كما في العديد من أعمال الفيديو خاصتها، تستعمل ديبورا ليجوريو صوتها لتحمل المُشاهد عبر الصور والأشكال والمساحات الذهنيّة. هنا، صور لمشاهد طبيعيّة مركّبة فوق رسومات متحرّكة "لاند كوفر" (غطاء الأرض) تعتمد على بيانات من برنامج الهيئة الأوروبيّة لتنسيق المعلومات عن البيئة (CORINE)، يظهر مسحا لمناطق مدينيّة أوروبيّة. بعد هذه المعلومات، يتبع المزيد، بجماليّات فيها حنين إلى الماضي كالتي قد نجدها في كتاب طبيّ قديم، مع قائمة من المعلومات، ملخّصات من تقارير الوكالة الأوروبيّة للبيئة عن أثر تغيّر المناخ الأوروبي.

غالبا ما تحدد الفنانة منطقة جغرافيّة أو مفهوميّة، وعليها تعيد ترتيب معان مختلفة، كما مثلا في الفيديو "مربوط بأسلاك تحت الماء" (وايرد اندر ووتر) (١٩٩٩) و"من كعكة دونت إلى لولب" (دونت تو سبايرل) (٢٠٠٤). بالإضافة إلى ذلك، يمكن لحبكة ذهنيّة أن تكون السبب الرئيس لتشكيل الأشكال والأجساد، كما في رسوماتها أو كولاجاتها وعدد من أفلامها الفيديو والرسوم المتحرّكة، "نمط" (باترن) (٢٠٠١) و"مشهد الحجم" (سايزسكيب) (٢٠٠٣) و"المشهد الطبيعي" (لاندسكيب) (٢٠٠٢).

يمكن وصف عمل ديبورا ليجوريو بأنه أسلوب شخصي في تصوير البيئة المحيطة من خلال إيقاع متواتر من السرد. يصفّ عملها طبقات الموضوع المختلفة جنبا إلى جنب، متلاعبا بالهرم التسلسلي والأبعاد، بحيث تتداخل القصص الشخصيّة والجماعيّة، والتي غالبا ما تقوم، في هذا السياق، مقام استعارة متبادلة. تبرز سلسلة ذهنيّة مميّزة ومثيرة للفضول من الكنايات التي تستخدمها لمكان ما. وتخلط ليجوريو بذلك ما بين الذهنيّ والإجتماعيّ والثقافي والحسيّ بينما تحافظ على احترامها للبيئة بكل تعقيداتها.

Irregular Configuration, 2005, video, double projection, 7 min loop, courtesy of the artist and Francesca Minini

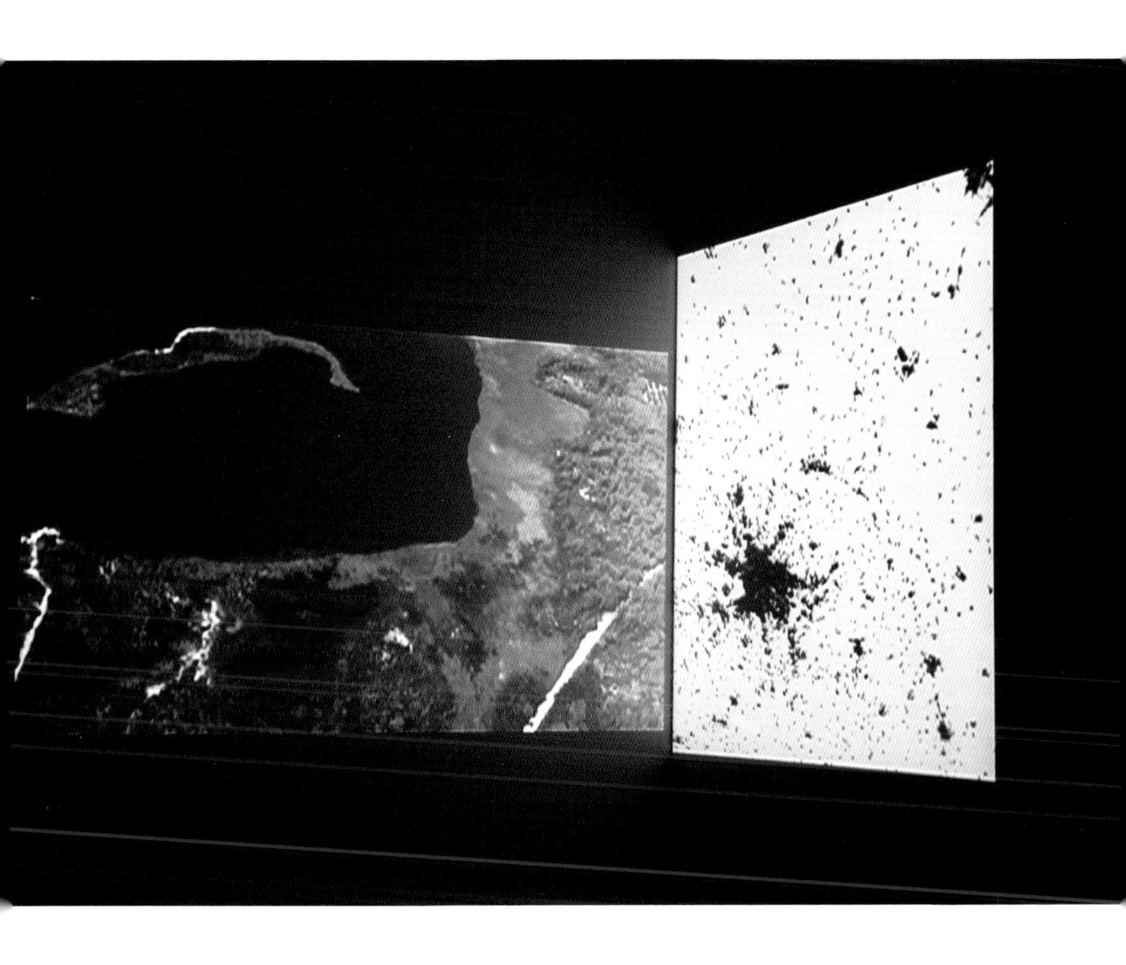

CLAUDIA LOSI

Claudia Losi's work, moving between an emotional approach and a more conceptual one, shows her strong interest in historical change and the complexity of natural phenomena, with attention to scientific and literary disciplines. Slowness and manual activity are important components of her research, consciously juxtaposed with restless daily contemporary reality.

In her works, Losi manages to gather and project certain tensions, conveying the fascination of someone discovering and observing each thing for the first time. Her works and projects are like life-forms, living beings with a particular condition and at a specific "time", which may vary from one organism to the next. For example, it might be a microscopic life-form like lichen (*Tavole Naturali*, since 1995), a woman slowly embroidering (*Places|Bidassero|Sardinia*, video, 2004), or the earth's largest living being (*Places|Bidassero|the Whale*). The artist waits patiently for each one, transforming encounters into experiential data, and therefore into a deeper knowledge of what she makes and describes. The *Balena Project* (since 2002) is one of Losi's most important works, for years now the backbone and manifesto of her artistic research. It constitutes a whale sewn in woollen cloth in real dimensions, 24 metres long, beginning, in 2004, its long journey as a platform for projects and actions that have traced an imaginary trail, leading this great aquatic mammal through Italy and other countries in very different contexts. It becomes a pretext for gathering stories, engaging the eyes, expertise and passions of many people.

Losi tries to underline the changing of things, life-forms in gestation, the formal destiny shared by everything that lives, grows and is transformed.

Arazzo, begun in 1996, is a work in progress. As certain lichens grow on the rocky surface of a boulder, so these archipelagos of wool expand and die on a woven surface. Sooner or later the threads will be pulled out, from the centre toward the edges, leaving only the contours and the "eroded" inner part, perishing, full of holes.

With the work *Formal Living Process*, realised for the 8th Sharjah Biennial, the artist, evoking the oily substance through an irregular form, highlights the intimate and often unknown story that accompanies the history and the nature of the precious liquid. The memory and the forms of the flora and fauna of millions of years ago intertwine and are placed on the puddle of fabric, as if in a silent dance that seems to go on forever, heedless of the meanings and the value that humans have assigned to this substance over the course of history, and that in more recent times have been the cause of tension and conflict – far from the apparent calm and elegance of these prehistoric forms.

Special thanks to Paolo Rumiz, Museo Tridentino di Scienze Naturali (and in particular Carlo Miaolini, Claudia Lauro, Christian Casarotto), Carlotta Casalegno, Iman Al-Sayed and all the embroiderers in Sharjah; Furkan, Rezwan, Ihtisham and Islam

كلوديا لوسي

يُظهر عمل كلاوديا لوسي الذي يتراوح بين الأسلوب العاطفي وذلك النظريّ بدرجة أعلى، اهتمامها الشديد بالتغيّر التاريخي وتعقيد الظواهر الطبيعيّة، مع التركيز على النُظم العلميّة والأدبيّة. البطء والنشاط الجسدي مكوّنات هامّة في بحثها، تتركّب بوعي مع الواقع المعاصر اليومي القلق.

تستطيع لوسي أن تجمع وتعكس في أعمالها توتّرات معيّنة تكشف عن انبهار أحدهم عندما يكتشف ويراقب كلّ شيء لأوّل مرّة. أعمالها ومشاريعها هي أشكال حيويّة، كينونات حيّة بظرف محدد و"زمن" معيّن، يمكن أن يتنوّع من نظام حيويّ إلى آخر. مثلا، يمكن أن يكون نظاما حيويّا ميكروسكوبيّا مثل الحزاز (طحلب فطريّ) (تافولي ناتورالي، منذ ١٩٩٥)، أو امرأة تطرّز ببطء (بليسيس(أماكن)/بيداسيرو/ساردينيا، فيديو، ٢٠٠٤)، أو أضخم الكائنات الحيّة على الأرض (بليسيس(أماكن)/بيداسيرو/الحوت). تنتظر الفنّانة كلّ واحدة منها بصبر، تحوّل اللقاءات إلى بيانات تجريبيّة، وبالتالي، إلى معرفة أعمق لما تصنعه وتصفه. "مشروع بالينا" (منذ ٢٠٠٢) هو أحد أهم أعمال لوسي والعمود الفقريّ لبيان عملها البحثيّ منذ سنوات حتّى الآن. يتكوّن من حوت مصنوع من قماش صوفيّ بقياسات واقعيّة، طوله ٢٤ مترا، بدأ، في ٢٠٠٤، رحلته الطويلة كمنصّة من أجل مشاريع وأفعال تتبّعت أثرا خياليّا مما أخذ هذا الحيوان الثديي المائيّ عبر إيطاليا وغيرها من الدول في مضامين متنوّعة جدا. يصبح حجّة لجمع القصص، وجذبا لأنظار وتجارب وعواطف العديد من الناس. تحاول لوسي أن تشدّد على تغيّر الأشياء، أشكال حيويّة تنمو، المصير الشكليّ الذي يشترك فيه كل شئ حيّ، ينمو ويتغيّر.

أراتسو، هو عمل قيد الإنشاء، بدأ في عام ١٩٩٦. ينمو نوع ما من الحزاز على السطوح الصخريّة لصخرة ملساء دائريّة، تتمدد أرخبيليّات الصوف هذه وتموت على سطح منسوج.

آنا أم لاحقا، سيتمّ سحب الخيطان من المركز نحو الأطراف، تاركة حدود الجزء الداخليّ "المتآكل،" يفنى مليئا بالثقوب.

في عملها (عملية حياة رسمية) المعدّ خصيصاً لبينالي الشارقة الثامن، تسلط الفنانة الضوء من خلال استحضار المادة النفطية في شكل غير منتظم، على القصة الحميمية الغائبة والتي ترافق تاريخ وطبيعة هذا السائل الثمين. ذاكرة وأشكال النباتات والجيولوجيا (فلورا وفونا) التي تتشابك منذ ملايين السنين لتجد نفسها في نسيج من حفرة وحل، وكأنها تقدم رقصة صامتة أبدية، دون أن تعير أي اهتمام للمعاني والقيم التي أعطاها البشر لهذه المادة عبر التاريخ: هذه المادة التي أصبحت، في العصور الحديثة، سببا للصراعات والتوتر مبتعدة عن هدوئها وأناقتها التي كانت تتحلى بها في مرحلة ما قبل التاريخ.

شكر خاص لباولو روميز، موزيو تريدنتينو دي سيونتس ناتشورالي (وبالأخصّ كارلو مايوليني، كلاوديا لاورو، كريستيان كاساروتو)، كارلوتا كاسالينو، إيمان السّيّد والخيّاطون في الشارقه: فرقان، رضوان، إحتشام، وإسلام

Celacanti, 2006, drawing, embroidery on light fabric and padding, 150 x 150 cm

LUTZ & GUGGISBERG

Brood

Brood was originally conceived by the artists as an army - ornithological stand-ins for a band of warfaring men. But as soon as they were placed in an orderly line of pairings in the museum it was obvious that the charred, wooden birds were less like soldiers than refugees, the traumatised victims of natural catastrophes or the targets of political purges.

Like every work by Lutz & Guggisberg, the reading of *Brood* cannot be confined to a single interpretation. Its deliberate openness and ambiguity allows for meanders of the subconscious and the irrational, engendering a deep uncertainty as to whether we should find the installation comically touching or threatening. It is not even clear whether the birds are undergoing a process of construction or deconstruction, for *Brood* is literally halfway between being completed and destroyed. In depriving the birds of wings, stalling the creative act and setting fire to the entire flock, the artists have played God in deciding when to quell the flames and allow their invention to cling, traumatised, to a purgatorial form of life.

Wood plays a major role in Lutz & Guggisberg's practice - whether in works composed either from fetish or kitsch objects assembled from flea markets or from gnarled branches and bulbous roots collected directly from the woods. Unlike these, the more mundane packing crates used for *Brood* are far removed from their original function and appearance in being roughly broken apart and reconstructed into the crude but clearly recognisable shapes of birds. From the horrors of the film *The Birds* to the humour of *Chicken Run*, the creatures have long held a fascination for us that is enhanced in *Brood* by their touchingly human quality. It is not the first time that Lutz & Guggisberg have appropriated and humanised the animal kingdom, but the mannerist bathos of the work renders *Brood* their densest metaphor yet for the fragility of life.

Felicity Lunn

لوتز وغوغيزبورغ

برود (تفكير قلق)

تجلى العمل الفني بعنوان: بْرود (تفكير قلق) في بداياته على شكل جيش. تمثل فيه مجموعة من الطيور فرقة من الرجال المحاربين. لكن بمجرّد وضعهم في صف منتظم من الأزواج في المتحف بدا واضحا أنّ هذه الطيور الخشبيّة المتفحّمة لا تبدو كجنود بقدر ما تبدو كلاجئين. ضحايا كوارث طبيعيّة أو عمليات تطهير سياسيّ.

كما هي جميع أعمال لوتز وغوغيزبورغ. لا يمكن حصر قراءة بْرود (تفكير قلق) بتفسير فرديّ. فانفتاحه وغموضه المقصودان يفسحان المجال أمام تعرّجات اللاوعي واللاعقلاني. مما يولد حيرة عميقة عما إذا كان من المفترض أن نجد في هذا التركيب الفنّي فكاهة أم تهديد. ليس من الواضح حتّى. إن كانت هذه الطيور تتعرّض لعمليّة بناء أو تفكيك. فـ "بْرود" (تفكير قلق) هو حرفيّا في منتصف الطريق. بين أن يتمّ الإنتهاء من صناعته أو تحطيمه. بحرمان الطيور من الأجنحة. ووقف الفعل الإبداعي وإضرام الحريق بالسرب بأجمعه. يلعب الفنانان دور الخالق في تحديد وقت إخماد الحريق والسماح لمخلوقاتهما بالبقاء معلقين. مصدومين. في مكان يتوسط الموت والحياة الأخرى.

يلعب الخشب دورا رئيسا في الأعمال الفنية للوتز وغوغيزبورغ. إن كان ذلك في أعمال تألّفت من أشياء إمّا مبتذلة (كيتش) أوهوسيّة رمزية (fetish) تمّ تجميعها من سوق البرغوث (سوق الجمعة) أو أغصان كثيرة العقد أو جذور بصلية جُمّعت مباشرة من الغابات. بعكس كل هذه. فإن صناديق الشحن العاديّة التي استعملت في بْرود (تفكير قلق) بعيدة كل البعد عن استعمالها وهيئتها الأصليين إذ تم تكسيرها بشكل عنيف وإعادة بنائها بأشكال غير متقنة ولكن يمكن التعرّف على أشكال الطيور فيها بسهولة. من الإحساس بالرعب في فيلم "ذا بيردز (الطيور)" إلى حس الفكاهة في فيلم "تشيكن رن (سباق الدجاج)". لطالما فتنتنا هذه المخلوقات. ويتعمق هذا الإحساس في بْرود (تفكير قلق) بسبب صفاتها الإنسانيّة المؤثّرة. وهذه ليست المرة الأولى التي يستملك فيها ويؤنسن لوتز وجوجيزبيرج مملكة الحيوان. إلاّ أنّ الأسلوب الإسفافي في هذا العمل يجعل بْرود (تفكير قلق) أكثر استعاراتهما كثافة حول هشاشة الحياة.

فيليسيتي لَن

Melting Snowman and Burning Bird, 2002, photograph, variable

AHMED MATER

أحمد ماطر

It is a savage world, Ahmed is aware of this. In his artistic works he cherishes the primitive structure of the human being, its primitive composition, morula, and a heap of bones. The beautiful proud face is nothing but a ridiculous skeleton under the X-ray. Nonetheless, Man thinks that he is something quite dangerous. That he is an absolute power just because he possesses the ability to display objects, carrying them, placing them, or pulling them out, just because he possesses the ability to inflict wounds on the body and similar wounds with his words on the soul, and just because of his ability to smash tiny things crawling beneath him, without realising that the real absolute power is the ability to be a flower.

Ahmed appears to be obsessed with the mercy that doesn't exist and the brutality that enwraps the world, and the arrogance of humans that smashes the green, the ripe and the fresh for the sake of everything that can be displayed on the shelves of commercial shops, or on the shoulders of military costumes, or around legendary thrones; taking advantage of everything, even the sacred (the yellow cow), simply to serve the logic of the market and the logic of politics and religion and whatever else one might think of. In this context the world is but a supermarket that makes you into a commodity. And how naive is the human being when he thinks that he is more valuable, when he drifts away from the mud out of which he was created.

While contemplating the commercials of the yellow cow's products, I tend to remember how much I hate markets, because there everything is for sale, nothing is just given away for the sake of God, out of compassion. A tradesman would laugh at this idea because markets know no God. And mercy is an attribute of God. Marketing everything means materialising everything. And when everything is materialised, everything becomes stony, even one's heart.

Mariam Alsaedi

العالم متوحش، أحمد يدرك ذلك. في أعماله يذكّر الإنسان بتكوينه البدائي، مضغة، وأكوام عظام. الوجه الجميل الوسيم المزهو بنفسه تحت الأشعة مجرد جمجمة سخيفة مضحكة. ويظن نفسه شيئا خطيرا (أقصد الإنسان وليس أحمد). يظن نفسه قوة مطلقة، فقط لأنه يمتلك القدرة على الحركة، على تغيير الأشياء من أماكنها، حملها ووضعها واقتلاعها، على إحداث الجروح في الجسد بيده، وفي الروح بلسانه، وسحق الأشياء الصغيرة تحته. لا يدرك أن القوة المطلقة هي القدرة على أن تكون "وردة".

أحمد يبدو مشغولا بـ "الرحمة الغائبة"، بالقسوة التي غلفت العالم، بكل هذه العجرفة التي تسحق الأخضر واليانع والندي، لصالح كل ما يمكن وضعه على أرفف محلات تجارية، أو على أكتاف بدل عسكرية، أو حول مقاعد حكم سلطوية. استغلال كل شيء حتى المقدس في "البقرة الصفراء" لخدمة منطق السوق التجاري والسياسي والديني، وكل ما رأت عين وخطر على قلب بشر. يجعل العالم سوبر ماركت، ويجعلك سلعة. ويا لحمق الانسان، حين يظن أنه بعيد عن الطين يصير أغلى.

وأتذكر وأنا أتأمل دعايات منتجات "البقرة الصفراء" كم أكره الأسواق، لأن فيها كل شئ يُشترى. "لاشئ لوجه الله". أو يضحك البائع. ففي منطق السوق وجه الله غائب، والرحمه إلهية. تسويق كل شئ يعني "تسليع" كل شئ، وحين يصير كل شيء سلعة... يتحجر كل شيء ، حتى قلبك.

مريم الساعدي

The Yellow Cow Products, 2006, mixed media, variable

TEA MÄKIPÄÄ

تيا ماكيبا

10 Commandments for the 21st Century

"10 Commandments for the 21st Century" is a 10-point list of simple rules of behaviour. If put into action, these wishes and rules could slow down and gradually erase some parts of the ecological disaster caused by human population.

The project refers to currently used technical solutions - not to the possibly better ideas of the future. In the best-case scenario, the future viewers of this artwork will find our current problems and these 10 rules of behaviour ridiculous, and evidence of our backwardness at this point in history around the year 2000, when human beings had not yet found an environmentally sustainable lifestyle.

The aim of the project is to awaken discussion and to appeal to the viewers' personal feelings of responsibility. It can also relieve the confusion, brought about by ecological issues, by recommending simple actions for everyday life.

وصايا عشر للقرن الـ ٢١

وصايا عشر للقرن الـ ٢١ هي قائمة من ١٠ نقاط لقواعد بسيطة للسلوك. لو فُعّلت، تستطيع هذه الأمنيات والقواعد أن تبطئ، وتدريجيّا أن تمحو أجزاء من الكارثة البيئيّة التي سببها السكّان البشر.

يشير المشروع إلى الحلول التقنيّة المستعملة حاليّا - ليس بالضرورة الأفكار الأفضل للمستقبل. في أفضل الأحوال، مشاهدو هذا العمل الفني المستقبليون سيجدون مشاكلنا الحاليّة وهذه القواعد العشر للسلوك سخيفة، وكمجرّد دليل على تخلّف تلك النقطة من التاريخ حول عام ٢٠٠٠، عندما لم يجد السكان البشر أسلوبا معيشيّا مستمرا بيئيّا بعد.

يهدف هذا المشروع إلى إيقاظ حوار ومناشدة المشاعر الشخصيّة لدى المشاهدين ذوي الإحساس بالمسؤوليّة. كما يمكن أن يزيل التشويش أمام القضايا البيئيّة بنصّه على أفعال بسيطة للحياة اليوميّة.

10 Commandments for the 21st Century, 2006, media and size variable

10 COMMANDMENTS FOR THE 21st CENTURY:

1 › Do not fly.
2 › Recycle.
3 › Use a bicycle or public transportation instead of a car.
4 › Avoid any products with plastic packages.
5 › Avoid heating and air conditioning, if possible.
6 › Avoid any products that come from far away.
7 › If you are not really sure you need it, don't buy it.
8 › Do not produce more than 2 children.
9 › Do not cultivate, build on or otherwise consume virgin land or water.
10 › Make all these steps easy and cheap for yourself and others to achieve.

HASSAN MEER

حسن مير

Art, for me, constitutes the language through which I discover the state of the human being and the contradictions he/she lives through in the shadow of the cultural conflicts between civilisations, and relating these to symbolic elements and concepts amongst these civilisations. Due to the severe conflicts in which our societies live, I realised the value of researching for and experimenting with new tools better describing our contemporary issues, utilising conceptual dissemination or conceptual art. I achieve this through the means of video art, based on delivering the idea in a clearer form than that of traditional means of expression. I then develop the experiment relying on roots rather than experimenting in a void.

Accordingly, my experimentation in recent years has been directed towards this unique mixing of the personal and the public, that is, the mixing of the personal and the public memory.

My works are to do with the contemplation of and research into the spiritual aspect and magic traditions of the deeply rooted heritage in our societies related to the convictions and mythologies of the East. This is a result of my marvelling at death and human extinction, as well as at some local rituals. I sometimes record the changes of pattern in social and political life and in human behaviour in the area, as well as the alienation in the city due to oil wealth and the oil-masters.

We cannot deny the role of the new wealth in changing the face of the area economically; however, we often find in our cities the "city within a city" model, where the inhabitants do not interact with their neighbours. For one reason or another, they have different lifestyles but they share environmental challenges resulting from oil production and refinement, breathing in the unhealthy air and within constant proximity of the burning flames. It is possible that the local refinery represents a strong challenge for local people to coexist with the environmental dangers resulting from pollution and toxicity; however, the people are unable to change or move the petroleum encampment.

الفن عندي هو اللغة التي أكتشف من خلالها حالة الإنسان والتناقضات التي يعيشها في ظل الصراعات الثقافيه بين الحضارات وربطها ببعض العناصر والمفاهيم الرمزيه لتلك الثقافات.

في ظل الصراعات الحادة التي تعيشها مجتمعاتنا أدركت أهمية التجريب والبحث بأدوات جديدة أكثر تعبيرا عن قضايانا المعاصرة باستخدام البذر المفاهيمي أو الفن القائم على المفهوم أو الفكرة باستخدام فن الفيديو لإيصال الفكرة بشكل أكثر وضوحاً من طرق التعبير التقليدية. ثم تطوير التجربة اعتماداً على الجذور. أي عدم التجريب في الفراغ.

لذلك تتجه التجربة عندي في السنوات الأخيرة. إلى المزج الفريد بين الشخصي والعام. أي بين الذاكرتين الشخصية والعامة.

أعمالي هي تأمل وبحث في الجانب الروحي وطقوس السحر للموروثات الراسخة منذ القدم في مجتمعاتنا والمتعلقه بمعتقدات الشرق وأساطيره. وجاءت أساساً من انبهاري بالموت وفناء الإنسان وبعض الطقوس المحلية. وفي بعض الأحيان أسجل التغيرات النمطية في الحياة الاجتماعية والسياسية. والتغير في سلوكيات الإنسان في المنطقة. والتغريب الذي حدث في المدن بسبب ثروات النفط وأساطينها.

قد لاننكر دور الثروة الجديدة في تبديل وجه المنطقة اقتصادياً. ولكن في بعض النماذج نجد في مدينتنا نموذج" مدينة داخل مدينة" سكانها لا يخالطون جيرانهم لسبب أو لآخر. أو لاختلاف أنماط حياتهم. ولكنهم يتشاركون في التحديات البيئية الناجمة عن تكرير النفط واستنشاق الهواء غيرالصحي ومنظر اللهيب المتصاعد طيلة الوقت. وقد تكون المصفاة تحدياً جدياً لسكان المنطقة التي توجد فيها للتعايش مع المخاطرالبيئية الناجمة عن تلوث واستنشاق الهواء غير الصحي. لانه ليس باستطاعتهم تغيير أو إزاحة هذا المعسكر النفطي.

The Oil Camp, 2006, video installation & documentary images, courtesy of the artist

GUSTAV METZGER

First we had Nature.

And then came the Environment.

Environment is the *smoke* humanity has put on Nature: the people who used Latin had no word for Environment – they only knew *natura*. There is an urgent need to redefine notions of Nature and Environment. The term Environment has been hijacked by the forces that are manipulating the world. When Mr. Bill Clinton stated that he would be the first "Environmental President" – what can this mean? Anything and nothing. The term Environment lends itself perfectly to telling lies and giving illusions. The people who run production and distribution, the controllers of media and Government, local and national, are systematically using the term Environment to hide realities, confuse the public, and distort their perceptions of reality. This has been done for the basest of motives: to maintain profits and power. The term Nature is dropped, and replaced by Environment. One way forward would be to *drop* the term Environment, and speak of Nature and *damaged* Nature. This could be an interim stage, while the air is cleared, and the discussion brought onto a higher and more realistic plane. The voidance of Nature and its substitution by Environment represent a grave threat to culture. The loose use of concepts, and their misuse, are first steps in the decline of culture. This is happening worldwide at present. We are faced by a gigantic task: the deconstruction, de-definition, demystification and redefinition of that term which sums up one of the big issues of our time – Environment.

...

Environmental destruction was part of an ongoing approach to maintain the viability of the system. The explanation as to why it has worked reasonably, when compared to the policies of the Communist Block, is in the preparedness and ability to incorporate the clean-up process as part of the long-term strategy. The Block countries have fallen flat on their faces because they never incorporated the clean-up as part of the profitability equation. Did they profit from the destructive process? There was one major miscalculation in the programme: the Greenhouse Effect and the Ozone Layer. No one, thirty years ago, was in a position to predict the extent of this development. It was the genie in the bottle. Just as no one would have predicted the worldwide AIDS scourge. Damage the Environment: OK. And then repair it: clean it up, change your technology. A viable path into the future. Like radiation from a nuclear reactor at the point of no return, the Ozone Layer and the Greenhouse Layer entered the equation and stand, like Chernobyl, before the world, as a warning and worse, as an uncontrollable event that can bring all down.

Gustav Metzger, excerpts from "Nature Demised Resurrects As Environment", 1992, in Gustav Metzger, *Damaged Nature, Auto-destructive Art*, Coracle Press, London, 1996

جوستاف ميتسجر

في البدء كانت الطبيعة، ثمّ جاءت البيئة.

البيئة هي الدخان الذي غطت به البشريّة الطبيعة: لم يكن لدى الناس الذين يتكلمون اللاتينيّة كلمة تعبر عن البيئة – عرفوا الطبيعة (ناتورا) فحسب. هناك حاجة ملحّة لإعادة تعريف مفهومي الطبيعة والبيئة. لقد قامت القوى التي تتلاعب بالعالم باختطاف مصطلح البيئة. عندما أعلن السيّد بيل كلينتون أنّه سيكون أوّل "رئيس بيئي"، ماذا كان يقصد بذلك؟ أيّ شيء ولا شيء. إن مصطلح "البيئة" مطواع تماما لقول الأكاذيب وبيع الأوهام. يستخدم أولئك الذين يسيطرون على الإنتاج والتوزيع، وعلى الإعلام، والحكومات، المحلية والعالمية، يستخدمون مصطلح البيئة لإخفاء الواقع وتشويش العامّة وتشويه إدراك الحقيقة. ويقومون بذلك لتحقيق أهداف خسيسة: المحافظة على الأرباح والسلطة. فتم إسقاطَ مصطلح الطبيعة، واستبداله بمصطلح البيئة. إحدى السبل المتاحة أمامنا هي إسقاط مصطلح بيئة، والحديث عن الطبيعة والطبيعة المتضررة. ويمكن أن نعتبر هذه مرحلة انتقاليّة، حتى يصفى الجوّ وتتوضّح الأمور، ويرتفع الحديث إلى مستوى أسمى وأكثر واقعيّة. تمثل عملية إفراغ الطبيعة واستبدالها بالبيئة تهديدا خطيرا للثقافة. أما الاستعمال الرخو للمفاهيم، وإساءة استخدامها، فهي الخطوات الأولى نحو انحطاط الثقافة. يحدث هذا على مستوى العالم ككل في وقتنا الراهن. تواجهنا مهمّة ضخمة: تفكيك، ونزع التعريف، وإزالة الغموض، وإعادة تعريف ذلك المصطلح الذي يلخّص إحدى أكبر قضايا عصرنا هذا – البيئة.

...

لقد كان الهدم البيئي جزءا من مقاربة مستمرّة للمحافظة على بقاء النظام. أما تفسير لماذا أثبت هذا النظام فعاليته بالمقارنة مع السياسات الشيوعيّة فيكمن في استعداديّته وقدرته على دمج عمليّة التنظيف في استراتيجيته طويلة الأمد. لقد فشلت الدول الشيوعيّة لأنّها لم تعتبر عمليّة التنظيف جزءا من المعادلة الرابحة. هل حققوا أرباحا من عمليّة الهدم؟

لكن هناك أمر واحد لم يحسب حسابه البرنامج: ظاهرة الاحتباس الحراري وطبقة الأوزون.

لم يتمكن أحد قبل ثلاثين عاما من التنبؤ بهذا التطوّر، كما لم يكن ممكنا لأحد التنبؤ بداء الإيدز العالميّ. إنّه مارد المصباح السحري. نعطب البيئة، حسنا، ومن ثمّ نصلحها: ننظفها، نغير التكنولوجيا... هذا مسار معقول نحو المستقبل.

لقد أصبحت طبقة الأوزون وظاهرة الاحتباس الحراري، مثل الإشعاعات المنبعثة من المفاعل النووي حين تصل نقطة اللاعودة، جزءا من المعادلة، وتقف مثل تشيرنوبل، أمام العالم، كناقوس خطر، فعل خارج عن السيطرة، سيتسبب بنهايتنا جميعا.

جوستاف ميتسجر، أجزاء مِن نصّ "نيتشر ديميزد ريزيركتس آز إنفيرومينت (طبيعة متوفّاة تُبعث بيئة)،" ١٩٩٢، نُشر في: جوستاف ميتسجر، "داماجد نيتشر، أوتو-ديستركتف آرت (بيئة مهدّمة، فنّ تلقائيّ-التهديم،" مطبعة كوراكل، لندن، ١٩٩٦

Model for Stockholm, June (Phase 1), 1972/2006, metal wire, plastic, toy cars, acrylic and mdf board. Courtesy of the artist. Photo: Terje Östling, Lunds Konsthall

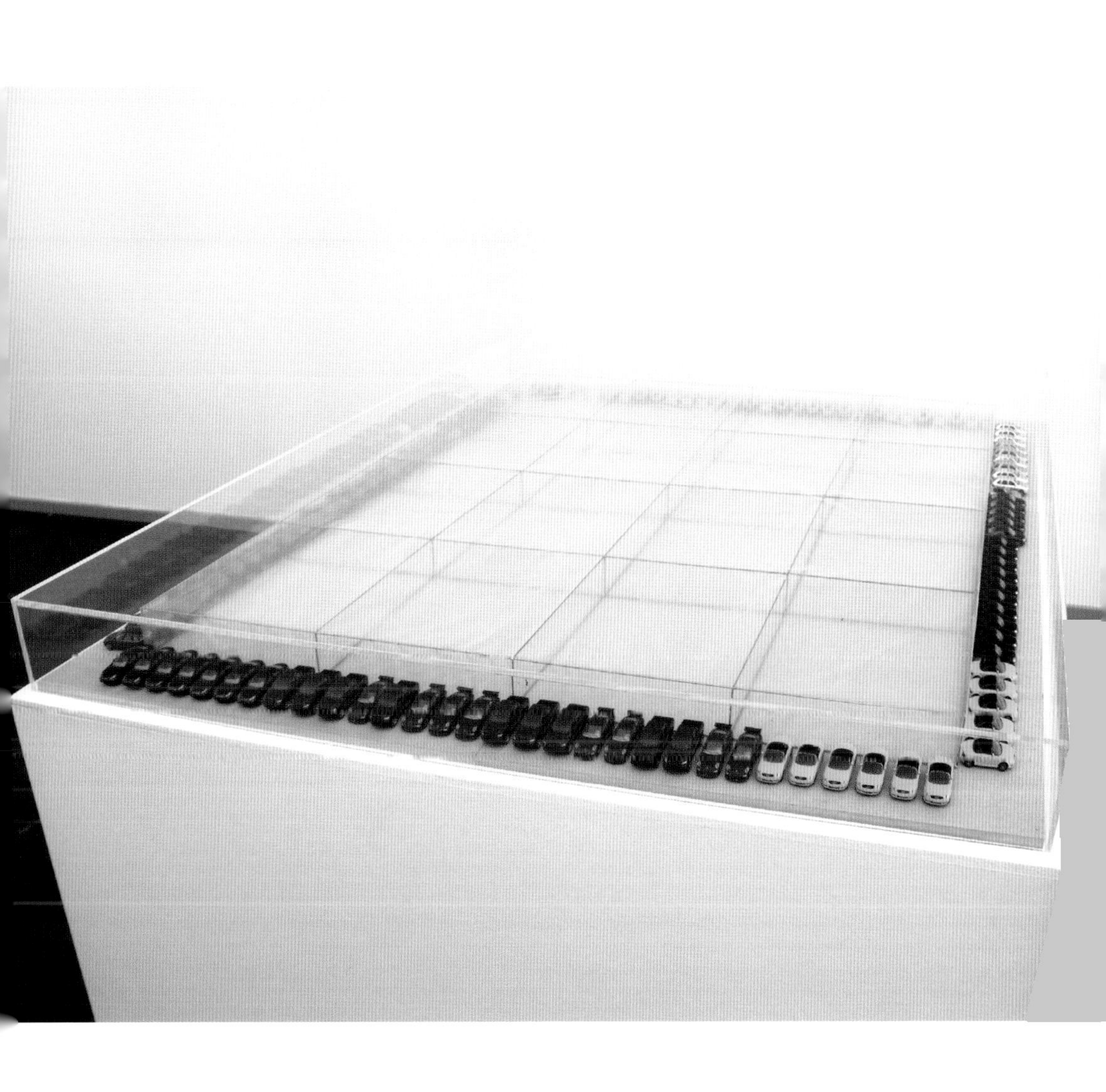

MIND BOMB

MindBomb started as the street postering project of a group of artists and friends in 2002 in Cluj, Romania. It was a pioneering action at the time, marking the reintroduction of the truly autonomous sociopolitical poster in Romanian culture. The ultimate purpose of this collaborative street postering action is the creation of an autonomous space for dialogue and debate that initiates social change around some of the more pressing sociopolitical issues that are shaping mainly contemporary Romanian society. MindBomb's belief is that an effective poster will be one that implicates each viewer as an active participant in the collective process of reshaping society that could lead to positive change, not in order to create a forum for consensus, but one for the clash of competing ideas and claims - a truly democratic space.

The MindBomb project gathered around it a community of volunteers, forming an organic space in which friendship and affinity were factors galvanising a network amplified by the internet: people took part in the actions without knowing each other and in the end this created opinions. For the MindBomb campaign in 2004, some 12,000 posters were printed and disseminated in 10 Romanian towns. This event was an opportunity to create a lively forum for online discussions about political and socio-economic issues in Romanian contemporary society.

The 2006 action - "MindBomb for Rosia Montana!" was a protest against Europe's planned biggest open cast gold mine at Rosia Montana which would make intensive use of cyanide. It was equally a protest against the publicity campaigns of Gabriel Resources and Rosia Montana Gold Corporation for this extremely dangerous project. This was the first time that such an action has been used for an environmental campaign anywhere in the world. Through this protest MindBomb aims to highlight the problem of environmental pollution in Romania and its relationship with the overwhelming corruption of the state and local authorities.

At Sharjah Biennial 8, drawing on its leading concepts, MindBomb will present a series of five posters through which we question the local context for the global and actual issues of our common world. We believe that, by asking some central questions, we can reach the intimate depth of each viewer and provoke active answers, whether these are observable or not. We are convinced that a person's deepest inner beliefs and concerns are the same the world over, no matter their apparent cultural differences.

We do not want messages with overly vague statements of criticism that are cynical and demoralising. We want to create critical but inspirational posters aimed at changing attitudes, not politics, and to inspire the individual to personal action, to the belief that the first step to change begins with changing oneself.

مايند بومب

بدأ مشروع MindBomb مجموعة من الفنانين والأصدقاء في مدينة كلوج، رومانيا، في عام ٢٠٠٢ وكان في بداياته مشروع لافتات - بوسترات - في الشوارع. كان في حينه عملا رائدا دشن في الثقافة الرومانية فكرة إعادة إحياء البوستر السياسي - الاجتماعي المستقل حقا. إن غاية ما يسمو إليه هذا العمل الجماعي، هو خلق مساحة مستقلة للحوار والنقاش للبدء بتغيير اجتماعي إزاء عدد من القضايا الإجتماعية الملحة التي تقولب المجتمع الروماني.

تعتقد MindBomb أن من شأن البوستر الفعال أن يورط المشاهد ليصبح مشاركا فعالا في العملية الجماعية لإعادة تشكيل المجتمع، بما يؤدي إلى التغيير الاجتماعي الإيجابي، وليس الهدف إيجاد منبر من أجل التوافق، وإنما منبر لتصادم الآراء والأفكار، أي خلق فضاء ديمقراطي حقيقي. إن الهيكل الجديد الذي بنيناه بعد حملة MindBomb الأولى في عام ٢٠٠٢ وقبل الحملة الحاسمة في عام ٢٠٠٤ حين تم البدء باستخدام الإنترنت، قد وفر الفرصة لتوسيع الممتلكات الإبداعية التي أخذت تتدفق على المشروع بسهولة أكبر، وأسهمت في توسيع مجال الرؤية.

وبهذا تمكن مشروع MindBomb من حشد متطوعين شكلوا مجالا حيويا، تحولت فيه الصداقات والعلاقات إلى عوامل تحفيز لشبكة توسعت بفضل الإنترنت، حيث صار الناس يشاركون في النشاطات دون معرفة بعضهم البعض. وفي النهاية، أدى ذلك إلى تشكل الآراء. في حملة عام ٢٠٠٤، تمت طباعة وتوزيع ١٢٠٠٠ بوستر في عشرة مدن رومانية، وقد وفرت تلك الحملة فرصة لتشكيل منبر حيوي للمشاركة في النقاشات، عبر الخط الإلكتروني المفتوح، حول المشاكل الاجتماعية - الاقتصادية للمجتمع الروماني المعاصر.

العمل الذي قدمناه في عام ٢٠٠٦ "MindBomb من أجل روزايا مونتانا"، كان عبارة عن احتجاج على مشروع أوروبي لافتتاح منجم للذهب في روزايا مونتانا، يعتمد بشكل رئيس على الاستخدام الكثيف لغاز السيانيد. كان أيضا احتجاج على الحملات الدعائية ل "موارد غابرييل" و"شركة روزايا مونتانا للذهب" بسبب هذا المشروع الخطير جدا. وكانت هذه أول مرة يتم استخدام مثل هذا العمل لحملة بيئية في أي مكان في العالم.

في بينالي الشارقة، ستقدم MindBomb، وانطلاقا من مفاهيمها الريادية، سلسلة من خمسة بوسترات تتضمن تساؤلات حول السياق المحلي الخاص بالقضايا الفعلية والعالمية المشتركة في عالمنا المعاصر. إننا نعتقد بأننا قادرون، من خلال طرح بعض الأسئلة المركزية، على الوصول إلى الأعماق الحميمية لكل مُشاهد، وإلى استثارة إجابات فعالة، سواء أكان ذلك واضحا أم لا. فنحن مقتنعون بأن معتقدات الفرد الداخلية وهمومه الخاصة، هي نفسها في كل العالم، بغض النظر عن الاختلافات الثقافية.

لا نريد رسائل نقدية غامضة أو ساخرة أو محبطة، وإنما إنتاج بوسترات نقدية ملهمة، تهدف إلى تغيير المواقف، وليس السياسة. نرغب بإلهام الفرد نحو المبادرة الشخصية، نحو الإيمان بأن الخطوة الأولى لإحداث التغيير، إنما هي تغيير الإنسان لذاته.

Inefficient, 2004, offset printing, 44 x 64 cm

INEFFICIENT

IN:

Liquidating illegal businesses and fraud ★ Eradicating alcoholism, indifference and family violence ★ Eliminating the trafficking of human beings and the abuse of power.

ABDUL RAHMAN AL MA'AINI

Abdul Rahman Al Ma'aini's works are fields of visual signals painted with accuracy and precision. Perhaps related to the historic science of alchemy – mystical, a form of the old 'Heratic' script or the magical 'Hermetic' symbolism – his painting is an impulse rooted in a special personal system that is at once ancient and contemporary. Possibly its source can be traced to the depths of the subconscious, or a collection of symbols, shapes, colours and marks that have remained in Abdul Rahman's memory since childhood, carved in the fabric of what he knows. Maybe it has been inspired by the fast-paced life of the modern city, its endless stream of sounds, the giant moving billboards in the crowded streets, and the malls and shops. Or it could be the byproduct of the movie or TV scenes or the advertisements that fill the daily papers we receive so quickly from all parts of the world. The point of Abdul Rahman's paintings is not to locate the sources of their symbols, but to look at them and convince ourselves that, yes, this is indeed a triangle painted in red, and that definitely is from a blue-square period. All Abdul Rahman has done is to make these elements visually tangible by placing them in the context of 'the art of photography'.

Abdul Rahman condenses the elements of life into simple symbols, painting them next to each other in a disturbed, paranoid manner. They magnify to the left, right, up and down, and they are coloured in a myriad of cold, warm, pale and bright colours. These colours and symbols intertwine to form an improvised musical visual fabric, moving along the surface at a great pace. They are the product of the excitement that dashes across the mental and visual tissues, though the nerves and muscles, creating a physiological activity; and they are transformed into the tangible elements of inspiring subjects and continue the ongoing infatuation with the new.

Hassan Sharif

عبد الرحمن المعيني

لوحات عبد الرحمن المعيني عبارة عن حالة من الإشارات البصرية مرسومة بدقة محكمة السد، كتيمة، ربما تتعلق بالكيمياء القديمة، كشكل كهنوتي من أشكال الكتابة القديمة، هيروغليفي Hieratic أو سحري، انها نزوة ناتجة عن نظام خاص قديم جدا ومعاصر، ربما مصدرها قيعان اللاوعي، أو هي عبارة عن رموز وأشكال وألوان وعلامات باقية في ذاكرة عبد الرحمن منذ الطفولة، محفورة في أعماقه، أو ربما مستوحاة من الحياة السريعة للمدينة المعاصرة بضجيجها ليلا ونهارا مثل الإعلانات الكبيرة والمتحركة في شوارع المدينة المزدحمة، وفي الأسواق والمحال التجارية، أو قد تكون نتاج مشاهد سينمائية أو تلفزيونية أو الإعلانات التجارية في الصحف اليومية التي تأتينا من كل حدب وصوب من العالم وبصرعات مفرطة جدا، الهدف من لوحات عبد الرحمن ليس البحث عن المصدر الذي أُخذت منه هذه الرموز، وانما أن نشاهد هذه الأعمال ونمتع أنفسنا بأن هذا الشكل مثلث وملون بلون أحمر، والآخر عبارة عن مربع وملون بلون أزرق فقط لاغير. فكل ما فعله عبد الرحمن هو أنه جعل هذه العناصر ملموسة بصريا من خلال وضعها في سياق (فن التصوير).

يقوم عبد الرحمن باختصار عناصر من الحياة الى رموز بسيطة ورسمها إلى جانب بعضها البعض بطريقة موسوسة ومضطربة، تكبر هذه الأشكال يمينا، يسارا، فوق، تحت، ملونة بألوان عديدة: باردة، دافئة، باهتة، مشعة، تتداخل فيها الرموز والألوان لتعطي في نهاية الامر نسيجا بصريا موسيقيا، وارتجاليا يتحرك على سطح اللوحة بسرعه فائقة، إنه نتاج موجة من الهياج تنتقل عبر الانسجه الذهنية والبصرية وعبر الأعصاب والعضلات، ينشأ عنها نشاط فسيولوجي يتحول الى عناصر ملموسة لإثارة مواضيع ملهمة، والتدحرج المستمر والافتتان بالجديد.

حسن شريف

Untitled, 2007, (detail), acrylic on canvas, 425 x 270 cm

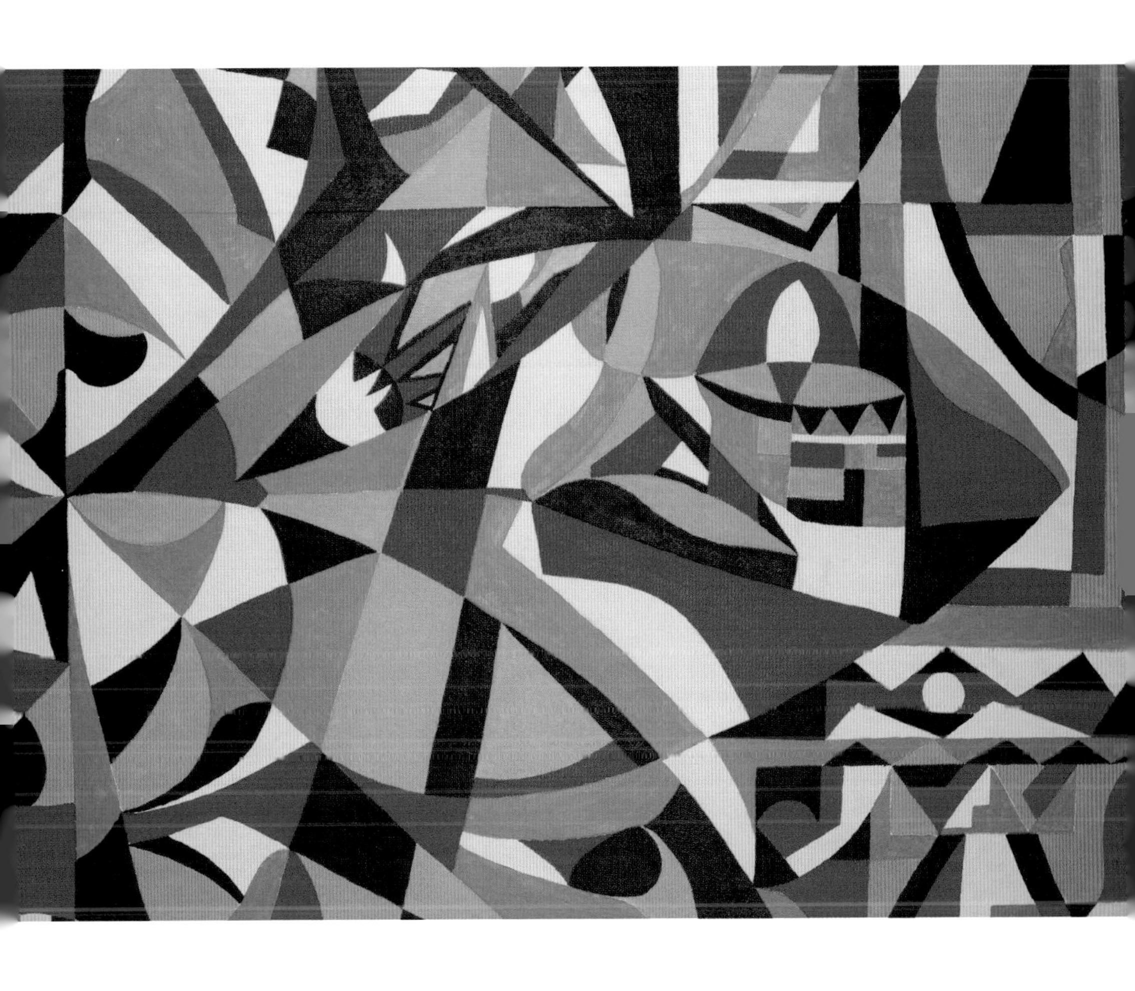

MAHA MUSTAFA

In the art of Maha Mustafa a tension appears physically between what you might call a "meteorological" and a "geological" perspective. They often confront each other within the same work – as in *Landscape Minus 37°C*, where the ice appearing on the ribs of a gigantic freezing unit arouses the illusion of a frosty mountain scene. The cold – a meteorological and therefore changing phenomenon – thus creates strata of a geological, that is, remaining nature, which is of course a pretty accurate description of how it actually happens. This, however, does not make the problem less acute. Survey at the same time demands a notion of the changeable – and an ability to look beyond it. Could this be possible?

You might say that art, as long as man has devoted himself to it, has been trying to show that this possibility exists. Yes – which indeed it is for the reason that man, since the beginning of history, has been creating art. In her book *Det umuliges kunst* (The Art of the Impossible) from 2005 the Danish author Solvej Balle expresses a view of art you might call anthropological, based on an understanding of art as a basically existential practice, where man is treating certain conditions consequential upon moving around "with body, identity and mind in a world of time, space and materiality". In the restrictions implied by this, artistic practice gives the opportunity for transgressions that provoke a feeling of totality, of survey: of, for a moment, being able to perceive the world in a way that suits our senses. The works of Maha Mustafa seem to me to be rooted in a similar basic outlook. Swinging between a human and a superhuman view, between the transitory and the remaining, they seem constantly to seek new outlooks: new ways of accomplishing this "impossible" mission.

مها مصطفى

إنني أسعى لاكتشاف العلاقة بين الطبيعة والضوء، بين الفن الزمني البيئي، الذي يتضمن العديد من المواد الإصطناعية وتقنيات الخليط (الضوء، الحرارة، الدخان). أقوم بجسر الهوة بين المتضادات، المفهوم، والواقع والخيال. لذلك، فإن أعمالي التركيبية الفنية تتراوح بين مظاهر كل أشمل، وغالبا ما تصل إلى العالم كما تصل الفكرة إلىً العقل. إنه" الفن كفكرة"، أو "الفن المفاهيمي".

في العادة تنمو إعمالي من السعي نحو درجة من السيطرة على، أو على الأقل الإحساس بالراحة إزاء، العالم المادي. في أعمالي، يستخدم الضوء الكهرباء بصفتها تحدث في الزمن، ويعمد إلى تنظيم سياق الحياة وأشيائها. إنها كما أصفها: "المطلق، كل شيء، ولا شيء". كذلك، فإن تجربتي تنبثق من ذكرى أنني قد تحركت في الفضاء، وكيف تكشف لي ذلك مع مرور الوقت. حين أبتكر تركيبا فنيا ما، فإنه من الأهمية بالنسبة لي أن أعبر عن تجربتي مع مكان عملي، أو موضوع العمل، مع تنويعاته الواسعة وفقا لكيفية التعامل معه، وما الذي أقوم به من أجل إنجازه، ومن يراقب. أما عملي التركيبي، فهو يتمثل في البنيان، المعمار، ففكرة المكان مثيرة لانه، على الرغم من حقيقته المادية، فهو لا يوجد إلا من خلال تعاملنا معه.

يمكن القول إن الفن ما زال يسعى، منذ كرس الإنسان نفسه له، لإثبات أن هذه الإمكانية موجودة. نعم، هذا ممكن حقا، وذلك لأن الإنسان ما زال يخلق الفن منذ بداية التاريخ. في كتابها "فن المستحيل" الصادر عام ٢٠٠٥، تعبر المؤلفة الدنماركية، سوليج بالي، عن رأي في الفن يمكن وصفه بالأنثروبولوجي، والمتمثل في اعتبار الفن ممارسة وجودية في الأساس، حيث يتعامل الإنسان مع ظروف مختلفة باختلاف انتقاله من مكان لآخر "بجسده وهويته وعقله، عبر عالم من الزمن والفضاء والمادة".

ووفقا لما يوحي به هذا من قيود، فإن ممارسة الفن توفر الفرصة لحصول تجاوزات تولد الشعور بالعمومية، بالاستعراض، وبكل ما تعنيه تلك اللحظة التي ننظر فيها إلى العالم على نحو يلائم حواسنا.

تبدو لي أعمال مها مصطفى متجذرة في نظرة أساسية مشابهة. تتأرجح بين نظرة إنسانية وخارقة الإنسانية، ما بين المؤقت والدائم، تحاول أعمالها دائما أن تبحث عن رؤى جديدة: أساليب جديدة لتحقيق المهمة "المستحيلة".

Landscape Minus 37°C, 2004, installation

JESUS BUBU NEGRON

The projects that I develop promote social interaction with authority and the structures of power in society. The outcome eventually emerges as an art work sometimes in the form of a "document". Thus, I maintain a vehicle between the relationships that I develop in the public sphere, and the sphere of the art world and art spaces.

Jesus Bubu Negron

A 'conceptual romantic', Bubu creates objects, performances and public sculptures that have a strong lineage in art history - Conceptual Art, Land Art, Arte Povera - but are linked to the place for which they are conceived in a very direct and deeply personal way. Often involving local communities, his work becomes a social event as much as it is a form of visual poetry, reflecting on social, environmental and political realities.

Whether he goes fishing with Lithuanian fishermen, using nets knitted from the thrown away plastic wraps of six packs (*Transmallo*, 2003); recreates Michelangelo Pistoletto's Minus Object *Rosa Bruciata* (*Burned Rose*, 1965) handcrafted by drug addicts from San Juan as a gigantic version of the little roses that they make from palm leaves to sell on the street (*Rosa Tekata* (*Junky Rose*, 2005), for the Turin Triennale) - or, like here in Sharjah, buries an old fishing boat with sand as an answer to Robert Smithson's iconic *Partially Buried Woodshed* (1970) - the simple gesture points beyond the sheer object and its art historical reference, bridging the gap between the social sphere and the secured realm of art.

Eva Scharrer

جيزوس بوبو نيجرون

الأعمال التي أقوم بها تنادي بتفعيل التواصل الاجتماعي بين الفرد والسلطة في المجتمع. ويظهر العمل في النهاية في صورة ما يمكن اعتباره "وثيقة". ومن ثم فإنني أحاول الحفاظ على وجود جسر من العلاقات بين المحيط العام ومحيط وفضاءات الفن.

جيزوس بوبو نيجرون

يقوم جيسوس بوبو نيجرون, هذا الفنان الذي ينتمي إلى المدرسة الرومانسية في الفن المفاهيمي, بتصوير أجسام وأعمال تمثيلية وتماثيل عامة لها علاقة وطيدة بتاريخ الفن - الفن المفاهيمي والفن الطبيعي وحركة الفن الفقير - غير أن أعماله في الوقت ذاته مرتبطة بشدة بالمكان التي صممت من أجله بشكل مباشر وشخصي للغاية. وتتحول أعمال هذا الفنان, التي هي غالبا ما تحتوي على إشارات و"إيماءات لمجتمعات محلية, إلى حدث اجتماعي بالقدر نفسه الذي تحمل فيه تأثير الشعر المرئي لتعكس الواقع الاجتماعي والبيئي والسياسي. هذا الفنان يذهب للصيد مع صيادين ليتوانيين ويستخدم شباك مصنوعة من مواد التغليف البلاستيكية (ترانسمالو, ٢٠٠٣) ويعيد تصميم تمثال مايكل أنجلو بيستوليتو "الجسم الناقص تحت اسم "الوردة المحروقة" -١٩٦٥- وهو التمثال الذي صنعه يدويا لمدمني المخدرات في مدينة سان خوان ليكون نسخة ضخمة للورود الصغيرة التي يصنعها تجار الخردوات في بورتو ريكو من أوراق النخيل من أجل بيعها في السوق (وردة تجار الخردة, ٢٠٠٥ - عُرضت في تريناًلي تورينو) - أو كما يفعل هنا في الشارقة عندما يدفن قارب صيد قديم في الرمال في رد يحمل طابع الفن المفاهيمي على عمل روبرت سميسون المعروف باسم "السقيفة نصف المدفونة (١٩٧٠)". إن أعمال هذا الفنان تجسر الهوة بين المحيط الاجتماعي والمحيط الآمن للفن.

إيفا شارير

Brite Bike, 2005, bikes and reflective tape, C-print, variable dimensions, courtesy of the artist

JACQUES NIMKI

Practice

I work from or within the urban environment, using mainly weeds and flowers to examine various ideas: plants looked at but not seen, forgotten in the backdrops of the everyday, inhabiting places that are usually neglected or unexplored. Researching and walking in these areas I gather information, collect plants for drawing, painting, flower pressing and seed propagation. During a survey, I record a variety of information that is stored on a Psion palmtop. This information is used as a reference tool to support my practice. It contains over twenty categories (from a plant's basic description, to its magical properties, social history, edibility, symbolic associations, etc). The type of information, the way it is stored and written, deliberately avoids and has no conventional scientific value; it is anti-botanical and written in a crude and simplistic manner.

All my works are entitled *Florilegium*. The original *Florilegium* (literally "flower book") is a category of books from the seventeenth century, where images were more significant than text. Many of the books contained a variety of styles by one artist, from the naturalistic and pictorial to the abstract and diagrammatic.

The picturing of plants in the form of a Florilegium had no scientific purpose, no intent to analyse, classify or explore its subject, no text, and no argument, it was primarily a portable device to exhibit one's possession and ownership of plants.

The collection of plants, as indeed other categories of exotica, was contingent upon wealth and leisure, and was motivated by curiosity, novelty, exoticism and rarity.

A Florilegium of weeds is more than a record of plants in a given area; it is a construction of "the unseen seen".

Weeds are perceived as plants in the wrong place, the unwelcome visitors in man-made environments, the underclass, the immigrants and vagrants of the plant world. Often described as wild, uncontrollable, tough, etc, they are in truth connected to a nature more natural than the "nature" that excludes them.

Many of them survive in the toughest of conditions, trodden upon, ignored and fed chemicals; they become extremely hardy and are almost impossible to eradicate. Not protected by any laws, they find their own ways of surviving. Regenerating themselves from tiny pieces of roots, many can produce thousands of seeds that can germinate, grow and set seed again in a few weeks

Weeds also have beneficial properties. Some improve the soil, attract wildlife and predators; many can be eaten, made into beverages and were used in the past for their herbal, medicinal, magical and cosmetic purpose. They are connected to the very root and fabric of societies, their names having strong connections in history and folklore.

By aestheticising what society finds unpleasant and insignificant we are made aware that the experience we want to experience as "nature" is one that is contrived and filtered. The "nature" we consider as desirable and other worldly is in truth simulated and manufactured and is as far removed from "nature" as possible.

جاك نيمكي

الممارسة

في عملي أستخدم بشكل رئيسي الأعشاب الضارّة والأزهار لاختبار مختلف الأفكار: النباتات التي ينظر إليها الجميع وما من أحد يراها، المنسية في قطرات الأيام، والتي تسكن الأماكن التي تكون في العادة مهملة أو غير مستكشفة.

باحثاً ومتجولاً في هذه الأماكن، أجمع المعلومات، والنباتات لرسمها، وتلوينها، وأضغط الأزهار وأنشر البذور.

وخلال المسح، أوثق مجموعة من المعلومات وأخزنها على الكمبيوتر المحمول على كفة اليد. أستخدم هذه المعلومات كمراجع لعملي، وهي تشتمل على أكثر من عشرين فئة من المعلومات (بدءا من الوصف الأساسي للنبتة، إلى خصائصها الساحرة وتاريخها). أما نوعية المعلومات وطريقة تخزينها وكتابتها، فهي تتجنب بشكل متعمد وجود أي قيمة علمية نموذجية لها.

أعمالي جميعها تسمى Florilegium - كتاب الأزهار. تشكل الكلمة الأصلية Florilegium (حرفياً كتاب الأزهار) صنفاً من الكتب التي شاعت في القرن السابع عشر، حيث كانت الصورة أكثر دلالة من النص. وقد اشتمل العديد من الكتب على مجموعة من الأساليب التي يعتمدها فنان واحد، من الطبيعية إلى التصويرية، فالتجريدية والتخطيطية.

تصوير النباتات على شكل "كتاب أزهار" لا يحمل أي هدف علمي، أو نيّة في التحليل، أو تصنيف أو استكشاف موضوع، لا نص، لا جدل. فهذا النوع كان بداية وسيلة محمولة لعرض ملكية الشخص وحيازته للنباتات.

هواية جمع النباتات، كما هو الحال بالنسبة لجمع لأصناف الأخرى الغريبة وغير المألوفة، كانت طارئة على الثروة والمتعة، يدفعها الفضول والجدّة، والغرائبية والندرة.

"كتاب الأزهار" للأعشاب هو أكثر من مجرد سجل أو توثيق للنباتات في منطقة معينة، إنه تكوين هيكلي لـ "غير المرئي الذي انكشف."

يُنظر إلى الأعشاب الضارّة على أنها نباتات في المكان الخطأ، إنها بمثابة الزائر غير المرغوب فيه في البيئات التي صنعها الإنسان، الطبقة المهمّشة، المهاجرة، والمشردة في عالم النباتات. وغالباً ما توصف بأنها بريّة، غير قابلة للضبط والسيطرة عليها، وخشنة الطباع...الخ. غير أنها في الحقيقة، مرتبطة بالطبيعة بشكل أكثر طبيعية من "الطبيعة" ذاتها التي تنبذها.

إنها غير محميّة بموجب أي قانون، غير أنها تجد سبيلها إلى البقاء والحياة. إنها تعيد إحياء نفسها من النتف الصغيرة المتبقية من جذورها، والعديد منها يمكن أن ينتج الألوف من البذور التي يمكن استنباتها، لتنمو وتنتج البذار من جديد خلال بضعة أسابيع.

وبعضها يحسّن من نوعية التربة، ويجتذب الحياة البرية والحيوانات المفترسة. وقد استخدمت لأغراض عدة، عشبية وطبية، سحرية وتجميلية. كما أنها ترتبط بالجذور العميقة للمجتمعات ونسيجها.

بتجميل ما يراه المجتمع غير جميل وخالياً من أي دلالة، نصبح واعين لحقيقة هي، أن التجربة التي نريد أن نعيشها على أنها "الطبيعة"، هي تجربة مرتّبة ومنقحة. فالطبيعة التي نعتبر أنها مطلب الجميع وكأنها من عالم آخر، هي في الحقيقة عبارة عن محاكاة وتصنيع للطبيعة، بعيدة كل البعد عن "الطبيعة".

Florilegium (June), 2003, acrylic and pressed flowers on laminated board, 196 x 145 x 4 cm, courtesy of The Approach gallery

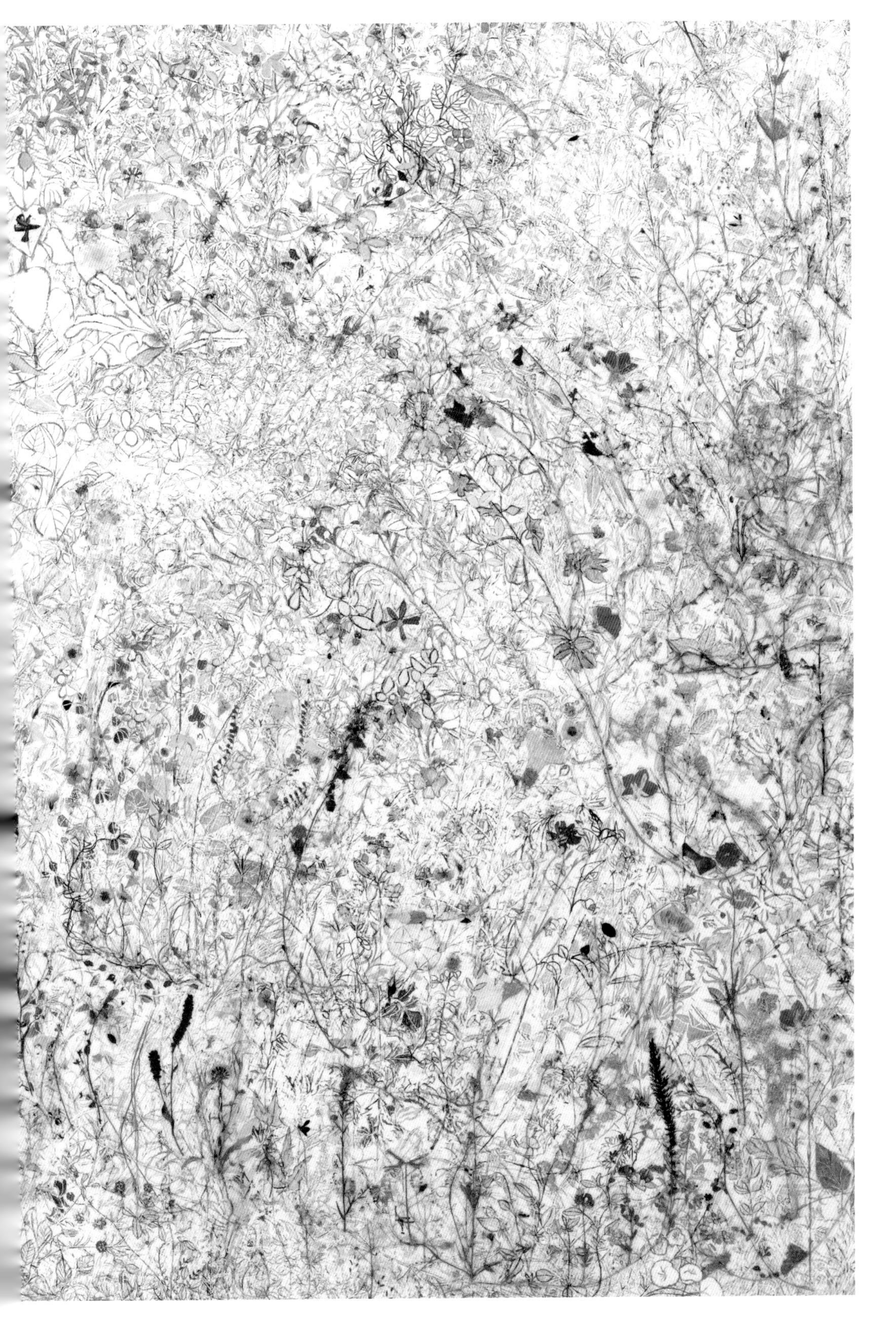

CORNELIA PARKER

For some years Cornelia Parker's work has been concerned with formalising things beyond our control, containing the volatile and making it into something that is quiet and contemplative like the "eye of the storm". She is fascinated with processes in the world that mimic cartoon "deaths" - steamrollering, shooting full of holes, falling from cliffs and explosions. Through a combination of visual and verbal allusions her work triggers cultural metaphors and personal associations, which allow the viewer to witness the transformation of the most ordinary objects into something compelling and extraordinary.

Cornelia Parker has become known for a number of large scale-installations including *Cold Dark Matter: An Exploded View* 1991 (collection Tate Modern) where she suspended the fragments of a garden shed, blown up for her by the British Army, and *The Maybe* 1995, a collaboration with actress Tilda Swinton, who slept in a glass case as part of an installation in the Serpentine Gallery. More recently she wrapped Rodin's Kiss with a mile of a string to make a new work, *The Distance (a kiss with string attached)*, 2003 for her contribution to the Tate Triennial.

In tandem with the large projects she has been realising an ongoing series of smaller works in various mediums, entitled *Avoided Object*, working in collaboration with numerous institutions including the British Army, Colt Firearms, Her Majesty's Customs & Excise, The Royal Armouries, The Alamo and Madame Tussauds.

Her work *Heart of Darkness* 2004, included in the Biennial, is an installation created with burnt wood retrieved from a forest fire in Baker County, Florida. The fire, dubbed 'Impassable I', was intended to be a controlled burn by the U.S. Forest Service, but due to extreme weather conditions quickly became a wildfire that consumed tens of thousands of acres.

كورنيليا باركر

لقد أولت كورنيليا باركر اهتمامها في السنوات الأخيرة إلى ترسيم الأمور الخارجة عن سيطرتنا، واحتواء الأشياء السريعة التغيير لتصبح هادئة وتأملية مثل "عين العاصفة". وهي مفتونة بعمليات معينة في العالم تحاكي "وفيات" الشخصيات الكرتونية- الآلات البخارية، والرماية الملأى بالثقوب، والسقوط من أعلى التلال، والتفجيرات. وتستطيع من خلال عملها ومن خلال الجمع بين التلميحات البصرية والشفاهية، أن تستحث الاستعارات الثقافية والروابط الشخصية، والتي تسمح للمشاهد أن يشهد التحول في الأجسام المعتادة تماماً، بحيث تصبح شيئاً جذابا خارقا للعادة.

أصبحت كورنيليا باركر معروفة من خلال عدد من التركيبات الكبيرة الحجم بما فيها: "مادة قاتمة باردة: نظرة متفجرة" (١٩٩١) (المجموعة الحديثة في متحف تيت)، حيث علقت شظايا سقيفة حديقة، نسفها لها الجيش البريطاني. أما "الممكن The Maybe" (١٩٩٥)، فهو بالتعاون مع الممثلة تيلدا سوِنتن، التي نامت في صندوق زجاجي كجزء من نصب في جاليري سيربنتاين. ومؤخراً، عملت على تغليف عمل رودن Kiss بأسلاك لصنع عمل جديد، "المسافة (قبلة مرتبطة بسلك)"، ٢٠٠٣، وكان هو مساهمتها في معرض متحف تيت الترينال (يعقد كل ثلاث سنوات).

وإلى جانب المشروعات الكبرى التي تقوم بها، هناك سلسلة مستمرة من الأعمال الأصغر باستخدام مختلف الوسائط، وهي بعنوان "الجسم الذي نتجنبه"، وذلك بالتعاون مع العديد من المؤسسات بما فيها الجيش البريطاني، وشركة كولت للسلاح، ودائرة الجمارك والمكوس، المدرعات الملكية، وAlamo ومتحف مدام توسو للشمع.

أما عملها "قلب العتمة" (٢٠٠٤)، والمشارك في بينالي الشارقة، فهو عبارة عن نصب صنعته باستخدام الخشب المحروق الناتج عن حريق غابة في مقاطعة بيكر، فلوريدا. كان الهدف من الحريق الذي لقب بـ "أنا غير سالكة" أن يكون حريقاً خاضعاً للسيطرة من قبل خدمة الغابات الأمريكية، ولكن، وبسبب ظروف الطقس السيئة، سرعان ما انتشر كالنار في الهشيم وقضى على آلاف الهكتارات.

Heart of Darkness, 2004, charcoal from a Florida wildfire (prescribed forest burn that got out of control), 3.23 x 3.96 x 3.23 m, installation view, Galeria Carles Tache, Barcelona

PABLO PATRUCCO

Global Facts and Waste

It is Benjamin who suggests that in order to truly know a society one has to look at the less privileged environs of its interstices, at the objects that are left behind as a result of human activity, at its waste and at the order that they represent or parody to some extent. For quite some time now Pablo Patrucco has assumed that view in his work, outlining the remains of a culture of precariousness such as the one that defines modern Peru.

Behind the popular/pop profile of its expression lies the vision of the agglomeration and saturation that characterises a part of the local pop culture transfixed by a modest, although explosive version of consumption and mass development: the intricate network of neighbourhood advertisement boards and publicity, the precarious self-construction materials, the consumer articles in the reduced scale of the retailer, or the multiplied bodies of the bathers at the public beaches - and within all that, the recycling culture as a form of underemployment and survival rather than a form of ecological awareness. It is there, in the specific approach, that the background of the debris itself appears as an allegorical sample of the digestion of the local processes of consumption and mass development. And so to some extent, the attentive look at the true process of decomposition as a still life, and at the same time as *vanitas*, in which the most visible forms of waste acquire, in Patrucco's work, the quality of being a symptom and a definition of the global consumption process and the re-concentration of current power - a process in which waste, garbage and poverty begin to look the same everywhere.

Rodrigo Quijano

بابلو باتروكو

حقائق العولمة والفضلات

يرى والتر بنجامين أنه لكي تعرف أي مجتمع بشكل متعمق، على المرء أن يبحث عن المناطق الفقيرة فيه، عن الأشياء التي يتم التخلي عنها بفعل الأنشطة البشرية، عن الفضلات، وعن النظام الذي يمثله، أو يعطي صورة ممسوخة عنه إلى حد ما. يطرح بابلو بيتروسو هذا الرأي في عمله الفني الذي يرسم فيه الخطوط العريضة لبقايا حضارة قائمة على حافة الهاوية، كما هي حال دولة بيرو الحديثة في الوقت الراهن.

فخلف مشهد موسيقى البوب الشعبية الذي يشكل تعبيرا لها، يكمن مشهد التكديس والإشباع، الذي يمثل جزءا من حضارة البوب الشعبية المحلية، بصفتها نسخة متواضعة، وإن تكن متفجرة، من ثقافة الإستهلاك والتنمية الشعبية: إنها شبكة معقدة من لوحات الإعلانات والدعاية المحلية، من مواد البناء الفردي غير المأمونة، من المواد الإستهلاكية لدى باعة المفرق، أو من الأعداد المتضاعفة لأجساد رواد المسابح العامة. في خضم كل ذلك، تنتشر ثقافة إعادة تدوير الفضلات - الريساكلينغ - تعبيرا عن حالة تضخم البطالة ودخل الكفاف، وليس تعبيرا عن وعي بيئي. هكذا، ووفقا لهذه المقاربة، تبدو تلك الخلفية من الحطام المتراكم، كعينة مجازية لعملية هضم العمليات الإستهلاكية المحلية والتنمية الشعبية. وإلى حد ما، فإن نظرة فاحصة سوف توضح أن عملية التحلل الفعلية بصفتها حياة ساكنة، وفي نفس الوقت كلوحة من طراز فانيتاس (أسلوب فني لرسم الحياة الساكنة مع إشارة إلى حتمية فناء الإنسان)، هي عملية تصبح من خلالها أكثر أشكال الفضلات وضوحا، وفقا لأعمال بيتروسو، أعراضا أو من مكونات التوجه الاستهلاكي العالمي، ومن عملية إعادة تركيز السلطة - وهي عملية، تبدو فيها مشاهد الفقر والفضلات والنفايات، هي نفسها في كل مكان.

رودريغو كويجانو

Esteras 1, 2004, oil on canvas, 110 x 110 cm

DAN PERJOVSCHI

Temporary projects with permanent markers

I use drawing to organise knowledge. Not fancy or sophisticated, but simple and direct. Direct on the wall. The drawings look like graffiti or cartoons but they are not. They are my way of understanding and reacting to the world. Globalisation, 3G, wars, culture, morning coffee, bird flu ...you name it. I address political and social issues alongside little everyday happenings on the same wall. I simplify things and then mass them together. There are entire stories concentrated into one image, a film into one frame. That frame matters to me. Maybe it will matter to you too. At first you may smile. Then ...

In recent years I just moved from one wall to another, from one city to another. Different sites and different times require different drawings. I keep adding new ones to my permanent repertoire. Let's see what happens in Sharjah ...

دان بيرجوفسكي

مشاريع مؤقتة باستخدام حبر دائم

أستعمل الرسم لأنظّم المعرفة. بطريقة بسيطة وعلى الحائط مباشرة. تبدو الرسومات مثل الجرافيتي (الرسم والكتابة المشاغبة على الحيطان العامّة) ومثل الرسومات الكاريكاتورية. إلاّ أنّها ليست كذلك. إنّها طريقتي في فهم العالم ورد فعلي بالنسبة إليه. العولمة والـ 3G والحروب. والثقافة. وقهوة الصباح. وأنفلونزا الطيور... وغيرها. أنا أبحث في قضايا سياسيّة واجتماعيّة على نفس الحائط وفي الأمور الصغيرة التي تحدث يوميّا. أنا أبسط الأمور وثمّ أكثفها معا. هناك قصص كاملة تتكثّفت في صورة واحدة. فيلم في لقطة. هذه اللقطة التي تهمّني. وقد تهمّكم أنتم أيضا. قد تبتسمون في البدء. وثمّ...

في السنوات الأخيرة. تنقّلتُ من حائط إلى آخر. من مدينة إلى أخرى. تتطلّب المواقع المختلفة والأوقات المختلفة رسومات مختلفة. أستمرّ بإضافة رسومات جديدة إلى مجموعتي الدائمة. فلنَرَ ما سيحدث في الشارقة...

White Chalk Dark Issues, 2003, chalk drawing on the wall, courtesy Kokerei Zollverein Kunst and Kritik Essen Germany, photo: Wolfgng Guenzel

THINK!
POSITIVE
HIV
TERRORISM
IN SARS TIME
UGLY
NICE
PATRIOT
KAPITAL
WEAPONS
FUTURE
IS CLOSE
KAMIKAZE
DON'T DIE
ALONE

DAN PETERMAN

Dan Peterman has been working since the mid-1980s as both an artist and an activist on the explosive intersection of ecology and aesthetics. Alternative economies, the production of "green" energy and eco-friendly recycling stand at the centre of his engaged aesthetic interest. An example of this art practice is Peterman's furniture that is made of recycled plastic, which on the one hand reminds us, through its strict geometrical form, of Minimal Art, and on the other hand is functional, thus calling into question the boundaries between free and applied art. Another example is the *Chicago Compost Shelter* (1988), a Volkswagen van body buried and being heated with warm, steaming horse dung, which was used in the cold winter as a shelter for homeless people. Dan Peterman also runs his Chicago project *The Building*, which is a complex that since 1996 has housed a bicycle workshop, an atelier for artists, an alternative agriculture project and the editing rooms of a leftist magazine. In spring 2001 *The Building* burned down to its fundaments. It was thought that this was an act of arson, since the piece of land had become interesting to property speculators.

Immediately afterwards the artist became engaged in the rebuilding of the area and new working groups began to appear. Amongst them were the same subjects that had interested Dan Peterman before the catastrophe of *The Building* happened; what is new, however - and this surely has to do with his experiences at that time - is the rather pessimistic view concerning the ecological turning-point, which he formulates consistently. So instead of presenting engaged and "applied" projects, as had been the case in the 1990s, the artist produces almost small works, which reflect the ecological momentum, first and foremost from the aesthetic, and no longer from the "real function" perspective. A typical example of this is his work *Beyond Chance and Skill* (2006), which is composed of discarded adhesive tape and paper that he recycled into small footballs. These balls now lie on a piece of artificial grass, which is again left over from the installation *The Happy End of Franz Kafka's America* by the artist Martin Kippenberger.

Peterman seems to state in an attitude of resignation that ecology in the era of neo-liberal globalisation only has a chance on the grounds of art. The work series *Things That Were Are Things Again*, which is composed of cast aluminium pieces, points in the same intellectual direction of an almost "negative Utopia". Discarded scrap was cast here and then re-shaped; the aesthetic result is abstract-filigree objects that again and again remind us of ornamental signs. Hung in a row on the wall of the gallery, these objects quickly become a decorative attraction; instead of recycling, one thinks only of market-oriented artistic handicraft. This very trend makes sense, unfortunately: recycling at exactly the time when survival is becoming increasingly difficult has entered - in the dual sense of the word - into the formal canon of contemporary art and so has become appreciated and saleable.

Raimar Stange

دان بيترمان

يعمل بيترمان منذ منتصف ثمانينيات القرن العشرين، كفنان وكناشط معاً، في نقطة التقاطع النزقة بين علم البيئة وعلم الجمال. ويقع في مركز اهتمامه الفني الملتزم الاقتصادات البديلة وإنتاج الطاقة "الخضراء" وإعادة التدوير. وخير مثال على هذا الفن أثاث بيترمان المصنوع من اللدائن المُعاد تدويرها، والذي يُذكّرنا بشكله الهندسي الدقيق بفن المنمنمات من جهة، كما يسائل من جهة ثانيه، في استخداماته العملية، حدود الفن الحر والتطبيقي. وثمة مثال آخر هو "ملجأ السماد العضوي بشيكاغو" (١٩٨٨)، وهو عبارة عن هيكل ميكروباص "فولكس فاغن" تتم تدفئته بواسطة الطاقة الناتجة عن إحراق رَوث الأحصنة، ويُستخدَم في الشتاء البارد كملجأ للمشردين. يدير دان بيترمان أيضا مشروعه المسمى "البناية" ("ذي بيلدنغ") في شيكاغو، وهو عبارة عن مجمّع اتخذت منه عدة جهات مقرا لها منذ عام ١٩٩٦، منها ورشة دراجات هوائية ومشغل فنانين ومشروع للزراعة البديلة وغرف التحرير لمجلة يسارية. وفي ربيع عام ٢٠٠١ احترقت "البناية" بالكامل حتى الأساس، وكانت الفرضية المرجحة بأنّ الحريق كان مفتَعلاً، لأنّ أرض المبنى باتت في تلك الأثناء مَدار اهتمام المضاربين في بورصة العقارات.

عقب ذلك اندمج الفنان في إعادة بناء المنطقة، وبدأت مجموعات عمل جديدة بالظهور، من ضمنها نفس القضايا التي شغلت دان بيترمان قبل كارثة "البناية". إلاّ أنّ ما استجد في ذلك الوقت – وهذا بالتأكيد له علاقة بتجاربه الراهنة – هو نظرته المتشائمة إلى نقطة التحول البيئية (الإيكولوجية)، والتي يثابر بيترمان على صياغتها. فبدلاً من تقديم مشاريع ملتزمة و"تطبيقية" – كما كان الحال في سنوات التسعينيات – بدأ الفنان بإنتاج أعمال صغيرة تعكس الزخم البيئي من وجهة النظر الجمالية أولا وآخرا وليس "الوظيفية". تماماً كعمله الفني "وراء الحظ والمهارة" (٢٠٠٦)، حيث قام دان بيترمان بإعادة تدوير أشرطة لاصقة مُلقاة وورق مُهمَل وجعَلها على شكل كرات قدم صغيرة. هذه الكرات موضوعة الآن على قطعة من الحشيش الاصطناعي، وهو بدوره عبارة عن بقايا التركيبة الفنية "النهاية السعيدة لأمريكا الخاصة بفرانتز كافكا" (١٩٩٤) للفنان مارتن كيبنبيرغر.

يبدو أنّ بيترمان يريد أن يقول، مستسلماً، بأنّ البيئة في زمن العولمة النيوليبرالية لم يعُد لها فرصة مطلقاً إلاّ على أساس الفن. وتشير سلسلة أعماله بعنوان "الأشياء التي كانت، هي أشياء مرةً أخرى" (٢٠٠٦)، والتي تتكون من قطع من الألمنيوم المسكوب، إلى نفس الاتجاه الفكري المتمثل في شبه "مثالية سلبية". في هذا العمل قام بيترمان بصَهر خردة مهمَلة ثم أعاد صبها وتشكيلها من جديد، والنتيجة الفنية هي قطع تجريدية مزركشة، تذكرنا بالرموز الزُخرفية، والتي سرعان ما تكتسب صفة تجميلية لدى تعليقها في صف واحد على حائط الجاليري. وبدلاً من أن تدعو إلى التفكير بإعادة التدوير فإنها تبدو عملا فنيا حرفيا صالحا للتسويق. إلا أن هذا الاتجاه، للأسف، له معنى: فلقد دخلت عملية إعادة التدوير إلى قواعد الفن المعاصر في نفس الوقت الذي أصبح البقاء فيه أكثر صعوبة – بالمعنى المزدوج للكلمة – وبهذا أصبحت لها قيمة تباع في السوق.

رايمر شتانغه

Adaptations, 2006, installation view, Klosterfelde, Berlin

MARJETICA POTRC

Personal responsibility is what is most important for the future. A much more radical phenomenon than the Western Balkans is represented by the new territories in Acre, an Amazonian state in Brazil on the border with Peru: these are great examples of 21st-century communities that are building a sustainable present and, if you will, the future. I spent two months there earlier this year as part of a Sao Paulo Biennial residency. Over the last 15 years, land in Acre has been distributed to individual communities. This is approximately the same period during which Yugoslavia fragmented into its separate constituent republics. But while the fragmentation in Yugoslavia was extremely painful, what happened in Acre has been a happy fragmentation.

The Acrean communities practice small-scale economies, and I might add that this is important not only for their survival, but also for the survival of the world. They also have a unique approach to land ownership. In the new territories, the emphasis is not on the individual owning land and extracting resources from it solely for his own benefit, but on the collective ownership and sustainable management of natural resources for the benefit of the whole community. One might say this smells of communism, or that it presents a direct critique of capitalism. Far from it. This strategy is not about ideology, but about local knowledge. Here, the existence of the individual is understood essentially as coexistence. Individuals and communities are accountable for themselves and to others. That's self-organisation for you, and yes, it is possible to practice an existence beyond ideological constructs.

Marjetica Potrc

From an interview with Anna Daneri, published in Italian as "Europe Lost and Found", Marjetica Potrc e Kyong Park: "Ritorno al futuro", *Flash Art Italy* (October-November 2006): pp.110-111.

ماريتيكا بوترك

المسؤوليّة الشخصيّة هي أهم ما نحتاجه لبناء المستقبل. وإذا أردنا ظاهرة أكثر تطرّفا من البلقان الغربية فإننا نجدها في الأراضي الجديدة في ولاية آكر. وهي ولاية أمازونيّة في البرازيل على الحدود مع البيرو. نجد في هذه الولاية أمثلة ممتازة لمجتمعات من القرن الحادي والعشرين تقوم ببناء حاضر مستدام، وإن شئتم، مستقبل أيضا. قضيت شهرين هناك في أوائل العام الماضي كجزء من برنامج الإقامة في بينالي ساو باولو. عبر السنوات الخمس عشرة الماضية ، تمّ توزيع الأرض في آكر لمجتمعات مختلفة. واكب هذا انقسام يوغسلافيا إلى جزيئات جمهوريّة منفصلة. لكن في حين كان الانقسام في يوغسلافيا مؤلماً للغاية، إلا أن ما حدث في آكر من تقسيم كان مفرحاً جداً.

تمارس المجتمعات الآكريّة نظما اقتصاديّة محدودة، وأضيف، أنّ هذا ضروري ليس لاستدامتهم فحسب، بل أيضا من أجل بقاء هذا العالم. لديهم كذلك مقاربة فريدة في ملكيّة الأرض. التركيز في الأراضي الجديدة ليس على الملكية الفردية للأرض والحصول على خيراتها للمصلحة الخاصّة، وإنما على الملكيّة الجماعيّة والإدارة المستدامة للمصادر الطبيعيّة من أجل مصلحة المجتمع ككل. يمكن للمرء أن يقول أنّ فكرة الملكية الجماعية هذه تبدو شيوعيّة، أو قد تمثّل انتقادا مباشرا للرأسماليّة. الأمر بعيد عن ذلك كل البعد، فهذه الاستراتيجيّة ليست عقائدية بل مستقاة من المعرفة المحليّة. هنا، يُفهم وجود الفرد على أنّه تعايش بشكل أساسي، والأفراد والمجتمعات مسؤولون أمام أنفسهم وأمام الآخرين. هذا هو التنظيم الذاتي، ونعم، من الممكن ممارسة وجود يتجاوز النظريات العقائديّة.

ماريتيكا بوترك

من مقابلة مع آنا دانيري، نُشرت بالإيطاليّة بعنوان "أوروبا فُقدَت ووجدَت: ماريتيكا بوترك إي كيونغ بارك: ريتورنو أل فوتورو." "فلاش آرت إيتالي" (تشرين أوّل أكتوبر - تشرين ثاني نوفمبر ٢٠٠٦)؛ ص. ١١٠-١١١.

Barefoot College: Power from Nature, 2005, energy infrastructure, Rajastan, India, in collaboration with Nobel Peace Center, Oslo, Norway, photo: Marjetica Potrc

MICHAEL RAKOWITZ

The invisible enemy should not exist, 2007 Michael Rakowitz's most recent project, was originally conceived for a solo exhibition beginning of this year at Lombard-Freid Projects in New York City. It is an attempt to reconstruct the archeological artefacts looted from the National Museum of Iraq in the aftermath of the American invasion in April 2003. For the Sharjah Biennial, an updated version of this work will be shown, featuring 17 objects produced in late February and early March 2007. To date, 70 artifacts have been replicated to scale.

The title of the exhibition takes its name from the direct translation of *Aj-ibur-shapu*, the ancient Babylonian street that was used as a processional way and that ran through the Ishtar Gate. This magnificent blue tile gate, which was excavated in Iraq in 1902-1914 by German archeologist Robert Koldewey, is on permanent exhibition at the Pergamon Museum in Berlin. In the 1950s, the Iraqi government rebuilt the gate; close by stands a reconstruction of the ancient city of Babylon, created by Saddam Hussein as a monument to his own sovereignty. Today the reconstructed Ishtar Gate is the site most frequently photographed and posted on the Internet by US servicemen stationed in Iraq.

The invisible enemy should not exist unfolds as an intricate narrative based on extensive research about the artefacts stolen from the Museum, the current status of their whereabouts, and the series of events surrounding the invasion, the plundering and related protagonists. Alluding to the implied invisibility of these artefacts–initial reports about their looting were inflated due to the "fog of war," stated Museum officials–the reconstructions are made from the packaging of Middle Eastern foodstuffs and local Arabic newspapers, moments of cultural visibility found in cities across the United States. The objects were created together with a team of assistants using the University of Chicago's Oriental Institute database, as well as information posted on Interpol's website. This version of the project represents the incipient stage of an ongoing commitment to recuperate the over 7,000 objects that remain missing.

A series of episodic drawings punctuate the installation. The drawings reveal a narrative that includes the story of Dr. Donny George, former President of the Iraq State Board of Antiquities and Heritage and Director General of the National Museum in Baghdad, who worked tirelessly to recover looted artefacts. Under Saddam Hussein, Dr. George worked at archaeological sites to avoid Ba'ath Party meetings and also sidelined as a drummer in a band called 99%, which specialized in covers of Deep Purple songs. A version of their "Smoke on the Water," recorded especially for this project by the New York-based Arabic band *Ayyoub*, becomes the sound background for the show.

Updated with newly reconstructed objects and installed in the Sharjah Art Museum, which is located only 800 miles away from the National Museum of Iraq, the project sheds light on the erosion and loss of humanity and cultural heritage due to greed, capitalism and thoughtless conquest - an irretrievable loss that can be paralleled with the loss of natural heritage due to similar interests, which go hand in hand.

مايكل راكوفيتش

"العدو لا يمر من هنا"، ٢٠٠٧... هذا هو اسم أحدث المشروعات الفنية للفنان مايكل راكوفيتش الذي كان قد صممه في الأساس ليكون معرضا فرديا يقدمه في بداية هذا العام في قاعات لومبارد-فرايد بروجيكتس الفنية في مدينة نيويورك. ويحاول الفنان من خلال معرضه هذا إلقاء الضوء على الأعمال الأثرية التي نُهبت من المتحف الوطني العراقي في أعقاب الغزو الأميركي لبغداد في إبريل ٢٠٠٣. وسيشهد بينالي الشارقة الثامن نسخة محدثة للمعرض الذي سيضم ١٧ عملا صممها الفنان في آخر شهر فبراير وأوائل مارس ٢٠٠٧. وحتى اليوم جرى تصميم ٧٠ عملا كَنُسخ فنية يحاكي بهم الفنان ما جرت سرقته من أعمال أصلية من المتحف الوطني العراقي.

وقد اُقتبس اسم المعرض من ترجمة للعبارة الشهيرة الموجودة على أحد شوارع مدينة بابليون القديمة، وهي العبارة التي حملت الحروف "أج أيبور-شابو" والتي تعني ترجمتها "العدو لا يمر من هنا"، وهو شارع كان يشهد الموكب الذي كان يمر ببوابة عشتار بمناسبة احتفالات العام الجديد. ومن المعروف أن هذه البوابة الخلابة ذات البلاط الأزرق والتي كشف عنها النقاب العالم الأثري الألماني روبرت كوليوي في الفترة من ١٩٠٢ إلى ١٩١٤.

ويدور المعرض حول الأعمال التي سُرقت من المتحف ويقدم معلومات حول حالتها الحالية وأماكن وجودها والأحداث التي صاحبت عملية غزو بغداد وما تعرضت إليه المدينة من أعمال سرقة ونهب. وقد جرى تصميم أعمال المعرض عن طريق جمع بعض المواد الغذائية الشرق أوسطية وبعض الصحف العربية ومن بعض المواد في بعض المدن الأميركية. وقد تم تجميع تلك الأعمال على يد فريق من المساعدين للفنان الذين استخدموا قاعدة بيانات معهد أورينتال التابع لجامعة شيكاغو بالإضافة إلى معلومات نُشرت على الموقع الإليكتروني للإنتربول. هذه النسخة من المعرض تمثل المرحلة الأولى من المشروع الجاري لإعادة أكثر من ٧٠٠٠ عمل لا يزال مفقودا حتى يومنا هذا.

وهناك سلسلة من اللوحات تحدد المسار الزمني لعملية التركيب. و هناك رسومات تكشف عن قصة تتعلق بالدكتور دوني جورج، الرئيس السابق لمجلس الآثار والتراث العراقي والمدير العام السابق للمتحف الوطني العراقي والذي لم يألو جهدا في استعادة عدد كبير من الأعمال التي تعرضت للنهب والسرقة. فإبان حكم صدام حسين كان الدكتور جورج يعمل داخل المواقع الأثرية أثناء عمليات التنقيب من أجل أن يتفادى اجتماعات حزب البعث. وكان يعمل أيضا طبالا في فرقة غنائية عرفت باسم "٩٩٪" كانت متخصصة في أداء أغنيات وعروض فرقة ديب بيربل. وقد استخدمت نسخة من العمل الغنائي لتلك الفرقة والذي يحمل اسم "دخان على الماء" والذي سجلته خصيصا للمعرض الفرقة العربية "أيوب" التي تقيم في نيويورك-تُستخدم كموسيقى تصويرية للعرض الذي يصاحب تقديم المعرض.

وقد تم تزويد المعرض، الذي يُقدم في متحف الشارقة للفنون، بأعمال جرى إعادة تصميمها حديثا. ويلقي المعرض بالضوء على ما تعرضت إليه الإنسانية من تشويه وخسائر فادحة بسبب الطمع والرأسمالية والطيش. وهي الخسارة التي لا يمكن أن يعوضها شيء وتضاهي في فداحتها خسارة التراث الطبيعي بسبب عوامل مشابهة.

The Invisible Enemy Should Not Exist (Recovered, Missing, Stolen Series), 2007, installation view, middle eastern packaging and newspapers, glue, variable dimensions, courtesy of the artist and Lombard-Freid Projects

Saudi Dates
SULTAN

NOGUCHI RIKA

To the desert

One day, I met dressed camels in a desert.
The camels live in the desert with the Bedouins.
The Bedouins compose poetry.
I will make a work about the camels and the Bedouins.

Noguchi Rika

It could be said that what Noguchi Rika tries to unfold is something like an open-ended potential, found in a simple on-going incident or situation. Noguchi's photograph capturing a situation is taken from afar or discreetly from behind. But it somehow reminds us of a situation in a novel.

Noguchi often photographs a scene of an activity, such as people working on a construction site or walking somewhere in silence. A photograph extracts one particular part of a situation. This gets separated from what happened before and after and from other surrounding circumstances. Therefore, a photograph is not necessarily able to convey correctly the situation that is actually happening in the frame. Noguchi conversely takes advantage of this defect and is eager to decipher again the suspended situation. By employing what might be described as a novelistic imagination, she creates an open-ended situation to establish what she calls "a new way of looking at the earth".

The series included here is entitled New Land and was taken on a new island reclaimed from the sea. The construction site itself is "a site where an incident is taking place" and what is being created there is new ground, i.e. "a site for something to be constructed", a site where something might happen, a site with an open potential of creation – Noguchi's photographs are always presented to us as scenes where such possibilities are formulated or as sites where a new way of looking at the world opens up. According to Noguchi, "Any place is capable of becoming somewhere."[1] What supports it is the photographer's imagination and our imagination receiving it.

Rei Masuda, "[sait] site/sight" / Photography Today 2 – [sait] site/sight, The National Museum of Modern Art, Tokyo, 2002, pp.90-91

[1] Although this statement was made in reference to a series entitled Dreaming of Babylon, it is also suggestive in appreciating other works by Noguchi.

نوغوشي ريكا

إلى الصحراء

في يوم ما، قابلت جمالا ترتدي الثياب في الصحراء.
تعيش الجمال في الصحراء مع البدو.
يؤلّف البدو الشعر.
سأصنع عملا عن الجمال والبدو.

نوغوشي ريكا

يمكن القول أن ما تحاول نوغوشي ريكا طرحه، هو شيء أشبه ما يكون باحتمال مفتوح النهايات، يمكن العثور عليه في حادثة أو وضع بسيط متواصل. إن الصورة الفوتوغرافية التي تلتقطها نوغوشي لحالة قائمة بذاتها، هي صورة ملتقطة عن بعد، أو من الخلف، بهدوء تام، وبما يذكرنا بوضع معين في رواية ما. كثيرا ما تقوم نوغوشي بتصوير مشاهد أشخاص يقومون بعمل ما، مثل مشهد أناس يعملون في ورشة بناء، أو مشهد أناس يمشون بصمت في مكان ما. تركز الصورة على جزء معين من الوضع المذكور، وبذلك تنفصل الصورة عما حدث قبلها أو بعدها، وعن أية ظروف محيطة بها. وهذه الصور الفوتوغرافية ليست قادرة بالضرورة، على النقل الأمين للحدث الفعلي الذي يجري في الإطار. تعمد نغوشي إلى الاستفادة من هذا العيب، وذلك باستيعاب الحالة المعلقة من خلال استخدامها لما يمكن تسميته بالخيال الروائي، لكي تخلق وضعا مفتوح النهايات، بهدف تأسيس ما تطلق عليه صفة "الطريقة الجديدة للنظر إلى الأرض". سلسلة الصور الموجودة هنا بعنوان "أرض جديدة" صورت في جزيرة جديدة تمت استعادتها من البحر. أما مكان البناء في حد ذاته، فهو "مكان يحدث فيه حدث ما". وما يتم تشكيله هناك هو أرض جديدة، بمعنى "موقع لشيء سيتم بناؤه". إنه مكان قد يحدث فيه حدث ما، فهو مكان مفتوح على كل احتمالات الخلق. يتم عرض صور نغوشي علينا كمشاهد مفتوحة على هذه الاحتمالات، أو أماكن يمكن منها الانفتاح على رؤية جديدة للعالم. ووفقا لنوغوشي، "أي مكان يمكن أن يكون هو المكان".[1] يدعم هذا العمل خيال المصور، وخيالنا المتلقي.

راي مسودا، من مجلة فوتوغرافي توداي ٢ — (سايت)، المتحف الوطني للفن الحديث - طوكيو، ٢٠٠٢، ص. ٩٠ — ٩١.

[1] رغم أن هذه الجملة ذكرتها الفنانة في الإشارة إلى سلسلة صور بعنوان حلم بابل، إلا أنها توفر إطلالة على أعمال نوغوشي الأخرى.

Catching Water #4, 2001, C-print, 94 x 240 cm, courtesy of the artist, D'Amelio Terras, New York and Gallery Koyanagi, Tokyo

BUDOOR AL RIYAMI

بـدور الـريامـي

Filled with thousands of commands each second, our brains can no longer be surprised. Everyone runs with a quickening momentum that confuses values and beliefs and the need to cope with the variables of the present and the past. A vortex contains a spread mixture of material and symbolic terms, clashing at times and bonding at others.

The feet do not halt their steps and move in all directions. The foot painted with the coloured shoes of modernity - surrounds us with the thump of its steps, exactly like the hubbub of the city. We do not notice the bare foot, the foot rooted in the earth, we will not hear its ancient pace, calm like the life that we lost long ago on the other side of the city asphalt! We will see how these toes will cleanse the pavements and the street's remains off the new foot, the worn shoes and the coming time!

The work attempts to create an atmosphere contrasting in terms: what we visually consume on a daily basis, side by side with symbolic terms incapable of materialising - despite our belief in the necessity of their existence - to face the deep struggle within ourselves regarding the exhaustion of our spiritual values by our contemporary material life and the true link to our balanced human roots on this earth.

لا شـيء بات يدهش أدمغتنا المحملة بآلاف الأوامر في الثانية الواحدة. فقد أصبح الكل يجري بتسارع يمزج القيم والمعتقدات. والحاجة الى التكيف مع المتغيرات في الحاضر والماضي... دوامة من خليط متناثر من المفردات المعنوية والمادية... تتنافر تارة وتتحد تارة أخرى.

الأقدام التي لا تتوقف خطواتها وفي كل الاتجاهات. القدم المطلية بأحذية العصر الملونة. يحاصرنا وقع خطواتها تماما كضجيج المدينة... لن نلاحظ تلك القدم العارية. النابتة من الأرض. ولن نسمع خطواتها القديمة الهادئة كالحياة التي فقدناها منذ زمن على اسفلت المدينة! وسنشاهد كيف ستغسل تلك الأصابع ما تبقى من أرصفة وشوارع على القدم الجديدة. والحذاء المهترئ والزمن القادم!!

يعتمد العمل على خلق جو من التناقض في المفردات التي نستهلكها بصرياً بشكل يومي. جنبا إلى جنب مع مفردات معنوية غير قادرة على الحضور - بالرغم من إيماننا بضرورة تواجدها - لنواجه ذلك التصارع العميق في أنفسنا حول استنزاف الحياة المادية المعاصرة لقيمنا الروحية والصلة الحقيقية لجذورنا الإنسانية المتوازنة على هذه الأرض.

The Charming Young Lady, 2006, video

RAEDA SAADEH

The woman as a recurring subject in my installations or performance work is represented as living in a state of occupation. This occupation or "occupying" force is effected through political conditions in her environment and impacts on the otherwise peaceful quality of her world. Both private and public elements manipulate this world.

In my art works, the woman I represent lives in a world that attacks her values, her love, her spirit on a daily basis, and for this reason she is in a state of occupation – and her world could be here in Palestine or elsewhere; yet despite all, she looks towards her future with a smile.

In *Untitled* (2005) I am photographed wearing a gentleman's suit complete with a formal tie, but I am wearing the suit backwards. In this work, I am attempting to express the masculine dominance that is so prominent within our culture; but my wearing the suit backwards is my own intervention, commenting on the necessity to view things otherwise and from a non-masculine-dominated perspective. The gentleman's suit does not have any particular cultural identity and could be worn by any man from anywhere in the world.

The subject/woman I represent in the majority of my work is weighed down with oppression but is filled with ambition; she is saner than she should be and yet she is also a little mad. She is both fragile and strong, she is fully aware and responsive, and she is constantly on the move. And every move she makes, every act, is an act that exhibits awareness of her surrounding environment, while simultaneously being an act of revolt against social orders/conditions.

In the new video project, *Vacuum* (2007), commissioned by Sharjah Biennial 8, I am seen in a desert landscape, attempting to vacuum the sand. It is an endless process, as I move across the sand in a continuous vacuuming motion in an attempt to question how much life is given and how much taken.

The actions of the subject I represent reflect an evaluation of the self and that of the subject's environment, submission and revolt – attempting to live a life alongside the forces of occupation in all its forms, and regardless of its geography. The subject is concerned with issues that "occupy" her individual spirit and the realities of her daily life, whether political or personal.

رائدة سعادة

المرأة موضوع يتكرر في أعمالي التركيبية أو عروضي، وتتمثل في امرأة تعيش تحت الاحتلال. يتأثر هذا الاحتلال، أو القوة "المحتلة"، بالظروف السياسية لبيئتها، ويؤثر على الطبيعة المسالمة لعالمها. وتتلاعب العناصر الخاصة والعامة، كلاهما، بهذا العالم.

السلطة المحتلة لها اوجه مختلفة: يمكن أن تتخذ شكل الواقع اليومي الملموس، مثل جدار من الاسمنت، سياج، حاجز عسكري، منع تجول، حاجز من الحجارة، أو يمكن ان تعيد تأكيد سلطتها في وجه طفل، أو منزل، أو لغة، أو ثقافة، أو توقعات تقليدية. ثمة محددات على حريتها الشخصية أيضا: المرأة، الأم، العشيقة، الدليل، حامية الحمى. تسعى نحو العدالة وتحلم بالتغيير، واعية لأعدائها من حولها وتدفع نفسها إلى الأمام بقوة وعزم. تشعر في بعض الأوقات وكأن عليها ان تبدو كالمجنونة، لكي تتجنب أذى الاحتلال وهي تحاول حماية من تحب من الآثار السلبية للخوف.

المرأة التي أمثلها في أعمالي الفنية تعيش في عالم يهاجم يوميا قيمها، حبها، وروحها. وهي لهذا السبب في حالة احتلال – عالمها قد يكون في فلسطين او في أي مكان آخر – ولكن بالرغم من ذلك، تبتسم في مواجهة مستقبلها.

في "بدون عنوان" (٢٠٠٥) التقطت لي صورة وأنا أرتدي بدلة رجالية مع ربطة عنق، ولكني أرتديها معكوسة. أحاول في هذا العمل أن أعبر عن السيطرة الذكورية السائدة في ثقافتنا، ولكن ارتدائي للبدلة بشكل معكوس، هي مداخلتي الخاصة وتعليقي على ضرورة رؤية الأمور بطريقة مغايرة، من منظور غير-ذكوري. البدلة الرجالية، لا هوية ثقافية محددة لها ويمكن لأي رجل في أي مكان في العالم أن يرتديها.

الموضوع/المرأة الذي أحاكيه في أغلب أعمالي مثقل بالقمع، لكنه مليء بالطموح. فهي أعقل مما يجب، ولكن فيها مسحة من الجنون أيضا. هي هشة وقوية في الوقت نفسه، واعية تماما ومتجاوبة، وفي حالة حركة دوما. كل حركة تقوم بها، كل عمل، هو عمل يظهر وعيا لبيئتها المحيطة، وفي الوقت نفسه هو عمل ثوري ضد الظروف الاجتماعية.

في مشروع الفيديو الجديد، "شفط الهواء" (٢٠٠٧) والذي صنع لبينالي الشارقة الثامن، ترونني في بيئة صحراوية أحاول أن أشفط الرمل. إنها عملية لا تنتهي، وأتحرك عبر الرمل في حركة شفط الرمل، في محاولة لطرح تساؤل حول، كم يعطى من الحياة وكم يؤخذ.

تعكس افعال هذا المشروع تقييما للنفس ولبيئة الموضوع، الخنوع والثورة – في محاولة لعيش حياة محاذية لقوى الاحتلال بكافة أشكاله، وبغض النظر عن موقعه الجغرافي. يعنى الموضوع بالقضايا التي "تحتل" روحها الفردية وواقع حياتها اليومية، السياسية والشخصية.

Untitled, 2005, photography, 120 x 90 cm

ABDALLAH AL SAADI

I have been going on bike rides since 1992 - in the Emirates as well as in other places such as Japan, France, Scotland ... On these trips I make sketches of natural scenes and document them in my journals. In other words, my trips are organised and deliberate; the one thing I am constantly seeking is the formation of a philosophy of my own. An understanding of life, the search for self - life for me is a continuous journey.

You find the element of movement in this work, where I have attached a sketched scroll to a boat. This scroll sticks at random during the boat's movement near the shore.

This movement is related to silence and contemplation. My works look for the "I" through collision and discovery. I do not attempt to deal with traditional drawing on its own, but I make of the surrounding environment a formative element, and not simply a set in which the drawing is embraced. The scroll here is an element, as are the boat and the beach; the visual aspect is an infinite dimension for the artwork.

عبد الله السعدي

منذ العام ١٩٩٢ أقوم برحلات بالدراجة الهوائية، سواء فى الإمارات أو في بلدان أخرى مثل اليابان، فرنسا، سكوتلاندا وغيرها، أو أقوم برسم الاسكتشات لبعض المناظرالطبيعية، أو أسجل في دفتر مذكراتي... أعني أن رحلاتي منظمة ومدروسة. هناك شيء واحد أبحث عنه في جميع رحلاتي، وهو تكوين فلسفة خاصة بي، مفهوم حياة، البحث عن الذات. فالحياة بالنسبة لي رحلة لا تتوقف أبدا.

في هذا العمل تجد عنصر الحركة، فلفافة الورق المرسومة والتي قمت بربطها وتثبيتها على القارب، تلتصق بشكل عشوائي أثناء حركة القارب بالقرب من الشاطئ، محدثة حركة مقترنة بالصمت والتأمل. أبحث في أعمالي عن الأنا عبر الصدم والاختراع، لا أحاول التعامل مع الرسم التقليدي فقط، بل أجعل من البيئة المحيطة عنصرا مكونا وليس مجرد موقع يحتضن اللوحة، فهذه اللفافة خامة، وكذلك القارب والشاطئ، فالبعد البصري هو بعد لا نهائي للعمل الفني.

Cologne, 2006, (detail), paper scroll, ink on paper, 10 x 500 cm, courtesy of the artist

HUDA SAEED SAIF

Huda Saeed's work adopts a movement by which she reorganizes our mental image frames. The element of movement in her work creates a new environment, a groundwork that allows us to reconstruct our understanding of the whole environment; it brings us into tune with the modern world we live in. The work liberates the thought of viewers from the shackles of convention and illuminates dimensions that allow for a greater perspective, using the idea of quantum mechanics.

Through her works, Huda stresses freedom of will and choice available to the viewer by using the theory of relativity: "the relativity of time and space allows art to transcend its limit."

Independent and subjective, Huda Saeed's work creates its own space, space that works within the historical progress of our time, and which is therefore different from and unbound by the old. Her emancipated space creates history because it dominates history; it doesn't reproduce it, it precedes it. Not only does it reject to grant it sanctuary, it places it at a precarious position. Her space is thus "free space". Huda saeed's work is sarcastic to the bone, mocking life in today's world. Yet she presents it within such extravagant, overdone layout, that it renders speechless those with ready anecdotes on the irony of life in our modern cities.

Though her work Huda Saeed critically scrutinizes a the human race. She refers to the notion of retuning to nature, which is not totally possible because of our present reality. It is also a hopeful look to the future because life, with all its noise and pitfalls, still has its positive side. This is the new dynamic; in fact this had always been the dynamic without which history would have been utterly superfluous.

Hassan Sharif

هدى سعيد سيف

عمل هدى سعيد يعتمد على الحركة التي من خلالها تقوم بإعادة ترتيب الصور العقلية لدينا. عنصر الحركة في عملها يخلق بيئة جديدة تمكننا من إعادة فهم البيئة الشاملة. ويوحدنا مع نغمة العصر الذي نعيش فيه. هذا العمل يحرر فكر المشاهد من القيود السائدة ويوجهه إلى الأبعاد الضخمة إلى أبعد الحدود عن طريق استخدامها النظريات الفيزيائية مثل (ميكانيكا الكم) وتؤكد هدى سعيد من خلال عملها على أهمية الإرادة والاختيار عند المشاهد لأن مقاييس المكان والزمان نسبية وبالتالي فضاء الفن هو الفضاء اللانهائي.

الاستقلالية والطبيعة الموضوعية هي من سمات عمل هدى سعيد. وهذه العناصر تخلق فضاءها الخاص. هذا الفضاء يعمل وفقاً للتطور التاريخي للعصر الذي نعيشه. وبالتالي فضاء عملها يختلف تماماً عن فضاء الأزمنة القديمة.

فضاء عمل هدى سعيد يخلق التاريخ لأنه يهيمن عليه. لذلك لا يكرره. بل يسبقه لأنه يرفض أن يستقبل التاريخ فقط. بل يضعه في مأزق. لهذا السبب فضاء عملها الشرعي هو "الفضاء الحُر".

هدى سعيد من خلال عملها تنظر إلى الحياة نظرة نقدية. وتعبر من خلال عملها عن الحياة الإنسانية التائهة وسط دهاليز الحياة. وهي تشير من خلال عملها إلى فكرة العودة إلى حضن الطبيعة ولكن هذه الحياة الجديدة لا مفر منها لأنها أصبحت جزءاً من (الحاضر) وهي حنيننا إلى المستقبل بكل ضجيجه. لأن الحياة الجديدة تمتلك في مضمونها إيجابيات مثلما تمتلك سلبيات. هذه دينامية الإنسان عبر القرون. ومن دون هذه الدينامية لم يكن للتاريخ أي أثر.

حسن شريف

Some vision, 2006, video, courtesy of the artist

MICHAEL SAILSTORFER

Several aspects are recurrent in the work of Michael Sailstorfer: the sculptural transformation of matter from one thing into another, the fascination with the laws of physics (and, ultimately, the construction of the universe), and the notion of mobility versus standstill – where the latter also translates into the notion of "home". As a sculptor, Sailstorfer is interested "in the idea of creating something new by taking something away". An early work, *Waldputz* (Forest Cleaning, 2000), exemplifies the idea of sculpting space through creating a void: the artist cleaned a 4.8 x 4.8 square metre of ground in a Bavarian wood by removing all needles, grass and everything else but the blank soil, creating a visual square flanked by three trees. By removing also the moss from the trunks of the trees up to a certain height, the square became an immaterial cube. This neat act of domestic maintenance was not only a visual interference in an existing ecosystem; it was also a sly reference to Land and Minimal Art, e.g. the spatial inscriptions of Richard Long, Robert Smithson or Jan Dibbets.

A house stands at the centre of the work *3-Ster mit Aussicht*, (3-Star with a view, 2002), in collaboration with Jürgen Heinert. The artists purchased a wooden chalet in the Bavarian countryside, just to feed it piece by piece into its own wood-stove, until only the smouldering stove and a smoking chimney remained. The outcome of this performance without audience, which lasted from dawn until dusk, is a series of photographs and a less than 2-minute film, which shows the architecture dismantling and engulfing itself in a slapstick-like act of self-destruction. Yet, the image itself is highly romantic – imagine Gordon Matta Clark meets Caspar David Friedrich for a picnic on a lawn. A similar twist on reverse entropy is performed in the work *Sternschnuppe* (Shooting Star, 2002), in which a Mercedes Benz W123 powers a street lamp, which sits on a launching ramp on the back of the car; the glowing lamp-post is then fired into the evening sky – a heartbreaking romantic image, but executed on a weapon-like apparatus. The flight of the lamp-post lasts only as long as a distant falling star appears on the iris, until it crashes to the ground just a few metres from the launching vehicle.

The notions of velocity vs. standstill, entropy and material transformation through gradual erosion, is once again exemplified in *Zeit ist keine Autobahn* (Time is not a Highway, 2005). Powered by an electric motor, one car wheel after another runs at high speed into a wall, until the rubber is pulverised by constant attrition and the tube finally bursts. The melancholy, or absurdity, of this piece could almost be seen as a laconic metaphor for society's never-ending demand for speed – and the waste (in both energy and matter) that comes with it.

Eva Scharrer

ميخائيل سيلستورفر

تتكرر عدة خصائص في أعمال ميخائيل سيلستورفر: التحوّل النحتي للمادة من شئ إلى آخر، الافتتان بقوانين الفيزياء (وبالنهاية تكوين العالم)، وفكرة الحركة مقابل السكون - حيث يمكن ترجمة الأخيرة إلى فكرة "الوطن" أيضا. كنحّات، سيلستورفر مهتمّ بـ "فكرة تكوين شئ جديد على أساس إزاحة شئ ما." أحد أعماله الأولى، والدبوتزس (تنظيف الغابة) ٢٠٠٠، يمثل فكرة نحت مساحة من خلال تكوين فراغ: نظّف الفنان مساحة ٤،٨×٤،٨ مترا مربعا من الأرض في غابة بافاريّة من خلال إزالة كل الأغصان الإبرية والعشب وكل شئ آخر ما عدا التراب العاري، فصنع مربّعا بصريا على أطرافه ثلاث شجرات. بإزالته الطحالب من على جذوع الأشجار حتى ارتفاع معيّن، أصبح المربّع مكعّبا غير ملموس. لم يكن فعل التنظيف المنزليّ الأنيق هذا تدخّلا بصريّا في نظام بيئيّ موجود فحسب، بل كان أيضا إشارة إلى الأرض والفن المنمنم، أي النقوش الفراغيّة لـِ ريتشارد لونغ أو روبرت سميثسون أو جان ديبيتس.

ويتوسط العمل ٣-ستير ميت أوسيخت (٣ مجسّمات مع مطلّة) ٢٠٠٢، الذي قام به بالتعاون مع يورغن هينيرت، بيت خشبي. فقد اشترى الفنانان بيتا صغيرا (شاليه) خشبيّا في الريف البافاري، وقاموا بتغذية موقده بخشب البيت قطعة بعد قطعة. في النهاية، لم يبقَ شئ إلاّ الموقد المشتعل والمدخنة. كان نتاج هذا الأداء الذي خلا من المتفرّجين واستمرّ من الفجر حتى الغروب، سلسلة صور فوتوغرافيّة وفيلم أقصر من دقيقتين، يعرض بناء معماريّا يفكك ويبتلع ذاته فيما يشبه التمثيل الهزلي لعملية التدمير الذاتيّ. بالرغم من ذلك، فالصورة بحدّ ذاتها رومانسية - تخيّل جوردون ماتّا كلارك يقابل كاسبر ديفيد فريدريك من أجل نزهة على العشب. يتمّ محاكاة انقلاب غريب في مجرى الأحداث مشابه للتحول الداخلي المعكوس في العمل ستيرنسشنوبّه(شهاب) ٢٠٠٢، حيث تمدّ سيّارة مرسيدس بنز W123 وحدة إنارة في الشارع بالطاقة. يرتكز عمود الإضاءة على قاعدة إنطلاق على ظهر السيّارة ومن ثمّ ينطلق عمود الإضاءة نحو سماء الليل - صورة رومانسية تنفطر لها القلوب ولكنّها تنطلق من آلة تبدو كالسلاح. لم تطل مدّة طيران عمود الإضاءة أكثر من المدّة التي يظهر فيها الشهاب أمام العين حتّى يسقط متكسّرا على الأرض على بعد بضعة أمتار من واسطة الإطلاق.

تتمثّل فكرة السرعة مقابل السكون، التحول الداخلي وتحوّل المادة من خلال التآكل التدريجي، مرّة ثانية في تسايت إست كاينه أوتوباهن (الوقت ليس طريقا سريعا) ٢٠٠٥. يتحرّك عجل سيّارة تلو الآخر بسرعة عالية باتجاه حائط بفعل طاقة مستمدة من محرّك كهربائي، حتّى يهترئ المطّاط بسبب الإحتكاك المستمرّ وينفجر في النهاية. يمكن أن نعتبر كآبة وسخرية هذا العمل كاستعارة موجزة عن حاجة المجتمع الأبدية للسرعة - والإسراف (في كلّ من الطاقة والمادّة) الذي يصاحبها.

إيفا شارير

3 Steres With a View, 2002, in collaboration with Jürgen Heinert, photos: Siegfried Wameser, courtesy of Johann König, Berlin and Zero..., Milan

TOMAS SARACENO

Following in the tradition of Buckminster Fuller, Tomas Saraceno's installation, sculpture, photography and video work challenge the conventional restrictions on the human habitat, and suggest new ways of perceiving nature. The possibility of moving cities from the earth's surface into the air is a central theme in his practice, and his futuristic urban models of floating metropolises are not just fantasy - Saraceno is working towards realizing them as a practical solution. In depicting these flying communities he points out the narrowness of traditional land-bound perspectives and creates, in Fuller's words a, "great and anticipatory vision of the future."

Saraceno's ongoing research concentrates on the project "Air-Port-City", which the artist has been conducting for some years now. Starting with the open patent application of the innovative material Aero gel, used for the construction of lighter-than-air vehicles, Saraceno is working on the possibility of building residential structures and urban settlements in the sky that exploit natural energies.

Moving like clouds, these habitations and flying gardens redefine geographical and political boundaries, generating human and political communities in continuous transformation. These Air-Port-Cities would be freely constituted in compliance with international laws, challenging the political, social, cultural and military restrictions presently in effect around the world. Toward the realization of this vision, Saraceno is conducting research and experimentation to investigate the possibilities of this future reality. One such experiment, confirmed by the Buckminster Fuller Virtual Institute, is the first solar-energy geodesic balloon ever built, utilizing trash bags ('59 steps to be on air - by sun power') and including instructions for do-it-yourself construction of a solar energy balloon.

As envisioned in his panoramic video installation of floating clouds recently commissioned by the Barbican, that was filmed on the surface of the world's largest salt lake, Salar de Uyuni in Bolivia, Saraceno's recent prototype of a molecular structure of air-filled pockets - step one of an experimental work-in-progress - aims to breach the limits of the horizon between sea-level and the sky. The structure would float on the water, lifted by solar energy and moved by its inhabitants. Operating on a functional as well as on a metaphorical level, like most of Saraceno's realized projects to date - e.g. the large-scale inflatable three-story balloon for the 2006 Sao Paulo Biennial - the possibility of navigating in such a scenario is based on people's ability to pay attention to and be responsible for their fellow inhabitants.

توماس ساراسينو

حسب تقاليد باكمينستر فولر، تتحدى أعمال توماس ساراسينو التركيبية والنحتية وفي التصوير والفيديو، المحددات التقليدية للموئل الإنساني، وتطرح أساليب جديدة لإدراك الطبيعة. إمكانية نقل المدن من على سطح الأرض إلى الهواء، هي فكرة مركزية في أعماله الفنية، ونماذجه المستقبلية الحضرية لمدن عائمة في الهواء ليست خيالات فقط - فساراسينو يعمل نحو تحقيقها باعتبارها حلا عمليا. من خلال عرض هذه المجتمعات العائمة في الهواء، يؤشر ساراسينو إلى ضيق الإدراك التقليدي المقتصر على الأرض، وبكلمات فولر يخلق: "رؤيا عظيمة واستباقية للمستقبل."

تركز أبحاث ساراسينو المستمرة، والتي دأب الفنان على القيام بها منذ سنوات، على مشروع "مدينة-ميناء (يحملها)-هواء" (أو مدينة محمولة في الهواء). بدءا من طلب مفتوح لبراءة اختراع للمادة الخلاقة (إيروجيل) والتي تستخدم في بناء مركبات أخف من الهواء، يعمل ساراسينو على إمكانية بناء هياكل سكنية في الهواء، ومستوطنات حضرية تستغل الطاقات الطبيعية.

تتحرك هذه المساكن مثل الغيوم، والحدائق الطائرة تعيد تعريف الحدود السياسية والجغرافية، وتولد مجتمعات إنسانية وسياسية متحولة بشكل مستمر. سيتم تشكيل هذه المدن-الميناء (المحمولة في)-الهواء، بشكل حر حسب القوانين الدولية، متحديا المحددات السياسية والاجتماعية والثقافية والعسكرية، التي تطبق حاليا في كافة انحاء العالم. لتحقيق هذه الرؤيا، يقوم ساراسينو بأبحاث وتجارب لفحص إمكانيات هذا الواقع المستقبلي. إحدى هذه التجارب، والتي يؤكدها معهد باكمينستر فولر الافتراضي، هو أول بالون يعمل بالطاقة الشمسية باستخدام أكياس القمامة (٥٩ خطوة لتكون في الهواء-بالطاقة الشمسية) مع تعليمات لمن يرغب في أن يصنع بنفسه بالونا يعمل على الطاقة الشمسية.

وكما تخيله في عمله التركيبي المبني على الفيديو لغيوم عائمة في الهواء بناء على طلب متحف باربيكان، والذي صور على سطح أكبر بحيرة ملحية في العالم، سالار دي أويوني في بوليفيا، فإن نموذج ساراسينو لهيكل جزيئي بجيوب هوائية-الخطوة الأولى لعمل تجريبي قيد الإنشاء- يهدف إلى اختراق حدود الأفق ما بين مستوى البحر والسماء. الهيكل سيعوم على الماء، تحمله الطاقة الشمسية ويحركه السكان. وعلى المستويين المجازي والعملي، كما هو الحال في معظم أعمال ساراسينو حتى اليوم - على سبيل المثال البالون الكبير من ٣ طوابق الذي يمكن نفخه، والذي قدمه إلى بينالي سان باولو عام ٢٠٠٦ - فإن إمكانية ملاحة مثل هذا السيناريو مبنية على أساس قدرة الناس على تحمل مسؤولية السكان الآخرين والانتباه إليهم.

Flying garden – Air-Port-City, 2006, installation

JOE SCANLAN

I

I never let my self get in the way of a good idea.

II

Several years ago I made some artworks related to Cubism. From across the room you couldn't tell the difference, but they were even better up close, where you could. Interesting as they were, though, I knew they would never be as compelling as they could be so long as I was perceived as their maker. So, in addition to making the artworks I had to create an artist to make them.

Enter Donelle Woolford, who has a better idea, better story to tell, than I do. Picture this: a young African American woman, well read and smartly dressed, sets out to reclaim an aesthetic legacy stolen from her ancestors 100 years ago. Working alone in a remote corner of a recycling facility on the fetid backwaters of a faded industrial town, she rekindles past glories by reconstructing them from memory.

Donelle Woolford, Cubist painter. Donelle Woolford, appropriation artist. Donelle Woolford, narrative sculpture. The possibilities are endless.

جو سكانلن

(١)

أنا لا أسمح لنفسي أبداً أن أقف في طريق فكرة جيدة.

(٢)

قبل عدة سنوات أنجزت بعض الأعمال الفنية المرتبطة بالتكعيبية. وما كان ممكنا عن بعد أن تتبين الفرق بينها وبين الأعمال التكعيبية، ولكنها تبدو أجمل عن قرب، حيث يتبين الفارق واضحا. وعلى غرابتها، عرفت أنها لن تكون جذابة بالقدر الكافي، ما دامت من صنعي. وعليه، فبالإضافة إلى صنع الأعمال الفنية، كان عليّ أن أختلق الفنان الذي سوف يصنعها.

إذن، فليتقدم دونل ولفوورد، فهو لديه فكرة أفضل، ولديه قصة يرويها هي أفضل من قصتي. تخيلوا المشهد التالي: سيدة أفريقية أمريكية شابة، مثقفة وأنيقة، تنطلق لاستعادة إرث جمالي سرق من أسلافها قبل مئة سنة. تعمل لوحدها في زاوية بعيدة في أحد مرافق إعادة التدوير على المياه النتنة في محيط بلدة صناعية محتضرة، فتعيد إشعال جذوة الأمجاد الماضية، من خلال إعادة تكوينها من الذاكرة.

دونل وولفورد، رسام تكعيبي. دونل وولفورد، فنان التخصيص. دونل وولفورد، المنحوتة السردية. الاحتمالات لا تنتهي مع هذا الفنان.

Donelle Woolford: A view of the artist in her studio, 2006, digital print, courtesy of Joe Scanlan

Saphir: video

The title *Saphir* (French for sapphire) evokes not only the pure maritime light typical of Algiers, but also those flickering glimmers on the horizon that symbolise people's dreams and aspirations. In Arabic, the word *safir* also means 'ambassador', a person who travels between different places, the representative of one country on the soil of another.

This play on meaning is extended through two central characters in the film. The first is an Algerian man who walks across town, with no apparent purpose, and silently watches the daily ferries arrive and depart from the port. His image is counterpoised by that of an older woman, a daughter of the noirs (a term for those European settlers who left Algeria after its Independence). She inhabits the Safir Hotel, one of the grand landmarks of French colonial Algiers, whose imposing architecture is a powerful and resonant reminder of a past that still casts its light and shadow over the city. Both characters circle within their own separate but parallel worlds, their paths often appearing to intersect, but without any conclusion.

Saphir: photographs

A series of panoramic images focus on the periphery of the city. Men stand before the immense, mist-shrouded sea, contemplating the horizon filled with ships in transit or awaiting permission to cross. The images can be seen as atmospheric, even poetic. But a further reality is also expressed: how individuals are directly and radically affected by social, political and environmental challenges. They suggest the longing of disenchanted young men, who often still dream of travelling across the water to Europe.

In other photographs, empty French colonial houses and dilapidated ruins appear to emerge out of the cliffs where they once stood overlooking the sea. Although ravaged by time and by the sea that has gradually eaten them away, the constructions have lost none of their elegance. Today the question is what will become of these French ruins? Will they eventually turn to dust amid widespread indifference? Or, in a few centuries will they become a symbol of national pride like the sites which bear witness to the hegemony of Rome during Antiquity?

Confronting the contemporary life of the city with an older and more ambivalent legacy, the project Saphir presents a portrait of Algiers in a transitional moment, the local character gradually becoming absorbed into the current of increasing globalisation.

سافير: فيديو

يعكس العنوان، "سافير" (بالفرنسيّة تعني الحجر الكريم)، مفهوم الكلمة ذاتها، فالفيلم لا يحاكي الضوء البحريّ المعهود للجزائر فحسب، وإنما تلك اللمعات المشعّة في الأفق التي ترمز لأحلام الناس وآمالهم. أما بالعربيّة، فكلمة سفير تعني من يسافر بين الأماكن المختلفة، ويمثّل دولة ما على أرض دولة أخرى.

يطول التلاعب بالمعنى من خلال شخصيتين رئيستين في الفيلم. الأولى شخصيّة رجل جزائريّ يسير عبر المدينة، بلا أيّ هدف ظاهر، ويتأمّل بصمت المراكب اليوميّة التي تغادر الميناء. تقابل صورته صورة امرأة أكبر سنّا، ابنة ما اصطلح على تسميتهم بأصحاب الأقدام السوداء pieds noirs (مصطلح للمستوطنين الأوروبيّين الذين تركوا الجزائر بعد استقلالها). تقيم في فندق السفير، إحدى المعالم الأنيقة لجزائر الإستعمار الفرنسي، والذي تمثّل هندسته المهيمنة تذكارا قويّا لماضٍ ما يزال يلقي بضوئه وظلاله على المدينة. محدقةً بالبحرّ من شرفات الفندق، قبل الإنسحاب نحو فخامة قاعاته، تحاكي المرأة حركات الرجل وتعزّز إحساسا أرحب من الوهن والجمود والانغلاق. تحوم كلّ من الشخصّيتين ضمن عالميهما المنفصلين المتوازيين، وكثيرا ما يبدو وكأن مساراتهما تتقاطع، ولكن دون جدوى.

سافير: صور فوتوغرافيّة

سلسلة من الصور الفوتوغرافيّة البانوراميّة تركّز على أطراف المدينة. يطل مجموعة من الرجال على البحر الواسع المغطى بالضباب، يتأمّلون خطّ الأفق المليء بالسفن العابرة تنتظر إذن المرور. وفي حين تبدو ظلالهم الصغيرة وكأنّها تربط السماء بالشاطئ، تنكشف روايات رقيقة ولكن معقّدة من خلال هذه الأشكال المجهولة التي تمشي وتراقب وتنتظر بمحاذاة الشاطئ وتحاكي السفن الساكنة. يمكن اعتبار هذه الصور حسية وحتى شاعريّة، ولكنها أيضا تعبر عن حقيقة أخرى: كيف يتأثّر الأفراد بشكل مباشر وكبير بالتحديّات الإجتماعيّة والسياسيّة والبيئيّة. تحيلنا هذه الصور إلى أشواق هؤلاء الشباب الذين ضاعت أوهامهم ولكن ما يزالون يحلمون بالسفر عبر المياه نحو أوروبا.

في صور فوتوغرافيّة أخرى، نرى بيوتا فارغة وخرائب متهالكة على الطراز الاستعماري الفرنسي تبدو وكأنها تبزغ من المنحدرات حيث وقفت يوما تتأمّل البحر. وبالرغم من أن الزمن قد عفا عليها والبحر أكلها تدريجيّا، إلا أن هذه المباني لم تفقد أناقتها. هذه بالذات حالة البناء المشهور "البيت المسكون" الذي يطلّ على البحر. على مر السنين السنين، وكغيره من المساكن، لم تتمّ صيانة هذا البيت أو حتى هدمه. واليوم، تبدو واجهاته وكأنّها تسأل: ما مصير هذه الآثار الفرنسيّة؟ هل ستتحوّل في النهاية إلى غبار وسط هذا الإهمال الواسع؟ أو، هل ستصبح بعد قرون قليلة مفخرة وطنية كما المواقع التي تشهد لفترة حكم الرومان؟ يبدو خطّ شاطئ العاصمة كنقطة انتقالية بين هنا وهناك، بين الماضي والحاضر، بين الذاكرة والنسيان.

يواجه مشروع "سافير" الحياة المعاصرة للمدينة بأسطورة أقدم وأكثر تناقضا، ويقدّم صورة للجزائر في لحظة انتقاليّة، تذوب فيها الشخصيّة المحليّة تدريجيّا في تيّار العولمة النامي.

Haunted House, 2006, panoramic C-prints, 100 x 80 cm, courtesy of the artist and Galerie Kamel Mennour, Paris

ANAS AL-SHAIKH

The work explores the idea of construction and destruction through the use of black and white symbolism to create a work space suggesting the opposition and complementarity between these two contrasts (the black and the white) as well as the degree of the influence of these relationships, whether complementary or opposing, on our lives, futures, environments, and societies. This is as a result of human decisions which are either for the benefit of the human being, society and the surroundings in which he/she lives or, on the contrary, where these decisions are detrimental to humanity, its freedom and integrity. Such decisions can also be detrimental to the environment, and everything related to coming generations and the survival of the human race, as well as to the future of earth. This means the maintenance and protection of earth from the extinction of its natural wealth and life forms, forests, trees and plants, which are its main resources and protect the air from natural pollution and also the industrial pollution caused by dark human interferences. Unfortunately, many such interferences are made to serve the interests of influential individuals and authorities, or for the benefit of some societies and powers. They exploit political, economic, social, and ethnic issues, as well as those related to civilisations and social class, with the aim of controlling many natural resources and national capabilities. Much of this control is done in the name of humanity and of preserving its freedom, integrity and progress.

أنس الشيخ

يتطرق العمل إلى فكرة البناء والهدم من خلال استخدام رمزية الأبيض والأسود لتكوين فضاء العمل للإيحاء بالتقابل والتعاكس والتكامل بين هذين النقيضين (الأبيض والاسود). ومدى تأثير هذه العلاقات سواء المتكاملة أو المتناقضة على حياتنا ومستقبلنا وبيئتنا ومجتمعاتنا بفعل قرارات الإنسان. هذه القرارات قد تكون لصالح الإنسان والمجتمع والمحيط الذي يعيش فيه وإما أن تكون عكس كل ذلك، وحينها تقوم على كل ما هو ضد الإنسانية وحريتها وكرامتها. وضد المحيط البيئي، وضد مستقبل الأجيال القادمة وبقاء الجنس البشري، وكذلك ضد مستقبل الأرض والمحافظة عليها وحمايتها من أي انقراض للثروات الطبيعية والكائنات الحية والغابات والاشجار والنباتات، والتي تعتبر المصادر الرئيسية والفائقة الأهمية في حماية الهواء من التلوث الطبيعي والصناعي التي نتجت عن تدخلات الإنسان الظالمة. وللأسف، فإن الكثير من تلك التدخلات تتم لصالح بعض الأفراد أصحاب النفوذ والهيمنة، أو لصالح بعض المجتمعات والقوى في هذا العالم من خلال استغلالها للقضايا السياسية والإقتصادية والاجتماعية والحضارية والطبقية والعرقية من أجل الهيمنة على العديد من الثروات الطبيعية ومقدرات الشعوب.

Confrontation 4, 2006, video, courtesy of the artist

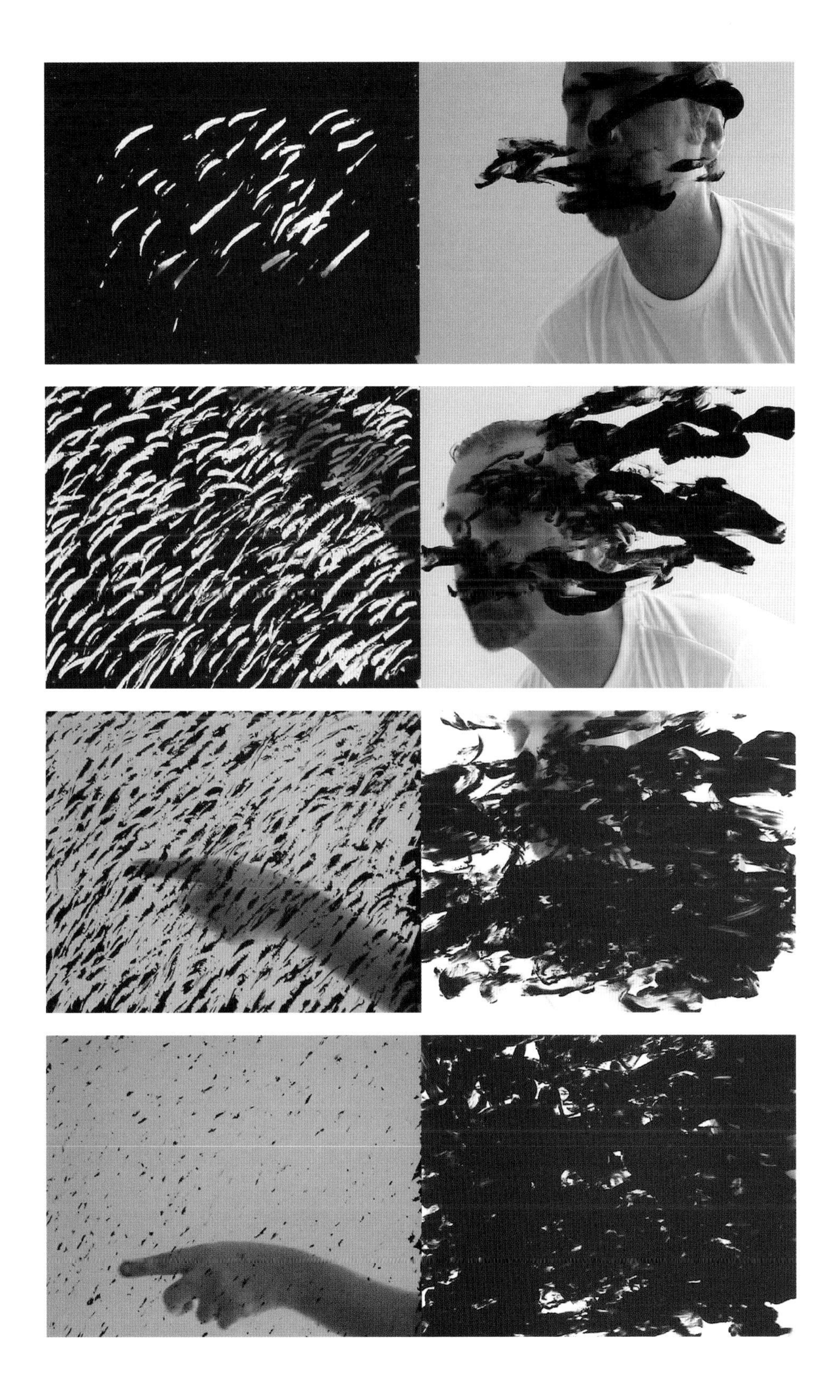

RANJANI SHETTAR

Having trained in sculpture at Chitrakala Institute of Advanced Studies in Bangalore, Ranjani Shettar creates three-dimensional works that explore the confrontation of the urban and the organic, the metaphysical and the mundane. Employing a wide range of common, everyday materials such as wax, Indian ink, paper, resin, cotton, PVC pipes, plastic sheeting, and mud. Shettar constructs sculptural artefacts that speak obliquely to the effects of urbanization in newly high-tech Bangalore. By using a formal language that invokes the organic and a material language that suggests the industrial, she operates in a manner similar to that of Bangalore itself, where industrial urbanisation is colliding with (and collapsing into) the once rural countryside. But above all else, Shettar's work asks phenomenological questions about the way in which we inhabit particular spaces in our built environment.

In her solo exhibition "Home" (2000), Shettar launched into a sculptural investigation of the concept of shelter. Employing a biological idiom in these works, the artist built a series of archetypal structures from nature that might be thought of as "homes", ranging from those of insects and birds to silkworms and even plants. *Invitations*, for example, is a series of pod- or cocoon-like resin forms that are piled rather haphazardly in a corner. Another work by Shettar, *Thousand Room House*, is reminiscent of a beehive, although its strangely organic honeycomb structure is constructed with the decidedly artificial materials of plastic sheeting, rope, and rivets. Each of these works speaks to what philosopher Gaston Bachelard has described as an "intimate immensity", in that each structure invokes a shelter that is poetically suggestive of our oneiric ability to invest spaces with our own desires and phenomenological memories. As suggested by Bachelard, "A house that has been experienced is not an inert box. Inhabited space transcends geometrical space." Such a specificity of inhabited space, of the space of a shelter invested with a particular kind of living and spiritual energy, is operative in Shettar's work. As she herself suggests, "Home is the body. The body is not the physical alone but the mental, emotional and the spiritual." In all of her work, Shettar maintains this explicit dialogue between the spiritual and the everyday.

By Douglas Fogle, Curator, Walker Art Center, 2003

رانجاني شيتار

تقوم رانجاني شيتار، التي تلقت تدريبها في فن النحت في معهد شيتراكالا للدراسات المتقدّمة في بانغالور، بإنتاج أعمال ثلاثيّة الأبعاد تستكشف المواجهة بين المدينيّة والعضويّة، وبين الميتافيزيقي والدنيوي. مستعينة بنطاق واسع من المواد ذات الاستخدام اليومي مثل الشمع والحبر الهندي والورق والصمغ والقطن وأنابيب وصفائح البلاستيك والطين، تكوّن شيتّار قطعا نحتيّة تتحدّث بشكل موارب عن آثار التمدن في بانغالور، المدينة التي غدت عالية التقنية. تستحضر شيتار العضوي واللغة الماديّة التي تحيل إلى الصناعيّ، وتعمل بكيفيّة تماثل تلك التي تعمل بها بانغالور ذاتها، حيث تتصادم المدينيّة الصناعيّة - وتنهار نحو- ما كان يوما ما ريفيّا. ولكن فوق كلّ شئ، تطرح أعمال شيتّار أسئلة ظواهريّة عن الطريقة التي نسكن فيها أماكن معيّنة في بيئتنا المعمارية.

يمكن قراءة الصفات العضويّة لعمل شيتّار بشكل إيجابيّ في سياقات الفن التاريخي لفنانة "الآرتي بوفيرا" ماريسا ميرتس، ونحاتي أسلوب ما بعد المنمنم في نفس الفترة مثل إيفا هيسّه، وفنانة الإسمنت-الجديد البرازيليّة ليجيا كلارك، أو الفنانة الإرجنتينيّة جيجو. تستعمل شيتّار مثل سابقاتها مواد صناعيّة تتناقض مع طبيعة الأشكال العضويّة في عملها، بحيث تعكس الشقاق بين الصناعي والطبيعي. وكسابقاتها، عملت شيتّار في سياق جيل متقدم من الفنانين الهنود في مجال النحت والتركيب الفنّي، مثل شيلا جودا وآنيتا دوبه. تتفاوض كل منهن في مساحة تشبه تلك التي تتفاوض حولها الفنانات اللاتي سبق ذكرهن، ولكن ضمن خصوصية هنديّة.

من كاتالوج: كيف تصبح المواقع أشكالا: الفن في عصر معولم، مركز ووكر للفن، مينيابوليس، الولايات المتحدة الأمريكيّة.

بقلم دوجلاس فوجل، قيم على معارض، مركز ووكر للفن، ٢٠٠٣

I am no one to tell you what not to do (installation at ARTPACE), 2006, 30 x 25 x 12 ft, cast silicon & carved mesquite wood, courtesy of the artist and Talwar Gallery, New York

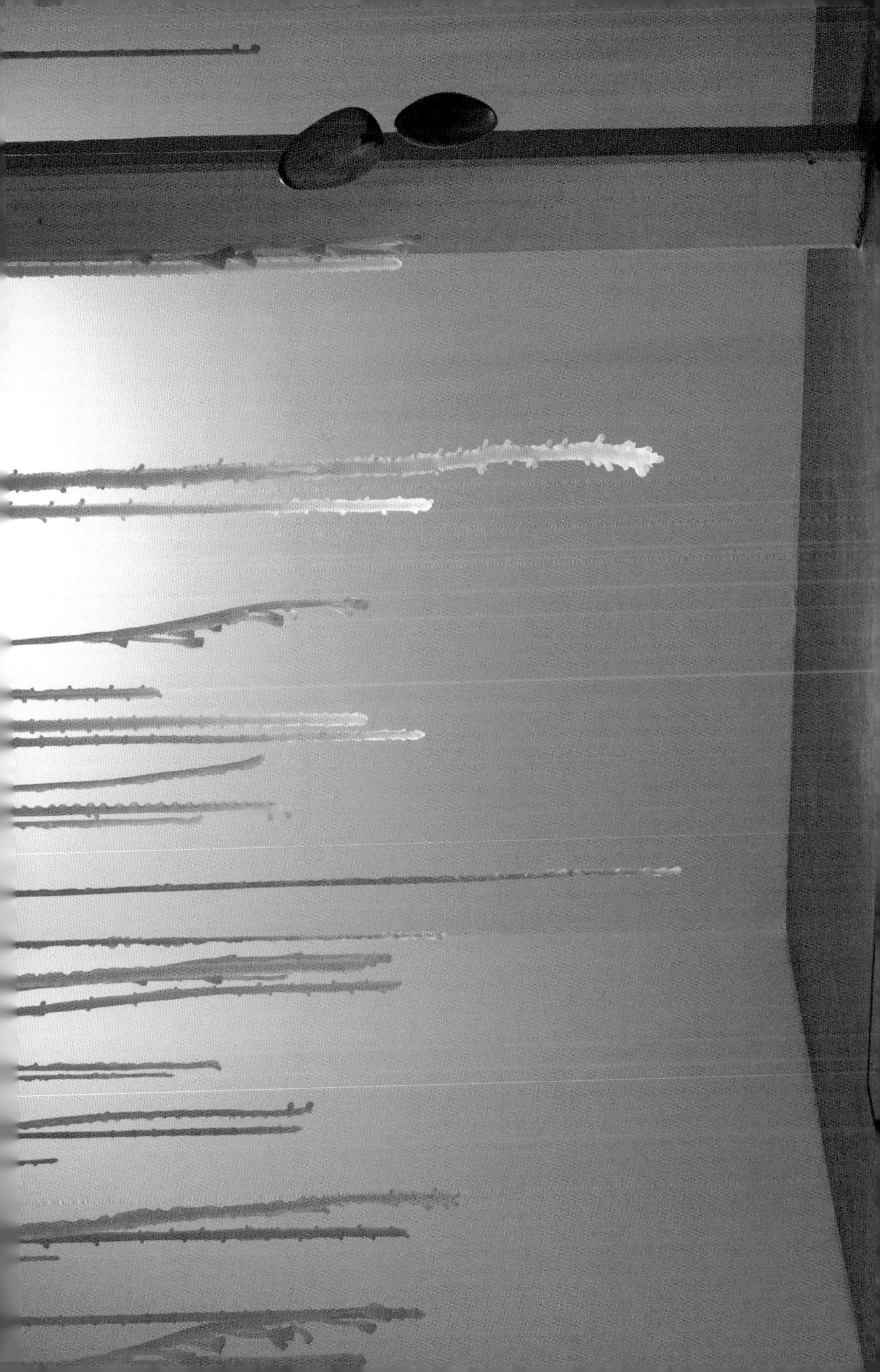

SOI PROJECT

SOI is a collective group of artists, designers and architects from Bangkok and Tokyo. The aim of SOI is to create and moderate multidisciplinary projects that connect creator and public audience from different disciplines. SOI uses an unofficial or informal manner as a bridging strategy with the aim of "connecting" rather than "directing", as well as slow and long-term establishment rather than immediate solutions. This relates to the meaning of "SOI": that is "little street" or "alley" in Thai. "I" also connotes to "secondary" rather than "main". The nature of SOI is one that supports a subconsciously expanded network of the city rather than urban planning and directed development; but at the same time it fills the gap of urbanscape that is missing from development.

SOI was established in 2003 by the Japanese architect, Jiro Endo. It started within the framework of music exchange between Thais and Japanese called the SOI Music Festival. In the early years, Jiro, in collaboration with Wit Pimkanchanapong, an artist/designer with an architectural background, used music as a collaborative platform for other artists/designers/creators. In 2005 "art" was emphasised in SOI as a platform for music as well as music for art. This was done under the name of "SOI Project" a special project for Yokohama Triennial International Contemporary Art Exhibition. SOI Project invited Thai visual artists to collaborate with musicians and exhibit the work for the three months exhibition. In the middle of the exhibition SOI Project re-installed the works for the music performance stage-set for a two-day music festival. In 2006, without the music elements the SOI project was expanded to include a platform for the Contemporary Thai Artists' Exhibition as part of the Thai Festival in France, "Tout à fait Thaï".

For Sharjah Biennial 2007, an uncanny context for Japanese/Thai culture, SOI needed to be redefined. Perhaps something even more simple and visible can connect public interest.

مشروع (اس او آي)

SOI (سوي) جماعة من الفنانين والمعماريين من بانكوك وطوكيو تهدف إلى ابتكار وإدارة مشاريع في الفروع المعرفية المختلفة والتي تربط ما بين المبتكر والجمهور العام من مختلف المجالات المعرفية. تتبنى SOI أسلوبا غير رسمي كاستراتيجية لمد الجسور بهدف خلق "صلات" وليس "التوجيه". وتعتمد أسلوب التأني بدلا من الحلول الفورية. لهذا النهج صلة بمعنى SOI، ألا وهو "شارع صغير" أو "ممر" في تايلاند. لذلك فهو قد يوحي أيضا، بما هو ثانوي وليس بما هو رئيسي. طبيعة هذه المجموعة تنحى نحو دعم شبكة في المدينة تتسع بشكل تلقائي غير واع بدلا من التخطيط الحضري والتنمية المباشرة. لكنها في نفس الوقت تعمد إلى سد الفراغ في المساحات المدينية التي لا تطالها التنمية.

تأسست "SOI" في عام ٢٠٠٣، على يد المعماري الياباني جيرو أيندو. وبدأت نشاطها في إطار التبادل الموسيقي بين تايلاند واليابان، حيث أقيم مهرجان SOI للموسيقي. خلال السنوات الأولى، ركز جيرو، بالتعاون مع ويت بيمكانشانبونغ، وهو فنان ومصمم ومعماري، على الموسيقى كمنبر تعاوني لفنانين ومصممين ومبدعين آخرين. في عام ٢٠٠٥، تقرر في "SOI" التركيز على "الفن" كمنبر للموسيقى والموسيقى من أجل الفن. وقد تم ذلك تحت عنوان"مشروع SOI"، كمشروع خاص لترينالي يوكوهاما الدولي للفن المعاصر. دعا مشروع SOI فنانين تشكيليين تايلنديين للتعاون مع الموسيقيين، وتم عرض الأعمال على مدى ثلاثة أشهر. وضمن العرض المذكور، تم إعادة تركيب الأعمال من أجل العرض الموسيقي ضمن مهرجان موسيقي لمدة يومين. وفي عام ٢٠٠٦، توسع "مشروع SOI"، وبدون العناصر الموسيقية، ليشمل معرضا للفن التايلندي المعاصر، كجزء من المهرجان التايلاندي الذي أقيم في فرنسا تحت شعار" تايلاندي مائة في المائة". أما في بينالي الشارقة لعام ٢٠٠٧، فقد أصبحت "SOI" بحاجة لإعادة تعريف نفسها من أجل سياق غريب على الثقافة اليابانية - التايلاندية. بالتالي قد يحتاجون إلى شيء بسيط وبصري ليجذب اهتمام المشاهدين.

Pru Pop Live Concert, 2005, installation, Bangkok

SAMIR SROUJI

سمير سروجي

A Hanging Garden

A Hanging Garden is a site-specific garden project that is informed by the tension at the far edge of growth and the desert. Grass, sand, gravel, and crude oil are the ingredients at play. This temporary installation is conceived as a composition of natural and man-made materials in vicarious balance suspended 145 cm above ground.

Viewing the peripheries of human development from satellite images, especially in the UAE region, one is struck by the seeming tenacity of green patches as well as by the fragility of their existence. There are no transitions; the shift from lush gardens to arid desert is a violent one. These gardens exist at a knife's edge proximity to their demise and return to sand. *A Hanging Garden* echoes these confrontations and reflects on their immediacy.

It is said that the ancient Hanging Gardens of Babylon were created by King Nebuchadnezzar to cheer his homesick wife, who came from a mountainous green region to the dry, flat lands of Mesopotamia. Referencing the Babylonian myth, *A Hanging Garden* is also a contemplation on the human desire to transform geography; on the heroism and futility of this endeavor witnessed at the tenuous line between sand and grass.

حديقة معلّقة

"حديقة معلّقة" هي مشروع حديقة في موقع محدد مبعثها التوتّر في أطراف الخضراء والصحراء. عشب ورمل وحصى ونفط خام هي العناصر التي تتفاعل في هذا المشروع. هذا التركيب الفنّي المؤقّت هو تشكيل من مواد طبيعيّة ومواد صنعها الإنسان في توازن صريح معلّق على ارتفاع ١٤٥ سم فوق الأرض.

تلوح لنا أقاصي التطوّر الإنساني في صور الأقمار الصناعية، خاصّة لمنطقة الإمارات العربية المتحدة، فيصعقنا عناد البقع الخضراء وهشاشة وجودها في نفس الوقت. لا توجد مرحلة انتقاليّة: فالتحوّل من الحدائق الغنيّة إلى الصحراء العاريّة هو تحوّل عنيف. هذه الحدائق تعيش على حافّة اندثارها وعودتها إلى الرمال. يحاكي مشروع "حديقة معلّقة" هذه المواجهات ويتأمل في قربها العاجل منا.

يُقال أن الملك نبوخذنصّر بنىّ الحدائق المعلّقة التاريخيّة في بابل ليُسعد زوجته المصابة بالحنين إلى بلادها الجبليّة الخضراء مقارنة بأراضي الرافدين المنبسطة الجافّة. وكما هو الحال في الأسطورة البابلية، فإن "حديقة معلّقة" هي أيضا تأمّل في الرغبة الإنسانيّة لتحويل الجغرافيا؛ في بطوليّة وعبثيّة، هذه المغامرة التي نشهدها عند الخطّ الرفيع الفاصل بين الرمل والعشب.

A Hanging Garden, 2006, architectural installation, virtual rendering of installation, courtesy of the artist

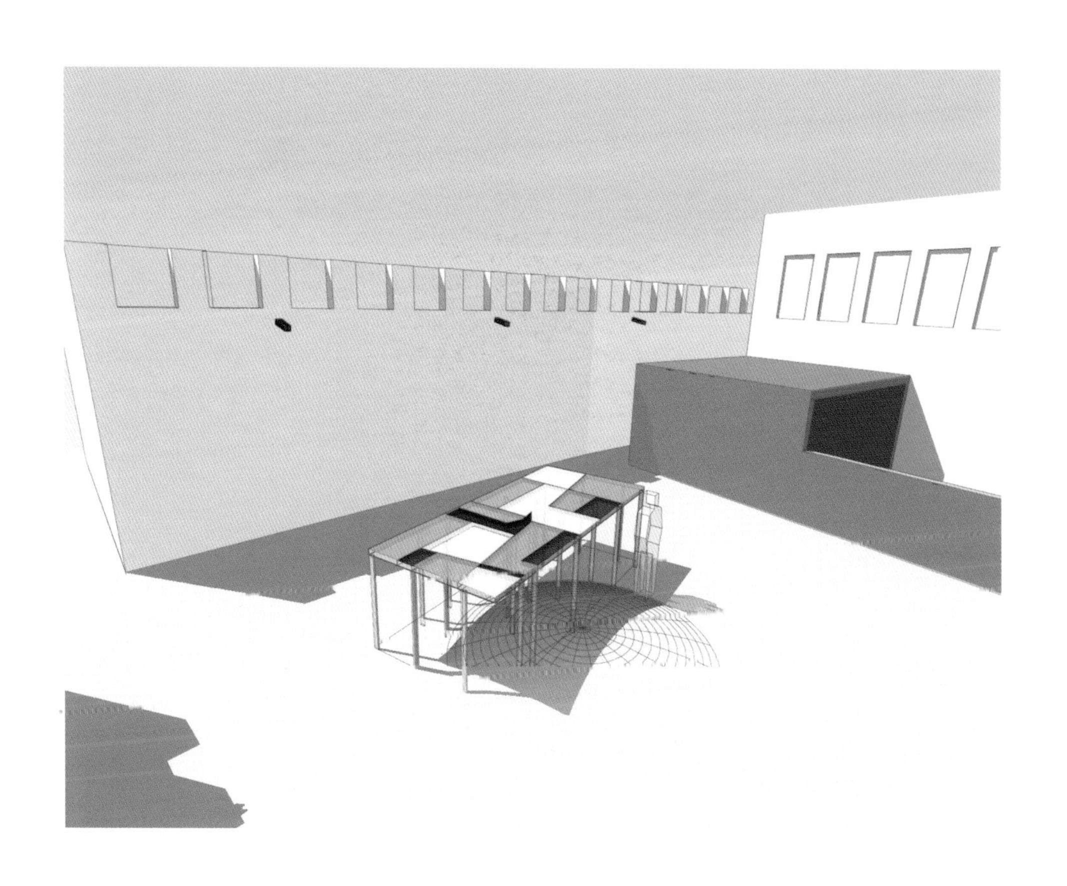

SIMON STARLING

Autoxylopyrocycloboros documents a performance or, perhaps better, an action that took place on, and ultimately in, the waters of Loch Long on the West Coast of Scotland. I was commissioned by Cove Park, a residency programme that is situated on the hills overlooking the Loch, to make a new work and what I came up with is in many ways a response to the very particular local situation and its history.

Loch Long is part of the Clyde Estuary and as such is where steamboats were first built and used successfully. It is also an extremely deep sea loch, in places as deep as 85m, and consequently became home to Britain's Trident submarine base at Coulport and Faslane. There is a sci-fi-style, hollowed-out mountain which contains dozens of nuclear warheads. With the introduction of the nuclear submarine base in the 1970s came the peace camp, which has for years doggedly kept the question of the existence of the submarine base in the press, holding demonstrations, campaigning and at times just being a niggling thorn-in-the-side of the Royal Navy. Loch Long and its surrounding countryside is also an extremely beautiful part of Scotland. So it's in this context that I decided to make a kind of slap-stick, self-defeating voyage using a restored wooden steam launch.

In 2003 I took my class from the Staedelschule to visit Cove Park and we were given a tour of the submarine base at neighbouring Faslane. On this tour we were shown a video presentation about the base and its workings; this presentation, however, included a number of sketches from British TV situation comedy, - Only Fools and Horses, that kind of thing. It struck me afterwards that these rather lame attempts to win over an otherwise rather sceptical audience, were in fact somehow extremely poignant. These simple slap-stick moments were, in some rather touching sense, the only way to deal with the implications of this crazy world that we were all glimpsing at first hand for the first and hopefully the last time. They were, on one level, perhaps an existential cry for help from this rather awkward naval officer, who had spent large chunks of his adult life under water in a weapon of mass destruction. It became clear to me that any attempt to deal with the "site" of Cove Park would have to involve large doses of slap-stick. I started to think back over those rather violent early cartoons I saw many of as a child - that scene when a cat or dog or duck or whoever cuts a Gordon Matta-Clark style hole in the floor, only to find right they are in the middle of the section that plummets to the basement below. These thoughts of painting myself into a corner, coupled with my sketchy knowledge of steamboat history on the Clyde, led me to Autoxylopyrocycloboros. In October I set out on a self-defeating voyage in a 23ft-long steam launch around the waters of Loch Long. The boat gradually, piece by wooden piece, was fed to the steam engine's boiler until, inevitably, it disappeared into the submarine infested depths.

سيمون ستارلنج

يوثق مشروع Autoxylopyrocycloboros لعرض، أو ربما لعمل، جرى تنفيذه على، وفي، مياه لوك لونغ في الساحل الغربي لاسكتلندا. وقد كلفتني الهيئة المسؤولة عن Cove Park، وهو برنامج إقامة موجود على التلال المطلّة على البحيرة، بأن أصنع عملاً جديداً، فكان ما خرجت به- وبطرق عديدة - استجابة إلى الوضع المحلّي، بكل خصوصيته وتاريخه.

البحيرة الطويلة (Loch Long) جزء من كلايد إستوري Clyde Estuary، وهي المكان الذي صنعت فيه القوارب البخارية لأول مرّة، واستخدمت بنجاح. كما أنها بحيرة عميقة جداً في البحر، يصل عمقها في أماكن معينة إلى ٨٥ متراً، وقد أصبحت لاحقاً مقرّ القاعدة البحرية البريطانية Trident في كولبورت وفاسلين. وهناك جبل تم تجويفه يبدو وكأنه من الخيال العلمي وزُرعت فيه العشرات من الرؤوس الحربية النووية. ومع ظهور القاعدة الغواصة النووية في السبعينيات من القرن العشرين، جاء مخيّم السلام، والذي أثار جدلا في الصحف ولسنوات طوال وبإصرار كبير حول مسألة بقاء القاعدة الغواصة، وقاموا بتنظيم المظاهرات، وشن الحملات، وفي بعض الأوقات كان يكفي أن يكونوا شوكة في خاصرة القوة الملكية البحرية. تشكل Loch Long وما يحيط بها من مناطق ريفية، منطقة خلابة من اسكتلندا. لذا، قررت ضمن هذا السياق أن أقوم بنوع من رحلة فكاهية للتدمير الذاتي، باستخدام زورق بخاري خشبي مرمم.

في عام ٢٠٠٣، اصطحبت طلبتي من ستادلشول لزيارة كوف بارك Cove Park، وقد نُظمت لنا جولة في أرجاء القاعدة الغواصة في منطقة Faslane المجاورة. خلال الجولة تم عرض فيديو حول القاعدة وما تقوم به من أعمال وأنشطة، اشتمل العرض على عدد من الاسكتشات المستلهمة من برنامج تلفزيوني بريطاني يعتمد على كوميديا الموقف - "فقط الأغبياء والأحصنة". ولقد ذهلت عندما عرفت فيما بعد، أن هذه المحاولات الواهية لكسب جمهور متشكك، كانت مؤثرة في حقيقة الأمر. هذه اللحظات البسيطة من التهريج، كانت على ما يبدو الطريقة الوحيدة للتعامل مع مضامين هذا العالم المجنون، الذي كنا جميعاً نلمحه بداية للمرّة الأولى، والتي أرجو أن تكون هي الأخيرة. كانت صرخة وجودية للمساعدة أطلقها ضابط البحرية هذا، وقد أمضى فترات طويلة من حياته كشخص بالغ تحت المياه في أحد أسلحة الدمار الشامل. لقد تبيّنت أن أي محاولة للتعامل مع الموقع - موقع Cove Park، لا بدّ وأن تشتمل على جرعات كبيرة من التهريج. وبدأت أفكر في أفلام الكرتون المشحونة بالعنف، والتي شاهدت الكثير منها عندما كنت طفلاً - وتذكرت ذلك المشهد الذي يحفر فيه قط أو كلب أو طير البط أو أي شخص، حفرة على غرار الفنان Gordon Matta - Clark في الأرض، ليجد نفسه مباشرة في وسط الجزء الذي يشده إلى طابق التسوية. هذه الأفكار التي تتعلق برسم نفسي في زاوية، مقترنة بمعرفتي البسيطة بتاريخ القوارب البخارية في Clyde، قادتني إلى الـ Autoxylopyrocycloboros. وفي تشرين الأول، انطلقت في رحلة تدمير ذاتي في زورق بخاري طوله ٢٣ قدماً حول مياه Loch Long، وبالتدريج كنت أطعم القارب - قطعة خشبية بعد قطعة - إلى مرجل المحرّك البخاري، إلى أن اختفى في أعماق البحر الملوث بالغواصة النووية.

Tabernas Desert Run, 2004, production still, Tabernas Desert, Andalucia, Spain, courtesy of the artist and The Modern Institute / Toby Webster Ltd., Glasgow

RALEIGH

GERDA STEINER & JÖRG LENZLINGER

The Desalination Plant Waste Garden

This garden is situated in one of the old courtyards of the heritage area in Sharjah. The nutrients for the garden are the waste products of the desalination plant. Huge quantities of energy are used to transform enormous amounts of seawater into freshwater. The leftover product of this process is brine: it consists mostly of water and salt, along with some chemical by-products, and is thrown back into the sea.

In our garden we transform this waste product into growing salt-crystal plants. Through a 3-metre-high hanging and branching-out hose system, the saltwater (brine) reaches used drinking bottles. From these points it drips slowly along ropes and fabrics onto vegetation that is made out of artificial flowers, garbage and real dried plants from Sharjah. During this dripping process the water evaporates and salt crystals begin to form, building up and extending these plants. The visitor can walk under the house system through the garden and have a close look at the amazing salt-crystal plants.

Salt is a symbol for life and death. The dead artificiality of plastic plants wakes up to new life. As Sharjah has not enough freshwater sources, the seawater has to get rid of the salt. But without salt there is no life either. Both salt and water are precious and a big issue in the worldwide environmental debate. The consequences of intensive agriculture are lack of water and over-salted earth. In Sharjah huge amounts of sweet water are used for uninspired decorative green areas.

Our blood contains the same amount of salt as you find in seawater (a memory of the origins of life). Salt is essential for the body's metabolism, but in higher concentration deadly to all life. In former times salt and gold had the same value - we still find this today in the word "salary". There have been salt wars. Salt is an old symbol for friendship in Muslim, Christian and Jewish cultures. Evaporating salt water cleans the air and is used as a treatment for breathing problems.

The Desalination Plant Waste Garden is a devotion to Salt and you would do well to inhale deeply!

جيردا شتاينر ويورغ لنزلينجر

حديقة أعشاب البحر

تقع هذه الحديقة في واحدة من الساحات القديمة في منطقة التراث في الشارقة. وقوت هذه الحديقة هو النفايات الخاصة بمصنع لتحلية مياه البحر. قدر كبير من الطاقة يجري استخدامه لتحويل كميات هائلة من مياه البحر إلى مياه عذبة صالحة للشرب. النفايات الناتجة عن عملية التحلية هذه تتمثل في كميات من ماء البحر، والذي يتكون في معظمه من ماء وملح بالإضافة إلى بعض المشتقات الكيميائية. وفي العادة يجري إعادة هذا الماء إلى البحر مرة أخرى.

في حديقتنا الشاعرية نقوم بتحويل هذه المخلفات إلى نبات معدني مالح. فمن خلال استخدام خرطوم مياه يصل طوله إلى ثلاثة أمتار في الهواء يجري توصيل الماء المالح إلى نقاط متعددة يتساقط منها هذا الماء ببطء عبر أحبال وقطع من القماش إلى أعشاب مصنوعة من البلاستيك ومن نباتات حقيقية جافة تنمو في الشارقة. وأثناء هذه العملية يتبخر الماء وتنمو بلورات ملحية تساعد على نمو وتكبير حجم هذه الأعشاب. يمكن للزائر أن يسير في هذه الحديقة ليتمتع بجمال منظر هذا النبات الخلاب.

ويرمز الملح إلى الحياة والموت في آن. فالطبيعة الميتة للجماد الموجودة في الأعشاب البلاستيكية تنهض إلى حياة جديدة. وباعتبار أن الشارقة تعاني نقصا في موارد المياه العذبة, فإن الحاجة تمُس إلى تحلية مياه البحر. غير أنه من دون ملح لن توجد هناك حياة. فالملح والماء يحتلان أهمية كبيرة على جدول المؤتمرات والاجتماعات التي تناقش قضايا البيئة في العالم .والتوسع الزراعي بدوره ينتج عنه نقص في المياه وازدياد ملوحة الأرض.

ويحتوي الدم البشري على كمية الملح نفسها التي يجدها المرء في ماء البحر. فالملح عنصر حيوي لعملية التمثيل الغذائي ولكن عندما تزيد نسبته فإنه يؤدي إلى قتل الحياة في أي كائن. وفي العصور القديمة كان الملح يتمتع بالقيمة نفسها التي يتمتع بها الذهب. وهو ما نجده اليوم واضحا في حروف كلمة "سالاري"، التي تعني بالعربية الراتب، باعتبار أن الملح بالإنجليزية يعني "سولت". واندلعت حروب كثيرة في الماضي بسبب الصراع على الملح. كما أعادت "مسيرة الملح" التي قام بها المهاتما غاندي إلى الهند استقلالها. وفي الثقافات الإسلامية والمسيحية واليهودية يرمز الملح إلى الصداقة. ومن المعروف أن الماء المالح المبخر يُنقي الهواء، ويُستخدم كعلاج لمشكلات التنفس.

ومن ثم فإنه في حديقة نفايات أعشاب البحر عليك أن تستنشق الهواء بكل قوة!

Root Treatment, 2004, installation, 4 x 5 x 8 m, courtesy of the artists

Less Oil More Courage

Some years ago I received an invitation card in the mail from a gallery in New York (Matthew Marks); it was an invitation to an exhibition by a young artist by the name of Peter Cain. Peter was a painter known for his anamorphic splicing of cars; they were coolly painted with the brushes of oil paint thinly applied to canvas. They were the marks of a realist (almost graphic) with the narrative of a surreal world; it was the world of surfaces and the surfaces of the metallic baked enamel of cars. But if cars were his fascination, the anamorphic world of biotechnological mutation was in the shadow of these cars – a world where Dolly the sheep was being cloned and Adobe Photoshop computer software about to be introduced into the world, offering a new landscape of photographic rendering beyond our imagination. But Peter's life was cut short and he did not see beyond the age of 37, and the invitation I received was for an exhibition five years after his death.

On the front of the invitation card was a reproduction from a page of Peter's artist's notebook: a text that read "More courage less oil". Taken in context, that message was clearly a note to himself about the dilemma of being a painter and the moral choices one faces in executing a painting. I kept the card on my wall all these years for what I thought was a very inspired thought, not just for a painter but also perhaps for all artists.

Today, in the present context, we face a different dilemma altogether. The question of courage and the thoughts of facing our present condition come ironically from the turn of Peter Cain's inspired message.

Less Oil More Courage asks us to face our own desires in the making, and to confront and question them, even as we try to achieve them. How do we, as a society and a community, face our weakness with courage and find the place in our consciousness to redirect the course and path we have been travelling? We will travel to our mortal end, but while we are on this road, perhaps a small detour off course can bring us closer, to face the facts and be inspired enough to change.

Chiang Mai, Thailand 2007

نفط أقل، شجاعة أكثر

تلقيت عبر البريد قبل بضع سنوات، دعوة من غاليري ماثيو ماركس في نيويورك لحضور معرض لفنان شاب يدعى بيتر كين. كان بيتر رساما اشتهر برسمه للسيارات بالأسلوب الواقعي المشوه بتحول استدلالي بحيث يصبح من الصعب التعرف عليه سوى من خلال انعكاسه في المرآة (anamorphic). وكان يعمد إلى رسمها بفرشاة الألوان الزيتية التي تغطي قماش اللوحة بطبقة رقيقة من الألوان. كانت تلك سمة رسام واقعي (أو حتى توضيحي)، يروي حكاية عالم سيريالي، هو عالم سطح الأشياء وسطح السيارات المطلي بالمينا اللامع. ولكن إذا كان بيتر مولعا بالسيارات، فإن العالم المتحول للتحور البيو-تكنولوجي كان في خيال هذه السيارات - عالم يتم فيه استنساخ النعجة دولي، كما يتم عرض برمجيات "أدوبي فوتوشوب" للعالم، والتي تقدم مشهدا جديدا لعالم التصوير يتخطى خيالنا.

غير أن حياة بيتر انتهت قبل أوانها، ولم يتح له أن يبلغ عامه السابع والثلاثين، والدعوة لحضور معرضه، كانت بعد خمس سنوات من وفاته.

كان على الوجه الأمامي لبطاقة الدعوة التي تلقيتها، صورة لصفحة من مذكرات بيتر الفنية، كتب فيها: "شجاعة أكثر، نفط أقل". تلك الجملة، في ذلك السياق، كانت ملاحظة خاصة موجهة لنفسه (أي بيتر)، لتعكس معضلة أن يكون رساما، والخيارات الأخلاقية التي يواجهها لدى تنفيذ لوحة ما. علقت هذه البطاقة على الجدار، ولم تزل هناك منذ عدة سنوات، إذ وجدت هذه الجملة ملهمة جدا، ليس فقط بالنسبة للفنان ذاته، وإنما لكل الفنانين.

أما اليوم، وفي السياق الراهن، فإننا نواجه معضلة مختلفة كل الاختلاف، فسؤال الشجاعة والأفكار التي تواجه واقعنا الحالي إنما تنبع، ويا للمفارقة، من الجهة المعكوسة لصيغة بيتر.

"نفط أقل، شجاعة أكثر"، إنها صيغة تتطلب منا مواجهة الرغبات المعتملة فينا، ومجابهة ومساءلة تلك الرغبات التي نسعى إلى تحقيقها. كيف يمكن لنا، كمجتمع أو كجماعة، أن نتغلب على ضعفنا بالشجاعة، وأن نجد مكانا في وعينا، لكي نتمكن من تحويل إتجاه سيرنا؟ إننا مسافرون باتجاه موتنا لا محالة، غير أنه طالما ما زلنا نسافر على هذه الطريق، قد نفكر بالسير في طريق جانبي قد يقربنا من مواجهة الحقائق لتلهمنا بما يكفي لإحداث تغيير ما.

تشيانغ ماي، تايلند ٢٠٠٧

Untitled 2003 "Less Oil More Courage", 2003, oil on canvas, 30 x 40 cm. Private collection

LESS OIL
MORE
COURAGE

MIERLE LADERMAN UKELES

I am wild about the public domain because we all own it; it is ours. Open up the streets, the parks, the infrastructure for urban energy systems and for the flow of urban material, the recycling plants, the airwaves. We need to stake our claim and to take our place.

Each person is unique. Period. Each person is an entire world and has infinite value.

Each person is different from all the people who ever lived. Each person owns her/his freedom. Each person is sacred.

Each person is inside the picture. This has never happened before in the history of the world. Before this time, it was only the special few, the owners, who were IN the picture: those to be pictured. They were held up by everybody else, the behind-the-scenes enablers and maintainers. But now that's all different. We are in a period of stupefying geometry whose scale of everyone-in-the-picture is only now beginning to dawn and unfold.

Art is freedom; freedom of unique human expression. Period. Its form, infrastructure, process, system, duration, location, its any material whatsoever is the choice of the creating artist.

Is there an automatic conflict between the innate spirit of freedom owned by each person and the resource limits of all of us living together on this planet? Of course. Can our powers of creation turn this into something workable, even something brilliantly workable? Our whole Earth is sacred. Living together on the Earth is sacred.

I focus on the city. The city is a living entity, our ecological home - or it could be. I aim for an art of mass urban scale, our scale today; yet, at the same time, where the limitless value of each individual human creature can become articulated, where the voice of an individual can be heard forever.

We have unlimited power to create transformation. The artist and the art manifest this power and bring it into reality.

I am showing you two works of mine: *Touch Sanitation Performance* (1977-1980), an early work with 8,500 sanitation workers; and current work - some of my proposals as Artist of the Fresh Kills Parkland (1989-2014), formerly the largest municipal landfill on earth; some involve up to a million people. Both works are for New York City. Both are an attempt to deal with what I see as a prime challenge of our age: to create a public picture at mass urban scale with the individual perceptible.

ميرل لادرمن

إنني أعشق المساحات العامة لأنها ملك لنا جميعا. إنها لنا. فلتفتح الشوارع والمتنزهات، والبنى التحتية لنظم الطاقة الحضرية، ولتتدفق المواد الحضرية ومعامل التدوير وموجات الهواء. نحن في حاجة لأن نراهن على حقنا في أن نأخذ مكاننا. فكل شخص هو فريد في حد ذاته، هو عالم بحد ذاته وله قيمة مطلقة. كل شخص مختلف عن جميع الناس الذين عاشوا في يوم ما. فكل شخص يمتلك/تمتلك حريته/حريتها. كل شخص مقدس.

كل شخص له مكانه داخل الصورة. لم يحدث مثل هذا من قبل في تاريخ العالم. فقبل الآن، كانت ثمة قلة خاصة: كان المالكون وحدهم في الصورة، وكان يجري تصويرهم وحدهم، هم من يحترمهم الآخرون وهم المتنفذون. أما الآن، فكل شيء مختلف. نحن في عصر هندسي جديد مدهش، مقياسه يكمن في أن الجميع داخل الصورة. لقد بدأ هذا العصر بالإشراق والانتشار.

الفن هو الحرية، حرية التعبير الإنساني الفريد. نقطة. شكل الفن وبنيته التحتية وعمليته ونظامه وأمده ومكانه، كلها نتاج اختيار الفنان الخلاق. هل هناك أي صراع تلقائي بين الروح المكنونة للحرية التي يمتلكها كل إنسان، وحدود الموارد الخاصة بنا جميعا، نحن الذين نحيا على هذا الكوكب؟ بالطبع! هل يمكن لطاقة الخلق أن تحيل ذلك إلى شيء عملي رائع حقا؟ إن كل أرضنا مقدسة، أن نحيا معا على هذه الأرض هو أمر مقدس. أركز على المدينة لانها كينونة حية، ولإنها بيتنا البيئي - أو يمكن أن تكون. إنني أتطلع إلى فن له مدى حضري شاسع، مدانا الحالي. لكن، في نفس الوقت، هو المكان الذي يمكن التعبير فيه عن القيمة اللامحدودة لكل إنسان، وحيث يمكن أن تسمع صوت الفرد إلى الابد.

إننا نمتلك طاقة غير محدودة تمكننا من إحداث التحول. إن الفن والفنان يفصحان عن تلك الطاقة، ويجسدانها في الواقع.

إنني أقدم لكم عملين من أعمالي: "عرض تطهير اللمس" (١٩٧٧-١٩٨٠)، وهو عمل مبكر مع ٨٥٠٠ عامل نظافة. أما عملي الحالي فهو عبارة عن بعض مقترحاتي كفنانة "فريش كيلز باركلاند" (١٩٨٩-٢٠١٤)، وهو كان سابقا أكبر مكب نفايات في العالم، ويرتبط بحياة نحو مليون شخص. مدينة نيويورك هي موضوع كلا العملين، وكلاهما أيضا محاولة للتعامل مع ما أعتبره أكبر تحد في عصرنا: تكوين صورة عامة بمقياس جماهيري حضري، يكون كل شخص فيها مرئيا.

Touch Sanitation Performance, 1977-1980, performance work, New York, NY, all 59 community districts, July 1979-June 1980. A citywide performance facing each of the 8,500 NYC Sanitation workers individually and saying to each: "Thank you for keeping NYC alive." Also includes: ROLL CALL, HANDSHAKE AND THANKING RITUAL, and FOLLOW IN YOUR FOOTSTEPS

sanitation
D28

SERGIO VEGA

Paradise in the New World

Once I found a mouldy old book abandoned on the lower shelves of a political science library. It was an edition printed in the 1940s of a manuscript from 1650 and published by the Peruvian government in celebration of the four hundredth anniversary of the discovery of the Amazon River. The title was *Paradise in the New World. Apologetic Commentary, Natural and Peregrine History of the Western Indies, Islands of Firm Ground of the Oceanic Sea by the Licentiate Don Antonio de León Pinelo of the Council of His Majesty and the Contracting House of Indies who resides in the City of Seville.*

The myth of South America as a "paradise found" started with Columbus when he asserted in a letter to the Queen that the entrance to terrestrial paradise was at the mouth of the Orinoco River. Columbus travelled with a copy of *Marco Polo's Voyages*. The Gulf of Paria resembled the description Marco Polo made of a place in Asia he had taken for the Garden of Eden. The confirmation of a previous text is a substantial part of discovery, which makes the newly discovered thing not exactly new.

In Pinelo's version, Eden was a circular territory of 160 leagues (510 miles) in diameter, and the Paraná, the Amazon, the Orinoco and the Magdalena were the four rivers of paradise. Pinelo's text reflected the intellectual transitions of the 17th century: it attempted to reconcile a theological account of creation with a scientific view of nature derived from the newly developing discipline of Natural History.

Eden turned out to be in Brazil. The area of paradise covers a section of the state of Mato Grosso with rainforests, rivers, swamps, mountains, archaeological sites, indigenous reservations, rural towns, shanty-towns, and cities. These various sites, along with their histories and tales, supplied the source materials for this project.

At the Sharjah Biennial 8 I am presenting a video entitled *Paradise on Fire*. This project addresses the controversy regarding the Chiquitano forest, one of the most endangered eco-regions on the planet. Last year Enron/Shell finished a gas pipeline that links the source in Bolivia with the city of Cuiabá in Mato Grosso (the centre of Pinelo's Paradise). The companies agreed with local and international environmental agencies to make reparations for the potential damage to the ecosystem as result of the construction of the pipeline. Instead, they finished the project and left.

Paradise on Fire examines contradicting views and expectations about paradise: pristine nature left alone versus modern artificial lifestyle. From this perspective, Arabia's investment in creating an artificial paradise from the profits of oil exploitation becomes a paradox. In the case of the Chiquitano forest, reliance on oil energy results in the opposite: the destruction of an existing paradise.

سيرجيو فيغا

الجنة في العالم الجديد

عثرت ذات مرة في مكتبة متخصصة بالعلوم السياسية، على نسخة من كتاب قديم بالي، مطبوعا في أربعينيات القرن العشرين، ويحتوي على مخطوطة تعود لعام ١٦٥٠، نشرتها حكومة البيرو بمناسبة الاحتفال بالذكرى الأربعمائة لاكتشاف نهرالأمازون. كان عنوان الكتاب "الجنة في العالم الجديد، رحلاتي والتاريخ الطبيعي للهند الغربية وجزر الأرض القوية في بحر المحيط"، بقلم المحترم دون أنطونيو دو ليون بينيلو، عضو مجلس جلالته ومجلس متعاقدي الإنديز الذي مقره في اشبيلية.

بدأت الأسطورة القائلة بأن أمريكا الجنوبية هي الجنة المكتشفة مع كولومبوس، الذي ادعى في رسالة وجهها إلى الملكة، بأن فم نهر أورينوكو هو المدخل إلى الجنة الأرضية. كان كولومبس يحمل معه في رحلته نسخة من كتاب ماركوبولو، وكان خليج باري يشبه الوصف الذي ذكره بولو عن مكان في آسيا ظن أنه جنة عدن. يشكل التأكيد الوارد في النص السابق جزءا أساسيا من الاكتشاف، الأمر الذي يجعل الاكتشاف الجديد غير جديد تماما.

وفقا لنسخة بينيلو، كانت جنة عدن منطقة مدورة تبلغ مساحتها نحو٥١٠ أميال، وكانت أنهار البرانا والأمازون والأورينكو والماغدالينا، تشكل الأنهار الأربعة في الجنة. يتأمل نص بينيلو في التحولات الفكرية التي جرت خلال القرن السابع عشر، محاولا التوفيق بين الرواية الدينية عن الخليقة، والنظرة العلمية إلى الطبيعة، والتي هي نتاج تبلور علوم الطبيعة الحديثة. هكذا تحولت جنة عدن لتصبح جزءا من البرازيل، ومساحة الجنة تغطي جزءا من دولة ماتوغروسو المليئة بالأشجار المطرية والأنهار والمستنقعات والجبال، والمواقع الأثرية والبلدات الريفية ومدن الصفيح والمدن الكبرى. إن كل تلك المواقع، إلى جانب تاريخها وحكاياتها، قد وفرت المادة المرجعية لمشروعي.

في بينالي الشارقة الثامن، سوف أعرض شريط فيديو عنوانه:" الجنة تحترق". يتصدى هذا المشروع للصراع حول غابة شيكوبتانو، وهي إحدى أكثر المناطق المهددة في العالم. فقد انهت شركة إينرون/شيل في العام الماضي مد أنبوب للغاز، يصل بين بوليفيا ومدينة كويابا في ماتوغروسو، التي تقع في وسط جنة بينيلو، واتفقت الشركة مع وكالات محلية ودولية على دفع تعويضات عن أية مخاطر قد تهدد البيئة نتيجة لمد ذلك الأنبوب، إلا أن الشركة ما لبثت أن رحلت بعد إكمال مشروعها.

يستعرض شريط" الجنة تحترق" الآراء المتضاربة والتوقعات حول الجنة: لقد تم إهمال الطبيعة النظيفة النضرة من أجل أسلوب حياة إصطناعي حديث. وانطلاقا من هذا المنظور، فإنه من المفارقة أن يتوجه العرب للاستثمار في بناء جنة اصطناعية باستخدام أرباح النفط، بينما بالنسبة لغابة شيكوبتانو، فإن أرباح النفط سوف تؤدي إلى نتيجة عكسية: تدمير الجنة القائمة.

Global Warming series, 2005, installation view, Arsenale, Venice Biennale

LUCA VITONE

Self-portrait

It is a sign - or a nemesis - of our times that one cannot easily isolate, abstract or purify the qualities from the defects, the lights from the shadows. In contemporary visual art, the dialectics of difference, including the ambiguity of reality, the moral bleakness of technique and the vertiginous corporeality of every idea, is a genetic fact and a crucial problematic horizon. But to debase images, to prevent them from drifting in the heavens of aesthetics by anchoring them to entropy, means also to expose the potential of resistance, the temporal and memorial density of a creative gesture that includes the limit and the dispersion, the platform of history *inside* that of the psyche, and the annihilation in *the act* of constructing. Therefore, if from the start this *dense* image measures itself against its lost potentiality or against the paroxysm of its "spectacular" inflation, it is capable of marking out a precarious path of mending, in short, of producing reality.

For his exhibition, Luca Vitone thus employs breath as his material and colour, or better still, the heavy breath of Sharjah. Linen canvases are filters on which the city deposits the dross of its metabolism, its shapeless slobber that stains and corrodes. What's filtered and what we see at the end is, therefore, also Time - long, real time - which both corresponds to and contrasts with the abstract time of inspiration and execution. Taking the place of the painter's provisionally omniscient position is the precarious position of the chance-seeker, of duration's anthropologist. And so the "monochromes" simultaneously become the self-portrait, imprint, *index* of a time and place, and the self-portrait of painting, the description of a territory and the epos of an identity, observed from a suspended but fortified position that lives the disparity between the ideal model and the concrete result. Painting is led back to literal fact - the contrast and integration between pigment and support, between the barren clean and the fertile dirty. And bereft of the artist's hand and style, painting is obliged to set its potential into motion and to make itself once again the epicentre of a condensation, of a turn in indifference, of an unexpected shift of the visible.

Stefano Chiodi

لوكا فيتوني

صورة ذاتيّة

إحدى إشارات أو لعنات عصرنا الراهن، أنّ المرء لا يمكنه بسهولة عزل أو تجريد أو تنقية الحسنات من العيوب أو الإضاءات من الظلال. أصول منطق الإختلافات في الفن البصريّ المعاصر، بما فيها التباس الواقع والانكشاف الأخلاقي للتكنيك والمادية الدّوامية لكلّ فكرة، هي حقيقة جينيّة وأفق أساسيّ إشكاليّ. ولكن احتقار الصور، ومنعها من التنقّل في سماوات الجماليّات بتقييدها بمرساة التحولات الداخلية، يعني الكشف أيضا، عن مدى إمكانيّة المقاومة، والكثافة الزمنيّة والتذكاريّة للفعل الإبداعي الذي يضمّ الحدود والانتشار، ومنصّة التاريخ داخل النّفس، والإبادة في فعل البناء. بالتالي، لو قاست هذه الصورة الكثيفة نفسها منذ البداية، بالمقارنة مع إمكانياّتها الضائعة، أو أمام نوبة تضخّمها "الرائع"، لكانت قادرة على رسم الطريق المحفوف بالمخاطر نحو التعافي، أو، باختصار، نحو إنتاج الواقع.

ولهذا يستعمل لوكا فيتوني في هذا المعرض النّفَس كمادته ولونه، أو أفضل بعد، نَفَسُ الشارقة الثقيل. قطع القماش الكتّانيّ هي المصافي التي تودع المدينة فيها مخلّفات عمليّاتها الحيويّة، ولعابها الذي يترك بقعا ويسبب التآكل. ما يترشح وما نراه في النهاية هو، بالتالي، الزمن أيضا - زمن طويل وحقيقيّ - والذي يتجاوب مع، ويغاير الوقت المجرّد للوَحي والتنفيذ. يحل الباحث عن الفُرَص، عالم الانثروبولوجيا (علم الإنسان)، محل الفنان العالم بكل شيء مؤقتا. وبالتالي تصبح "أحاديّات الألوان" في ذات الوقت صورة ذاتيّة، بصمة، فهرس الوقت والمكان، وصورة ذاتية للوحة، وصف مساحة وملحمة هويّة، تمّت مراقبتها من موقع، معلّق ولكن مدعّما، يحيي التفاوت بين النموذج المثاليّ والنتيجة الملموسة. تمّ إعادة توجيه الرسم نحو الحقيقة الحَرفيّة — التناقض والتشابك بين الصبغة والدعم، بين العقيم النظيف والخصب الوسخ. ومحروما من يد وأسلوب الفنان، يضطر الرسم إلى إعادة تحريك إمكانيّاته، أن يجعل نفسه ثانية مركزا لعملية تكثيف، ولتحوُّل في اللامبالاة، ولتحرّك غير متوقّع للمرئي.

ستيفانو كيودي

Finestra VI grande (Isola dell'Arte), 2004, acquerello di polvere su carta, 205 x 155 x 5 cm incorniciata, photo: Roberto Marossi, Collezione privata, Milano, courtesy Galleria Emi Fontana, Milano

SHATHA AL-WADI

شـذى الـوادي

Similarity or just complexity?

Humans can never be alike,
Nor can trees .
A man and a tree form
An entity with a unique quality!

I am a human, and I am a tree;
I have a body, and I have a trunk.
I have hands, and I have branches.
Together we share
Earth, sand, love, and generosity
Between strength, anger, and embrace,
Sheltered under shadow, complexity, and suddenness,
Amidst originality, toughness, but also incomplete solidity.
Watered,
By one Creator...

Now, does this make us
More similar or complex?

أهو تشـابه أم مجـرّد تعـقيـد؟

لا يمكـن لبنـي البشـر التشـابه،
ولا يمكـن للأشـجار التشـابه،
هـكـذا يصبح الإنسـان، كـمـا الشـجـرة - وحـدة فـريدة
الخـصـائص!

أنا بشـر كـمـا أنـي شـجـرة
لـدي جسـد ولـدي جـذع
لـدي يدان ولـدي أغـصـان
معـاً نشـترك
بالأرض، والرمل، والحب، والكـرم،
وبيـن القـوة، والغـضـب، والعـنـاق،
نأوي رأسـنـا تحـت الظـل، والتـعـقيـد، والفـجـاءة
وفـي خـضـم الأصـالـة، والخـشـونـة، بل الخـشـونـة التـامـة
يسـقينا خـالـق واحـد أحـد!

فـهـل يجـعـلنـا هـذا، أكـثـر تشـابهـاً
أو أكـثر تعـقيـداً؟

Similarity or Just Complexity, 2007-2006, installation, courtesy of the artist

CAMILLE ZAKHARIA

Cultivate Your Garden

> To be rooted is perhaps the most important and least recognised need of the human soul
>
> Simone Weil

"Cultivate Your Garden" is a spiritual journey that I undertook in response to my sense of helplessness faced with my inability to change the world around me. My idyllic childhood was ripped apart by the Lebanese civil war, the same war that forced me to leave Lebanon as a young adult. I haven't returned since.

Everyone reacts differently to traumatic events. Some choose to confront them in the form of political or social activism. I reacted by embarking on a very personal journey of self-discovery. Having failed to find or create a sense of security on the outside, I constructed a safe spiritual retreat within myself.

The "Cultivate Your Garden" suite is an autobiographical work that examines the intrinsically intertwined concepts of home, identity and belonging. It is inspired by Voltaire's literary classic, Candide, in which Voltaire ridicules the optimistic theory of "all is for the best in this best of all possible worlds". Candide, the naïve hero of the story, learns this philosophy of life and goes on a series of adventures where he experiences the disasters of war, hunger, sickness and torture. He settles down at the end of the novel to cultivate his garden and seek fulfillment from the modest routine of everyday life.

In this work though, there is a twist to the original story. Because of the Lebanese civil war, I had to leave Lebanon and look for a garden to cultivate. Drawing upon my early vernacular photography, I constructed a mythical landscape. This monumental photographic installation composed of seven panels is populated by sombre, monochromatic, Modigliani-esque figures that dominate the foreground in stark contrast to the rich and colorful background. A hybrid of Beirut, New York, Paris, Bahrain, Turkey, Greece and Canada – places that at one point or another in my life I called home, the dreamscape represents my surreal home and resonates a sense of displacement.

كميل زخريا

فلتزرع حديقتك

> قد تكون الحاجة الأكثر أهمية للروح الإنسانية، والأقل إدراكاً من قبل الآخرين، هي حاجة الإنسان لأن يكون له أصل، وجذور تضرب في مكان ما من العالم.
>
> سيمون ويل

"فلتزرع حديقتك" عبارة عن رحلة روحية قمت بها، استجابة إلى إحساس تملكني بأني شخص عاجز، لأنني غير قادر على تغيير العالم من حولي. لقد مزّقت الحرب الأهلية في لبنان طفولتي المطمئنة الهانئة. إنها الحرب ذاتها، التي أجبرتني على مغادرة لبنان كشاب يافع، ولم أعد إليها منذ ذلك الحين.

يتصرف كل واحد منا بطريقة مختلفة إزاء الصدمات والأحداث المأساوية التي يتعرض لها. البعض يختار مواجهتها على شكل نشاط سياسي أو اجتماعي. أما أنا، فقد اخترت مواجهتها بالشروع في رحلة شخصية جداً لاكتشاف الذات. وإذا ما أخفقت في أن أخلق إحساساً بالأمان في محيطي الخارجي، أعمد إلى بناء خلوة روحية آمنة داخل نفسي.

جناح "فلتزرع حديقتك" عبارة عن عمل يوثق لسيرة ذاتية تتفحص المفاهيم المؤتلفة في دواخلنا للبيت، والهوية، والانتماء. وهو عمل مستلهم من أحد الأعمال الأدبية الكلاسيكية لفولتير، Candide، والذي يسخر فيه من النظرية المتفائلة القائلة، بأن "كل ما يحدث هو الأفضل في هذا العالم الأفضل." يتعلم Candide، وهو البطل الساذج للقصة، فلسفة الحياة، ويخوض سلسلة من المغامرات حيث يعيش كوارث الحروب، والجوع، والمرض، والتعذيب. وفي نهاية الرواية، يستقر لزراعة حديقته، ويسعى إلى تحقيق ذاته من خلال الروتين المتواضع للحياة اليومية.

غير أن هذا العمل يقدم تحولا في أحداث القصة الأصلية. فبسبب الحرب الأهلية في لبنان، كان علي أن أغادر بحثاً عن حديقة أزرعها. بالاستناد على أعمال التصوير البدائية في بداية حياتي الفنية، عملت على بناء مشهد أسطوري. أما شخوص هذا النصب الفوتوغرافي التركيبي الذي تألف من سبع لوحات، فتتمثل بمجسمات على طراز موديلياني Modigliani-esque، كئيبة، أحادية اللون، تسيطر على الواجهة، في تباين كبير مع الخلفية الغنية والمليئة بالألوان.

إنها نتاج لتلاقح بين مختلف الثقافات: بيروت، نيويورك، باريس، البحرين، تركيا، اليونان، وكندا، وجميعها كانت بمثابة الوطن لي، في فترة ما من فترات حياتي. ومساحة الحلم هذه، هي وطني الذي لم أعرفه سوى في أحلامي، وتعبر عن إحساس بالإزاحة والنزوح.

Cultivate Your Garden, 1998, (panels 4 & 5), photocollage on paper, 100 x 152 cm

Sharjah Biennial
بينالي الشارقة

الدليل المرافق لبينالي الشارقة الثامن، ٤ أبريل - ٤ يونيو ٢٠٠٧

دولة الإمارات العربية المتحدة • حكومة الشارقة • دائرة الثقافة والإعلام
United Arab Emirates • Government of Sharjah • Department of Culture & Information

الفن والبيئة وسياسات التغيير

طبيعة صامتة

بينالي الشارقة ٨

Pay Phone
Pay Phone

بينالي الشارقة ٨

رئيس البينالي
سمو الشيخة حور بنت سلطان القاسمي

مدير البينالي
جاك برسكيان

مساعدة
فرح شاور

المقيمون
محمد كاظم
إيفا شارير
جوناثان واتكنز

لجنة التحكيم
نيغار عاظيمي
تشارلز إشه
جيتا كابور

المنسق العام
هشام المظلوم

سكرتاريا
فاطمة أحمد
مريم علي

منسقة البينالي - الإعلام والشحن
مهيتا الباشا أوريتا

الشحن
فراس عودة
علياء الصابي

المشرف الإداري
ريم شديد

شؤون الفنانين
لارا الخالدي

تصميم المعرض (هندسة معمارية)
منى المصفي (م.م)

مساعدون
سمر المصفي (م.م)
ميس نافوخ
مي ميرزا
رشا ضاهر

مشرف عام على تجهيز وإعداد المعرض (هندسة الكتروميكانيك)
حسن علي الجدة

تجهيزات وتقنيات
نيكولاي بنيدكس سكيوم لارسن

مساعدون
إيمان السيد
لطيفة مكتوم

الإعلام العربي
إسماعيل الرفاعي

الشؤون المالية
أحمد كمال

تقنية المعلومات
نوف يوسف

إدخال المعلومات
حسام أبو باشا

تصميم الموقع الإلكتروني
هاني شرف - كيوريس للتصميم
غسان السوداني

تصوير فوتوغرافي
بيتر ريدلينغر
ألفريدو روبيو

البرنامج التعليمي والمرشدون
ذكريات معتوق
هند بن درويش
علياء الملا
عنود الخضر
باسم صالح السايد
فاطمة علي محمد
حليمة سليمان طارش
إسماعيل السويدي
جواهر السويدي
محمد أحمد محمد
محمد فايز
سعاد إسماعيل طارش
وفاء عبد الله علي
وليد سيد البغدادي

الورش الفنية - الإشراف
طلال معلا
سكرتاريا
دينا الغصين

مدرسون
جعفر دويلة
محمد بدر
رياض معتوق
وسام حداد
ياسر صافي

منسقة المتطوعين
يسرى صالح

فنيون وتقنيون
أحمد عبد الجبار
كانكوران سليمان شاجان
كمال سعيد محمد
أطلس خان أمير دوار خان
عبد أمير دوار خان
عبد الرحمن
أنيل كومار
حبيب اولا سلطان
حسن درويش
خالد سامي
محمد خان ميرا خان
محمد عتيق
رمضان محمد
رشيد حسن
شكير بوثيا
سمير ك.ب
سراج علي
محمد إقبال

تنسيق الحركة
علي النمر
سيف الدين ك.ف
منصور أحمد ضياء
محمد غالب
أمجد خان
محمد كان فضل كول

مخازن
يوسف طه

أمانة المكتبة
مريم عبد الله
هدى سالم الناصر

تصميم الميداليات والدروع (الجوائز)
كارلوس مرينوس

العلاقات العامة والإعلام (الدولية)
برنزويك للفنون - لندن
ماريا فيندرز
بن رولينغسون بلانت
جوانا بولص
كاتي تيلور
ألكس روبا

العلاقات العامة والإعلام
(الوطن العربي)
جيوين - شركة علاقات عامة
مأمون صبيح
ماجد واصي
جين ميكيل

الدعاية والإعلان والمطبوعات
كيوريس للتصميم
عبير بركات
هاني شرف

الإعلانات الخارجية
غولدن بالون
فهد الشريف

الشحن
كراون للفنون الجميلة
أرنود بوزيناك

التأمين
شركة البحيرة الوطنية للتأمين

المواصلات، الإقامة والحجوزات
الشرق للسياحة
تيتو ماتشان
سنيال فيجيال

حجوزات الطيران
سكاي لاين للسفر
ساديا باشا

الفنادق
روتانا الشارقة
أيمن غريب
مناع العيد
هوليداي إنترناشونال الشارقة
ناصر ناصف
منتجع ماربيلا
أنيل سينغ
عاصم بدر

خدمات الطعام
شركة ألبرت أبيللا الشارقة
ليندن مارك اناندا

دائرة الثقافة والإعلام - حكومة الشارقة

المدير العام
عبد الله محمد العويس

سكرتاريا
ماريا محي الدين طورمش

مدير إدارة الفنون
هشام المظلوم

سكرتاريا
عائشة ساعد حمد
خديجة محمد علي

مدير إدارة التراث
عبد العزيز عبد الرحمن المسلم
عبد الستار العزاوي
بدر محمد
محمد خميس
أمينة أحمد
خليل إبراهيم

الحسابات والمالية
أحمد إبراهيم ركاض
أحمد محمد أحمد حسن
محسن عبد الرحمن فضلي
أمل عبد الله المرزوقي
مريم علي خميس

المشتريات
علي محمد الجروان
عمران أحمد القطري
عبد الوهاب عبد الغفور البلوشي

شؤون الموظفين
عبد الله حسن المناعي
فيصل حسن الزرعوني

العلاقات العامة
حسن جاسم أحمد
حسين مصطفى محمد
عبد اللطيف عبد الله
حسين خان فضل الرحمن

القسم الإعلامي
اسامة طالب مره
عائشة مصبح العاجل
وفاء ناصر المازمي

الحجوزات والحركة
موهان كومار

تقنية المعلومات
رائدة مخامرة
فدوى السويدي

شكر خاص

سمو الشيخ عصام بن صقر القاسمي
رئيس مكتب سمو الحاكم، الشارقة

سمو الشيخة بدور بنت سلطان القاسمي
رئيس مكتب تطوير قناة القصباء

سالم بن محمد العويس
رئيس هيئة مكتب المجالس البلدية لإمارة الشارقة
رئيس المجلس البلدي لمدينة الشارقة

محمد مصبح خلفان السويدي
مدير عام مكتب سمو الحاكم، الشارقة

صلاح علي المطاوع
مدير عام شرطة الشارقة

صلاح طاهر الحاج
مدير عام بلدية الشارقة

رندة كمال

نتقدم بالشكر إلى

عبد الله الشويخ
عبد الله كروم
عبد الرحمن أبو بكر أحمد
عبد الرحمن محمد بوخاطر
عادل المتولي
أحمد عبد السلام
أحمد أبو نجا
الحر محمد النور
الوليد بن خادم
أنس شومال
اندريا روز
انيكا لينسون
أروى لوتاه
سيزر إسبادا
شنتال كروزيل
كرس دركن
كولن جي. ريني
ديريك أوغبورن
ديانا ستيفنسون
ابتسام عبد العزيز
فاتن حج إبراهيم
فاطمة يوسف بن صندل
غازي بقجة جي
حيدر الأمين
حماد ناصر
هيزل بيج
حازم صواف
هند خير
هشام عبد الكريم
إيناس أبو سيدو
أيرس لنز
إيريت روغوف
إسماعيل البشري
جاسم المظلوم
جون مارتن
جودي بولنجتون
جمعة إبراهيم السويدي
جمانة إميل عبود
خديجة كنمبو
خالد بن بطي المهيري
خالد إسماعيل صفر
ليان ميلا
مريم الدباغ
مروان السركال
ميره السويدي
مايكل براي
معتز محمد حسين
محمد العامري
محمد حسن عوض
نور العمران
نوريا أوسكوز
أسامة محمد سمرا
بي رافي
بول هنسسي
رائدة سعادة
ريموند بروتشر
رينا كرفهال
روبرتو لوباردو
روبالي كرنك
سيف محمد المدفع
صلاح بن بطي المهيري
صالح طاهر الحاج
سامر كمال
سهام محمد الشريف
سو أندرووود
سوزن روبرتس-منياناللي
طارق الغصين
طارق سلطان بن خادم
توفيق القماطي
تري إفنز
ثاني الشامسي
ثيو فون ديبشتز
وليد ديماس
وندي شانغ
يعقوب عبد الله
يسر الدباغ
زينا فرحات
زياد صبح

وزارة الداخلية - إدارة الجنسية والإقامة في الشارقة
وزارة الداخلية - الإدارة العامة لشرطة الشارقة
وزارة التربية والتعليم - منطقة الشارقة التعليمية
بلدية الشارقة
بلدية الذيد
إذاعة وتلفزيون الإمارات العربية المتحدة - الشارقة
دائرة التخطيط والمساحة، حكومة الشارقة
هيئة كهرباء ومياه الشارقة
جامعة الشارقة - كلية الفنون الجميلة والتصميم
الجامعة الأمريكية في الشارقة
إدارة متاحف الشارقة
مركز اكسبو الشارقة
قناة القصباء
المعمل، مؤسسة للفن المعاصر، القدس
دار الخليج للصحافة والطباعة والنشر، الشارقة
الجامعة الأمريكية في دبي
مدرسة الشفاء بنت الحارث
مركز البحوث البحرية وحوض الأسماك - أم القيوين
النادي البحري للفنون والسياحة

الدليل

المحرر
سيرين حليلة

المحرر المساعد
لارا خالدي

الترجمة
بسمة الفار
ديالا خصاونة
اعتدال عثمان
حسن أبو لبن
حاتم حسين
محمد الوضاح عيدابي
مراد رمضاني
سلافة حجاوي

محرر اللغة العربية والتدقيق اللغوي
إسماعيل الرفاعي

محرر اللغة العربية
غازي الخليلي

محررة اللغة الإنجليزية
آن رودفورد

الصور الفوتوغرافية
جاك برسكيان
القسم العربي ص. ٤-٥، ٢٤-٢٥
القسم الإنجليزي ص. ٤-٥، ٦-٧، ٨-٩، ٢٨

ترتيب الأسماء المدرجة في الدليل، جاء حسب الأبجدية في اللغة الإنجليزية. ترتيب أسماء الفنانين جاء حسب الكنية، وحسب الاسم الأول في حالة وجودهم كمجموعة فنية. ترتيب الأسماء في لائحة الشكر، جاء حسب الاسم الأول.

تصميم
لينا صبح

مصمم مساعد
خالد عبد الله خليفة مزينة

إدارة الطباعة
محمد خليل

الطباعة والتجليد
مطبعة الإمارات

الدليل
العنوان: بينالي الشارقة ٨، طبيعة صامتة: الفن والبيئة وسياسات التغيير
٣٦٠ صفحة ٢٣٣ × ١٦٥ ملم
الغلاف: كونكرر تكتشر ٣٠٠ غم
الورق الداخلي: اوفست خالي الخشب ٨٠ غم وآرت مات ١٣٥ غم

الناشر: بينالي الشارقة

ISBN 9948-04-328-6

العنوان
بينالي الشارقة
ص.ب. ١٩٩٨٩ الشارقة
الامارات العربية المتحدة
هاتف: ٥٦٨٥٠٥٠ ٦ ٩٧١+
براق: ٥٦٨٥٨٠٠ ٦ ٩٧١+
العنوان الالكتروني:
info@sharjahbiennial.org
www.sharjahbiennial.org

يقدم البينالي بالغ امتنانه لإسهامات الفنانين والكتاب، غير المحدودة .
مقتطفات النصوص التي اختارها الفنانون أو الداعمون لهم، تعدّ جزءاً أساسياً، لعرض وتقديم مشاريع الفنانين والبرنامج التعليمي في المعرض.
بذلت كافة الجهود للاتصال مع الفنانين وأصحاب حقوق النشر لإدراج النصوص والصور التي أرسلت من قبلهم، ضمن محتويات الدليل.
جميع النصوص المنشورة في الدليل تعبر عن رأي أصحابها ولا تعبر بالضرورة عن رأي المحررين أو إدارة البينالي.

كافة المعلومات الواردة في الدليل صحيحة حتى تاريخ صدوره.
اعتمد السنتيمتر كوحدة قياس، لمختلف الأبعاد (الطول، العرض، العمق).

الرعاة

هيئة المنطقة الحرة لمطار الشارقة الدولي
Sharjah Airport International Free Zone

مصرف الشارقة الإسلامي
Sharjah Islamic Bank

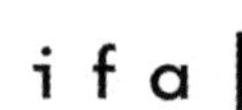

Institut für Auslands-
beziehungen e. V.

IKON

الراعي الإعلامي

عرض موجز لبرنامج الأفلام

مارك ناش
مقيم
هذا البرنامج هدفه إلقاء نظرة طويلة على موضوع (طبيعة صامتة: الفن والبيئة وسياسات التغيير). من جهة ، فإن الفيلم الوثائقي "كابوس داروين" يعالج القضايا الملحة للمناخ والتغيرات البيئية. بينما تتطرق أفلام الفنانين لقضايا واسعة المدى من الطبيعة الحسية والرمزية لمادة الماء(في فيلم زدرافتش). وحالة قطاع المناجم في الصين (في فيلم شاوبن) إلى تأملات أكثر شاعرية على ميراث الكفاح للتحرير والاستقلال.

قائمة الأفلام

أندريش زدرافتش
نهر الزجاج، باليه النهر في الفصول الأربعة، ١٩٩٧
يتجلى التوظيف المجازي البليغ للماء في فيلم تجريبي روائي وتسجيلي يفحص العلاقات الإنسانية المرتبطة بأراض/ أماكن بعينها عبر التركيز على المياه والصراعات حول حقوق المياه وذلك من خلال سينما تجريبية غير روائية ونشطة.
نهر الزجاج فيلم فيديو يستغرق ٤١ دقيقة يغوص بالمشاهدين بصريا في المياه الزمردية لنهر ستوشا بسلوفينيا. ويتطلب طول الفيلم ومقاربته من المتفرجين أن يغيروا وعيهم وخبرتهم بعالم الطبيعة.
إن نهر الزجاج يشق فضاء يجعلهم يتأملون علاقتهم بالعالم الطبيعي وكيف يوظف هذا العالم في الفيلم وفي الحقيقة.
لقد اعتاد المشاهدون النظر إلى المشاهد الطبيعية في السينما باعتبارها لا تستحق منهم اهتماما متواصلا. لكن الفيلم يتحدى مثل هذا الاعتياد حين لا يقدم سوى تدفق النهر من داخل النهر نفسه على امتداد الفصول الأربعة. ففي خلال ٤١ دقيقة إما أن يصبح النهر مهما أو لا يستحق الاهتمام. نهر الزجاج يجبر المشاهدين أن يكون لهم الاختيار، وأن يدركوا أنهم قاموا بهذا الاختيار.

بريجتج فان دير هاك
لاجوس متسعة وقريبة، ٢٠٠٢
يعتمد هذا الفيلم على بحث قامت به جامعة هارفارد حول مدينة لاجوس بإشراف رم كوولهاس.
يقدر عدد سكان لاجوس بحوالي ١٥ مليون نسمة. وعلى الرغم من الجريمة، ومشاكل الصرف الصحي، والاختناقات المرورية المستعصية على الحل، ونقص المياه والكهرباء، إلا أن لاجوس تنمو بسرعة كبيرة حتى أنه من المتوقع أن تصبح ثالث أكبر مدينة في العالم عام ٢٠٢٠. لقد قرر المهندس المعماري رم كوولهاس أن يدرس لاجوس من أجل أن يفهم ما الذي يجعل كل هذا الاختلال الوظيفي يؤدي وظيفته بنجاح. وعن طريق الاعتماد الشفاف على مسار سائق حافلة يمنحنا الفيلم لمحة من حيوات ثماني شخصيات من سكان لاجوس والعلاقات الخلاقة التي يكونونها مع مدينتهم المركبة. ويضيف كوولهاس ردود أفعاله وتفسيراته خلال خمس سنوات استغرقها البحث الذي قام به في لاجوس. لقد كان تصوير الأفلام محظورا في نيجيريا، لذلك لا توجد سوى صور قليلة للاجوس. وهذا الفيلم يفصل بين المشاهد (المتسعة) البعيدة وتلك (القريبة) الحميمة للمدينة. مما يسمح للمشاهد بالانتقال بين هذه المشاهد وتلك على التوالي بصورة فعالة. هناك أيضا ثلاثة شرائط صوتية مختلفة يمثل أولها تعليقات رم كوولهاس، ويقدم الثاني أحاديث مع السكان، إلى جانب أصوات المدينة نفسها.

هيوبرت ساوبر
كابوس داروين، ٢٠٠٤
"كابوس داروين" عبارة عن قصة تدور حول البشر في الشمال والجنوب، وحول العولمة، وحول السمك.
في وقت ما خلال عام ١٩٦٠ جرت في بحيرة فيكتوريا تجربة علمية محدودة تتمثل في تقديم نوع جديد من الأسماك ليعيش هناك. وفي المقابل أدت هذه التجربة إلى كارثة بيئية شملت البحيرة. إن البرش النهري، وهو ضرب من السمك المفترس الضاري، كاد أن يقضي تماما على الفصائل السمكية المحلية. وبرغم ذلك تكاثر هذا النوع الجديد بسرعة مذهلة أدت إلى أن أصبحت شرائحه البيضاء تصدر اليوم إلى كافة أنحاء العالم.
لقد باتت طائرات الشحن الضخمة التابعة للاتحاد السوفيتي السابق تأتي يوميا لجمع حصيلة الصيد مقابل حمولة تخص بلاد الجنوب، وتتكون من الأسلحة والذخيرة المغذية لحروب لا حصر لها تجتاح قلب القارة السوداء. إن هذا الرواج لصناعة متعددة الجنسيات تتكون من السمك والأسلحة خلق تحالفا عولميا شريرا على شواطئ أكبر بحيرة مدارية في العالم، وارتبط ذلك بجيش من الصيادين المحليين، وعملاء البنوك العالمية، وأطفال مشردين، ووزراء أفريقيين، وسماسرة أوروبيين، وبغايا تنزانيات، وطيارين روس.

إجلولك إيسوما / زاخاريوس
كونك،ونورمان كون، يوميات نود راسموسن، ٢٠٠٦
قدم زخاريوس كونك و نورمان كوهن ويمثلان فريق فيلم "أتانارجوات" أي العداء السريع، أول فيلم بلغة الإسكيمو من منطقة إنوكتيتت. ويعد الفيلم سبقا جديدا، إذ ينطلق من داخل مجتمع الإسكيمو وهو أيضا من إنتاجهم.
لقد استلهم المخرج زخاريوس كونك فيلمه "يوميات كنود راسموسن" من حياة جمهوره الأول وهم الإسكيمو، ويتراوح هذا الجمهور بين كبار السن الذين ما زالوا على قيد الحياة، والشباب الباحثين عن مسقبل يجاوز السأم والبطالة والانتحار. ويحاول الفيلم الإجابة عن سؤالين ظلا يلحان على المخرج طوال حياته: من كنا؟ وما الذي حدث لنا؟
أما هذه المرة فمحور السؤالان هو لحظة فارقة في تاريخ الإسكيمو تعود إلى اللقاء الأول بالمكتشفين الأوروبيين والمسيحية. فحوالي عام ١٩٢٢ ارتحل المستكشف وعالم الأنثروبولوجيا الدنماركي كنود راسموسن إلى القطب الشمالي الكندي ليسجل قصص ومعتقدات القبائل المحلية هناك، ولقد أصبحت هذه الرحلة نقطة انطلاق

لرواية هذه القصص داخل الفيلم. فيما ركز الفيلم على قادة الإسكيمو مثل آفا. آخر الكهنة العظام (يلعب دوره حفيده باكاك إنوكشوك) وأومك الذي قاد اعتناق المسيحية. أما القصص فترويها ابنة آفا واسمها آباك. ويقدم الفيلم كله من خلال وجهة نظر شعب الإسكيموفي حين يبدع كونك وكوهن رؤية باهرة للماضي القريب ولزمن غريب وأليف. كانت فيه الطبيعة والجوانب الروحية تتحكمان في السلوك. بينما كانت العناصر السحرية جزءا من الحياة اليومية. ويعتمد الفيلم على الروايات الشفوية التي تعلمها كونك وكوهن من المسنين. ويستخدمان تقنيات سينمائية مدهشة. قدما من خلالها فيلما ممتعا ومثيرا للمشاعر والتأمل في آن واحد.

أيزك جوليان

الشبح الأفريقي. ٢٠٠٥

ينسج "الشبح الأفريقي" مرجعيات سينمائية ومعمارية من خلال تصورات غنية للحياة المدنية في أواجادوجو. مركز السينما في أفريقيا. والمساحات القاحلة في المنطقة الريفية حول بوركينا فاسو. تتخلل وقائع الفيلم فواصل مستمدة من مادة أرشيفية لأحداث الحملات الإستعمارية المبكرة واللحظات التاريخية الفاصلة في التاريخ الأفريقي. ويلعب مصمم الرقصات المعروف ستيفن جالوواى (باليه فرانكفورت) والممثلة فانيسا مايري (بلتيمور) دوري "الشبح المخادع" و"الشاهد" في هذا العمل المتقن الذي يتأمل انتزاع الطابع القومي عن مناطق وفضاءات ولدت نتيجة اللقاء بين الثقافة المحلية والثقافة العالمية. بينما تظل أشباح التاريخ محومة وسط حقائق الزمن الراهن.

كومار شاهاني

شار أد يهياى. ١٩٩٧

يعتمد فيلم شاهاني على رواية قصيرة كتبها رامبندرانات طاغور عام ١٩٣٤. ويتناول المرحلة الإرهابية التي تخللت حركة الحرية الهندية. لقد سمحت امرأة اسمها إيلا لنفسها أن تصبح تميمة حية متحركة ومتكلمة بين مجموعة من الإرهابيين. إنها تمثل حضورا أنثويا مريحا لشابة تمزق احترامها لذاتها بسبب تجربة السيطرة الاستعمارية. ويوظف الجانب الأيديولوجي جمال أيلا واعتزازها بنفسها ليكشف روح البعث الجديد في البلاد.

هؤلاء الفرسان آثروا التشرد وتركوا أمهاتهم وأخواتهم وزوجاتهم لكي يقترفوا النهب والانتحار والقتل من أجل قضيتهم. تبتهج إيلا أول الأمر بهذه الحالة. ثم تبدأ في المساءلة عندما يظهر أتن. أحد أفراد المجموعة. مقاومة هذا المنحى التلقيني. إنه يرفض أن يتسامى بمشاعره تجاه إيلا ويظل ممتلئا بالنفور إزاء الأعمال الإرهابية. وعندما توصلا إلى سعادة بسيطة كان تورطهما عميقا بحيث ظلا يلعبان دورهما حتى الثمالة.

أوكي هيرويوكي

شكل قصر إخوة ماتسوماى كون - ١. ١٩٨٨

إن المسلسل الذي نشأ مع العمل الذي أطلق عليه "يوميات ماتسوماي كون" (١٩٨٨) كان مخططا لمدينة ماتسوماي في هوكايدو. قدمه هيرويوكى أوكي كمشروع للتخرج خلال دراسته للعمارة بالجامعة. وإلى جانب المسودة الخاصة بالتصميم المعماري قدم التصميم نفسه من خلال وسائط متعددة مناظر طبيعية فيما يشبه اللوحات المستقلة المعروضة من منظور الشخصية الخيالية "ماتسوماى كون". وفي العام التالي (١٩٨٩) قدم فيلم الافتتاح "فيلم لماتسوماى كون". أما الأجزاء الأولى من المسلسل فقد وظفت في الفيلم في شكل يوميات تبدأ بيوم بداية العام. فيما تميزت حركة الكاميرا بنقل إحساس فيزيقي بالارتجال. وعلى حين توقف المسلسل السنوي عام ١٩٩٦ إلا أنه بدأ مرة أخرى عام ٢٠٠٢ ب "رؤية لموت ماتسوماي كون". ولقد عكست هذه الأعمال الأحدث تغيرات أخذت تتطور مثل استخدام كاميرات الفيديو. وإحضار الممثلين إلى مدينة ماتسوماى لتصوير المشاهد. أما بالنسبة للمادة الفيلمية المأخوذة من حلقات المسلسل السابقة. فقد تم استيعابها لكي تطيل الفيلم بينما اتخذت أشكالا تختلف عن تلك التي كانت عليها في الماضي. ولقد استغرق فيلم "شكل قصر إخوة ماتسوماى كون ١" وهو رقم ١٣ من المسلسل. أكثر من شهر بداية من ٢٢يناير ٢٠٠٦. بينما تراوحت مواقع التصوير بين هاكوديت وسابورو وطوكيو وكوشي. إضافة إلى مدينة ماتسوماى.

يانغ شاوبن

٨٠٠ متر تحت السطح. فوق سطح الأرض - تحت سطح الأرض.٢٠٠٥

يتكون الفيلم من محورين يدوران حول حياة عمال مناجم الفحم. فيتناول أعماق المناجم و مجتمعات العمال ومساكنهم. يركز جانب "ما تحت الأرض" على عمليات الإنتاج في مناجم الفحم. فيما يمثل الجانب الآخر ما هو "فوق الأرض" فيقدم رؤية ممتعة لحياة عمال المناجم حين يخرجون إلى سطح الأرض. إنها حياة ماتزال محجوبة في الظلام تغيب فيها إمكانات الهرب. ومن خلال التجربة الشخصية والسفر تلتقط رهافة إحساس الفنان قضايا معقدة تكشف الجانب الإنساني داخل دورة الإنتاج.

يتعلق الأمر هنا بالجانب التاريخي وببصيرة كاشفة لأبعاد التنظيم السياسي. وبالتغير المتسارع للنظام الاجتماعي. والقدرة على البقاء. والقوة. ويعيد المشروع فحص تاريخ التصنيع والفضاءات المدنية والذاكرة الاشتراكية. وعلاقة ذلك كله بالتاريخ المعاصر للفن الصيني.

موازنة ٧٠ طناً من الكربون

الندوة الفكرية: ٥ - ٧ أبريل ٢٠٠٧
برنامج الجمعية الملكية للفنون والبيئة (RSA) ولاتيتيوذز (Latitudes) بالتعاون مع الجامعة الأمريكية في الشارقة.
المكان: مركز اكسبو الشارقة.

منظمو الندوة:
ميكايلا كريمن (الجمعية الملكية للفنون)
ماكس آندروز (لاتيتيوذز)
ماريانا كانيبا لونا (لاتيتيوذز)
رودريك غرانت (الجامعة الأمريكية بالشارقة)
أمير بربيك (الجامعة الأمريكية بالشارقة)
منسقة الندوة:
شرن أهيماز (بينالي الشارقة ٨)

تهدف الندوة المصاحبة لبينالي الشارقة إلى البحث في ملامح العلاقة بين الثقافة والبيئة وما في ذلك تحديات وتناقضات. كما سيركز الحدث على العمل المتميز في مجال العمارة والفنون البصرية عبر التكنولوجيا الجديدة في التصميم وعلى الشاشة. يشارك في النقاشات فنانون وأكاديميون وطلاب ومعماريون ومصممون محليون وعالميون. كما ستستفيد الندوة من وجهات نظر أشخاص يتعاملون مع قضايا البيئية بشكل يومي. تطرح الندوة محاور جريئة في دولة تهيئ نفسها للمستقبل وللتغيرات التي يتوجب علينا جميعاً التفاعل معها.

الخميس ٥ أبريل

الكلمة الافتتاحية يقدّمها بروس ستيرلنغ بعنوان البيئة وسياسات التغيير

جلسة نقاش حول جاذبية المصطلحات البيئية
فن البيئة - أزياء البيئة - سياحة البيئة - سياسة البيئة - قرى البيئة.... رسّخ مفهوم البيئة نفسه في كل مجالات حياتنا. كيف تغيّر وتطور مفهوم البيئة من خلال ممارساتنا اليومية؟
الجلسة برئاسة جيرمي بيندك - كيمر: مدرّس فلسفة بالجامعة الأمريكية بالشارقة
سارا ريتش: رئيسة تحرير Worldchanging وinhabitat.com موقع يركز على التصاميم والمدن الصديقة للبيئة.
سيرجيو فيغا: فنان مشارك في بينالي الشارقة ٨.

سيوبان ليدن: منتج ومقدّم البرنامج اليومي (سيوبان على الهواء) في محطة راديو عين دبي - ١٠٣,٨ إف إم.
ستيفاني محمود: طالبة تسويق وإدارة بالجامعة الأمريكية بالشارقة.

مقتطفات من برنامج الأفلام:
ريفرغلاس: باليه النهر في أربعة مواسم. أندريه زدرافيك - ١٩٩٧م (٤١ دقيقة)
"يمثّل ريفرغلاس مادية النهر سوكا وهو علامة مهمة في الثقافة السلوفانية ويمثّل قوة ونقاء المياه من وجهة نظر النهر، أي وجهة نظر غايا (الأرض الأم). يذّكر محتوى ومواد التصوير بصانعي أفلام آخرين مثل مايكل سنو (La Region Centrale ١٩٧٠) وروبرت بيفر (The Stoas ١٩٩١-٩٧)". مارك ناش

المحاضرات المصاحبة:
١- الطوارئ والمخاطر
ما هو دور المعماريين والمصممين والفنانين في شؤون الإسكان والمجتمع؟ مع تزايد الضغوطات على الموارد والمساحات وتقلبات المناخ السياسي، كيف يمكننا محاولة تقليل المخاطر قبل وقوع الكوارث بدلاً من التعامل مع تبعاتها؟ هل يمكن للتصميم والمعمار أن يكونا أعمال سياسية؟
الجلسة برئاسة مهدي سابت (بروفيسور معمار وتصميم بالجامعة الأمريكية في الشارقة)
سوزي بلات (المعمار للإنسانية والمصمم الأول لأعمال إعادة بناء ما بعد التسونامي)
مايكل راكوويتس (فنان مشارك في بينالي الشارقة ٨)

٢- الموارد: الحقيقة والمواد
هل يقبل الفنانون والمصممون والمعماريون على المواد المعاد تصنيعها؟ وكيف يؤثر ذلك على وجهة نظرنا تجاه المادية في الفن والعمارة؟ وما هي علاقة ذلك بأسئلة أعمّ حول الموارد والمياه والطاقة... الخ؟
الجلسة برئاسة منى المصفي (معمارية في بينالي الشارقة وأستاذة في الجامعة الأمريكية بالشارقة).
مايكل برونغارت (مصمم وكيميائي - مؤلف مشارك ل: "من المهد إلى المهد. إعادة تصنيع الطريقة التي نصنع بها الأشياء" هامبورغ / شارلوتسفيل)
توماس ساراسينو (فنان ومعماري من فرانكفورت مشارك في بينالي الشارقة)

حوار:
كومار شاهاني: السياسة وبيئة التغيير
مارك ناش (قيّم برنامج الأفلام في بينالي الشارقة ٨ ومدير MA Curating Contemporary Art في الكلية الملكية للفنون بلندن) وغيتا كابور (ناقد وقيّم في نيودلهي وعضو في اللجنة التحكيمية لجائزة الفن في بينالي الشارقة ٨ - ٢٠٠٧م) في حوار حول أعمال صانع الأفلام الهندي كومار شاهاني.

الجمعة ٦ أبريل

جلسة نقاش حول موازنة/اختلال توازن "الفن في مواجهة القضايا"
زادت غزارة إنتاج الأعمال في مجال الفن والبيئة حول موضوع الأعمال التحسينية في المواقع الصناعية. تم طرح تجارة الكربون وموازنته كوسيلة لإعادة التوازن للمناخ. كيف يمكن لهذين التحركين أن يكونا متصلين؟ كيف يمكن اعتبار أعمال بعض الفنانين نوعاً من الموازنة أو الإصلاح؟ كيف يبحث بعض الفنانين عن نتائج واقعية بينما يطرح الآخرون استراتيجيات للمواجهة أو المقاومة؟ ما هو الأهم: القضايا أم الفن؟
الجلسة برئاسة ستيفاني سميث (مديرة المجموعات والمعارض، قيّمة الفن المعاصر، متحف سمارت للفنون، جامعة شيكاغو)
كويو كووه (ناقد وقيّم - داكار)
بيتر فند (فنان مشارك في بينالي الشارقة ٨)
تشارلز أشه (مدير Van Abbemuseum، ايندهوفن وعضو اللجنة التحكيمية لجائزة الفن في بينالي الشارقة ٨)

مقابلة عبر الفيديو مع نوآم تشومسكي
جوناثان واتكنز (قيّم مشارك في بينالي الشارقة ٨) وكورنيليا باركر (فنانة مشاركة في بينالي الشارقة ٨) للتعريف بمشروع باركر لبينالي الشارقة ٨:
تتبعها جلسة أسئلة وأجوبة من الحضور.

السبت ٧ أبريل

عرض الفنانين: إي-أكس بلو مع أيرين أنستاس

جلسة نقاش حول التخطيط المدني والمدينة المستقبلية

ما هو مستقبل المدينة كموطن للإنسانية؟ فالبيوت تزداد كثافة والمساحات التجارية والثقافية والاجتماعية والمخصصة للبنى التحتية تتضاءل مما يتناقض مع رغبتنا في التواجد في مساحات مفتوحة ومليئة بالحرية. ما هو مستقبل المدينة ككائن غير حي متفاعل ثابت تقطنه كائنات حية؟

الجلسة برئاسة جورج كاتودرايتس
سمير سروجي (فنان مشارك في بينالي الشارقة ٨)
رولا صادق (مديرة التصميم والتخطيط في مجموعة التصميم، نخيل)
سامر كمال (مؤسس بيئة، شركة الشارقة للبيئة)

المشاركون في ندوة بينالي الشارقة ٨

بروس ستيرلنغ (مشارك رئيسي في الندوة)
جيرمي بيندك - كيمر(مدرّس دراسات دولية بالجامعة الأمريكية بالشارقة)
سارا ريتش (رئيسة تحرير Worldchanging وinhabitat.com موقع يركز على التصاميم والبنى الصديقة للبيئة)
سيرجيو فيغا (فنان مشارك في بينالي الشارقة)
سيوبان ليدن (منتج ومقدّم البرنامج اليومي (سيوبان على الهواء) في محطة راديو عين دبي- ١٠٣،٨ إف إم.)
ستيفاني محمود (طالبة تسويق وإدارة بالجامعة الأمريكية بالشارقة)
رم كولهاس (معماري ورئيس مكتب العمارة المتروبوليتية بروتردام)
فاتح رفقي (عميد كلية المعمار والتصميم بالجامعة الأمريكية بالشارقة)
مهدي سابت (بروفيسور معمار وتصميم داخلي بالجامعة الأمريكية في الشارقة)
سوزي بلات (المعمار للإنسانية والمصمم الأول لأعمال إعادة بناء ما بعد التسونامي)
مايكل راكوفيتس (فنان مشارك في بينالي الشارقة ٨)
مايكل برونغارت (مصمم وكيميائي)
منى المصفي (معمارية في بينالي الشارقة وبرفيسورة في الجامعة الأمريكية بالشارقة)
توماس ساراسينو (فنان ومعماري من فرانكفورت مشارك في بينالي الشارقة)
مارك ناش (قيّم برنامج الأفلام في بينالي الشارقة ٨ ومدير MA Curating Contemporary Art في الكلية الملكية للفنون بلندن)
غيتا كابور (ناقد وقيّم في نيودلهي وعضو في اللجنة التحكيمية لجائزة الفن في بينالي الشارقة ٨ - ٢٠٠٧م)
ستيفاني سميث (مديرة المجموعات والمعارض، قيّمة الفن المعاصر، متحف سمارت للفنون، جامعة شيكاغو)
كويو كووه (ناقد وقيّم - داكار)
بيتر فند (فنان مشارك في بينالي الشارقة ٨)
تشارلز أشه (مدير Van Abbemuseum، ايندهوفن وعضو اللجنة التحكيمية لجائزة الفن في بينالي الشارقة ٨)
جوناثان واتكنز (قيّم مشارك في بينالي الشارقة ٨)
كورنيليا باركر (فنانة مشاركة في بينالي الشارقة ٨)
جورج كاتودرايتس (معماري وبروفيسور معمار في الجامعة الأمريكية بالشارقة)
سمير سروجي (فنان مشارك في بينالي الشارقة ٨)
رولا صادق (مديرة التصميم والتخطيط في مجموعة التصميم، نخيل)
سامر كمال (مؤسس بيئة، شركة الشارقة للبيئة)
ميكايلا كريمن (مديرة الجمعية الملكية للفنون والبيئة)
إي-أكس بلو (فنانون مشاركون في بينالي الشارقة ٨)
ايرين اناستاس (فنانة مشاركة في بينالي الشارقة ٨)

برنامج اليونسكو

يشترك بينالي الشارقة ٨ مع اليونسكو (المنظمة العالمية للتربية الثقافية والعلوم)، في توسيع دائرة المشاركة والانخراط في التطوير الحضري المستدام، ومضامينه الثقافية، بدعوة فنانين شباب من مختلف أنحاء العالم، للتفكير وتصميم مشاريع خلاقة تنبع من صميم تصوراتهم وتفكيرهم عن الحيز الحضري والمجتمعات، تلك الأعمال التي نتجت عن التحولات الفنية والأشكال الجديدة في الفنون الرقمية.

وفي هذا الصدد سخرت المنظمة جائزة اليونسكو لترويج الفنون، للتكريم والاعتراف بالعمل الفني الفذ والمقدم من ضمن الأعمال الفنية المعروضة في بينالي الشارقة ٨

ستقوم لجنة التحكيم الدولية، المعينة رسمياً من قبل الأمين العام لليونسكو والمكونة من خمسة أعضاء يمثلون المناطق الجيو/ثقافية (آسيا/الهادي، أمريكا اللاتينية/الكاريبي، أفريقيا، العالم العربي، أوروبا/ شمال أمريكا)، باختيار العمل الفائز، وذلك بمشاركة ممثلين اثنين من اليونسكو ومن بينالي الشارقة.

منسقو البرنامج
تيريزا فاغنر
دويان لي

لجنة التحكيم الدولية
عبد الله كروم (المغرب)
بيرني سيرل (أفريقيا الجنوبية)
يوجينو تيسلي فاليز (المكسيك)
جون غانيون (كندا)
سو يونغ رو (كوريا)

وضمن إطار التعاون بين اليونسكو وبينالي الشارقة، ستنظم ورش دوليه للمدربين خلال فعاليات البينالي، حيث ستمر الورش لمدة خمسة أيام، تحت إشراف، فنان/مدرب في مجال الميديا، والذي كان قد حاز على جائزة اليونسكو لترويج الفنون ٢٠٠٧ في مجال الفنون الرقمية.

يشارك في الورش ستة مدربين، ثلاثة من المحليين والعرب، وثلاثة من أماكن مختلفة من العالم، والمدربون هم من المدرسين في المراحل العليا، لمواد مثل الإنجليزية، التاريخ، الجغرافيا، الفنون، الموسيقى، الكومبيوتر، العلوم.. كما يدرس بعضهم في نوادي ومراكز تدريبية.

المدربون
أحمد نابلي
فرانشيسكا ماركيز
جمانة عبود
نيلفون أريكان
شيرين سعيد
سودهيتش ماتيلاكه

الهوّيات الإبداعية والفكرية، متنوعة بتنوع البيئات والثقافات الإنسانية، إلا أن الخطاب الإبداعي يحاول دائماً أن يشكل نقطة التماس بين مختلف الشعوب، إنه خطاب متجرد عن الانتماءات الضيقة وملتصق بجوهر الإنسان ووجوده الكلي على سطح الأرض.

ودائرة الثقافة والإعلام ضمن توجهاتها تحاول أن تساهم في هذا المشهد الإبداعي الإنساني، بما يتماهى مع التصورات الحكيمة ذات الطابع الإنساني الشامل، والتي يطرحها ويؤسس لها حضرة صاحب السمو الشيخ الدكتور سلطان بن محمد القاسمي عضو المجلس الأعلى للاتحاد حاكم الشارقة، ولعل بينالي الشارقة يعكس وبجلاء الرغبة الدائمة في الانفتاح على النتاجات الإبداعية المتطورة، وفي سياق اللحمة الإنسانية والبحث عن الجوهري في الفنون البصرية الجديدة وطروحاتها الفكرية، والتي تتبنى في كل مرة موضوعة وثيقة الصلة بالهموم الإنسانية وإشكالياتها الملحة، كموضوع البيئة التي يطرحه بينالي الشارقة ٨، تحت عنوان (طبيعة صامتة: الفن والبيئة وسياسات التغيير) والذي يشير إلى حيوية الموضوع وأهميته، خصوصاً في هذه الأوقات الحرجة من تاريخ البشرية والتي أصبحت فيها الحياة مهددة بالعديد من الأخطار والكوارث البيئية، والتي يحاول البينالي أن يقدم فيها إسهاماته الخاصة، بالمعنى الجمالي والوجداني والفكري، وبما يربط الاجتماعي بالإبداعي والعالمي بالبيئة المحلية الخاصة.

دائرة الثقافة والإعلام
حكومة الشارقة

المحتويات

خارج الأقاليم الضيقة

حور القاسمي

الحلم هو المعنى الذي يحققه الإنسان وهو يطارد إلماحاته في اليقظة والغياب.

الحلم هو المحرك الأول الذي جعل المبدعين يصيغون نشيدهم الأسطوري عن الأرض، وهم ينوسون بين شفافية الصورة المتخيلة وقسوة الواقع.

الحلم الذي يشدنا إلى أمنا الأرض، ويضعنا على تخوم الكون كي نتوحد مع إيقاعه الكلي.

الحلم بأرض آمنة تتسع لنا وللأجيال القادمة التي ستعمّر الأرض بماء الحلم ذاته.

والحلم هو ما يدفعنا في هذه الدورة من بينالي الشارقة، لأن نطالب الإنسان في الأصقاع كلها، برفع يد القسوة عن ظاهر الأرض وباطنها، فقد أوشكت أن تزفر الغضب الذي يحتبس في عروقها، وأن تفرغ حممها في وجه الإنسان الذي تمادى في استنزافها، بعد أن أشعنا الاضطراب في مجالنا الحيوي وفي بيئتنا، التي أعطتنا دون حد، فتمادينا دون حد، احتضنتنا، فانقلبنا عليها.

إنها أرضنا تئن تحت ثقل المعاول التي تحاول استنفادها، حتى بات من الضرورة، إشاعة الوعي البيئي والتعريف بحجم الأهوال والكوارث المحتملة، فهل ثمة من يشاركنا هذا الحلم لرسم صورة أخرى لوجودنا بشكل أكثر غنى وفاعلية؟

لقد حاولنا في هذه الدورة أن نقرن الحلم بالفعل وأن نتقصّى عن صيغ إبداعية متميزة، تصب في عمق هواجسنا وتشاركنا الرغبة في تغيير أساليب تعاملنا مع البيئة بمائها وترابها.

من هنا يتعدى بينالي الشارقة ٨ سياق العروض العابرة، فالبينالي ليس مجرد فسحة بصرية، أو محطة عابرة للفنانين ومحبي الفن.. إنه طريقة للتفكير والتأمل، صيغة متكاملة ومنسجمة مع رغبتنا في فتح آفاق جديدة للحوار، وسياق ثقافي وإبداعي، منفتح على مكونات هذا العصر وعلى قضاياه الملحة.

وليس من قبيل المصادفة أن تحتضن الشارقة هذا الحدث الكبير، فإمارتنا مبنية على احترام التقاليد والثقافة المحلية، وعلى تكريس ثقافة ذات طابع إنساني قادرة على ربطنا بهمومنا الكبرى، واجتراح أسئلة جديدة، تكشف النقاب عن خبايانا.

وفي هذا الإطار يحاول البينالي أن يوسع حدود العادات والأفكار المكرسة لفتح آفاق جديدة، ومد وشائج تزيد من لحمة الكائن على هذه الأرض.

وهذا الحيّز هو عبارة عن حوار دائم بين التقاليد المتوارثة والقيم الجديدة، وإشاعة ميكانيزم النقد في هذا الجدل الدائم. ولهذا كان البينالي محور حديث مفتوح في مختلف أنحاء الوطن العربي والعالم.

وكي ننأى بحلمنا عن الزوال، آثرنا السير في دروب أكثر وعورة، بعد أن حدث تغير عميق في العلاقة بين الأرض وساكنيها، وأصبحت عرضة لانتهاكات دائمة ومنظمة، جعلتنا على حدود كوارث وشيكة، فنحن جميعاً نعيش في محيط حيوي واحد للإبقاء على حياتنا، ومع ذلك فإننا ندمر الطبيعة ونستهلك مواردها، بطريقة لن نترك معها سوى احتمالات الخراب.

ومن هنا يكون البينالي، محاولة لاتخاذ موقف إزاء ما يحدث والإسهام في تعرية السياسات الجائرة تجاه كوكبنا، ولهذا أيضاً نريد لبينالي الشارقة أن يكون جزءاً من النسيج الثقافي والاجتماعي لبيئتنا المحلية، وشرفة نطل منها على التجارب المعاصرة خارج الأشكال الجاهزة والمفاهيم المكرورة. ووسيلة لإقامة حوار خلاق مع مبدعي العالم خارج الأقاليم الضيقة. إنه سانحة للبحث والتجريب وطرح الأسئلة التي تفضي بدورها إلى أسئلة أخرى.

(وليس خلاصنا)

جاك برسكيان

لقد تولى بينالي الشارقة الثامن المهمة الملحة المتمثلة في تناول بعض التحديات البيئية التي تواجه العالم اليوم، وذلك من منظور فني، ومن خلال إشراك فنانين من مختلف المجالات وعلى مستويات متعددة: بيئية، واجتماعية، وسياسية، وثقافية، وفردية...الخ. للوهلة الأولى، قد تبدو هذه المحاولة محدودة أو لا تتسم بالحساسية، أو أن لا حول لها ولا قوة أمام القضايا الملحة والكوارث الفاجعة التي تنال منطقتنا في الوقت الحاضر (الشرق الأوسط والعالم العربي). الزمان فصل الشتاء لعام ٢٠٠٧، والقائمة زاخرة: فلسطين، لبنان، سوريا، العراق، إيران، أفغانستان، السودان، "الحرب على الإرهاب"، التسليح النووي، نزع السلاح، العنف الطائفي والمذهبي، الاغتيالات، الفساد، التسيب الأمني، الأميّة، الفقر، عمالة الأطفال، حقوق الإنسان، الديموقراطية، والقائمة تطول. وكما كتب جان لوك نانسي في صيف ١٩٩٥ في المقدمة التي استهل بها كتابه (أن تكون جمعاً مفرداً)

> "إنها قائمة لا نهائية، وكل شيء يحدث بطريقة تجبرك على إدارة الحسابات فقط دون أن تصل إلى المجموع النهائي. إنها ابتهال، أو صلاة الأسى الصافي والفقدان الخالص، إنها نداء يسقط من بين شفاه ملايين اللاجئين كل يوم، سواء كانوا مبعدين، محاصرين، مشوهين، جوعى، مغتصبين، منبوذين، مقصيين، منفيين، أو مطرودين".[١]

في عالمنا هذا، تصبح حتى أبسط المصطلحات التي نستخدمها لمناقشة موضوع البيئة كعلم وكحيز مكاني محيرة. ففي فلسطين، على سبيل المثال، "الأرض" - العزيزة والعظيمة دوماً - هي الحافز الأكبر الذي يجعل الناس، في أغلب الأحيان، يموتون، ويُقتلون، مقدمين أرواحهم فداء لها، وها هي قد أصبحت بمثابة مكبّ للنفايات، إذ أُفرغت من محتواها الأصلي لتملأ بالأنقاض والنفايات. وبإفراغ الكلمة من معناها على هذه الشاكلة، نجدها قد أصبحت، مجرد معنى اصطلاحي استراتيجي لمصلحة الخطاب السياسي، لا يكتسب صفة الشجاعة والاحترام سوى في لعبة البلاغة، أو في صياغة وإطلاق الشعارات القومية. كما أن العديد من الدلالات التي تشكل وجودنا، والبيئة التي نعيش فيها، والمعايير التي تتشكل بموجبها إنسانيتنا، قد أصبحت جميعها "مكبات للنفايات" أيضاً. فالجريمة المنظمة تقوض العلاقات الاجتماعية؛ والعنف والعدوان والخيانة، أصبحت جميعاً هي المفردات التي تسيطر على تجربة حياتنا اليومية، والتي استشرى فيها التلوث السمعي والبصري.

أما "تهكمات مرحلة ما بعد السياسة"[٢] وهو المصطلح الذي استخدمه جاري جينسكو، فإنها تبث التقاعس والخمول بين المواطنين، وأما مجموعة المبادئ الأخلاقية التي وضعناها حجر أساس لعالمنا، فقد انتهكت بشكل عرضي لدرجة، بات فيها النسيج الأخلاقي للأنظمة الاجتماعية، مهدداً بالانهيار.

عندما نشهد كارثة، سواء كانت طبيعية أو بفعل البشر، سرعان ما تكرر أمّي قولها: "لقد اقتربت نهاية العالم" وإذا حاولنا أن نتخطى اللامبالاة في التعامل مع أثر أعمالنا على البيئة، وعلى الانتقاص المستمر من احتمالات ديمومة الكائن على هذا الكوكب، فإن اعتقاد أمّي الدائم بقرب يوم القيامة يكشف عن الوجه السوداوي لإنسانيتنا، ألا وهو تلك الرغبة في التدمير.

وعند الحديث عن الدمار، أخبرتني منى مصفي- المهندسة المعمارية

[١] أن تكون جمعا مفردا، ترجمة روبرت دي رتشاردسون وآن إيي أوبيرن. ستانفورد، كاليفورنيا: مطبعة جامعة ستانفورد، ٢٠٠٠، ص. ١٣

[٢] "احتمالات البيئة متعددة الأنظمة." ورقة مقدمة في الجمعية الملكية للفنون، لندن، ٢٧ نيسان ٢٠٠٥

لبينالي الشارقة السابع والثامن- في إحدى حواراتنا، أن التهديدات والمخاطر التي يجب حماية الإنسانية منها، قد تغيّرت بشكل ملحوظ على مدى السنوات المائة الماضية، إذ تحوّلت من المخاطر الناجمة عن الطبيعة، إلى تلك الناجمة عن فعل البشر. لا بدّ من حماية الإنسان من نفسه إذاً. ومن منظور نفسي-عاطفي (والذي يحدّنا ويقودنا أيضاً إلى التسليم بحتمية القدر)، يمكننا العودة إلى ما كتبه جان بودريار عندما شرح أن نزعات التدمير لدى البشر تنبع من رغبتهم في مشاهدة النهاية (نهاية العالم)، آخذين بعين الاعتبار أنهم لم يكونوا حاضرين عند بدايته ونشوئه:

> إننا لن نصل أبداً إلى معرفة الفوضى الأصلية، الانفجار الكبير... لأنه حدث محجور. ونحن لم نكن موجودين هناك أبداً. ومع ذلك، بإمكاننا أن نحافظ على الأمل، الأمل بأن نشهد اللحظة الأخيرة، أو السقوط الكبير، يوماً ما. إنه ذروة المتعة، فرح الانفعال بالنهاية تعويضاً عن بداية لم يؤذن لنا بمشاهدتها [المنشأ]. هاتان هما اللحظتان الوحيدتان اللتان تشكلان أهمية بالنسبة لنا، وحيث كان نصيبنا الإحباط في اللحظة الأولى، تجدنا نبذل المزيد من طاقتنا للإسراع في الوصول إلى النهاية، أو في تحقيق اللحظة الثانية، لتسلك الأشياء أو الأحداث، طريق فنائها الأخير...[٣]

هذا العالم الشجاع الجديد الذي كان يفترض بنا أن نحققه من خلال التقدم العلمي والتكنولوجيا، لم يؤد بنا في نهاية المطاف إلا لإخضاع الطبيعة، واستغلال مواردها، وافتراس جسدها، والتنبؤ بموجات غضبها. وإذا حاول أحدنا أن يوضح ويشرح مواطن الخلل، لا بدّ وأن تقوده الإجابة إلى مصدر واحد، ألا وهو العنصر البشري، الإنسان الذي أدى استغلاله الجشع والمنفلت للطبيعة ومواردها إلى الاستعمار، والإمبريالية، والعنصرية، والرأسمالية.

ويمكننا أن نوضح هذه النقطة من خلال مثال واحد وهو حوادث تسرّب النفط، (غير متناسين بالطبع أن شعلة هذا المشروع، هذا البينالي، قد اتقّدت بفضل الموارد النفطية الهائلة للإمارات). إننا نعرف أن ناقلات النفط وخزّاناتها عرضة للحوادث، وأنها تتعطل بسبب العطش الذي لا يرتوي إلى النفط. ومع ذلك، وبتكرار الحوادث، ما زلنا نعتبر تسرب النفط مجرد حوادث، ومصادفات مقبولة لاقتصاديات تجارة النفط وأسلوب حياتنا. والأسوأ من هذا وذاك، هو اعتبار نتائج حوادث تسرب النفط أمراً واقعاً لا يمكن تغييره، بل نتعامل معه بهزة كتف غير مبالية ولسان حالنا يقول: "الحياة مستمرة في كل الأحوال."

وفي حين يتعين علينا أن نتصدى للقضايا الكبرى الظاهرة والمرتبطة بالبيئة مثل الكوارث الطبيعية وارتفاع درجة حرارة الكون، يجب ألاّ تؤدي هذه إلى خسف أو تقزيم القضايا التي تصادفنا على مستوى العلاقات الاجتماعية، والثقافية، والسياسية. وفي هذا المقام، يقترح فيلكس غوتاري في كتابه البيئات الثلاث نهجاً "كليّا" للتفكير في البيئات التي يعرّفها:

> الآن، أكثر من أي وقت مضى، لا يمكننا فصل الطبيعة عن الثقافة. ولاستيعاب التفاعلات بين النظم البيئية، والميكانيك الكوني، والعوالم الاجتماعية والفردية للإحالات والإشارات، علينا أن نتعلم كيف نفكّر بطريقة "كليّة"... وتماماً كما تغزو الطحالب الوحشية والمشوهة مياه البندقية، كذلك تغزو شاشات تلفازاتنا وتغرقها الصور والبيانات "المنحطة".[٤]

وأشكال التلوث المتقاطعة هذه، والتي تغذي بعضها بعضاً، وهي: التلوث العقلي، والبصري، والسمعي، ما زالت لا تلقى اهتماماً على مستوى الهيئات الرسمية وغير الرسمية، والتي يقع من ضمن اختصاصها ومسؤولياتها حماية

٣ جان بودريار، هسترة الألفية، وهم النهاية: أو شدة الأحداث، ترجمة، تشارلز دودا، باريس: Galilee، ١٩٩٢

٤ فيلكس غوتاري، البيئات الثلاث، ترجمة، أيان بندار وبول ساتون، نيو برنزوك، نيو جيرسي، مطبعة أثلون، ٢٠٠٠ ص. ٤٣

البيئة الحيّة. إنها ليست مرئية تماماً. بالتالي لايمكننا قياس أثرها الضار على الأشخاص، والموائل، والمجتمعات، ولكن لا بدّ من تحديد هذه الأضرار ووضعها في مقدمة الاهتمامات والأولويات. كما أن بيئة النطاق الاجتماعي أو ما يعرف بـ "البيئة الاجتماعية" تحتاج إلى بعض الاهتمام. وقد حذّر غوتاري من هذا الأمر، وبشكل لا يخلو من المبالغة، مستخدماً مثالاً محدداً ألا وهو شركات التطوير العقاري:

> يسمح لرجال مثل دونالد ترامب بالتكاثر بحرية، ومثل السلالات الأخرى من الطحالب، يقومون بالاستيلاء على مقاطعات بأكملها في نيويورك وأتلانتك سيتي؛ وهو يقوم ب "إعادة التطوير" من خلال رفع الإيجارات، مما يدفع بعشرات الآلاف من العائلات الفقيرة، والتي حكم على معظمها بالتشرد، والحرمان من سقف يأوي رأسها، لأن يصبحوا كالأسماك النافقة في البيئة الطبيعية.[٥]

إننا نعيش لحظة تاريخية تشهد تغيرات سريعة، قد تأخذ شكل حوادث غير متوقعة. وتحل المرجعيات التي تمخّضت عنها العولمة محل مرجعيات الحداثة وما بعد الحداثة. وقد أصبح عصر البرمجيات قادراً على تحوير الأفكار الطبيعية والمصطنعة، وإعادة النظر في علاقات المكان بالزمان. نحن نستطيع الآن، أن ننفصل رقمياً عن العناصر التي كوّنت يوماً ما ذاتيتنا (التخلق الرقمي من خلال الإنترنت أو ألعاب الكمبيوتر).

لقد أجبرنا على الدخول في "عالم الفوضى"، كما لاحظ إدوارد غليسون، "نوع من النمو العالمي المتعرج، واحتفاء لا نظامي بالفوضى والضلال."[٦] هكذا هو النظام العالمي الجديد. "نحن نعيش في زمن لم يعد بمقدورنا أن نفرض فيه شروطنا على العالم."[٧] أين يتركنا هذا الوضع، وما الذي علينا القيام به؟ بين فكرة محاولة تغيير العالم وإعطائه مستقبلاً ما، والسير وسط المعمعة. نحن- فريق بينالي الشارقة- نرى دورنا في فتح الباب أمام احتمالات متعددة، في توفير وسائل، وإعطاء منبر للأفراد والجماعات (فنانون، مثقفون، مفكرون، نشطاء، سياسيون، بيروقراطيون، علماء، والناس بعامتهم)، لزيادة الوعي حول المسائل والقضايا البيئية الحرجة، وأن ندق ناقوس الخطر. لقد آن الأوان الذي نأخذ فيه هذه المسائل والقضايا على محمل الجد، ليس فقط من قبل المختصين والجهات المهتمة، بل أيضاً، من قبل الجمهور العام. وكما يرى غوتاري، علينا أن "نتوقف عن النظر إلى هذه القضايا على أنها مرتبطة بأقليّة تعشق الطبيعة، أو بمجموعة أخصائيين مؤهلين."[٨] نحن نميل إلى بناء "كتلة حرجة" من المقترحات غير المتكلفة، تهدف إلى خلخلة حالة الارتضاء السائدة وتقويض بريق التقدم المصطنع، ووعده الخيالي بتحقيق نشوة الفردوس على الأرض. وفي الوقت ذاته، نحن ننوي عرض أعمال تجسد منهجيات بديلة في الفكر والتقييم، ونماذج متوافقة مع الوعي المتزايد لبيئتنا المهددة. إننا نرغب في أن نعيد الفن ليحتل موقعه الملائم في عملية التنمية الاجتماعية، والاقتصادية، والثقافية، والمستدامة، دون أن نتخلى عن اعتباراتنا الأخلاقية والجمالية.

إننا نرى دور الفنان أساسياً ومحورياً. وبالمقارنة مع العلماء والمحللين، يحق للفنانين تجربة الأشياء من خلال التساؤل والبحث الذهني، بما يتجاوز ضغوطات السوق ومتطلباته، حيث النماذج "ليست بحاجة إلى الاختبار ليتبين أنها منقوصة، من حيث ربحيتها أو حصتها في السوق، ذلك انه ليس [لديهم] قدرة على الشراء بموجب هذه الشروط."[٩]

ومع ذلك، تبقى المنطقة الحرة المستقلة للفنانين مرتبطة باقتصاد السوق، (الذي يمتطي صهوة كل موجة من موجات الازدهار التي تشهدها

[٥] المرجع نفسه.
[٦] مقتبس في بيتر هولورد Absolutely Postcolonial، مانشستر، إنجلترا: مطبعة جامعة مانشستر، ٢٠٠١، ص. ١٧

البورصة وأسواق المال، وكل فيض دافق من المليونيرية والبليونيرية) وإن كان التعبير عنها يأتي بعبارات مختلفة. ودون الالتزام بالمقدمات الضيقة لمجالات الاختصاص والالتزام الصارم بالمعادلات والصيغ، يمكن للفنانين أن يجسروا الأنظمة ويربطونها بعضها ببعض بطريقة متكاملة، ويمكنهم أن يقترحوا شبكات عمل، ونماذج تستجوب أساليب الحياة وممارساتها بشكل ناقد.

إن الفرضية الأساسية لهذا البينالي بسيطة ومباشرة: وجهنا الدعوة لعدد من العروض المتواضعة التي تتناول مسألة البيئة (الايكولوجيا) في السياقات الاجتماعية، والاقتصادية، والسياسية، والبيئية. وتوقعنا التعرض لموجة عارمة من الانتقادات والأحكام على أسلوب الحياة المغرق في الاستهلاكية، واللامبالاة، والتطوير الحضري المتسارع في الإمارات. وكان هذا حال معظم الفنانين الذين أتوا إلى هنا في زيارات استكشافية. وعليه، يبقى التحدي أمامنا، هو الحفاظ على حوار مستمر ومتواصل، مع الحرص على إنجاز أعمال نقدية، وإيجابية في الوقت ذاته، والاستثمار المستمر في القدرة الخلّاقة للفنانين، لدفعهم إلى الإنجاز وتخيّل أعمال جريئة، ومستدامة، وملتزمة. وكان أحد الأجوبة المحتملة هو ما تلقيناه من خارج المحيط المباشر للأنشطة والمعارض في البينالي، إنه تحديداً (معادلة التلوث الكربوني) "ثاني أكسيد الكربون". وعندما اجتمعت مع إحدى الفنانات المشاركات في البينالي، فرضت هذه المعادلة كشرط لها للصعود إلى متن الطائرة التي ستنقلها إلى الشارقة، وقد ذكرت لي أسماء بعض الشركات التي تحسب كلفة كمية ثاني أوكسيد الكربون الذي تنفثه الطائرة في الجو نسبة إلى طول الرحلة، ومن ثم تحدد بعض المشروعات التي يستثمر فيها مبلغ مساو لإيجاد وسيلة لتنقية الجو من الكربون الذي خلفته الرحلة، وذلك بزيادة امتصاص غاز ثاني أكسيد الكربون.

يهمنا توعية نطاق أوسع من الناس بمقتضيات حماية البيئة، التي تدعو إلى إجراءات فورية على المستويات الأساسية لسلوكنا الحياتي اليومي، مما دعانا إلى الاتصال بسامر كمال، وهو أحد رجال الأعمال الرياديين المقيمين، والذي يحاول أن يطرح وينشر ممارسة إعادة التدوير في الشارقة، في مبادرة ترتبط بشكل وثيق وذو مغزى برغبتنا في التعويض عن مساهمتنا في التلوث العالمي.

كان كمال يبحث عن منهج جمالي لتحويل عبوات إعادة التدوير إلى عناصر جذابة لسكان الشارقة، واستطاع أن يحصل على موافقة الهيئات الرسمية لهذا المشروع، بالإضافة إلى كسب تأييد الشركاء من القطاع الخاص لقضيته هذه. هذه الفنانة المعنية بمعادلة التلوث الكربوني، وسامر كمال، لم يكن ممكناً أن تتقاطع محاولاتهما إلا في سياق البينالي، والتي تشير إلى الطريقة التي يمكننا من خلالها النظر إلى البينالي على أنه يطرح سيناريوهات تعطي نتائج إيجابية، بالإضافة إلى طرق ونماذج للتعامل مع الضرورات البيئية التي تلقي بظلالها على حياتنا.

غير أنه قد يبدو من السذاجة أن نعتقد بأن بينالي للفن يمكنه أن يعكس أو يقلب هذا هذه النزعة التدميرية لإحداث أثر إيجابي ملموس. نحن نعي، أن الزيادة الكبيرة في أعداد السكان وبخاصة في المناطق الأقل حظاً، تحجب النور عن جميع المحاولات الرامية إلى إصلاح الضرر، أو قلب اللامبالاة وطريقة التفكير "الإقطاعية التي عفا عليها الزمن، والعادات المحلية البالية، والمحلية العنيدة."[١٠]

وللوقوف إلى جانب بودريار في نظرته النفسية-الاجتماعية، ومع الحفاظ على التزامنا بالفرضيات المنطقية، وفي ضوء الوضع الحالي الذي يمنعنا من التنبؤ بالمستقبل، فإني أعتقد أنه بغض النظر عما نقوم به، سواء كان إضراراً،

٧ نفسه.

٨ غوتاري، المرجع السابق، ص. ٥٢

٩ تشارلز إشة، مقترحات متواضعة، أو لماذا كان "الاختيار مقتصراً على كيفية تبديد الثروة وهدرها." إدينبيرغ: ٢٠٠١

١٠ بيتر هولورد Absolutely Postcolonial، ص. ٧

أو استنزافاً، أو تجريفاً، أو استهلاكاً، أو طمراً، أو تلويثاً، أو تدميراً، أو تشويشاً، أو تغييراً لوجه الأشياء، أو إخفاءً له، أو احتواءً، أو خنقاً، أو إشغالاً، أو ترهيباً، أو إيذاءً، أو إفساداً، أو تسريباً، أو توسيخاً، أو تعفيناً، أو تسميماً، أو محاولة للإصلاح، أو التعديل، أو التبديل، أو إزالة الخلل، أو تحقيق الأفضل، أو التغيير، أو التحسين، أو التكييف، أو الضبط، أو اللصق، أو التطوير، أو التأمين، أو الترميم، أو التجديد، أو الابتكار، أن يكون للكون تدابيره الحمائية الخاصة به ومنطقه في استدامة التوازن، الذي يتجاوز أفعال وقدرات البشر.

إن خلخلة التوازن بشكل منتظم والتسبب في اضطراب آليات هذا التوازن المستدام سوف يطغى على قدرة الكون على تعديل وتكييف ذاته بذاته. وعليه، إن كنا سنشير إلى قانون نيوتن الثالث- بأن لكل فعل رد فعل مساو له بالمقدار ومعاكس له بالاتجاه- فإن توارينا (وليس خلاصنا) من غضب الأرض سيكون من خلال أن نفعل كل ما في وسعنا لإرجاء النهاية، منكرين ما أشار إليه بودريار بأنها "ذروة المتعة"، وآملين الخلاص من نبوءة نهاية الكون.

القيّمون

السياق البيئي

محمد كاظم

يتزايد عدد سكان الكرة الأرضية في الزمن الحاضر بشكل مطّرد يومياً، ويتزايد استنزاف الموارد والمواد الخام الطبيعية في العالم يوماً بعد يوم، والتي لم تعد تكفي لسد حاجة الإنسان على هذا الكوكب "الأرض". جميع الكائنات الحية، الصغيرة منها والكبيرة، أصيبت بالإنهاك بسبب الحروب وعدم الاستقرار السياسي والاقتصادي على المستوى العالمي، والمخزون الاحتياطي للطاقة الطبيعية في تناقص مستمر. الجو العام للبيئة ملوّث، الأمراض بأنواعها وأشكالها وبمسمياتها المختلفة لا تصيب الإنسان فقط، وإنما الحيوانات والطيور والأسماك. وحتى الحديد والنحاس وغيرها من المواد الطبيعية مهددة. البحار، الغابات، الوديان، والأنهر جميعها ملوّثة، وحتى الغيوم والأمطار. ولا تقتصر المشاكل البيئية على سطح الكرة الأرضية، وإنما وصلت الأمور إلى تأكسد فكري للدماغ البشري، بمعنى أن هناك مستويات ذهنية تختلف من فرد إلى آخر، ولا يمتلك الجميع القدرة على هضم واستيعاب الأمور الفكريه والثقافية التي تؤثر على البيئة السياسية، والاجتماعية والاقتصادية في المجتمع، أي مدى قدرة الفرد على طرح مواضيع ذاتية، ومدى قدرة المؤسسات الاجتماعية بمختلف فروعها تحويل هذه الذاتية إلى إنجاز اجتماعي. عدا عن تلوث الفضاء والغلاف الجوي بالصور والمعلومات والأحاديث والخطابات والأخبار الكاذبة والرخيصة. وهي تسبح في الفضاء الخارجي وتأتينا كالعفاريت ليلاً ونهاراً.

من المعروف أن الطبيعة، "كوكب الأرض"، هي مصدر الثروة كلها، ومليئة بمواد وأماكن مختلفة، ثمة أماكن نحبها ونزورها ونعطيها الصفة الشرعية باعتبارها أماكن طاهرة، ونقدسها لأغراض دينية، نحافظ عليها ونحبها ونزينها بالذهب والأحجار الكريمة والروائح الطيبة، وندافع عنها ونحارب من أجلها ونقترب منها. وثمة أماكن أخرى على كوكب الأرض قاسية في صرامتها ومخيفة، وهي أيضاً جزء من تكوين الطبيعة الذي لا مفرّ منه، كالجبال العالية، والشلالات، والصحاري الخالية من النباتات والماء، والحُمَم البركانية، والأماكن الكثيرة الزلازل والفيضانات، نحاول قدر الإمكان الابتعاد عنها وتجنبها. نقوم بتدمير بعض الأماكن في هذه البيئة الطبيعية التي نعيش فيها مثل الجبال، الهضاب، الوديان والشواطئ الطبيعية وغيرها لغرض بناء إنشاءات جديدة، مثل الأبراج العالية، الموانيء، والمزارع المزودة بالأجهزة الحديثة والمدن العصرية ومنشآتها الجديدة، لكي نتحمل الحياة المعاصرة. مثلما نقوم بتفكيك بيئة العادات والأساطير القديمة في الانثروبولوجيا المحيطة بالإنسان عن طريق دراسة أصل الجنس البشري، تطوره، أعراقه، سلالاته، عاداته وتقاليده ومعتقداته، ونقوم بصياغتها من جديد لنتحمل نقد الذات ولخلق علاقة متبادلة مع البيئة التي نعيش فيها، ونقوم بتفسير جميع الأمور البيئية بلغة وسياق القيم العصرية والخبرات الإنسانية الجديدة، ندرس علم "التبيُّؤ" لمعرفة العلاقات بين الكائنات الحيّة وبيئتها.

يمتلك محيط كوكب الأرض في فحواه الحياة، والموت، واللحظات الجميلة، واللحظات الكئيبة. نعيش نحن وجميع الكائنات الأخرى في ريعان شبابنا وفيما بعد نموت ونتعفن في جوف هذا الكوكب الأم، نطمح إلى ترك آثارنا ونقوشنا، نحفر ونكتب على سطح هذا الكوكب ملاحظاتنا وإيماءاتنا وأمنياتنا وندمجها مع المشاهد الطبيعية، وبالرغم من كل ذلك، نقوم بانتهاك فضاء هذه البيئة التي وجدنا أنفسنا فيها.

منذ بداية القرن العشرين حتى الآن ظهر أكثر من خمسين مدرسة أو مذهب فني أو أسلوب فكري ثقافي تنتهي مصطلحاتها بحروف "ism"، هل حققت هذه "الإيزمات" بيئة مناسبة لحياة الفرد والكائنات الحيّة الأخرى؟ هل الانزواء والجلوس في ورشة العمل المغلقة والانهماك في رسم لوحة لمشهد مأساوي عن الحالة الحاضرة ينقذ الإنسانية من الهلاك؟

موضوع البيئة موضوع متشعب جداً ومعقد، هناك بيئة سياسية، اقتصادية، نفسية، صحية، تجارية، استهلاكية، هكذا نعيش في فضاءات بيئية مختلفة ومحفوفة بالمخاطر "Risky environment". هل نتوقع "أحداثا بيئية جديدة"؟ هل بإمكان السياق الفني المعاصر أن يخلق "بيئة ملائمة" "Risky environment"؟ الإجابة على جميع هذه الأسئلة تكمن في أن البيئة هي المجازفة والخوض في عملية التجربة نفسها، واختيار البيئة قصداً "للمهمات جمالية معاصرة".

بين القرنين الثامن عشر والتاسع عشر نشطت الابتكارات التكنولوجية والتي كانت تهدف إلى تخفيف أعباء إنسان ذلك الزمان، وتكمن هذه الابتكارات في كل من الآلات البخارية، الكهرباء والقطار وغيره. وتطور خطاب ومفهوم الإنسان في ذلك الزمان تماما، استجابة للتغير الاجتماعي الجديد وظهور أفكار جديدة في تاريخ البشرية، وأصبح العمل الفني يتوافق مع العلوم الأخرى.

ولا يتحقق ذلك دون أن نكافح بجهد وإدراك التلوّث الثقافي السائد في المجتمع عن طريق إعادة النظر في المناهج التعليمية، لأن السلطة التعليمية هي التي تُقرر مستقبل الأجيال القادمة. ومن أجل أن تكون الاجيال القادمة مهيئة لاستقبال كل جديد، لا بد من تطوير المؤسسات الثقافية والتربوية وادخال الخطاب الثقافي للفن المعاصر في المناهج التعليمية وتقديم الفنون التي تتميز بالمعاصرة وتواكب الزمن الحاضر.

مستعدون لارتفاع حرارة الأرض؟[1]

إيفا شارير

لا يخلو تنظيم بينالي حول موضوع "الفن والبيئة" في الإمارات العربية المتحدة من المفارقة، أو على الاقل تحد ما. فالتغير المناخي العالمي لم يعد مجرد نبوءة مستقبلية، حيث حلّ، ومنذ فترة طويلة، محلّ الإرهاب العالمي في العناوين العريضة للصحف، كونه التهديد والخطر الجديد الكبير الذي يواجهه العالم اليوم. ولعلّ احدث البراهين الرسمية الأخيرة على ذلك، هو ظهور ونشر التقرير المناخي الصادر عن اللجنة الحكومية حول التغير المناخي التابعة للأمم المتحدة في الثاني من شباط ٢٠٠٧. ينظّم البينالي في مكان شيّد أساساً من الصحراء، في مكان يعتمد اقتصاده، كما ثروته، اعتماداً رئيساً على الوقود، وفي مكان بالقرب منه وفي دبي، تحديداً، تنشط حركة العمل والعمال في إنشاء العمارات العملاقة والضخمة، دون أي حساب لعواقب مثل هكذا تدخل في النظم البيئية. فلماذا الاهتمام بالأرض إذا كنت تستطيع بناء أرض أخرى؟[2] هذا، دون أن نغفل الكم المتزايد من السفر الجوّي من أجل الفن، وبخاصة في سنة تشهد أنشطة ثقافية ضخمة مثل بينالي موسكو، وبينالي فنيسيا، ودوكيومينتا Documenta 12، ومشاريع النحت في Munster، وبينالي استانبول، بالإضافة إلى بيناليات ومعارض فنية أخرى لا تعد ولا تحصى في هذا السباق العالمي المحموم وغير المسبوق الذي يشهده عالم الفن. ولقد اشتركت مؤخراً أنا نفسي، وكنتيجة لزياراتي الميدانية للشارقة، في "المسافر الدائم"، وعليّ أن أعترف هنا أني شعرت بالذنب لهذا الاشتراك. فالمعضلة إذن، تكمن في أيدينا نحن، ومن الواضح أنه لا يمكن لنا مواجهتها بالنوايا الحسنة فقط. أو، بعبارات أخرى: كيف لنا أن نشكل مفهوم الوعي البيئي، وأكاد أزعم أننا جميعاً نحمل هذا الوعي في مكان ما، كيف لنا أن نشكل هذا المفهوم بفرح الفن المعاصر، وشكوكه الناقدة، وجمالياته؟

لقد ألقت مؤخرا العديد من المعارض الضوء على مختلف النواحي التي ينخرط فيها الفن في الهموم البيئية. من هذه المعارض: "أعمال أرضية: التعاون البيئي في الفن المعاصر" في جامعة كارنيجي ميلون في بيتسبيرغ حيث عرضت أعمال فنية ك "حالات دراسية في التغير الاجتماعي والبيئي،" و"ما هو أبعد من الأخضر، نحو فنّ مستدام" في متحف سمارت للفن في شيكاغو الذي يستكشف الاستراتيجيات المستدامة في الفن والتصميم المعاصرين، بالتركيز على الأعمال المشتركة والمجتمعية. وتحت عنوان Ecotopia أو طوباوية بيئية، عرض ترينالي ICP الثاني للتصوير الفوتوغرافي والفيديو في نيويورك رؤى بعض الفنانين المعاصرين للعالم الطبيعي في مناخ من التغيير. وفي معرض السفينة - فن التغير المناخي" في متحف الحياة الطبيعية في لندن، دعيت مجموعة من الفنانين لرحلة إلى الكتل الجليدية الآخذة بالذوبان في القطب المتجمد في قاعدة كيب فيرويل Cape Farewell؛ وقد نظمت جميع هذه المعارض عام ٢٠٠٥/٢٠٠٦. ومؤخراً، نظم معرض بعنوان "أكثر من هذا: أصوات وتعبيرات حول الاستدامة" في جاليري KIT في النرويج، وذلك بهدف استكشاف دور الفن وعلاقته مع التنمية المستدامة. بالإضافة إلى ذلك، ثمة مبادرات مثل برنامج الفنون والبيئة، الذي تنفذه الجمعية الملكية البريطانية لتشجيع الفنون RSA والذي جمع بين الفنانين والعلماء لمناقشة إمكانية تطوير ممارسات بيئية واجتماعية مسؤولة في مجالات الفن، والهندسة المعمارية، والتخطيط الحضري، من خلال ندوات ومنشورات في هذا الإطار.[3]

ويبقى السؤال: هل يمكن للفن أن ينقذ الكوكب؟ وهو العنوان الرئيس

[1] هذا العنوان مأخوذ من حملة دعائية لملابس من ماركة ديزل والتي، للمفارقة، تعرض موضة الهيبيين في فترة التغير المناخي.

[2] لجزر "العالم" وحدها في الجبهة المائية لدبي، هناك بليون متر مكعب من الرمل يتم العمل على إزالتها الآن، وجبال بأكملها تحمل وتزاح من جانب ما من البلاد إلى جانب آخر. إقرأ أيضاً مايك ديفيز، الفردوس المشؤوم، ٢٠٠٥

[3] مؤتمر الفنون والبيئة الذي نظمته RSA بعنوان "لا عودة إلى الوراء؟" وقد عقد في كلية لندن للاقتصاد في كانون الأول ٢٠٠٦، والذي أعلن فيه أيضاً عن صدور كتاب: الأرض، الفن: كتيب بيئي ثقافي، تحرير ماكس آندروز ومن منشورات RSA بالشراكة مع مجلس الفنون في إنجلترا، لندن ٢٠٠٦. وسينظم الجزء الثاني من المؤتمر في الجامعة الأمريكية في الشارقة بالتعاون مع RSA، لندن، وLatitudes، برشلونة في نيسان ٢٠٠٧

الذي تصدر الصفحة الأولى من إصدار شهر آب في العام الماضي من مجلّة مراجعة الفن Art Review، وهو الإصدار الذي عرف أيضاً بالعدد الأخضر. ومن الأمور الملفتة فعلاً، هو هذه الموجة من شعبوية البيئة أو موضة البيئة، التي اكتسحت وسائل الإعلام في الفترة الأخيرة.[٤] بعد أن كان موضوع البيئة ينازع ويحتضر على هامش الاهتمام الاجتماعي لفترة طويلة. وبعد أن تصدرت الاستدامة الاهتمام في التصميم، قامت مجلات عديدة في الموضة الراقية وأسلوب الحياة المتميز مثل مجلات Elle, Vogue, Vanity Fair، بإطلاق "عددها الأخضر" كذلك عام ٢٠٠٦. لذا، إذا كان السياسيون واختصاصيو البيئة قد أخفقوا في إنقاذ الكون حتى الآن، فقد تفلح مجموعات الموضة الضاغطة، أو ما يعرف بلوبي الموضة، في ذلك، لأنها تمتلك أفضل الحجج والآراء . كما جاء في التحليل المرير لعالِم المستقبل بروس ستيرلنج Bruce Sterling.[٥]

وبغض النظر عن مدى شعبية ورواج أو عدم شعبية هذا الموضوع، فإنه ما زال موضوعاً جادّاً. وللأسف، فالاحتمال الأكبر للجواب على السؤال أعلاه، هو "لا، لسوء الحظ". ولكن، حتى وإن لم يغير الفن بالضرورة الطريقة التي يتصرف بها البشر - ونحن لسنا مؤهلين لنقول لهذا أو ذاك ما هو الصح وما هو الخطأ - إلا أنه يبقى الأقدر على استنهاض فكرهم والتسلل إلى تفكيرهم. كما أننا نود أن نؤمن بدور الفن كمحفّز للفهم العاطفي، فهو بمثابة الشرارة والوسيلة الكفيلة بوضع الإطار اللازم للتجربة البصرية و/أو الاجتماعية.[٦]

لقد أصبحت ممارسة الفن المعاصر عبارة عن حقل عملي يتسع باطراد، وهو متعدد المذاهب كما هو متعدد العلوم. بالإضافة إلى أنه بحد ذاته، يحمل كمية من التنوع كما في الفهم الثقافي لمصطلح "بيئة" أو إيكولوجيا بمعناه الجمعي، وهو المعنى الذي اكتسبته في العقود الماضية. ويفرّق الفيلسوف الفرنسي، والناشط والمحلل النفسي فيليكس غوتاري، في عمله البيئات الثلاث بين البيئة الطبيعة، والاجتماعية، والعقلية.[٧] وهو نطاق يتراوح من المستوى الكلّي إلى المستوى الجزئي، والذي من الممكن أن يتوسع بشكل أكبر ليشمل حقولاً أخرى مثل البيئة السياسية، والثقافية... الخ. فالتلوث ليس فقط غازا منبعثا في الهواء، إنه يسكن في ويؤثر على كافة جوانب وجودنا الإنساني. وبشكل مماثل، يشير الفنان يواكيم كوستر Joachim Koester، إلى مساهمته في بينالي الشارقة الثامن وهي عبارة عن فيلم يعتمد على رسومات متحركة متفرقة من أعمال هنري ميشو باعتبارها "بيئة العقل"، على أنها رحلة إلى أقاصي العالم الداخلي. وبالإضافة إلى خرق مفهوم البيئة (الايكولوجيا)، فإن مفهوم "البيئية" و"البيئة" بحد ذاتهما يتعرضان للتساؤل والتحدي.

لقد تم تفكيك مفاهيم "الطبيعة" و"البيئة". إلا أنها ما تزال تحتفظ بقوتها الميثولوجية والمضعضِعة ضمن الحركة البيئية وما بين الجمهور العام. وإذا فهمنا فكرة "البيئة" على انها تشمل الإنسان، نجد أن طريقة تسمية المجتمع البيئي لبعض المشاكل على أنها بيئية والبعض الآخر على أنها ليست بيئية أمرا اعتباطيا. لماذا، على سبيل المثال، تصبح ظاهرة صنعها الإنسان مثل ارتفاع حرارة الكرة الأرضية والتي قد تتسبب في مقتل مئات الملايين من البشر خلال القرن القادم مشكلة بيئية؟ لماذا لا نعتبر الفقر والحرب مشاكل بيئية بينما ارتفاع حرارة الكرة الأرضية تعتبر كذلك؟[٧]

وقد ذكر جوستاف متزجر في عام ١٩٩٢ أن مصطلح "البيئي" يعني في يومنا هذا "كل شيء ولا شيء"، ما يجعل من الأفضل لنا التخلّي عنه مقابل الحصول على تعريفات أكثر تحديداً.[٩] باختصار، نحن نواجه فوضى ناتجة عن مصطلحات متداخلة ذات معان متعددة، ومفاهيم مرتبكة، وأيديولوجيات فاشلة، بالإضافة إلى الظاهرة الحديثة المتمثلة في "مناصرة الأخضر" أو

٤ مثال واحد فقط وهو فيلم آل غور بعنوان الحقيقة غير الملائمة والذي أعتقد أن الجميع قد شاهده على متن الطائرة مما يجعل المفارقة مكتملة وتامة.

٥ بروس ستيرلنغ، اتجاهات ساخنة: *Climate Change in the Glossies* في: الأرض، الفن: كتيب بيئي ثقافي، المصدر نفسه ص. ١١١-١١٥

٦ استعير هذا التعبير من لوسي ليبارد، ما هو أبعد من قطعة الجمال، في: الأرض، الفن: كتيب بيئي ثقافي، المصدر نفسه، ص. ١٤

٧ فيلكس جاتاري، البيئات الثلاث، لندن (٢٠٠٠) أيضاً للإطلاع: "إحتمالات البيئة متعددة الأنظمة"، ورقة مقدمة في الجمعية الملكية للفنون، لندن، ٢٧ نيسان ٢٠٠٥

٨ مايكل شلنبيرجر وتد نوروس، موت البيئة، سياسة الإحماء الكوني في عالم ما بعد البيئة، ٢٠٠٤، www.thebreakthrough.org

٩ يقترح جوستاف متزجر إسقاط مصطلح "بيئة" والحديث بدلاً عنه عن "الطبيعة" و"الطبيعة المدمرة/الخربة" كما جاء في مقاله الطبيعة الميتة تنبعث على شكل بيئة، في العمل الموسوم: جوستاف متزجر: الطبيعة المدمرة، الفن الذاتي التدمير، لندن ١٩٩٦، وقد استخدم اقتباس منه هنا كتصريح للفنان.

"الغسيل الأخضر". بينما نحن نواجه وضعا عالمياً يشير فيه عقرب الساعة الافتراضية إلى خمس دقائق قبل الثانية عشرة. أو لربما. تجاوز هذا العقرب ساعة الصفر فعلاً؟!

ربما تتكون لدى الفنانين القدرة على تناول الأشياء بطريقة مختلفة في هذه الأوقات التي تشهد انفعالات شديدة وتعطيلاً للتغيير الجذري من قبل السياسيين المشهود لهم بالعناد. بالإضافة إلى اللاعبين بحبال السلطة العالمية والمجموعات الضاغطة المناصرة لهم. ويمكن للفن. ومن خلال الوسائل الكامنة فيه. بغض النظر عن محدوديتها. أن ينتهج في بعض الأحيان الطريق المختصر بالالتفاف حول الحواجز المؤسسية أو حتى الانزلاق والتسرب من بينها. ويمكنه في الوقت ذاته. توظيف العلم دون أن يثقل بصرامته وتشدده. أو ربما. يمكنه الإبطاء من خطوته من خلال طرح معنى شعري. أو ربما العصيان الشعري. ضد أساليب الاقتصاد العالمي. فالأمر هنا لا يتعلق بتقديم حلول مؤقتة لإنقاذ الكوكب. وإنما بخلق صورة وتجربه ملائمة لتهذيب حساسية علاقتنا بالأرض وتأثيرنا عليها. متذكرين دوماً الأبعاد الاجتماعية. والسياسية. والاقتصادية. والعقلية لل "بيئة".

وعليه. هل سيتمكن بينالي الشارقة الثامن تحت عنوان "طبيعة صامتة: الفن والبيئة. وسياسات التغيير" من أن يكرس نفسه "البينالي الأخضر". وهي الفكرة التي طرحتها بعض المجلات؟ أشك في ذلك. فعلاً. في الحقيقة. قد تبدو الأمور أحيانا عكس ذلك تماما. والنشطاء البيئيون الجديون سيخالفوننا الرأي في الأرجح. فكما أن نموذج الطبيعة الصامتة في تاريخ الفن هو تذكرة الموت memento mori بقدر ما هو مديح لعطايا الطبيعة. يأتي عنوان بينالي الشارقة الثامن ليلقي بظلال معناه على قراءات متعددة واحدة. وإذا اعتبر الفن مرآة المجتمع. فقد لا يكون هذا البينالي ذاتي التدمير. أو ملوِّثا بما فيه الكفاية ليؤدي هذه الوظيفة.

بالطبع. هذه فكرة نظرية. وفعليا. تجدنا- نحن المنظمون والقيّمون على البينالي - نتحمل مسؤولية معينة عندما نتناول مثل هذا الموضوع الجدّي. الذي يحمل لنا المخاطر والحساسيات الفعلية في آن معاً. فبعض المسائل والقضايا مثل الاستدامة. يجب أن تكون مجرّد أفكار رئيسة في كل خطوة من خطوات التكوين. والإنتاج والنقل. وليس فقط فيما يتصل ببينالي الشارقة الثامن. وإنما لجميع المتاحف. والمعارض الفنية. و البيناليات على حد سواء. وحتى كل شركة وكل إنسان منذ الآن فصاعداً. دون أدنى شك. فإن الأمر يتطلب انعطافة ١٨٠ درجة ويشكل تحديا كبيرا حين تعمل ضمن ظروف معدة مسبقا وضمن إطار زمني محدد. وعليه. يثير هذا النفر العديد من الفنانين المختارين وكذلك المشاريع. أسئلة دون أن يسعفوننا بحلول. أو لعل في هذا الاختيار ما يعطينا إجابات على أسئلة لم نعبّر عنها بعد!

تتراوح المشاريع التي تم التعاقد عليها لبينالي الشارقة الثامن من الطوباوي إلى المقلق. ومن المستتر إلى الاحتفالي. ومن الإيماءة السريعة الزوال إلى الكتلة الحرجة. تنطلق إلى الغيوم. وتغوص في اعماق البحر. ومن خلال استراتيجيات التفكيك والتلويث. وبتطبيق الابحاث. وأساليب ناشطة وتوثيقية. وأيضاً من خلال استخدام الاستعارة. والدعابة. واللعب. يعلّق الفنانون المختارون على طرقنا في الإنتاج والاستهلاك. كما يلقون الضوء على بعض السخافات اليومية التي يعيش فيها مجتمع اليوم.

لم يكن من السهل أبداً اختيار الفنانين للتعامل مع هذا الموضوع المفروض على البينالي. والذي يشكل في الوقت ذاته تحد كبير لا يقبل أنصاف الحلول. كانت ثمة خيارات واضحة وأخرى أقل وضوحاً. بعض الفنانين الذين تمت دعوتهم إلى بينالي الشارقة الثامن عمد إلى تناول مسائل معينة. مثل

تدمير الطبيعة، وإعادة التدوير، والاستدامة، والنظم البيئية، والاقتصاديات العالمية على مدى وقت طويل، ومن خلال مختلف الاستراتيجيات والمحاور، وإن لم تكن لدى أيّ من هؤلاء الرغبة في أن يصنف بالضرورة على أنه فنان "بيئي" أو "اخضر." وفي حين أن العديد منهم قد عمل في حقل موسع على تقاطعات الفن، والفعالية، والتصميم، كان الهدف من هذا البينالي، وكما هو واضح، التركيز على العمل الفني الفردي، بدلا من أن يكون معرضا للطاقة البديلة، أو الحدائق المجتمعية، أو التصميم المستدام أو أساليب البناء الجديدة. نحن نعي بأن هناك بعض المحاولات الفنية الفردية والجماعية (مجموعات مثل الارض الحرة Free Soil، ومزارعو المستقبل Futurefarmers، والمجموعة التعليمية Learning Group، سوبر فلاكس Super Flux، والمساحة الابداعية فيتامين Vitamin Creative Space) والمعنية بالقضايا البيئية ولكنها ليست ممثلة في هذا البينالي، والسبب في ذلك أنهم عرضوا أعمالهم في بعض المعارض والمنشورات المذكورة سابقا.

وعلى الرغم من أن الضرورة حتّمت استثناء العديد من الحركات الفنية السالفة والتاريخية التي ظهرت في الستينيات والسبعينيات هنا، إلا أن مسار الممارسة الفنية المعنية بالبيئة، يعود حتى إلى أزمان ما قبل البيئية. وفي هذا المقام، وعندما نتحدث عن الحركات الفنية السالفة والتاريخية، فإنني أتحدث عن فن الأرض، وفنانين مثل روبرت سمثسون، ورتشارد لونغ، وجوردن متى-كلارك، وجوزيف بويز، أو هانس هاك.

ويجيء فنان مثل جوستاف متزجر، والذي قام بتطوير مصطلح "الفن الذاتي التدمير" وهو بحكم التعريف، عبارة عن "شكل من الفن العام للمجتمعات الصناعية"[١٠] ليكون عام ١٩٥٩ فعلاً بمثابة الجواب على الظروف التي سادت بعد الحرب والحرب الباردة في وقته، وهو ما يبدو في يومنا هذا بمثابة النبوءة. كما أنجزت ميرل ليدرمان أوكلز عملها بعنوان "طقس تعقيم لمسة المصافحة باليد" Touch Sanitation Handshake Ritual، وجهت فيه الشكر الشخصي إلى كل عمال النظافة في مدينة نيويورك لإبقائهم مدينة نيويورك على قيد الحياة في الفترة ما بين عامي ١٩٧٧ - ١٩٨٠، وما زالت مندمجة في قضايا العمالة واستخدام مكب النفايات.

أما بيتر فند - وهو الذي أنشأ مؤسسة تطوير المحيط والأرض عام ١٩٨٠- فقد عمل ومنذ ذلك الحين، على تكريس أبحاثه المستمرة والمعمّقة للمياه والموارد الطبيعية في حوض الخليج. أما الفنان دان بيترمان والذي يعيش في شيكاغو، فقد عمل أيضاً على تطوير أعمال فنيّة ملتزمة بيئيا واجتماعيا منذ بدايات الثمانينيات من القرن العشرين، وكان مؤثراً على جيل من الشباب اليافعين مثل تو جرينفورت، الذي يجيب على تماسكات اقتصادية وبيئية بإيماءات تحليلية لعوبة، وبسيطة، لا تخلو من الحدة. كما أن مفاهيم الطاقة والأنتروبيا هي أفكار مركزية في العمل الشعري-المفاهيمي الذي أنجزه سايمون ستارلنغ، والذي طرح فيه رحلة انكفاء ذاتي باستخدام القارب تسير باتجاه تحقيق الفكرة الرئيسية لبينالي الشارقة الثامن. ويعمل الفنانون مارجتيكا بوترك، ومايكل راكوفيتز، وتوماس ساراسينو على تقاطعات الفن، والتصميم، والهندسة المعمارية: أعمال بوترك تركز على الاستدامة الذاتية والعمل الميداني، ويعمل راكوفيتز على توأمة الهندسة المعمارية مع الحقيقة التاريخية وتدفق الهواء المحسوس كاستعارات للعبة القوى السياسية والاقتصادية. أما ساراسينو، فيتبع رؤى الأيديولوجيين المعماريين، مثل بكمنستر فولر، لإنشاء سيناريوهات طوباوية - وإن كانت ممكنة في نهاية المطاف - لحياة مستقبلية في المكان.

ويركز كل من هاكانسون، وإلينا هالبرن على مختلف نواحي العالم

[١٠] جوستاف متزجر، الفن الذاتي التدمير، لندن، ٤ تشرين الثاني، ١٩٥٩، نشر في: جوستاف متزجر، كتالوج متحف الفن الحديث، أوكسفورد، ١٩٩٩، ص. ٢٦

الطبيعي - هاكانسون من خلال بحثه الدقيق والشعري في الوقت ذاته. في مصير السلالات المهددة بالانقراض وظروف الحياة التي يحيكها لها الإنسان، وهالبرن من خلال انشغالها الشخصي المعمق والذي يكاد يكون انشغالاً حميماً بالجيولوجيا - في حين أن لارا آلمارسيغي تستكشف وتوثّق فضاءات غير معرّفة في هذا الاضطراب الذي تشهده المسطحات الأرضية الحضرية.

وقد قمنا بدعوة فنانين آخرين، ومجموعات فنية أخرى للمشاركة في الموضوع والسياق المحلي للشارقة. وخلال زياراتهم وجولاتهم، التي كانت بالنسبة لمعظمهم هي الأولى إلى هذا الجزء من العالم-قد قرر أحدهم وبكامل وعيه أن يقوم بهذه الرحلة دون أن يصعد إلى متن الطائرة- ظهرت بعض المشاريع التي لا تخلو من الإثارة، والتي لا تعالج موضوع البحث من الوجهة الخارجية المعولمة وحسب، بل أنها انشغلت بالمدينة، وببنيتها التحتية، ومحيطها، ومجتمعاتها المحلية المتعددة، طارحة إيّاها كحقل واسع للبحث والتجربة. فيستخدم كل من جيردا شتاينر ويورغ لنزلنغر منتجات الفضلات الناتجة في محطة تحلية المياه الموجودة في الشارقة لخلق حديقة ملح خلابة، ويقوم جيسوس بوبو نيغرون بدفن قارب صيد قديم في رمل الصحراء، وتصور لوكا فيتون المدينة وبيئتها من خلال تلك الخطوط التي استقرّت لأشهر طويلة على أقمشة اللوحات الزيتية. أما دان بيتروفتشي، فيقوم بخربشة تعليقاته المرحة واللاذعة في الوقت ذاته على الجدران معتمداً على ملاحظاته الخاصة والأخبار اليومية. وأخيراً، هناك مجموعة الفنانين e-Xplo (بالتعاون مع آيرين أناستاس) الذين يرفعون صوتهم عاليا للتعبير عن العمال الذين يقومون بسواعدهم ببناء الإمارات لتصل إلى ما وصلت إليه اليوم، وهم يرفعون هذا الصوت من خلال جميع أغانيهم وأشعارهم، والتي تشيع بمختلف اللغات المستخدمة في هذا البلد.

وبينما أقوم بطباعة هذا المقال، ما زالت التجربة مستمرة، وثمة صعوبات ما زالت تستدعي المعالجة، وثمة حدود عديدة ما زالت تحتاج إلى الالتفاف حولها. لقد أثبتت التجربة حتى الآن، أنها تجربة التعلم والتفاوض المستمرين، وهذه العملية التي تترك نفسها مفتوحة على مختلف الاحتمالات، قد أهملت جميع المخاطر التي تتضمنها، وساعدت فعلاً على إثراء خبرتي وتجربتي، وهذا ما أرجو أن يكون عليه الحال بالنسبة لجميع الأطراف الأخرى المعنية بها.

هكذا، إذن، يمكننا أن ننظر إلى هذا البينالي على أنه استعارة للنظام البيئي بحد ذاته، نظام تتفاعل فيه مختلف المناهج ولربما، تتحاور وتتناظر مع بعضها البعض، ولكنها في نهاية المطاف، تنجو وتنجح بشكل عام، وهذا هو المرتجى!

وفي النهاية، ورغم كل شيء، لن نصل إلى تقليل كمية الكربون المنبعث في الهواء من خلال هذا البينالي. بدلا من ذلك، سنكون قد جمعنا آثارا كربونية لا بأس بها. ولن تساهم الأعمال الفنية المعروضة كثيرا في حل مشكلة ارتفاع حرارة الكرة الأرضية، ولن ترفع الظلم الاجتماعي، ولن تعيد تدوير نفسها. معظم هذه الأعمال سيتم تغليفها وشحنها إلى مكانها الأصلي، مثل الفنانين والقيّمين والضيوف الدوليين الذين سيركبون الطائرات ويتجهون إلى أماكن أخرى. لكننا نأمل أنهم سيحملون معهم بعض المشاهد التي، بالرغم من الضعف الظاهري للفن في مواجهة تحديات التغيير البيئي، إلا أنها قوية بما يكفي ليكون لها حياة تتخطى البينالي وتجعل الناس يفكرون أكثر بالأثر الذي يتركونه حين يتحركون على سطح هذا الكوكب.

اعترافات قَيِّم - ١ ديسمبر ٢٠٠٦

جوناثان واتكنز

أكتب هذا وأنا على متن طائرة بوينغ ٧٤٧، مسافرٌ من لندن إلى ميامي. لم أدفع ضريبة مقابل الغازات المنبعثة التي تشكل مساهمتي في ظاهرة ارتفاع حرارة الكوكب. أشرب عصير البندورة في كأس بلاستيكيّ، بعد أن أكلت وجبة شهيّة في علبة بلاستيكيّة ملفوفة بورق القصدير - وقد أصبح هذا الكأس والعلبة قمامة على طاولتي. وجبتي القادمة؟ ستؤكل على الأغلب بأدوات بلاستيكيّة في أوعية متعددة يتمّ التخلص منها، وتصاحبها أشياء مغلّفة أكثر، تشتمل على منديل وملح وفلفل ونكّاشة أسنان وسكّر ومنديل مرطِّب. سيتمّ إزالة ما لم أستهلكه عندما تنتهي هذه الوجبة. وعندها، ماذا سيحدث لهذه الأشياء؟ كما يتوقّع المرء في هذه الأوقات المستنيرة، يُعاد تدوير الكثير من الأشياء، ولكن يتنهي الأمر ببعضها في المكبّ بالتأكيد، أو تُحرق. لا أعرف ولن أستفسر عن هذا التفصيل بالذات في حياتي.

أنا أطير إلى ميامي لأنضمّ إلى نقاش طاولة مستديرة، مقدِّمة لبينالي الشارقة القادم. الموضوع: البيئة والفن المعاصر. طبعا لا تناقض بالأمر، على الأقل، أن أكون راكبا على الطائرة لتنظيم حدث كهذا - حقيقة لم تغب عن المنظمين - خاصة وأن المعرض سيقام في مدينة تزدهر على مدخولات النفط.

التناقض المضاعف هو أنّ الطيران الإماراتي، الذي أخذني مؤخّرا إلى الشارقة لزيارة الموقع، يعرض فيلم آل غور الإستثنائيّ، آن إنكونفينينت تروث (حقيقة غير مناسبة). كان الأمر بمثابة فريضة منزليّة إلى حدّ ما - فرصة لي لأراجع وأستذكر موضوعنا - ويشبه كثيرا مشاهدة اجتماع كنسيّ إحيائي. الصيغة والخطاب في آن إنكونفينينت تروث (حقيقة غير مناسبة) مألوفان للغاية، يغرسان شعورا بالذنب، في حين يقدِّم الغفران من خلال سلسلة من الوصايا في هيئة تلميحات بيئيّة سهلة تتوضّح عند نهاية الفيلم وظهور الأسماء. يميل غير - المنظمين، أمثالي، إلى الشعور بعدم الراحة عندما يكون التلاعب مكشوفا إلى هذه الدرجة، مهما كانت الرسالة صادقة. وخرجت من هذا الفيلم الترفيهي بقلق بلشفيّ متمرّد. طلبت شرابا آخر - زجاجة صغيرة من النبيذ الأحمر، مع وجبة مغلّفة أخرى وكأس بلاستيكيّ ومنديل - وعدت إلى روايتي ذات الغلاف الورقيّ، بوسيبيليتي أوف آن أيلند (إمكانيّة جزيرة) لميشيل هويليبيك.

يُلقي هويليبيك سحره بطرق تختلف كثيرا عن آل غور. أغلب شخصيّاته غير متعاطفة، وصفه للسلوك الإنحطاطي المنسوجة مع العلميّ المتخصص مصحوبة باحتكام إلى النزق. يتمثّل هذا النزق في نهاية بوسيبيليتي أوف آن أيلند (إمكانيّة جزيرة) في تشدق مرهف ضدّ "البيئيّة." يشخّص الحركة البيئيّة التي نشهدها الآن على أنها نتيجة دافع ماسوشي متديّن، مدفوع بالنكران أكثر منه تطبيق المنطق العام. رؤيته للمستقبل متشائمة، تتألّف من عالم تبخّرت فيه المحيطات إلى حدّ ما، وتتجوّل فيه أجيالنا القادمة مجموعات من الصيادين وحيث تعيش المنسوخات الإنسانيّة حياة من العقم.

أعترف أنني فضّلت كثيرا قراءة هويليبيك عن مشاهدة آل غور. لعلّ ذلك لأنّ هويليبيك يدعونا لتخيّل شئ ما بدل الإيمان به. بكلمات أخرى، قد يكون آل غور على حقّ، إلاّ أنّ هويليبيك يدفع بنا ويشدّنا من خلال الخيال لتفهّم أمور تتوازى مع التشكيك الفلسفي الذي يناسبني بشكل أكبر. وهذا برأيي ما يصنع الفن المعاصر الأفضل.

في هذا النسق، أفضَلُ المعارض الفنيّة هي غير التعليميّة. إنّها كحاورات، لا يتّفق فيها جميع المشاركين، على "رسالة" تصوّر وتوضّح أفكارهم. من الخطأ أن نتوقّع أن يكون بينالي الشارقة الثامن نموذجا للممارسة البيئيّة الصائبة. أيّ ادّعاءات كهذه ستواجه اتّهامات حتميّة بالنفاق، وأيّ هيئة متكاملة يتخذها البينالي سيناقضها عدد من الأعمال المشاركة في البينالي. تاريخ الفن ليس تاريخا للقدّيسين، وبالتالي أتأمّل في هذا الإطار بالذات، أن لا أكون الوحيد الراغب في الاعتراف بذلك.

هشام المظلوم

المنسق العام للبينالي

مدير إدارة الفنون، دائرة الثقافة والأعلام

تفعيل التواصل الاجتماعي والإنساني، وتعميق القواسم المشتركة التي تربط بين الإنسان في مشرق الأرض ومغربها، كان ومازال من الأولويات التي حققها الفن ومنذ فجر التاريخ.

إنه الرسالة التي تخاطب الجميع والتي تنطوي حروفها على اللغة الكونية التي تنتظر من يكتشفها في كل مرة ، حين تكون الأسئلة هي أسئلة الوجود والهاجس هو هاجس الإنسان.

ومنذ تأسيس البينالي كنا نحاول في دائرة الثقافة والإعلام وفي إدارة الفنون، أن نستقطب نوعية متميزة من الفنانين والمفكرين والتي تسمح بتعميق الرؤى الفكرية والجمالية وتتيح المجال للإطلاع على نتاجات تنطوي على قيم إبداعية كبيرة، ولعل البينالي عبر مسيرته، أخذت أهدافه تتسع، وطموحاته تزداد ورؤاه تتعمق وتتطور، بما يستجيب ويتماهى مع رؤية حضرة صاحب السمو الشيخ الدكتور سلطان بن محمد القاسمي عضو المجلس الأعلى للاتحاد حاكم الشارقة، في إيجاد روابط إنسانية وفكرية وإبداعية، بين مختلف الجنسيات وفي تحذير أفق معرفي يشترك في صياغته الجميع.

بهذا البعد الإنساني تجلى خطاب صاحب السمو الفكري، وبذلك العمق كانت توجيهات سموه دليلا لعملنا في الإعداد والتجهيز ومتابعة مختلف الفعاليات الفنية والثقافية، وخصوصاً بينالي الشارقة، والذي اكتسب أبعاداً جديدة منذ أن ترأسته سمو الشيخة حور القاسمي وربطته مع آخر التطورات في الفنون المعاصرة، واستطاعت أن تحقق له وجوداً مميزا بين مختلف البيناليات في العالم. ومما يشير إلى ارتباطها الوثيق بالقضايا الإنسانية والاجتماعية الملحة، هو تبني سموها في هذه الدورة لموضوعة البيئة التي تشكل ضرورة إنسانية، وحاجة جمالية والتي وجدت لها أرضاً خصبة في إمارة الشارقة، حيث البنية التحتية المناسبة والتوجيهات الحكيمة في الحفاظ على بيئة آمنة وتعدد المحميات الطبيعية والعديد من الهيئات المعنية بموضوع البيئة وكيفية الحفاظ عليها من استنزاف الموارد. وبالنظر إلى مختلف العوامل والظروف التي تؤثر على البيئة، من حروب وتصحّر واستهتار واستنزاف للموارد البشرية، وهذا ما يجعل البينالي تظاهرة إبداعية واجتماعية وإنسانية تدخل في نسيج القضايا الجوهرية التي يحاول الإنسان إيجاد الحلول لها، وتحاول أن تضيء عبر المشاريع الفنية والعروض المتنوعة، وعبر الورش والندوات الفكرية، بعض الجوانب المتعلقة بكيفية الحفاظ على البيئة وجعل سؤال البيئة هوالسؤال الذي نطرحه على أنفسنا يومياً وبشكل فاعل. فالبينالي يطرح موضوع البيئة وعلاقتها بالفن على اختلاف جوانبها، من بيئة بصرية، اجتماعية، ذهنية، طبيعية.... وبالتالي يصبح للبينالي العديد من المهام التي يؤديها في وقت واحد والتي تبقيه على صلة بالإنسان وهمومه وتطلعاته أينما وجد، وتعكس في الوقت نفسه بنيته كحالة فكرية وفنية متكاملة في جميع دوراتها بحيث تعبر عن رؤيته.

تصميم المعرض

منى المصفي

يهمني من المواقع، تلك التي تمتلك ميزة مدهشة على تكوين علاقة مع المواقع الأخرى، لكن بطريقة تشكّك، تحيّد، أو تخترع فيها، مجموعة من العلاقات التي تحيل إليها، أو تعكسها. هذه الفضاءات، المرتبطة بجميع الفضاءات الأخرى، والتي تناقضها في الوقت نفسه هي، نوعان رئيسيان. أولا هناك الطوباويات. ومن الأرجح أن يكون هناك في كل ثقافة، في كل حضارة، أماكن حقيقية - أماكن موجودة فعلا قد تشكلت لدى تأسيس المجتمع - تبدو كمواقع مضادة، نوع من الطوباوية المثبتة فعلياً حيث أن المواقع الحقيقية، كل المواقع الاخرى الحقيقية الموجودة في ثقافة ما تكون ممثلة ومتعارضة ومقلوبة في آن واحد.

ميشيل فوكو[1]

مقدمة

توجّه بينالي الشارقة الثامن، يطرح الفن كوسيلة لتشكيل فهم أفضل عن علاقتنا بالطبيعة والبيئة، آخذين بعين الاعتبار أبعادها الاجتماعية والسياسية والثقافية بشكل متداخل. وكتجاوب مع هذا التوجّه، نظرنا إلى البيئة كنظام للتعايش المشترك والتعاون. واخترنا تصميما للمعرض يعمل كحقل للتفاوض والتعاون ما بين الفاعلين المختلفين من الفنانين، والقيمين، والمصممين. لبينالي الشارقة الثامن ثلاثة مواقع رئيسيّة: متحف الشارقة للفنون، مركز إكسبو الشارقة، ومنطقة التراث. تم تطوير هذه الاستراتيجيات المشار اليها أعلاه بشكل أكثر تكاملا في مركز الاكسبو، حيث أنّ رحابة المساحة شكلت تحديا حقيقيا لكافة المعنيين. كان المفهوم المعماري لهذا المكان، متابعة للفضاء المديني الداخلي الذي بدأناه في بينالي الشارقة السابع، ولكن، بدلا من تكوين محاكاة نقية لقطعة مدينية مع مساحات مغلقة أو مفتوحة، قمنا بتطوير استراتيجيات موقع داخلي لا مركزي قابل للتفاوض.

استراتيجيات التفاوض

مفاهيم اللامركزية، التوزيع والتنظيم الذاتي مرتبطة بفكرة عن الحياة المدينية. وبتوليف ذلك مع تصميم المعرض، تم تطويرالسيناريو لإشراك الفنانين في القرارات المرتبطة باحتياجاتهم من الفضاء وتأثير أعمالهم عليه . ضمن هذا السيناريو، أصبح القيمون والمصممون مثل المجسات والوسطاء ما بين الفنانين الذين يساهمون في تصوير مساحاتهم الخاصة وفي علاقاتهم مع البنى المجاورة.

العناصر المعمارية

الاستراتيجيات أعلاه كانت مدعمة برؤية تكوينية مرنة تتحقق من خلال مشاركة الفنانين. تتجسد هذه المواقع، التي يتم التموضع فيها بحرية ونظام سهل، بواسطة مجموعة من الفواصل الجدارية السائبة . بعرض ٩ أمتار وارتفاع ٤.٥ أمتار وهي موزّعة بنظام مرن عبر خمسة مسارب واسعة بنفس العرض، بحيث يمكن رؤيتها من الواجهة. وتحدّد هذه المنصّات الأماكن حسب الحاجة بمقاييس مختلفة وبنسب إضاءة متفاوتة الحدة. وتم تركيب سطح من قطع من القماش المشدود شبه الشفاف بارتفاع ٩ أمتار عن

[1] مفهوم الهيتروتوبيا كان موضوع محاضرة قدّمها ميشيل فوكو عام ١٩٦٧ ونشرت عام ١٩٨٤ تحت عنوان "الفضاءات الأخرى" في الصحيفة الفرنسيّة "العمارة/الحركة/الإستمراريّة" رقم ٥ الصادرة في باريس، وترجم نصّ المحاضرة إلى الإنكليزيّة تحت عنوان "من فضاءات أخرى" في مجلّة دياكريتكس ١٦ رقم ١ عام ١٩٨٦ عن دارنشر جون هوبكنز الجامعيّة في ماريلاند.

سطح الأرض وببعد متر واحد عن هيكل السقف المعدني بحيث ينشر إضاءة النهار والإضاءة الكهربائية بشكل متسق. الفراغات بين قطع القماش تماثل المخطط على الأرض لكن مع بعض الإنزياح بحيث تسمح بتعليق سكك الإضاءة الإضافية، كما تسمح برؤية الهيكل المعدني للسقف.

حركة النسج

تتخذ الاستراتيجية المتعلقة بفضاء المعرض شكلها من خلال أدائها. يمكن للزوار أن يحددوا مسارهم، وعندما ينسجون طريقهم بحرية عبر فضاء المعرض يحسون بالبنية التشكيليّة المرنة للمخطط ويكتشفون مع كل انعطافة، طبقة جديدة من التراكيب. وبينما يسير الزائر نحو عمل تركيبي معين، يتحوّل المشهد البعيد المبعثر تدريجيّا إلى مشهد قريب محدّد وتصبح المشاهدة في بعض الأحيان، اندماجا كاملا في مساحة مغلقة جزئيّا أو كلّيا. وبذلك يتشكّل حول التراكيب المتباينة حقل من التوتر، والعلاقات والتساؤلات، وكل مشاهد يتفاعل بشكل مختلف مع الأعمال المألوفة والأقل إلفة، بينما يندمج مع مضمونها المعروف أو المتصوّر. اماّ الرؤية من فوق الجسور المعدنية المتعامدة مع العناصر المتموضعة بشكل حر على ارتفاع ٤، ٥ أمتار فوق مستوى الأرض، فهي تحيل إلى نسيج ضخم وهيكل شبكي، وتمكن الزائر من رؤية التراكيب في الاسفل، من زاوية واسعة أو محدّدة، وترسم له طريقا مباشرا يعود به إلى المدخل.

هيكل الصقالة

لربط الموقع مع سياق محيطه المديني، وهو عبارة عن موقع بناء محموم، استخدمنا نظام هيكل الصقالة كبنية اساسية للمعرض، مع تحريف استخدامه الأصلي، ويمكن رؤية الصقالات جزئيا فقط عبر حواف بعرض ١، ٢ متر للفواصل الجدارية السائبة. استأجرنا الصقالات من شركات المقاولات واستعرنا بعضها من المؤسسات العامة في الشارقة، في مساهمة بسيطة منا لنشر وعي صديق للبيئة، وإيماءة رمزية لعمليات البناء المحمومة في الخارج، ورغبة في استثارة فنّاني بينالي الشارقة الثامن للاسهام في مواقع مستقبليّة مختلفة.

الخلاصة

نشارك العديد من الفنانين المشاركين الوعي، بأن الهندسة المعمارية يمكن ان تقدم مساهمة من خلال توسيع نطاقها، نحو ما هو أبعد من العلاقة ما بين الشكلي والرمزي، بأن تتضمّن الأبعاد الاقتصادية والسياسية والاجتماعية والثقافية وتغنيها. اردنا عبر الاستراتيجات التعاونية المختلفة التي تبنيناها أن نجعل بينالي الشارقة الثامن مفتوحا على اللامركزية والتفاوض و حاولنا أن نتفاعل مع جانب محدد من موضوعة البينالي الطموحة.

مشهد عام لمجسم عروض بينالي الشارقة٨ في إكسبو الشارقة الذي يتضمن أماكن عرض الأعمال التركيبية والفيديو، الداخلية، وأماكن العرض المفتوحة. مجسم: ميس نافوخ. صورة: بلامن غالابوف

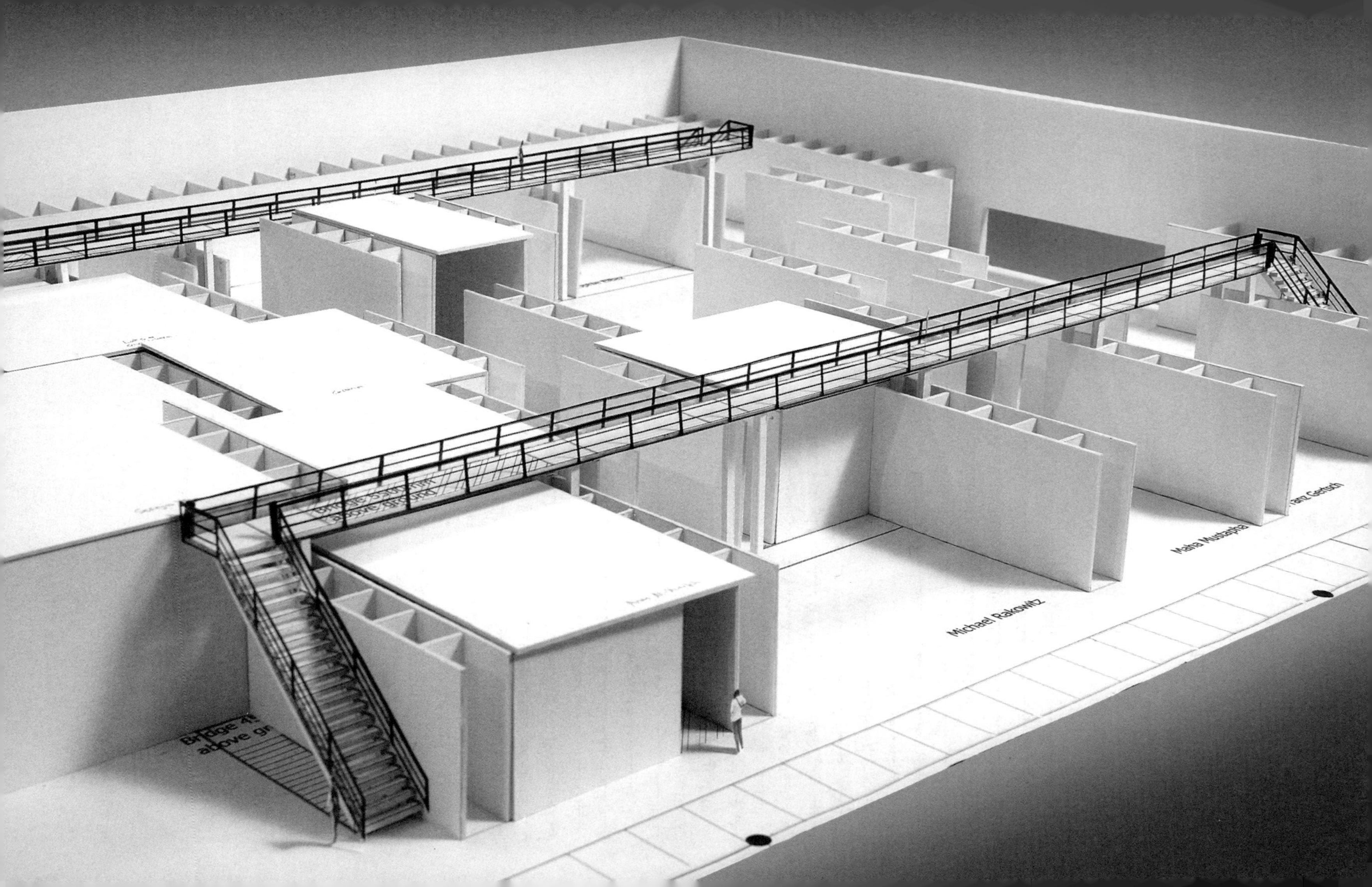
Michael Rakowitz
Maha Mustapha

نربي الأمل

سيرين حليلة
محررة كتالوج بينالي الشارقة ٨

نعيش في زمن المليون معيار، زمن الجماهير الغفيرة، حيث لا يتحدى أحد مقولة جورج أورويل الشهيرة: جميع الحيوانات متساوية، لكن بعض الحيوانات متساو أكثر من غيره. الفنانون هم الإثبات الوحيد بأنه يتبقى لنا، بعد أن تنجلي الرؤيا، بعض المبادىء التي لا يمكن إساءة تفسيرها أو قلبها: مثل قيمة الإنسان والحياة الإنسانية، وضرورة التفكير في المستقبل حين نتصرف اليوم.

المقالات وبيانات الفنانين الواردة في هذا الدليل، هي محاولة متواضعة لإضافة "المعرفة إلى السّلطة" قبل أن يترك الجمهور/القاريء/الفنان، مكان العرض. هناك الكثير من الاحتمالات المفتوحة للتساؤل والتأمل والنقد وإعادة التقييم. أن يكون لنا أثر، هذا هو خيار كل منا. قد يكون هذا الأثر سلبيا أو إيجابيا، لكن بما أننا ولدنا، وتمكنا، بمعجزة ما، من الاستمرار في الحياة، لا بد وأن نترك أثرا. هذه هي الفكرة الأساسية من المقالات وأعمال الفنانين في هذا البينالي. ما هو الأثر الذي نتركه؟ ما هي عواقب أعمالنا؟ فإذا لم تكن مرئية بالشكل الكافي، سنضخمها بشكل يفوق كافة المقاييس، كي لا يدعي أحد أنه لم يفهم أو لم ير أو لم يسمع. كيف يمكن لنا أن نقلل من الأذى الذي نسببه للبيئة، وكيف يمكن أن يكون تأثيرنا إيجابيا؟ هذا هو السؤال الأكبر، والذي تتم الإجابة عليه بأكثر من مائة طريقة وطريقة في هذا البينالي.

أن نحدث فرقا، هذه هي مسؤوليتنا، وهذا ما يقوله كل فرد يشكل جزءا من هذا البينالي. نريد أن نحدث فرقا، هذا هو سبب تواجدنا هنا، سواء أكان ذلك انطلاقا من مسؤوليتنا، أو واجبنا، أو حبنا في البقاء.

إذا أجرينا بحثا سريعا في الانترنت سنجد ما يلي: ٥٠ طريقة لإنقاذ الكوكب، ١٠١ طريقة، ١٢ طريقة، ١٠ طرق... ١٦ طريقة غير مؤلمة للمساعدة في إنقاذ الكوكب. تفترض كلها بالطبع، أنك تمتلك سيارة، بطاقة اعتماد، دوش، وأموالا كافية لتشتري بكميات كبيرة. من الواضح أن المسؤولية في التلويث وفي الإنقاذ تقع على عاتق الأغنياء. ما الذي يتوجب علينا نحن الباقين أن نفعله؟ توضح لنا بعض المقالات في هذا الدليل، إجابات توصل إليها الكتاب الذين يحاولون في الوقت الراهن أن يفحصوها في أجزاء مختلفة من القسم الجنوبي من عالمنا.

الطبيعة الصامتة، البيئة، والتزامنا لا يغطي فقط البيئة الطبيعية أو المادية، فنحن نركز في هذا البينالي أيضا، على الطاقة البشرية، والتي هي أهم مصدر متجدد للطاقة يتم استنفاذه بالطريقة التي نعيش فيها حياتنا، بالحروب والصراعات، بالسفر الدائم والقلق، بوسائل الإعلام والاحتلال بأشكاله المختلفة. وفي نهاية المطاف، إذا ما كانت هناك فعلا طرق عديدة لإنقاذ العالم، ما علينا سوى التركيز على ثلاثة: نفكر بالسّلم، نأخذ زمام المبادرة، ونربي الأمل.

الفنون والإدراك

منير فاشي

يبدأ نص البيان العام بأن بينالي الشارقة الثامن قد "اختار الموضوع الغامض حول علاقة الإنسان بالكرة الأرضية كمحور أساسي". يتضمن المحور كلمات سأناقشها في هذه المقالة: الغموض والإنسان والأرض والعلاقة بينها وبين الفنون. فالأيديولوجية المعاصرة السائدة تركّز على أهمية اليقين، وعلى السيطرة والمسار الأحادي للتقدم، بدلا من فن العيش مع الغموض والتعددية والحيوية. ويتضمن الإدراك ضمن الأيديولوجية السائدة النظر إلى الإنسان كفرد[1] منفصل عما حوله، بدلا من النظر إليه كشبكة من العلائق والعلاقات. تنطلق هذه المقالة من الإدراك بأن الفنون تشكل وسيلة رئيسية لوقف - ومن ثم معالجة وعكس - عملية التخريب والأذى، التي لحقت بالعلاقات بين الناس وبالطبيعة، نتيجة السير السريع للعلوم دون أي واعز من أية حكمة خلال ال ٤٠٠ سنة الفائتة. فالتحدي الجوهري الأكبر الذي نواجهه في عالم اليوم ليس سياسيا أو اقتصاديا أو اجتماعيا، بقدر ما هو تحولٌ في إدراك الشخص لذاته ولعلاقته مع العالم، وأيضا، إدراكه للعلوم والمعرفة ولموقع الأدوات والمنطق والقيم، والتي جميعها تحكم أفعال الناس وتفاعلاتهم. إذ بدون مثل هذا التحول، تكون التغيرات على المستويات الأخرى - في أفضل الأحوال - تغيرات شكلية وضحلة. إن دور الفنون كبير في البدء بمثل هذا التحول وإثرائه. أستعمل كلمة "فنون" في هذه المقالة بالشكل الذي نمت وترعرعت فيه ضمن الحضارة العربية الإسلامية - بمعنى علاقتها الحميمة مع الأدب، ومع الرؤى الكلية التي يجسّدها الناس في حياتهم.

تبدأ الفنون من نقطة مضادة للنظرة إلى الإنسان كموظف ومستهلك (مستهلك لسلع وبضائع ومعان ومقاييس جاهزة ولقوانين يطبقها الناس بطريقة آلية). سأستعمل مثالا لتوضيح هذه الخاصية. ذكر لي صديق فلسطيني كيف أن أباه الفلاح كان يذهب إلى الحقل كل صباح لينظر بعيون تملؤها المحبة إلى كل شجرة، ليرى فيما إذا كانت تحتاج إلى عناية خاصة. تشكل تلك العناية مظهرا جميلا، ليس فقط للتناغم بين عقله وقلبه وعمله، وإنما أيضا، لعلاقته مع المكان والأرض والشجر والتاريخ والحضارة، وفي نفس الوقت لعلاقته مع عائلته والناس في مجتمعه. وكان التعبير الناتج عن تلك العلاقات انتعاش نباتاته وأشجاره، كما كانت مصدر معرفته وفهمه وبقائه ومعنى وجوده. علّمَته أن يعيش مع الغموض (المرتبط بالتقلبات الجوية)، وساعدته على تكوين صورة ذاتية للمستقبل. لقد كوّنت تلك العلاقات أساس حيويته وانتباهه الشديدين للعالم من حوله، واللذين تجسدا في اهتمامه اليومي بحماية الأشجار من أي ضرر، وتوفير ظروف تساعدها على النمو والعطاء. لم يحاول والد صديقي أن يسيطر على نموها وأشكال نموها، فهو - عكس الموظف والمستهلك - كان حرا، بمعنى أن عمله كان نابعا من منطلق ذاتي، ومن الاستماع للطبيعة والتناسق مع قوانينها، وليس من اتباع قوانين عشوائية. كان إدراكه لدوره يتلخص بتوفير ظروف صحية للنباتات والأشجار لتنمو وفق طبيعتها، وبطريقة تحترم قدرتها الطبيعية على النمو. هو تماما مثل الرسام "الناضج" الذي يترك العنان ليده لتخط ما تخطه مدفوعة بدوافع "طبيعية". وهذا هو الحال - كما يظهر - مع والد صديقي الذي ترك العنان ليد الطبيعة "ترسم" المخلوقات النامية.

في المقابل، فإن العلماء الذين ساروا وفق الإدراك الذي صاغه "فرانسس بيكن"، يحاولون السيطرة على نمو النباتات وأشكال ذلك النمو. فالغرض من

[1] ربما تجدر الإشارة هنا إلى أن استعمال كلمة "فرد" لترمز إلى كلمة individual ليس دقيقا لأن الكلمتين لا تشيران إلى نفس المعنى.

العلوم - حسب "بيكن" - هو "قهر الطبيعة وإخضاعها".[2] ضمن هذا المنطلق، لا توجد "صداقة" بين العلم والحكمة، ولا يوجد اهتمام لدى العلوم لاحترام الطبيعة، إذ يكمن غرضها الرئيسي في استكشاف "قوانين الطبيعة"، لاستعمالها في خدمة مصالح ذاتية ومصالح من هم في موقع السلطة والقوة - والتي عنت عمليا خدمة قيم السيطرة والجشع والانتصار على الآخرين. وتشكل علوم الكيمياء والفيزياء النووية والهندسة الجينية مظاهر صارخة لقهر الطبيعة وإخضاعها. نشهد في الوقت الحاضر النتائج الكارثية لمفهوم العلوم هذا، والتي تظهر على شكل فوضى وتفتت وتمرد (بما في ذلك تمرد الطبيعة). ومن الجدير بالذكر، أن هذه النتائج نابعة من الإدراك والفهم السائدين للعلوم وليس لسوء في تطبيقها. لا شك بأن العلوم والمعرفة والتكنولوجيا بمفاهيمها السائدة قد حلت العديد من المشكلات والقضايا، ولكنها في الوقت نفسه، خلقت مشكلات أكثر وأخطر بكثير. فالتهديد النووي بإفناء الحياة على الأرض، وتلويث البيئة لدرجة تبدو استعادتها لعافيتها السابقة شبه مستحيلة، والسعي للهيمنة على العالم أجمع، هي من أخطر التهديدات التي نواجهها حاليا. فتلويث الجسم والبيئة خلال القرن العشرين يعادل أضعافا مضاعفة تلويثهما عبر العصور. من هذا المنطلق، من الضروري أن يقدم للطلبة في المدارس أناس مثل "إينشتاين" ليس كأمثلة يُقتدى بها، وإنما كأمثلة لعلماء اتبعوا مفهوما للعلوم خاليا من الحكمة والمسؤولية - وهو طريق من الضروري عكسه. لقد فعلوا ما فعلوه وهم واعون كاملا للنتائج. لذا، فإن أي محاولة لتبرير ما فعلوه إن هي إلا دلالة على تشويه العقول.

إن اقتناع الناس بأن هذا المسار هو الطريق الوحيد لفهم العلوم، يجعل الأمور أكثر سوءا. فأي شخص يحيد أو يتساءل عنه يجري تهميشه ووصفه بالرومانسية والمثالية، أو كمثال لشخص يرفض التنافس ويرغب في البقاء متخلفا عن الركب. إن تحرير الذات من الاعتقاد بمسار أحادي يشكل في رأيي، أحد التحديات الجوهرية التي نواجهها حاليا لاستمرار الحياة على الأرض؛ وهو تحدٍّ يمكن للفنون أن تلعب دورا رئيسيا في التعامل معه. ولكن، من الصعب جدا أن تلعب الفنون هذا الدور، إذا ما واصلنا الإدراك أن إخضاع الطبيعة هو الغرض من العلوم . ربما من الأنسب أن ندرك أن الغرض من العلوم هو السعي لمعافاة الطبيعة البشرية والطبيعية، من التخريب الذي يلحق بهما جراء طرق العيش التي نتبعها.[3] بعبارة أخرى، نحتاج إلى علوم تساعد على تنظيف التلويثات التي أنتجتها العلوم السائدة - بما في ذلك إعادة النظر في المفاهيم والممارسات والإدراكات المرتبطة بها.[4] فمثلا، تشكل الطاقة الشمسية والهوائية أمثلة على أنواع لا تلوث الحياة ولا تضر بها. بعبارة أخرى، يمكن إدراك العلوم على أنها زيادة فهم وقدرة الناس على حماية ومعافاة الطبيعة مما نلحقه بها من أضرار. لذا، من الممكن إدراك العلوم على أنها اختراع أدوات تجعل حياة الناس أكثر راحة دون أن تلحق ضررا بالطبيعة البشرية أو الطبيعية. سأختار مثالا من بيان SB8 لتوضيح هذه النقطة: "إن مشاهدة الصحراء تتحول خضراء نضرة، يشير إلى أن الناس الذين يعيشون في هذا المكان [الإمارات العربية المتحدة] يحاولون بشكل واضح استعمال الموارد التي يملكونها لخلق مكان على الأرض أكثر راحة، وأكثر ترفا ورفاهة مما كان عليه الحال، أي خلق جنة عدن من صنع الإنسان". من المفهوم أن لا يرى شخص من أوروبا الجمال والإلهام والغنى والوضوح والبساطة والأصالة الموجودة في الصحراء ، وما لايمكن تبريره أو فهمه أن لا يرى العرب فيها ذلك. فإدراك العرب للصحراء ينعكس في الكلمة الجميلة التي كانوا يستخدمونها للإشارة إليها: البادية، والتي تجسّد الحياة بصفائها وبساطتها ونقائها. إن تحويل البادية إلى أمر لا يعكس طبيعتها، ويجعلها تعتمد دوما على "تغذية

[2] أنظر Carolyn Merchant, The Death of Nature (New York: Harper Collins, 1983). See also Yusef Progler in http://www.multiworld.org/m_versity/articles/yusef.htm

[3] أنظر Ivan Illich, Shadow Work, Chapter IV... والذي هو مصدر هذه الفكرة، والتي وجدها ما زالت تُناقش في القرن الثاني عشر، قبل أن تُطمس وتُستبدل بالتدريج بفكرة "فرانسس بيكن".

[4] بالطبع، يمكن أن تساعد بعض الأدوات السائدة في هذه العملية.

من خارجها". هو مثال على إدراك أن العلوم إخضاع للطبيعة وليس فنّ العيش بطريقة متناغمة معها وحامية لها. إن تحويل البادية إلى "جنة عدن" يشبه وضع أرجل للحيّة: نجعلها كسيحة غير قادرة على الحركة! إن تحويل البادية إلى جنة عدن يحول أهلها إلى أناس غير قادرين على العيش في بيئتهم بدون عناصر غريبة يتغذون منها باستمرار، أي تبنيهم طريقة حياة لا يمكن استدامتها على المدى البعيد. مثل هذا التبني يهمل الحكمة المتضمنة في قصة الغراب (في كتاب "كليلة ودمنة") الذي حاول تقليد مشية الحجلة مما أدى به في النهاية إلى أن يخسر الاثنين: تقليد الآخرين والأصالة. إن العيش بطريقة متناغمة مع الطبيعة لا يعني عدم محاولة جعل الحياة أكثر راحة ورفاهة، وإنما يعني اتباع طرق قادرة على "توليد ذاتها" ومتعاونة مع الطبيعة ومتوافقة مع حكمة الخالق. فالعلم الذي يفتقر إلى حكمة يمكن أن يؤدي إلى خراب.إن كون العلوم الحديثة نمت في رحم "قوى إمبراطورية" كأدوات لسرقة قارات وإبادة شعوب ونهب مواردها. كذلك، ربما هو أحد الأسباب التي تفسر عدم اتباع العلم هذا الطريق. فالعيش بطريقة متناغمة مع الطبيعة تتناقض مع النمط الاستهلاكي، في العيش معه ومع قيمه: الربح والجشع والسيطرة والفوز.

تصوروا - كاقتراح يوضح ما جاء أعلاه - أن النظام التعليمي في مدارس "الإمارات العربية المتحدة" اعتمد القوارب الشراعية كأساس لتصميم العملية التعليمية! سيتعلم الطلبة أمورا غائبة كليا عن أفضل المدارس التي يطلقون عليها "عالمية". سيكوّنون معاني لكلمات مثل معرفة وتعلم ومنافسة وتقييم تختلف جذريا عما هو سائد. سيتعلمون كيف يتعايشون مع الغموض وبطريقة غير متناغمة مع الحياة والطبيعة - قدرات مهملة في المؤسسات التعليمية (والتي تتبع عادة مناهج جافة ذات بعد واحد ومحكومة من قبل خبراء أجانب باهظي التكاليف). بالإضافة إلى ذلك، فإن البحر وعلاقة الناس به سيكونان إلهاما طبيعيا لفنونهم. (إنه لمن المثير فعلا التفكير في العالمين المختلفين المتمثلين بالقوارب الشراعية والقوارب المسيّرة بالمحركات).

في عالم تتزايد فيه سيطرة العلوم المرتبطة بقهر الطبيعة وإخضاعها، يمكن أن توفّر الفنون طرقا للحياة، وإدراكات ومفاهيم وعلاقات تجسد قيما تختلف جذريا عن المنافسة والربح والسيطرة والفوز والجشع. لقد أساءت المفاهيم والممارسات والقيم السائدة إلى جسم الإنسان ونفسيته، كما مزقت النسيج الاجتماعي والروحي في المجتمعات، ولوّثت الطبيعة. من هنا، يمكن أن تعمق الفنون قيما لعل من أهمها قيمة العافية - عافية الإنسان والعلاقات والطبيعة. بالإضافة إلى ذلك، يمكن أن تجسد الفنون الطيبة والمتعة والاستمتاع كقيم جوهرية في الحياة. فالطبيعة موجودة للاستمتاع بها وليس لإخضاعها، للإعجاب بها وليس لسوء استعمالها. من الضروري استعادة التمتع بأعجوبة الخليقة وبتعبيراتنا عنها. هذا هو جوهر الفن في رأيي. لقد عبر فنان صيني يعمل بالفخّار عن ذلك بقوله: إن اهتمامه الأكبر لا يكمن في القطعة التي يصنعها، وإنما فيما يبقى بعد أن تنكسر القطعة. شاهدت مرة امرأة تكوّن أشكالا جميلة في الرمل وكان الناس يتجمعون حولها وينظرون بإعجاب إلى رسوماتها ويستمتعون بها. كانت كلما تنتهي من رسمة تمسحها بيدها وتبدأ رسمة جديدة. فالفن تعبير عما يحدث داخل الشخص، ويكمن في العلاقة بين عالمه الداخلي والعالم خارجه، كما يكمن في المتعة والمعنى اللذين يستمدهما من التعابير التي يكوّنها نتيجة تلك العلاقة. وربما أروع العلاقات هذه ،هي تلك التي تحدث دون وعي ودون سابق تخطيط، عندما يكون من الصعب فصل الشخص عن الخبرة أو التعابير التي

يكوّنها. عندما يخرج التعبير بشكل تلقائي وطبيعي. لا أتكلم هنا عن المتعة التي يمكن أن تُشترى وتُباع، وإنما عن تلك المتعة التي يندهش لها الشخص ، أي بطريقة ليست مبرمجة ومخططة، وإنما تنبع من حيوية واندماج كبيرين. ولكن، حتى يعكس الفن احتراما للحياة والطبيعة والناس والحضارة، على الفنان أن يبقى على اتصال مع الألم في العالم. إن الفترتين اللتين شكلتا أكثر الفترات إلهاما في حياتي كانتا عقد السبعينيات والانتفاضة الأولى (كلاهما في فلسطين). عاش الناس خلالهما بكل انتباه لما حولهم وتعاملوا معهما بكل حيوية. عاشوا بما هو متوفر لدى جميع الناس، بما في ذلك قدراتهم وطاقاتهم، كان ما فعلوه كليا تحت سيطرتهم. لا يزال في العصر الحاضر متسع للناس ليعملوا ما يرغبونه في مجالات الفنون أكثر مما هو في مجال العلوم. لذا، من الضروري حماية الفنون من أن تقع فريسة للمؤسسات والمهنيين والهيمنة التجارية. فالحرية المرتبطة بالفنون لا تعني التحرر من الارتباط، بل من الأطر والمعاني والرموز الجاهزة والمغلقة. يحدث الفن عندما ينتقل الاحترام من اتباع تعليمات وقوانين إلى كون الشخص مخلصا لما يجري داخله ولارتباطاته بالحياة، عندما تكون حياة الشخص غير منفصلة عما يعمله ويعبر عنه. هناك فرق شاسع بين حكّاء يحكي حكاية بنفس الطريقة كل مرة، وحكّاء يحس كليا بما ومن حوله. هناك فرق بين مدرّس يحضّر خطة التدريس ويقدمها بطريقة آلية، ومعلم - مثله مثل فنان - يندهش بما يخلقه. هناك فرق - كما قلت سابقا - بين مركب شراعي ومركب آلي، بين مزارع عضوي ومزارع يتبع وصفات جاهزة ويعتمد على اليات. بوجه عام، هناك فرق بين العيش كـ"فنان" والعيش بطريقة آلية.

يرتبط ما ورد أعلاه بخاصية تتعلق بالمؤسسات تجدر الإشارة إليها: في الحالات التي يحدث فيها تعلم لا نلاحظ ذلك ولا نستعمل كلمة "تعلم" للإشارة إليها. وفي الحالات التي لا يحدث فيها تعلم نستعمل كلمة "تعلم" للإشارة إلى ذلك! مثلا، إذا كان هناك أولاد يلعبون بالرمل أو يتمشون في الأحراش أو يطبخون أو يتحادثون أو يسبحون أو يزرعون، ويتعلمون الكثير من خلال ذلك، نقول بأنهم يلعبون أو يزرعون الخ، ولا نقول أنهم يتعلمون. نستعمل كلمة "تعلم" للإشارة إلى ما يحدث في المؤسسة التعليمية، حيث تقتصر على عملية مليئة بقياسات وتقييمات يسيطر عليها مهنيون مرخّصون.[5] في مثل هذه الأوضاع، يقول الناس ما لا يعنون، ويعنون ما لا يقولون، ويصبح التعلم في أفضل الأحوال، عبارة عن مجموعة مهارات آلية ومعلومات متناثرة ومنفصلة.

تماما مثل ما يحتكر التعليم المؤسسي عملية التعلم، ويلغي التعلم النابع من الحياة، تحتكر الفنون المؤسسية (والمسماة بالفنون الجميلة، وكأن هناك فنونا قبيحة!) معنى الفن وتلغي التعابير الفنية الإبداعية الغنية والمتنوعة الموجودة لدى الناس. من هنا يكمن التحدي في التعرف على الفنون التي تكوّن جزءا هاما من حياة الناس وطرق عيشهم، وفي حماية تعابيرهم الغنية والمتنوعة من سيطرة المؤسسات والمهنيين. فأي منحى في الحياة (سواء أكان لغة أو فنا أو علما يفقد مع الوقت روحه وحيويته) إذا ما عتمد في استمراره على أن يُدرّس من خلال أطر رسمية. يعكس الفن عادة علاقة الشخص بما حوله. فالشاعر الفارسي "حافظ"، مثلا، عاش معظم حياته في مدينة شيراز، التي كوّنت بجمالها وعيه وتعبيره وجعلته عبر مئات السنين أحد أكثر الشعراء إلهاما في العالم. كذلك فإن الفنان المصري "سيد درويش" لا يزال يلهم الملايين في العالم العربي.

في العام ١٩٧٨ كنت عضوا في اللجنة المسؤولة عن تأسيس كلية الفنون في جامعة "بيرزيت" بفلسطين. لسوء الحظ لم تر النور، لأن الاحتلال الإسرائيلي لم يسمح بذلك.[6] من الجدير بالذكر هنا، أن الكلية كانت مصممة

[5] ما يمكن قياسه هو أمور محسوسة مرئية. مثلا نستطيع قياس عدد المرات التي يصلي فيها الشخص ولكن لا يمكن قياس تقواه. كذلك يمكن قياس مدى قدرة الطالب على حلّ معادلات ولكن من الصعب قياس قدرته على ملاحظة أنماط وعلاقات.

[6] من الجدير بالذكر أن نفس الاحتلال أعطى بسرعة إذنا لبناء كلية هندسة! الفنون أخطر بكثير من الهندسة! لذلك أيضا، لم تعترف سلطات الاحتلال ببرنامج دليلي سياحة في جامعة بيت لحم.

حول أشخاص يجسدون في حياتهم تعابير فنية مختلفة. تشكل الأساس لحاملي الشهادات. [ربما فرقة "الورشة" المصرية أقرب ما تكون إلى هذه "الفلسفة".]

من أهم وأكثر التحديات إلحاحا في وقتنا الحاضر (في مختلف المجالات). هو كيفية توفير وحماية مساحات (مادية و معنوية) حيث يعيش الناس ويعملون ويتفاعلون ويعبّرون خارج تدخّل المؤسسات والمهنيين. مساحات لا يُعامل فيها ما ينتجه الناس كسلع. فما يشار له بمعاهد فنية مهنية تكون عادة مكدّسة بكتب ومواد فنية من مختلف الأنواع (والتي تكون عادة باهظة التكاليف). ولكنها غير قادرة على رؤية فنانين يصنعون من نفايات يرميها الناس منتوجات جميلة خلاقة. مثل هؤلاء الفنانين هم أقرب ما يكونون إلى المزارعين العضويين الذين ينظرون إلى كومة من نفايات الخضروات ويرون زهورا تنمو وسطها. فالفن ليس مهنة بقدر ما هو طريقة حياة. ونظرة إلى الحياة والتعبير بصدق عن الخبرة معها. طريقة لرؤية العالم - بكل الجمال والألم فيه. فبدون فنون. ينمو اعتقاد بأن من الممكن فهم كل نواحي الحياة عن طريق العقل والفكر. وأن الحياة مدفوعة بشكل رئيسي بقوى السوق. أجد نفسي مرة أخرى مدفوعا لأن أذكر أمي الأمية كمثال على ما أود قوله. كتبت عنها كـ"رياضية"[٧] و كـ"معلمة" و كـ"مجسدة لروح جميلة في الأديان". وعيت خلال كتابتي هذا المقال أنها فنانة أيضا. فيما يتعلق بالأنماط والأشكال والقياسات. إذ تعاملت. كخياطة. مع أشكال وقياسات غير موجودة في الكتب المقررة في الرياضيات. ولا ينطبق ما كانت قادرة على فعله على أدوات اخترعها الرياضيون والمهندسون. فالرياضيات الرسمية تتعامل مع مستقيمات وزوايا ومربعات ودوائر وأشكال هندسية أخرى لها معادلات... في المقابل. كانت أمي تتعامل مع منحنيات جسم امرأة خاصة بها. ولا يشاركها أحد فيها. لم تستعمل أنماطا جاهزة وإنما كان لكل امرأة خصوصيتها. كل ملبس صنعته (خلال ٤٥ سنة) كان خلقا فريدا! كان جميع ما فعلته أعمالا فنية بكل معنى الكلمة. وليس تطبيقات آلية لمعادلات ومقاييس. قدرتها هي قدرة فنان. وليس قدرة رياضي أو مهندس - قدرة لا يمكن اكتسابها عن طريق تدريس منظم أو معرفة عقلية صرفة. بالرغم من ذلك. لم أسمع أحدا يشير إليها كفنانة! هذا ما عنيته بقولي: إن فنون الناس لا يمكن أن تُرى من خلال عيون رسمية أو مهنية.

* * *

إن إدراكي لما يحدث في العالم (رغم ظواهر تشير إلى غير ذلك) هو انحسار المنطق (في مجتمعات كثيرة) المبني على السيطرة والمنافسة والانتصار والهيمنة. فالأزمات التي نراها تتزايد حول العالم هي أزمات ناتجة عن مؤسسات وعن النمط الاستهلاكي في العيش. والأخطار التي ذكرتها سابقا والنابعة من المنطق السائد ومن طرق العيش السائدة - التهديد النووي بالفناء وانحلال البيئة ومحاولات الهيمنة على العالم - هي أخطار حقيقية. إلا أنه بالرغم من الوعي بذلك. يشعر كثيرون بالشلل نحو ما يمكن عمله. إن إفقار الخيال يسهم في عملية الشلل هذه. من هنا. تشكل الفنون طريقا هاما في إغناء الخيال وتوفير مسارات انتقالية صحية.

من وجهة النظر هذه. فإن دور الفن كبير جدا في توسيع وتعميق مدى الحرية لدى الشخص - ليس حرية الامتلاك والاستهلاك. وإنما حرية خلق أشياء ومعان وتعابير ومساحات. ربما توجد أشياء وخدمات أكثر لدى الناس في الدول الغنية. ولكن دوما مع تعليمات بكيفية استعمالها. والتي تسقط الناس عادة في فلك نمط الاستهلاك. فالحرية تعني. تفاعلات إبداعية بين أشخاص مدفوعين من داخلهم. ومن تفاعلات مع مجتمعاتهم وبيئاتهم.

[٧] أنظر مثلا المقال Community education is to regain and transform what has been made invisible. Harvard Educational Review, Feb. 1990

[٨] زرت عام ١٩٧٠ متحفا في مدينة كزكو Cuzco في البيرو والتي كانت عاصمة الإنكا Incas وكان هناك تمثال لفرس يمتطيه شخص إسباني يدفع برمحه نحو شخص راكع على ركبته. ذكر لنا الدليل (والذي كان نفسه من الإنكا) بأن الشخص الراكع هو عربي في الأندلس. وطلب منا أن نلاحظ كيف أن الشخص الراكع يبدو على هيئة إنكا وذلك لأن الفنان الذي نحت التمثال (والذي كان أيضا من الإنكا) لم ير عربيا في حياته ولكنه تخيل أن يكون يشبهه ما دامت العلاقة مع الإسباني تشبه علاقته بالإسباني! كذلك أشار الدليل إلى أن نظرة الراكع وطريقة إمساكه بالرمح تعكسان روح مقاومة لم ينتبه لها الجنود الذين كانوا يراقبون النحات...

[٩] فهم لا يرغبون في لعبة المنافسة ومعرفة اللغة الإنكليزية...

من هنا، تجسد الحرية قيمة أخلاقية واجتماعية. ومن بين الحريات الهامة، والمهملة، حرية المشاركة في تكوين المعاني والمعايير، وفي تكوين صور عن المستقبل. عندما أزور مدارس يوجهوني عادة إلى غرفة الكمبيوتر، فأسأل "أرغب في رؤية غرفة الطبلات". [تماما كما أن القارب الشراعي والقارب الآلي يجسدان عالمين مختلفين جذريا، كذلك تعكس الطبلة والكمبيوتر عالمين بعيدين عن بعضهما بعد الثرى عن الثريا.]

عندما أتكلم عن أهمية تحرر الفنون من الموضع الإدراكي الدوني لنفسها، نتيجة حشرها في زاوية من قبل المجتمع، لا أتكلم فقط عن أهميتها في حياة الناس، وإنما أيضا - وربما الأهم - عن أهميتها في بقاء الحياة على الأرض، فالفن والثقافة والحكمة هي ما يلهم الناس حاليا حول العالم. سأذكر باختصار بعض الأمثلة للتوضيح. بعد ٥٠٠ سنة من محاولات القتل والتدمير وطمس طرق العيش لدى السكان الأصليين في جنوب المكسيك، برزت حركة "الزباتيستاز" كأمل من أكثر الحركات إلهاما لكثير من الناس حول العالم.[٨] كذلك فإن صموئيل هنتنجتن Huntington في كتاب جديد، يعتبر أن أكبر خطر على أمريكا هو الهسبانيكس Hispanics أي الذين جاءوا من المكسيك وكوبا. من الواضح أن خطرهم ليس سياسيا أو عسكريا أو اقتصاديا، بل ثقافيا. فخوف هنتنجتن ينبع من الطريقة التي يديرون فيها حياتهم، والطريقة التي يتعاملون فيها ويتحادثون ويرقصون ويغنون ويرون، كما أن مصدر قيمتهم ينبع من داخلهم ومن مجتمعاتهم ومن علاقاتهم ببعضهم.[٩] [من هنا تبرز عنصرية البرنامج التلفزيوني "افتح يا سمسم" Sesame Street ودوره في تكوين الإدراك.] كذلك الحال بالنسبة لإفريقيا وأواسط آسيا وشبه القارة الهندية والعالم العربي، إذ أن العمود الفقري لها جميعا هو الثقافة. من الضروري النظر إلى الفنون من هذه الزاوية.

* * *

في حياة كل شخص ناحية هامة تكمن في مصدر قيمته. أود أن أنهي هذا المقال بالمبدأ الذي نستلهم به فكر وعمل "الملتقى التربوي العربي"، والذي أقترح أن يكون المبدأ الذي يمكن أن يكون مصدر قيمة الفنانين (بدلا من لجان رسمية)، هو المبدأ المتضمن في عبارة للإمام علي يقول فيها: "قيمة كل امرئ ما يحسنه". ولكلمة "يحسن" في اللغة العربية خمسة معان: يشير المعنى الأول إلى مدى إتقان الشخص لعمله (البعد المعرفي المهاراتي)، ويشير الثاني إلى مدى حسن العمل للناس والمجتمع (بُعد المسؤولية). أما المعنى الثالث فيشير إلى مدى ما يعطيه الشخص من ذاته (بعد العطاء، بدلا من الأخذ فقط، أو ما هو أسوأ، الاستهلاك). ويشير المعنى الرابع إلى مدى الجمالية التي يبعثها العمل في الحواس (البعد العاطفي). ويشير الخامس إلى مدى احترام الآخرين وحسن المجادلة (بعد النسيج الاجتماعي الروحي)... هذه المعاني تجسد حكمة وتنوعا وإيمانا بالناس. من الصعب التفكير في مجال يتجسد فيه معنى هذا المبدأ بأكثر مما هو في مجال الفنون.

الأمل في حقبة كاليوج

مانيش جين

في الغرب، يتحدث الخبراء عن عصر العولمة- الفرص والأزمات التي تمخض عنها هذا الحجم والسرعة غير المسبوقين في تاريخ الاقتصاد العالمي. ويعرّف كبارنا وحكماؤنا في الهند الأزمان الحالية بزمن كاليوج Kalyug. ويعنون بهذه العبارة "العصور المظلمة" أو الزمن الذي يكون فيه البشر أبعد ما يكونون عن "الله". إنها الفترة الأصعب للسلالة البشرية يتوقع فيها أن تسود وتنتشر فظائع عديدة في المجتمع. وتحذر الكتب المقدسة بأنه خلال هذا العصر: "يقبل الناس أولئك الذين يتصرفون كطغاة ويؤيدونهم". "أما الرجال الذين يوهمون الناس بأنهم متعلمين فسيقومون باختزال الحقيقة وإخفائها بحكم ما يقومون به من أفعال وتصرفات."

طالما فكّرت بالمعنى الذي تحمله كلمة Kalyug بالنسبة لي إلى جانب معناها في الأسفار المقدسة. في بعض الأيام، اشعر أن دلالته تكمن في الانفصال التام الذي أصبح يعيشه الرجال والنساء في العصر الحديث عن الطبيعة (والغرور التام الذي يحرّك أي تفاعل يبادر إليه بطل الاقتصاد مع أمّنا الأرض). في يومنا هذا، لم يعد أطفالنا يعرفون مصدر غذائهم، ومياههم، وملابسهم، ووقودهم...الخ؛ أو أين تطمر عبواتهم البلاستيكية، وبطارياتهم، وألعاب الفيديو القديمة التي استخدموها...الخ. نعلمهم بأنهم مواطنين صالحين إذا رموا الأشياء في حاويات إعادة التدوير دون التساؤل عمّا يحدث لها عندما تغادر الحاوية. لقد جعلتهم طرق التدريس الحديثة في المدارس ووسائل الإعلام غير قادرين على رؤية الروابط والنتائج التي تترتب على خياراتهم، مثلاً، كيف أن النفط الذي يعتمدون عليه كثيراً في حياتهم يرتبط بالحرب. والمفارقة هي أن الدول التي لديها ما يسمى بأفضل النظم التربوية والتعليمية هي التي تركت أكبر قدر من أثر أقدامها على البيئة.

وفي أيام أخرى، أفكر بأن دلالة kalyug تتمثل في الخسارة العظيمة لقيمة ما يعرف بـ jabaan أي الفجوة بين ما نقول إننا نؤمن به وما نقوم به فعلاً ومعها خسارة الشخص لعزّته أو كرامته وإحساسه المقدس بالوجود في هذا الكون. إحساسنا الخاص بقدرة البشر على التدخل ومسؤوليتنا الشخصية عن أفعالنا وخياراتنا قد تراجع وتآكل في مواجهة المؤسسات الضخمة. وقبل سنوات عديدة، لاحظ لويس ممفورد وبإدراك مرهف أن أنسنة الآلة ستؤدي إلى مكننة الإنسانية أو البشرية. وما هو مخيف فعلاً هو أننا غير قادرين على (أو بما يبعث على قلق أكبر هو أننا لا نريد) أن نكيّف ذلك الصوت الملح للمنطق الواعي المشترك الذي يتغلغل في وعينا وفي بوصلتنا الداخلية والخارجية ليتواءم مع ذلك الصوت الذي يكبح وهمنا بعظمة الذات ويساعدنا على فرض الحدود الذاتية الخاصة بنا. وقد أصبحت قدرتنا على تقييم الأشياء أو الوصول إلى الخيارات من منظور بعيد المدى مشوّهة تماماً. لقد درّبنا على الاعتقاد بأن كل ما هو قيّم في الحياة يمكن أن يقاس بشكل دقيق وفعال من خلال النقود. وقد درّب أبناؤنا من خلال المدارس على الاعتقاد بأن النجاح هو القدرة على الحصول على الأموال دون الإخلاص في عمل اليوم؛ وكلما كان عدد الأشخاص الذي يمكن للمرء استغلالهم أكبر، كان ذلك في صالحه وأفضل له. نحن نضع رقعة سعر للغابات، والمياه، والجبال، والنظم البيئية برمّتها، ونعتقد أننا نستطيع أن نتحمّل المسؤولية المالية المترتبة على تخريبها ودمارها. ولا يكون لحياتنا أهمية سوى عندما يتعلق الأمر بالاستهلاك والناتج القومي الإجمالي؛ وفيما عدا ذلك، يبقى وجودنا عبئاً على كاهل الحكومات

والمخططين. وربما في هذا ما يلقي بعض الضوء على السبب الذي يجعلنا نستمر في ترك المجال لمنطق السوق ودولة الأمة أن يسود على عمليات صنع القرار لدينا وأن يتحكم في علاقاتنا ببعضنا بعض- ويفسر لماذا نعتبر التسليح العسكري العنيف، والنمو الاقتصادي غير المستدام، والتقتنيات السادية، مساوية للتقدم.

من الملفت أن نلاحظ هنا أنه في مواجهةالـ Kalyug، وبشكل خاص الأزمة البيئية المشوّهة التي تنتج عنها، يدعو قادة العالم إلى وضع أجندة عالمية لأهداف الألفية للتنمية، من حقوق الإنسان، والتعليم للجميع، وتكنولوجيا المعلومات والاتصالات...الخ - جميع الحلول المقننة-التكنوقراطية التي تجعلنا متآلفين تماماً ضمن نظم الحداثة ومؤسساتها. ومرّة بعد مرّة، يطالبوننا بأن نعتقد بأنه في يوم ما سوف تعمّ المكاسب على الجميع؛ أو أنه سيتم تطوير تقنيات جديدة لتنظيف وإزالة جميع مظاهر الفوضى والخراب التي تمخضت عنها هذه القوة الاقتصادية الماحقة؛ أو ببساطة علينا أن نقبل بالأمر الواقع ألا وهو أنه ما من بديل لهذا الوضع. وحتى ما يسمّى بالملتقيات الراديكالية، فإنها تتركز بشكل رئيس على تثبيت السياسة الأمريكية الخارجية أو قوانين منظمة التجارة العالمية. غير أن طبيعة الأزمة التي نحن بصددها الآن تبدو وكأنها تشير إلى الحاجة إلى المزيد من التحول العميق للوعي والذي يمكنه أن يلهمنا لرؤية واستشراف الاحتمالات الخفيّة/الجديدة. وكما قال آلبرت إينشتاين في إحدى المرّات، أنت لا تستطيع أن تحل المشكلة باستخدام الأطر المرجعية ذاتها التي شكّلتها. لذا، علينا أن نتخطى التفكير بمناهج معزولة تركز على حل قضية ما. بكلمات أخرى، يستدعي الأمر رؤيا بعيدة المدى بمنظور أوسع نطاقاً.

وعليه، أود أن أفترض هنا أن الكوارث البيئية التي يواجهها كوكب الأرض في يومنا هذا لا يمكن أن تحل ببساطة من خلال التدابير القانونية أو وسائل التحايل التكنولوجي. إنها مسألة ثقافية بالتأكيد، ولا بدّ من مقاربتها من خلال هذه الرؤيا. وكما تصف مارغريت ويتلي الأمر: "العالم لا يتغير فردا فردا، إنه يتغير عندما تتشكل شبكات العلاقات بين الأشخاص الذين يشتركون في القضية والرؤيا ذاتها لما هو ممكن. هذه أخبار جيّدة لأولئك الذين يرغبون من بيننا في خلق مستقبل إيجابي. وبدلاً من القلق بشأن الكتلة الحرجة، لا بدّ لعملنا من أن ينصبّ على تعزيز الروابط الحرجة." وتتطلب منا الجهود المتنوعة التي تبذل في التجديد الثقافي أن نعمل على تغذية وتعزيز الحوار بين الثقافات. كما أن الوعي ينمو ويتطور بينما نحن نتعلم كيفية التفاعل مع مختلف الحقائق- سواء كانت داخلية أو خارجية. ويشكل الحوار بين الثقافات أداة مهمة للكشف عن مختلف منظورات الحقيقة وسبر أغوارها. ولفهم الحياة التي يختبرها الآخرون علينا أن نمتلك مهارات الحوارات التأملية والتي يمكننا من خلالها وبها أن نختبر الفرضيات الخاصة بنا ونتساءل عن فرضيات الآخرين.

ويصف جوستافو إستيفا الأمر قائلاً: "عبارة ما-بين- الثقافات تلمح إلى وضع ديناميكي يتشكل فيه وعي خاص بأن ثمة أشخاصاً آخرين موجودين، وقيماً، وثقافات قائمة، وأن العزلة مستحيلة. وعي كهذا يعني ضمناً الاعتراف والإقرار بمحددات كل ثقافة وفهم لجميع ما هو إنساني. وبدلاً من اللجوء إلى ثقافة الشخص الخاصة في محاولة لعزل نفسه، والابتعاد عن الآخر أو قمعه، يلهم الشخص إلى التفاعل مع الآخر مدركاً وواعياً لكينونته الآخرية الراديكالية... وهذا يتضمن الانفتاح على هموم وانشغالات الآخر، وعلى الإرشاد، والشكوك، والإلهام، والمثاليات أو أي عنصر آخر يمكن للطرفين الاشتراك به وما من أحد منهما يسيطر عليه."

وفي يومنا هذا، لم يعد هذا الحوار بين الثقافات مقتصراً على الشرق مقابل الغرب أو الشمال مقابل الجنوب. والآخر لم يعد مجرّد ظاهرة خارجية، بل أنه قد نشأ في داخل كل واحد منّا. إذن، لا بدّ لحوار الثقافات من أن يبدأ من عندنا نحن- بين منطقنا، وذواتنا التحليلية، وحدسنا، وذواتنا الخلاّقة، وبين الكائنات القديمة، غير المرتبطة بزمان معين وبين ذواتنا الحداثية. ويجب أن يتكرّس في عائلاتنا ومجتمعاتنا المحلية، وبين مجتمعاتنا الحضرية وتلك الريفية، وبين الرجال والنساء، وعبر الأجيال، والطبقات، والطوائف الاجتماعية...الخ. وثمة حاجة ملحّة للتفكير بشكل أكثر عمقاً في كيفية تحويل مستوى وسرعة تفاعلاتنا لتوفير المزيد من الوقت للأمور الحميمة، والحساسة، والخفيّة.

وثمة دور حساس ومهم يؤديه الفنان في خلق مثل هذا الحوار بين الثقافات والمشاركة في استضافته. غير أنه من المحزن أن نرى دور الفنان هذا وقد أهمل وأصبح موضع افتراء في معظم أوساط ودوائر التغيير الاجتماعي. فقد احتل السياسيون، ونشطاء الإدارة، والمروجون الإعلاميون وغيرهم من النشطاء. لقد ألهمتني كلمات آناندا كوماراسوومي بأن "الفنان ليس نوعاً خاصّاً من البشر. كل إنسان هو نوع خاص من الفنان." وفي الوقت ذاته، أعتقد أن تحقيق خصوصية الشخص كفنان تحمل معها نوعاً أعلى من المسؤولية الاجتماعية. وبكلمات أخرى، القول بأن كل شخص هو فنان في الحياة لا يعني بالضرورة أن "الفنان" قد افرغ من أي أو كل الأدوار الاجتماعية. والحقيقة هي أنه يجب النظر إلى الفنان بموجب معايير عالية. وعلى كل منا، كما على الفنانين، المشاركة بشكل حيوي ونشط في عملية الخلق المشترك وعدم الاكتفاء بالملاحظة أو التكيف بشكل سلبي وساكن مع هذه المجموعات أو مجتمعات التعلّم هذه. خلافاً لذلك، نكون عرضة لخطر الانزلاق إلى مصيدة أخرى للعالم الجاهز الصنع إذا توقعنا من الآخرين أن يخلقوا لنا مجموعات التعلّم هذه. غير أن الفنون والآداب تشكل أداة قوية للتحول الشخصي والجماعي ولا بدّ من إخراجها من حيّز "الكماليات". لقد وصلت البشرية إلى حدود العقل التحليلي والمنطقي. وهذا الالتزام بالفن يساعد على تيسير الوضوح بشأن الهوية الفردية (من أنا؟)، المعنى (ما هو السبب الذي يجعل حياتي تستحق العيش؟) والعلاقة (كيف أرتبط بالآخرين؟). يمكن للفنون أن تساعدنا على الانتقال إلى ما هو أبعد من الشعارات والدعاية والانتقال إلى ما قال عنه رومي مرة بأنه العوالم التي توجد فيما هو أبعد من "الصح" و "الخطأ". ويمكن للفنون أن تساعدنا على كسر آلية الأسود والأبيض التي تصطبغ بها البشرية- أطر الكفاءة، وتوحيد الأشياء، والثقافة الأحادية- والبدء من جديد برؤية المساحات الرمادية التي تملأ جميع مجالات الحياة وحقولها. عندها، نستطيع أن نرى في الشك فرصة لخلق روابط ذات مستوى أعلى للتوسع في الوعي وتطويره، بدلاً من اعتباره مصدر خوف يحسن بنا السيطرة عليه أو حتى محوه من على الوجود.

أود أن ألقي الضوء هنا على مجالين يبدو أنهما متناقضين- ارتداد-التعلّم unlearning والتذكر re-membering[١]؛ ويمكن لأولئك المعنيين بموضوع الفن والفنون التركيز عليهما بهدف التشجيع على المزيد من مجموعات التعلّم للحوار بين الثقافات.

ارتداد- التعلّم أمر ضروري لنا إن رغبنا في استعادة إيماننا بالخير الموجود في الآخرين وفي المعتقد بأن العديد من الاحتمالات الجديدة قائم ومن الممكن خلقه- إنهما شرطان أساسيان لتشكّل حوار الثقافات. وما أعنيه بعبارة "ارتداد-التعلم" هو تلك العمليات التي تساعدنا على إعادة اختبار نماذجنا العقلية أو تكيفنا. وحتى نرى الأمور بمنظور جديد، علينا أن نصبح واعين للراشحات العقلية التي تحكم طرقنا في فهم الأمور. ولا يترادف

١ والتر بنجامين، "ثيسيس أون ذا فيلوسوفي أوف هيستوري (بحث في فلسفة التاريخ)،" إليومينيشنز (نيويورك: شوكين بوكس، ١٩٦٩)، ص. ٢٥٥

"ارتداد- التعلم" مع النسيان. فحتى يفتح لنا "ارتداد- التعلّم" احتمالات لحوار الثقافات، علينا أن نفهم حقيقة ما وهي أنه يمكن أن توجد في دواخلنا نحن العديد من العقبات التي تحول دونه بما فيها: الخوف من النقد والانتقاد، وعدم الثقة، والتنافسية، والتفكير المجزّأ، والأنا الكبرى. وثمة عقبات أخرى عميقة تنبع من عجزنا "المدرّس" على احتمال الغموض أو الرؤية بشمولية أكبر (بما هو أبعد من النظم المصطنعة). لقد تم تكييفنا على التفكير بمعادلة "إما...أو" (مثلاً: الرأسمالية مقابل الشيوعية، والمجتمع مقابل الطبيعة). كما تضعف قدرتنا على الحوار بسبب تصنيفات معيّنة نلصقها بأنفسنا وبالآخرين. وتصنيفات الهويّة هذه- والتي تقوم في أغلب الأحيان على أساس المهن، والطائفة الاجتماعية، والنوع الاجتماعي، والطبقة الاجتماعية، والمستوى التعليمي...الخ- تخلق لنا حواجز مصطنعة تحد من استكشافنا للأشياء ونمائنا. ويتملكنا الخوف من التفاعل مع أشخاص معينين والذين نعتقد أن الفضل يعود إليهم في تكوينهم لأنفسهم أو حتى في تكويننا نحن. و"ارتداد-التعلم" لا بدّ وأن ينطوي على مواجهة هذه العقبات والحواجز.

أما بالنسبة للتذكّر، علينا أن نعيد ربط أنفسنا بأعضائنا- اليدين، القلوب، الأرواح، أجيالنا المختلفة، روابطنا المقدسة مع النار والمياه، والأرض، والتراب. نحن جميعاً نمتلك حدساً عميقاً لا يخضع لمحددات الزمن، كما نمتلك الحكمة والخيال. علينا أن نستصلح نظم التعلّم الفردي الخاصة بنا وننتزعها من "المصانع الدراسية أو المدارس". كما علينا أن نعالج أموراً أخرى وسمها السرعة (تعلم الأشياء بشكل أسرع ليس هو دوماً بالأمر الأفضل لإبداعنا)، والذكاءات المتعددة، والحالات العاطفية، والتجارب، والنظم المعرفية...الخ. علينا أن نستعيد عضويتنا في الجماعة أيضاً لنرى القوة والسلطة خارج مؤسسات الدولة والسوق. ففي هذا ما يمكنه أن يلهمنا لنكون قادرين على إدراك المساحات الخلّاقة والفرص الماثلة أمام أعيننا والتي لم نعرها اهتماماً وتقديراً من قبل- بكلمات أخرى، أن نرى من جديد ما كنا نسيناه.

وفي الوقت ذاته، علينا أن نتذكر كيف يمكن لقدراتنا أن تتعزز من خلال التعاون والمشاركة مع الآخرين. والأهم من هذا وذاك، علينا أن نتذكر كيفية ربط المعرفة والتكنولوجيا مع الحكمة والأخلاقيات. فهذا سوف يوفر لنا التواضع المطلوب لمعرفة حدودنا والمنطق العام لفهم حقيقة أنه لا يتعين علينا أن نفعل الأشياء كلها فقط لأنه بمقدورنا ذلك (أي أنه ليس من الضروري متابعة وتحقيق جميع المبادرات العلمية والتجارية "الخلاقة"). والتذكر أمر ضروري لإمدادنا بالإلهام اللازم لنباشر أحلامنا الخاصة من جديد (لا أن نستقبل أحلام الآخرين الجاهزة) وأن نستعيد ثقتنا بأنفسنا من حيث أننا نستطيع تحقيق هذه الأحلام على أرض الواقع. عندما نبدأ بالتذكر، سنبدأ من جديد في رؤية الحقيقة بأن كل واحد منّا هو جزء من عملية الخلق المشترك للكون ككل. وهذا الخلق المشترك يتناغم ويتصل بعمق مع الحياة ككل. وهذا ما نطلق عليه في الهند عبارة *Tat-twam-asi* (أنت هو ذلك).

أودايبور (Udaipur) كمدينة تعلُّمية

على مدى السنوات الست الماضية، عملنا، وبطرق مختلفة، على استكشاف الطرق الكفيلة بإعادة إحياء حوار الثقافات في إطار حياتنا الخاصة وبيئة التعلم المحلية كجزء من مشروع "أودايبور كمدينة تعلُّمية." نحن نرى في المدينة كائناً حياً فيه العناصر الطبيعية، والثقافية، والروحية، والفيزيائية ويشترك فيها الأشخاص ببناء المعاني، والعلاقات، والمعرفة. وتوفر المدينة مجموعة منوّعة من السياقات للتوسع في وعينا وتعزيز قدراتنا على تقدير نقاط القوة والمواهب الموجودة لدينا، ومعالجة المشاكل البيئية والنفسية

المرتبطة بالتطوير الحضري الذي لا يخضع للضوابط اللازمة ولبناء الثقة والصداقات الحميمة. هذه المدينة عبارة عن دعوة مفتوحة للأشخاص من كل الأعمار والخلفيات في أودايبور لاستكشاف طرق العيش والتعلّم التي تعتمد بشكل أكبر على الطبيعة والبيئة الطبيعية. إننا نسعى من خلالها إلى استعادة السيطرة على عملية التعلّم بحيث تبقى بين يدي المتعلِّم. وهذا ما قادنا إلى صياغة هذه المدينة بحيث تشمل كل شيء من السياحة التي لا ينتج عنها أي مخلّفات إلى العمل مع المعالجين التقليديين، إلى إنتاج الأعمال المسرحية والأفلام عن المجتمعات المحليّة.

تركز هذه المدينة على العائلات، والمنازل، والأحياء من حيث كونها فضاءات راديكالية للتغيير الاجتماعي. ونحن ندرك أن التفاعل بين الأجيال أمر ضروري ومهم إن نحن أردنا للحكمة أن ترى النور وأن نعمّق الفعل وأثره. ولعلّ أحد المبادئ الرئيسية الموجهة بالنسبة لنا هنا هو أن الأشخاص يطلعون بعضهم بعضاً على ما لديهم وباختيار طوعي منهم وبروح الامتنان مما يجعلهم متوافقين مع مبدأ هندي قديم يرفض ويلعن تحويل المعرفة إلى سلعة تباع وتشترى. وما من إكراه على شيء هنا. وما من مبنى منفصل قد بني خصيصاً لمدينة التعلم هذه؛ بل نحن اخترنا أن نستخدم وبشكل مبدع ما هو قائم وموجود فعلاً: منازل الأشخاص، قطع الأراضي الفارغة، والحدائق والمتنزهات العامة، والمعابد، والمساجد، والمعتزلات الدينية (الأشرام)، وأماكن العمل، أو مكاتب المنظمات المحلية. وتحاول المدينة أن تتجاوز التصنيفات المؤسسية للعام والخاص وأن تعيد للاهتمامات الأصيلة وطاقات أفرد المجتمع المحلي أهميتها ودمجها في إطار عمل المدينة. بكلمات أخرى، في أودايبور كمدينة تعلُّمية، يكون الأفراد والسياقات الفعلية هم نقطة البداية-لا أفكار مجرّدة، أو مشاريع لتقطيع البسكويت، أو مؤشرات قائمة على النتائج.

لم تجهّز مدينة أودايبور التعلُّمية لتلبية طلبات السوق؛ إنما كان تجهيزها لتحقيق الفهم الشخصي وحوار الثقافات. وهذا لا يعني أن الأسئلة المتعلقة بالمعيشة غير موجودة فيها؛ بل هي موجودة وإنما في سياق الفهم والعلاقات. تساعدنا هذه المدينة على أن نعيش المفاجآت بكامل قوانا وحيويتنا وأن نستشعر إثارة مستمرة في رحلتنا نحو المجهول.

وعلى مدى مسار العمل في عملية المدينة التعلُّمية هذه، أتيحت لي الفرص العديدة للانخراط في العمل الفني في مناسبات مختلفة في أودايبور وحول الهند. وهناك اتجاهات وتيارات عديدة لاحظت أنها تحمل تهديداً عظيماً للطاقة الراديكالية المتجددة لدى الفنان وقدراته على فتح حوار الثقافات.

أولاً، رأيت أن الترويج لفن الأطفال دائما ما يكون في إطار المسابقات؛ لقد خلق هذا الأمر وضعاً غير صحي حيث يصل العديد من الأشخاص، بمن فيهم أنا، إلى الاعتقاد بأنهم ليسوا فنانين "جيدين". كما يدفع هذا بالأطفال إلى البقاء في صندوق ما هو "آمن" لإرضاء الحكّام مما يثنيهم عن خوض المخاطر في الفن. وتتجلى روح المنافسة هذه فيما بعد ضمن عالم الفن لوضع حدود على الطريقة التي يتفاعل بها الفنانون مع بعضهم بعض.

ثانياً، رأيت فصلاً خطراً بين الفنان المحترف والمجتمع المحلّي لصالح السياح أو الأغنياء. سمعت العديد من الفنانين يعلقون قائلين: "لا يفهم المجتمع المحلي الفن الذي ننجزه كما لا يقدرونه، فما جدوى التفاعل معهم، إذن؟" إنه وضع غريب يرسم فيه الفنان الذي نزع من أصوله وجذوره الأفكار، والتصاميم (الموتيفات)، والصور مستلهماً البيئة المحلية المحيطة به؛ غير أنه لا يعود ليشارك الأشخاص في هذه البيئة هذه الرسومات ولا يساعد على إثراء الثقافة المحلية وحياة المجتمع المحلي.

ثالثاً، ثمة تجزئة حادة للفنان إلى ثلاثة أدوار منفصلة هي: المصمم، والمنتج، والمسوّق. فعلى سبيل المثال، قمت مؤخراً بزيارة عائلة في الهند كانت تنتج ورقاً ومنتجات ورقية يدوية على مدى أكثر من أربعمائة عام. وكانت عمليات التصميم، والإنتاج، والتسويق كلها تتم داخل المنزل ومن قبل أفراد العائلة أنفسهم. إلا أن الأمر الآن أخذ بالتغير في حقبة التخصص والإنتاج الجماهيري. فهناك شخص يأتي من الولايات المتحدة لوضع التصاميم، ومجموعة أخرى من العمال تقوم بالإنتاج فقط، وآخرون يقومون بأعمال التسويق أو المشاركة. ومع هذه الاتجاهات الثلاثة جميعها، يتم إنتاج المنتجات غير أن الفنان يضيع ككائن متكامل، كمؤطّر، وجامع لحوار الثقافات.

وفي عملنا، حاولنا أن نتصدى لهذه الاتجاهات من خلال مجموعة من الأنشطة المنوّعة في أودايبور. وعلي أن أوضح منذ البداية أن جزءاً كبيراً من تفكيرنا واستراتيجياتنا قد استوحى روح (حركة فن الغريب). وعبارة (فن الغريب) تستخدم هنا لوصف الفن الذي يفهم في معناه الفضفاض على أنه "خارج" الثقافة الرسمية (للمزيد من المعلومات، أنظر www.rawvision.com. وفي العادة يكون اتصال هؤلاء الفنانين المصنفين على أنهم فنانين غرباء ضئيلاً أو حتى معدوماً مع مؤسسات عالم الفن المنظم ومنها الجامعات، والمحترفات، والمتاحف...الخ. إنهم لا يحملون شهادات متخصصة في الفن. وتنمو أعمالهم وتصدر عن دافعيتهم الداخلية وتجربتهم المكنونة، سوظّفين في الغالب مواد متفرّدة أو أساليب تصنيعية. ولعلّنا نشجع في هذا المقام المزيد من الفنانين ليظهروا من جديد في المجتمع المحلي دون تدريب عملي أو شهادة.

لقد واصلنا استضافتنا للعديد من ورش عمل ارتداد- التعلّم حول الفن مع الأطفال واليافعين. وتعقد مثل هذه الورش ضمن المدارس والأحياء السكنية. وما من فرض أو إكراه فيها، ولا يترتب عليها رسوم، أو امتحانات، أو شهادات. والغاية الكامنة لمثل هذه الورش هي تنمية قدرات الأشخاص وبشكل حيوي على تعريف، ومقاومة، وقول "لا" للمؤسسات/الاتجاهات/السلوكيات/الهياكل الإجبارية المشجعة على الاستهلاك، والتنافسية، والتي تسترقنا؛ وبدلاً من ذلك، علينا أن نبدأ من جديد ونبني العلاقات والفضاءات الطبيعية التي تساعد على تعزيز التعلّم بناء على مبادرة ذاتية وحوار ثقافات. ومثل هذه الورش تسعى إلى استكشاف إجابة على السؤال: كيف يمكننا أن نشترك وبشكل أصيل في مشاعرنا، وتجاربنا، وأفكارنا من خلال تعبيراتنا الخاصة؟

عندما بدأنا باستضافة هذه الورش، كان أحد أول الأمور التي لاحظناها هو التكيف العميق الذي تحدثه المدرسة داخل كل طفل. لقد درّس الأطفال أن يتبعوا تعليمات المدرّس والاعتماد على الكبار لتزويدهم بالقوالب التي تناسبهم. فعلى سبيل المثال، وفي اليوم الأول من الورشة، رسم ٢١ من أصل ٢٥ طفلاً الموضوع ذاته- الجبال، الشمس، الكوخ، والنهر- وما درّبوا على رسمه في المدرسة. وفي اليوم الثاني، قال معظم الأطفال إنهم لم يعرفوا كيف يرسمون شيئاً آخر. وتطلب الأطفال أيضاً مديحاً مستمراً، وكان يهمهم الحصول على موافقة وتطمينات العامل الخارجي: وكانوا يعرفون حق المعرفة كيف يحصلون عليها، وكان يمكنهم القيام بأي شيء يرغبون فيه، وكان ما يرسمونه "جيداً". ولاحظنا أن الأطفال غالباً ما كانوا يسخرون من العمل الفني لأقرانهم؛ ولم تكن لديهم المعرفة بكيفية دعم أو تقدير بعضهم بعضاً. ووجدنا أن الأطفال الذين لم يذهبوا إلى المدرسة كانوا أكثر انفتاحاً على التعبير عن مختلف الأشكال والصور وتجربتها.

وفي سياق ورش العمل، هناك موضوعات معيّنة نشأت كموضوعات مهمة. وأحدها يشتمل على المساحة الكافية "لجعل الشخص يقبل باتساخ يديه

مرة أخرى"- بعيداً عن أفكار الطبقة الوسطى العقيمة حول "النظافة". وموضوع آخر هو فتح فضاء آخر للانخراط في المسائل الحساسة المتعلقة بأشكال الوسائل المسيطرة مثل الكتب الدراسية، والتلفزيون، والصحف. إننا نمضي الوقت في مناقشة من الذي ينشئ الصور التي نراها وكيف يمكن للأجندات والصور النمطية المختلفة أن تروّج من خلال صور محددة.

وثمة موضوع ثالث ألا وهو استكشاف الطريقة التي نفهم من خلالها "الموارد" أو "الجذور" التي ينبع منها فننا. ولهذا أبعاد عديدة. إننا نحاول أن نشجع الشباب اليافعين على الاطلاع على تجاربهم الشخصية المختلفة وكذلك القصص المحليّة المفضلة. كما أننا نمضي الوقت محاولين الولوج إلى الأشكال التقليدية للفن والتصميم المحلّي. والطريقة الأسهل للقيام بهذا الأمر هي التفاعل مع أمهاتنا وجدّاتنا الأميّات (واللواتي لم ينسب إليهن الفضل اللازم كمدرّسات مشروعات في إطار المدرسة). إنهن من يمتلك أدوات الأساليب التقليدية مثل المندانا والتي رسمت على روث البقر والبيوت المشيّدة من الطين. كما أننا نطرق باب ذاكرة اللاوعي لجماليات اللغات المحليّة والـ Lokavidya أي معارف الناس وذلك من خلال العمل في المهرجانات المحليّة وباللغة المحلية والتي يحظر تداولها في المدرسة عادة.

أما بالنسبة للموارد، فقد كان تركيزنا على استخدام الألوان المحلية (المصنوعة من مواد طبيعية تستخدمها الأسرة في حياتها اليومية مثل الزعفران، والحنّة، والفحم..الخ). كما أننا نشجع على "رفع التدوير". ومن المظاهر الرئيسة لهذا الأمر كان بناء العلاقات مع أشخاص معينين مثل الخياط للحصول على قطع القماش المستخدمة، وميكانيكي الدراجات الهوائية للحصول على الإطارات الكاوتشوكية، ومالك الدكان للحصول على الصناديق الكرتونية الفارغة.

ونحاول من خلال موضوع رابع أن نستكشف انفتاحنا على ارتكاب الأخطاء بدلاً من إخفائها. وكذلك، التغلّب على الخوف من العقاب أو السخرية أو النقد الذي نواجهه ونحن نحاول استكشاف أفكار جديدة والدخول في تجارب وعلاقات جديدة.

ومن المبادرات الأخرى التي أطلقناها ونفذناها هي إعادة ربط الأطفال والشباب مع الفنانين والحرفيين. إننا نحاول أن نصطحب الأطفال إلى مواقع الفنانين بدلاً من دعوة هؤلاء لزيارة المدارس. وكان أحد آمالنا هو محو الأسطورة التي جعلت من المحترفات مكاناً يقتصر على الأغنياء فقط. وكذلك، يحصل الأطفال على الفرصة لإشراك الفنانين بشكل أكبر في عملهم، وإلهاماتهم، وتجاربهم. كما أنهم يمضون وقتاً كبيراً يسألون الفنانين عن المعنى الذي يسكن في فنّهم، وبشكل خاص الأساليب الأكثر معاصرة. والأهم من هذا وذاك، أنهم يعيشون تجربة وجود العديد من الأساليب المختلفة للفن إلى جانب الواقعية. كما نزور المزيد من الفضاءات التقليدية مثل قرية صناعات خزفية تعرف باسم موليلا. ففي هذه الأوضاع، يعيش الأطفال مع العائلات بهدف تجربة المزيد من الطرق المتكاملة للعيش- الفنان الذي يعيش ضمن حكمة المجتمع المحلّي، والفنان بتناغم مع الطبيعة. وفي نهاية المطاف، وبعد أخذ صفحة من هذه التجارب، نأمل أن نستطيع تحليل المحترف وإعادته من جديد إلى المنزل والحي السكني. ولعلّ الأمر الذي كان على جانب خاص من الإثارة حتى الآن هو أن بعض الفنانين قد بدأوا فعلاً في الخروج من الحدود الآمنة لمحترفاتهم وجامعاتهم متطوعين بوقتهم لأنشطة المجتمعات المحلية.

ولخلق المزيد من الفرص للتفاعلات الدراسية ذاتية التنظيم بين أفراد المجتمع المحلّي والفنانين، قمنا أيضاً بنشر كتابين للأطفال وعائلاتهم. أحدهما بعنوان Rang Bharay Jeevan Mein أي "الحياة تضج بالألوان"؛ وفيه مقابلات مشتركة حول مختلف الفنانين والأشكال الفنيّة في أودايبور. ويلقي الكتاب الضوء على عمل ١٢ فناناً تتراوح أساليبهم من المنمنمات التقليدية إلى القبلية، فالمعاصرة. كما يعرض الكتاب عناوين المحترفات الخاصة بمختلف الفنانين إلى جانب دعوات لزيارتها. ومن الأمور الملفتة بشكل خاص في هذا الكتاب هو أنه جاء نتيجة لبحث قام به شباب لا معرفة لديهم بالفنون. ويعرض الفصل الأخير من الكتاب تأملاتهم وأفكارهم حول الطريقة التي تحوّلت فيها مدركاتهم حول الفن والفنانين.

أما المبادرة الثالثة التي كنا نعمل على تجربتها فهي أن نعيد الفن إلى المساحات العامة مثل المتنزهات، وواجهات المنازل والمتاجر المحلية. كنا نطلب إلى الفنانين المحليين أن يعملوا بشكل تعاوني مع الأطفال والعائلات من سكان الحي المحلي لإنتاج جداريات، ولوحات فسيفسائية، ومنحوتات باستخدام المواد المتوفرة محليّاً، وبشكل خاص المهملات.

وفي العديد من المشروعات، كنا نستخدم أساليب التقدير مع العائلات في المجتمع المحلّي لاستكشاف اللحظات الممتعة في حياة الأشخاص وكذلك المعرفة المهمة، والأسئلة، والعواطف، والمهارات المتوافرة لديها. ودخلنا أيضا في العديد من النقاشات بشأن التغييرات الطارئة على مجتمعاتهم المحليّة وفي أودايبور.

أما بالنسبة لما استطعنا الوصول إليه من خلال هذه المبادرات المختلفة، فهو القناعة بأن الفن كمنتَج والفنان كمنتِج للفضلات الفنية يجب أن يتحولا إلى أسئلة العيش الفنّي أي، ما نأكل، وما نلبس، وكيف نتحرك باتجاه الأشياء، والطريقة التي نختار التواصل فيها، والطريقة التي نعنى بها بصحتنا، والطريقة التي نربّي بها أطفالنا، والطريقة التي نعتني بها بمواردنا الطبيعية.

وعلينا أن نفهم هنا أن الفنّ لا يقتصر على المخرجات بل هو يعنى بأسلوب حياتنا- وبالطرق التي نتبعها في استكشاف الأماكن والارتباط بها، وكذلك الأشخاص والأفكار؛ وفهم أنفسنا وتطوير مواهبنا اللامحدودة؛ وتغذية حساسيتنا تجاه الآخرين والطبيعة. وكما يرى كارلوس بتريني وهو مؤسس حركة الطعام البطيء: "أن تكون بطيئاً يعني أنك تسيطر على إيقاعات وقوافي حياتك الخاصة. فأنت الذي يقرر السرعة التي عليك أن تسير بها في سياق معين. وإذا كنت أنا اليوم أريد أن أسير بسرعة، فإني أسير بسرعة؛ أما في الغد إن أنا رغبت أن أسير ببطء، فإني سأسير ببطء. فما نحن بصدد الكفاح والقتال لتحقيقه هو الحق في أن نقرر نحن بأنفسنا الإيقاعات الخاصة بنا."

حلمي هو أن تتمكن الفنون من إيقاظ الجرأة الكامنة في كل منا - الجرأة التي تشجعنا على إحياء أعمق مبادئ الحياة. أذكر هنا قصة من تراث السكان الأصليين لأمريكا حين طلب منهم أن يرسلوا أولادهم إلى مدارس المستعمرين البيض. إجابتهم كانت مليئة بالحب والحكمة. قالوا، "بعد أن أرسلنا بعض أطفالنا ليتعلموا علومكم، اكتشفنا لدى عودتهم بأنهم لم يعودوا يصلحوا ليكونوا صيادين، محاربين، أو مستشارين. لم يعد لهم نفع. بالتالي علينا أن نرفض باحترام عرضكم الطيب. ولكن، وبما أنكم أظهرتم هذا الاهتمام بنا، علينا أن نرد لكم الجميل. فإذا رغبتم بإرسال دزينة من أولادكم إلينا، سنعلمهم كل ما نعرفه ونحولهم إلى بشر." كل ما أستطيعه الآن هو أن أصلي ليتمكن الناس في كافة أصقاع المعمورة من التصدي للآلة بمثل هذا الوضوح والقناعة.

المراجع:

كوماراسوامي، أ. ١٩٩٤. الفن وسواديشي. مونشيرام مانوهارلال، ناشرون. نيو دلهي، الهند.

إستيفا، ج. المجتمعات التعلمية الناشئة وعائدة النشوء: حكمة قديمة ومبادرات جديدة حول العالم. اليونيسكو. فرنسا.

مامفورد، ل. الفن والتكنيك. ١٩٥٢. مطبعة جامعة كولومبيا، نيو يورك.

بيتريني، س. كما أخذ النص من هونوري، س. ٢٠٠٤. في مدح البطء. هاربر كولنز، ناشرون. نيويورك.

سري غورو غرانت صاحب.

ويتلي، م. ود. فريز ٢٠٠٦، "استخدام الظهور لرفع الابداعات الاجتماعية إلى مدى أوسع." معهد بركانا.

http:// www.berkana.org/pdf/Lifecycle.pdf

اللاعودة، التبديد،
الفوضى الشاملة وآلات الضجيج

فرانشيسكو ماناكوردا

يشارك الإنسان - وبدرجات تتجاوز جميع المخلوقات الأخرى التي يعرفها- مشاركة واعية وإن كانت ضئيلة، في انتقائية التغييرات ووتيرة الإسراع في تطوره. وهذا ما يتحقق على شكل تعديل تابع ووظيفة مكونة لإجمالي توازنه الديناميكي النسبي، عندما يزيد من سرعته في الاستجابة إلى التفاعلات الشاملة والمعقدة للكون (والتي يُشار إليها محلياً بـ "البيئة").
بكمنستر فولر

من الصعب تجنب الانطباع بأن التفريق بين ما يقوم في الوقت، وما لا عودة عنه، ومن ناحية أخرى ما هو خارج إطار الزمن، ما هو خالد، هو في صلب النشاط الرمزي البشري. وربما يكون الأمر كذلك بشكل خاص فيما يتعلق بالنشاط الفني. وفي حقيقة الأمر، ثمة اتصال وثيق بين واحد من تجلّيات التحول والأثر الذي نحدثه في شيء طبيعي، كالحجر، إلى تحفة فنّية مرتبط بشكل وثيق بتأثيرنا على المادة. فالنشاط الفنّي هو الذي يكسر التناسق المؤقت للشيء، إنه يترك العلامة التي تترجم عدم تساوقنا المؤقت إلى عدم اتساق مؤقت في الشيء. ومما يمكن العودة عنه إلى شكله الأصلي، يكاد مستوى الضجيج الدوري الذي نعيش فيه، يرفع صوت الموسيقى العشوائية وموائمة للوقت في آن معاً.
إيليا لريجوجين و إيزابيل ستنجرز

ثمة مسار غريب لتعلّق الفنون البصرية بنظرية الأنظمة وعلم السبرنتيك(cybernetics)، والذي بدأ في الخمسينيات، تحديداً مع اهتمام مؤسس المجموعة المستقلة Independent Group جون مكهيل بالبيئة المتعلقة بالتصميم والهندسة المعمارية (من خلال وساطة مباشرة لبكمنستر فولر). ويعود من جديد في السبعينيات في صلب علاقة الفن المفاهيمي مع نظرية المعلومات، في أعمال هانس هاك أو مارثا روسلر لمحاكاتهما النحتية للأنظمة الحيّة، وأعمال ستيفن ولاّتس لأنها تمثل نهجاً سبرنياً أكثر انفتاحاً. لقد كان الفنان والناقد جاك بيرنهام وما زال، المترجم الأكثر تفوقاً لمثل هذا النهج إلى الحقل الجمالي. ويرسي النص التطوري الذي وضعه بعنوان جماليات الأنظمة ونشره في ملتقى الفن Artforum عام ١٩٦٨ الإطار النظري المتمكن: "لقد كانت وظيفة الفن الإرشادي الحديث هي الكشف عن حقيقة أن الفن لا يقيم في الكينونات المادية، وإنما في العلاقات بين الأشخاص وبين الأشخاص ومكوّنات بيئتهم."[1] قد يستند مثل هذا الاهتمام الطويل الأمد إلى افتتان ميتافيزيقي بعض الشيء بالنموذج الذي يحتوي كل ما حوله، والذي قد بيّن لنا كيف يمكن لمختلف أجزاء الحياة، وكذلك مختلف مجالات المعرفة، أن تترابط وأن تعتمد على بعضها البعض، تماما كما هو الحال بالنسبة لأي جسم حيّ في بيئته. لقد أشعل هذا الشكل من البلاغة النظرية فهم الإنسان، وهو يحلم بالوصول إلى رؤية شاملة للحالة الإنسانية بعلاقتها بالكون. وبما يشبه المعتقد الديني، كان الهدف من نظرية النظم، وإلى درجة كبيرة أيضاً، قريبتها من الدرجة الثانية الهيكلية، إيجاد إطار لغوي قادر على تفسير الكمية الكبيرة من الظواهر البيولوجية، والذهنية، والاجتماعية بنظرة واحدة. كما تجذّرت هذه الميزة غير المسبوقة للنهج النظامي في علاقته بعلم الأحياء،

[1] جاك بيرنهام، "جماليات الأنظمة"، أعيد نشره في جاك بيرنهام، أعمال غريبة عظيمة- مقال حول معنى فن ما بعد الفن الشكلي، جورج برازيلر، ١٩٧٤، ص. ١٦؛ وبالنسبة لأعمال هاك المبكرة، يقول بيرنهام: "بعض الميول الأخيرة في أعمال هاكتبرهني. ويتمثل أحدها في الإرادة لاستخدام جميع أشكال الحياة العضوية من أكثرها ثانوية وبداءة إلى أكثرها تعقيداً. ويبدو أن هذا امتداد منطقي لفلسفته المتعلقة بالنظم الطبيعية. وقد اشتمل أحد الأعمال ونشر في فصل الشتاء الماضي [نشر هذا النص عام ١٩٦٩] على احتضان صغار الدجاج كعملية مستمرة. وقد بدأ هاك فعلاً بالتخطيط لنصوص بيئية على لسان الحيوانات حيث تستمد المعلومات من الأنشطة الطبيعية للحيوانات ضمن بيئاتهم."؛ جاك بيرنهام، "أنظمة الوقت الفعلي" في جاك بيرنهام، Great Western Salt Works، المرجع ذاته، ص. ٣٠؛ أنظر أيضاً معرض معرض بيرنهام من خلال برنامج تكنولوجيا المعلومات: إنه معنى جديد للفن، المتحف اليهودي، نيويورك، ١٩٧٠

ما قد يرسي له أساساً بعيداً عن الادعاء الميتافيزيقي باستناده إلى ترجمة النماذج الملحوظة من العلوم إلى تخمينات نظرية، مما أتاح المجال أمام إعادة صياغة المشاكل القديمة، وكذلك شرح نظرية المعلومات الحديثة النشوء، بالإضافة إلى ربط الماضي والمستقبل من خلال نهج تعاوني. وهذا هو الحلم بقانون كوني واحد، والذي يمكن استخدامه لترجمة المعطيات عبر مختلف النظم، والأحياء، والبيئات.

وبالنسبة لـ جون مكهيل، كان الفن المعاصر- كما هي الهندسة المعمارية المعاصرة- أداة تستشرف المستقبل. إنه أداة كمالية تسمح للإنسان أن يتكامل مع المشهد الثقافي والبيولوجي للمستقبل. وفي مساهمته في المعرض التطوري (الرشيمي) الموسوم "هذا هو الغد"، يشرح الوظيفة التي يشترك فيها الفن مع الهندسة المعمارية: "في مرحلة ما من الشؤون الإنسانية تكون الطبيعة الفعلية لمثل هذه الحقيقة التي يستدل عليها عادة بالحواس موضع تساؤل، ويصبح من العبث واللا جدوى استشراف الغد من خلف أقنعة المصنوعات الفنية لليوم، والتي ندركها ونطرزها وفقاً لفرضياتنا الحالية بشأن ملاءمتها للإنسان. فأي تغيير في بيئة الإنسان يكون مؤشراً على تغيير في علاقته بهذه البيئة، وفي طريقته الفعلية لإدراك وترميز تفاعله معها.[2] وفي نهاية المطاف، سيبلور الإنسان من خلال تطبيق التكنولوجيا فهماً أفضل لوضعه الحالي والمستقبلي في العالم. غير أن ذلك لن يتحقق إلا إذا كان هذا التطبيق متخذاً لموقعه الملائم في النظام الاقتصادي الأوسع نطاقاً، والذي لا يحتاط للمزايا قصيرة المدى وحسب، بل يضع النشاط البشري في مركز شبكة من العلاقات البيولوجية، والاجتماعية، والثقافية المتبادلة. وفي هذا الإطار، نجد أن المستقبل يمثل فرصة للعمل نحو التزام بيئي طويل المدى تجاه الإنسان وكونه، والزمان/المكان لإشعاع الطاقة الجمالية.

أما الجانب المظلم للإلحاح ذاته بشأن تناول الوقت وعدم تساوقه، فلا بدّ أن يدور حول فكرة الأنتروبيا (عامل رياضي يعتبر مقياساً للطاقة غير المستفادة في نظام ديناميي حراري) والتحلل، والتي استولت على عقول الفنانين منذ روبرت سميثسون إلى جوستاف متزجر، بالإضافة إلى تجلّيها في ممارساتهم. ويأتي القانون الثاني لديناميكيات الحرارة thermodynamics ليشكل الافتراض الأكثر روعة، والذي يتقاطع مرة أخرى بين مختلف الأنظمة ويمكن أن تكون له صلة بأي من نظريات الأنظمة، من البيولوجيا إلى نظرية المعلومات، إلى الاقتصاد والتدوير. ووفق هذا القانون، تعتبر الأنتروبيا نظاماً مغلقاً يكبر عبر الزمن، مما يؤدي إلى المزيد من اضطرابات النظام. وتتجاوز مضامين هذا القانون مجرد التطبيق الواقعي له، من حيث أنه ترك المجال مفتوحاً لتأويلات مجازية لموضوعات دينية مثل حتمية الكارثة المستقبلية، والموت، ومشكلة اللاعودة في الوقت، والتي يتعين على كل لاهوت كما على كل غائية (الاعتقاد بأن كل شيء في الطبيعة موجه إلى غاية) تقبله. وإذا كان لنا أن نتتبّع أصول النهج النظامي البحت نجده لدى مناصري التطبيقات المبحثية المتنوعة مثل بكمنستر-فولر (الهندسة المعمارية والتكنولوجيا)، لودفيك فون بيرتالانفي (البيولوجيا)، وجريجوري بيتسون (علم النفس)، ومارغريت ميد (الأنثروبولوجيا)، ونوربرت فينر (مؤسس السيبرانية أو علم التُّربين)؛ وأبطال الجانب الأنتروبي مثل جورج باتاي، وإيليا بريجوجين، ومايكل سير، نجد أن لديهم فتنة أعمق بالفوضى، والاضطراب، والتشتيت اللعين.

وفي نظرة أعمق إلى نظريه النظم، نجد أنه من الممكن وبسهولة، تجريد علائقية النظام البيئي من حيث هو فكرة نهجية ليصبح هيكلاً حياتياً معمماً، نستطيع من خلاله تفسير جميع أنواع الظواهر الطبيعية البعيدة، والظواهر

[2] جون مكهيل، "هل هم مثقفون؟"، في "هذا هو الغد"، جاليري وايت تشابل للفنون، ١٩٥٦، ص. ٣٠. أنظر جون مكهيل لمعرفة المزيد عن التحقيق المتقدم لمكهيل حول فن التصميم ونهج النظام البيئي وذلك من حلال المؤلف الموسوم، مستقبل المستقبل، ستوديو فيستا لمتد، ١٩٦٩ بالإضافة إلى جون مكهيل، السياق البيئي، ستوديوا فيستا لمتد، ١٩٧١

[3] جريجوري بيتسن، الخطوات نحو علم بيئة للعقل، جيسن آرونسن، ١٩٨٧، ص. ٤٣٧-٤٣٨

[4] "هناك ما أسماه فرويد بالطريق الملكي إلى اللاوعي، وكان يشير بذلك إلى الأحلام، لكنني أعتقد أنه علينا أن نجمل إبداع الفن إلى جانب الأحلام في هذا المقام، على جانب مدركات الفن والشعر وما إلى ذلك. كما قد أدخل معها أفضل ما في الدين. فهذه جميعاً عبارة عن أنشطة يشارك فيها جميع الأفراد. وقد يكون لدى الفنان غاية واعية لبيع صورته، أو حتى غاية واعية لصنع تلك الصورة. غير أنه عند صناعتها، عليه بالتأكيد أن يريح ذلك الغرور لصالح تجربة إبداعية يكون فيها لعقله الواعي مساهمة صغيرة وحسب. ونستطيع القول إنه يتعين على الإنسان أن يعيش حقيقته في الفعل الإبداعي- أن يعيش حقيقته بالكامل- كما لو كان نموذجاً سيبرنيباً." المصدر نفسه، ص. ٤٤٠. ويتعزز هذا النهج بشكل أكبر من خلال الممارسة السيبرنية المنفتحة لستيفن ولاتس: "كقوة مقابلة للتوافق الإدراكي، يقدم العمل الفني للجمهور بيئة رمزية، يمكن من خلالها تنفيذ الروابط والتفاعلات بين المعلومات اليائسة وبطرق قد لا تكون مسموحة ضمن حقيقة عالمها الخاص." ستيف ولاتس، "المجموعة كنظير اجتماعي في الممارسة الفنية"، في عمل ستيفن ولاتس الموسوم، اتجاهات ضمن العلاقات الأربع، جاليري ساثمتن للفنون، ١٩٧٧، ص.٤. هذه كانت الطريقة التي يمكن من خلالها أن يوضع الفن في ريادة التحول في الأنظمة. "السيبرانية- شرارة تطوير علوم الحاسوب - مجموعات مقدمة من الأفكار (التغذية الراجعة) نظام الضبط الذاتي التنظيم، نقاط التشابه بين الظواهر العلمية والاجتماعية) التي مكنت الفنان أو الباني من صنع النماذج (الرياضية وغيرها) للأعمال التي يشارك فيها الجمهور مشاركة حيوية." رتشارد فرانسس، "ستيفن ولاتس"، في ستيفن ولاتس- ثلاثة مقالات، آي سي إيه لندن، ١٩٨٦، ص. ٧

المصطنعة بالإضافة إلى عقل الإنسان نفسه: "دعوني أبدأ الآن بالحديث عن الكائن الحي الفرد. فالكينونة شبيهة بخشب البلوط وتتمثل ضوابطها في العقل الكلي، والذي قد لا يكون أكثر من انعكاس للجسم الكلي. غير أن النظام مجزءا بطرق متباينة، بحيث أن آثار شيء في حياة غذائك على سبيل المثال، لا يغيّر في حياتك الجنسية، كما أن الأشياء في حياتك الجنسية لا تغير حياتك الحركية أو الناشطة...وهكذا. وثمة كمية ما من التجزيء الذي هو-دونما أدنى شك- أحد حيثيات الاقتصاد الضرورية.[3] وفي النموذج السيبريني، يكون للفن وظيفة تأكيدية، ومن الممكن أن تكون رسالته تبيان الترابط المتبادل الذي نميل إلى إغفاله ونسيانه.[4] وبالاستفادة الكاملة من نهج نظام البيئة، يمكن أن يتوسع نطاق التشابه ليشمل الممارسة الفنية، وليس فقط لتوضيح نقطة ما تتعلق بمستوى محتوى العمل الفني فحسب، بل أيضا لتطبيق المفاهيم والنتائج النظرية على الخطاب الفني، من حيث هو نظام بيئي في قدرته على إنتاج المعاني.[5] ولعلّه يكون من المفيد عندها، وضع المزيد من التفاصيل للأنظمة ضمن الأنظمة، عند دراسة التفاعل بين الأعمال الفردية بصفتها وحدات نظامية، يعتمد معناها كما تعتمد وظيفتها بشكل مشدد، على الخطاب الفني كونه كائنا حيا في حالة من التكيف الديناميكي الدائم.[6] هل يمكننا اعتبار نموذج النظام البيئي "وسيلة" يستخدمها الفنانون لبناء أعمالهم؟ هل يمكننا أن ندفع بهذه الفكرة إلى حد استيراد بعض التقييم البيئي إلى النظرية الجمالية، في محاولة لصياغة الأحكام الجمالية بفضل هذه "الترجمة" والتي قد لا تكون ملائمة؟

وفقاً لروزالند كراوس، والتي عبّرت بوضوح وشفافية ن ما يمكن اعتباره التعريف المقبول ذا التخصيص المتوسط، فإنه "لتحقيق استدامة الممارسة الفنية، لا بدّ من أن يكون الوسيط هيكلا داعما، وأن يولّد مجموعة من التقاليد، والتي سيكون البعض منها "مقتصراً" بشكل كامل على الوسيط، على فرض أن الوسيط نفسه هو موضوعها. وهذا ما يؤدي إلى خوض تجربة فرضتها الضرورة الخاصة بها.[7] ويمتاز هذا التعريف (الذي يترك جانباً للحظة خصوصيته) بالانفتاح إذا نحن توسعنا في تعريف "الهيكل الداعم"، موسعين حدوده مما يمكن اعتباره دعماً فنيّاً (قماش الرسم الزيتي، الرخام، التصوير، والنص)، بالإضافة إلى السمة البارزة للعمل (مثل محتوى العمل أو المسائل أو مجموعة الاهتمامات التي تعود إليها، مثلاً: التناقض في عمل مارسيل برودثايرز). وفي الحقيقة، يمكن للهيكل الداعم أن يكون فكرة، أو مفهوماً، أو اهتماماً، شريطة التعامل معه من خلال التقاليد التي تولده، وأن يتم تناوله بشكل متكرر. ويبدو، أنه من المشروع لنا مقارنة فكرة الهيكل الداعم بفكرة النظام ضمن تعريف كراوس، والتي لا تختلف عن تعريف الهيكل الحيّ، وبخاصة في فكرة ماتورانا وفارلا المتعلقة بآلة التكون الذاتي.[8] وبالمثل، يعرّف النظام البيئي على أنه التفاعل بين أحيائه الذين يتبادلون الطاقة والمواد مع بيئاتهم المحيطة، في حالة من الاستقرار الديناميكي والتناغم.[9]

ويمكن اعتبار العمل الفنّي الذي يحمل دلالة النظام البيئي، عملاً قادراً على إنشاء خريطة مرئية، أو خريطة تنطوي جزئياً على أربعة أبعاد، وتعمل- سواء بالمعنى الحرفي للكلمة أو بمعناها المستعار- ككائن حي في التفاعل مع بيئتها الثقافية والفنية التاريخية. وإن نحن قبلنا بهذا التعريف، كان بإمكاننا استكشاف المزيد من الطرق المتاحة للحكم على العمل الفني بطريقة "النظام البيئي"، والتحقيق فيما إذا كانت القيم التي يحركها هذا الحكم، يمكن وصفها بشكل مبدئي.

إذن، ما الذي يشكل بالضبط الخريطة رباعية الأبعاد، وكيف تصبح جليّة ومفهومة؟ إن العمل الفنّي يدخل نفسه سواء بوعي أو بلاوعي، إلى شبكة من

٥ "علينا أيضاً أن نوسّع من المفاهيم الفيزيائية والبيولوجية لعلم البيئة بحيث يشمل السلوكيات الاجتماعية للإنسان- كعوامل على القدر نفسه من المساواة ضمن النظام البيئي. فالأرض لم تتغير فقط بفعل التحولات العلمية والتكنولوجية لمهام اقتصادية وصناعية معينة وإنما كانت هناك اتجاهات قيمية محددة حفّزت هذه التحولات، من خلال الأنظمة السياسية-الأخلاقية، والفن، والدين، والحاجة إلى الاستمرارية الاجتماعية والتواصل المعلن في المدن، ونظم الطرق السريعة/وما إلى ذلك." جون مكهيل، السياق البيئي، المصدر ذاته، ص. ٣

٦ بطريقة الـ matrioska، نستطيع أن نحلل وإلى ما لا نهاية الأنظمة التي تشتمل على أنظمة أخرى، والتي ربما تنتهي بافتتان سيبريني يغشى الأبصار، وهو ما حدث بالفعل في حقبة السبعينيات:" أحد الأوهام الرئيسة لنظام الفن هو أن الفن يسكن في أجسام معينة. ومثل هذه الحقائق الفنية هي الأساس المادي لمفهوم "عمل الفن." ولكن وفي حقيقة الأمر، فإن جميع المؤسسات التي تعالج معطيات الفن، وبالتالي تصنع المعلومات، هي مكونات لعمل الفن. ودون نظام دعم، لا يعود للجسم تعريف محدد له." جاك بيرنهام، "أنظمة الوقت الفعلي"، في جاك بيرنهام، *Great Western Salt Works*، المصدر ذاته، ص. ٢٧

٧ روزالند كراوس، رحلة في بحر الشمال: *Art in the Post-medium Condition*، تيمز وهودسن، ٢٠٠٠، ص. ٢٦

٨ "آلة الشعر التلقائي عبارة عن آلة منظمة (معرّفة كوحدة) على شكل شبكة من عمليات الإنتاج (التحول والتدمير) للمكون الذي ينتج المكونات التي: (١) من خلال تفاعلاتها وتحولاتها تعيد وباستمرار خلق وتحقيق عمليات الشبكة (العلاقات) التي أنتجتها؛ (٢) تكونها (الآلة) كوحدة ملموسة في المساحة التي توجد فيها المكونات من خلال تحديد المجال الطوبوغرافي لتحققها على شكل شبكة من هذا النوع. ويتبع هذا أن آلة التكون الذاتي تعمل وباستمرار على توليد وتحديد تنظيمها الخاص من خلال عملها كنظام لإنتاج المكونات الخاصة بها، وتؤدي هذا بتحول لا نهاية له للمكونات في ظروف التشويش المستمر والتعويض عن التشويش." همبيرتو ر. ماتورانا وفرانسيسكو جي فارلا، التكوّن الذاتي والمعرفة، شركة دير يدل للنشر، ١٩٧٢، ص. ٧٨-٧٩

المعاني لها قيمها التاريخية، والاجتماعية، والرمزية، بالإضافة إلى مضامينها وعلاقاتها المترابطة. والعمل الذي يوظّف فكرة النظام البيئي ليكون الهيكلية الداعمة له، ينجح في توضيح مجموعة من العلاقات واحتمالات تغيرها بمرور الوقت (البعد الرابع). وكما هو الحال في التصميم الرباعي الأبعاد لديناميكية بكمنستر-فولر *dymaxion* أو الهندسة المعمارية القائمة على الزمن، والتي طرحها سدرك برايس، يمثل الزمن عاملاً رئيساً في خلق هياكل قابلة للتعديل، وفي حالة مستمرة من التوازن الديناميكي. مع ذلك، فإن إضافة البعد الرابع تعيدنا مرة أخرى إلى عاملين اثنين مهمين: فمن جانب، مسألة العودة إلى الحالة الأصلية المرتبطة بالقانون الثاني لديناميكيات الحرارة، ومن جانب آخر، الخريطة رباعية الأبعاد، وكلتاهما تبدوان وكأنهما تشهدان في نهاية المطاف على فكرة التعقيد بدلاً من التبسيط التعليمي، والذي هو أحد المؤشرات التي يمكن من خلالها، الحكم على عمل فنّي من منظور النظام البيئي. والعمل المعقد، هو الذي يكون مناقضاً للتواصل الشفاف والتوضيح: وقد لا يكون للفن دور في التواصل حول مسألة أو حالة من الحالات، بل أن يجعلها أكثر تعقيداً وغموضاً، مع التعبير عن مضامينها المتعددة، وفي بعض الأحيان، الغامضة والمتعددة الأوجه. وفي هذا المقام، يذكرنا لودفيك فون بيرتالانفي بأنه: "يقال أن الطاقة هي عمله الفيزياء، تماماً كما أن القيم الاقتصادية تعبر عن ذاتها من خلال الدولار أو الجنيه." وفي فعل آخر من أفعال الترجمة، تجدنا نتساءل إن كنا نستطيع أن نعتبر التعقيد، هو عملة الجماليات البيئية المؤقتة.[10] وتؤدي بنا هذه الاتجاهات إلى تقييم وتقدير الأعمال، التي بدلاً من أن تشير إلى الحلول، تتمحور حول نظامها الداخلي الداعم، بتوازن إجمالي ديناميكي دائم التغيير، بحيث تقوم في بعض الأحيان بتغذيته، وفي أحيان أخرى تركز على اضطراباته (وهنا يعود سميثسون إلى الظهور بشكل ساحر لإنقاذنا)، وهنا يمكننا بالضبط، أن نجد مفتاحاً أكثر تعقيداً نستطيع من خلاله أن نجد لأنفسنا موضعاً في الخريطة الرباعية الأبعاد.[11]

إذن، لم تعد الإشارة إلى العلاقات الكامنة في نظام ما كافية، وهذا ما كان حلماً بالنسبة للتطبيقات المبكرة للسيبرانية في الفن، وربما اتصلت بشكل غامض بافتتانه التكنوقراطي بمضمون علم الحاسوب.[12] ويجب أن تبقى العودة إلى الحالة الأصلية ومضامينها الأنتروبية، أحد النقاط المركزية في النقاش الجمالي بسبب احتمالاته الرمزية. وعندما يدخل الوقت في الصورة، نجد أن النهج الغائي يندمج في النهج اللاهوتي، حيث تبرز المؤقتية أفكار الموت والتحلل. ويقوم جورج باتاي بتعريف سريان الطاقة في كتابه الموسوم الحصة الملعونة- مقال حول الاقتصاد العام، على أنه القوة الرئيسة للنشاط البيولوجي الحيوي وكذلك النشاط البشري. إنه يسمّيها ظاهرة كونية تنظم الحياة على الكوكب وفي الكون. إنه يوجه افتتانه بهذا الأمر إلى فائض الطاقة الذي لا يمكن استخدامه، ويجب أن ينفق دون فائدة في حركة تبديدية إسرافية.[13] وفي خطته الكبرى، تعتاد الطاقة على الاستهلاك الاقتصادي العادي، في حين أن فائضها يبدد في ظروف متطرفة مثل الحرب، أو أنه يوجه ضمن قنوات من الرفاهية الجمّة. وفي التصنيف الأخير، تجده يجمع ثلاث طرق طبيعية للـ "تبذير المرفّه": الأكل، الموت، والتناسل الجنسي، ويضع بمقابلها، طريقتين مخصصتين لضبط مصروف الطاقة: العمل والتكنولوجيا.[14] تصبح الأنتروبية وضرورتها التي لا يمكن العودة عنها في رؤية باتاي، استعارة نظرية فاتنة للظروف المأساوية، التي لا يستطيع الإنسان تجنبها. ويقيّم باتاي التبديد أو الإسراف على مستوى رمزي، كحالة متناقضة ومشرقة للوفرة، ويحوّل معتقده ما يقيّم على أنه موضع خزي أخلاقي- تحديداً هدر- ضمن عمل رمزي، ينشأ فيه المعنى من خلال الوفرة والتبديد.

٩ النهج النظامي لعلم البيئة ورائده هوارد ت. أودم بشكل خاص وهو الذي وضع هذا التعريف البسيط: "تتصل الكائنات الحية ببيئتها غير الحية بشكل غير قابل للانفصال كما أنها تتفاعل مع بعضها بعض. وتكون أي كينونة أو وحدة طبيعية تشتمل على الجزء الحي وغير الحي المتفاعلين لإنتاج نظام مستقر يتم فيه تبادل المواد بين الأجزاء الحية وتلك غير الحيّة عبارة عن نظام بيئي." هوارد ت. أودم ويوجين بي. أودم، أساسيات علم البيئة، شركة دبليو ب. ساندرز، ١٩٥٣، ص. ٩؛ وفي نظرية الفن، وصف النظام الذي طرحه بيرنهام كمفتاح لفهم الفن المفاهيمي والمعلومات على أنه: "لقد درسنا النظام- مركب من القوى المرئية وغير المرئية في علاقة مستقرة- وقد أصبحت شكلاً متصاعداً للتعبير البصري. والنظام كما هو الجسم الفني عبارة عن حضور فيزيائي وإن كان لا يحافظ على ثنائية المشاهد-الجسم وإنما يميل إلى دمج الاثنين ضمن مجموعة من الاحداث التفاعلية المتحولة." جاك بيرنهام، ما هو أبعد من النحت الحديث- آثار العلم والتكنولوجيا على النحت في هذا القرن، آلن لين، مطبعة بنغون، لندن، ١٩٦٨، ص. ٣٧٢

١٠ لودفيك فون بيرتالانفي، نظرية النظام العام، المصدر ذاته، ص. ٤١

١١ "بالطبع، في بداية السبعينيات، كان هناك العديد من الفنانين الذين بدأوا فعلاً بالتحقيق في الأسئلة المتعلقة بالتفاعل والإصلاح البيئي- وكان الأشخاص يتباينون بالأسلوب والاتجاه كهيلين ونيوتن هاريسن، وهانس هاك، وبتي بومن، وآلن سونفست. يبدو أن هناك القليل من الأدلة في كتابات سمثسون أو تعليقاته العامة التي استشعرت انجذاباً لهذا النوع من العمل. ففي نهاية المطاف، كان طموحه الرئيس وهو في الحقيقة ما يوحد جميع نبضاته الأخرى يبدو أقل من أن يقترح كيفية إصلاح موقع معين؛ بل كان طموحه هو دراسة الطرق التي أدت إلى خراب ذلك الموقع. وكان يبحث دائماً عن السبل الكفيلة ربما بأن تجعل هذه الأعطال، وهذه الاضطرابات مفيدة في استرجاع الرواسب الأنتروبية الرنانة ضمن اللحظة الحاضرة." جيفري كاستنر، "هناك، الآن: من روبرت سمثسون إلى جوانتنامو"، في ماكس آندروز (طبعة منقحة)، الأرض، الفن، كتيب ثقافي في علم البيئة، الجمعية الملكية للفنون والآداب، ٢٠٠٦، ص. ٢٨

باتاي ليس هو المفكر الوحيد الذي حاول تغيير استيعابنا المكتسب لخسارة النظام (الأنتروبي) من أثر سلبي إلى مورد إيجابي. كما أن ظهور فكرة الديناميكيات الحرارية غير الخطيّة قد أتاح المجال أمام نشوء الفكرة العلمية لـ "النظام التبديدي". ويشتمل هذا التعريف الذي يوضحه، الكيميائي إيليا بريجوجين الحائز على جائزة نوبل وفيلسوفة العلم إزابيل ستنجرز، على أي نظام مفتوح، مثل الأعاصير والزوابع، التي تتبادل الطاقة والمادة مع البيئة ضمن شرط "بعيد عن التوازن الديناميكي الحراري"، والذي يمكن ترجمته مبدئياً إلى نظام فوضى إيجابية.[15] ويحدث هذا، عندما يتذبذب النظام بهذه الطريقة القوية بسبب التغذية الراجعة الإيجابية، حتى أنه يدمر التنظيم الذي كان قائماً مسبقاً؛ ومن الممكن أن تكون النتيجة غير المتوقعة لهذا الانقسام الثنائي، مستوى أعلى من الفوضى أو التنظيم. في مثل هذه الظروف، يفقد الاستقرار والتوازن، وهما العاملان اللذان يحظيان بقيمة عالية حسب نظرية النظم العامة القديمة، وضعهما الغائي للتفوق غير المشروط، بحيث تبقى فسحة للعمل الإيجابي بسببه الحظ، والفوضى، والضرورة، والاضطراب. وإذا كان باتاي يقيّم الوفرة والتبديد كنشاط رمزي ضروري، يتم فيه الاحتفاء بحماسة الحياة احتفاء طقوسياً، يبتعد بريجوجين عن إطلاق أحكام أخلاقية وأحكام القيمة الجمالية على الفوضى، والهدر، والأنتروبيا. فحسب مفهومه هو، لا توجد خسارة علمية في عدم التنظيم، بل على العكس، قد يكون ثمة كسب ما في التعقيد، وهو القيمة التي تنتج-في تناقض منطقي- من خلال الفوضى بعيداً عن التوازن. ولا يعطي بريجوجين الخسارة قيمة سلبية على المستوى الرمزي (التكويني)- كما هي بالنسبة لباتاي- بل هي على المستوى العملي (التطبيق العملي) مبنية على تقييم علمي.[16]

هل يمكن للعمل الفني أن يكون هيكلية تبديدية بدلاً من أن يكون نظاماً عاماً؟ وهل يمكن لهذه الهيكلية أن تكون وسيطا؟ هنا، قد يكمن الفرق الرئيس ضمن آمال بيرنهام في جماليات الأنظمة والفن السيبريني الذي ساد في السبعينيات. عندها، وفّرت قيم معينة مثل استقرار النظام وضبط مكوناته لأنصارها، الحجة المناسبة لمرشح أو فلتر يمكن الحصول عليه في نهاية المطاف للسيطرة على النظام الحقيقي، الذي قبل بحلم تكنولوجيا المعلومات والمضامين شبه الدينية للهيكلية: "لن يصبح النظام الديناميكي المستقر مجرد رمز للحياة، بل هو الحياة بكل ما في الكلمة من معنى- الحياة بين يدي الفنان والوسيط المسيطر على المشاريع الجمالية المستقبلية."[17] وبعيداً عن توجيه التفاؤل ذاته إلى النهج النظامي المطلق، يمكننا أن نقارب بين قيمة الاضطراب والتعقيد، أو حتى نضيفها إلى التعقيد كونها عاملاً رئيساً في حكمنا الجمالي، واثقين أننا إذا لم نعتبرها عاملاً سلبياً، فإنها قد تؤدي بالعمل الفني إلى درجة أعلى من التنظيم، وهي بالتأكيد، نظام أكثر تعقيداً ولا يسير ضمن خط واحد.[18] وفي هذا، علينا أن نتذكر دوماً نموذج الهياكل التبديدية. ويضع بريجوجين وستنجر في اقتباسهما الاستهلالي الثاني، النشاط الرمزي للإنسان في قمة نقطة التلاقي بين النظام واختلال النظام، وبين ما لا عودة عنه وما يمكن أن يعود إلى حالته الأصلية، وبين الخلود والسهم الزمني للأنتروبيا. ووفقاً لهما، يمكن للإنجاز الفني أن يتكون من خلال ترجمة عدم تساوقنا المؤقت (السقف الزمني الخطي للأنتروبيا الذي لا عودة عنه)، ووضعه ضمن عدم تماثل الجسم بطريقة شمول وبمثل هذه الحركة، جميع التناقضات والتضاربات الكامنة في العملية. وعليه، يشكل الفن الجيد نشاطاً رمزياً يحفر مضامينه المتعددة الطبقات في عملية تحول/ترجمة الطاقة، والمادة، والمفاهيم دون تطهيرها من الضجيج، الذي يمكن أن يصدر عن عملية تحوّل من هذا القبيل.

[12] "لاستخدام محاكاة سيبرانية أخرى، الفنانون عبارة عن أنظمة "التكبير التحول"، أو أنهم أفراد مضطرون- وبحكم تركيبتهم النفسية- لأن يكشفوا عن الحقائق النفسية على حساب الاتزان البدني المجتمعي، وبجرأة متزايدة. تكون إحدى وظائف الفنان، في اعتقادي، هي أن يحدد الطريق التي تستخدمنا فيها التكنولوجيا." جاك بيرنهام، "أنظمة الوقت الفعلي"، المصدر ذاته، ص. ٣٨

[13] "سوف أبدأ بحقيقة أساسية: الكائن الحي، وفي وضع يتحدد بموجب لعب الطاقة على سطح الكرة الأرضية، يحصل بشكل طبيعي على طاقة تفوق ما هو ضروري للحفاظ على الحياة؛ ويمكن استخدام الطاقة الزائدة (الثروة) لنمو نظام ما (مثلاً: العضو الحي). وإذا لم يكن بإمكان النظام أن ينمو إلى درجة أكبر، أو إذا لم يكن بالإمكان استيعاب الفائض بالكامل، فبالضرورة أنه يتبدد دونما فائدة لأحد؛ لذا يجب أو أن ينفق هذا الفائض سواء بإرادة من الشخص أو دون إرادته بشكل مفرح أو بشكل كارثي." جورج باتاي، الحصة الملعونة- مقال حول الاقتصاد العام، كتب زون، ١٩٨٨، ص. ٢١

[14] مجلدات باتاي الحصة الملعونة مقسمة بشكل معروف إلى المجلد (١): الاستهلاك، المجلد (٢): تاريخ الشهوة الجنسية، والمجلد (٣): السيادة.

[15] "تزداد الأنتروبية فقط بسبب عمليات العكس. وخلال القرن التاسع عشر، كانت الحالة النهائية للتطور الديناميكي الحراري في صلب الأبحاث العلمية، وكان هذا توازن الديناميكيات الحرارية. وقد تم النظر إلى العمليات غير القابلة للقلب أو العكس على أنها أذى، وإزعاج، ومواضيع غير جديرة بالدراسة. لقد تغير هذا الوضع في يومنا هذا. إننا نعرف أنه بعيداً عن التوازن، يمكن لأنواع الهياكل أن تنشأ آنياً. وفيما يتعلق بظروف التوازن، يمكن أن يكون لدينا تحول من الاضطراب، ومن الفوضى الحرارية إلى نظام. ويمكن لحالات الديناميكية الجديدة للمادة، إنها الحالات التي تعكس تفاعل نظام معين مع محيطه. وقد أخبرنا هذه الهياكل الجديدة بـ الهياكل التبديدية للتأكيد على الدور البنّاء للعمليات التبديدية في تكوينها." إيليا بريجوجين وإزابيل ستنجرز، النظام من رحم الفوضى- حوار الإنسان الجديد مع الطبيعة، هاينمان، ١٩٨٤، ص. ١٢

[16] "لم تعد زيادة الأنتروبيا مرادفة للخسارة، بل هي تعود الآن إلى العمليات الطبيعية

إذن، هل يكون اختلال النظام عملة أخرى لتقييم الجماليات؟ قد يكون من المتاح لنا، أن نجعل الحقل الجمالي هو الحقل الذي تنفق فيه أكثر من عملة واحدة. إنه الحقل الذي يتمخض فيه خليط محدد من التبادلات المستمرة عن صيغة معينة، من الحلقات فردية التي لا يمكن تكرارها. تجمع بين العملات مع بعضها البعض، والتي يكون "الضجيج" بالتأكيد، عملة أخرى فيها. عندها، يمكننا أن نجمع اختلال النظام، والضجيج، والتعقيد تحت العديد من الترجمات المحتملة للأنتروبيا ونتائجها الرمزية والمادية. وتحديداً، في التداخل الذي نتج أثناء بناء نظام ديناميكي رباعي الأبعاد يسعى جاهداً لتحقيق توازنه، بحيث يمكننا أن نعرّف مؤشراً للتحول الجمالي: في سياسة التغيير، يجب أن يقيّم الضجيج والتداخل كوسائل إضافية للنقل، لا كهدر غير مستغل لعملية التحول أو الترجمة. وواسطة نقل كهذه، لا بدّ وأن تؤدي إلى تواصل آخر في أوقات معينة من خلال تعاملها مع النشاط الرمزي، وفي أوقات أخرى، من خلال بث رسالة تكون أكثر شفافية. يركز العمل الفني على تشوهات التوازن مهما يكن نوعها، ويبحث في عدم التساوق، ويستهدف التناقضات، لأنها بالنسبة له تجليات قيّمة للاضطراب الإيجابي.

وكما يرى فيلسوف ما بعد الهيكلية- ميشيل سيير، الشعر هو ضجيج العلم، وفي الزاوية بين النظام واختلاله، يستطيع الإبداع الإنساني أن ينتج معنى جديا، ونظاماً جديداً يكون أكثر تعقيداً: الضجيج يدمر ويرعب. لكن النظام والتكرار المسطح يعيشان في حاضرة الموت. والضجيج يغذّي نظاماً جديداً والتنظيم، والحياة، والفكر الذكي يحيون بين النظام والضجيج، وبين الاضطراب والتناغم التام. ولو كان لدينا النظام فقط، ولو كنا لا نسمع سوى التناغمات التامة، فسرعان ما سيغرق غباؤنا في نوم لا حلم فيه. ولو كنا محاطين دوماً بأغاني الحب الساخرة الصاخبة (shivaree)، ستنقطع أنفاسنا ونفقد ثباتنا، وسننتشر بين جميع ذرات الكون الراقصة."[19] لا بدّ لنا إذن من أن نضع الفن البيئي النظامي في حالة عدم التوازن المتأرجح بين الضجيج والتناغم. وهنا، يؤيد سيير الترجمة بين الأنظمة، كونها عملية تتحول فيها الرسالة من خلال استخدام قناة معينة. ولا بدّ لهذا النشاط التحوّلي من أن ينتج التداخل، وهو الضجيج الذي يمكن أن نجد له قيمة بدلاً من اعتباره مجرد هدر.

هذه العملية الموصوفة في هذا المقال، وكذلك في الفن الذي يناصره هذا المقال، يشكلان كلاهما آلات ضجيج، وترجمات، تؤدي إلى التداخل الذي يرى كنشاط رمزي، يبدو متموضعاً بشكل خاص وفريدا من نوعه في الخطاب الفني.[20]

ترفض آلة الضجيج أن تكون قناة لمعالجة المسائل مباشرة، وبشكل جليّ لا لبس فيه. بل إنها تترك مهمة التواصل الواضح للتصميم الجرافيكي والصحافة الشفافة. ونحن نترك للفنانين مهمة بناء آلات الضجيج الملائمة، وتوليد الغموض أو اللاشفافية بدلاً من التواصل الكفؤ، مما يؤدي في نهاية الأمر، إلى تعقيد رؤيتنا بالغموض والصعوبة، بالإضافة إلى تعقيد فهمنا لموقف بني البشر، ضمن النموذج النظامي البيئي ذي الأبعاد الأربعة، التي لا تنتظم خطّاً محدداً.

ضمن النظام. وهذه هي العمليات التي تؤدي في نهاية المطاف بالنظام إلى "التوازن" الديناميكي الحراري" الموافق لحالة الأنتروبيا القصوى." إيليا بريجوجين، وإيزابيل ستنجرز، نفسه، ص. ١٢٠

١٧ جاك بيرنهام، ما هو أبعد من النحت الحديث، المرجع أعلاه، ص. ٣٧٦

١٨ النظام غير الخطي هو النظام الذي لا يكون سلوكه مساوياً لكمية أجزائه.

١٩ ميشيل سيير، الطفيلي، جون هوبكنز، ١٩٨٢، ص. ١٢٧

٢٠ "كان هذا صحيحاً بالنسبة للفكرة المنهجية للرمز: فإذا كان التحليل الرمزي هو صنع ما أسميناه بشكل عام النقد الرومانسي، إنه ما عرفه القرن التاسع عشر برمّته وبعلماء الرياضيات والفيزياء فيه...الخ. وفي الواقع العملي، فإن هذا النمط من التفكير، والحساب الرمزي، والنماذج الفيزيائية، والاقتصادية... الخ. ميرلو-بونتي، في عين الروح، قد قدّس هدا النوع من ترجمة الوقائع الممنهجة، إلا أنه أضعف عموميته من خلال زعمه للطريقة واعتباره أن المثال يمكن أن يكون دالاًّ على خفض التركيز. وفي الواقع، ليس هناك طريقة حقيقية يمكننا من خلالها أن تطبق قانوناً معيناً للأنتروبيا عقب الاستعارات المتلاحقة والتي يمكن في نقطة معينة في هذا التعاقب، أن يضيع القبول القوي للمفهوم، سواء في جزء منه أو كله، وألا نتكلم بعد ذلك عنه بكلمة نعم، كما الطفل يجرّب النطق بكلمات الكبار." ميشيل سيير، هيرمز أو التواصل، طبعة منتصف الليل، ١٩٦٨، ص. ٢٨

بين الرغبة الإنسانيّة وقانون الطبيعة: أمثلة عن علاقة الإنسان والكوكب في ممارسات فنيّة حاليّة

أكيكو ميكي

موضوع علاقة الإنسان بالأرض ليس جديدا في تاريخ الفن. منذ بداية وجود الإنسان على هذه الأرض، ومن لوحات العصر الرومانسي في القرن التاسع عشر إلى بعض الأعمال الضخمة على طراز فن الأرض ومشاريع الفن البيئي في الستّينيات والسبعينيات، إلى نشاطات الفن البيئي الحديثة، استكشف العديد من الفنانين هذه القضية الأساسية.

إلا أن هذا الموضوع أصبح حاسما جدّا في السنوات الأخيرة. واتّخذت المقترحات الفنيّة التي تطرح مشاكل القضايا المتعلّقة بالموضوع مثل التطوير الحضري الزائد عن حدّه، والتلوّث وسوء الإستعمال والإعتداء، واستنفاذ مصادر الأرض الطبيعيّة وغيرها، اتّخذت اتّجاهات تزداد تنوّعا. مؤخرا، توقّع بعض المختصين أن يتم في المستقبل، ترحيل ٢٠٠ مليون إنسان بسبب ارتفاع منسوب المحيطات، بالإضافة إلى انقراض ٤٠ بالمائة من الأجناس الحيوانيّة.[1] ويحذّر آخرون من موجات الحر المتوقعة في ٢٠٤٠، أو من انتشار الحمّى الإستوائيّة حتى في المناطق المناخية المعتدلة في ٢٠٨٠، أو اختفاء الغابات الإستوائيّة وتصحّرها خلال ١٠٠ سنة من الآن. في ظروف مريعة كهذه، لا يمكن لأحد يعيش على الأرض، ومن ضمنهم الفنانين، تجاهل سؤال علاقة الإنسان مع الأرض كليّا: كيف يمكننا معاملة كوكبنا؟ ما الذي ندين به للأرض، وما الذي تدين به لنا؟ ما هو موقعنا في العالم، وما هي مسؤوليّاتنا وامتيازاتنا؟

أخذ العديد من الفنانين على عاتقهم مواجهة هذه المشاكل. المشروع المعنون بـ "ويند كارافان - أوبزيرفيشن أوف أور بلانيت (كارافان الريح - رصد كوكبنا)" للفنان الياباني سوسومو شينجو، هو من ضمن بعض الأمثلة على ذلك. هذا المشروع الطويل الأمد هو محاولة لاستكشاف إمكانيّة عيشنا بتناغم مع الطبيعة، وما هي السعادة الحقيقيّة، من خلال أنشطة فنيّة وتبادل ثقافي مع السكان محليين. مثال آخر هو "كيب فارويل (رأس برّ الوداع)" للفنان البريطاني ديفيد بكلاند. نظّم بكلاند رحلات إستكشافيّة إلى القطب الشمالي الأعلى، دعا إليها فنانين مثل جاري هومي وآنتوني جورملي وريتشيل ويتريد وعلماء وتربويين، لمخاطبة وزيادة الوعي بشأن التغيّر المناخي. في هذه الأثناء، يطرح آخرون، تحديدا الجيل الأصغر من الفنانين، هذه الأسئلة بطرق غير مباشرة ومجرّدة بدرجة أكبر، بخلطها التحليل الناقد مع الطبيعة الشكلية للفن التشكيلي وتقديمهما في سياق فنّي. أرغب في أن أناقش هنا، بعض الأمثلة المذكورة الأخيرة للفنانين القادمين من بقاع العالم المختلفة، بشكل منفصل عن الفنانين المشاركين في البينالي هذا العام.

تعايش

قد يبدو الأمر غريبا إن بدأت بالحديث عن الإيكيبانا، تنسيق الزهور الياباني التقليدي والذي تطوّر كثيرا في القرن الرابع عشر، وما يزال يُمارس بشكل واسع في بلدي اليوم. بالرغم من ذلك، فإن بعض أفكار الإيكيبانا تبدو ذات مغزى محدد حين نفكر بالتطبيقات العملية لبعض فناني الجيل الأصغر. عادة ما يُقال أنّ الإيكيبانا هي ممارسة فنيّة، ولكنها ليست لاعبا أساسيّا. تكمن قيمتها الفنية في ترتيب الزهور بعلاقتها بالمزهرية، وبالتناغم بين هذه العناصر. بالإضافة إلى ذلك، فإن الإتّجاه الأساسيّ في هذا العمل هو تقدير ما خلقته الإلهة الطبيعة. بكلمات أخرى، إنها تشير إلى أنّه لا يمكن عزل

[1] نيكولاس ستيرن، "رؤية نقدية لاقتصاديات التغير المناخي"، الخزينة، بريطانيا، تشرين أوّل ٢٠٠٦

أيّ نشاط إنسانيّ عن بيئته أو عن الطبيعة. ولا يمكن لانسان أن يخلق شيئا بشكل كامل. يمكن أن يلقى المرء عقلانيّة وأسلوب تناول للأمور. تشبه ما ذُكر سابقا في صلب نشاطات الفنان السويديّ هنريك هاكانسون.

هاكانسون هو غالبا أول الفنانين الذين يخطرون بالبال حين نتحدث عن علاقة الإنسان مع الأرض، وبالذات مع الطبيعة. منذ بدايات مهنته في أوائل التسعينيات، استعمل هاكانسون بفعاليّة نباتات حقيقيّة كمواد أساسيّة، بالإضافة إلى تركيزه على الحياة اليوميّة للحيوانات والطيور والحشرات لصنع أعماله الفنيّة. حائط تغطيه نباتات أثيثة توفر بيئة مناسبة ترتع فيها الحشرات، وغابة استوائيّة مقلوبة رأسا على عقب حيث يُدعى زوّارها للسير تحت وبين النباتات، وغابة من مائة أوركيدة طفيليّة تنمو كل واحدة منها على قطعة من فرع شجرة معلّقة في الهواء. جميع هذه من أفضل الأمثلة، وهي مجهّزة بالسقاية والتدفئة والأنظمة الشمسيّة حتى تشكّل كل واحدة منها وحدة حيويّة مستقلّة. هاكانسون، وبأسلوب بحث شبه علميّ، يراقب ويوثّق، ويصوّرها بالفيديو باستعمال أكثر الأجهزة التكنولوجيّة تطوّرا، كما في الأبحاث العلمية الزائفة. لا يقدّم في أعماله تصويرا مثاليّا للطبيعة، كما أنها لا تطرح تحليلا إرشاديا، وإنما ينتزع أجزاء من الطبيعة ويقدّمها في إطار فنّي، ولكن بطريقة محددة، بهيئة عالم العروض، مع مسارح وإضاءات خاصّة وملصقات إعلان وتسجيلات صوتية على اسطوانات الفينل وغيرها، وكأنّ هذه النباتات الآيلة إلى التحلل والأجناس الآيلة إلى الانقراض نجوم غناء مثل هورين. تستقرّ اهتماماته عادة على المشاهد الغريبة عنّا، مثل الفيلم عن الأناكوندا (أفعى ضخمة) النائمة والذي سجّله بواسطة كاميرا مراقبة، صورة موجودة حقّا، إلاّ أنّها بعيدة عن حياتنا الحضريّة اليوميّة. هل يقدم هاكانسون من خلال الطريقة البطيئة التي يبيّن فيها تهتّك الطبيعة من خلال وضع النباتات تحت ضغط وفي ظروف حياة منافية للعقل كناية على كيف يعامل الإنسان الطبيعة؟ وهل الحيوانات، التي تبدو في أعماله قريبة جدا ولكن من المستحيل التخاطب معها، تحيلنا إلى عزلة الجنس البشريّ عن الطبيعة؟ تُثار الكثير من الأسئلة ومن خلالها ، يوقظ الفنان حساسيّتنا تجاه الظواهر الطبيعيّة والتنوّع، ويذكّرنا بأننا جزء من نظام بيولوجيّ أكبر، أي كوكبنا.

كل ما عليها يتفاعل

بالنسبة للفنانين السويسريين جيردا شتينر ويورجه لينزلينجر، يبدو الرابط بين العوامل المختلفة أكثر أهميّة. بدأت صناعتهما للفن بالسفر إلى مختلف أركان العالم. كما يمكن للمرء ملاحظة ذلك بوضوح في كتابهما "ستيوبد آند جود ميراكلز (معجزات غبيّة وجيّدة)" (٢٠٠٣)، والذي مزج المشاهد/الغرائب التي رأياها وتركيباتهما الفنيّة التي حققاها خلال فترة سفرهما - والتي امتدّت فترات طويلة غالبا. يعتقد الفنانان أنّ طريقة صنع الفن هي تلقّي الوحي من موضوعات مختلفة قابلاها أثناء ترحالهم، وتطوير العلاقات ما بينها. في كلّ مرّة يزوران أماكن للتفكير بعمل فنيّ محدد وتطويره، يتعلّمان عن الثقافة المحليّة ومختلف تقنيات الزراعة، والنظم المحليّة للبستنة، واكتشافات علماء كل منطقة من خلال النباتات. يرى الفنانان كلّ أسرار العالم في كلّ ما يدور حول النباتات والمواد المختلفة، ويحاولان فهم العالم بطريقة أكثر عمقا، بالإستمرار في التعلّم عنها وعن تنوّعها.

يجمع شتينر ولينزلينجر مختلف الأشياء من السكان المحليين، بما فيها الفضلات مثل الأسلاك الكهربائية والألعاب المكسّرة وغيرها، ويدمجانها في تركيبات فنيّة معقّدة وشاعريّة مع النباتات والمواد الأخرى التي اشترياها في الموقع. في تركيبهما الحديث "نايت موثس إن ذا ويل بيلي (عثّ ليليّ في بطن

الحوت)"، ٢٠٠٦. في اليابان، اختلطت مواد جديدة وقديمة، مثل عشّ عصفور وجداه أثناء سفرهما في أفريقيا، وشبكة صيد وبلاستيك ستايروفوم متروك وجداه على الشاطئ القريب، بالإضافة إلى عيّنات من الطعام، وأزهار اصطناعيّة اشترياها من أسواق محليّة، جميعها معا. وما يثير اهتمامهما في عمليّة الإبداع هو أسلوب "إعادة التدوير." لا يعيد الفنانان تدوير المهملات فحسب - والتي تتحوّل إلى كينونة غامضة بوضعها في سياقات مختلفة، وإنّما يعيدان تدوير أعمالهما السابقة، يصنعان ورق حائط من تفاصيل صور لتراكيب فنية سابقة، مثلا. غالبا ما يختار الفنانان موادا عضويّة مثل البلور، ينمو البلور بمرور الوقت، وبالتالي تظهر جوانب مختلفة باختلاف المواقع/الأوقات التي تُعرض فيها. يتّصل الفنان بالآخر بشكل لا متناه في أعمالهما.

يمكن وصف العمل الفني لشتينر ولينزلينجر كنسج قماش أو تجميع خيوط لقصة لا تنتهي أبدا. تخلق تركيباتهما الفنيّة تأثيرات تحويليّة بين الخيال والحقيقة، الخارج والداخل، الحميميّة والانفتاح، المكبّر والمصغّر والنظام والفوضى. تراكم التفاصيل في أعمال شتينر ولينزلينجر بحدّ ذاته يمثّل العالم بالفعل. من خلال الغرائبيّة الدقيقة والجمال الرقيق، يحكي لنا الفنانان أن العالم يمكن أن يكون ساحرا إذا غيرنا نظرتنا إلى بيئتنا.

مصدر الشفاء والطاقة

أكثر ما يُشتهر به كاي جوكيانغ هو مشاريعه الفنيّة الضخمة التي تستخدم الألعاب الناريّة والتي اختُرعت في موطنه الصين. وهي مادّة غير تقليديّة للتعبير. ويبني كاي أعماله علَى الملاحظة النقدية للعالم المعاصر وتقدم ملاحظات مباشرة عليها. وكثيرا ما تأخذ شكل الأحداث سريعة الزوال مثل الغيمات بشكلها الفطري (التي تحيل مباشرة إلى القنابل النوويّة) باستعمال الألعاب الناريّة. في التسعينيات، قدم عدة أنشطة في أماكن مختلفة من الولايات المتحدة الأمريكية، من ضمنها موقع التجارب النوويّة في نيفادا. تمّ توزيع العديد من الصور الفوتوغرافيّة للأحداث على شكل بطاقات بريديّة، وبالتالي أصبح السلاح النووي تخصص الولايات المتحدة الأمريكيّة. قام كاي مؤخرا بتجهيز تركيب فنّي يتكون من قطيع من ٩٩ ذئبا معصوبي العيون يهرعون عميانا نحو حائط فيصطدمون به، وبالتالي يقتلون أنفسهم بذاتهم، إحالة نقدية إلى تصاعد الشعور القومي وإلى انقراض الحيوانات كذلك.

تركز أعمال كاي على التعامل بحساسيّة مع الطبيعة، والتاريخ الثقافي والروحاني، ويتّصف عمله بالمقياس الجريء والحكمة الآتية من الشرق، وروح الدعابة الفريدة، والأهم من ذلك، يجب أن لا ننسى أنّه غالبا ما يقصد أن يكون العمل مصدر شفاء وطاقة لأولئك الذين يختبرونه. يظهر ذلك بوضوح في عمله الأوّل "برينغ تو فينيس وات ماركو بولو فورجوت (أحضر إلى البندقيّة ما نسيه ماركو بولو)" (١٩٩٥) حيث ضمّ كاي التركيب الفنّي، الذي يمزج بين التصوير من ممارسة الأبر الصينيّة، وبين الجغرافيا المحلية لمدينة البندقيّة التي تتجلى في الماء من القناة الكبرى (جراند كنال) والتي يُقال أنّها من أكثر المياه تلوّثا في العالم. وباعتبار البندقيّة كائن حي، يقدّم الفنان الأدوية لعلاج الأمراض المعاصرة التي أصابت المدينة. تحدّث الفنان عن المشروع وقال: "جلب ماركو بولو معه إلى الغرب الكثير من الأشياء الجديدة والنادرة والقصص المثيرة. إلاّ أنّه لم يجلب معه الروح أو الرؤيا الشرقيّة للسماوات والكواكب وللحياة. باستعمال الطب الصيني كأحد رموز هذه الروح، سأحضر معي الأشياء التي لم يتمكن ماركو بولو من جلبها."[٢] من أعماله الحديثة الأخرى "كاريتّا فاونتين (نافورة كاريتّا)" ٢٠٠٢، وهو عبارة عن نافورة على شكل

بيت السلحفاة موضوعة في قلب مجمّع تجاريّ في طوكيو. يسلّط الضوء على الروابط مع الطبيعة من خلال إدخال حجر طبيعيّ إلى المدينة وأن يطبّق بفعاليّة أفكار الفنغ شوي. بالحقيقة، يجب تفسير عدد الأعمال التي تستعمل الألعاب الناريّة على أنّه تنوي خلق مصدر للطاقة. استُعملت الألعاب الناريّة كأسلحة على مرّ العصور. ولكن كاي لا يستعملها من أجل العنف، بل يستعملها من أجل التعايش بين الطبيعة والكائنات البشريّة بنقله الاتهامات الموجهة للأسلحة النوويّة، من خلال تمثّل الذبذبات المتعاطفة ما بين أمنا الأرض والفنان وغيرهما.

تشكيل منصة

"لاند مارك (مَعلَم)" هو مشروع للفنانة الأمريكيّة جينيفر ألّورا والفنان الكوبي جويرمو كالزاديّا طوراه معا بين عامي ٢٠٠٣ و٢٠٠٦. يتعامل المشروع مع السؤال عن علاقة الإنسان والأرض بطريقة محددة جدا، بتفحّص الطرق المتنوّعة والمعقّدة التي "تحدد" فيها الأرض. يأخذ المشروع كحالة دراسية مشاكل جزيرة فييكويس في بويرتو ريكو التي احتل الجيش الأمريكي أراضيها لأكثر من ستة عقود. كان لاستعمال الأرض كمضمار لتجارب البحريّة الأمريكيّة للقنابل تأثيرا كبيرا على الأوضاع الإقتصاديّة والإجتماعيّة والثقافيّة والبيئيّة لفييكويس، والتي كانت فيما مضى جزيرة ذات جمال استوائيّ يستوطنها صيّادون محليّون. ومع أن الأرض لم تعد تستخدم من قبل العسكرية الأمريكية منذ ٢٠٠٣ بناء على جهود حركات المقاومة المدنيّة، إلاّ أنّ مصير الأرض غير معروف بعد. بالاعتماد على القصّة الحقيقيّة في فييكويس، وبالتواصل القريب مع نشطاء حملة المطالبة باستعادة الأرض ومع المحليّين، حقق الفنانان المقترحات الفنيّة على هيئة فيديو وكتاب وسلسلة من الصور الفوتوغرافيّة ونحت أرضيّ. يذكروننا بحقيقة أنّ الأرض تكتسب معالمها من خلال تاريخ الوجود الإنساني عليها، مما يثير الأسئلة التالية: ماذا يعني لأرض ما أن تكون عليها معالم؟ كيف نضع المعالم على أرض ما؟ من الذي يقرر مايستحقّ الحفاظ عليه وما يستحقّ تدميره؟[3]

من أجل سلسلة من الصور الفوتوغرافيّة صمم الفنانان نعالا مفصّلة لإضافتها إلى أحذية أناس منخرطين في حملات إستعادة الأرض. من خلال الطريقة التي يمشي بها المتظاهرون عبر الأرض العسكرية، يُعلّم حضورهم على شكل بصمات أقدامهم. قصدت ألّورا وكالزاديّا أن تصوّر بصمات الأقدام هذه المواقع (جغرافيّا وجسديّا ولغويّا وغيره) وأن تكون وظيفتها معاكسة-التمثيل لوظائف الموقع في ذلك الوقت. كما أنّهم يستذكرون العلامة التي تُركِت على القمر نتيجة سباق الوصول إلى الفضاء، وبصمات أقدام المستعمرين الذين رسوا في أرض جديدة. قطعة أخرى، النحت الأرضيّ الضخم، هو محاكاة جماليّة ومفاهيميّة لقسم من مضمار فحص القنابل، باستعمال تكنولوجيا التصوير ذاتها التي يستعملها الجيش: استملاك ناقد للوسائط التي يستعملها الجيش.[4] يتفاجأ المشاهدون أوّلا بالجمال الهندسيّ للأنماط. لكن، عندما يدركون أنّهم يمرّون بتجربة فعلية لعملية تدمير الأرض بدخولهم إليها مباشرة (بنفس الطريقة التي تدمر فيها اختبارات القنابل الأرض)، يباغتهم شعور غير مريح بتخيّلهم أن البركة الاستوائيّة الرائعة التي غطّت يوما ما أرضيّة البحر قد اختفت الآن تقريبا. أضف على ذلك أن هذه الأرضيّة ليست ثابتة، وتتكوّن من عدد من الأجزاء مصفوفة ببساطة جنبا إلى جنب، وبالتالي يمكن تقسيمها وإعادة تركيبها أو إعادة تشكيلها، وهي تنقل إلينا الإحساس بعدم استقرار الوضع الحالي. وفي نفس الوقت، تقوم مقام منبر للمستقبل.

[2] حوار مع القائمين على المعرض من ضمنهم الكاتبة. كاتالوج (نشرة مصوّرة) للمعرض، ترانسكالتشر (عبر الثقافة)، بينالي البندقيّة، ١٩٩٥

[3] جنيفر ألّورا وغيلرمو كالزاديّا، لاند مارك (معلَم)، متحف بالي دو توكيو (متحف قصر طوكيو، موقع الإبداع المعاصر/ متحف باريس)، ٢٠٠٦

[4] كالسابق.

يفسّر الفنان لنا هذه الفكرة بالشكل التالي: "بشكل عام، يتأمّل العمل كيفيّة صنع مضمار لتجربة أسلحة المقاومة ضدّ قوى الإستعمار والعولمة والعسكرة والتهديم البيئي. إنّها منبر حيث للحوارات الأساسيّة عن الأخلاق وحقوق الإنسان والعدل في مجتمع عالميّ يزداد عرضة لأشكال هدّامة من العنف والعدوان أعظم وأكثر دمارا. بالتالي، يمكن لإعادة تمثيل هذه المنطقة المجروحة أن تصبح أرضا خصبة ومادة خام لتخيُّل وتطوير واستكشاف هذه القضايا، جغرافيا وسيطة وانتقاليّة بين الدمار والشفاء."[٥]

حقيقة الأرض

صاروخ في السماء الزرقاء، آراء متنوّعة حول مركز إطلاق الصواريخ الصناعي، غطّاس في بركة تدريب، رافعة على شاطئ البحر، فريق من الرجال والنساء يسبحون معا في ظروف متجمّدة. هذه هي المواضيع التي تلتقطها المصوّرة الفوتوغرافيّة اليابانيّة ريكا نوجوشي من خلال عدسة كاميرتها. مع بعض الإستثناءات، الصور مجهّزة في مشاهد واسعة لآفاق عريضة من شرائط للأرض والبحر والسماء، مع حضور قليل أو معدوم تماما للبشر. الصور مأخوذة على نمط توثيق المشاهد العاديّة، تحاكي أسلوب المصورين المفاهيميين الألمان. بعكس أساتذة هذا الجنس الفني، لم يتم التلاعب في أيّ من صور نوجوشي من أجل تحسينها، أو التغيير فيها على الإطلاق. إنّها ببساطة مضاءة بإنارة يوميّة خفيفة، وتكمن المفارقة في أن هذا الأسلوب المباشر يضفي أثرا غريبا على صورها. بالإضافة إلى ذلك، لا تبدو المشاهد التي تلتقطها مهمّة لعيوننا المعاصرة. وبالتالي، فإن صورها غالبا ما توصف بأنّها رؤية للأرض بعيون كائنات فضائيّة.

يتعايش في صورها مناخان متضادان معا بشكل مثير للفضول: العادي وفوق العادي، الوسخ والجميل، الدنيويّ والروحانيّ، الصناعيّ والسماويّ مثل المشاهد الطبيعيّة لمركز تانيجاشيما الفضائيّ، مجمّع يُطلق منه برنامج الفضاء الياباني جميع رحلاته تقريبا، موجود في جزيرة جنوبيّة ذات طبيعة خلاّبة. في حين تميل الصور لأن تكون هادئة ومليئة بالجمال الأثيريّ، تركّز نوجوشي رؤاها على أماكن من زوايا الأرض الأربعة، ومناطق ذات طبيعة قاسية، أو الحدود الجغرافية للإنسان مثل السماء أو جبل عالٍ أو بحيرة متجمّدة. بالحقيقة، فإن إطلاق الصواريخ أو الغوص أو السباحة، جميعها أفعال تتحدى الجاذبيّة الأرضيّة. الفنانة بتركيزها على هذه المناطق والأفعال لعلّها تذكّرنا، أنّه في حين أنّ الكواكب والسماء وما تحت البحر عوالم رغباتنا وأحلامنا فإنّها ليست مواطن عيشنا الطبيعيّة. وبالرغم من أنّ صورا تمثّل أمورا ومواضيع عاديّة كهذه متوفرة جدّا في الإعلام، تصرّ نوجوشي على التقاط موضوعاتها بذاتها. من أجل تصوير غطّاس، حصلت على رخصة غطس خصّيصا، ومن أجل صور في مركز الفضاء، عملت في المطعم المحليّ مقابل النوم في بيت صاحب المطعم لانه لا توجد فنادق في المنطقة. ومن أجل سلسلة صور ضبابيّة لصاروخ وذيله الدخانيّ، صنعت لنفسها صواريخ ورقيّة وأطلقتها بذاتها. تعتمد صور نوجوشي تماما على الفضول والرغبة في استكشاف الحقيقة كما تراها هي، باتّصال مباشر مع البيئة، وتفسّر الفنانة ذلك بقولها: "أرغب في تصوير الحقيقة، أن أجد طرقا جديدة للنظر إلى الأرض."[٦] تقترح صورها أنّه ما يزال هناك عجائب وغموض وجمال على كوكبنا، ويمكن رؤيتها ببساطة من خلال إرادة المرء وجهده.

غالبا ما يوصف الزمن الذي نعيشه في بداية القرن الـ ٢١ على أنّه حقبة من الشك والقلق والإحساس بأنّه ليس هناك من مخرج. تساءل جان بول سارتر عما يمكن للأدب أن يفعله من أجل تخطّي المرحلة القلقة في الستّينيات،

[٥] كالسابق، ص. ٥٤

[٦] وثيقة إعلاميّة، معرض ريكا نوجوشي، سمبوديز (بعضهم)، جاليري إكون، ٢٠٠٥

الآن، يتساءل العديد من الفنانين عما يمكن للفن أن يفعله لتغيير وضع كهذا. فالفنان قد يكون هو من يملك الحل من منظور مختلف عن منظور السياسة والعلم. وبالتأكيد، فإن الفن هو أحد المجالات القليلة التي تتجاوز الحدود القوميّة والتي نجحت الإنسانيّة في بنائها. ويمكن للفن أن يملك سلطة أكبر كوسيط مما تملكه السياسة أو وسائل الإعلام والتي ما زالت محددة جغرافيا. وفي حين ليس هناك فعل نحو خلق نوع من الحكومة الكوكبيّة تتصدى للمشكلات البيئيّة، بالرغم من الإقتراحات العديدة التي تقدّم بها المفكّرون، فإن كلّ فنان وفنانة طرحته هنا كمثال، يستكشف بيئتنا الحيّة بطريقته، ويحاول الكشف عن الكثير من تناقضات وتعقيدات الواقع من وجهات نظر تاريخيّة وسياسيّة واجتماعيّة واقتصاديّة وثقافيّة. والأهم من هذا، أنّ أصوات الفنانين تصل إلى العامّة بشكل مباشر أكثر من أصوات السياسيين.

إذا كانت الرغبة الإنسانيّة قد جلبت معها تطوّرا حضريّا مفرطا، وتلوّثا، وسوء استعمال واستنفاذا لمصادر الأرض الطبيعيّة، فإنّها الرغبة الإنسانيّة كذلك التي تبحث أبدا عن الجنّة على الأرض. تمثّل الرغبة التعلّق الدنيويّ، كما تمثّل الكارما (القدَر) من وجهة النظر الدينيّة. لكنها أيضا النبع الذي لا ينضب للتطوّر وتحقيق الإمكانات الإنسانيّة. يجب النظر إلى كلّ أمر من منظورات متعددة. لربما السبب وراء إعجابنا البصري بهذه الأعمال الفنيّة اليوم، هو أنّها توحّد وتصور بشكل جميل الصناعيّ والسماويّ والروحانيّ والماديّ، والطبيعيّ والاصطناعيّ، والدمار والشفاء، والرغبة الإنسانيّة وقانون الطبيعة، ولعلّ في بعضها مفاتيح مستقبلنا.

في مدح محدّداتنا

تريفور سميث

الحديث عن الماضي تاريخيّا لا يعني معرفته على ما هو عليه حقا.
يعني أن يتمسّك المرء بذكرى ما، كما تومض في لحظة غضب.
يجب المحاولة في كل حقبة زمنيّة، وفصل التقاليد بعيدا
عن الامتثاليّة التي تكاد تسيطر عليها.

والتر بينجامين[1]

مؤخّرا، تلاحقني صورة لذاتي الشابة.

قبل عشرين عاما، في نهاية الثمانينيات، كنت في العشرينيات من عمري، وقد انتقلت مؤخّرا إلى فانكوفر لأدرس تاريخ الفن. الصورة التي تخطر ببالي الآن، ليست لمناسبة حافلة معيّنة أو حدث مؤلم، هي لتفصيل ما من حياتي اليوميّة. أنا أمشي بين الصفوف، ألفّ وأدير مظلّتي - لونها بنيّ ولها يد خشبيّة - تاركا ورائي المناخ القاسي والجاف لطفولتي في البراري. أنا أحتفي بالمطر الخفيف في هذه المدينة على الشاطئ الغربي وبالمظلة. لو كنت اليوم مثل العديد من أهل المدن المغتربين، أربط بين المظلّة والسماء المبللة والمزاج السيئ والرغبة العميقة في البقاء في الداخل. لم تكن تخطر ببالي علاقة كهذه أبدا. رائحة أرض الغابة المبللة تتناقض بحدّة مع الإنطلاق المفاجئ لعاصفة البراري. تحترق فتحات أنفي والسحابات تكفهر، لتصبح رعدا في حرارة ما بعد الظهيرة.

لقد كان هاجس الوعي البيئيّ الذي يعالجه بينالي الشارقة الثامن مفهوما واضحا في نهايات الثمانينيات في فانكوفر. أتذكّر زملائي الطلاب، والأساتذة حتّى، وهم يحملون أكوابا معزولة معلّقة بحقائبهم، وهم يهرولون بين قاعات الدراسة. الجميع كان يعلم أنّ الاستمرار باستهلاك أعداد من الأكواب الورقيّة والبلاستيكيّة بلا نهاية، ليست فكرة جيّدة. كانت المحال التجاريّة تشجّع استخدام أكياس يمكن إعادة استعمالها. كانت المواصلات العامّة أمرا محبذا. كانت هناك حركة بيئيّة قويّة تعترض على تقطيع أجزاء كبيرة من الغابات المطريّة.

في إحدى عطل نهاية الأسبوع، سافرت وأصحابي إلى الخطوط الأماميّة، قدنا السيّارات ببطء طوال ساعتين في طرق تحطيب وعرة. أتذكّر تحرّكنا عبر مشاهد غابات كثيفة جدا، حتّى وصلنا إلى موقع تحطيب فارغ. الطاقة الأنثروبومورفيّة أمر يصعب علي التعبير عنه، ولا يسعني إلاّ أن أقول، إنّ الأمر كان أقرب ما يمكن لساحة حرب. بالنظر إلى الوراء أتساءل، لمَ لم تصدمني الأسمدة والأدوية التي سمحت للزراعة الأحاديّة أن تحتلّ بنفس القوّة محلّ البحار الرائعة من عشب البراري الأصليّة؟ لعلّ السبب، أنّ دورة حياة الأعشاب تُقاس بالسنة، مقابل العقود وربما القرون التي يمكن لشجرة أن تستغرقها لتكبر.

لطالما كانت الشجرة موضوعا هامّا للفنانين في فانكوفر. صوّرت إميلي كار في أوائل القرن العشرين الغابات المطريّة في مقاطعة كنديّة مقُصيّة، ويظهر العديد من أشهر صورها قرى السكان الاصليين (الأبوريجينال) المهجورة ومشاهد لغابات المطريّة. إحدى أكثر لوحاتها إثارة للمشاعر "سكورند آز تيمبر، بيلوفد أوف ذا سكاي (مُحتقر كالخشب، معشوق السماء)" ١٩٣٥، حيث صوّرت شجرة منحنية، ومنفردة تُركت وحيدة وسط مساحة تحطيب أفرغت من الأشجار.

[1] والتر بنجامين، "ثيسيس أون ذا فيلوسوفي أوف هيستوري (بحث في فلسفة التاريخ)،" إليومينيشنز. (نيو يورك: شوكين بوكس، ١٩٦٩)، ص. ٢٥٥

صوّر الفنانون المعاصرون من جيلي فانكوفر كمدينة بحدود لا متناهية، أكثر منها مركزا عالميّا. أحياء لا نهائيّة على أطراف المدينة تبتلع المساحات الريفيّة، أو تتوقّف بشكل فجّ عند طرف غابة. إنّ الشجرة، والتي تكاد تتفوّق في ذلك على مجمّع مكتبيّ حديث أو مبانٍ بنكيّة، رمز أساسيّ في الوعي المديني الفانكوفري فصّله جيف وال في مقالة كتبها في الوقت ذاته تقريبا، حين كنت لا أزال أشمّ رائحة الغابة وألفّ المظلّة تحت المطر.

"ضمن العمليّة الإجتماعيّة ذاتها، حيث يعدّ شجر الغابة الجميل المنتِج متجها إلى زوال بسبب الحصاد الفائض غير المنظّم، يصطفّ شجر المدينة غير المنتِج مثل صفوف العسكر في مواقعها الاستراتيجية في هذا الصراع الأيديولوجي. كم هو سهل الوقوع ثانية في براثن الإيمان بتناغم لا يزال موجودا في المدينة والدولة، عندما تبدو فانكوفر كأنّها ما تزال مستقرّة في دورة الحياة للآلاف من نقاط الحراسة المزيّنة هذه. تركّز الزراعة المدينيّة على تشكيلات النباتات الخضراء التي تتألّف من أعداد من الطُبع الشجريّة، مرتّبة بشكل تكراريّ على أطراف الشوارع، أو مجمّعة بشكل جميل صوريّ في المساحات المفتوحة والحدائق. نادرا ما نرى شجرة منفردة في المدينة، والسبب محض أيديولوجيّ. الشجرة الوحيدة، هي الرمز القديم للإنسان الفاني، متجذرة في كلّيّة الطبيعة، إلاّ أنّها تعاني من مصيرها وحيدة. في عهد تبدأ فيه كلّيّة الطبيعة بالمعاناة بشكل مميت، يصبح بإمكاننا أن نراها كإنسان."[٢]

في إحدى رسومات رودني جراهام المعتادة، كانت طبعة الشجرة الوحيدة مقلوبة رأسا على عقب. ابتداء بـ "كاميرا أوبسكورا" (١٩٧٩)، عاد جراهام إلى هذا الموضوع في عدّة مناسبات خلال الخمس وعشرين سنة الماضية. في عمل الفنان وول الموسوم "باين أون ذا كورنر (شجرة صنوبر حائطيّة على الزاوية)"، ١٩٩٠، نشاهد مثالا على شجرة منفردة كهذه في المدينة، "متجذرة في كلّيّة الطبيعة، إلاّ أنّها تعاني من مصيرها وحيدة." شجرة صنوبر وحيدة تطل على بيتين بسيطين إلى يسارها. عمل آخر من ١٩٩٠، لوحة كين لوم المشهورة "آي وودكتر آند هيز وايف (قاطع أخشاب وزوجته)"، هي تصوير هزليّ قاس للعلاقة الإقتصاديّة والإجتماعيّة في اقتصاد كولومبيا البريطانية المعتمد على الموارد الطبيعية. يرتدي الزوجان قميصين مقلّمين بخطوط متقاطعة، وأحذية عمل طويلة الأعناق، وقبّعتين وبنطاليّ جينز. يقفان أمام جذع شجرة أعرض منهما معا. في الوقت ذاته تقريبا، بدأ روي آردن بإنتاج صوره الفوتوغرافيّة، التي تصوّر "المشهد الطبيعي للإقتصاد"، مثل "تري ستامب (جذع شجرة)" و"نانايمو" و"B.C."، (١٩٩١)، حيث يمكن رؤية جذع شجرة منبطحا على الأرض، يواجه القطع في الشجرة حيث بُترت عدسة الكاميرا، مثل جسم مقطوع الرأس. بعد ذلك بقليل، صوّرت سلسلة إيان والاس "كليوكوت بروتست (احتجاج كليوكوت)"، (آب أغسطس ٩، ١٩٩٣)، ١٩٩٣-٩٥ المظاهرات السلميّة التي أثارتها محاولة الحكومة المحلّيّة فتح أكثر من نصف منطقة البراري النقيّة في كليوكوت ساوند على الشاطئ الغربي لجزيرة فانكوفر أمام عمليّات التحطيب.

إذا كنت سأنظر من خلال عدسات ورديّة، أرغب في القول أنّ هؤلاء الفنانين ألهموا فيّ الوعي البيئيّ، إلاّ أنّني أعتقد، أنّه من الأدق القول أنّهم زرعوا فيّ إحساسا بالتناقضات السياسيّة والسخريات الثقافيّة، التي تجعل سوء استخدام البيئة ممكنا. لم تكن هناك علاقة مباشرة بين هذه الأعمال الفنيّة والحركة البيئيّة، إنّما وفّرتا الرموز الضروريّة للتأمّل الناقد الغائب عن شعارات الإعلام والدعوات الصارخة لتفعيل الرأي العام. في حين لم يكن (قلّل وأعِد استعمال وأعِد تدويرا) مبدأ سيئا للحياة، إلا أنه كان بالتأكيد مهدّئا أكثر منه علاجا. على اي حال،

[٢] جيف وال، "إنتو ذا فوريست: تو سكيتشيز فور ستديز أوف رودني جراهام ورك (إلى داخل الغابة: رسمان لدراسات في عمل رودني جراهام)" في رودني جراهام، (فنكوفر: جاليري فانكوفر للفن، ١٩٨٨) ص. ١٦

كسبت من خلال أعمال هؤلاء الفنانين فهما أعمق للطبيعة المعقّدة للنظام البيئيّ، ومن ضمنه يرتبط الخيار الأخلاقيّ والجماليّ بعلاقة معقّدة مع البيئة.

بالرغم من حقيقة أنّ عددا من الفنانين في فانكوفر يتمتّعون بسمعة عالميّة قديرة، وغيرهم قد بدأ بالحصول على الشهرة، فإن ما يدهشني بوضوح شديد كما أذكر لم يكن الشعور بالعالميّة الذي انتابني، بقدر محدودية الأفق الحتمية التي واجهتها. مهما كانت درجة ريفيّتي، لم تكن - كما يُعتقد في الغالب - حاجزا أمام انجذابي لأكثر أشكال الفنّ تقدمّا وطموحا من حولي، بل على العكس، أعتقد أنّ حدودا كهذه، كانت أساسيّة في تعطّشي لما هو جليّ بأنّه معرفة عالميّة جديدة - مثل ذلك الذي شعرت أن الفنانين يمثلونه في أعمالهم وكتاباتهم.

لقد عشت في ستّ مدن وفي قارّتين حتّى اليوم، وقد أتيحت لي الفرصة للعمل وللسفر بشكل مكثّف في أنحاء العالم، ومن الغريب أن أتذكّر أنّه في نهاية الثمانينيات كانت فانكوفر أكبر مدينة عشت فيها وأكثرها عالميّة - أكبر بمرات عديدة من ريجينا حيث ولدت وكبرت. لم أذهب إلى بينالي البندقيّة أو دوكيومنتا من قبل. لم يكن الثورة التي شهدناها خلال العقد الأخير في عدد البيناليّات قد حدثت بعد - بينالي الشارقة ذاته تأسس في ١٩٩٣، وبعد سنة كاملة من ذلك التاريخ زرت نيويورك للمرّة الأولى.

بطبيعة الحال، عندما استمرّت الإشاعات أن نيويورك تفقد مركزها في قلب السوق الفني أمام مدن مثل كولون، لم يكن لديّ أيّ منظور في هذا الشأن. وحين بدأت التعرّف إلى الفن المعاصر الذي كان يزدهر من حولي، لم أقم بذلك من خلال السوق الفنّي - حيث لم يكن هناك سوق محليّ يُذكر للأعمال الفنية التي تعتمد المفاهيم والتصوير الفوتوغرافي الذي بنى سمعة فانكوفر العالميّة - وإنما من خلال جاليري فانكوفر للفن، ومن خلال طلاّب زملاء وأصحاب كانوا منخرطين في مساحات يديرها فنانون، حيث كان صلب تشكيل الفنّ المعاصر. بتعلّمي المزيد والمزيد عن الفن والسينما والفلسفة والسياسة والخليط المعتاد لتجارب الفنّانين، طوّرت إحساسا اكتسبته بصعوبة، إلاّ أنّه متقلقل، وكأنّ ذلك يؤكّد قول الفيلسوف ميشيل فوكو: المعرفة = القوّة. في الوقت ذاته، أكّد فيّ مبدأ الحركة البيئيّة العالميّة، "فكّر عالميّا وتصّرف محليّا"، إحساسا بالقيمة والهدف.

رغم أنّ كل هذا كان مثيرا للغاية، إلاّ أنّ الأمر وصل إلى نقطة تناقصت عندها المكاسب، حيث بدا في المحصّلة، أنّ كلّ المعرفة العالميّة هذه، تزيد من تعقيد، أو تظهر التناقض في كل الأفعال. بدأ الإيمان الذي تقمّصته فكرة "فكّر عالميّا وتصّرف محليّا" ينهار سريعا بعد أن انتقلت إلى أستراليا في بداية التسعينيات. هناك، بدأت باستيعاب الجانب المحافظ بشكل عميق لهذا المبدأ. بتصرّفك محليّا، لا يمكنك أبدا أن تناقش موقعك عالميّا. إذا كنت على الهوامش تبقى مسلوب القوى، وإن كنت في المركز، من السهل جدا أن تكون راض عن ذاتك في قوّتك وقيمة ثقافتك. بالرغم من ذلك، في السوق الذي يزداد عولمة، فإن مبادرات محليّة بسيطة مثل إعادة التدوير، يمكن أن يكون لها تأثير اقتصادي عميق، ولكن، ليس التأثيرات التي تتوقعها، بالضرورة. حديثا، كانت المصوّرة الفوتوغرافيّة زوي ليونارد تصوّر أكواما من بالة الملابس المعاد استعمالها، مكوّمة خارج مراكز التصنيف الصناعيّة في نيو يورك. متتبعة رحلتها، صوّرت ليونارد الملابس ذاتها التي بيعت في أسواق قرويّة في أفريقيا. تُباع القمصان القطنيّة المستعملة وجاكيتات البدلات وغيرها، برخص يُنافس صناعات الأقمشة المحليّة التي أصبحت عرضة للخطر، ويعد ذلك حلقة من التبعيّات العالميّة. في المرّة القادمة عندما ترى طفلا من الكونغو يرتدي قميصا مرسوما عليه العلم الأمريكي، يجب أن تعلم أن لا علاقة لذلك بحبّه

لأمريكا (أو ديف ليبارد أو سلير) بل يتعلّق الأمر كليّا بالإقتصاد.

لبعض الوقت، اعتقدت أنّه من الممكن مراجعة هذه المصطلحات مثل "فكّر عالميّا وتصرّف محليّا". أردت أن أستعمل اهتمامات محليّة وخصوصيّات معيّنة تحديدا، كالعامل المحفّز لتطوير معارض وفي نفس الوقت الاندماج في حوارات يمكن أن تكون أكثر عالميّة بنطاقها - وهو، بشكل أو بآخر، مدفوعا بعملي كقيّم للمعارض نحو تطوير العديد من البيناليّات خلال العقد الماضي.
حين كنت في بيرث، لربما كنت على هوامش مراكز الفن المعاصر العالميّة، إلاّ أنني أردت أن أعمل وأتصرّف كأنّني في مركزها في المطلق. لم يكن من الضروري أن يصبّ كل معرض في خصوصيّة محليّة أو اهتمام فحسب، بل أن يحاول بطريقة ما، التدخّل على مستوى النقاش الأوسع. لم أعد أرى نفسي شخصا إقليميا، وأردت أن أخط طريقا إلى ذلك الحوار الأوسع ما بين كل المهتمّين، كما أتاح لي الفنانون والأساتذة في فانكوفر قبل عقد من الزمن.

من الواضح أنّه يمكن لاستراتيجيّة المعرض أن تستوعب الاهتمامات والقضايا البيئيّة بسهولة. جذب عمل الفنانة الأدائيّة السنغافوريّة تانغ دا وو "آم سوري ويل آي ديد نت نو ذات يو وير إن ماي كاميرا (أنا آسفة يا حوت، لم أعلم أنّك في كاميرتي)" ١٩٩٨، ردّا عاطفيّا قويّا من الزوّار.[٣] تمّ إنشاء تمثال لحوت بالحجم الطبيعي من شبك الدجاج المعدني وأوراق الصلاة، حيث تم حث الزوّار على إلصاق أشياء أو ملاحظات تتعلّق بعلاقتهم أو استعمالهم للبيئة. في نهاية المعرض، بدا الحوت مثل أيّ كائن بحريّ يخرج من الأعماق، تغطّيه الأصداف والقشور.

استدعى تقديم "ماكرولاب (مختبر كبير)،" وهي وحدة معيشة وتواصل مستدامة ذاتيا، في محميّة طبيعيّة على جزيرة تبعد ١٨ كم عن شواطئ بيرث في عام الـ ٢٠٠٠، مستوى جديدا من التفاعل مع الاهتمامات البيئيّة بالضرورة.[٤] التناقضات الساخرة في محاولة وضع عمل فنّي بطول ٤٠ قدم وعرض ١٠ أقدام عدا عن اللوحات الشمسيّة والبنية التحتيّة اللاسلكيّة في منطقة بيئيّة عالية الحساسيّة، أمر فيه تحدّي ويثير التفكير. وضعت الأحاديث اليوميّة عبر الإنترنت اللاسلكي زوّار الجاليري في الصورة، وتمكّن أولئك الذين يزورون الجزيرة من زيارة الموقع في أوقات محددة من اليوم، للتحدّث مع أفراد الطاقم. وأنا أكتب هذه المقالة كنت أزور الموقع الإلكتروني لـ I-TASC
(<Interpolar Transnational Art Science Constellation <http://www.interpolar.org)، وهو مشروع نتج عن الـ مايكرولاب. يتواجد حاليّا فريق من الأشخاص في أنتاركتيكا يجرون البحوث في إمكانيّة تأسيس مركز أبحاث هناك. يثير هذا المشروع طويل الأمد الاهتمام جزئيّا، بسبب الصورة الخيالية العلميّة التي يقدّمها - في وسط البيئة، والغريب عنها في الوقت ذاته.

أما الأهم في كل هذا فكانت الحوارات التي تطوّرت بين أفراد الطاقم، ليس من أجل رؤية فلسفيّة عميقة، وإنّما، للمحاولة الصادقة لفهم امتيازات وتناقضات وجودهم المؤقت هذا، على القارّة الأخيرة على الأرض. في المراحل الأولى لإقامتها، عبرت أماندا رودريجيز آلفيس، أحد أفراد الطاقم، عن إحباطها تجاه النفاق في المعايير، بالنسبة لقضايا التأثيرات البيئيّة التي أثارها هذا المشروع:

> "أجد أن الأمر بشكل عام لايخلو من نفاق. عندما يقول الناس أننا يجب أن نحافظ على أنتاركتيكا، لأنّها البريّة الرائعة الأخيرة. بدون أن يكونوا على الأقل، مهتمّين بالحفاظ على البيئة من حيث نأتي. إن كنّا سنكون راديكاليين في أنتاركتيكا، يجب أن نكون كذلك في أوطاننا. من السّهل أن نرغب بالمحافظة على شئ بالكاد تمّ لمسه، ولكن من الصعب الحفاظ على ما دمّرناه فعلا."[٥]

[٣] قُدّم عمل تانغ دا وو في المعرض "ديفايد آند ملتيبلاي: تانغ دا وو آند لوكاس جودوني (قسّم وضاعف: تانغ دا وو ولوكاس جودوني)،" جاليري غرب أستراليا للفن، ١٩٩٨

[٤] قُدّم مايكرولاب كجزء من "هوم (وطن/ بيت)" في جاليري غرب أستراليا للفن في بيرث، أستراليا ٢٠٠٠. قمت على المعرض وتوم مولكير وجاري دوفور. استمرّ موكلير ليتشارك مع ماركو بيلجان ليؤسسا I-TASC (Interpolar Transnational Art Science (Constellation

قد تكون المعرفة قوّة. لكن من الواضح أنّ الحصول على المزيد والمزيد من المعلومات والحنكة، لا يعني أنك ستمتلك المَخرَج أو السلطة لتحويل المعرفة العالميّة إلى فعل. شاهدت مؤخّرا فيلم "إنكونفينينت تروث (حقيقة غير مناسبة)" لـ آل غور، من موقع ينطوي على مفارقة، إذ كنت جالسا على متن طائرة تطير فوق المحيط الأطلسي بعشرات الآلاف من الأمتار. غور رجل سلس، مقنع وهادئ، في وجه ما قد يبدو على أنها إحصاءات تثير غمّا لا يفوقه غمّ. يقدّم الصورة الأولى في العالم على الإطلاق، والتي أخِذت من الفضاء بواسطة روّاد فضاء السفينة أبوللو، ويتحدّث عن موجة الوعي البيئي الذي أوحت به هذه الصورة في أواخر الستينيات. رؤية الأرض كاملة في صورة واحدة يضع الأمور في نصابها، فتبدو الأرض في صحة جيّدة ولكنها هشة. بالرغم من ذلك، وبشكل متناقض، فإن الصعوبة الكبرى بالنسبة إلى كلّ هذه المعرفة العالميّة التي نملكها بشأن الفن والبيئة كليهما، أنّ القضايا تبدو ضخمة وعصيّة، بحيث لا تملك إلاّ أن ترفع يديك استسلاما وتسير بعيدا. كما تقول رودريجيز آلفيس دائما "من الصعب المحافظة على ما دمّرناه فعلا."

إن كانت شخصيّتي المحليّة هي التي تلوح أمامي في لحظات الغضب، فالسبب هو أنيّ أتذكّر كيف تكون البراءة أحيانا الدافع للفعل. إننا نملك معرفة زائدة عن الحاجة أحيانا، فتبدو المهمّات نصب أعيننا مستحيلة. وبالرغم من سعينا وراء الحكمة العالميّة من خلال مشاريع مثل بينالي الشارقة، أعتقد أننا جميعا محليّون حتما، ورؤيتنا جزئية، متورّطون عميقا ضمن أفق تجاربنا وتغيب عنا عادة القوّة لتحويل رؤيتنا إلى فعل. يمكن لفن رائع بالطبع، أن ينتج عن هذه الفجوة بين الأهداف السامية والإمكانات المتناهية. عرّف توماس كرو هذا بأنّه تعريف الجنس الأدبي الرعوي.[6] المؤشرات غير واعدة فيما يتعلّق بالبيئة. ومحاولات العودة إلى الممارسة الريفية محددة في ظروف محلية - التفكير عالميّا أثناء التصرّف محليّا. ولكن، عندما يتعلّق الأمر بأن تتحمّل أشكال وأدوات أكبر من السلطة والنفوذ - أمثال بروتوكول كيوتو - هذه القضايا، فإنّ إمكاناتها تقّوض عن قصد، بسبب المقاومة العنيفة لرغبات واهتمامات محددة، تفكّر محليّا، في حين تتصرّف عالميّا.

إن في الأمر ضرب من التناقض. فالفن الذي رأيته كبوّابة لعالم يزيد اتّساعا، يبدو الآن، للأسف، وكأنّه قوّة ضعيفة، في وجه التحديات التي يسببها التغيّر البيئي. إن كان دافع المعرفة هو الذي يصنّف العديد من فناني فانكوفر العظماء، أو كانت المشاركة الجماليّة في الحد الأعلى هي التي تدفع بالمشاريع التي شاركت بتقديمها في بيرث، فإن الفن يقف متهالكا أمام الطبيعة. بالطبع، لطالما كان الأمر كذلك، فإن تقاليد المشاهد الطبيعيّة العظيمة، حتّى في أكثرها ادّعاء، كانت دائما بطبيعة الحال سلوكات نمنماتيّة. ضع هذه اللوحات خارجا في المشاهد الطبيعيّة وراقب، حتّى أعظم الأعمال الفنيّة تختفي وأنت تقود سيّارتك بمحاذاتها بسرعة ١٠٠ كم/ساعة.[7] بالطبع، نحن لا نشاهد إلى هذه اللوحات بهذه السرعة. وهذه هي إحدى الأمور المهمة المتعلقة بتقبّل الفن كقوّة اجتماعيّة ضعيفة. إنّها تذكرنا بأن علينا أن نخفف من سرعتنا ونتقبّل محدّداتنا.

يجد كلّ جيل طرقا جديدة لمنح صفة الأهميّة للمشاركة بمتع بسيطة ورؤى صغيرة، وحتّى محليّة. بتراكمها تدريجيّا، تمثّل محاولات كهذه، مجموع محاولاتنا للنجاة في زمن طموحات عظيمة تفيض عن حدّها.

تريفور سميث هو قيم على المعارض مقيم في مركز دراسات القيام على المعارض، كليّة بارد.

[5] <http://www.interpolar.org> </www.interpolar.org>. يمكن الوصول إلى يوميّات الطاقم تحت عنوان "ناو NOW." نُشرت تعليقات رودريجيز آلفيس في ٣١ ديسمبر كانون أوّل، ٢٠٠٦.

[6] توماس كرو، "ذا سيمبل لايف: باستوراليزم آند ذا بيرسيستانس أوف جنر إن ريسنت آرت (الحياة البسيطة: الرعويّة وعزم الأجناس الأدبية في الفن الحديث)"، نيو هافن ولندن: مطبعة جامعة ييل، (١٩٩٦)، ص. ١٧٧

[7] هنا أعيد صياغة كلمات روبرت ماك فيرسون، وهو فنان عظيم ومصدر وحي وأحد الأسباب التي تدفعني للقيام بما أقوم به.

منطقي/بيئياً؟
تأملات في العلاقة بين الفن والبيئة

رايمر شتانغه

١) تفكيك أم تزيين؟

هناك نهر يغمره ضوء أخضر فاهٍ. ويُعزى هذا اللون إلى وجود مادة "اليورانيوم". الكلام هنا هو عن العمل الفني "تيارات في نهر الفيزر" (١٩٩٨) للفنان الايسلاندي اولافور الياسون. ولكن ما هو الموضوع فعلا؟ هل هي قطعة من فن الأرض "السائل"؟ أم هو تدخل لريشة رسام في المشهد الطبيعي؟ هل هي "صورة عابرة أحادية اللون" تكشفها حركة النهر"؟ أم هي تحذير ضد التدمير البيئي، "الآفة النفطية"؟ المثير في هذا العمل الفني، هو أن جميع القراءات السابقة ممكنة، وبذلك يكون لهذا العمل الحق بان يُوزَن بميزان الجماليات، أو أيضا، بميزان النشاط البيئي البحت. اولافور الياسون نفسه تحدّث عن "الإرهاب اللطيف". ولكن، أليست هذه هي نقطة ضعف هذا العمل؟ ألا يتأرجح هذا التركيب الفني السائل العابر، دون إرادة منه، بين كونه عملا تفكيكيا وعملا تجميليا، بين الفن المبتذَل والنقد المبهَم؟

للإجابة على هذا السؤال، من الضروري أن نلقي نظرة على عمل ثان للفنان، هو "إضاعتك للوقت" (٢٠٠٦)، وهو عبارة عن خمس كتل جليدية موضوعة في معرض نوي غهيم شنايدر في برلين. تم جلب هذه الكتل التي تزن ستة أطنان من الساحل الجنوبي لأيسلندا، ويصل عمرها إلى ١٥٠٠٠ سنة. نُقلت القطع إلى اليابسة الأوروبية لكي تُعرض هناك، في وسط ألمانيا، ويتم "إبقاؤها على قيد الحياة" بواسطة نظام تبريد مُكلِف. بعد العرض، سيتم إطفاء نظام التبريد الباهظ التكاليف، سينصهر الجليد، وسيتكوّن العمل الفني عندها "فقط" من فكرته (القابلة للتكرار)، إنه إذن رغم "نهايته" قابل للبيع. هذا العمل، هو من ناحية، جميل للغاية بسطوحه الجليدية البرّاقة وكُتَلِه الموزعة والمبردة جيدا، وهو يذكّر سريعا بلوحات الرسام الألماني الرومانسي كاسبار دافيد فريدريش، أو بفيلم هوليوود الشهير "تايتَنِك". وهو من ناحية أخرى، يطرح أسئلة، مثل السؤال عن لا معقولية مفهوم أن "كل شيء يمكن نقله"، وبتكلفة قليلة، إلى درجة أنه بات مربحا لكل عمل تجاري متنقل في البلاد ذات الدخل المنخفض، وهو أحد نتائج الليبرالية الجديدة في الوقت الراهن. يطرح العمل أيضا، ذلك السؤال عن انصهار الجبال الجليدية والكارثة المناخية، تلك المشكلة التي لا يسببها فقط، انفصال الكتل الجليدية الشديدة القِدَم وانصهارها فيما بعد، وإنما أيضا، أجهزة التبريد المستخدمة، والتي باستهلاكها المرتفع للطاقة، تقوم بتسريع هذه العملية أكثر فأكثر.

يَعرِض لنا إذن اولافور الياسون مرة أخرى التوتر ما بين الفن الجمالي والالتزام (البيئي) - ومع ذلك، ألا تبقى هذه الأعمال في النهاية عالقة بين ما هو قابل للتأويل بذكاء، وما هو قابل للتذوق بلذة؟ ألا نفقد بالذات، دقة التحليل وقوة الموقف، التي يمكن أن تؤدي فعلا إلى عواقب سياسية؟ أم أنّ هذه العواقب، ربما، لم تَعُد أمرا يمكن التفكير فيه اليوم. هل فات الأوان، والضغط النيوليبرالي العالمي قد أصبح فعلا قوي جدا، للقيام بتحول بيئي؟ هل مقاربة الياسون المتواضعة، والتي قد تكون غير مؤذية، هي المقاربة الوحيدة (مع الأسف) الممكنة ؟

٢) استطراد: مقتطفات تاريخية من الحركات البيئية

إن الحضارة الإنسانية، برأي كثير من الناس، تُنتزَع من الطبيعة. فالماهيّة التقنية والماهيّة الفنية هي إذن (برأيهم) الماهيّة الإنسانية. ومنذ منتصف القرن التاسع عشر يُحتفى بهذه الماهية اللاطبيعية على أنها "الحداثة"، خاصة في فرنسا. فمثلا كتب الأخوان ادموند وجيل دي غونكور في مذكراتهم في الأول من تموز عام ١٨٥٦: "صبّت الشمس وهي تغرب ذهبا على لوحات الإعلانات المذهّبة الكبيرة فوق ممر البانوراما. لم يسبق أن ابتهج قلبي وعيني لشيء أكثر من رؤية الواجهات المدهونة والمتراصة... ولا حتى شجرة بائسة، نابتة بالكاد في شق في الإسفلت. وهذه الواجهات البشعة تخاطبني، كما لم يسبق أن خاطبتنيً الطبيعة أبدا." من هذه الزاوية، تظهر الطبيعة على أنها "بائسة"، وعلى النقيض، فما هو اصطناعي (مهما بلغت بشاعته) هو مدعاة للابتهاج. فيما بعد، صار شارل بوديلير الأب الروحي لهذه النظرة من الحداثة. ولكن نقاد هذه التفوهات المعادية للطبيعة لم ينتظروا للرد: "دعونا لا نطري أنفسنا بسبب انتصاراتنا البشرية على الطبيعة. فبعد كل انتصار كهذا تثأر الطبيعة لنفسها منا. وفي الحقيقة، نحصل في البداية على النتائج التي توقعناها، ولكن ما يأتي بعد ذلك يختلف تماما، وله تأثيرات غير متوقعة وفي أغلب الأحيان تلغي النتيجة الأولى. إن الناس في بلاد ما بين النهرين وفي اليونان وآسيا الصغرى وأماكن أخرى، والذين قاموا بإبادة الغابات للحصول على إراضٍ صالحة للزراعة، لم يحلموا أنهم بهذا إنما وضعوا حجر الأساس للتصحرّ الحالي في تلك البلدان، فبإزالتهم للغابات، أزالوا مراكز تجميع وحفظ الرطوبة هناك"، هذا ما كتبه فريدريش انغلز في ١٨٧٦.

وفي الوقت نفسه تقريبا، قدم "الفن الحديث" و"حركة الجوالة والشباب الألماني" مشروع "عودة إلى الطبيعة"، عودة جمالية وملتزمة بالإصلاح. هذه الحركة الأخيرة تربط وبوعي منذ عام ١٨٩٦، سمات من الرومانسية مع تأثيرات معادية للطبقة الوسطى، ومقاربة تربوية نحو الإصلاح الاجتماعي مع إفراط في الإيمان بالشباب المتحرر. إن نقد الحضارة الذي قام به الفن الحديث Art Nouveau عند بدايات القرن الماضي ذو أهمية أيضا. إن استخدامه للزخرفة الخطية والأشكال المأخوذة في الغالب من بواعث نباتية، كانت نقدا واسعَ المدى "الانتصارات" التقنية الحديثة. والتر بنيامين، الناقد والفيلسوف، يشرح الأمر في كتابه "مشروع ممرات القناطر" على خلفية كيفية عرض المرأة في الفن الجديد Art Nouveau كالتالي: "إن الفكرة الأساسية من الفن الجديد هو تمجيد العقم. إذ يتم رسم الجسد (على نحو التفضيل) بالأشكال التي تسبق سن البلوغ." "العقم": إنها الطبيعة التي أفقدتها التكنولوجيا توازنها.

والآن، ننتقل بسرعة إلى ما بعد الحرب العالمية الثانية حيث دخل إلى الضمير الجماهيري وعيا بيئيا نقديا. وبالطبع، قام علماء الاجتماع والفلاسفة مبكرا بالتعامل مع هذه الأفكار، مثل مدرسة فرانكفورتر في الولايات المتحدة الأمريكية وألمانيا. إلا أن هذا التفكير النقدي لم يتحول إلى وعي جماهيري بيئي إلا في منتصف الستينيات، من خلال ما يسمى بـ "جيل قوة الزهور" أو من يسمون "الهيبّون" ومن شابههم، والذين التزموا بإعادة الصلة ما بين البشرية والطريقة الأساسية في الحياة مع الطبيعة. وانطلاقا من هذه الحركة وغيرها تأسس في السبعينيات في كل مكان في أوروبا ما سُمي "أحزاب الخُضْر" والتي تصدت للطاقة النووية، ولأنواع أخرى من الأنشطة الصناعية المدمرة للبيئة. وفي بداية هذا العقد تم أيضا تأسيس المنظمة العالمية للبيئة "غرين بيس" (السلام الأخضر)، تلك المنظمة الناشطة منذ ذلك الحين في التنبيه إلى مشاكل تدمير البيئة اليوم.

٣) غوستاف متسغر، ولاحقا سانتياغو سييرا

في سنوات الستينيات السالف ذكرها، طوّر الفنان غوستاف متسغر - وهو من مواليد عام ١٩٢٦ في نورنبرغ بألمانيا لعائلة يهودية بولندية، وهاجر إلى لندن عام ١٩٣٩ - فنَّهُ الملتزم سياسيا، كما كان أيضا نقديا من منظور بيئي. يتكون فن غوستاف متسغر الذي أسماه بنفسه "فن ذاتي التدمير" (كما يدل الاسم) من منتجات يدوية يدمرها (هو بنفسه) في عملية جمالية، على سبيل المثال عن طريق "لوحات العمل الحامضي". تم تنفيذ أحد أعماله عام ١٩٦١ في ساوث بانك في لندن، وبمساعدة حامض تم دهن الشاشات به، قام الفنان بإحداث ثقوب في قماش الرسم بشكل متوال، نتج عنها آثار فنية تماما. ولكن متسغر في "مانيفستو الفن ذاتي التدمير" (١٠ مارس/آذار ١٩٦٠) لم يؤكد على الجمال الحسي لهذا النوع من الفن بقدر ما أكد على الطابع التحليلي - التحذيري له، حيث ذكر: "إنّ الفن ذاتي التدمير يبعث الحياة من جديد في هَوَس التدمير: ذلك الدافع الذي يقع تحت تأثيره الفرد والجماعات. إنّ الفن ذاتي التدمير يوحي بقوة الإنسان، في تسريع وتوجيه عمليات تحلل الطبيعة، ويعكس المثالية القهرية لصناعة الأسلحة - مصقولة حتى التدمير. إنّ الفن ذاتي التدمير هو تحويل التكنولوجيا إلى فن الأماكن العامة." وكان الفنان قد توصل في بداية الستينيات في جزر شدلاند البريطانية، إلى فكرة "تسريع وتنظيم عمليات تفكك الطبيعة". وقال متسغر عن ذلك بعد أكثر من ثلاثين عاما: "في ذلك المكان ساد هدوء لم اشهد مثله من قبل، وقد كتبت حينها مذكرات يومية، وسجلت في تلك المذكرات نقاطا كانت ذات أهمية بالنسبة لي، منها، أنه يجب التخلص من السيارات. بالنسبة لي، كان هذا اختراقا مفاجئا في اتجاه جديد، وكان في غاية التطرف: يجب التخلص منها! لقد أشغلت نفسي بموضوع تدمير السيارة كطريقة للتصدي لتدمير الإنسانية، تدمير الطبيعة."

هذا الجانب من تدمير البيئة كان النقطة المركزية لمشروعه "ستوكهولم يونيو" (Stockholm June) (١٩٧٢)، والذي كان قد تم التخطيط لعرضه في شكله المبكر "كاربا" KARBA (١٩٧٢/٧٠) في دوكيومنتا ٥ (documenta 5) في مدينة كاسل بألمانيا. ولكن حتى الآن، بقي "ستوكهولم يونيو" غير متحقق، كما هو حال الكثير من أعمال متسغر. كان المشروع يتصور وضع ١٢٠ سيارة حول هيكل مستطيل الشكل بارتفاع يتراوح ما بين ٢،٥-٤ أمتار، ومن ثم تغليف هذا الهيكل الفراغي ببلاستيك شفاف، وأحداث ثقوب فيه على أبعاد متساوية، ثم يتم تشغيل محركات المئة والعشرين سيارة من الصباح وحتى الليل، منتجة بذلك غازات عادمة يتم توجيهها إلى داخل الهيكل، الذي يتحول وبشكل متزايد إلى "كابوس" سام رمادي اللون. المرحلة الثانية من المشروع كانت وضع السيارات المعبأة بالوقود بالكامل، وبمحركاتها الدائرة في ذلك الهيكل الفراغي المغلّف بالبلاستيك، ولكن هذه المرة بدون ثقوب فيه. وفي حال أن النيران لم تشتعل في السيارات بحلول ظهر اليوم التالي، فقد كانت الخطة أن يتم رمي الموقع بأكمله بقنابل صغيرة. إجمالاً، اكتشف متسغر بهذا العمل صورة استفزازية لما يحدث يوميا في شوارعنا: إنّ البيئة يتم تدميرها عن وعي. وبالمقارنة مع إلياسون، فإنه لا يمكن التحدث هنا أيضا عن "الإرهاب اللطيف"، بسبب الطبيعة العدوانية والهدّامة لأعمال متسغر.

وفي الوقت نفسه -ويمكن أن يكون هذا مفاجئا للوهلة الاولى - يشغل غوستاف متسغر نفسه بأعمال فنية، يمكن وصفها بأنها "منحوتات للطبيعة، متحركة، ومجرّدة، وتبدو غير عدوانية مطلقا". فمثلا، في معرضه المنفرد "فن الكريستال السائل" (١٩٦٦) عرض متسغر منحوتته بعنوان "أرض من الفضاء" (Earth from Space) في واجهة متجر الكتب "بِتِر بُكْس"

(Better Books) في لندن، والمصنوعة من صفائح زجاجية مركبة على شكل صليب يتخللها قطع كريستال سائل. يتم تسخين هذا الكريستال بواسطة سلك متوهج إلى أن ينصهر. نتيجة لهذه العملية، تتحول قطع الكريستال أولا إلى قطع شفافة، ثم رمادية، وأخيرا وبعد أن تبرد، تكتسب ألوانا كثيفة. ما يحدث هنا هو أيضا تدمير، إلاّ أنه يحدث في عملية بصرية ذات طبيعة تجميلية شاعرية. تقنية "الكريستال السائل" هذه، والتي شارك متسغر في تطويرها، أصبحت تُستخدم في العروض التصويرية الشبيهة، وذلك كديكور للخلفية في عروض فرق الروك مثل فرقة The Who.

الفنان المكسيكي سانتياغو سييرا، هو الآخر قام بتنفيذ عمل تركيبي في ربيع ٢٠٠٦ مبنيا على أساس المشروع المذكور أعلاه، "ستوكهولم يونيو" (Stockholm June): ففي وسط المدينة الألمانية الصغيرة شتوميلن، تم وضع ٦ سيارات تدور محركاتها، وتم تحويل مسار الغازات العادمة المنبعثة إلى داخل كنيس يهودي باستخدام خراطيم مثبتة على فتحات العادم (الاكزوست)، وأمام الكنيس كانت كمامات واقية ضد الغازان جاهزة لكي يستخدمها من يريد الدخول إلى الكنيس، لضمان المرور الآمن.

وبسبب الانتقاد الشديد من قِبل الرأي العام وجب إزالة العمل بعد أيام قلائل. ثمة سوء فهم أدى إلى هذا الانتقاد، فسانتياغو سييرا لم يقصد مطلقا بعمله هذا الانتقاص من قيمة معاناة اليهود الذين تم خنقهم بالغاز من قِبل النازيين الألمان، وكل ما كان يقصده هو إظهار أن الغازات العادمة المنبعثة من استخدام السيارات اليوم تسمم البيئة، وعلى وعي منا بذلك، وبهذا، فان هذا الاستخدام يحمل عن وعي أيضا، ذنب نشوب الكوارث الطبيعية وتبعاتها المدمرة. وتماما كما كان الأمر خلال فترة "الرايخ الثالث"، فإن لا أحدا اليوم يريد أن يتقبل تحمل ذنب تلك الكارثة، رغم العلم بها. وهذا الأمر بالذات يجعل من التشابه الذي يطرحه سييرا ما بين عملية قتل اليهود بالغاز والغازات العادمة المنبعثة من السيارات مقاربة استفزازية، ولكن منطقية في نفس الوقت.

من المؤكد أنّ قَتْل اليهود الاستهدافي والجماعي يختلف عن تدمير البيئة الواعي الراهن. ومع ذلك فاليوم كما بالأمس، هناك ضحايا يصيبهم الضرر رغما عنهم ودون أن يُسألوا. إضافة إلى ذلك، لا مفر اليوم كما بالأمس، فلا يمكن الهرب من الكارثة البيئية العالمية. كذلك، فإن ثمة مصالح رأسمالية معينة كانت بالأمس كما هي اليوم سببا للكارثة (وتلك المصالح لا زالت جزئيا هي المصالح نفسها). فليس صدفة أن النازيين هم من بنوا الطرق السريعة (الاوتوبانات) في ألمانيا، وأن سيارة "الخنفساء" الأسطورية صنعتها فولكس فاغن في ذلك الوقت أيضا. ويظهر استطاعة زائري الكنيس وضع الكمامات الواقية، أنّ ما أراده الفنان بوضوح، لم يكن تجربة مهوِّنة (بلا نهاية) للقتل الجماعي في ذلك الوقت، وإنما كان دور مقترف الجريمة المحمي، لأنه من المرجح أن تكون أغلبية زوار ذلك العمل التركيبي من سائقي السيارات ويلبسون الكمامات!

إن متسغر وسييرا يعرضان فنا بيئيا ليس صريحا سياسيا فحسب، وإنما استفزازيا أيضا، ورافضا للحلول الوسط. وبالمقارنة مع الياسون بالذات، تطرح هذه الاستراتيجيات العدائية اسئلة مثل: هل يجب ان يكون الفن السياسي إشكاليا وشرسا بشكل صريح؟ أو: هل يحتاج إلى المواضيع الاستفزازية؟ ومتى تصبح المواضيع بيئية بشكل صريح؟ في الفصل التالي سوف أتعرض لهذه الأسئلة.

٤) ما هو „الحس الجمالي البيئي"؟

لطالما كان "الفن اليساري" النقدي الملتزم فنا مجردا، فنحن نذكر قليلا "الطلائع" في النصف الأول من القرن الماضي: الدادية والسريالية، وكلاهما شيوعي التوجه، إلى حد كبير، وقد مارستا الثورة ضد البرجوازية. إنّ هاتين الحركتين ليستا جزءاً من الفن التجريدي بالتأكيد، إلاّ أنهما إما تفككان الواقعية بعدوانية كما هو الحال لدى الداديين، أو تحوّلان الواقعية إلى سريالية، أي إلى "اللاواقعي". إن الفن الأكثر تأثيرا من الناحية السياسية في ذلك الوقت، هو على الأرجح "البنائية" (الروسية) والباوهاوس الألمانية، وكلاهما يحبذ التجريد. وكرفض لثقافة وسياسة المحاكاة البرجوازية، فان هذين التيارين كانا يراهنان على التشكيل المباشر لما هو حقيقي، ولهذا يبدو لهما وكأن حقل التجريد قد خُلق من أجلهما. مثال على ذلك "المربع الأسود" (١٩٢٩) لِكاسيمير ماليفيتش، والذي يعني مربعا أسود فقط، وبذلك فهو لا يمثل شيئا، وإنما نفسه هو، وتصبح هذه الصورة "اللا صورة" تقريبا نموذجا لتفاهم بين المجتمع والسلطة، لا يمثل فيه القيصر الشعب، بل يمثل الشعب الشعب، يمثلون ويحكمون أنفسهم بأنفسهم. وأكثر من ذلك بعد: إن لغة التجريد الواضحة تسمح على ما يبدو، بالإعراض عن الشعوريات والإيديولوجيات البرجوازية المكروهة، والتي أدت في النهاية إلى الحرب العالمية الأولى. ولاحقا صَلُح التجريد الجمالي أيضا، كنقد "للواقعية الاشتراكية" المستبدة، حيث أن تجارب "البنائيين" الروس مع الاشتراكية والشيوعية الموجودتان واقعيا، كانت كارثية (وتختصر بكلمة واحدة: الستالينية)، وكثير من البنائيين نأوا بأنفسهم في النهاية عن الفن الملتزم سياسيا.

إن لغة البنائية المرتكزة على الاختزال والتجريد، تم التقاطها من قبل "الحركة المنمنماتية" الأمريكية (Minimalism) على طريقة دونا لد جَد وروبرت موريس. هذا المذهب الفني يعتبر نفسه أيضا ضد الطبقة الوسطى تماما، ويدافع عن نفسه ضد الماهية التجميلية للفن التجسيدي. وهذه الماهية التجميلية بالذات، جعلت هذا الفن، في سوق الفن، والذي كان قد تطور بشكل كامل في حينها، بضاعة رخيصة، تجد لنفسها بسرعة مكانا في غرف الجلوس وضمن الأعمال الفنية التي يجمعها الهواة. إلا إن المنمنماتية (Minimalism) فقدت بعد قليل قدرتها على الصمود السياسي، وصارت تُستخدم لفائدة النظام الرأسمالي. وكما أن المنمنماتية رفضت أن تقدم الفن الذي يحاكي الصورة، فإنها رفضت أيضا، أن تصنع صورة مضادة ناقدة، وهذا بالذات ما جعل من الممكن إدماج لغتها الرسمية في الحس الجمالي للرأسمالية، بمعنى، إن المنمنماتية صَلُحت بحسها الجمالي الهادئ لأن تُعطي تعبيرا للأناقة الهادئة للشركات الدولية - المنمنماتية أصبحت بذلك "أداة التصميم التجاري". استجابة الفنانين كانت فورية: فمن جهة تم الاندفاع باتجاه مزيد من الاختزال في أعمال مثل "نزع مادية الشيء الفني" (dematerializing of the art object) (لوسي ر. ليبارد)، ومن هذه العملية نشأ "الفن المفاهيمي" (Concept Art). من جهة أخرى، تم هز أساليب المنمناتية وتعبئتها بتركيبات سردية تحريضية، وهنا تجدر الإشارة بالدرجة الأولى إلى غوستاف متسغر وهانس هاكه، ولاحقا عمل سانتياغو سييرا السالف ذكره بهذه الطريقة أيضا. وتماما كغوستاف متسغر، فإن هانس هاكه على ما يبدو، كان له أيضا مرحلتا عمل مختلفتين: مرحلة مبكرة وشبه تجريدية يندرج تحتها مثلا "مكعب التكثيف" (١٩٦٣-١٩٦٥)، وهو مكعب شفاف يتكثف ماء في داخله. في هذا العمل يتم عرض نظام (بيئي) مغلق، تتواصل فيه عمليات بيولوجية مع بعضها البعض. المرحلة الثانية كانت الأطول وهي معروفة على أنها مرحلة سياسية تحريضية، تمثلت بعمل مثل "صندوق العزل، غرينادا" (١٩٨٣). لدينا

هنا مرة أخرى مكعب مغلق، ولكنه من الخشب وله شقوق ومطبوع عليه العبارة التالية: "صندوق عزل كالمستخدم من قِبل الجنود الأمريكان في معسكر الاعتقال بوينت سالينس في غرينادا". إن الشكل المحض قد تم تلويثه إذن بالتنوير السياسي. وقد استمر هانس هاكه بالعمل على فكرته عن النظام وأخذها خطوة إلى الأمام بتطبيقها على السياق السياسي. هناك استراتيجية جمالية أخرى للفرار من هيمنة الرأسمالية، وهي "مشروع الفن" المُتأتّي من "فن الفكرة". فجوزيف بويز (وغيره) وإنجازاتهم البيئية السياسية، سيصبح لها وزن هنا في وقت قريب. وبالنسبة لجيل الفنانين الاصغر سنا، فسوف يكون من سماتهم في النهاية، استخدام كل هذه الاستراتيجيات في أعمالهم بشكل جيد. والأمريكي دان بيترمان والدانمركي توي غرينفورت مثالان جيدان هنا. (سأتحدث عنهما أكثر في الفصل القادم)

إن الأسئلة المفتوحة عن جودة الفن السياسي (بالإشارة إلى السؤال عن جودة الفن البيئي) لها تأويل آخر أيضا، هو: هل يجب أن يكون الفن البيئي ناقدا للمجتمع بشكل علني، أو بالمعنى الضيق: هل يجب أن يكون سياسيا؟ الفيلسوف الألماني بورغهارت شميت مثلا، يَعتبر في هذا السياق "إدراك الطبيعة" و"مواجهة الطبيعة" فنا بيئيا. وزميله غيرنوت بويمه يمضي في "غَزْل" هذه الفكرة، واضعا "التحالفات الطبيعية" هذه "كأجواء" تتوسط أي فن بيئي. ففي رأيه أن الأمر في هذه "الأجواء" يدور حول "التغلب على وجهة النظر الذاتية"، وأن الإنسان عندها لا يعود يرى نفسه، متفردا وأنانيا، أو أنه أفضل ما خلق اللّٰه، بل يدرك أنه جزء من البيئة المحيطة به، والتي تسمح له أصلا بالحياة أو بالبقاء على قيد الحياة. حسب بويمه، فإنّ هذه الرؤية البيئية للعالم هي التي تعطي الإنسان قدرته على التأمل واستخدام اللغة. كتب بويمه: "إن الإنسان ككائن لغوي بشكل خاص، هو على الأرجح ليس مستقبلا فقط للتواصل (الكلامي) الموجه إليه، وإنما لتلفظ الحضور (يعني حضور أي شخص) في حد ذاته. إن الإحساس بجمال الطبيعة سيكون عندها، ليس فقط الإدراك المشترك لما هو مقبول له/لها، وإنما تجربة الوجود الذاتي محمولا ومعززا من قبل الطبيعة المحيطة في تعبيرها عن حضورها." من هذا المنظور سيكون فن اولافور الياسون (الذي انتقدته سابقا)، وجماعات العمل "الجمالية التجريدية" لمتسغر وهاكه (التي اشرت أنا إليها) فنا سياسيا بيئيا.

٥) دان بيترمان، ولاحقا توي غرينفورت

يتوسط إنتاج الطاقة البديلة وإعادة التدوير أعمال الفنان الأمريكي دان بيترمان. يعالج الفنان بعض جوانب هذا الموضوع في "ملجأ السماد العضوي بشيكاغو" (١٩٨٨)، وهو عبارة عن سيارة فولكس فاغن عادية، تتم تدفئتها في الشتاء القارس بواسطة روث أحصنة الشرطة الخيالة في شيكاغو، وتُستخدم كمكان للنوم لمن هم بلا مأوى، منقذين بذلك حياتهم. هذا الترتيب يخدم كنموذج حقيقي لاستخدام جميع مصادر الطاقة الممكنة (الغاز الحيوي هنا)، ولكن أيضا، كنموذج للتعامل الملتزم والإنساني مع المستضعفين، أي من يُسمَّوْن "المجموعات المهمشة اجتماعيا".

إعادة التدوير تظهر عند دان بيترمان بمختلف الطرق، مثلا على شكل بلاستيك يتم إعادة تدويره ليصنع منه لاحقا الأثاث. فهناك "الطاولة المهرولة" (١٩٩٧) التي يمكن استخدامها من قبل المارة في شارع متشيغان في شيكاغو على سبيل المثال. وفي الوقت نفسه يقنعك العمل بشكله الهندسي الواضح على أنه منمنماتي. إن "الطاولة المهرولة" هي إذن فن مستقل ومفيد في الوقت نفسه.

منذ عام ١٩٩٦ يعمل دان بيترمان في مجمّع، اسماه "البناية" (The Building)، تشمل فناء لإعادة التدوير، كما يوجد في "البناية" مشغل الفنان، وكذلك مكتب الجريدة اليسارية „ذي بافلر (The Baffler). وتتمم الزراعة البديلة سلسلة النشاطات هذه. يدير بيترمان هنا أيضا، ورشة لتصليح الدراجات الهوائية "الخردة"، كمشروع فني، وفي الوقت نفسه كإجراء براغماتي (واقعي) يعمل بشكل حقيقي. وبذلك فإنّ الشباب العاطل عن العمل لا يمكنه هنا تعلم مهارات مهنية والقيام باحتكاكات اجتماعية فحسب، بل يمكنه أيضا، الحصول على دراجة هوائية صالحة للركوب كأجر له. هذا العمل الفني يتكون من الفكرة اللا-مادية لاقتصاد بديل، ومن المعاوَنة الأدائية للشباب العاطل عن العمل، والنتائج الشبيهة بفن النحت، والمتمثلة بالدراجات الهوائية التي جُعلت صالحة للاستعمال من جديد.

في عام ٢٠٠١ احترقت "البناية" بالكامل، وقد أُعيد بناؤها اليوم من جديد، وتستطيع أن تُثبت نفسها وسط شيكاغو حاضرة الرأسمالية، وذلك كدليل على أنه يمكن للأنماط البديلة من الاقتصاد وعلم البيئة في القرن الحادي العشرين أن تكون موجودة بالكامل.

الشاب الدانمركي توي غرينفورت (وبهذا أصل إلى نهاية نَصي) يناقش في عمله الفني موضوع إعادة التدوير كذلك. فهناك على سبيل المثال عمله "إنتاج كيلوغرام واحد من بلاستيك البي اي تي (PET) يتطلب ١٧,٥ كيلوغرام من الماء" (٢٠٠٤)، حيث يشير بعنوانه هذا إلى فن بيترمان. في هذا العمل يمكن رؤية زجاجة ماء معدني سعة ١,٥ لتر، صُهرت تحت تأثير الحرارة ليصبح حجمها ٠,٥ لتر فقط. يراد بهذا العمل الإشارة إلى أن إنتاج الزجاجة التي تُستخدم لمرة واحدة فقط (disposable)، يستهلك كمية من الماء تفوق بكثير الكمية التي يمكن تعبئتها فيها لاحقا. إشكالية الاستهلاك وإعادة التدوير واستهلاك الطاقة المرتبط بذلك تقع هنا أيضا، في بؤرة اهتمام التفكير الفني، ولكن مع تفاؤل أقرب نسبيا إلى التحفّظ، فيما يتعلق بإمكانية تغيير الوضع الآخذ في التفاقم.

وضع توي غرينفورت التجربة حيز التنفيذ بمشروعه "من الأخضر إلى الرمادي" (٢٠٠٦)، والذي جعل من خلاله إمداد الطاقة لمبنى معرض „فيته دي فيت" في روتردام (هولندا) موضع تفكُّرٍ ناقدٍ. نقطة الانطلاق في ذلك، هي رغبة الفنان بأن يتم خلال مدة عرضه لعملهِ الفني في مبنى المعرض إمداد المبنى بكهرباء "خضراء"، أي أن يكون توليدها غير ملوث للبيئة. وتشير الرسائل المتبادلة حول هذا الأمر بين معرض "فيته دي فيت" وبين الجهة الهولندية التي تزوده بالطاقة، أن ذلك (ولأسباب تتعلق بالعقود المبرمة) سيكون ممكنا فقط ابتداءً من العام ٢٠٠٧، وسيكون الإمداد عندها للعام بأكمله فقط. بعد ذلك قام غرينفورت بإجراء الترتيب التالي فيما يتعلق بعرض عمله الفني: تُركت القاعة رقم ١ في المبنى، والبالغة مساحتها أكثر من ١٠٠ متر مربع فارغة، وبذلك عُرضت كمكعب ابيض محض، تُنيره أضواء النيون الساقطة عليه من السقف ليصبح متوهجا ومستهلكا شديدا للطاقة. لا يُرى في هذا العرض (الفني) "العقيم" والواضح في آن معا، سوى تبادل الرسائل الذي ذكرناه للتو، المطبوع على ورق من حجم DIN A3 رمادي اللون وبلا إطار، موضوعا على الواجهة الأمامية للقاعة. إن ما يحدث هنا هو توثيق بسيط و"نزْعٌ ذكيٌ للمادية" في أفضل تقاليد "الفن المفاهيمي". وما يوَثّق هنا هو المحاولة غير المجدية (في بادئ الأمر)، للانتقال بمساعدة مشروع فني، من الزمن "الرمادي" للكهرباء "التقليدية" غير الحكيمة إلى الإمداد بالطاقة "الخضراء". ما تبقى هو المطالبة بتغيير بيئي فعلي وطويل الأمد يتخطى النظام (المغلق) لمصنع الفن.

سير ذاتية

حور القاسمي
رئيس البينالي
مقيّمة مشاركة لمعرض "نير" ١٩٩٨ مع كل من ديريك أوغبورن و بيتر لويس ومقيّمة مشاركة لمعرض" أندي وورهول" ٢٠٠٢ مع بريجيت شينك من غاليري بريجيت شينك، مدينة كولون، اللذين أقيما في متحف الشارقة للفنون. رئيسة ومقيمة مشاركة لبينالي الشارقة السادس مع بيتر لويس ٢٠٠٣. رئيسة بينالي الشارقة السابع ٢٠٠٥. أستاذة التصوير الزيتي والرسم في مركز الشارقة للفن التشكيلي ١٩٩٧. درست الفنون التشكيلية في كلية سليد للفن التشكيلي بلندن وتعد حاليا رسالة الماجستير في تقييم الفن المعاصر من الكلية الملكية للفن في لندن.

جاك برسكيان
مدير البينالي
مقيِم ومنتج والمدير المؤسس لغاليري أناديل ومؤسسة المعمل للفن المعاصر في القدس. القيم العام لبينالي الشارقة السابع (٢٠٠٥). عمل مقيّما في السنوات الأخيرة لمعارض عديدة منها: معرض "إعادة النظر في الفن الفلسطيني"، مؤسسة أنطونيو بيريز في أسبانيا ٢٠٠٦. معرض "بلا مسار" - فنانون عرب معاصرون من الشرق الأوسط، البيت الثقافي العالمي - برلين ٢٠٠٣، معرض عن الفن الفلسطيني الجديد في غاليريهات بون وشتوتجارت وبرلين، ٢٠٠٢. التمثيل الرسمي لفلسطين في بينالي ساو باولو الرابع والعشرين. نشاطات إضافية تتضمن: الأمسية الثقافية الفلسطينية في المنتدى الاقتصادي العالمي في البحر الميت بالأردن ٢٠٠٤، مبادرة جنيف، فعالية الالتزام الشعبي ٢٠٠٣، احتفالات الألفية في بيت لحم ٢٠٠٠. إنتاج أفلام قصيرة وأعمال مصورة بالتعاون مع مخرجين فلسطينيين: "كرة وصندوق ملون"، "ولدي"، "آخر خمسة أفلام قصيرة في الألفية"، "أفضل أربع أفلام قصيرة في الألفية".

محمد كاظم
قيّم
مواليد الإمارات ١٩٦٩. عضو جمعية الإمارات للفنون التشكيلية في الشارقة منذ ١٩٨٥. شارك في بيناليهات متعددة منها بينالي الشارقة في جميع دوراته هافانا بنجلاديش، سنغافورا، القاهرة ومعارض في هولندا وموسكو. وعمل كاظم في ٢٠٠٥ كمقيّم لمعرض جمعية الإمارات الذي أقيم بالتوزاي مع بينالي الشارقة ٧. عمل مقيّما لمعرض "ويندو" (١٦ فنانا إماراتيا) في توتال آرت غاليري بدبي ٢٠٠٦. شارك في معرض الخمسة ومعرض الستة في الشارقة، ومنتدى لودفيج للفنون ومعرض الأرقام وعلامات الزمن في ألمانيا ،معرض لغات الصحراء في متحف بون ويُدرّس كاظم فن التصوير في مسرح الشباب منذ ١٩٩٩.

إيفا شارير
قيّمة
مقيّمة وناقدة فنية. مقيمة حاليا في بازل في سويسرا. تعمل في معارض تنظمها مؤسسات فنية عالمية مثل مركز بي إس ١ للفن المعاصر بنيويورك ومعرض بيت الفن في بازل ومعرض بازل/موتينتس. شاركت في مشاريع فنية مثل "سابميرج". مقيّمة لمعرض "الفن الجديد من نيويورك" في نورمبيرغ. مقيمة للمهرجان الخامس للفن الشاب في برلين و براغ و نيويورك. كتبت مقالات في كتالوجات فنية عن الفنانين الجدد وتساهم بشكل منتظم في مجلة "آرت فورم انترناشونال" وفي موقع أرتفورم الإلكتروني في نيويورك وفي نشرة "كونست" الفنية الصادرة من زيورخ ومجلة "سي ماجازين" في تورنتو وصحيفة "بي إيه زيد" اليومية في بازل إلى جانب مطبوعات أخرى كثيرة.

جوناثان واتكنز
قيّم
مدير إيكون جاليري برمنجهام منذ ١٩٩٩. وفي السابق عمل لأعوام عديدة في لندن كمقيّم لغاليري سيبرنتين (١٩٩٥-١٩٩٧) - مدير غاليري شيسنهالي (١٩٩٩-٢٠٠٠). مدير فني لبينالي سيدني ١٩٩٨. مقيّم زائر لمعرض كوتيديانا، كاستيلو دي ريفولي في مدينة تورينو الإيطالية في (١٩٩٩-٢٠٠٠) وبينالي البندقية (يونيو ١٩٩٧) ومعرض ميلان أوروبا ٢٠٠٠ وترينالي ميلان نوفمبر ٢٠٠٠ ومعرض "حقائق الحياة" للفن الياباني المعاصر في غاليري هايورد بلندن في خريف ٢٠٠١، ومعرض "أيام كهذه:" وترينالي الفن البريطاني المعاصر في لندن ٢٠٠٣. وعمل ضمن فريق المقيمين لبينالي شنغهاي (سبتمبر ٢٠٠٦). كتب مقالات عديدة عن الفن المعاصر وكتب دراسة نقدية عن الفنان الياباني أون كاوارا.

منى المصفي
مهندسة معماريّة
حصّلت منى المصفي على خبرات تخصصيّة في فرنسا وإيطاليا والولايات المتحدة الأمريكية. خلال عملها التخصصي في باريس اهتمّت بترميم الأبنية ثمّ بتصميم المعارض. شاركت في عدّة مسابقات لتصميم المعارض والمتاحف وفازت كمشاركة في تصميم جناح فرنسا في معرض إشبيليا الدولي لعام ١٩٨٩.
وكمصمّمة لبينالي الشارقة الفنّي السابع الذي افتتح في نيسان/ أبريل عام ٢٠٠٥ أكّدت على مفهوم المشهد المديني الداخلي المتبدّل بما يؤكّد على التأمّل وتبادل الأفكار حول الفن التركيبي المعاصر وموضوعة البينالي "الإنتماء". كما أسهمت في تطوير تصميم معرض البحيص الأثري الثامن عشر في متحف الشارقة للآثار. تم تصوّر هذا المشروع مع علماء آثار من جامعة تومبنغن لسبر استراتيجيّات مبتكرة في معارض الآثار ولجسر الشجوة بين التعليم والتطبيق . يتضمّن عمل المصفي الأكاديمي التعليم في قسم الهندسة في جامعة جورجيا للتقنيات (أتلانتا-الولايات المتحدة الأمريكيّة) من ١٩٩١ إلى ١٩٩٢. وفي البرنامج الباريسي التابع لنفس القسم بين ١٩٩٣ و٢٠٠١.حيث طوّرت دروسا حول مواقع محدّدة تتراوح بين الفضاء المديني والداخلي بما يسمح باكتشاف علاقة الفضاء بمختلف المساحات .وهي تدرّس منذ عام ٢٠٠٢ في قسم الهندسة والتصميم في الجامعة الأمريكيّة في الشارقة. تركّز حاليا في تدريسها وأبحاثها على الفضاء في عصر ما بعد الحداثة مع الإهتمام بتصميم المعارض، الإضاءة ودراسة علم إدراك الظواهر .

سيرين حليلة
محررة كتالوج بينالي الشارقة الثامن مستشارة في الإدارة الثقافية، صحفية، وكاتبة مندمجة في العديد من المشاريع الثقافية في فلسطين والأردن منذ ١٥ عاما. عملت في الفترة ما بين ١٩٩٩ - ٢٠٠٠ كمحررة لمجلة This Week in Palestine، وهي مجلة شهرية لترويج الثقافة والفنون والسياحة الثقافية في فلسطين، كما عملت مستشارة ثقافية لبرنامج الأمم المتحدة الإنمائي لإنشاء دائرة ثقافية في بلديتي أريحا ورام الله. منذ عام ٢٠٠٠، أنشأت المكتب الإقليمي للملتقى التربوي العربي في

الأردن وهو مشروع عربي تأسس في عام ١٩٩٨ ويركز على التعلم وبناء المعرفة على الخبرات الفردية والمحلية. بادرت في عام ٢٠٠٤ بمشروع أزكى دنيا وهو موقع على الانترنت لتسويق وتوزيع المنتج الثقافي غير التجاري للجمعيات والأفراد في العالم العربي. وفي عام ٢٠٠٥ أسست مشروع "سفر" وهو صندوق لتجوال الشباب العربي المبادر، وكلاهما مشروعين ضمن أعمال الملتقى التربوي العربي. عملت كمنسقة الاحتفالات في مشروع بيت لحم ٢٠٠٠ بتركيز على احتفالية رأس السنة الألفية الثانية وبرنامج الاحتفالات. في الفترة ما بين ١٩٩٢ - ١٩٩٨ نشطت في الهيئة الإدارية بمهرجان فلسطين الدولي للموسيقى والرقص بمناصب متنوعة. وفي عام ١٩٩٩ أقامت مهرجان أريحا الشتوي بالتعاون مع بلدية أريحا. في الفترة الممتدة بين عام ١٩٩٠ - ١٩٩٨ قامت بالمساهمة في تطوير حملة تشجيع عادة القراءة في المجتمع الفلسطيني ضمن مؤسسة تامر للتعليم المجتمعي (فلسطين). وفي عام ١٩٩٤ قامت بتأسيس وحدة النشر ضمن المؤسسة لتنشر كتبا للأطفال والشباب ومن إنتاجهم. هي عضو مؤسس في مجلس أمناء فرقة الفنون الشعبية الفلسطينية منذ عام ١٩٨٠ وفي الجمعية الدولية للمترجمين الفوريين AIIC (جنيف) منذ عام ٢٠٠٥ وفي مجلس أمناء مسرح البلد (الأردن) منذ عام ٢٠٠٦.

منير فاشي

كاتب مشارك

ولد منير فاشي في فلسطين في ١٩٤١. وأبعد عن المدينة مع عائلته في ١٩٤٨ واستقر في رام الله. وتعلم منير ودرس أيضا الرياضات والفيزياء ومادة التربية التعليمية في كل من فلسطين (خاصة في جامعة بيرزيت) والولايات المتحدة. وحصل على درجة الدكتوراة في التعليم من جامعة هارفارد وأنشأ مؤسسة تامر في فلسطين في ١٩٨٩. وظل منير يعمل على مشاريع تعليمية لمدة أربع عقود في فلسطين وفي العالم العربي. ويشغل منصب زميل بحثي في مركز الدراسات الشرق أوسطية في جامعة هارفارد منذ ١٩٩٨ حيث أسس منتدى التعليم العربي. وله مؤلفات عديدة باللغة العربية عن التعليم والرياضيات والاستعمار. تولي مؤلفاته اهتماما خاصا بمركزية التعبير الفني في تنمية وتعليم المجتمع. ونشرت له مقالات عديدة في إصدارية ".هارفارد إديوكيشنال ريفيو" وعدد من الصحف والمجلات الدولية. وهو عضو نشط في شبكة المجتمعات التعلمية للمعلمين ونشطاء المجتمع المشاركين في النقاشات الخاصة بالحاجة إلى تطوير الربط بين الأنماط المختلفة للمساحات والفرص المتاحة لإنماء مدى أوسع من القدرات الإنسانية.

مانيش جين

كاتبة مشاركة

يعمل مانيش جين حاليا منسقا ومؤسسا مشاركا لمعهد شيكشانتار، "معهد الشعوب لتعليم إعادة التفكير والتنمية" و يعمل رئيس تحرير صحيفة "فيرموكت شيكشا" التي تعني ترجمتها "تحرير التعليم".
وقام بتحرير خمسة كتب عن موضوع المجتمعات المتعلمة تناقش مستقبل التعلم وسبل تغيير النماذج الحالية للتعليم. ومانيش مهتم بشدة بمدينة أودايبور الهندية، باعتبارها تمثل نموذجا لكيفية تعليم المدن حيث يعمل بشكل نشط مع الأطفال والعائلات المحلية حول عدد من المشروعات التعليمية والزراعية. وقبل تأسيسه لمعهد شيكشانتار، قضى مانيش عامين في فرنسا حيث عمل كأحد كبار المخططين للمبادرة العالمية لليونسكو التي حملت اسم التعلم بلا حدود. وعمل مانيش أيضا مستشارا في مجالات التخطيط التعليمي وتحليل السياسات والبحوث وتصميم البرامج التعليمية واستخدام وسائل الإعلام والتقنية الحديثة مع منظمات اليونيسيف وهيئة المعونة الأميركية وبرنامج الأمم المتحدة للتنمية والبنك الدولي وأكاديمية مركز التطوير التعليمي في عدد من الدول في أفريقيا وجنوب ووسط آسيا. وعمل مساعد رئيس تحرير لنشرة منتدى تطوير التعليم الأساسي ومحو الأمية مع معهد هارفارد للتنمية الدولية. وعمل مانيش لمدة عامين كمصرفي استثماري مع مؤسسة مورغان ستانلي حيث تركز عمله في قطاعي التقنية العالية والاتصالات. وخلال الاثنى عشر عاما الماضية يسعى مانيش إلى الحصول على درجة الماجستير في التعليم من جامعة هارفارد ودرجة البكالوريوس في علم الاقتصاد والتنمية الدولية والفلسفة السياسية من جامعة براون وذلك بهدف أن يتمكن من رؤية العالم بعيون أكثر إبداعية وواقعية. وتشمل اهتمامات مانيش الطبخ ولعب الشطرنج والإخراج السينمائي وألعاب الفيديو وكرة السلة والسير لمسافات طويلة والزراعة.

فرانشيسكو ماناكوردا

كاتب مشارك

يعمل فرانشيسكو ماناكوردا مدرسا في الكلية الملكية للفنون في لندن في قسم الفن المعاصر وهو كاتب ومقيّم غير متفرغ مقيم في لندن. وفي ٢٠٠٤ عمل مقيما لمعرض "الآلة المنهجية" في غاليري ميد بجامعة ووريك وفي ٢٠٠٥ ومعرض" اتجاه معين في التمثيل الفني - نادي السينما في توماس دين" غاليري توماس دين بلندن. كما نظم أيضا ندوة "البيئة والتدريب الفني" لبرنامج "الفنون والبيئة" في الجمعية الملكية للفنون بلندن. وفي ٢٠٠٦ عمل مقيّما لمعرض" شبه الجزيرة الهندية في الفن المعاصر" في مؤسسة ساندريتو ري ريبودينجو في مدينة تورينو الإيطالية ومعرض" ستالايتس" في غاليري تانيا بوناكدار في نيويورك. وقد نشر مؤخرا دراسة متخصصة عن ماوريزيو كاتيلان (إليكتا، ٢٠٠٦) و يساهم بشكل منتظم في مطبوعات "فلاش آرت" و"ميتروبوليس إم" و"دوموس".

أكيكو ميكي

كاتبة مشاركة

تعمل أكيكو ميكي مقيمة رئيسية في متحف "بالى دي طوكيو" للفن المعاصر منذ عام ٢٠٠٠. وقد عملت ميكي مقيمة ومقيمة مشاركة في العديد من المعارض، منها: "عبر الثقافات" في بينالي البندقية ١٩٩٥ و"الثبات والأزياء: الفن الصيني المعاصر وسط محيط متغير" ١٩٩٧ و"موقع الرغبة" في بينالي تايباي ١٩٩٨ و"حياة الفن ٢١-تلفزيون سبيرال" ١٩٩٩ و"الخدار: أفلام يابانية معاصرة" ٢٠٠٠، "توبياس ريهبيرجر: التغير الليلي" ٢٠٠٢، و"ريفين نوينشفاندر: تماثلات سطحية" ٢٠٠٣، "نوبيوشي أراكي: النفس والحياة والموت" ٢٠٠٥. وعملت مديرة مشاركة لمشروع دينتسو للفن (وهو عبارة عن عدد من الأعمال الفنية مركبة في مجمع من المباني الحديثة صممها كل من جين نوفيل و جون جيردي في طوكيو وأنجزت في ٢٠٠٢). كتبت مقالات عديدة لعدد من الكتالوجات الخاصة بمعارض عالمية وعدد من المجلات اليابانية مثل "بيجوتسو تيكو" و"باريس فوتوز" و"تيما سيليستي"، الخ. شاركت في تأليف

عدد من الكتب مثل "فن جديد جدا" في عام ٢٠٠٠ وكتاب "ملف فناني العالم" ٢٠٠٤.

تريفور سميث

كاتب مشارك

تريفور سميث هو مقيّم فني مقيم في مركز الدراسات الراعية للفن التابع لكلية بارد في نيويورك حيث عمل مقيما مشاركا مؤخرا لمعرض "ريسل" الذي كان المعرض الذي افتتح به متحف هيسل. و في السابق كان مقيّما لمتحف نيويورك للفن المعاصر في نيويورك حيث عمل مقيّما مشاركا لمعرض "أندريه زيتل: المساحة النقدية" في الولايات المتحدة الأميركية. وقد وُلد سميث في كندا ودرس تاريخ الفن في جامعة بريتش كولومبيا. وفي الفترة من ١٩٩٢ إلى ٢٠٠٣ كان يقيم في أستراليا حيث عمل في البداية في بينالي سيدني ثم عمل مديرا لمعرض كانبرا لمساحات الفن المعاصر. وفي الفترة من ١٩٩٧ إلى ٢٠٠٣ عمل مقيّما للفن المعاصر في غاليري غرب أستراليا للفن. وشارك بأعمال في العديد من المعارض منها: الكوميديا الإلهية: فرانشيسكو غويا، باستر كيتون، ووليام كنتريدج". وقد نُشرت له مقالات عديدة في كتالوجات فنية وصحف في أوروبا وأستراليا وأميركا الشمالية.

رايمر شتانغه

كاتب مشارك

ولد رايمر شتانغه في هانوفر في ١٩٦٠ ويقيم حاليا في شرق برلين حيث يعمل مقيّما وناقدا. وقد عمل مقيما لمعارض عديدة منها: "جاست دو إيت" (فقط افعل هذا الأمر-كما تشير الترجمة) في متحف لينتوس، في لينز - ٢٠٠٥ (مع فلوريان ولدفوجل)، ومعرض "لوكيشن شوتس" في غاليري إيرنا هيسي، بروكسل ٢٠٠٥، ومعرض "داس جروسي راسينشتوك" في نورمبيرغ (مع فلوريان ولدفوجل). وله مؤلفات عديدة منها "وجوه" و"فرانكفورت ٢٠٠٢"، و"العودة إلى الفن" و"روجنر أند بيرنارد" و"هامبورج ٢٠٠٣" و"الغاليريهات الدولية". ويساهم شتانغه بشكل متواصل في مطبوعات "باركيت"، في زيوريخ و"فلاش آرت" في ميلاند و"مودرن بينتيرز" في نيويورك ونشرة "كونست" في زيوريخ و"سبايك" في فيينا و"زويا ريفيو" في برلين. وهو أيضا مغن ذو صوت جهوري في أوركسترا أرت كريتيك في برلين.